CW00448649

Michelle Vernal

Prologue

T he red fox poked his head through the hole he'd dug under the bricks. This was his secret point of entry. A closely guarded gap between the brick wall separating the gardens in which he had his den and his favourite dustbin.

The bin was located around the back of a handsome Georgian townhouse, one of a long row of identical buildings opposite St Stephen's Green. This particular bin, with its scraps of bacon, black and white pudding, sausage, fried potato, toast crusts, and on occasion, soda bread, had the best pickings in the area.

His ears were pricked for any sounds alerting him to danger, and his black nose twitched as he sniffed the night air. It was crisp with a tang of chimney smoke and the remnants of late-night suppers. The only sound was the odd car winding its lonely way home. He waited for a beat or two longer, and only when he was certain it was safe did he squeeze his bristly body through the gap.

The one and only time he'd been bold enough to investigate the bin's contents in the early morning hours, he'd encountered a fierce round woman wielding a rolling pin. She'd shouted at him and waved that wooden baton in a way which meant to do him harm. Thankfully her cumbersome size told him she wasn't quick enough to catch him, and he'd shot back

Michelle Vernal

The Guesthouse on the Green Series, Books 1-3 with bonus content

Copyright © 2018 by Michelle Vernal

O'Mara's, Moira Lisa Smile, What Goes on Tour , The Guesthouse on the Green
series

All rights reserved.

No portion of this boxset may be reproduced in any form without written permission from the publisher or author, except as permitted by U.S. copyright law.

through his hole into the sanctity of his gardens—safe. He'd heard her muttering about setting a trap, but none had ever been laid. His prowess when it came to keeping the mice at bay had been his saving grace. It had been a lesson learned, though, and calling as those first shards of morning light broke was a mistake he'd not made twice—until now.

His yellow eyes darted about the courtyard inspecting the shadowed corners. A chink of light peeped through the curtains of the room closest to the back door despite the lateness of the hour. The temptation of what he might find in the bin, however, was too strong. He couldn't turn back now, and he crept stealthily over to it, nudging at the lid with his nose. As he felt it budge, he was grateful it never sat as firmly over the lip as it should, and with one last good push, it slid off, clattering to the ground.

He had to move fast now, and he dived in head first, emerging victoriously, having snared a piece of bacon rind and a sausage. They would make a tasty addition to the grasses, berries, and odd squirrels he dined on in the gardens. The curtains to the room were wrenched open, flooding the courtyard with light. The fox snaffled his rind and scrambled from the bin, jubilantly dragging the sausage he'd found with him. It would make for a feast to be enjoyed back in his den.

He glanced back to see how the land lay. A woman of indeterminable years stood at the window, her tear-stained face peering out into the courtyard. They were a strange lot these humans, he thought, squeezing back through the cavity and slipping away into the darkness.

Chapter 1

♥

1999 Dublin

Aisling O'Mara had a gift. It hadn't been bestowed on her by three meddlesome fairies like Princess Aurora's gifts of beauty, song, and being awakened by her true love's kiss. Oh, she was an attractive enough woman, or so she'd been told on occasion. Marcus, whom she'd thought was her true love, used to give her an admiring once-over from time to time and tell her she was a fine-looking woman. He'd never been the effusive sort, but then again, he did work in banking.

As for beauty, well, now it had bypassed her and blessed the face of her younger sister, Moira. She'd been Maureen O'Mara's 'surprise' baby. The day she arrived, Maureen told her husband, Brian, he could forget about giving her the glad eye in the future. She'd be keeping her legs crossed until the end of her days ta very much.

Aisling had been nine when she and Roisin, to their disgust, had to push their beds closer together to make way for their baby sister. Whether her sister's beauty was a gift, Aisling was unsure because things came easily to Moira, far too easily, and she was headed for a fall. Aisling could feel it in her bones.

She'd had the same feeling in the weeks leading up to her wedding; only she'd ignored it, more fool her.

So, that left song. Celine Dion, she was not. Shortly after her tenth birthday, she'd auditioned for the children's choir at St Teresa's and been told in not so many words, don't call us, we'll call you. Suffice to say, they'd never called, not even when Mammy had tried to bribe the choirmaster with one of her famous Porter Cakes.

No, Aisling's gift was a simple one. There was no magic involved. Hers was a practical gift. She'd been born with an innate ability to listen to and fix other people's problems. Talk to Aisling; she'll know what to do. How many times had she heard that sentence uttered over the years? It was to her that family and friends turned when they needed a shoulder, and sometimes it could be a heavy burden. Aisling often thought instead of managing the family's guesthouse, O'Mara's Manor House, she should have had a newspaper column. It would be called Dear Aisling or Ask Aisling. Not original titles by any means, but effective and straight to the point. She would be the Irish version of the agony aunt over in the States; what was her name? Dear Abby—that was it.

Yes, she sighed, sipping her coffee and looking at the letter lying open on the table; her talents were wasted.

'I'm off now.' Moira popped her head around the doorway. 'Don't wait up for me tonight; I'll be late.' She strode over to the table and snatched a piece of Aisling's toast, stuffing the triangle into her mouth before Aisling could shriek at her to give it back.

Moira was employed as a receptionist for one of Ireland's largest law firms, Mason Price. Seeing how Friday had rolled around, Aisling knew Moira would be staying behind for the customary end-of-week drinks.

'If you got up earlier, you'd have time to make your own toast.'

'Yours tastes better.'

'It's toast, not cordon bleu cooking.' Aisling took stock of her younger sibling, her mouth curving as she spied the white runners peeking out from under the hem of her black trousers. They were very Minnie Mouse, but Aisling knew as soon as Moira got to work, they'd be swapped for a pair of heels. As long as they weren't her heels.

'You've not got my black Miu Miu's in your bag, have you?' She stared hard at Moira; whose left eye twitched when she fibbed.

'No, and would you leave off about your stupid Miu Miu's. I borrowed them once.'

'And got a scratch on the heel.'

'It was microscopic.' Moira's hand snaked out for another piece of toast, but Aisling was quicker and held the plate up out of her reach. She hadn't detected a twitching eye; she'd let the Miu Miu's go for now. It made sense for Moira to walk the short distance to the multi-storey office building near the Grand Canal. The traffic was bumper to bumper of a morning, and it was faster to get there on foot.

Moira looked particularly lovely today, footwear aside, with her dark hair scooped back into a low ponytail. The moss green coloured blouse she was wearing under her suit jacket brought out the flecks of gold in her hazel eyes. To be fair, the black Miu Miu's would have worked a treat with her sister's black trousers.

Moira and their older sister Roisin both took after their Mammy. They'd inherited her olive skin, which obligingly turned mahogany when they went on their holidays. Aisling had Nanna Dee on their dad's side, long gone now bless the old harridan, to thank for her strawberry blonde mop. The green eyes, a smattering of freckles, and skin that refused to tan no matter how long she sat out in the sun meant she'd drawn the short straw, in her opinion. Not that she got many opportunities for sunbathing these days anyway, and it wasn't just down to Dublin's inclement weather.

Aisling couldn't remember the last time she'd taken a holiday. There'd been no opportunity for time off since she'd taken over the running of the guesthouse nearly two years ago. It was a job that needed her at the helm seven days a week, three hundred and sixty-five days of the year. Of course, Moira, Mammy, and Roisin would argue this wasn't the case. They'd be quick to say Aisling chose to see herself as indispensable. Perhaps it was true. She needed to keep herself busy after everything that had happened. God, she'd had a hell of a twelve months.

Chapter 2

'**A**sh, did you hear me?' Moira waved a hand in front of her sister's face.

'What? Oh yes, you said you'll be late. Well, have fun, but don't go getting hammered or anything.'

This received a frown. 'You're such a sourpuss these days, and you're not my keeper, Aisling O'Mara. I'm twenty-five, not fifteen.'

Aisling sighed; she never used to be a sourpuss. 'Sorry. It's habit, but we've got lunch with Mammy tomorrow, remember, and you don't want a sore head, or you'll never hear the end of it from her.'

'Oh, feck it, I'd forgotten all about that,' said Moira. I've arranged to meet Andrea on Grafton Street for eleven o'clock tomorrow. I was looking forward to it too. We're going shopping. I'm due some retail therapy.'

Money burned a hole in her sister's pocket. Aisling decided she was allowed to be self-righteous. She'd managed to kick her designer-shoe shopping habit when she'd arrived back in Dublin. Marcus and his thrifty ways had seen to that. Truth be told, she hadn't had much choice in the matter; a disposable income was needed to maintain a designer-shoe habit. The wage she drew from O'Mara's, while a living one, was not a patch on her old salary. The old Aisling had packed up her frivolous side when she'd packed her bags and returned to O'Mara's after Dad got sick.

'Don't roll your eyes, Ash. I need a new dress because Posh Mairead from the Finance Department's gotten engaged to Niall. He's a senior partner, and how she snared him with those buck teeth of hers, I don't know—there's hope for us all. Personally, I think he's only marrying her because of her family name. The Horan's are old money, and everybody knows Mairead only works because her daddy thought it would be good for her to see how the other half live. Anyway, the engagement party's only a couple of weeks away, and I've got absolutely nothing to wear. I have to look my best because all the partners have been invited, and I have it on good authority Liam Shaughnessy from Asset Management is going to be there.'

Aisling was exhausted by the time Moira finished her monologue but not so tired she hadn't seen the predatory gleam in her eyes as she mentioned Liam Shaughnessy. 'Be careful, Moira,' she warned for the second time that morning.

'What?'

'From what you've told me, yer man, Liam, sounds like a player.'

'Ash, just because you made a bad call doesn't mean all men are tarred with the same brush as Marcus fecking coward McDonagh. He was a selfish eejit.' She shuddered for effect. 'I didn't like the way he'd give you that look.'

'What look?'

'The look that said you were being loud. It made me want to kick him. It was the same look Mr Mathias used to give me in the juniors. He always described me as a disruptive member of the class. I wanted to kick him too, remember?'

'Vaguely.' Alright, so Marcus didn't like her drawing attention to herself, but that was because he was reserved. He liked to sit back and observe, not be thrown in the mix.

'And the way that man used to hog the remote control for the tele spoke volumes, an only child, used to getting his own way.'

Aisling looked at her sister. She'd forgotten how he did that. The channel surfing had driven her mad. She'd be happily involved in Melrose Place, and the next, she'd be confronted by that mad Australian wrestling crocodiles. An annoying habit she'd add to her list of reasons as to why she should continue ignoring his letters. Maybe Moira was right when she said she was bitter from having been burned. She was bitter like an unripe lemon.

'Anyway,' Moira prattled on, 'Mairead's only gone and hired The Saddle Room at the Shelbourne for it.' She breathed, 'Shelbourne' with reverence before looking hopefully at Aisling. 'Maybe you could explain to Mammy for me? Sure, look it, we could always make it for the following week.'

'I will not. You've got plenty of things you can wear. Your wardrobe's overflowing as it is. Mammy doesn't ask a lot from us, Moira, you know that.' Seeing Moira open her mouth, she warded her off. 'Alright, I'll grant you she tells us what to do a lot, but she's had such a horrible time of it, the least you can do is front up for lunch. She looks forward to seeing us.'

'We've all had a horrible fecking time,' Moira huffed. 'And it's bloody inconvenient. She's a whirling social dervish that fits us in to suit her social calendar.' Moira's hazel eyes regarded her sister steadily. 'And don't start because it's true, and you know it.'

She could be a selfish mare, sometimes thought Aisling as she shut her mouth. They would go to lunch to keep the peace even if she did have a point.

'What's that you've got there?' Moira pointed to the letter lying next to Aisling's plate, her face lighting up as she asked, 'Is it from Pat?'

Moira adored Patrick, their handsome big brother. Aisling, however, had his number. Although, she was the only one in the family who did. He was a chancer. Mammy thought the sun shone out of her eldest child and only son's arse. She could make an excuse for his behaviour faster than a magician could pull a rabbit out of a hat. Roisin sat on the fence. She'd side with Mammy and Moira when it suited and agree with Aisling when she wanted to borrow a pair of her shoes.

Patrick O'Mara was a selfish so-and-so with notions about himself. Look at how he'd thrown his toys out of the cot after Dad died. He'd flown off to the States without a backward glance when he hadn't got his way over O'Mara's being sold, right when Mammy needed him most. Aisling frowned. As far as she was concerned, America wasn't far enough. Her brother always had his own best interests at heart. If he were chocolate, he'd eat himself.

'No, not Patrick, it's from the ESB, that's all, gas is going up again.' The lie tripped smoothly from her tongue, and she felt a flash of anger towards Patrick as she saw the look of disappointment on her sister's face. He hadn't been in touch since Christmas, and then he'd only sent a card and a photograph of himself and his new girlfriend, Cindy. She was the perfect appendage—arm candy with big blonde hair and a perfectly aligned, white, toothy smile. Moira, upon seeing the photograph fall from his Christmas card, had announced, her boobs weren't gifted to her by God, that's for sure.

'That reminds me I forgot to tell you, Roisin rang yesterday,' Aisling said. 'Noah's getting a certificate for 'good work' at his school assembly this morning.'

Their nephew had only started at his primary school in the affluent London suburb of Highgate a month ago and was already getting a pat on the back. Aisling felt a surge of pride as though she had something to do with him being awarded an accolade. There'd be no hope for her in years to come if he went on to graduate from university.

Moira's smile was wistful. 'Ah, I wish we could be there cheering him on. His little face will be a picture. Mind you,

Colin; the Arse will be puffed up like a peacock saying it's down to the Quealey genes, eejit that he is. Do yer know the last time I spoke to Roisin, she told me he'd got it in his head that Noah's the next Beckham because he scored a goal at toddler footie. I'll bet you anything; he's one of those awful parents who stands on the side-lines shouting and bawling.' Her mouth formed a startled 'O' as the old grandfather clock in the corner chimed the half-hour. 'Feck, is that the time? I've got to run, or I'll be late.'

A twinkling later, their front door banged as Moira left and no doubt hurtled down the stairs two at a time. Hurricane Moira. If Mammy had been here, Aisling knew she'd have called after her; slow and steady wins the race, Moira! She was full of pertinent idioms. Aisling wondered at times whether she kept a book hidden about her person to always have the right saying on hand at the right moment!

Alone once more, Aisling turned her attention back to the letter she'd been reading before her sister appeared. She kept returning to it. It was rather like picking at a scab for want of a nicer turn of phrase. The plain white envelope it had arrived in a few days earlier had been addressed in the handwriting that always sent a piercing stab straight through her heart. She picked it up from where she'd leaned it against the salt shaker and eyed the carefully written address for a few moments.

How much easier things would have been if she could have packed her bags and run far away when it happened. Preferably somewhere warm with balmy breezes and coconut palms, lots of coconut palms. She shivered. It was nothing a hot shower wouldn't fix.

Aisling folded the letter, placing it back inside the envelope, before pushing her chair back and getting up from the table. She tucked it away in the hidden drawer at the back of the bureau where Mammy used to stuff the letters that came from the hospital. It was as if she'd believed by ignoring the infor-mation they contained; she could make what was happening to her husband go away. These days there was a new pile of letters there which Aisling wished she could make go away. She locked the drawer, returning the key to its hook on the inside of the desk. Her talents were wasted, she thought, for the second time that morning mentally composing a Dear Aisling letter.

Dear Aisling,

I was due to get married this time last year only my fiancé disappeared a week before our wedding. He left me with no explanation as to why he'd left other than a brief note saying he was sorry, but he couldn't go through with the wedding. Three months ago, he began writing to me from Cork, his bolthole asking me to forgive him. He says it was all a huge mistake, he got cold feet, and he wants a second chance. Blah, blah, blah. What should I do?

Yours faithfully,

Me

The problem was, while she was a wonder at sorting out the lives of those around her, Aisling didn't have the foggiest how to fix what was wrong in hers.

Aisling shook her head in an effort to clear it. Marcus fecking coward McDonagh, as Moira so charmingly referred to him, didn't deserve to occupy any more of her thoughts today. With that, she banished him and moved over to the windows. The sky, she saw, drawing the curtains and hooking them back, was pale blue with fat scudding clouds. A cool wind had been blowing most of the week. Still, it wasn't raining; that was something.

She stared through the panes of glass. There were six of them in total. She could recall their Mammy effing and blinding when it was time to give them a good polish. Now the job fell to her she knew how Mammy had felt; they were a sod to clean. Across the road, the leafy tops of the trees in St Stephen's Green danced as they tried to cling valiantly to the boughs.

Autumn had always been Aisling's favourite time of the year. She loved to watch the greenery give way to the fiery oranges, reds, and yellows of autumn. Since Marcus had left, the season had lost its allure. Now it was a reminder that a year ago, she'd been jilted. Her gaze dropped to the traffic on the road below.

It was heavy with the early morning rush, people hurrying here, there, and everywhere. The streets were so congested these days. She was glad she didn't have to travel far to work—three flights of stairs down to reception, and she was there. And on that note, she thought, moving away from the window, it was time she got her a into g. O'Mara's was mad busy of a Friday with the influx of travellers arriving for the weekend. Aisling liked to keep on the go; being busy was an all too welcome distraction from Marcus.

Chapter 3

♥

'Morning, Aisling,' Bronagh Hanrahan mumbled. 'Love the suit, very you.' Her mouth was full as she looked up from the computer where she was processing a reservation with one hand and holding a spoon in the other. It was something she could do with her eyes closed given how long she'd worked for the O'Mara's—nearly thirty years! Mind you, when Maureen O'Mara had first gotten the Macintosh, Bronagh had been dragged kicking and screaming into the computer age. A mug of tea was next to the keyboard along with a bowl of cereal, Bronagh's requisite box of Special K next to her in-tray.

Bronagh was a serial dieter and could often be heard lamenting no matter how hard she tried; she couldn't seem to lose any weight. 'It's the menopause, so it is. It gets us all in the end,' she'd state before pointing a finger. 'Just you wait, Aisling. You'll hit your forties, and that lovely slim waist of yours will vanish, and you'll be left with a roll around your middle like that short bald fella's.'

'What short bald fella?'

'Ah, you know, yer man, the Buddha chap.'

This amused Aisling because she knew, were she to open the drawer in the desk at which Bronagh sat, she'd find a half-eaten packet of custard creams in there. It also surprised her to hear her waist being referred to as slim. She'd always been the well-padded one in the family. There was nothing like a broken heart to curb one's appetite, though, and the pounds had fallen off her in the weeks after the wedding was cancelled.

Aisling greeted Bronagh, confiding in her that while her shoes had cost the earth, the suit had been a steal at Penneys. She was a firm believer in anything looking a million dollars so long as it was paired with the right shoes. It was how she justified the ludicrous sums she'd splurged on them over the years.

She peered over Bronagh's shoulder and ran a finger down the diary's open page to see who was checking out that morning. Their receptionist might be au fait with the Mac, but she still didn't trust it and insisted on keeping all their guests logged in her diary as well. Behind them, the fax whirred into life and began churning its message out as the phone simultaneously began to ring. Aisling grinned as Bronagh's jaw went into overdrive before she swallowed and composed herself.

'Good morning, O'Mara's Manor House; you're speaking with Bronagh. How can I help?'

Ever the professional. Aisling was still smiling as a commotion sounded on the stairs a second later. Her head swivelled in that direction. Mr Miller, larger-than-life, was standing on the landing. His suitcase was beside him, as was a large holdall. He had a baseball-style cap pulled down on his head; his t-shirt bore the slogan "Kansas: Not Everything is Flat", and a camera was slung around his neck. He was urging his wife to get a move on in his booming Midwestern American accent.

'June-bug, for the love of God, woman, get down here! I can't carry all of this on my own.'

'I'm coming, Jacob, don't rush me. You know I hate being rushed.'

'Can I help with anything, Mr Miller?' Aisling moved over to the base of the stairs looking up at him as she rested a hand on the rail, ready to go to his aid.

'You could put a rocket up my wife, Aisling. That would help. The tour bus will be stopping by to pick us up any minute.' He gestured to the holdall. 'Do you think you could manage that? This case weighs a ton. June's been shopping for the kids and the grandkids, as well as half of Kansas City, and we're only three days into our tour.'

Aisling made her way up to the first-floor landing, taking the bag and hefting it up over her shoulder. Mrs Miller had proudly displayed all her treasures in the guest lounge for her to admire last night. She'd made the appropriate enthusiastic noises as the American woman had shaken a glass dome demonstrating how snow fell on the little leprechaun trapped inside. She'd bought tea towels with four-leaf clovers and Irish blessings printed on them, along with a Foster and Allen CD. She had a selection of thimbles, wishing jars, and luck stones. Her precious Belleek pottery was bubble-wrapped, but Aisling hoped the delicate china didn't break between now and when she arrived home.

Mrs Miller's pride and joy, though, she declared, was a traditional Irish dancing costume. It had come complete with a red ringlet wig. 'I did Irish dancing as a girl, Aisling, and I always wanted the proper dress and shoes to wear. There was no money for frivolities when I was a young'un though—not with eight mouths to feed in the family.'

Aisling had bitten her bottom lip to stop herself envisaging the well-endowed Mrs Miller jigging about in her short green dress, white tights, and black shoes to her Foster and Allen CD, reliving her childhood dream. Each to their own!

'I checked out already, so once my wife decides to grace us with her presence, we're good to go. Ah, speak of the devil. Here she comes.'

June Miller's tread sounded lightly on the stairs, and she appeared behind her husband. 'It was my hair, Aisling,' she said, spotting her. 'Flat as a pancake after I blow-dried it this morning. The water's so soft here. I looked like I had a helmet on, and I've been trying to zhoosh it up a bit.'

'Well, you succeeded. You look like you stuck your finger in an electric socket, woman. You should have left it alone.'

He wasn't wrong, but Aisling gave her a reassuring smile. 'It looks lovely, Mrs Miller. There's loads of body in it. Now then, I hear you've got a bus to be catching. So, we'd best get down these stairs.'

The couple, cases thudding behind them, followed her down to the foyer where a tall, thin man in a tweed cap and clobber that would look right at home on a farm in County Middle-of-Nowhere, had appeared.

'Ah, here they are now,' said Bronagh.

'Mr and Mrs Miller?' the man said, stepping forward.

Mr Miller took his outstretched hand and shook it. 'Please call me Jacob, and this is my wife June.'

The man nodded and smiled at June, revealing a missing front tooth before taking her suitcase from her.

Jaysus! Aisling wondered what the tour company was called, Boondocks Bus Breaks, perhaps?

'I'm your tour guide, Ruaraidh. The bus is outside.'

'Say your name again, son?'

'Ruaraidh.'

'I think I'll just call you Roy if that's okay.'

Jacob Miller didn't wait for a reply, turning his attention to Aisling and Bronagh. 'Thank you, ladies, for your wonderful hospitality. We've enjoyed every minute of our time here in your capital city, haven't we, June? It's a fine establishment you run, Aisling.'

'We sure have. You made us so welcome. We appreciate it, and we'll spread the word about your beautiful manor house, won't we, Jacob?'

'We will indeedy.'

This was what it was all about, giving their guests happy memories of their time here in Dublin. Aisling thanked them for their kind words and for staying with them before wishing them a fabulous time tripping around Ireland.

Ruaraidh moved toward the door, eager to get his two charges onboard the bus. Aisling tried not to laugh at the look on his face as Mr Miller boomed, 'Lead the way, Roy, my boy.'

'Enjoy the craic!' Bronagh called after them.

There was a whoosh of cool air as Ruaraidh opened the door, and they heard Mrs Miller lament as she stepped outside. 'Darn it, Jacob, if you hadn't been rushing me, I would have put a scarf over my hair. That wind will flatten it faster—'

'Oh, put a sock in it, woman.'

Any further exchange was lost as the door shut behind them. Bronagh and Aisling grinned at each other. There were some guests who made you laugh, the Millers a case in point, and some that made you pull your hair out. Aisling threw a glance over her shoulder to Room 1. It was the only room on the ground floor, a single, and given the courtyard outlook, its nightly rate was cheaper than their other nine rooms. The door was firmly shut.

Miss Brennan had complained about other guests keeping her awake with their chatter in the lounge. The guest lounge was behind reception to the left, and the stairs were all that separated Room 1 from it, but no one had complained about the noise being a problem before. She'd also complained about the foot traffic up and down the stairs of a morning as other guests made their way down to the dining room below for breakfast.

She'd only been here for two nights and had found something to moan about each morning. Aisling wondered what today's problem would be. Then she frowned, remembering what Moira had called her this morning, a sourpuss. She didn't want to be like Miss Brennan. She'd always had a positive outlook on life and had been rewarded for this with a good life. It had been marching along in the direction she'd thought it would—the altar. Marcus had snatched her happy-go-lucky attitude away, though. He'd shattered not only her trust but her heart too. Stop it, Aisling, don't go there.

She focussed on the diary instead and flicked a couple of pages until she found what she was looking for. Their problematic guest wasn't checking out until Monday, three more days! Her mother's old mantra ran through her head, Just like the customer's always right, Aisling, our guests are always right. Even when they're not!

It was this attitude toward the people that chose to stay at O'Mara's that had turned it around from a tired old manor house and establishment that had seen better days to the quaint but plush accommodation offered today. So, Aisling resolved no matter what Miss Una Brennan from County Waterford pulled out of her hat this morning, she would smile sweetly and promise to sort the problem for her. Just as well, it was she and not Moira who'd stepped up and taken over running the guest house. Her sister had never mastered the art of smiling sweetly. She'd be likely to tell the old wagon—the particularly Irish epithet reserved for the most awkward of their female guests was a favourite of her sister's—that the tide wouldn't take her out or that the sea wouldn't give her a wave or some such insult.

Smiling at the thought of what Moira, with her repertoire of sharp retorts, would say, she set about her morning routine. It began with a customary sweep of reception to take note of what needed a tidy-up. The phone was ringing once more, and Aisling left Bronagh to answer it. The cushions on the elegant rolled arm sofa with its cream and green stripes could do with a plump. She saw to those first before straightening the magazines on the antique mahogany coffee table. A few of the brochures were out, and she refilled the Wicklow Tours slot with the glossy Slane Castle pamphlets ensuring there were no empty spaces.

There were only two of Quinn's flyers advertising his restaurant of the same name left. It was as good an excuse as any to call on him. Not that she needed an excuse! She'd known Quinn and had been firm friends with him since their wayward student days.

Maybe, she'd even take him up on his offer of dinner on the house. His way of saying thank you for recommending his traditional Irish fare to their guests. It would be nice not to cook for a change. Moira's culinary skills were limited, so unless Aisling wanted to dine on beans on toast each night, preparing the evening meal fell to her.

Yes, she decided, once breakfast was finished, she'd stroll over to Quinn's. Her eyes roved over the stand one last time, and when she was satisfied all was shipshape, she turned her attention to the blooms on top of the front desk. Bronagh, she saw, was off the phone and scraping out the remnants from her breakfast bowl.

The bouquet arrived fresh from Fi's Florists once a fortnight on a Monday morning. They'd need a freshen up if they were to continue looking their best between now and then. Aisling knew the trade tricks, trim the stems and add a little sugar to the water. She picked up the vase and carried it out to the poky but 'sufficient for their needs' kitchenette at the very back on the ground floor. The door beside it held a chunky old-fashioned brass key which, when turned, allowed the door to open up onto the steps outside. They led down to the concreted courtyard. Nobody used it, nobody except Mr Fox and Mrs Flaherty when she took out the rubbish.

The little red fox was rarely seen but often heard as he checked out what had gone into the bin that day. His calling card was the rubbish he'd leave strewn about the courtyard. Their breakfast cook, Mrs Flaherty, who despite her rosy apple cheeks and pensionable age could drop the 'f' bomb with the best of them, was often heard shrieking, That fecking fox! Ita, in charge of housekeeping, was terrified of her, and Aisling wished she had the same effect on the young woman because she might actually do some work then.

There was no need for a garden at the rear of the house for two reasons. Firstly, St Stephen's Green was their front garden. Sure, a busy road separated them from the Green, but it was only a hop, skip, and a jump away. Secondly, the back wall of O'Mara's housed a secret. A gate which, if ventured through, welcomed you into the Iveagh Gardens, Mr Fox's home.

Aisling took the flowers, their scent still heady, from the vase and set about her task. It was in this little kitchenette that Bronagh would heat her leftover dinner for lunch or make herself a cup of tea. She was on the front desk from eight am until four pm Monday to Friday, and then Nina, the young Spanish girl who'd started a year ago, would arrive to do the evening shift. On the weekend, James and Evie, two students, split the front desk shifts. Aisling spent her days overseeing them all.

Satisfied the arrangement would continue to brighten reception until Fi's next delivery, she carried the vase back to the front desk. The guest lounge was next on her agenda. It was her favourite room in the whole house. Aisling loved the cosy yet elegant sunny space. She'd conjure up images of the well-heeled people who'd have been received there when it had served as a drawing-room. The ladies she pictured all looked suspiciously like they'd stepped from the pages of a Jane Austen novel, and the men bore an uncanny resemblance to Colin Firth as Mr Darcy.

She stood in the doorway of the lounge for a moment. Her Mammy had combed the antique markets for the furnishings in here, including the gilt-framed artworks that lined the walls. The light-flooded in through twin floor-to-ceiling windows in keeping with the era of the house. The original fireplace was nestled between the windows. It was laid but never used these days, thanks to the wonders of central heating. She liked to envisage the visitors of old gathering around that fire in the wintertime as it roared and spat, with a glass of something warming and welcoming in their hand.

Aisling fluffed the cushions on the three-seater sofa identical to the lounger in reception. She straightened the magazines on the coffee table before checking the milk bottles and tea and coffee sachets in the tray on top of the buffet opposite.

The Earl Grey teabags needed replenishing; they were always popular, and, opening the cupboard, she took out the box and refilled them. Next in her morning routine was the room freshener. She spritzed each morning, walking around the expansive room, giving it a couple of bursts. If she closed her eyes, she could imagine she was in a grassy meadow, but without being afflicted by hay fever!

A teacup sat on the coffee table with a ring of red lipstick around the rim, and picking it up; she took it out to the kitchenette to wash. She'd draped the tea towel over the rail and had decided to pop downstairs to see how the land lay with Mrs Flaherty this morning when the door to Room 1 opened.

Chapter 4

'Oh, good morning, Miss Brennan. I trust you slept well.'
Aisling tried to keep the note of hope from her voice.
She could hear Mammy's voice in her ear; *She's the sort if you
give her an inch, she'll take a mile.* Mammy might not be here,
but she was right. Miss Brennan was a woman who'd sense
weakness and exploit it, and from the tight-lipped look Aisling
was receiving now, it seemed she already had.

'I didn't as it happens. There was a dreadful carry-on outside my window in the small hours.'

Aisling silently cursed Mr Fox, wishing he could have chosen to raid someone else's bin last night. 'I'm so sorry Miss
Brennan. That would be our resident fox. He comes a calling
from the Iveagh Gardens. They're behind the wall to the rear
of the house. She donned her brightest smile and told herself
to rise above Miss Brennan's pettiness and find something
nice to say. She was going to have to dig deep.

'That blue's such a lovely colour on you.' It was true. The
pale blue blouse Una Brennan wore under her cardigan was
the same shade as her eyes. She'd have been pretty once, but
now her features were pinched. Her face spoke of internal
unhappiness, and the harsh line of her tight bun from which a
few silver curls escaped did nothing to soften her appearance.

'Are you on your way to breakfast?' Aisling didn't expect an acknowledgement of her compliment.

'I am. I hope it doesn't take as long as it did yesterday. I think the cook was waiting for the hen to lay the egg. I have an appointment at ten o'clock this morning.'

'We do have the continental option available if you're in a hurry, Miss Brennan.'

'I prefer a cooked breakfast.' And with that, the older woman marched off down the stairs.

Awkward so-and-so. Aisling would put money on her, having been a headmistress or something of the like in her younger days. Her cardigan and skirt ensemble teamed with sensible shoes reminded her of the bad-tempered English teacher she'd had in secondary school. She stole a glance at her own impractical but oh-so-pretty Walter Steiger shoes as she recalled the awful woman. She used to frisbee the school books across the room to her students. She'd also had a habit of slamming her ruler down on the desk of any pupil who looked like they might be daydreaming about their latest favourite pop star rather than conjugating their verbs. Given Aisling had been smitten with Jon Bon Jovi that year, her desk had gotten a hammering! Now she poked her tongue out at Miss Brennan's retreating back. Mammy wouldn't approve, but Mammy wasn't here.

A handful of people were seated at the tables Aisling saw as she descended the stairs to the basement dining room. They were laid with white cloths and silver cutlery. Mr and Mrs Freeman from Australia with their teenage sons were tucking into their breakfast. They'd obviously risen bright and early. The family had toured Britain and had tagged on Ireland for the last two weeks of their holiday. The younger of the two brothers had finished high school, and this was the last hurrah before he too flew the nest and went off to university, Mrs Freeman had confided in Aisling.

The boys, who looked similar apart from their haircuts, were seated at a separate table to their parents. Aisling watched for a second as they shovelled down their bacon and eggs like they hadn't seen food since leaving Australia. It made her smile as she remembered Mammy going on about Patrick having hollow legs when he was a teen.

Her gaze flicked over to the young couple from Cork, the Prestons. They were seated in the far corner of the room beneath a large black and white print of Grafton Street in the twenties. Upon hearing they were from Cork, Aisling had been tempted to flash them a photo of Marcus. She wanted to ask if they'd seen him, and if so, how did he look? It was a crazy thought, but then sometimes, where he was concerned, she felt as though she had indeed gone crazy.

She'd managed to rein herself in and had learned that the reason behind the Prestons' visit was down to his being courted by the Dublin branch of the firm he worked at. The company had high hopes of tempting him and his wife to relocate to the Fair City. By the looks of their clean plates, they'd enjoyed their breakfast and were savouring a cup of tea before getting on with whatever the day had in store for them.

The retired and portly Mr Walsh, who'd left Dublin for Liverpool many moons ago, was seated at a table near the door to the kitchen. He was buttering his toast and casting about the table. He was missing Mrs Flaherty's homemade marmalade, Aisling guessed, and she ducked on through to the kitchen to spoon some into a dish for him.

'Good morning,' she greeted Mrs Flaherty, whose cheeks were even pinker than usual thanks to the heat from the frying pan, and received a nod in return. Aisling wasn't offended. One didn't disturb Mrs Flaherty when she was near a hot stove. She set about scraping the chunky orange marmalade from the jar into a dish, and, leaving the cook to her bacon and black pudding, she carried it through.

'Here we go, Mr Walsh. I think this is what you were missing.' She set the dish down.

'Aisling, pet, you're a wonder.'

'Well, now if I didn't know how partial you were to Mrs Flaherty's marmalade after all the years you've been coming to stay, I'd be a poor hostess indeed.' Mr Walsh had been booking into his favourite room on the third floor of O'Mara's for five nights in the first week of September for as long as Aisling could remember. He had a standing order to come back each year to visit his older sister, who lived in Rathmines. She'd never married, he'd told Aisling once, and had never moved from what had been their family home. He refused to stay with her despite her living in the house he'd grown up in because he said she drove him batty!

'Will you join me?' He gestured to his teapot. Mr Walsh liked her to sit down and share a cuppa with him of a morning. He reckoned her and Bronagh were the only sane people he spoke to once he left O'Mara's for the day.

'Give me two ticks,' she smiled. It faltered as she spied Miss Brennan. She'd settled herself as far away from the other guests as she could manage. Aisling wondered what her problem was. What made a person so cantankerous? She was spared from pondering her question by Mr Freeman waving her over.

'Good morning, Mr Freeman. What can I do for you?'

'So, you really don't say 'Top of the morning to ye' then?'

'Only in the films, Mr Freeman. Do you say, hmm, let me see—strewth?'

He winked. 'Fair dinkum, I do.'

Aisling laughed, 'Your gas.'

'Gas! I shall add that to my repertoire of Irish sayings.' His eyes twinkled as he went back to dipping his toast in his egg.

'Aisling,' Mrs Freeman said. 'We're going to see Riverdance tonight.'

It amused Aisling hearing one of her sons groan at the thought of an evening watching Irish dancing. His mother ignored him. 'We thought we'd have an early dinner before the show. Is there anywhere you recommend?'

'There is actually. I know of a lovely place just around the corner from here where the craic is great.' She grinned, seeing Mr Freeman sound out the word. 'It's called Quinn's, and they serve traditional Irish fare in a cosy setting. The food's delicious. Would you like me to make a reservation for you?'

'That would be wonderful, thank you.'

'Say five-thirty? Would that give you enough time before the show?'

'What do you think, honey?'

Mr Freeman nodded. 'Bang on.'

It was funny hearing Irishisms in such a broad Australian accent, Aisling thought giving him a thumbs up.

'Five-thirty would be perfect.'

'Five-thirty it is, Mrs Freeman. Mr Freeman, hoo-roo.' He roared with laughter. 'You got me with that one.'

She left them to get back to their breakfast, heading over to clear the Cork couple's plates. 'How was everything?' she asked, stacking the two plates.

'Lovely, thank you. Mrs Flaherty's soda bread is better than my nana's but don't tell her I said that,' Mr Preston chuckled.

As she carried the dishes out to the kitchen, Aisling hoped Miss Brennan had overheard his high praise. She stacked the dirty dishes in the dishwasher and then, retrieving an extra cup and saucer, went to join Mr Walsh, hearing Mrs Flaherty muttering behind her as she did so.

As she sat down opposite him, the cook pushed through the swinging door. She wiped her hands on her apron, her buttonlike blue eyes narrowed and her ample bosom heaving as she drew breath. She looked as though she were going into battle, a plump Boudica as she strode fearlessly across the dining room. Her voice rang out loudly as she asked Miss Brennan what she would like this morning.

Aisling turned her attention to Mr Walsh, who set about pouring the tea as he told her all about his mad sister's refusal to throw anything out. 'She's got that much gear piled up in there she could open a junk shop because most of it is rubbish.'

Aisling relaxed, listening to his banter. She liked his Liverpudlian accent. Mrs Flaherty was more than capable of handling the likes of Una Brennan.

Chapter 5

♥

U na eyed Aisling for a moment. Why she felt the need to totter about the place as though she were about to hit the runways of Paris was beyond her. They were in a Dublin guesthouse, for goodness sake. An upmarket one, but a guesthouse, nevertheless. She turned away and cut a sliver of her white pudding, spearing it with her fork. She could sense that formidable cook hovering, and she knew Aisling was wary of her. She'd been a short-tempered old bite, but she couldn't help herself. She put her fork down.

The pudding was golden and looked crisp to the bite. It was cooked just the way she liked it, and the only reason she wasn't relishing the full Irish breakfast on the plate in front of her was because her stomach was in knots. It had been from the moment she'd packed her bags and left her little terraced house in Ferrybank to board the Waterford to Dublin train. It had only worsened as the train chugged closer to the city, and it was this that was making her ill-tempered.

She'd caught the bus from Heuston Station to St Stephen's Green and had peered out the window unsure of what to expect. Dublin was the city of her birth. She was born in 1932, the year of the world's largest Eucharistic Congress. Una's mam had talked of a live broadcast from Pope Pius XI all the way from Vatican City to Phoenix Park at the Sunday mass. Imagine that, she used to say, his voice travelling all the way from Vatican City! She wondered what her mam would have made of the internet had she lived long enough for its invention.

It had been fifty years since Una had last walked the streets of this city. Back then, she'd known them like the back of her hand. From what she could see, not much had changed. The layout was still the same; she'd be able to find her way around despite the addition of the big, shiny glass monstrosities, so-called progress. What had changed, she'd sensed from the moment she stepped off the train, was the atmosphere. There was a buoyancy in people's steps that hadn't been here when she was a girl. The faces she passed as her case bumped along behind her weren't set in a hard, grim line of scraping by. There was a buzz in the air, lots of foreign accents, and the foot traffic! Well, it had to be seen to be believed. The streets were alive with activity.

She watched a double-decker bus pass by. The moss green buses of her youth that had belched their way around the streets with their open platform at the back were long gone. She recalled Leo leaping from that platform as the bus slowed despite the conductor's warning, and he'd held his hand out to her daring her to do the same. She'd put her trust in him and taken a leap of faith.

Her decision to book into O'Mara's had been deliberate. She remembered the old guest house from her younger days. She'd walk past it each morning on her way to where she was employed as a secretary for an accountant. What a funny little man Mr Hart had been with his round glasses and habit of reciting passages from James Joyce's works at random. The work had been straightforward, and it had also afforded her enough money to pay her board to her mother. The small amount left aside went towards her and Leo's wedding fund.

The job was dull, though, certainly not what she'd imagined herself doing when she was a little girl full of big dreams.

This was why as she passed by O'Mara's with its pretty window baskets and shiny nameplate, she liked to imagine all the glamorous lives led inside the grand old townhouse. The la-di-da ladies who'd graced the rooms inside the Georgian manor house wouldn't have had to scrimp and save for their weddings—the weekly treat, a fish and chip supper at Beshoff's.

Oh, the stories those brick walls could tell! Now of a pensionable age, while not wealthy by any means, she was comfortable. She only had herself to look after, and that had meant she'd been able to put aside a tidy amount to ensure she didn't have to go without in her retirement. It was time she saw the inside O'Mara's for herself. There was nowhere else she wished to stay in Dublin—certainly not with her sister, Aideen. At the thought of Aideen, her stomach knotted further, and she put her fork down.

'Is everything alright, Miss Brennan?'

Una was startled. She hadn't seen Mrs Flaherty approach her table once more. She'd been too lost in the past.

'I hope you're enjoying your white pudding. I buy in only the best from Brady's. They're craftsmen when it comes to stuffing their sausage casing.' The overbearing woman in her silly, frilly white apron challenged Una to disagree with her. Her pudgy arms crossed over a ridiculously oversized bosom.

She didn't have the energy to be argumentative, not today. 'It's perfectly fine, thank you.' To prove her point, she picked up her fork and popped the pudding in her mouth. She was sure it was more than perfectly fine. She was sure it was sweet and creamy and delicious, but to her, it tasted like sawdust. Nevertheless, she chewed resolutely, willing Mrs Flaherty to bustle off back to where she'd come from.

The pantomime obviously satisfied the cook because with a curt, 'I'm glad you're enjoying it,' she waddled off back to the kitchen, leaving her to dwell once more on what lay ahead today. There was no window to gaze out of here in the dining room. She supposed it would have once been used not just as the kitchen area but for service and laundry too. Either way, the black and white photographs of bygone days in Dublin lining the walls weren't proving enough of a distraction.

Her mind wouldn't stop pondering how fifty years had passed so quickly. They had, though, and Christmas after Christmas had rolled by without her spending it with her family. She'd always assumed she'd patch things up at some point, but there had never been a right time. Sometimes it felt like she'd simply closed her eyes for a moment, and when she'd opened them, she found herself transformed into the woman she was now. Where had that girl whose future was mapped out as bright and shiny as a new penny vanished to? That girl had taken what she thought lay ahead for granted, hers for the taking. There'd be a handsome husband, children clinging to her skirts, and a house with an electric cooker and no outdoor privy! Instead, she was a woman with aches and pains, pushing seventy, who, if she were to be honest with herself, was lonely.

She'd vowed fifty years ago to never set foot in Dublin again. A promise she'd made in anger and one she hadn't felt able to shy away from until now.

Chapter 6

T he dining room began to empty, and Mr Walsh announced to Aisling he needed to get a move on too.
Although he confided, he'd much prefer to while away his
day relaxing in O'Mara's with herself or the bonny Bronagh
to keep him company. Oh yes, he lamented theatrically, if
his time was his own, he'd happily whisk his favourite ladies
across to the Green for a quiet meander around the gardens.

Aisling told him good-naturedly to get on his way and to be
sure to pick up some cakes from the not long opened Queen of
Tarts on Dame Street. 'It's out of your way, but it's a lovely day
for a walk, and if their chocolate fudge cake doesn't sweeten
your sister, nothing will!' She sensed beneath all his bluster
where his sister was concerned there was an abiding affection.
Why else would he come so religiously each year?

'Chocolate fudge cake, you say?'

'The best chocolate fudge cake.'

He tapped the side of his nose before doffing his hat.
'Thanks for the tip, pet. I'll bring you a slice back.'

Aisling set about helping Mrs Flaherty clear the remaining
tables—all the while listening to her mumblings about that
wagon of a woman. Aisling assumed she was referring to Miss
Brennan, who'd barely touched her breakfast. She knew Mrs
Flaherty always took it personally if food was left on a plate.

By the time she'd moved on to her familiar monologue on that fecking fox, Aisling had begun to wipe the tables down. She glanced at the time; the breakfast service had another hour to run. By her count, there was only the businessman in Room 7 and the Petersons in Room 3, who were yet to make an appearance. She promised Mrs Flaherty, as she always did, to do something about the fox while fully intending to do nothing. Their bin had been visited regularly of a night time for as long as Aisling could recall. If not by Mr Fox exactly, then by his predecessors.

She'd seen him a handful of times, furtively edging his way across the courtyard before industriously nudging the bin lid off and helping himself to the day's leftovers. Sure, his untidy habits left a lot to be desired, but he did keep the mouse population down, and she'd loved Roald Dahl's Fantastic Mr Fox as a child. The fox was staying.

'Aisling, go and check on that lazy lump, Ita. I can manage here now. I need to write my shopping list.'

Aisling knew when she was being dismissed, and she knew better than to protest. It was supposed to be making up Room 9, the double Mr and Mrs Miller had vacated. The thought of geeing her up did not put a spring in her step as she climbed the stairs to the third floor. There was no lift in O'Mara's, and for those that couldn't manage the stairs, Room 1 was the best option. Aisling reckoned running up and down between floors all day was more effective and economical than any gym. Her heels had the bonus of not just giving her several inches in height but giving her calves a jolly good workout too. If Mr Walsh kept his word and brought her back a slice of cake, she'd best pick up her pace.

The thought of gooey chocolate fudge cake revved her up and she wished, not for the first time, Ita would move at a quicker pace. Moira called her Idle Ita, and it was fitting because, as Mrs Flaherty had just said, she did err on the side of laziness. Aisling strode down the corridor. A close eye had to be kept on her if the rooms were to be made up to O'Mara's high standard.

Ita Finnegan had worked at the guesthouse for just over two years. It had been her Mammy who'd taken her on shortly before retiring from the business. Aisling would argue, given how sick their dad had been at the time, Mammy hadn't been in her right mind when Ita's mam, Kate, approached her. She and Maureen O'Mara were friends of old, so when Kate asked Maureen if she could see her way to find something for Ita to do about the place, she'd felt obliged.

Aisling always got the impression from the younger girl she felt cleaning was beneath her. This was probably due to her insistence on not being referred to as the guesthouse's house-keeper. As it stood, it was a job description Aisling though undeserving, but Ita was adamant she be called by the more grandiose, Director of Housekeeping.

To be fair, she only kept her on because she hadn't done anything wrong per se, and she hated the thought of having to give anyone their marching orders—especially not someone whose mam was friends with her, Mammy.

She wasn't good at confrontation. It came, she reckoned, from her position in the family. Patrick and Roisin had been the rabble-rousers in their younger years, Moira the baby, and so it had fallen to her to be the peacemaker. Mind you, Ita sailed close to the wind at times, but Aisling knew too, given the current climate in the city, a replacement would not be easy to find. Jobs were plentiful, and beggars couldn't be choosers. So, unless she wanted to take on the housekeeping role and explain herself to Mammy and Kate Finnegan, Ita, for the foreseeable future, was here to stay.

She found her sitting on the wingback chair by the window, ignoring the gorgeous view of the Green as she leafed through a magazine. Mrs Miller must have left it behind. She jumped up from the chair when Aisling appeared in the doorway.

'Morning, Ita.' Aisling managed to bite back the snarky, 'hard at it, as usual, I see,' on the tip of her tongue.

'How're you, Aisling? I've done the bathroom, and I was just about to sort the bed.' At least she had the grace to look sheepish as Aisling began pulling the sheets off it in an effort to galvanise her. It had the desired effect.

'Once you've finished in here, Ita, could you check on Rooms eight, six, four, and two, make sure they're all re-stocked, please? We're full occupancy tonight.' She shouldn't have to spell it out after all this time, but if she didn't, their guests were likely to find themselves indisposed with no toilet paper!

Ita made a huffing noise as she balled the sheets and dumped them on the floor.

Give me strength! Aisling rolled her eyes and left her to it. Mammy had made a serious error in judgment when she took that one on. Friendship or no friendship.

———*ell*———

'Bronagh, I'm going to call around to Quinn's. I promised the Freemans I'd make a reservation there for dinner this evening for them, and we're nearly out of his brochures.' She could have just telephoned and made the booking, but truth be told, she needed some fresh air. She was feeling irritated—Ita's snail-like pace always had that effect on her. Bronagh brushed the biscuit crumbs off her sweater and waved Aisling off.

'Be sure and tell Quinn I said hello.'

Bronagh had a soft spot for Quinn Moran. She got giggly and played with her hair a lot whenever he called. He was oblivious to her flirting, which only served to make her even more giggly. Aisling found it amusing to watch, unlike Moira, who was appalled by anyone over the age of thirty engaging in flirtatious banter. 'Sure, it'd be like Mammy trying to have her way with him so it would,' she'd shuddered. 'Bronagh needs to find a man her own age. I might suggest she joins lawn bowls; it's a sea of silver heads.' Moira's tongue could clip a hedge at times, but she did make her laugh. Aisling had told her that Bronagh was only in her mid-fifties and that lawn bowls was having a resurgence with the younger generation, to which she'd replied tongue firmly in cheek, 'it would be right up Bronagh's alley then.'

'I will,' Aisling tossed back over her shoulder now as she turned the brass knob and opened the door. She shut it behind her before the wind got a chance to catch it. One of the familiar Hop-on Hop-off red Dublin tour buses whooshed past. There was a handful of hardy tourists huddled upstairs, cameras at the ready as they braved the elements. She paused to gaze wistfully across the road to the tree-lined park. It wouldn't be long before the leaves began to fall. When was the last time she'd taken a book and stretched out on the grass on the Green? She'd missed the boat there this year; it was too cold to do so now.

She used to love losing herself in a good story. She'd let the world pass her by making the most of the sunshine like any good Irish woman would—turning a blind eye to the luminous white male chests on display. Aisling knew the answer to her question. The last time she'd picked up a book and whiled away a leisurely few hours on the Green lost in someone else's story was when she'd come home to O'Mara's on her holidays. This was an anomaly, given her job had always felt like one big holiday to her.

Back then, Dad had been well, and Mammy would shoo her away once she'd helped out with the breakfast, telling her, 'Look, you're due a break Aisling, go read your book.' She'd shake her head, 'How I wound up with such a bookworm is beyond me. You've never been any different, though—always a dreamer. Right from when you were little, your nose was buried in some book or other.'

It was true. She'd once hidden in the old dumb waiter with a torch to escape her chores—that's how desperate she'd been to finish whatever it was she'd been reading at the time!

Those were happy days before Dad got sick, and she'd come home for good. She'd stopped reading then, and there'd been no time for lazy afternoons laying on a grassy, sunlit patch on the Green because Mammy's time had been sucked up taking care of Dad, and she'd needed all Aisling's help.

There was only one person to blame for her lack of work/life balance this last year, though. Well, two, herself and Marcus. Mammy and her sisters were right when they said she wanted to be busy. It was her choice to throw herself into the routine of the guesthouse's daily tasks. She did so to avoid thinking. It hadn't worked, of course. You couldn't bury your hurts.

The breeze was arctic, and she shivered before deciding if she walked briskly enough; she'd soon warm up. She set off following the Green around to Baggot Street. She was oblivious to the admiring glances from the women she passed who'd love to be able to stride along like Aisling O'Mara could in her blue patent leather high heels.

Chapter 7

♥

Aisling had always felt the tie to O'Mara's more keenly than her siblings. It was funny then that she'd been the first to leave it. She'd needed to get away after college, make a fresh start somewhere else.

She continued on her way, dodging a young man whose nose was buried in a guidebook. His backpack was so big it made her think of a tortoise with a shell on its back. For a moment, she felt a pang, envying his freedom.

As a child, it had been her, in between frantically turning the pages of a book who'd followed their Mammy and dad as they went about their daily routine. She was eager to learn the ropes of running the popular guest house. She figured it was her love of stories that made her feel so strongly about O'Mara's. The old manor house abounded with them thanks to their guests. All of whom came from different walks of life and had different tales to tell as to their reasons for coming to stay. She'd felt, and still did, for that matter, such a sense of pride that the house had been in their family for so many generations.

Aisling was lost in her thoughts as she reached the busy intersection and joined the cluster of people all waiting to cross. If she hadn't come home, then she wouldn't have met Marcus and put old ghosts to rest. Was it better to have loved and lost, as the old saying went, than never to have loved at all? She'd loved twice, and she didn't know the answer. As her eyes alighted on Boots, her deep thoughts were diverted as she remembered she was currently using her finger to gouge out what was left in her lipstick. She'd pop in now and buy a new one—and that was when she saw him.

Chapter 8

O h, Jaysus, it was Marcus; she was sure of it! It was as
though just by thinking of him, she'd conjured him up.
What was he doing in Dublin? He was supposed to be miles
away from her in Cork—not waiting at the lights to cross
Baggot Street. She must be seeing things. When he'd first left,
she used to think she saw him all the time. There'd been times
she'd thought she was going around the twist seeing these
Marcus look-alikes everywhere. The mind can play funny
tricks, and that was what it must be doing now.

Aisling peered around the burly man she was standing
behind, but a bus rumbled past, obscuring her view. It had
only been a glimpse; maybe it wasn't him. She was having
a Marcus-look-alike relapse, that's all. She'd close her eyes
for a tick, and when she opened them again, she'd realise it
was a stranger who had a similar look about him. It was her
subconscious telling her to stop poring over his letters and
move on.

She squeezed her eyes shut and, then opening them,
peeped around the burly man again. Feck, feck, feck. It was
definitely him; he was wearing the Oasis shirt she'd bought for
him from their concert under his jacket. It was the most rock
'n' roll he ever got wearing that shirt. She felt herself spiral
into fight-or-flight mode as her senses went into overdrive.

Her heart began pounding and her skin prickled with cold, clammy sweat. What should she do? She'd never been much of a fighter, and instinctively she wanted to run. To turn and run as fast as she could, back to the guesthouse, locking the door behind her to keep the big bad wolf out.

Marcus would see her if she made a holy show of herself by sprinting down St Stephen's Green. He hadn't spotted her yet. She was sure of it and, without thinking it through, Aisling veered off to her right. She kept her head lowered as she ducked and dived her way down the road heading into the sanctuary of O'Brien's sandwich bar.

The lunchtime queue was stretching long but thankfully hadn't reached the door, and she tagged onto the end of it behind two girls in office wear. The mundaneness of their conversation, what would have more calories a chicken Caesar wrap or a tuna melt? helped her to breathe and focus her thoughts. He must have been going to see her at the guesthouse. There was no other reason for him to be on fecking Baggot Street, for feck's sake! Calm down, Aisling.

She should have replied to his stupid letters and told him there wasn't a hope in hell of them getting back together, not after what he'd done. She hadn't, though; she'd let them pile up. Locking them away in the bureau drawer to pull out and angst over when no one was around, and now he was fecking well here.

She'd have to face the music sometime. She couldn't go home. Besides, a spark of anger flared; why should she feel like she had to go into hiding because he'd decided he'd made a mistake? Look at her now, for feck's sake. Swearing her head off, albeit silently, but if Mammy could hear her, she'd be threatening to wash her mouth out, and she was hiding in a fecking sandwich shop!

She shouldn't allow him to affect her like this. She should have brazened it out, greeted him coolly, and made him feel foolish for wasting his time coming back to Dublin. Now the shock was wearing off; she mulled the situation over. Perhaps it was a good thing him coming to see her. If she talked to him face-to-face, it might give her closure, and she'd finally stop having nightmares about white dresses with bodices of Irish lace and people staring at her sympathetically before whispering about her behind her back.

The queue shuffled forward. It was all well and good being brave and having bold thoughts of bringing her ex-fiancé down a peg or two as she hid in O'Brien's. How strong she'd be when they did meet was an entirely different matter altogether. His very presence had always affected her, given her a thrill each time she saw him.

She had no intention of ordering a sandwich of any description, so excusing herself, she pushed past the people who'd lined up behind her and ventured back out to the street. The coast was clear, so she continued down the road. Despite no sign of him, she was relieved when she spied the brass nameplate, Quinn's Bistro arching over the doorway of the whitewashed, ground-floor restaurant.

There was a gorgeous profusion of pansies decorating the windows on either side of the entrance, and she knew credit for the beautiful floral displays didn't lie with Quinn. The hanging baskets overflowing with vibrant, pink, and purple lobelia were lovingly tended by his maître d', Alasdair. He'd told her when she'd complimented him on his green fingers that he'd been head gardener for the lord and lady of a great house in a previous life.

A dose of Alasdair would take her mind off Marcus. He was one of a kind, with his flamboyant style and insistence on sharing the details of his past lives with anybody who cared, or didn't care for that matter, to listen. He was, also, Quinn said, fabulous at his job. The punters loved him even if he had been a Viking warrior back in the days when they'd plundered Dublin!

She paused to eye the blackboard outside, liking the sound of slow-cooked beef and Guinness stew. Her mouth watered, despite the fright she'd just had as her gaze darted down the handwritten menu, settling on a Baileys Irish cheesecake for dessert. She'd always loved her food and been prone to comfort eating. She was the girl who would get caught with her fingers raking through a tub of ice cream after a teenage drama. When Dad had been sick, she'd piled on the pounds. Then when he'd passed, she'd lost all interest in food despite Quinn's best efforts to keep her fed. He'd been such a good friend to her, to all the family. She'd lost her appetite when Marcus left too. Quinn had been a steady shoulder then as well.

She'd gotten her appetite back eventually, and sometimes comfort eating was the order of the day. She'd take Quinn up on his offer of dinner on the house. She needed a heart-to-heart with Leila. Her pragmatic friend would tell her what she should do where Marcus fecking coward McDonagh was concerned. Besides, it had been too long since they'd last caught up.

The cheery red door to the bistro opened, emitting a burst of noisy chatter from inside. A girl around Moira's age, in a skirt so tight it would surely split if she bent over, tottered out. An older man in a well-cut suit, looking very pleased with himself, followed behind her. There was a furtiveness about them, and Aisling watched them from under her lashes. She'd put money on wandering hands under the table as they waited for their Quinn's burger and bangers 'n' mash. She found herself composing one of her letters. The image of a world-weary, middle-aged woman who'd been let down by her husband sprang to mind. She was sitting at her kitchen table, pen poised over a writing pad.

Dear Aisling,

My husband often takes his young secretary out for lunch. He says it's thanking her for being so efficient. He comes home smelling of perfume and bangers 'n' mash. It's a cliché, but I think they're having an affair. What should I do? Confront him about my suspicions or continue to bury my head in the sand?

Yours faithfully,

Wronged Woman

God, Mammy always said her talents were wasted—with your imagination, Aisling, and your love of books, she'd say, you should have been a writer. Sure, look at the success that Keyes woman is having. She also said she should have been on the stage when she had one of her dramatic outbursts. She said it quite a lot come to think of it. Instead, she'd qualified with a much more practical Diploma in Tourism. It didn't stop her imagination from running riot, though, and it was getting out of hand. She was seeing philanderers everywhere these days. These two had probably had a perfectly innocent business luncheon. She changed her mind a beat later as the man planted his hand firmly on the girl's derrière—dirty old sod.

Shaking her head, she pushed open the bistro door and stepped inside the humming interior. She loved Quinn's with its exposed bricks and low timber beams. The atmosphere was always inviting, especially come winter when the log fire was roaring. What she loved most of all, though, was the aroma of garlic and onions that hung in the air. It called to her to take a load off and make herself at home.

Alasdair looked up from where he was flicking through the reservation book. 'Aisling O'Mara, my Dublin Rose! My one true love.' He clapped his hands like a small child, having been told they were going to McDonald's for dinner, before mincing toward her. He lunged at her cheeks, kissing the left, then the right side, before resting his hands on either side of her shoulders. 'You know, ours was the greatest love affair of all.'

This was what she needed; Aisling smiled at him, playing along with the banter.

'I was a penniless artist. You were the beautiful daughter of wealthy parents. We met on an epic voyage at sea, but sadly it ended in tragedy.' His hand fluttered to his chest.

'Hmm, tell me, Alasdair, did your name happen to be Jack and mine Rose?'

'You feel the connection too.'

'I saw Titanic twice.' She grinned. He was a tonic. 'Now then, Jack, would you have a table for four available for tonight at five-thirty? It's short notice, but our guests asked me for a dinner recommendation at breakfast this morning, and you know Quinn's is always my first port of call.'

'For which we are eternally grateful, and if there is no room ma petite fleur, we will make room.'

'Thank you. Oh, and I need some brochures while I'm here too; we've nearly run out.'

His dark head bobbed beneath the counter, and Aisling waited while he crouched down to peer inside the cupboard under the cash register. He popped back up like a jack-in-the-box with a stack of pamphlets for her as the phone began to trill and the door to the street opened.

'Sorry, Alasdair, silly time to call in. You answer that, and I'll say a quick hello to Quinn.'

He blew her a kiss before calling out a 'Hello, darlings; I'll be with you in two ticks,' to the man and woman who'd just walked in.

Aisling left him to multi-task with the phone and customers as she weaved her way around the tables. She smiled hello at Paula, the waitress, whose notepad was in hand as she made her way over to a table full of boisterous women. Seeing them all laughing, having a great craic, reinforced Aisling's resolve to make a date with Leila the moment she got home. She crossed her fingers. Hopefully, Marcus would be long gone when she got back, for today at least.

Chapter 9

A isling pushed open the swinging doors and was assailed with a deliciously rich waft of meats and vegetables simmering away inside the frenetic kitchen. Quinn was over by the gas hobs, his head down in conversation with the sous-chef as they discussed whatever it was bubbling in one of the many pots being tended to. His blond hair was just visible beneath his hat. The sous-chef spotted her first, giving Quinn a nudge.

His face she saw was flushed from the steam, and he needed a shave, which she'd be sure to tell him, but it was nice that his blue eyes lit up at the sight of her. 'Aisling! How's the form?' He wiped his hands on his chequered pants before striding over to wrap her in a hello hug. She hugged him back just as warmly.

'Grand,' she lied. 'It's a bad time to call, I know, right on lunchtime. I don't know what I was thinking other than I fancied a bit of air. I had to make a reservation for some guests and pick up more of these, so that's my excuse.' She held up the pamphlets. She wouldn't mention having seen Marcus from afar less than fifteen minutes ago. She knew Quinn's opinion of him, and it wasn't high. Come to think of it; it hadn't exactly been glowing before Marcus had jilted her. The feeling between the two men was mutual, and she'd never figured out why. Neither had said anything, but she could tell by their macho posturing when they were in one another's company.

'How's your mam getting on?' she asked. Mrs Moran had suffered a stroke a month back. Aisling had dropped a bunch of flowers around a few weeks ago. It had been a shock to see her looking frail and well, old, especially when she'd always been so sprightly. Aisling hoped, given time, she would get back to how she was before it happened.

He rubbed at the stubble on his chin. 'Alright. She's definitely slowed down, and she gets frustrated, you know, having to rely on Dad or me to take her everywhere. The doctor's not given her the all-clear to drive yet.'

'Give her my love, won't you?'

'I will do. And what about your mam—is she enjoying being by the sea?'

It was a sign they were getting older, Aisling thought, them asking after each other's Mammy's like so. There was a time—it didn't seem all that long ago—they'd have been moaning how banjaxed they were after Thursday night's rave-up.

'Ah, she loves it, Quinn. I swear everything in her wardrobe is nautical stripes these days, and she's even taken to wearing boat shoes. I never thought I'd see my Mammy in flats, but fair play to her, she'd look a bit odd in her striped tops and white pants with a pair like this on her feet.' She gestured to her impractical footwear.

'The thing is, she's never even been on a boat other than the Dún Laoghaire to Holyhead ferry. Mind you, I've heard her making noises about sailing lessons, so; it's only a matter of time.' Aisling shook her head. 'She's gone a bit mad taking up art classes and joining everything from the golf club to bowls. Oh, and she's on about the yacht club too now. She's managed to slot Moira and me into her busy calendar for lunch tomorrow.'

Quinn smiled gently. 'She's a good woman, your mam, and to be fair now, she nursed your poor dad until the end. Losing someone you expected to spend your retirement with would change your perspective on things. I expect she needs to keep herself busy.'

'When did you get so wise?' Aisling's eyes prickled unexpectedly with tears, and she blinked them away. She didn't want to stand here snivelling in Quinn's busy kitchen, but Dad's death, even though it had been a blessed relief when the time came, was still raw, and the pain snuck up on her when she least expected it. For Mammy to have grabbed life by the horns with quite as much vigour as she had was a shock too. She'd no desire to spend the rest of her days mouldering in O'Mara's with her memories, she'd said. Then she'd signed on the dotted line for a modern two-bedroom apartment with views out over Howth Harbour.

'I don't know about wise,' Quinn said, his eyes flicking over to the kitchen hand, who was taking advantage of his boss being occupied to check his mobile phone instead of cracking on with the chopping of vegetables. 'Observant maybe.'

'You're that alright. You never did miss much. Remember when you told me that Diarmuid and Orla from our old college gang had the hots for each other?'

He nodded.

'And I said you needed your eyes checking because Orla fancied Diarmud about as much as I liked Bono.' Aisling could never understand what all the fuss was about where the Irish rocker was concerned. It was something she'd been verbal about after a few pints of Guinness from time to time.

'And now they're married.'

'With four children, no less.'

They both laughed.

Paula pushed past, calling out an order.

'Does your dinner on the house offer still stand? Because I'm due to catch up with Leila, and I was eyeing the slow-cooked Guinness and beef stew on the board out the front before I came in.'

'Of course! Let me know a time, and I'll make sure we've got a table.'

'Thanks, Quinn, and you'll join us, I hope,' she said, before adding, 'It'd be good to sit down and have a proper natter. Anyway, I'll leave you to it.'

'I'd like that. It's been too long since we three had a catch-up. It was good to see you, Aisling. Take care now. Remember me to your mam too.'

'And me to yours. Oh, and Quinn—'

He raised a questioning eyebrow.

'Be sure and shave tonight, won't you?'

'What? Are you not keen on my rugged Brad Pitt Fight Club look? All the girls love him.'

'You're more a Ronan Keating type than Brad Pitt.'

'Ah well, the girls love him too.'

Aisling grinned. There was a time when she'd been smitten with Quinn Moran back in their college days. She still had a soft spot for him. It was something she'd learned to live with because he'd never looked at her in that way. She never let on how she felt for fear of ruining their friendship. Then she'd gone abroad for work, needing to put some space between him and her mixed-up feelings. All of that was a lifetime ago, ancient history. 'Bronagh sends her best. And remember to shave!' She mimicked shaving her jawline before turning and exiting out the swinging doors.

Aisling waved goodbye to Alasdair. She had to laugh hearing him tell a snappily dressed customer that he was sure they'd met each other before when they'd both been gentry landowners in the seventeenth century.

—ell—

Quinn watched Aisling leave, a wistful look on his face. Despite his swagger, there was only one girl he wanted to love him, but it had never occurred to her to look at him in that way. His love for Aisling had been a slow burn on his part. He'd been aware she was gorgeous, but still, their relationship had begun platonically with a friendship formed at college. They got around in the same group, and all had a great craic together. Then the realisation had hit one night as they neared graduation. Somewhere along the way, his feelings had taken root and grown into something deeper.

It was a million little things, like the way she tossed her head back and laughed, the slight dimpling in her cheek when she smiled. The sparkle in her eyes when she told a story or the way she'd leap off her stool to do the actions whenever the Macarena came on.

He could have said something back then on one of their many nights out, but he was scared. If she didn't feel the same way, he'd lose her friendship because there'd be no going back to the way things were once he'd crossed that line. So, he said nothing.

'Quinn, the water's boiling away on the potatoes.'

He jerked out of his reverie and did what he always did after he'd seen Aisling, threw himself back into his work.

Chapter 10

Aisling dragged her heels all the way up St Stephen's Green, feeling like Mr Fox as she furtively scanned the faces heading towards her. All three storeys of O'Mara's loomed over her, and she was relieved to have reached the guest house with no sighting of Marcus. She stood outside staring at the window box with its profusion of purple and yellow pansies, debating whether she should try to sneak a peek in through the windows. The problem was solved for her when the door opened and Mr Peterson, camera in hand, appeared. 'I forgot this,' he said in his posh Queen's English as he held the door for her. She had no choice but to venture inside.

'Thank you,' she said. 'You and Mrs Peterson be sure to have a lovely afternoon.'

'We will, thank you, dear.'

'There you are!' Bronagh's jet-black head with its tell-tale zebra stripe at the roots bobbed up from behind the computer. Her brown eyes, rimmed with a generous application of black liner, were ginormous and round. 'You'll never guess who had the brass neck to bowl in here while you were out.'

'Let me take a wild stab in the dark. Marcus?'

Bronagh's eyes shrank back to their normal size. 'Have you seen him then?'

'No. Well, yes, but from a safe distance, and he didn't see me. He was crossing Baggot Street, so I guessed this was where he was heading. I went and hid in O'Brien's.'

'If I'd known you were ducking in there, I would have got you to pick me up one of their chicken wraps. They're lovely.' She looked down at the plate next to the keyboard on which a sad-looking sandwich triangle sat. 'I don't even like tomato, but its low calorie.'

'Bronagh, food was the last thing on my mind. What did you say to him?'

'I told him you'd gone to live in an ashram in India.'

'You didn't?'

'I'd have liked to. I'd have liked to tell him to feck off too, excuse my French but, after what he did—'

'Bronagh, just tell me what you said.'

She picked up her sandwich. 'I told him you were out doing errands and wouldn't be back in until later. And I might have told him you were out tonight too. I didn't want him thinking you spend your nights sitting up there,' she pointed to the ceiling, 'pining for him.'

'I don't.' She did. 'But thanks.' She couldn't stop herself asking, 'How did he seem?'

'Not his usual cock o' the walk self.' Her eyes narrowed. 'Aisling, do not feel sorry for the man. He doesn't deserve it.'

'I wasn't.' That much was true, at least. 'I'm going to head upstairs for a bit, make a few phone calls while it's quiet. I'll leave you to your tomato sandwich.'

Bronagh muttered something about soggy bread and feck-less men under her breath as Aisling powered up the stairs. She'd phone Leila now while she was on her mind. Besides, she needed to offload her news on someone who'd helped pick up the pieces after he left.

—ee—

'Good afternoon, Love Leila Bridal Planning, Leila speaking.'

'Leila, it's me.'

'Who? I don't recognise that voice?'

'Don't be an eejit. I know it's been a while. I just saw Marcus.'

'No!'

'Yes.'

'Feck.'

'Exactly.'

'He looked the same. I was hoping he might have turned into a short fat garden gnome, but he hasn't.' Aisling curled up in her favourite chair. It was dappled with pools of sunlight from the window behind it, and she filled her friend in on her last few hours.

'Think Bono, Ash. I can't believe the nerve of the man. Why's he back now?'

'Well, there's something I haven't told you. I haven't told anybody. He's been writing to me.'

'Aisling. You're a soft touch, so you are. I hope you haven't replied.'

'No, but that's the thing. If I had, I mean, if I'd spelled it out, there wasn't going to be a second chance he might have stayed in Cork. Oh, Leila, what am I going to do? I don't trust myself to be around him. I'll either rage at him, or sob and I don't know what would be worse.'

'Definitely the sobbing. Run with the rage. Tell him the truth, Ash, tell him how much he hurt you, how he broke your trust, and it can't be fixed.' Her friend's tone was steely.

But could it? Aisling wondered. What if he meant what he'd been saying in his letters? What if she were to forgive him and try again?

'Look, I'm sorry, Ash, but I have to go, I've a bridezilla to meet in fifteen minutes, and she's already teetering on the edge. She went overboard with the teeth whitening, and her poor fiancé is going to have to wear sunglasses on their big day.'

'Tell her to drink lots of coffee and red wine between now and then.'

They both sniggered.

'Before you go, the other reason I rang was to invite you to dinner on Quinn at Quinn's. When are you free?'

'As incredible as it might seem, my social calendar is surprisingly empty aside from attending other people's weddings. How about Sunday?'

'Seven?'

'See you then.'

Aisling hung up. The three-bedroomed space, with its kitchen and a large living area, had always seemed full to the brim when they were growing up, despite the generous proportions. Right now, though, it just seemed empty and full of echoes.

The apartment had once upon a time, in the Georgian's heyday, been the top floor servant quarters. The O'Mara's had been quite well-to-do back then, but those days were long gone, and it was hard to imagine leading such a pampered life now. Aisling spied Moira's dressing gown. It was in a crumpled heap at the end of the sofa, her breakfast bowl and coffee mug abandoned on the coffee table. It was a lifestyle her sister, with her penchant for not picking up after herself, would adapt well to.

It had been her grandparents who'd converted the many rooms into a guest house. Hard times had hit, and it was the only way to keep the grand old building in the family. When they'd died, it had passed down the line to her father when Cormac, his older brother, had left for America.

She was too small to remember a time when she hadn't called the manor house home. She loved it. The rooms possessed an olde-worlde charm with their myriad nooks and crannies. Even the dumb waiter was still in working order. It ran all the way from the basement kitchen to their apartment and had been a favourite hiding place as a child. Most of all, though, she loved the view from their living room to the bustling street below and the peaceful Green beyond.

Her eyes settled on the bureau drawer, and she unfurled herself from the chair, feeling an almost magnetic pull toward it. She wandered over and retrieved the key on automatic pilot as she unlocked the drawer. She stared at the bundle of letters for a moment before picking them up. Sitting down at the table, she opened the last one Marcus had sent her.

She knew the sentiments by heart; they all said variations of the same thing. He was sorry. He should never have left her. The biggest regret of his life was not having the courage to marry her, but the biggest cliché of them all was Marcus had gotten cold feet.

Her eyes misted over as she read over the words she'd already reread time and time.

Chapter 11

♥

One year earlier or thereabouts

'**B**reathe in, Aisling. I'm wondering if you should have gone for size twelve,' Leila said, wriggling the zipper slowly up Aisling's back.

Aisling gulped in air and held her tummy in as tightly as she could. 'No, I've still got two weeks to lose a few pounds. I'll stop sniffing around Quinn's kitchen, and I might try the soup diet. I like a bit of leek and potato soup.' She looked at her maid of honour. She was a picture in the soft blue, almost grey dress she'd picked out for her bridesmaids. The colour suited Leila's light blue eyes and blonde hair. It was down around her shoulders now, but on the day, it would be worn up.

Moira, who'd wanted her, Leila, and Roisin to wear her favourite colour lilac, was sitting in the chair in the corner of the expansive plush dressing room of Ivory Bridal Couture. She looked bored as she fiddled with her phone. She was always on the thing, thumb frantically pushing buttons. Aisling couldn't see the attraction of always being contactable and had not succumbed to a mobile phone. Meanwhile, Roisin, who'd carefully relayed her measurements over the phone, was arriving in Dublin next week and would have her final fitting then. She'd wanted pink dresses, but Aisling had stuck to her guns because as soon as she'd laid eyes on the simple, blue silk cowl neck dress, she'd fallen in love. Besides, the colour would look well on all three of them.

Leila moved Aisling's hair out the way as she finally wrested the zip into place. She stepped back to admire her friend's reflection in the big floor-to-ceiling mirror at the far end of the dressing room. 'There, now look at you. I think you're the most beautiful bride-to-be I've ever seen—and I've seen a few.'

'Even if I do need to lose a couple of pounds,' Aisling laughed. 'And besides, I think you might be a little biased.'

Moira piped up, 'Five pounds at least, Aisling, and if you're going to do the soup diet, I think they're supposed to be clear soups, not potato and cream-based.'

Aisling poked her tongue out at her. She did have a point, though, and Moira was in her good books for putting Mammy off. She'd not wanted her coming along with them to this their final fitting. Mammy meant well, but Maureen O'Mara was a woman of many words. Which was a polite way of saying sometimes she had too much to say for herself.

She was bossy where her three girls were concerned. A tiger mama. She'd driven poor Roisin demented in the lead-up to her big day. When her sister had rung to congratulate Aisling on her engagement, she'd added sagely, 'As your big sister who's been there and done that, Ash, I want you to promise me something.'

'What is it?' Aisling wasn't promising anything until she knew what she was in for.

'Trust me on this. Don't let Mammy come with you to choose your dress or to any of your fittings. Do you remember our holy communion?'

'How could I forget? Mammy turned into a monster. We had to have the biggest and best dresses. We looked like tiny versions of Princess Diana on her wedding day. Dad was going mad over the cost of it all. Who knew she was so competitive?'

'Exactly, she was terrible when you were seven years old and committing yourself to Christ. Imagine what she'll be like now you're thirty-four marrying a flesh and blood man—*and* she had you pegged as being on the shelf. That's extra interfering points right there, and it'll be worse for you now her time's her own. Mark my words, you give her an inch when it comes to your wedding; she'll have you in a frothy white monstrosity. If she'd had her way, I would have wound up wearing a blancmange. Jaysus, the row we had in Abigail's Brides to Be, I thought Abigail was going to bar the pair of us.'

She'd heeded Roisin's words of wisdom despite feeling a little mean at not including Mammy. To be fair, though, she had plenty to keep her otherwise occupied. There was her plethora of social groups, and in her rare downtime, she was throwing a lot of energy into her mother-of-the-bride dress. She'd confided this was because she wasn't going to be outdone by Mrs McDonagh, who, what with Marcus being an only child, was sure to go to town with her outfit. So, with Moira's help, the first opportunity Mammy would have to see her in her dress was on the day itself.

Aisling felt a frisson of sadness as she turned to the left and then to the right. She'd wanted Dad to walk her down the aisle, but instead, his brother Cormac would do the honours. It still took her by surprise from time to time that Dad was no longer with them. It was also hard to believe if she hadn't come back to Dublin to take over O'Mara's, she'd never have met Marcus. Perhaps it was fate's way of softening the blow of losing her father. She blinked back the sudden smarting of tears and turned her mind to the guesthouse for a second. Bronagh would have everything under control, and Nina was perfectly able to manage the quieter evenings. She was grateful to the two women; their reliability and capability left her free to concentrate on this, admiring her dress.

She'd fallen in love with it the moment Niamh, Ivory Couture's owner, had pulled it from the rack. The mermaid trumpet style with its overlay of white Irish lace was not what she'd gone for initially. When she'd daydreamed of her big day, she was always in something princess-like with a tiara; there was always a tiara. Niamh's well-practiced eye had taken in Aisling's curves, however, and gently steered her away from her first choice.

She was so glad she had because Roisin's terminology of looking like a blancmange sprang to mind now. This mermaid trumpet gown was the most gorgeous dress she'd ever worn. It even eclipsed her love for the Prada satin pumps she'd picked out to wear with it. This was her Cinderella dress, and it embraced her hourglass form. Even if she didn't manage to lose those pesky few pounds, she'd be fine on the day so long as she didn't breathe or sit down!

Niamh popped her head in and tweaked the bodice of Aisling's dress so she wasn't revealing quite so much cleavage. She turned her attention to Moira's hem, gesturing for her to stand. Her sister obliged, and a debate raged as to whether it might need to be taken up half an inch. Moira convinced her to leave it as it was by telling her she planned on wearing heels higher than the ones she presently had on so the length wouldn't be an issue.

All the O'Mara women were short. The height gene had gone directly from Dad to Patrick. As such, Maureen, Roisin, Aisling, and Moira all insisted on wearing ankle-breaking heels to even up the odds.

Once Niamh had finished her final titivations, the girls got changed back into their civvies. Leila, pulling on her jeans, suggested a drink on the way home to run through the day itself one last time. Her wedding planning service was her gift to Aisling and one for which she was grateful. There was nobody else she would have trusted to help her pull off the most important day of her life. Certainly not her Mammy!

Moira bowed out, having already made plans to catch up with her friends at a pub where a new band they'd heard good things about was playing. So, Aisling and Leila, arm in arm, made their way down busy O'Connell Street with its Friday night vibe in full swing as people finished work for the week.

'The Gresham? We'll be able to hear ourselves think in there,' Leila suggested, and Aisling agreed.

They found a table in the civilised Writer's Lounge and sat opposite one another chatting until their drinks arrived. A low-calorie vodka soda for Aisling and a pint of Guinness for Leila. She'd ordered a honey-glazed ham sandwich too, and Aisling watched on enviously as she scoffed it down. Leila had hollow legs and never gained a pound. She also never stopped. She was one hundred miles an hour darting here, there, and everywhere as she made sure her clients had the best day of their lives.

Aisling was hardly sedentary, but no matter how many times she trooped up and down the flights of stairs at home, she always seemed to hold on to an extra few pounds. They clung to her rather like a toxic friend she couldn't get rid of. She dabbed at the crumbs left on Leila's plate and popped her finger in her mouth.

Leila produced the folder she'd compiled for Aisling and Marcus's nuptials, and Aisling pored over the booklet for Lisnavagh Castle. The princess dress might have gone, but the castle hadn't, and she was having a tiara that went without saying. Lisnavagh Castle, nestled against the lush green and gold countryside of Wicklow, was dreamy. It was the stuff of fairy tales. She flicked through the glossy pages eagerly, sighing over the picturesque setting. The sun would shine on her day; she was sure of it, just like it was in the pictures she was gazing at.

Mammy had suggested having the reception at O'Mara's like Roisin had. Their guesthouse had done her sister proud on the day, but Aisling lived and worked there; she didn't want to hold her wedding there too. Marcus, who would be moving in after their Maldives honeymoon, agreed with her. At least he hadn't disagreed when she'd stated that as they were paying for the wedding themselves, they should be able to hold it where they wanted. She hadn't felt the least bit guilty booking the extravagant venue. She only planned on doing this once, and she wanted it to be perfect.

Leila and Aisling whiled away a companionable hour discussing seating arrangements. The hot topic; where to put her dad's bite of a sister Aunt Delia? 'I think we should sit her next to Great Aunt Maggie; she's a bit doolally, so Aunt Delia's moaning about the soup not having enough salt or the duck skin not being crispy enough won't faze her.' Aisling announced, pleased with her solution.

Aisling had a slight flush to her cheeks by the time they left the bar and made their way home. It was partly due to the vodka soda, but it was also excitement. She couldn't wait for the sixth of September when she would become Mrs Marcus McDonagh. Leila walked with her across O'Connell Bridge before hugging her goodbye. She would catch the DART from Tara Station to her Blackrock home. The evening was warm despite it officially being autumn now, and the streets around Grafton Street were buzzing with early revellers. The joviality was infectious, and Aisling had a spring in her step. She paused to watch a young violinist playing near Marks & Spencer, fishing around inside her purse for some coins to throw him.

She'd have liked to learn to play an instrument. Mammy had sent her off to piano lessons after school, but like her singing, she'd no natural aptitude for it. She could, however, dance, and standing there caught up in the music, she lost herself in memories recalling how she'd first crossed paths with Marcus.

Aisling had been installed back in her old room at O'Mara's—which she thankfully now had to herself—for two weeks when she met the man she was going to marry. Moira had commandeered what had been Mammy and Dad's bedroom, the largest of the three, and had already managed to make it look as though some sort of clothes bomb had detonated in there.

It was unsettling being home. O'Mara's

felt different without Mammy and Dad buzzing about the place. It was hard to accept that Dad, their lovely, calm, steady father, had passed. That he wasn't here filling the spaces, a strong shoulder always there for them all to lean on.

Aisling didn't like to dwell on the empty spot he'd left behind. It was like poking at the pain with a lance. It would ooze fresh and raw with each prod. It was strange too accepting this new Mammy, a mam without Dad at her side tempering her. The life Aisling had known since gaining her diploma, of flitting from one glorious sunshine destination to another, already seemed a distant memory.

She loved the city she'd been born in, but she hadn't planned on coming back, not for a while at any rate. Hania, where she'd been managing a resort in need of being brought up to speed alongside its competitors, had been a little piece of paradise. The beautiful old town with its brilliant colours and that sky! It melded with the sea in a never-ending panorama of blue.

That was her old life, she told herself. It had never been her real-life, she realised now. Merely a stopgap. There would have come a time when all that globetrotting had gotten tiresome; it was just the decision to come home had been made sooner than she'd planned. It didn't matter how she tried to convince herself coming home was inevitable though, settling back in was easier said than done.

Thinking back on it, the company she worked for had been generous, more than generous, really. They'd allowed her an extended period off to come home and help when Dad's illness was too much for Mammy to cope with. It had helped they were heading into the quiet shoulder season, and she would soon have found herself winging her way to a busier climate anyway—job done. She supposed, in a way, the timing had been convenient for them.

She'd arranged to stay on in Dublin for a week longer following Dad's funeral. It had been, as per his wishes, a simple affair. For once, Mammy had not tried to go bigger and better; she'd honoured his wishes. It was two days later when Maureen O'Mara had thrown a spanner in the works with her announcement that she would not be staying on at the guesthouse without her husband.

They were all there gathered around the dining table, Patrick, Roisin, Moira, and herself—oh, and Colin the Arse had squeezed himself in beside his wife. It was like a scene from a film where the wizened lawyer reads the patriarch's last will and testament. Only there was no lawyer and no will, just Mammy, and she was firm and resolute in her decision. She claimed it wasn't rash; she'd had plenty of time to mull over her future while sitting at Dad's bedside these last few months. They'd discussed it while he was still well enough, she told them. Together they'd amassed a tidy sum over the years; all put away for a rainy day. Now that rainy day had come, and she wanted out.

The cards were laid on the table. Mammy refused to entertain the idea of a stranger managing the place, her argument being O'Mara's had always been a family business. She'd rather sell and divvy up the proceeds than trust their family name to a stranger. If, however, one of her children wished to take over the day-to-day running of the guesthouse, it would stay in the family. This was, of course, the preferable option, although she understood that while building O'Mara's into what it was today had been her and Dad's dream, it might not necessarily be theirs.

Children had a right to follow their own dreams, she proclaimed. It would be sad to sell, to lose the family connection with the building, but when it came down to it, O'Mara's was just a building after all. They were not to feel beholden, she said. Dad had made his peace with whatever choices were made once he'd gone.

Moira was far too flighty for the role, and Mammy had enough trouble without adding her to the list. Roisin had stayed out of the negotiations, not offering an opinion on what should happen with the family business one way or the other—unlike her husband. Her life was in London with the Arse and with little Noah. Her feisty wilful big sister seemed to have morphed into a meek and moany sort since she'd gotten married. Mind you; he was a bossy so-and-so, her brother-in-law. He'd stamp all over single-mindedness. She supposed her sister found it easier to acquiesce than to rock the boat, which left Patrick.

Her brother referred to himself as an entrepreneur. A job description, from what Aisling could see, on a par with being a Director of Housekeeping. It too entailed doing a lot of not very much at all. He spent his time swanning around the city in a flashy car, and in his world, it was important to be seen at the best restaurants and bars on offer somehow though he seemed to make shed loads of money.

Aisling's blood had boiled as she spied the predatory gleam in Patrick's eyes. He looked positively gleeful at the thought of all that freed up equity if the building were sold. Her gaze had swung in Colin the Arse's direction, and she'd seen the greedy glimmer in his eyes too. That same afternoon once everybody had dispersed to mull over what had been said, Aisling had taken herself quietly off. The decision had been an easy one. She telephoned her employers to thank them for their generosity and kindness toward her during her father's illness. She had, however, decided she was needed permanently at home. She wouldn't be coming back.

Thank goodness for Leila and Quinn. She'd have been lost without their friendship and support. The years away had given her perspective on those mixed-up feelings she had for Quinn. They were friends—it was all they'd ever be, and it would have to be enough. So, she'd picked up with her two old pals as though she'd only seen them yesterday.

It was Leila who'd suggested they head along and check out Monday night salsa dance classes. It would do them all good to stretch their cultural boundaries, she said. And that's where she'd met Marcus.

Chapter 12

♥

To learn Latin American dance was not something Aisling had ever thought about doing, but it could be fun. The exercise would be good too, a much more fun way of keeping fit than pounding it out at a gym. Not that she had any intention of doing that! Salsa could be something positive that would take her away from her grief and O'Mara's for a few hours at least.

'C'mon, Ash, it will be a good craic, so it will,' Leila pressured. 'And Quinn won't come unless you do; he said he's two left feet and he's only prepared to humiliate himself if you are too. Say you'll give it a go.'

'But what would I wear?'

'Something comfortable and practical, but sexy and evocative at the same time—you know, like Latin music. Then again, you don't want to distract your partner by wearing something too sexy. He might be so busy staring down your top he stamps on your foot or something.'

'Not if I'm partnering with Quinn, he'd be oblivious if I were dancing the tango topless, and that really didn't help, Leila.'

Leila giggled. 'I just imagined him in tight black trousers shaking a castanet and wiggling his hips around like yer man Ricky Martin. And who said he's going to be your partner? I'm the one trying to convince him to come.'

'Ah, but he won't come unless I agree to go too.'

'Fair play. I hope you're coordinated. Whoever you wind up partnering with could lose a toe with one of your stiletto heels.'

'Shake your bon-bon!' Aisling sang, and she and Leila collapsed in a fit of snorting giggles. When they'd sobered, Leila announced, 'I'm going to get in the swing of it by wearing a fitted black dress, and I might put a rose behind my ear.'

'You're thinking of the tango, not salsa, you eejit.'

'Oh, so I am. Ah well, we'll figure it out,' she laughed.

'Looks like I'm going to be learning salsa. You'd better tell Quinn there's no getting out of it now!'

The classes were held in a dance studio hidden away above a cluster of shops on Dame Street. The businesses were all closed for the day by the time Aisling, Leila, and Quinn, who'd been dragging his heels all the way there, arrived at the address. They opened the door with the nameplate that said they had come to the right place, Lozano's Dance Studio, and Leila led the way up the stairs. Aisling brought up the rear, making sure Quinn, who thankfully had opted for sweat pants, not tight trousers, and was not carrying a castanet so far as she could tell, didn't try to make a getaway.

A light shone under the double doors at the top of the landing. They could hear a fast Latin beat reverberating as they hovered for a moment. They looked from one to the other, uncertain as to whether they should knock or barrel straight in. Leila opted to be bold and pushed open the doors. The trio blinked as they found themselves in a brightly lit studio. There was a vast polished parquet dance floor, a mirrored floor to ceiling wall, and on the side of the room with the windows overlooking Dame Street below, a stretch of bar.

Aisling's eyes alighted on a woman who looked like she should be at a ballet class. She was dressed in a leotard and tights, with a wraparound skirt worn over, her right leg stretched out along the bar as she warmed up. *Just how physical was this going to be?* She wondered, eyeing the rest of her classmates; they were a mixed bag.

A group of girls around Moira's age were giggling in the far corner, aware they were being eyed by the cluster of twenty-something young men. There were two middle-aged couples in deep conversation, here to spice up their marriages, perhaps. A younger couple had their heads bent together, and she looked as though she was giving him a talking to. Aisling could see the light catching the sparkly diamond on the girl's finger as she prodded him in the chest, and she automatically penned one of her imaginary letters.

Dear Aisling,

My fiancé and I are getting married in two months. I want us to perform salsa at the reception to entertain our guests, instead of a boring traditional first dance. I've enrolled us in lessons, and he is making the biggest song and dance about going. If he can't do something simple like learn a few new dance steps for me, how does that bode for our married life together?

Yours faithfully,
Getting Cold Feet

—— *ele* ——

A couple who looked to be around Mammy's age were taking a twirl on the floor at the far end of the studio. She watched them for a beat, their ease with each other giving away the fact they'd danced like this in their youth. It made her think how unfair it was Mammy and Dad had been robbed of the chance to while away their golden retirement years together learning to salsa. Mind you, Moira would have had something to say about her parents gyrating against one another on a dance floor. The thought of the look on her face were she here now made her smile and chased off the sad thoughts.

She sensed Quinn tense next to her and reached over and squeezed his hand. 'It will be gas, you'll see.'

She refrained from telling him Moira had erupted in laughter upon hearing her sister's plans for the next six Wednesday nights. 'Three sad-arsed thirty-plus singletons learning salsa together!' she'd shrieked. Aisling had flicked a pea from her plate across the table at her. She might be a thirty-something, but she could be just as childish as her sister. Besides, there was nothing sad-arsed about it. The three of them had been too busy building their careers to devote time to serious relationships. She said this to her sister, who looked unimpressed as she picked up the pea that had just landed on her lap.

They'd all taken different paths upon leaving college. Quinn had opted to serve under a demanding Michelin starred chef at a top London eatery, learning his trade from the bottom up. He'd come back to Dublin five years ago, having decided he was ready to open his own restaurant. Leila, meanwhile, had worked as a bridal designer's assistant for one of Dublin's leading lights in the industry until she decided the time had come to build her own business. Aisling had taken to travel like a baby bird discovering its wings. She'd worked at resorts in the Whitsunday's in Australia, then Fiji, Hawaii, the Seychelles, and her last position in Crete.

They were all married to their jobs and had gotten very serious in their post-college years. You'd never believe the hijinks they used to get up to now. Yes, putting themselves outside of their comfort zone by doing something different, like learning a Latin American dance, would do them no harm whatsoever.

'It's a fecking meat market; that's what it is,' Quinn muttered, his eyes moving toward the glamorous duo currently pressed together in the centre of the room.

'I think that's Maria and Antonio Lozano,' Leila whispered, her eyes wide. 'They're good, aren't they?'

Aisling nodded, watching them. They were so lithe, so graceful. And yes, okay, they did look as though they should get a room but wasn't that what this dance was all about? Shouldn't you feel as though you were watching something deeply intimate and sensual? She glanced down at her plain black skirt. She'd teemed it with a white t-shirt. She felt frumpy and short, despite her heels, compared to the elegant instructor in her daring red dress.

The skirt she'd chosen might be plain, but it did billow out satisfyingly when she twirled. She knew this from having practised in front of the mirror in her bedroom. At least her Louboutin's (knock-offs but nobody needs know) added a touch of glamour. Leila had opted for a simple green dress with a nipped-in waist that, for some reason, made Aisling think of Tinkerbell.

The song wound down, and those who weren't on the dance floor applauded those that were. Maria and Antonio bowed, well used to the admiring glances. Antonio, in his accented English, welcomed them all, introducing himself and his wife, Maria, who both had Cuban ancestry. He explained the origins of the dance they'd come to learn.

Aisling hadn't known it had originated in Eastern Cuba. Nor had she known that the name salsa was a broad term for many forms of Latin American dance. They would be learning to a fast beat called the timba, which had its roots in the Afro-Cuban community. 'Salsa,' Antonio stated passionately, 'connects you with others. It is sexy and energetic. We come together to be our true selves and to be in the moment. Salsa is magic.' He performed some fancy and fast footwork before grabbing Mrs Lozano and spinning her around.

'Jaysus, feck,' muttered Quinn.

Leila whispered to Aisling, 'Will we be doing that bottom wobbling thing they do, do you think?'

'It's called twerking.'

It was then that the door opened, and Marcus walked in.

Chapter 13

♥

'I'm Marcus. Hi.'

'Aisling,' she smiled as the music started, and Maria Lozano began to shout instructions over the top of it.

'I'm going to apologise in advance for crunching your toes.'

'Apology accepted.'

'I'm only here because I'm the best man at a wedding next month. The bridal party is doing a Latin American dance at the reception for some unfathomable reason. Apparently, I don't have a natural aptitude, so the bride-to-be booked me a lesson,' Marcus said. 'And I feel ridiculous.' He was jiggling his hips in her direction at the instruction of Antonio Lozano.

Aisling grinned to herself, glancing over at the couple who'd inspired her 'Dear Aisling' letter. They'd been at odds when they first arrived, but he was looking even less impressed now. It didn't look like he had a natural aptitude for hip swivelling either. She hoped they made it down the aisle. It must be a new trend, she decided—salsa dancing at weddings—and she made a mental note to ask Leila later. 'You're not alone, feeling ridiculous, I mean,' she laughed, turning her attention back to Marcus and quickly straightening her face upon receiving a glare from Mrs Lozano.

Salsa was not just magic; apparently, it was a serious business too or at least learning the basic steps was. This sexy man thrusting himself awkwardly at her could pass for a Latino, she thought. Her pupils had dilated the moment he'd walked into the room apologising for being late. Leila had elbowed her, telling her to close her mouth, which she did. She'd already taken stock of his dark hair and serious eyes as they connected with hers.

He'd come to stand next to her, and so it had been natural that he partner with her. Quinn and Leila had paired up. Aisling was too scared to look over at them lest she and Leila have one of their giggle attacks. She wouldn't have been able to keep a straight face were it Quinn currently gyrating in front of her. It was all very well and good getting down and dirty when you had fiery Cuban blood rushing through your veins. It was a little trickier above a shop on Dame Street in Ireland, home to the Irish jig.

'What brings you here?' Marcus asked, attempting to spin her around.

'My friend, the blonde girl over there in green, thought it would be fun,' Aisling whispered, shuffling her feet along to the tempo. To her surprise, she was picking up the steps and managing to keep time with the rhythm. She was, she realised, having fun. She risked a glance at Leila and Quinn. Leila was gazing down at her feet as though surprised to discover she had two left ones. Quinn, though, she noticed, watching him for a few beats, was a natural. Who'd have thought?

She was glad Marcus was no Fred Astaire and had wound up here at Lozano's Dance Studio. She'd already decided tonight was going to be worth her not being able to move in the morning. It wasn't going to be down to her having used new muscles as she attempted moves she hadn't known existed. It had been a long time since she'd shaken her booty with as much enthusiasm as she was currently doing. No, her immobility would be because of her poor feet. She'd already lost count of how many times Marcus had trodden on them!

Ah well, she thought, stealing a glance at him from under her lashes, he had warned her.

'How do you manage it?'

'What?'

'Dancing in those shoes. Staying upright must be a challenge in itself.'

'Practice.' Aisling grinned. She really was enjoying herself and was pleased she'd let her friend talk her into coming. Wednesday night, salsa classes were going to be fun.

'Ah, I see. That's the secret, then. So, what do you do?' Marcus asked.

'I manage my family's guest house on St Stephen's Green, O'Mara's.'

'I know it.'

She wasn't surprised. O'Mara's was a fixture on the Dublin landscape.

'Until a couple of months ago, I was working in resort management. My last post was near Hania in Crete. It's a stunning part of the world. Have you been?'

He shook his head and frowned. 'No, I usually head for Cyprus. You came back to take over the family business?'

'It was that, or it was going to be sold. My dad died, and Mammy decided she needed a fresh start. It's taking a bit to settle back in, but the guesthouse is home.'

'I'm sorry about your dad.'

She smiled to let him know it was okay. 'What about you, what do you do?'

'I'm a manager at AIB.'

'A salsa dancing bank manager.'

He groaned, 'That was never on my CV, but you know I think I might have to thank Madeline for making me come along tonight.'

They smiled at one another, and Aisling felt a shiver of anticipation that tonight was the start of something special.

Across the room, Quinn was amazed. His feet had taken on a life of their own once the music had started, and he was following Antonio's instructions with ease. He glanced over at Aisling. He'd only agreed to come to these classes because it was a chance to be close to her. He could see how this was going to go, though. He'd seen it the moment her face had lit up when that eejit, Ricky Martin wannabe, who was wiggling his hips in front of her, had walked into the room.

'Quinn get off my foot,' Leila yelped.

Chapter 14

'**A**isling O'Mara, how long until Marcus makes an honest woman of you?'

Aisling blinked, realising she was still holding the coins she'd dug out of her purse for the busker in her hand. She tossed them into the violin case acknowledging his grateful smile before turning her attention to her old classmate, Orla.

'Hi, Orla. Gosh, it's been ages.' She hugged her old chum. 'Two weeks to go. I've just been for my final fitting tonight.' She filled Orla in on what was planned for the day itself, feeling a stab of guilt that she hadn't invited her. The cost per head for the meal meant she'd had to be ruthless and bypass friends she didn't see on a regular basis. Mammy had twittered on about inviting Mrs so-and-so and Mrs you-remember-her Aisling—but she'd stood firm. She'd done the same with Mrs McDonagh. She'd had to because Marcus seemed to have taken a backseat where their big day was concerned. Content to let her do all the organising, and that included dealing with his mam!

Orla's husband, Eddie, appeared alongside them with a familiar green M&S bag in his hand. He said hello to Aisling and stood listening to her and his wife catching up, beginning to shuffle his feet impatiently after a while. Orla took the hint and wished Aisling the best of luck for her big day before the two women said their goodbyes.

Nina was manning the front desk when Aisling breezed through the door, having made a mental note to polish the brass nameplate in the morning.

'How's things, Nina?' she asked the younger Spanish girl who was clipping papers into a ring binder. She'd worked at O'Mara's for the last few months.

'Ola. We're quiet tonight, Aisling. Marcus called in, though, and he left this.' She produced an envelope which Aisling curiously took from her outstretched hand.

Marcus had known she wasn't going to be in this afternoon. She'd told him she was meeting Moira and Leila for their final fitting. He was supposed to be going for the suit fitting she'd arranged for him. His pants were too long and would definitely need taking up. It surprised her he'd found time to swing by O'Mara's. She itched to get upstairs to see what was inside the envelope, not wanting to open it in front of Nina in case it was something that would make her blush. Unlikely, given Marcus's practical nature, but you never knew.

'How did the fitting go? I can't wait to see your dress,' Nina smiled.

'It went well, not much to tweak at all, although it is a little snug around here.' She patted her middle, and Nina laughed.

'I'm sure it'll be fine.'

The envelope was like a hot potato in her hand, but she hovered a tick longer to ask Nina how her family was. There was a quiet sadness about the young girl at times, and Aisling put it down to her being homesick. Her pretty face always grew animated when she spoke of her family. She knew that work was scarce in the small town where Nina came from, especially in the cooler months. Dublin, with its boom, had guaranteed her employment and a chance to perfect her English.

'My madre and padre are talking about extending their restaurante,' she said. Aisling had heard all about the small family-owned restaurant in the old town of Toledo where they lived. She also knew Nina sent money home to her parents. She worked two jobs, the evening shift here at O'Mara's Monday to Friday from four until ten pm. It was Nina who locked up of an evening, getting a taxi, on O'Mara's tab, home to the house she shared with six others. In the day, she waitressed a lunchtime shift at popular Pedro's in Temple Bar.

Nina began telling her about how her mother made the best cocido madrileño, and that there was nothing better to warm yourself with when the weather grew cool. Aisling's mouth watered hearing all about the pork stew with its chorizo sausage and chickpeas, which simmered for hours. She hadn't had any dinner, and the crumbs she'd snaffled from Leila's plate hardly counted. The phone rang, and their conversation drew to a close.

Aisling gave Nina a wave and raced up the stairs to the apartment. She let herself in, flicking on the light as she closed the door behind her. It wasn't quite dark yet, but rather that hazy in-between greyish light that signalled night was drawing in. The street lights had yet to come on, she noticed, quickly drawing the curtains before kicking her shoes off and curling up in her chair by the window. Only once she was comfortable did she open the envelope, then she tore into it in anticipation of what it might contain.

Perhaps Marcus had picked up the tickets for their honeymoon. They'd booked ten days of lazing in the sun, snorkelling, delicious food, and languid lovemaking in a luxury villa in the Maldives, bliss.

It wasn't tickets, however, and she unfolded the plain piece of white paper curiously, her eyes skimming Marcus's familiar neat handwriting. She could read the words, but she couldn't comprehend what they meant.

Ash, this isn't an easy letter for me to write, and I know that not telling you to your face is cowardly. I'm ashamed of myself for writing this, but if I tried to sit down with you to say I can't go through with the wedding, I'd bottle it. I wouldn't be able to stand the hurt on your face. You see, I knew I'd made a mistake from the moment I slid the diamond on your finger, but I couldn't see a way back.

My only excuse is things spiralled out of control these past months. I've felt like I was on a conveyor belt, and I couldn't get off. I do love you, please know that, but I shouldn't have proposed to you. It was too soon, and I wasn't ready. I'm not sure I'll ever be ready, to be honest. I've seen what marriage has done to my parents. They've lived a life of bitterness and sniping. I was always stuck in the middle of it, and I'm sure they only stayed together for my sake. Then when I grew up, they stayed out of habit. I don't want us to wind up like that.

Why did I ask you to marry me then? All I can say is I knew it was what you wanted, and I wanted to make you happy. In doing so, I've only succeeded in ultimately making you unhappy. Leaving Dublin seems the kindest thing to do. I'm transferring to Cork. I'm sorry from the bottom of my heart, and I hope one day you'll see it was the right thing for me to do.

Marcus

Chapter 15

Present Day

Aisling peered at her face in the bathroom mirror. Her eyes were swollen thanks to the tears she'd shed poring over Marcus's letters last night. If she had a dollar for every tear she'd cried since he'd left, she'd be a wealthy woman; she thought as she cursed him under her breath. She'd sat at the table last night, unable to stop torturing herself, again reading through every word he'd written to her these last few months until she reached the beginning, or the end, however you wanted to look at it.

All those hard-edged raw emotions at the knowledge he was leaving, and her life was not going to move forward from the sixth of September as Mrs McDonagh had rained down on her once more like cold, wet sleet.

There would be no fairy tale day with a happily ever after. There'd be no husband at her side, helping her run O'Mara's in the same fashion Mammy and Dad had. The third bedroom in the apartment would remain empty and untouched. It wouldn't be painted in a sunny yellow with a Winnie the Pooh border in anticipation of needing a nursery. She would continue to live here with Moira; her life would go on as it had before she'd attended that salsa class and met Marcus.

Aisling knew she'd survive, but she felt like a rug had been wrenched out from under her feet. Those first couple of months after Marcus had run away with his tail between his legs had been a period in her life she'd never have navigated her way through if it wasn't for Leila and Quinn. Again, they were the two sane constants who were there for her when life had let her down.

It was all well and good with Mammy, Roisin—who'd caught the first flight out of London upon hearing the news—and Moira railing against Marcus, but it didn't achieve anything. Although she'd admit, there was a certain satisfaction to be gleaned from hearing them call him everything under the sun while she sat and cried. It didn't change the facts, though; she'd still been deserted. While her family had ranted and raved in between consoling her, it was Leila who'd stepped up and taken practical control of the situation.

'This is the story, right?' she'd told the O'Mara women looking fierce for such a delicately boned woman. 'Aisling and Marcus the fecker, you're not to actually say that, by the way, mutually concluded they weren't right for each other after all.' They'd all nodded gratefully at Leila, glad somebody was telling them what they should say and do.

It was like one of those official celebratory breakup announcements—all very civilised and mutual. Aisling was clinging to the word 'mutual'. Mutual was her mantra because it meant she could continue to show her face around town. Despite her fragile state of mind, she still had enough wits about her to tell her friend if she ever got fed up with the wedding business, she'd make a fortune in public relations.

Leila had set about telephoning their guests, and if anybody had questioned the eleventh-hour cancellation notice, she'd replied smartly with, 'Sure look it, isn't it better this way than realising they weren't right for each other six months down

MICHELLE VERNAL

84

the line?' She'd negotiated the return of deposits through the promise of recommending future business to those left in the last-minute lurch. In short, she'd pulled Aisling out of a very big hole with her dignity intact. So, while her heart may have been broken, at least she could hold her head up.

'Should I go to Cork, see if I can make some sense out of all of this?' Aisling had asked over the top of her sugary cup of tea the third morning after Marcus had absconded. She'd been living on sugary cups of tea and not much else since she'd read the note. Quinn, upon hearing she wasn't eating, had been acting as *Meals on Wheels*. He was adamant he could tempt even the most finicky of eaters, but all she could think about was Marcus. The urge to confront him—to see him one last time and ask him how he could do this to her, was all-consuming.

'No, you should not!' Moira, Roisin, and Mammy chimed. 'Have some pride!'

'If anybody's going to Cork, it's me. I'll sort the fecker.' Fighting words from Moira.

'And me,' added Mammy, not to be beaten. 'I'll show him what I think of him.'

Roisin simply shrugged, 'I'm not going. I'm a lover, not a fighter. I'll stay here and look after you, Ash, while those two go and deal with him.'

'Nobody is going to Cork. Marcus made himself quite clear in the note as to how he felt. What's our catchphrase, Aisling?' Leila looked to Aisling like a conductor of a choir.

'If someone you love hurts you, cry a river, build a bridge, and get over it.'

'Ooh, that's good. Where did you find it?' Roisin asked.

'Online, under quotes to heal broken hearts, it's anonymous. Aisling's to keep repeating it to herself. The power of positive thinking and all that.'

Now, Aisling wiped away the steam her breath had left on the mirror as she said the words out loud to the face staring back at her. She'd cried the river, she'd spent the last year building a bridge, but having seen Marcus yesterday, she knew she was far from over it. Ah, God, a thought occurred to her, would he call this morning? He would be back—she knew he would, and the uncertainty of when he would next appear had her nerves jangling.

Why couldn't he have stayed in Cork? she asked herself again as she was filled with an urge to run away. Oh, to pack a bag and head for the hills, or even better, back to Crete. She closed her eyes for a beat, picturing herself back walking the streets of Hania's shaded old town, pausing to buy olives and a loaf of crusty bread. She couldn't run away because she'd made a commitment to her family by coming back and stepping into Mammy's shoes. She'd been raised to keep her promises, and if she were to break hers now, she'd be no better than Marcus fecking coward McDonagh!

Aisling turned away from the mirror. She needed to get moving, starting with a hot shower. That would surely have a restorative effect. It did, and she felt better once she'd towelled off and dressed. Her careful make-up application made her look much more herself, and she was hopeful her puffy eyes would have gone down by the time she got on the train to Howth. She'd pop downstairs and see how the land lay shortly. Hopefully, Mr Fox had behaved himself last night, and there would be no disgruntled Una Brennan to deal with. First things first, though, she'd wake Moira and remind her they were off to meet Mammy for lunch.

She knocked on her sister's door and waited. In days of old, she would have barrelled on in, but she'd learned her lesson the hard way, having caught her sister in flagrante delicto with her ex-boyfriend. Her face still flamed at the memory—*when had her baby sister grown up? And more importantly, what was she doing bringing her boyfriend back here to the family home?*

Moira, once dressed and with the boyfriend sent packing, had pointed out loudly that she afforded Aisling the courtesy of knocking before entering, and she should do the same. She'd also said what was good for the goose was good for the gander. Which in English meant if Aisling was happy to ride Marcus as though she were trying to win the Irish Derby under the O'Mara family roof, then Moira was entitled to do the same.

Aisling had protested that Mammy would go mad if she'd known all this riding was going on, and at least Marcus was making an honest woman of her. Moira had tossed this remark aside with a casual, 'Well, what Mammy doesn't know won't hurt her.'

The ground rules for living together as adult siblings with no parents to lay down the law was murky territory; indeed, Aisling concluded, backing down.

Today thankfully, there was no sound of anything untoward coming from her sister's room other than her familiar snores. The loudness of which meant she'd given it a good nudge last night. Aisling shook her head. She'd always kept a wary eye out for Moira, and it was a hard habit to break. She knew too that Moira would have loved to have been out from under her overprotective feet, free to do what she wanted without her sister eyeballing her disapprovingly, but the soaring rents in the city since the Celtic Tiger had begun to roar and the economy boomed made sure it wasn't an option.

Aisling was secretly glad, even if Moira and her diva attitude did drive her mad sometimes. She wouldn't have liked to have been left to rattle around in the manor house's apartment on her lonesome.

She knocked louder and waited a few seconds longer before opening the door.

'Jaysus, it smells like a pub in here.' She waved her hand under her nose before opening the curtains so that she could let some air into the room.

Moira stirred, squinting at the light before pulling the sheet over her head. 'Shut the curtains.'

'I will not. We're meeting Mammy for lunch, remember?'

'But I'm in bits, Ash. I can't possibly go. I think I've picked up a tummy bug.'

'You'll feel better after a shower.'

Moira disentangled herself from the sheet and sat up.

She would not win the Rose of Tralee at this moment in time, thought Aisling.

Moira groaned. 'I feel sick like a small hospital.'

'The best cure for the brown bottle flu is a hot shower, some paracetamol, and one of Mrs Flaherty's full Irish's.' Aisling was annoyed, she'd told Moira not to overdo it, and so she served her ace. 'Hmm, I'll ask her to whip you up a nice runny egg with lashings of black pudding, shall I?'

Moira turned green, but it had the desired effect, and she leapt from her bed.

Chapter 16

U na sipped her tea, and her eyes flicked to the younger
O'Mara sister sitting across the dining room from her.
Mrs Flaherty was fussing around her, clearly fond of the girl.
She was pretty, that was for sure, with her flashing dark eyes
and shiny hair. A real head-turner, but then so was Aisling,
the manageress. They certainly weren't peas in a pod, though.
If Una were a betting woman, she'd say there'd been lots
of jokes about the milkman having come-a-calling over the
years. Although stealing another glance over, if you looked
closely, you could tell the two were sisters. It was in the shape
of their faces and the tilt of their noses.

It was also apparent from the younger sister's greenish
tinge; she was under the weather. Out on the sauce last night,
no doubt, serves her right. Una, who never touched a drop,
was prim. The younger generation was far too fond of getting
on the, *what did they call it?* She searched for the word she'd
overheard the two young lads use on the train—*lash,* that was
it.

Una liked to listen in on young people's conversation. She'd
tune in as she stood in the queue at the Tesco's or when she
was waiting at the station. The bus and the train were good
places in which to catch snippets of banter. She was out of
touch with their generation in a way, when she was young,

she'd never have dreamed possible. Language was a funny thing the way words came and went like hem lengths over the years. So was age, she thought, eyeing the liver spots on the back of her hand.

She wondered if this young lass, who under Mrs Flaherty's watchful eye was dipping her toast into her egg yolk, knew what it was to have her heartbroken. Or was she the one who did the heart-breaking?

Una had been a pretty girl once too. Leo used to tell her she was beautiful. He used to say to her she made his heart sing. He was a man of hearts and flowers was Leo. Why then, if he'd thought her beautiful and she made his heart sing, hadn't she been enough?

She sighed and put her teacup down in the saucer. It was all such a long time ago, but if she shut her eyes, the pain was as fresh as the day it had been inflicted. Her mind was prone to drift, and she'd find herself back in that moment. Why was it so hard to remember if she'd put the cat out before she went to bed of a night, but the events of April 12, 1950, were as vivid as a film being projected onto the big screen?

She could hear the rustle of fabric as Mrs Flaherty made her way over, pulling her from her thoughts as she nodded her greeting. The cook's smile was tight as she asked if everything was to her liking. Una felt a pang. She didn't want to be this awkward old woman whom people tiptoed around. It was a role; however, she'd begun to play with such tenacity she'd forgotten how to let her guard down.

'It's fine, thank you,' she replied, pleased she'd had the foresight to order the Continental today. She'd managed the small bowl of cereal she'd helped herself to from the buffet as well as a slice of wholemeal toast. She could have complimented the woman on the marmalade, which she was certain was homemade, but she remained tight-lipped. Mrs Flaherty looked as if she'd liked to say something but thought better of it, taking herself off to the kitchen instead.

Today Una vowed she'd knock on Aideen's door. She wouldn't while away the hours sitting in the park across the road from her sister's house. Sitting on the bench like some sort of stalker as she watched the comings and goings—trying to catch a glimpse of her nephews. They'd be approaching middle-age now with children who were no doubt at that age where they had their parents tearing their hair out. What a thought! She a great aunt.

The problem was, once she got to the street on which Aideen had spent the last thirty or so years of her life, she couldn't bring herself to knock on her door. She'd told herself that she'd brazen it out yesterday and the day before. Time was running out, but each day sitting on that hard bench, she'd felt like she'd gazed at Medusa's face and been turned to stone.

Chapter 17

A isling stared out the window at the pocket-sized gardens rushing by below. Their smalls, and not so small's, blowing on the breeze for all to see. Her view beyond these yards was blocked by row after row of pebble-dashed houses all whizzing past in uniform design. She was facing backwards and feeling queasy on it. She hated not sitting facing the direction in which she was travelling on any kind of public transport, but the train had been packed when they'd boarded it. The only two seats left were situated diagonally from each other. She and Moira had stared at the empty spaces for a beat before having a standoff over who was sitting where. They were obliviously providing entertainment to the bored passengers as they bickered back and forth.

'For the love of Jaysus, sit down the pair of you.' A man with a missing front tooth wheezed.

Moira looked as though she were going to tell him to mind his own business as she glanced at him sharply. She closed her mouth, though, deciding to save her depleted energy reserves for her mammy and not waste them on a verbal exchange with a stranger. Aisling finally conceded to sit where she was currently perched because her sister was clearly still green around the gills. She didn't want to have to help clean it up if she lost the contents of her stomach, a very real possibility. Mind you; she wasn't feeling too flash herself.

She'd clambered over the elderly woman with her handbag on her knee, resolutely refusing to move across and make her life easier. 'I like an aisle seat,' she said, once Aisling collapsed, huffing and puffing into her seat. *Bully for you*, she said to herself, trying not to think about the slice of chocolate fudge cake she'd wolfed down not half an hour ago. Mr Walsh had left the promised piece of cake at reception for her, and she'd shovelled it down when James took himself off to the gents because she didn't want to share.

As the train lurched forward, she glanced over to where Moira was sitting. Her legs were twisted toward the aisle, and she had a look of concentration on her face as she breathed in and out slowly. She met her sister's gaze, and Aisling shot her a look that said she'd kill her if she showed them up by hurling on public transport.

Despite the odds being stacked against them, they made the journey without incident. Aisling exhaled, relieved as the train slowed and came to a halt in Howth Station. The sisters joined the throng exiting the train, hearing the excited chattering of plans being made for the day. They were keen, Aisling guessed, to make the most of the glorious weather and spend the day with the whiff of salt air in their nostrils.

The crowd carried them along until they exited down the steps of the pretty station building, its hanging baskets on either side of the wooden doors a profusion of tumbling pinks and reds. Aisling looked down the street; she could hear the snapping of the flags flying outside The Bloody Stream, its front beer garden and spiky cabbage palm trees lending a festive and determined air to hang onto the last vestiges of summer.

She averted her eyes away from the pub. Marcus had brought her there once not long after he'd proposed. She'd admired the diamond in her ring as it caught the light, waving her hand about in conversation far more than was necessary. The interior, she recalled, was rustic and cosy, and the craic had been great. There'd been live music; she'd wanted to dance, but Marcus wasn't keen. She'd also tasted the best bowl of chowder she'd eaten in her life. If Mammy suggested they go there for lunch, though, she'd have to refuse on the basis of painful memories. It was a shame because the chowder had been delicious. She realised she was feeling better now as her mouth watered at the thought of the creamy soup. She scanned the faces of people walking toward the station, and her eyes soon fixed on Mammy, who was waving out like a mad thing.

'Ahoy there, me hearties,' Moira muttered.

'Shush, she looks very well on it.' Aisling couldn't help but grin, though; she did look like a feminine version of Captain Birdseye, without the beard, of course! Still, it was nice to see her with her rounded figure of old. She'd gotten awfully thin after Dad died. She was looking much more her old self these days, even if this new version did insist on wearing casual sailing get-up for every occasion. It was a blessing she didn't wear a white cap and smoke a pipe to complete her look.

'Hi, Mammy! I like your hair.' Aisling eyed her mammy's shoulder-length bob, the hair lightened to a mid-brown with reddish undertones. It was softer than her natural dark, almost black, colour, which she guessed would be peppered with grey these days. Aisling hugged her as she caught up to them.

Mammy appeared to have shrunk in the few weeks since Aisling had last seen her. It took a beat for her to realise it was the flat shoes. She'd taken to wearing them since moving to the seaside village. Maureen released her daughter before giving her the once over. 'You're looking good, Aisling. I like the shoes, although probably not the most practical pick for a stroll along the pier. And you could do with getting those ends trimmed yourself.' She picked up a handful of her daughter's reddish-gold hair and frowned. 'Yes, a little trim, I think. Treena, my stylist, is marvellous. A little pricey but well worth it.' She swished her hair around for Aisling and Moira to admire.

Aisling had to smile at her mammy's use of the word stylist. She obviously thought it sounded posh because she'd rolled the sentence off her tongue with a plummy tone. 'Alright, Mammy, I'll book myself in for a cut.' Thirty-four years old, and she was still doing as she was told!

Mollified, Maureen O'Mara turned her attention to her youngest child, pulling her down into a busty embrace.

'Mam, let me go. I can't breathe,' Moira's muffled voice wafted up from the depths of her cleavage. 'Jaysus,' she muttered once released, 'you just about knocked me out. I can see the headline, 'Dublin girl rendered unconscious in a seaside village by mammy's overuse of Arpège. You'll have Ireland's bee population trying to pollinate you smelling like that.'

Maureen ignored Moira's diatribe as her eyes raked over her, narrowing as they settled on her face. 'You've a look of Princess Fiona about you—the ogress version. On the lash last night, were we?' She didn't wait for a reply. 'Just the other day, I was reading an article in the paper about the young people of our country's disturbing drinking habits. To think my own daughter plays a part in those drunken statistics.' She shook her head. Aisling wasn't sure if it was done in dismay over her daughter's drinking habits or whether she just wanted to swish her hair around again.

'You're a fine one to talk, Mammy. I can remember you singing Danny Boy at the top of your lungs when you'd knocked back a few sherries with Kate Finnegan.'

'Don't be cheeky, t'was only the once. Come on, now we've a reservation at Aqua. It's only been opened a year. I've not been before, but I've heard good things about it from my golfing ladies.'

The sisters linked arms with their mammy and, to Aisling's relief, bypassed The Bloody Stream as they turned toward

Dublin Bay instead. The water was calm and blue despite the wind that whipped around them as they stepped out onto the pier. Aisling filled her lungs with the tangy air. The fresh sea breeze would sort Moira out too. She watched the fishing boats jiggling against one another on their pier-side moorings. On the other side of the walkway, smart sailing boats were showcased in the marina. Determined anglers were fishing off the side of the pier, and families were strolling its length. The lighthouse loomed at the end of the jetty guarding the entrance to Howth Harbour. It was a symbolic welcome and farewell to weary travellers, Aisling always thought somewhat romantically.

Aqua was housed inside the former Howth Sailing Club building. 'You should feel right at home in here, Mammy, what with you looking the part and all,' Moira said, holding the door open for her.

Maureen wasn't sure whether Moira was being sarcastic or not, so she shot her a fierce look to be on the safe side. They were ushered to a table near the expansive windows, and she announced loudly for the benefit of the other diners that they had a prime table. 'Just look at that sea view, would you girls.'

As Moira and Aisling skimmed over the menu, she filled them in on her latest news. Derbhilla, her golfing partner, was having her knees done on Thursday. She was going to be out of action for a month or so. Maureen had been making up meals to pop in her friend's freezer for her to have when she got home from the hospital. 'Her husband's as useless as a chocolate teapot,' she confided, moving swiftly onto her frenemy, Agnes. She was a fellow widow who was making noises about stepping into Derbhilla's shoes while she was out of action. 'She's got far too much to say for herself, in my opinion, and I'm on the fence about her scoring abilities. I've a sneaking suspicion she doctors her results to better her handicap.'

Things could get ugly on the Deer Park Ladies golf course, Aisling smiled to herself, deciding on pan-fried fillet of fish. She'd be strong and bypass a starter, but she thought, perusing the desserts, she'd share the sticky toffee pudding with Mammy for afters. It was their favourite.

By the time the waiter came to take their order, they'd also received a blow-by-blow account of Rosemary Farrell's—a member of Mammy's rambling group—recent hip operation. *Who knew the metal orthopaedic implant could set the airport detectors off?* Apparently, Rosemary had learned this the hard way—holding all and sundry up at Dublin Airport as she tried to pass through security. She'd been patted down three times by the overly enthusiastic security guard, although Maureen said it was probably the most excitement Rosemary had had in years!

Moira not surprisingly ordered the fish and chips with pea puree. A good dose of stodge to soak up her sins.

'Sure, the puree will match your face,' Mammy muttered before announcing that she'd like the steak. 'And shall we get a bottle of wine, girls?'

Moira groaned.

'That'd be nice, Mammy,' Aisling said. It wasn't as though she'd be driving anywhere, and she hadn't overdone it last night, far from it. She'd taken herself off to bed, all cried out, with a mug of sweet tea, hoping it would send her off to the land of nod. Not that she'd needed any help sleeping, she'd been exhausted. The waiter scurried off with their orders and the promise of a chilled bottle of house white upon his return. Aisling decided now would be as good a time as any to tell her mammy and sister that Marcus was back in town.

Chapter 18

M oira choked on the water she'd just taken a sip of as Mammy thrust a napkin at her. 'You've dribble on your chin, Moira, wipe it up.'

'Did you just say Marcus is back in town?' She turned her attention to Aisling.

Aisling nodded; the shock had worn off in the ensuing hours that had passed since she'd seen him. But she could see how it had taken them by surprise. She filled them in on how she'd spotted him making a beeline for O'Mara's and how she'd successfully avoided him.

'Good woman,' Mammy said when Aisling told her how Bronagh had embellished her social life by telling him she wouldn't be home later either. Thus, getting her off the hook yesterday at least.

'I need this,' Aisling said as the waiter returned and set about pouring the wine.

Moira, having decided the news that had just been imparted warranted a hair of the dog, held her glass up to be filled too.

'He's a chancer, that one.' Mammy shook her head, doing the hair swishy thing once more.

'It's a good thing I wasn't there when he called,' Moira rasped. 'I'd have eaten the head off him, so I would.'

'I'm going to have to see him.' Aisling owned up to the letters he'd been sending her. 'If I'd replied, he might have stayed away.'

'I don't think it would have made any difference, Ash. He's a spoiled only child who's far too used to getting his own way. Just tell him to feck right off next time he shows up.'

Aisling couldn't help but think Moira's take on Marcus was a touch ironic given her uncanny ability of getting what she wanted when she wanted it. Still, that was their faults for running around after her the way they had when she was a tot. Marcus perhaps *was* used to things going his way, but that didn't make him a bad person.

'Aisling, what is running through that head of yours?' Mammy's eyes narrowed. 'You get the same expression on your face whenever Mrs Flaherty makes noises about seeing that auld fox off. You're a soft touch. Always have been.'

Aisling took a big gulp of her wine. She needed fortification if she was going, to be honest about what was on her mind. 'Mammy, I need to see him. I don't expect either of you to understand, but it might give me the closure I need.'

Moira muttered under her breath, and Aisling was sure she caught the words feck and sake in there.

Mammy was more vocal. 'You're not guest-starring on Oprah,' she shouted. 'We don't use words like journey and closure in our family. They are banned, bad words, do you hear me? We say things like on your bike you weasel and, and—'

'Feck off, fecker with the little pecker.' Moira waggled her little finger for effect.

Aisling shot Moira a look. 'Not helpful and not true, as it happens.'

'Well, what do you expect?' Moira said.

'But what if he is genuinely sorry? I mean, he wouldn't be the first man to get cold feet before his wedding now, would he? What if he wants to put things right between us? He might want to apologise to my face, Mammy. I'd like to hear him say he was sorry.' Her words sounded cringeworthy even to her ears.

Several diners' heads spun in their direction at Moira and Mammy's eruption, but Moira wasn't finished. 'That gob shite flicked you off with a note, Aisling. A note! He didn't even have the decency to call the wedding off to your face. We were there to pick up the pieces, not him. He does not deserve a second chance of any kind!'

Aisling's face flamed. 'Would you two lower the volume. The whole of Aqua does not need to know I was dumped, thank you very much.'

Their waiter, arriving with her pan-fried fish balanced in one hand and Moira's fish and chips in the other, was a welcome distraction. Aisling wasn't sure if she was imagining it or not, but he seemed to be extra solicitous toward her. He fluffed about shaking out her napkin and draping it on her lap before asking if she'd like an extra serving of tartare sauce on the house, or a top-up of her wine, perhaps?

She knew she wasn't imagining it when he patted her shoulder and said, 'The same thing happened to my sister one week before she was due to walk down the aisle. She's moved on now, married a fella from up the road in Malahide. He's a face on him like a bag of spuds but plenty of dosh.' He pointed out the window, 'That's his yacht there, the big shiny one. So, you see, life does go on. You'll be alright, love.'

Oh, for God's sake! Aisling was puce. So, the moral of his story was she could look forward to marrying someone ugly with pots of money and a yacht—bloody great!

Mammy jumped in, 'And tell me now—' she cast around for his name.

'Boyd,' he offered up.

'Boyd. What would your sister have done if that eejit ex of hers had made noises about patching things up?'

He looked around to make sure no guests were within earshot and leaned in toward the party of three. 'She'd have told him he was a ballbag and sent him packing. With said bollocks between his knees.'

'There you go, Aisling. That's what you're to do.' Mammy and Moira were united in victory.

Then like the sun coming out from behind the clouds, Mammy's face cleared. She turned toward Boyd, giving him the benefit of her smile set at full wattage as she asked him, would there be any chance of an introduction to his sister and her husband. 'Only I'm after sailing lessons and was looking to meet some like-minded boaties.'

It was later sitting on the DART home, bellies full and with that warm glow of having partaken of a tipple at lunchtime, that Aisling thought to ask her sister how her night had been. They were both in better spirits on the return journey thanks to Aisling facing forward and Moira's hangover having disappeared over the course of lunch. She'd texted her friend Andrea to see if she still wanted to catch up after checking with Aisling whether she wanted her to come home with her in case Marcus was there.

Aisling knew Moira was desperate to look for a dress to wear to the snooty engagement party she'd been invited to. Besides, Moira bopping Marcus on the nose if she came face-to-face with him wouldn't do any good. She had to be the grown-up he'd failed to be and talk to him face-to-face. It was inevitable he'd show up at some point, and she refused to skulk around like she had yesterday while she waited for him to reappear.

She told Moira this, and knowing the shops would still be open by the time their train rolled back into the city, her sister arranged to jump off at Connolly Station. Andrea would meet her there, and they could hunt for their outfits before going for an early dinner and then seeing where the evening led them. It was Saturday night, after all—she looked meaningfully at Aisling when she said this.

Aisling ignored the look. How Moira could think about food after the lunch they'd just put away was beyond her. Come to think of it, how she could think about hitting the town again after the state she'd been in this morning was incomprehensible. Oh, to be young and have stamina, she thought before moving on. Her curiosity piqued as to whether Moira had had any success in batting her eyelashes in Liam Shaughnessy, the Asset Management bigwig's direction.

'What did you get up to last night then?' she asked. 'Did you try your luck with yer man?'

'Liam?' She pulled a face. 'No, he fancies the pants off himself, so he does, and besides, he copped off with Mary from litigation. There's no accounting for taste.'

'That's an about-turn. Yesterday you were all googly-eyed over him.'

Moira's look was withering. 'Ah well, now that's because I've seen the light. Good luck to Mary, I say. She's batting above her weight there, but I've got my eye on a more mature man. A silver fox no less.'

'Jaysus, Moira, you're not after getting yourself a sugar daddy, are you?' Aisling mentally flicked through the images of the managing partners she'd seen on the company's website. The only lawyer who stood out amongst the montage was the fella she'd thought looked like he should be wearing a tall green hat. 'Please tell me it's not yer man I said looked like a leprechaun?'

'No, and Mr Sweeney looks like Mr Wonka, not a leprechaun, you're confused. We had that discussion.'

'Well, who then?' She'd expected an angry, or at the very least quick off the mark, rebuttal as to her suggestion of a sugar daddy. Moira, however, smiled enigmatically, reminding Aisling of the Mona Lisa.

She knew she wouldn't glean anything further from her; her sister was enjoying being mysterious too much. So, she turned her attention to the rows of pocket-sized gardens once more. She hoped the owners of the sheets billowing on the breeze brought them in before that dark cloud she could see lurking ominously on the horizon blew over top of their gardens. A shiver passed through her, and she hoped that cloud wasn't an omen.

Chapter 19

Una Brennan sat on the bench with her cardigan wrapped tightly around her. The sun might be out, but the breeze had a bite. There was a cloud in the distance too. It was dark and heavy. She didn't like the look of it and hoped it didn't decide to blow over in her direction. Despite the unusual clemency of the day, she was cold, chilled to the bone from sitting in the same spot as she had done each day since arriving in Dublin.

The park was gated, and the bench where she was seated was overhung by a tree from which the odd orange leaf floated down to land at her feet. Small children were shrieking as they clambered up the slide or bounced on the see-saw. Beyond the gates and across the road was a row of red brick houses, not dissimilar to the one in which she'd grown up. In the middle of that row was the house that belonged to Aideen.

What was it like inside? she wondered, recalling how Aideen always kept her side of their bedroom neat as a pin, whereas she'd driven her sister potty with her habit of leaving things wherever they happened to fall. She leaned forward, watching as a car pulled up outside the house, performing a parallel park. It was skilfully done. She'd never mastered the art herself, and many a time had driven straight on, ending up miles from where she wanted to be.

A tall chap with a shock of sandy, reddish hair and a middle that was just starting to soften got out of the car. Una gasped. He looked exactly like their da when he was in his middling years. He had to be one of Aideen's lads; there was no doubt. He opened the back door, bending down to re-emerge with a small child in his arm. The wee kiddie had overalls on, and his tousled hair, the same colour as his father's, gave away the fact he'd fallen asleep in the back of the car.

Una felt a physical pang, a yearning to call out to them. She wanted them to know her. They'd recognise her certainly, but what would she say? She wished she could push rewind, go back and do things differently this time around.

Behind her, a swing creaked, and she remembered how she'd loved the swings as a girl. *Higher, higher!* She'd order Aideen, who'd obligingly push her. She'd kick her legs out, imagining she could see over the stacks of chimney pots to the seaside beyond. If she swung hard enough, her magic swing would take her to the pebbly shore, and she'd dip her toes in the icy water, playing catch me if you can with the waves. Una closed her eyes, remembering.

Chapter 20

♥

1942

'That boy in Mrs Greene's front garden is staring at us again, Una,' Aideen whispered. Her lowered voice full of excitement at this unusual turn of events. 'I wonder why he's not in school.' She paused once they were out of his earshot to bend down and pull her ankle sock up. It kept rolling down and disappearing inside her Mary Jane in the most annoying manner. 'I wish my shoe would stop trying to eat my sock,' she said, straightening and jiggling her satchel, so the strap would stop digging into her shoulder. It was heavy with the weight of the books she carried.

The Brennan twins were on their way home from school. Mrs Greene lived six doors down from their house in the row of red brick terrace houses where the sisters had lived their entire lives to date. All the houses had bay windows and front doors with shiny brass knockers. It was a matter of pride, Una knew, to make sure your door knocker gleamed. She'd been sent out to polish theirs often enough! To say the boy was standing in the front garden was a stretch of the imagination too. He was leaning on the railings in front of the square patch of grass to the left of the path leading to Mrs Greene's blue door. It had been green until a month ago.

Una risked a glance back over her shoulder. He was still watching them, and she quickly looked away. 'I meant to tell you, but you fell asleep before I could, and then I forgot. I heard Mammy telling Daddy last night; he's Mrs Greene's nephew. His mammy's not well, so he's come to stay with her. He looks lonely if you ask me. I'd hate to be sent away if our mam was sick. Imagine if we had to go and stay with Aunt Finola?' The thought of their thin-faced spinster aunt, who was a firm believer if you spared the rod, you spoiled the child, made both girls grimace.

A thought occurred to Una. 'Perhaps they don't have twins where he comes from. Maybe that's why he's staring at us. We're a novelty.' She felt very grown-up using a big word like novelty. She'd seen it in a book and had asked Daddy to explain what it meant, storing it away to use at the appropriate time—like now.

'Where do you think he's from?' Aideen's ringlets bounced as she walked the short distance to their front door. She was the quieter and more reserved of the sisters.

'I don't know, but I think we ought to find out. If Mammy says we can, let's see if he wants to come to the canal with us to look for eels.'

The smell of stewed tea and the cabbage remnants of last night's colcannon assailed their nostrils as they stepped inside their door. The tea, Una deduced, her nose twitching, meant Mammy's friend Maire had called. She liked her tea brewed strong enough for a mouse to trot on! Tea, Una had overheard her mammy saying had been rationed; Maire would not like that. Una liked to keep an ear out. Adults didn't tell their children very much about anything, and listening in was the only way she learned what was going on.

She was sorry she'd missed Maire or Mrs Reynolds as she and Aideen called her. She was a source of wonderment to the sisters. It was in the way she'd weave a story. Even the dullest titbit sounded interesting when relayed by Mrs

Reynolds. Whenever she paid a visit, the twins tried to make themselves invisible in the corner of the room so as to be privy to whatever tale she was telling.

The last time she'd called, it had been to show their mam her new coat. She'd leaned in toward Alice and whispered, 'I paid,' she'd looked over her shoulder. Who she thought might be eavesdropping was a puzzle to the girls who were suddenly desperate to know how much she'd paid for her coat. Annoyingly her hand had gone up, shielding her mouth as she whispered the figure to Mammy, who made an appropriate, oohing sort of noise. It was terribly frustrating but fascinating all at the same time.

Mam had spotted her daughters breaking their necks to try to hear what was being said. 'Maire, we've got ears flapping. Girls go and play.' Yes, most frustrating. The smell of tea had been strong that afternoon, too, Una recalled.

Sister Mary Clare had been explaining all about the emergency at school. She said it gave the government special power. She also said that Ireland might be neutral in the war, but they were still feeling the effects with food and fuel shortages. Finbar O'Shea had told them at break he'd heard his parents talking about deer going missing from Phoenix Park. Una wasn't sure if she believed him. So far, her tummy hadn't felt the effects of rationing, and right now, all she cared about was eels and her soda bread and jam.

Mammy was peeling potatoes at the sink; she had an apron tied around the waist of her floral frock—it seemed to Una she had a frock for each day of the week.

Alice Brennan put her peeler down, wiping her wet hands on her apron as she turned to greet her girls. They'd both swooped on the soda bread she'd put out for them, with its thick smearing of butter and jam, and between bites were full of noisy news about their day at St Mary's. She smiled as Una chattered on over the top of her sister, her eyes wide with the drama of Deirdre O'Malley's misdemeanours. Deirdre, Una said, was always scratching her head, and her fingernails were dirty—she hailed from a part of Phibsborough where they didn't care if their doorknockers were shiny. Today she informed her mammy in the self-righteous manner of someone who would never feel the thwack of Sister Mary Clare's wrath; she'd used the ruler when Deirdre answered back.

Una had barely finished relaying her tale before she'd moved on in her typical style.

'Mam, can we go down to the canal to look for eels? We thought we'd ask Mrs Greene's nephew if he wants to come with us. He looks lonely, doesn't he, Aideen?'

Aideen nodded, she'd given up on trying to get a word in edgeways, and so she contented herself with nibbling on her bread.

'What about your homework?'

'We'll do it as soon as we've helped clear away the dinner things later, won't we, Aideen? Sure, we only have a little maths to do, anyway.' This wasn't true, they had rather a lot of maths to do, but it could wait. She had some very complicated sums to work out in the guise of a shopping list, but first things first. Eels!

Alice looked out the window. It was lovely out. It had been so for the last few days; summer, it would seem, had come early. The fresh air might burn off Una's boundless energy, she decided, agreeing they could head out so long as they were back in plenty of time for dinner. 'Your daddy better not have to come looking for you.' She tried to sound menacing, but their lovely sandy-haired giant of a father was not in the least bit frightening.

'And Una,' Alice added frowning, 'go and put your old cardigan on if you're going to be playing about by the canal. I didn't see you wearing that this morning when you left the house, or I'd have made you go and change.' Her elder daughter could be sneaky at times. She must have smuggled it out in her satchel when she left for school.

'Sorry, Mammy, I only wanted to show Clodagh how pretty it was and how clever you are.' She gave her mammy a winning smile.

When Mammy wasn't cooking or doing some household chore, she had her nose buried in the latest edition of Woman's Own. It was her treat, she maintained. It kept her abreast of the goings-on in the Royal family and also provided her with the patterns from which she knitted the girls woollens.

'You know better.' Alice didn't come down in the last shower, but she had no wish to take things further this afternoon. She was in too good of a mood; the weather had seen to that. Una, tinker that she was, was walking a thin line after her antics with little Aoife next door, though and would be brought into line if she crossed it again.

It was not even a week since Mrs Kelly had rapped on their door as Alice scraped the dinner plates. The woman, who always looked harried, and rightly so given her brood of seven, had her baby dangling off her hip and a tearful Aoife at her side.

'Your Una left Aoife trussed like a chicken to the lamppost and went in for her dinner,' she'd said, and Alice could see where Aoife got her tattletale tendencies from.

'Una!' She'd called over her shoulder. She'd heard Bridie Kelly bellowing at her lot next door often enough. An apology was called for from her daughter if she didn't want to feel the lash of her sharp tongue too.

Una had appeared looking sheepish. 'We were only playing cowboys and Indians, Mam.' She demonstrated her war cry before continuing, 'Aoife was my prisoner. I was going to untie her after dinner, only I forgot. Sorry, Aoife.'

Alice bit her lip to stop herself from smiling. Una didn't fool her. She knew young Aoife had told on her one time too many, and her daughter knew how to bear a grudge. 'Well, I think you need to tell Aoife you're sorry and sound like you mean it this time, don't you?'

Una had grudgingly acquiesced, and peace had been restored but not before she'd gotten a cursory telling off from Alice. She was a wild one at times was Una.

Alice picked up a potato and her peeling knife once more. Una had been told she'd miss out on the family's annual trip to Dublin Zoo if she put one more foot wrong between now and then. That girl of hers thought all she had to do was flash her smile, and she'd get off scot-free. She shook her head and went back to peeling the spuds.

Una thundered up the stairs; she had no intention of changing. She loved the cardigan's pretty blue colour and its flower border. The soft wool Mammy had knitted it with didn't itch and scratch like her clumpy old yellow one. Oh, she knew alright she wasn't supposed to wear it to school or for playing in, but she also knew it looked well on her, and she wanted to impress Mrs Greene's nephew. She looked down at those pretty flowers and felt torn, but only for a second and leaving the hated yellow one in the drawer, she raced back down the stairs.

'Una! How many times have I told you not to run down the stairs? When you break your legs, don't come running to me,' Alice's voice floated out from the kitchen.

Aideen was waiting by their front gate, still chomping on her soda bread. Her eyes widened as her sister flew out the front door. 'Why are you still wearing it? You heard Mammy.'

'My old one's itchy.' She shrugged off Aideen's concern. 'C'mon, he's still there.' She set off down the street, keen to make her getaway and find out more about this newcomer.

Aideen did what she always did and followed behind her sister.

'I'm Una Brennan, and this is my sister Aideen. We're twins, in case you didn't know. We're both ten,' Una stated boldly, coming to a halt outside Mrs Greene's front gate. Her nephew had moved to sit on the front step and was swinging a chestnut tied to a piece of string back and forth. 'And you can't play conkers on your own.'

'I know that, and it's not called a conker. It's a chessie, and I'm the champion at home.'

'Have you not seen twins before?' Aideen piped up, keen to get off on the right foot with this boy.

'Of course, I have. I'm not a culchie.'

Una wasn't sure if she believed him. 'Where are you from then?'

'Cork City. My mam's not well, and Da can't look after me as well as her, so I've come to stay with my aunt until she's better.'

'Are you an only child then?' This was incomprehensible to Una.

He nodded.

'Well, what's your name?'

'Leo.'

'We're going to look for eels in the canal. Do you want to come, Leo?'

His eyes lit up, and shoving his chestnut back in the pocket of his shorts, he stood up.

'You'd better tell Mrs Greene you'll be back in time for your dinner,' Una bossed.

Leo disappeared into the house, reappearing a beat later, followed by his aunt.

'Hello, girls.' Mrs Greene's matronly form appeared in the doorway.

'Hello, Mrs Greene.'

'So, you've met young Leo here,' she said, looking pleased he'd made some friends. 'He's staying with me awhile and will be starting at Saint Theresa's on Monday.

'You can walk with us to school, Leo, and watch out for Sister Mary Clare. She's very fond of her ruler, so she is.'

Ida Greene's mouth twitched, 'Oh, I'm sure Leo won't be on the receiving end of that now, will you, Leo? He's a good lad.'

Una wasn't so sure. He had a twinkle in his eye that said otherwise.

'Well, you'd best get on your way if you're going to be back for your dinner, and don't fall in the canal any of you! That cardigan's far too pretty to be getting a soaking in there, Una.'

The trio made their way down the street. As they rounded the bend, a huddle of pigeons fighting over slops flapped indignantly back to the rooftop from which they presided over the neighbourhood. Aideen didn't like the pigeons; she thought that they might try to peck her. Una informed Leo of this, adding that it wasn't the pecking you needed to worry about it was the other sort of deposit that was more of a problem. He laughed, and she felt very pleased with herself.

They kept their eyes open for sticks on the way which could be used to poke at the water, settling for sturdy twigs at the foot of a willow tree. The twins lead the way across the expanse of grass—it was long and tickled their shins—that would take them to the towpath.

'Oh, look at the swans.' Aideen pointed to two regal birds gliding down the water towards the reeds on the other side.

'Here looks a good spot,' Una declared, more interested in eels than swans. She made her way to the water's edge and, kneeling down, began poking at the water with her stick. The other two followed suit.

'I saw a fish!' Leo exclaimed, and the girls gathered around him as he pointed into the green water. Bubbles rose to the surface, and Una fancied she caught sight of a tail, but she couldn't be sure.

'What's it like in Cork City then?' she asked, keeping her eyes trained on the water.

Leo told them that from what he could see, it wasn't altogether that different from Dublin.

'What's wrong with your mammy?'

'She's something wrong with her heart.'

Aideen squealed. 'There!' A sinewy black shape was just visible before it slithered down into the murky depths.

'Don't lean too close, Una.'

Mindful of falling in, Una poked her stick back in the water to see if she could get it to move again, but nothing happened. Time was getting on. They'd best head home if they didn't want to get into trouble. She didn't want to be marched home by Daddy because Mammy would be sure to see her and know she hadn't done as she was told.

Una didn't know how it happened, but one minute she was clambering to her feet, brushing the dirt from her knees; the next, she had the sleeve of her cardigan snagged on Leo's stick. He jerked it, and the wool pulled away with it.

'Stop!' Una shrieked as Aideen got in the mix and tried to disentangle the stick. It was too late, though. The damage was done. 'Look what you've done. It's my best cardigan,' Una wailed, staring at the hole. She burst into tears. There'd be no hiding it from Mammy.

'Sorry, I didn't mean to.' Leo was stricken. 'It was an accident.'

'You should have been more careful!'

Leo walked off, not wanting the twins to see him upset.

'It's not Leo's fault, Una. You shouldn't have shouted at him. You should have worn your old one like Mam told you to.'

Una knew her sister was right, but it didn't help matters. She'd have to sit home on Saturday while the rest of them went to the zoo. She wouldn't get to see her favourite animals, the elephants, and she would not get an ice cream from the hokey-pokey man. She felt sick. Why, oh why hadn't she done as she was told?

It was a subdued duo who made their way back down the streets from which they'd come. They could see Leo in the distance, half running, half walking. Una knew she would have to say sorry for the way she'd behaved toward him. She hadn't meant to be horrible. She was angry at herself, not him. The fun had gone from the afternoon just like the sun was slipping behind the clouds. Una dragged her heels, feeling sicker with each step that took her closer to home.

'I'll tell Mammy it's my one, sure they're identical, aren't they?'

Una felt a flare of hope flicker and then splutter out. 'She won't believe you, Aideen. She'll know it was me not listening and doing as I was told.'

'I'll tell her I was showing off,' she nodded toward Leo, and Una knew that was exactly what she'd been doing. She'd been showing off by wearing the cardigan. Her sister had her pegged. Aideen knew her as well as she knew herself. 'Come on,' she said. 'Give it to me, and I'll put it on.'

'Thank you.' Una's voice was muffled as she shrugged out of the cardi, knowing she'd never admire the pretty flower border without feeling sick again.

'I wouldn't want to go to the zoo without you anyway,' Aideen said, taking it from her and handing Una her old yellow one that itched.

Present Day

Una's thoughts returned to the present, roused by a child's ear-piercing shriek. She glanced over to see the culprit's arms flung out, sliding down the slide to where her mammy was waiting to catch her at the bottom. She brushed a leaf away that had fallen onto her lap. Aideen had indeed taken the blame for her over the hole in that cardigan, although Una was certain Mammy had her suspicions about what had really happened. She hadn't said a word, though, as she set about darning it, mending it so you'd never know it'd been there. Una knew, though.

Her gaze flicked back to the house across the road. She and Aideen had always looked out for each other. It was the way it was. Until one day, they hadn't. The shadow from the tree in the patch of grass out the front of the house was stretching long, signalling it was getting late in the day. Una got to her feet, taking a moment to ease her aching joints, which had seized from sitting too long. She'd go and see Aideen tomorrow. She definitely would, she vowed.

Chapter 21

Aisling pushed open the guesthouse door, holding her breath in anticipation of Marcus being sat in reception. The nervous tension must be coming off her in waves, she thought. Would he be there, or wouldn't he? She was almost disappointed to see that the sofa was empty. Young Evie, looking even younger than her eighteen years with her hair pulled back in a ponytail, and no make-up save for a slick of gloss, was checking a couple in. Their clothing was somewhat eccentric. The woman was in a voluminous tie-dyed dress with a long floaty cardigan over the top, and a scarf draped around her neck, and he, with his silver beard and long wispy hair, reminded Aisling of a wizard. Merlin sprang to mind.

Evie glanced up from the computer and caught Aisling's eye, looking as though she wanted to say something. Whatever it was would have to wait until the new arrivals had been shown to their room. Their guests always came first, and, with that in mind, Aisling gathered herself, pushing thoughts of her ex aside as she came to stand alongside the bohemian pair.

'Good afternoon.' She held her hand out in greeting. It was given a warm shake in return by the gentleman. 'I'm Aisling O'Mara. Welcome to O'Mara's,' she smiled and shook his wife's hand as the gentleman introduced them both as Branok and Emblyn Nancarrow.

It was Emblyn who began to chat. She had a sing-song accent, and the way in which she rolled her 'r's' made Aisling pick them as hailing from Britain's West Country. She was right. Emblyn told her they were from Falmouth in Cornwall. Privately, Aisling couldn't help but think that the Cornish had even stranger sounding names than the Irish. Emblyn and Branok? They sounded like something from *King Arthur and the Knights of the Round Table*. To be fair, he looked like something from the old Arthurian legend, and he was supposed to have been born in their neck of the woods.

'And what brings you to Dublin? If you don't mind my asking?'

'Oh, I don't mind at all, dear. We're both artists. We own a gallery at home. Branok and I spent time in Dublin when we were young free spirits. Branok got it in his head that he wanted to relive his youth for a few days and visit our old haunts so,' she smiled, 'here we are.'

'It's a lot busier than I remember it,' Branok said, picking up their case, and Aisling was sure she heard him mumble and expensive.

'When were you last here?' Aisling asked.

'Oh, sometime in the late sixties. I had even longer hair then, and so did she. We spent a lot of time sitting in a semicircle in St Stephen's Green with other long-haired young people talking about the meaning of life.' He made a peace sign, and Aisling and Evie laughed. 'Remember how we crashed on the floor of that communal flat at night, Emblyn?'

'I do. We'd never get up again if we did that now. The emergency services would have to be called.'

'Well now, I think you'll find your bed here much comfier than the floor. I imagine you'll find Dublin quite different on this visit, but the heart of the city is still the same.' Aisling offered to help with their case and show them to their room.

'No, we'll be fine, thank you. We travel lightly. Sketchbooks and a few changes of clothes. Evie here has informed us of where we'll find everything we need. Now then, first floor, three doors down on the right. Come on, Emblyn, let's get settled in and then see about having a pint of Ireland's finest.'

Aisling recommended they check out Quinn's. She knew there was live music there tonight, and it was only a short walk from the guest house. 'Don't hesitate to ask if you need anything. We're here to help, and have a wonderful stay,' she called after them as they trooped up the stairs.

'I'm going to head up myself, Evie. Give me a buzz if you need me.'

Evie grabbed hold of Aisling's arm before she too disappeared up the stairs startling Aisling with her vice-like grip. She inclined her head toward the guest lounge, her eyes popping as she whispered, 'He's in there.'

'Who?'

'Yer man, Marcus.' Evie's voice was full of the drama of it all.

Aisling's breath caught in her throat as the thoughts raced through her head. He knew she was back. He'd have heard her voice. She'd have to go through and see him because she couldn't very well leave him sitting there. If Moira were to come home and spot him reclining on their sofa, there'd be hell to pay. For the briefest of seconds, she wondered about hiding and sending Evie in to do her dirty work, but she knew that would be beyond childish.

Be calm, be civilised, breathe slowly, and tell him to feck off, Aisling! she told herself, licking her lips. They'd gone paper dry. She'd not put lipstick on since finishing her lunch, and her hair had been whipped by the seafront wind. She wished Evie wasn't sitting there because she'd have dug out her make-up purse and tidied herself up before throwing herself into the lion's den. She didn't want to give the younger girl gossip fodder, though, knowing she was friendly with Ita. She could just imagine what the pair of them would say if they got their heads together. *Aisling was all concerned with looking her best! She obviously wanted him to see what he'd missed out on. That or she wants him back.*

No, she'd been humiliated enough when he'd left, and Evie, for all that the guests thought she was marvellous and for all her feigned wide-eyed innocence, was quite the scandalmonger. For that reason, she wiped the panicked look off her face. She took a steadying breath and thanked Evie for letting her know in a voice that did not betray the fact her insides had jellified. She held her head high and marched past the front desk and through into the guest lounge.

Chapter 22

T here he was. Larger than life, seated in one of the wingback chairs flicking through a magazine as though he
didn't have a care in the world. His lack of interest in the
magazine's content was evident in the speed with which he
was flicking through the pages.

'Hello, Marcus,' she said, coming to a halt behind the sofa
opposite him. His physical presence filled the room, and she
held onto the back of the sofa to steady herself. She'd deliberately blocked the path between them by standing where she
had. There would be no cordial hello kiss. Not on her watch.

He put the magazine down on the coffee table and stood
up. His smile was wide—too wide, and he looked delighted to
see her. He was wearing the same Oasis shirt as yesterday, she
noticed, wondering if he'd done so deliberately, given it had
been a gift from her. A subtle reminder of happier times. Now
he was at closer proximity; she could see his face looked a little thinner, and she watched as he rubbed at the stubble on his
chin. It wasn't like him not to be clean-shaven, and she forced
herself to meet his gaze. His hair was longer too, curling at
the collar instead of the short back and sides he favoured for
work. As for those swoony dark eyes, they might look tired,
but they were still having that same knee-weakening effect on
her.

'Ash! God, it's good to see you. I hope you don't mind me waiting for you here?' He lowered his voice to a conspiratorial level. 'I couldn't face listening to Evie going on about how her trip to London to see Boyzone perform at the Party in the Park was the best thing that's ever happened to her any longer.'

She wanted to smile, but she refused to. His easy-breezy way irked her. Why wasn't he on edge like she was? When she'd first met him, it was this natural confidence of his that had attracted her to him. He had a practicality about him, an ability to take control of situations. His swarthy looks had whispered of a broodiness she'd wanted to tame. Those looks were deceptive; she'd soon realised. Her imagination had outdone itself because Marcus worked with numbers at the bank. He was not a swashbuckling pirate. Nor did he have an intense deep side to him. What you saw was what you got with Marcus. Or at least that's what she'd thought.

She supposed with everything going on in her life when she'd moved back to Dublin, Marcus had been what she needed. Someone who'd take control and steer her down the unfamiliar path she'd found herself on because after Dad's passing, she'd been well and truly lost. Looking at him, it occurred to her she didn't know what she'd expected of him—that he would have changed in the year since they parted? A grovelling apology wasn't his style. Already he'd managed to put her on the back foot, which was ridiculous given he was on her territory.

'Why are you here, Marcus?' she managed to rouse herself to ask.

'You haven't replied to any of my letters.' He shrugged as though this were the obvious answer.

'Because I had nothing to say to you. You said what you wanted to say in the note you left me when you took off to Cork. You spelled things out pretty clearly.'

'Ah, Ash, that's not true. There's loads to say.'

Those eyes held hers, and her heart began to beat a little too fast. She didn't want to still find him attractive. *Pretend he's Bono, Aisling.* She hummed the first few bars of Pride, but the phone ringing jolted her, and she lost her thread. Evie would be cursing it, no doubt. She'd not be able to eavesdrop and talk on the phone. That level of multitasking wasn't in her repertoire. Aisling weakened as Marcus continued to look pleadingly at her.

'Not here.'

He glanced at his watch, 'Dinner?' then back at her hopefully.

She didn't want to sit in some cosy little restaurant listening to him blather about fresh starts. She needed to stay here on her own turf and tough it out.

'Moira's not going to be home for a while. We can talk upstairs.'

He got to his feet, and Aisling turned away, not wanting him to see her face lest the thoughts she couldn't control were written all over it. He was a fine-looking man, alright. She used to imagine what their babies would look like. Wonder whether they would have her strawberry blonde colouring or his dark features? She'd figured they'd have his, having read somewhere that brown was the dominant gene, and that was fine by her.

Evie's eyes bored into her as she informed whoever was on the phone that they did indeed have a double room available for the twenty-first overlooking the Green. *Let her think what she likes. It's none of her business.* Aisling didn't look back as she headed up the stairs. Her spine tingled with each step, aware of Marcus's proximity to her as he followed behind.

She flicked the lights on as soon as she walked into the apartment and drew the curtains out of habit. Not once did she allow her gaze to flicker in the direction of the bedroom she'd once shared with him.

He shut the door and hovered in the entranceway, seemingly not knowing where he should put himself. It must be strange to feel ill at ease in a place that had been like a second home. It was the first glimpse Aisling had had of uncertainty beneath his casual demeanour.

'It's weird being back here, Ash. If I'd handled things differently, I'd be living here with you now, as your husband.'

She wished he would stop calling her Ash. It was an intimate abbreviation; only her family and friends called her by it. His words stung. As if she needed reminding how, a year ago, her life had veered sharply off the track it had been happily tootling down. 'Well, you're not, and I'm going out soon. So why don't you sit down and say whatever it is you need to say.' She wasn't going anywhere, but he wasn't going to clutter her Saturday night. She pulled a chair out from the table and sat down. He did the same, sitting opposite her.

She could smell him, she realised. It was the spicy musk scent she'd fallen in love with when the girl on the counter at Brown Thomas had sprayed it onto a piece of card, wafting it back and forth ceremoniously before handing it to her. She'd bought the expensive aftershave for his birthday. She wondered if he was still using the same bottle or if it had long since dried up.

Should she offer him a drink? Aisling shifted in her seat. If it were any other guest, she would, but she didn't want him getting comfortable. She had no intention of making him feel at home.

'You at least read my letters?'

She nodded.

'Then there's no point in me saying I'm sorry again; you already know I am.'

The silence stretched long. Aisling feigned interest in her fingernails, and Marcus cleared his throat. She wasn't going to make this easy for him.

'I was scared, Ash. It's no excuse, but it's the truth. I panicked, and I took off.'

'Why didn't you tell me how you were feeling? I would have understood.' Her voice cracked, and she hated it for letting her down.

'No, you wouldn't have—don't pretend you would. I loved you. I still love you. That's why I'm here. So how could I tell you I shouldn't have proposed? How was I supposed to say it was too soon to get married? I'd made a mistake because I wasn't ready—didn't know if I'd ever be ready,' he shrugged. 'I tried to convince myself it would all be okay. I was clear about how I felt about you, so we'd be grand, but you got so caught up in your plans. Each time I saw you, the day was getting bigger, more elaborate. It felt like you'd forgotten what really mattered. Getting married was supposed to be about us making a commitment to each other. It terrified me, but it was a commitment I was prepared to go through with for you.'

'Stop right there.' How dare he? 'Don't you try to put the blame on me. I know what commitment is! What did you think I'd been spending all my time organising? A bloody wedding, so we could make that commitment! I was doing it for us.' Was she?

'I don't mean to sound like a condescending eejit.'

'Well, you fecking do.' She was breathing heavily.

He laid both his hands down on the table, palms facing up. 'What I said in the letter I left was true.'

'What? You asked me to marry you because you thought it was what I wanted?'

'No, yes.' He shook his head. 'Kind of. I'm digging a hole for myself. I knew I shouldn't have proposed, but it was too late I had. So, I tried to get swept up in all the plans like you were, but somewhere along the line, it stopped being about us. It was about the wedding. The castle, the menu, the photographer who was coming. It was all you ever talked about. I couldn't handle it.'

'Okay, so let me get this straight. Because I wanted a lovely day, the kind of day memories are made of, like a lot of women might I add, you thought I'd lost sight of what getting married meant?' Aisling would have liked to throw something at him, but there was only the salt and pepper shaker within reach, and she couldn't face cleaning up the mess.

'Everything snowballed, Ash. I couldn't think clearly, and so I ran. I'm so, so sorry for leaving you to face the aftermath, but I can't turn back time.'

'No, you can't. What's done is done, and I still don't understand why you've come.'

'I want you to think about giving me another chance.'

His eyes held hers, and she dropped her gaze before she lost herself. He couldn't just walk back into her life and expect to pick up where he'd left off.

'I get it must be a shock for you, me showing up like this, and you don't have to say anything, not tonight. But know this. I love you, and the biggest mistake of my life was leaving you. I'm not going to make that mistake twice. Can we try again, take things slower this time around?'

They sat in silence which Marcus broke. 'Are you happy, Ash?'

Was she? She felt like she'd been going through the motions of living since last September, nothing more.

'Please, promise me you'll think about what I've said.'

Aisling knew that now was her cue to stand up and tell him that hell would freeze over before she'd give him another chance. She should say he was a ballbag and send him packing with those bollocks of his between his knees like her mammy and sister said she should. The words, however, wouldn't come out of her mouth.

'Ash?'

'Okay.'

'You'll think about it?'

She nodded, hating herself at that moment.

'I'm staying with my mam if you want to talk or, you know, meet up. I'm in Dublin for a week.' His voice was hopeful as he got up from the table.

Aisling didn't say anything as he left, closing the door behind him. She sat at that table for a long time staring at the wall but not seeing anything other than Marcus's hopeful expression as he asked if they could try again. Her mental pen began to scribble.

Dear Aisling,

My ex-fiancé broke my heart. I thought I was moving on, but now he says he wants me back, and I'm not sure I've moved on at all. There's a part of me sorely tempted to give him a second chance because, if I'm honest, I'm lonely. I think he's genuine and means what he says. Maybe we did move too fast first time around. I just don't know if I could trust him not to leave me again. My head says send him packing, but my heart is wavering because I can't help but wonder if what he says about me having tunnel vision when it came to our wedding was true. What should I do? Follow my heart and see where it leads me or my head?

Yours faithfully,

Me

Chapter 23

Una had dozed off early. She'd had an early and agreeable dinner at a restaurant not far from the guesthouse, Quinn's. The food was simple fare, but simple fare cooked well. At her age, she couldn't be doing with spice, and there seemed to be an abundance of it about these days. The Irish digestive system was not designed for the likes of chilli. It had crossed her mind to give her compliments to the chef, but she decided not to. Her clean plate was compliment enough.

She'd laid her knife and fork down as the band had begun to unpack and had been sure to settle her bill before they could so much as strike a chord. She was not in the mood for music. The maître d' had said the most peculiar thing to her as she counted out the notes from her purse. He'd said he'd known her when she was a girl and that she and her twin sister used to love playing down by the Royal Canal. Impossible, of course, given he was only somewhere in the vicinity of his late thirties, but peculiar all the same, and the hairs on the back of her neck had stood up.

The fresh air from her day spent observing Aideen's house had made her sleepy, and she'd climbed into the double bed with its crisp white linen sheets and plump pillows in eager anticipation of a restful sleep.

She was almost grateful tonight for the now-familiar rattle and clatter that stirred her from her sleep. It had dragged her from a dream where Leo was berating her; he was calling her a stubborn, selfish fool of a woman. Each time she opened her mouth to ask him to stop, no sound would come out. It was most upsetting. She roused herself to peer out the curtains to the darkened courtyard below in time to spy the shadowy outline of a small creature creeping back toward the wall.

The moon came out from behind the clouds, and for a moment, it was as though a light had been switched on in the courtyard. She could see the fox had something in his mouth, a sausage she was fairly certain. It paused for a beat and looked up at her window. Their eyes locked, and then with a flick of his tale, he seemed to vanish into the wall. Una let the curtain fall and sighed.

She lay back down and watched the bedside clock, its red digits teasing her as they counted the seconds, the minutes until finally, the digits rolled over to three am. The dregs of the dream lingered like a painful hangover, and she tried to focus her mind on something other than Leo's angry face. There were happy memories, lots of them, and she chose the happiest of them all.

Chapter 24

♥

1948

'I love you, Una. I have done from the moment I first saw you. You were, are the most beautiful girl I've ever seen.'

'I feel the same way. I love you too, Leo.' Una gazed adoringly into his eyes before leaning forward and planting a kiss firmly on the nose of Mr Ted, her teddy. She picked the old brown bear up; his fluffy fur had rubbed away in places from all the years of holding him close to her like she was about to do now. She hugged him tight to her chest before releasing him and pressing her index finger to her lips. She was surprised to find they were cool and dry and not on fire at the memory of Leo's lips on hers.

Leo Greene might not have said those words to her this afternoon, but he had kissed her as they meandered home alongside the banks of the canal. The weather had been overcast with persistent light rain, the kind that eventually got its way and soaked you through to your skin. Neither of them was in a rush to get home, though, and so had set their own pace despite the rain.

It was her first kiss, and the butterflies it had set off in her tummy were still beating their wings madly. He'd walked her to her door, and they'd coyly let go of one another's hands before saying goodbye. His hair was plastered to his forehead, and her waves that she'd spent so long taming would now be corkscrews once more. Una had reached up and wiped away the droplet of water beginning to slide down his temple. Their eyes had locked briefly in a silent exchange that this was how it would be between them from now on before she'd ducked inside.

She'd called out a hello before charging up the stairs two at a time. She would catch a chill if she stayed in her wet things any longer, and Mam would go mad if she saw the state of her. Most of all, though, she wanted to relive that kiss in the privacy of her bedroom.

Leo was her and Aideen's second-best friend in the world; first place was reserved for each other. When his poor mammy died not long after he'd come to stay at his aunt's, his dad, unable to cope, had asked his sister if the arrangement could be made permanent. The sisters had taken him under their wing, and where they went, he went.

There'd been a subtle shift in their relationship this last year. Una had begun to see him in a different way. At sixteen, he was no longer that gawky boy who was all sharp elbows and knees. He'd filled out, and somewhere along the way, his features had become chiselled, defining the man he was becoming. Una, too had become aware of heads beginning to turn in her and Aideen's direction, of the boys, men even, eyeing them in a new manner. She hadn't returned those admiring glances. Nor, to her knowledge, had her sister, who didn't seem to have much interest in the opposite sex. Una's reasoning was different; she only had eyes for Leo. She supposed it had been that way since they were ten years old, and she'd first seen him leaning on his aunt's gate.

She'd declare all these pent-up feelings to Aideen each evening, and if Aideen wasn't to hand, then Mr Ted became her confidant. Now she thought about it, Aideen had been moody of late—quieter than usual. Una shrugged thoughts of her sister aside; she was too full of the afternoon and the feel of Leo's lips on hers.

When he'd asked her to come to the cinema with him on Saturday afternoon, there was a new film people were raving about, *The Three Musketeers*. She'd declared excitedly to Aideen that this was to be a date. A proper date. She could tell in the way he had shifted nervously when he'd asked if she'd like to go. This was no wander down to the canal to look for eels!

She'd hoped he would kiss her from the moment his arm had slipped around her shoulder in the darkened theatre. The smell of damp wool hung in the air, mingling with cigarettes, and Gene Kelly and Lana Turner filled the screen in front of them. Try as she might, Una couldn't remember a single thing that happened in the film after that. All she could concentrate on was the warmth where Leo's hand rested over her shoulder. She'd moved a little closer to him and leaned her head against his shoulder like the couple in front of them.

That damp Saturday afternoon, as the credits rolled down and people noisily exited the theatre chattering about the swashbuckling adventure they'd just watched, Leo had taken Una's hand. It felt natural; she'd thought, smiling up at him without guile.

It was near their old childhood haunt on the canal bank that Leo pulled her under the shelter of a tree. His face had softened as he looked at her, and she'd known then that he was going to kiss her. Their lips met and began a gentle exploring dance. She didn't want him to break away, but she was frightened by where the kiss might lead if he didn't. They'd both jumped apart as though scalded as a young lad on a bike raced past, calling something cheeky that was lost on the breeze.

Una put Mr Ted down, hearing Aideen's weary footfall on the stairs. Her sister pushed the door open and kicked off her shoes. She hung her coat up and quickly changed into dry clothes, draping her damp things over the end of her bed. She'd take them downstairs to hang near the fire later. Una's wet clothes lay in a puddled heap on the floor.

Aideen flopped down on the bed. 'Ah, God, my feet are killing me.' She lifted one stockinged leg and rotated her foot in small semicircles, to the left and then to the right, before doing the same with the other leg. Aideen had started work in the ladies' wear department of Brown Thomas a month back, and she was finding being on her feet all day hard work.

'I wonder if I'll get those horrible veins in my legs when I'm older like Miss Harrington. She's worked in haberdashery forever, and her legs are like gnarled tree roots. No fancy stockings can hide those.' She shuddered and eyed her slender calf, her nose wrinkling at the thought. Watching her sister, Una didn't regret her decision to apply for secretarial work upon leaving school. Being employed as a typist for an accountant might not hold the glamorous allure of selling the latest fashions showcased in Brown Thomas, but at least she sat down most of the day. And there was the bonus of not having to work on a Saturday!

Aideen had always hankered after employment in the grand department store. It stemmed from their annual trip to the store's sale to buy new shoes and a coat when they were smaller. Mammy was a stickler for quality, and if it meant knitting and sewing, everything else in her daughters' wardrobe, so be it. The Brennan girls were always well-turned out—apart from when they went looking for eels, poking about by the banks of the canal!

Aideen was the quiet, dreamy sister who loved inventing stories around the lives of the well-heeled ladies with furs draped across their shoulders they'd see on those outings. She'd gawp at them swanning around the store, like gazelles at home in their natural environment. Now here she was working there, six days a week—and her feet and legs had never ached so much in her life.

It was then she saw Mr Ted, and she looked from the stuffed toy to her sister, noticing the silly expression she had on her face. 'What've you been doing?'

Una giggled. 'I told you I was going to see *The Three Musketeers* with Leo.'

Aideen nodded. 'Was Lana Turner gorgeous?'

'I don't know.'

Aideen's face creased in irritation. She'd had a long day and wasn't in the mood for playing silly games. 'What do you mean?'

Una giggled, oblivious to how this silly girly version of herself was annoying her sister. 'Leo put his arm around me, and I don't remember much about the film at all after that. He held my hand when we walked home, and we got soaked to the bone, but we didn't care. When we reached the big tree by the canal, he pulled me to him like this,' she demonstrated by picking up Mr Ted once more, 'and he kissed me.' Mr Ted bore the brunt of her affections once more, and when she released him, she turned to look at her sister and said, 'Aideen, it was perfect.'

ell

Present Day

Una realised she was smiling as she lay in the darkness. Her index finger was resting on her lip as it had done all those years ago when she'd sat on her bed remembering Leo's sweet kiss. Now she wondered why she hadn't noticed the way her sister's face had crumpled as she relayed the story of her and Leo's outing. How had it escaped her notice that her sister too was in love with Leo Greene and just like her had been since they were ten years old? How her disobeying her mam all those years before could have had ripples like a stone being thrown in a pond. She knew the answer. She'd had plenty of time to think on it.

It was because she hadn't wanted to see it. She was sixteen and in that way of young girls far too absorbed in her own feelings to want to acknowledge anyone else's. Her sixteen-year-old self-had been caught up in the thrill of her first love, enthralled by it, and she hadn't seen Aideen, not really. Una blinked away the burn of tears and sighed, partly in frustration at her lack of sleep and partly in sorrow at the way things had turned out for them.

If she were at home, she would get up and make herself a cup of tea. She listened out, but there was nothing to hear. The guesthouse was silent. Would it matter if she were to go and make herself a cup of tea in the guests' lounge? It wouldn't disturb anyone, and it had to be better than lying here wide awake being tormented by things she couldn't change. Yes, she decided, pushing the covers aside and sitting up, she'd make herself a cup of tea. Mammy's friend Maire had always said a good strong brew could fix anything.

Chapter 25

A isling's mind was whirring with thoughts of Marcus's visit and what she should do. She'd been tossing and turning for hours. This was hopeless, she sighed, pulling herself upright. She flicked on the bedside light. She might as well get up and make herself a cup of tea. It would be better than spending another hour thumping her pillow in frustration.

Moira's door was open a crack, and she could hear her sister snoring lightly. It had been late when she'd gotten in. Aisling had already been in bed for what felt like hours when Moira peered around her door whispering loudly, 'Ash, are you awake?' She'd stayed silent and lain still, in no mood to talk to her inebriated sister. She knew if Moira had gotten wind of Marcus having been to see her, she would be in for a tipsy tirade, and the language would not be pretty. Moira gave up after a few beats and stumbled off to bed.

Aisling knew she'd be sleeping like a log, so there was no need to tiptoe as she made her way through to the darkened kitchen and switched on the light. There was a slight chill in the air, and she was glad of her fluffy dressing gown as she set about retrieving a mug from the dishwasher. The central heating wouldn't come on until five, timed to be toasty for the morning. It was the time of year when the early mornings and evenings were a reminder of the march of autumn toward winter.

Aisling went through the motions of filling the kettle and switching it on. She cursed under her breath as she opened the tea canister and saw it was empty. She stood there for a moment. Should she forget the tea and go back to bed? The thought of lying awake until daybreak held no appeal. There were plenty of teabags in the guest lounge. She knew this because she'd restocked them again that morning.

Should she brave going downstairs? No one would be about at this time. She wouldn't disturb anyone, not if she was quiet. Her decision made; she went and searched out her slippers and, being careful not to lock the apartment door behind her—she'd have to set off the fire alarms if she locked herself out and needed to wake Moira—she set off down the stairs. Every creak of the old timber beneath the carpet seemed magnified in the silence of the old house, and she stood cringing for a second or two on the staircase before taking the next step.

She finally reached the bottom and stood frozen by the realisation that a light was on in the lounge. The door was pulled to but not shut, and in the darkness, she could see the glimmer creeping out through the cracks. It wasn't like Evie to forget to turn everything off. Her dad picked her up faithfully at ten pm, and she always did the rounds before locking up for the night of a weekend.

Who would be sitting in there at this hour of the night? Perhaps one of their guests had had one too many and fallen asleep on the sofa. She'd take a peek. It wouldn't be fair for James to be confronted by some drunkard when he arrived in the morning—that was not in his job description!

Aisling pushed the door open and peered into the room, blinking against the sudden brightness. It took her a second to realise Una Brennan was staring back at her. She was sitting in one of the antique wingback armchairs. A small figure shrouded in her dressing gown, which was green like the fabric Mammy had chosen to recover the chairs in. *To tie the curtains in and bring the whole look together,* she'd said. A cup of tea was cooling on the teak occasional table, and the light came not from the chandelier dangling from the middle of the ceiling but rather the freestanding reading lamp. It illuminated Miss Brennan somewhat spookily from behind.

Una's eyes mirrored the same surprise as Aisling's, cats' eyes caught in headlights at finding one another awake at this time.

Aisling spoke first. 'I'm sorry to disturb you, Miss Brennan,' she stepped into the room. 'I've run out of teabags upstairs. I'll just grab a couple and leave you in peace.' She'd given the woman a fright she knew, but then she'd gotten one herself.

'You couldn't sleep either?' Una asked, her heart beginning to slow to its normal rate of beats per minute once more. She hadn't known who was going to appear when the door had squeaked open, and she was acutely aware that she was in her robe and slippers.

'No, things on my mind and the harder I try not to think about them, the worst it gets.' Aisling smiled ruefully, making her way over to the buffet to retrieve the teabags.

'I'd like the company if you care to join me.' Una was surprised at the words that popped unbidden from her mouth.

Aisling, too was taken aback. This was not the same shrewish woman she'd been encountering these last few mornings.

'Thank you. I'll make myself a cuppa. Would you like a top-up?'

'Yes ta.'

Aisling set about making the tea, all the while wondering over the peculiar situation she found herself in.

'My mam had a friend who always said a cuppa could fix anything.' Una repeated her earlier sentiment out loud this time as Aisling placed the cup and saucer down next to her and, picking up her own cup, sat down in the chair on the other side of the occasional table.

Aisling blew on the steam rising from her teacup. 'I don't think a cup of tea is going to fix my problem.'

'Nor mine,' Una said. 'When I was little, I used to think tea must have magical properties if it could fix things.'

Aisling raised a smile. 'My mammy always says that a problem shared is a problem halved.' It was one of Maureen O'Mara's favourite sayings.

'Hmm, simplistic but possibly more helpful than tea alone.'

Aisling stole a glance at the older woman. Her face looked gentler than it had this morning. She realised it was because she wasn't wearing the disgruntled expression she'd perpetually had in place since arriving at O'Mara's. It would be nice to confide in someone who could view her situation from a neutral vantage point.

'You could be my Switzerland,' she said.

'I beg your pardon?'

'Oh, sorry, I was thinking aloud. What I meant was that if I talk to you, you'd be neutral. You won't have a pre-existing opinion like my family and friends. They all think my ex, Marcus is a selfish eejit.'

'Ah, I see.'

They sat in silence for a minute or two, sipping their respective tea. It was Aisling who spoke up.

'This time last year, we were going to be married. We hadn't known each other long, but I knew as soon as I met him, he was the one for me. Or, at least I thought I did.' Aisling began haltingly at first and then decided, as her mammy would say, in for a penny in for a pound.

'He wasn't because he took off for Cork two weeks before our wedding with a bad case of cold feet. All he left behind was a note saying he loved me, but he didn't want to marry me. I was beside myself, but I threw myself into managing this place, and I was beginning to see that my life would go on without him when he started writing to me. He'd made a mistake, and he wanted me back. I ignored his letters, but they kept coming, and then yesterday he came here, to the guesthouse to see me. I wanted to hate him or at the very least still be angry with him, and I tried as hard as I could to conjure up those emotions, but I couldn't.'

'And now part of you wants to give him a second chance, and part of you feels that to do so would be letting yourself down.'

'Exactly.' Aisling drained her tea. 'Listening to him yesterday, it became clear why he never wanted to get married. His parents have an unhappy life together, and he's scared of winding up like them. He got caught up in the idea of it because he says, *it's what he thought I wanted.*'

'And did you?'

She nodded. 'My dad hadn't long passed, and I was pleased to have something else to focus on. So yes, I suppose I got swept up in the idea of a perfect day, but now, I'm not sure now whether it was for Marcus and me at all. I've had plenty of time to think, and I can see I was using the wedding as an antidote for me, Mammy, Roisin, and Moira to Dad dying. Only there is no antidote to grief. We were all reeling from his illness and the fact he wasn't with us anymore when I met Marcus. I think that's why our relationship moved as fast as it did. Maybe I did bully him along. Oh, I don't know.' Aisling shrugged. 'What he did leaving the way he did, I just don't know if I can ever move past that.'

'Yes, I can quite see your problem.' Una took a sip of her tea as she mulled over Aisling's predicament. 'The solution's really rather simple, though.'

It was? This was promising. Aisling leaned toward Una, eager to hear what she would say next.

'You must follow your heart, dear. There's a lot to be said for forgiveness, Aisling. It isn't always an easy thing to do, but it is the right thing to do. You don't want to live a life of regrets because you were too proud to find a way back.'

Aisling got the distinct impression they were no longer talking just about her and Marcus.

'I was engaged once too. A long time ago now.' Una's voice snagged as she found herself wheeling back in time to 1950, telling Aisling the story of that year and how what had happened had changed the course of her life irrevocably.

Chapter 26

♥

1950

U na pushed open the front gate and made her way up the path. She'd finished work early, having asked Mr Hart if she might go home. She'd woken that morning feeling odd, and as the day had stretched on, she'd begun to feel decidedly unwell. The contents of her breakfast had been tossed up in the toilet, and her throat was hot and aching. Her eyes were burning, and she couldn't focus on the paperwork she was supposed to be typing. She was chilled one minute and fiery the next. A pink rash, too, had appeared in the creases of her arms. It alarmed her, and she'd desperately tried not to scratch at it.

A bout of flu no doubt, Mr Hart had tutted, his tone suggesting she shouldn't have come into the office at all spreading her germs. He sent her home. She'd sat with her aching head resting against the window of the bus as it wound its way through the streets to the stop closest to home. She could do without getting sick. Her plan had been to race down to Dawson Street on her lunch break to pick up the copy of Modern Bride she'd ordered in. It was due to arrive today. Mammy had offered to sew her wedding dress, and she wanted to get some ideas as to the latest styles.

The wedding dress could wait, and she shut her eyes briefly, willing the bus to hurry up. All she wanted was to sleep.

How she made it up the stairs to her bed was a blur. So too were the events that transpired from then until her fever broke and she found herself in a hospital bed. She was in a ward with only one other bed. It was occupied by a young girl of about six or seven years who hailed from a small village in County Clare. She was tucked up in the bed across from Una. Her large eyes in her head showed she was very poorly. It was a mystery to Una as to what she was doing there.

It was explained by one of the kindlier nurses, her voice muffled by the mask she wore; she had scarlet fever. She was to stay in the Cork Fever Hospital in isolation for the next three to four weeks at least. It was a mystery where she'd caught the illness.

Her only visitors during that time were her mam and her dad. They came once a week, but even they were not allowed in to see her. They could merely stand at the glass and tell her the news. Mam told her they'd burned her bedding on the advice of the doctor who'd made the diagnosis before she was whisked away in the ambulance. Neither they nor Aideen were showing any symptoms, thank the lord. Leo, too was fighting fit. They sent their love.

Una was grateful for those visits. They were her only link with the outside world. Her world consisted of hushed, no-nonsense voices, an all-pervasive smell of carbolic soap, and scratchy sheets. She knew too her mam would struggle bringing herself to the less than salubrious part of the city where the hospital was located. This wasn't out of snobbery but rather fear—fear of catching something like the dreaded tuberculosis which was raging through the city. The rest of the wards in the hospital would have been full of people afflicted with the illness.

It was such a strange time. She was sick, yes, but still lucid enough to be lonely, homesick, and terribly bored. What it must have been like for the little girl who shared the small space with her Una couldn't comprehend. To be so little and so far away from home must have been terrifying. The nurse had confided that the girl, Maggie, had rheumatoid fever on top of scarlet fever and would be staying longer than Una. If indeed Maggie had felt frightened by the alien space she found herself in, she never said. In fact, she barely strung a sentence together the whole time Una was there despite their proximity.

With nothing else in which to occupy her time, Leo filled her thoughts. It was a form of torture not to be able to see him, and she missed Aideen terribly, even if she had been a moody mare this last while. She'd felt a distance growing between her and her sister over the course of the year. Una put it down to the difference in their circumstances. She was a young woman with a fiancé while Aideen, despite several advances, had declined all her potential suitors. She was too picky by far, and if she weren't careful, she'd wind up an old spinster Una would think, plucking at her sheets in irritation.

She thought it likely, although she'd never ask and Aideen would never say, that she was envious of her situation. She was jealous of how Leo took up so much of her time these days. It was time previously reserved for each other, and of course, Leo too had been as much a part of Aideen's world as he had Una's from the time they were ten years old. The old saying three's a crowd was true, however. One couldn't conduct a romance with a third party in tow. Perhaps her sister had felt pushed out. She put herself in her sister's shoes and decided that this must be the case.

She'd been so caught up in her own love affair she hadn't spared the time to think about Aideen and how it must have affected her. She'd merely found her twin's moodiness a selfish irritant designed to dampen her happiness.

It was the way of life, though, wasn't it? Things had to change. People grew up and fell in love. They got married and started families of their own. She made up her mind that she would talk to Aideen once she was well and home once more to explain all of this to her. Tell her that just because she was going to start a new chapter with Leo didn't mean that there wouldn't always be a special place reserved for Aideen. They were part of each other, after all. Two halves that made a whole.

Yes, she resolved, she would smooth the waters over once she got home.

In between these musings, she'd lie on her bed, fed up with herself and her bland surroundings. She'd imagine where Leo was and what he'd be doing at different times during the day. Her mind would drift toward their wedding. No date had been set, but still, she'd imagine herself in a dress similar to that worn by Elizabeth Taylor in her May wedding to Conrad Hilton Jr. Aideen as bridesmaid would wear blue, it was her favourite colour. She'd get swept along in a tide of images depicting horse-drawn carriages and magnificent cathedrals where she and Leo would exchange vows.

She was not delusional, though; she and Leo were not royalty or Hollywood stars, and the reality was her dress would be handmade by her mother. It would not be as voluminous as Elizabeth Taylor's shimmery, satin affair, but it would be pretty. The gown would be made with the sort of love money could never buy, and she would feel every inch the beautiful bride. The ceremony would take place in St Peter's Church, where they had attended Mass for as long as they'd resided in Phibsborough—forever! As for her carriage, she had her fingers crossed Dad would be able to borrow his boss's Bentley to drive her and Aideen to the church.

A honeymoon would be nice too. Una hadn't seen much of life outside of Dublin. She didn't think the odd stay down at her cousin Janet's near Wexford counted for much. Connemara would be pretty; she'd seen pictures of it in springtime in a magazine when the purple heather had formed a glorious carpet around the lakes. Or, if they saved enough money, they could cross the water and visit Wales; she had a second cousin who lived on a farm there.

Una would flush as she thought about what her nights might be like on her honeymoon. The lovemaking was something she didn't know much about. She and Aideen had gleaned what little information they did have from the whispered conversations of girls at school. It was something she suspected that, while initially a little frightening, would ultimately be something she'd enjoy very much—if those yearnings she felt when she and Leo kissed were anything to go by!

The time passed as time does, and the day came when Una left that white-walled hospital room. She felt sad to be leaving little Maggie on her own, but she couldn't wait to escape the confines, and she didn't look back as she walked away from the building. Her dad picked her up in his new Anglia. This was something that had changed in the time she'd been in hospital. The family now had a car. It made Una aware that while she had been shut away, life had indeed gone on.

The car was her dad's pride and joy, and he gave her a running commentary of the mechanics behind it as they pootled home. Mam, he mentioned, in between explaining how the gears worked, had organised a party tea. A celebration of their girl being well and coming home. Una walked through their front door, already tired from the exertions of leaving the hospital and listening to her dad. She was pale and thin and felt like she'd been away for months, not weeks, but she was home.

She was greeted warmly, and if things were off with Aideen and Leo, she didn't pick up on it. She never saw her mammy's worried frown as she glanced from each of her daughters and back over to Leo. Nor did she hear the forced joviality in her dad's voice as he tried to ward off the storm he knew was coming. The illness had left her drained and oblivious to the shifting sands of their relationship. They'd been sifted through and redefined while she'd been in hospital. But she knew nothing of this.

Chapter 27

♥

Present Day

The clatter of Aisling's teaspoon against her saucer as she placed her cup back down startled Una from her story. It was jarring in the silence, a quiet only broken by Una's murmuring voice. 'Do you know, even thinking about my spell in hospital conjures up the smell of carbolic soap. I couldn't get the stench of it from my nostrils for the longest time.'

Aisling stared into her empty teacup, there were no tea leaves at the bottom, and she didn't believe in that sort of thing, anyway. Nevertheless, she had a fair idea what was coming. She was so caught up in the emotion of what she'd been listening to; she hadn't been aware of her eyes beginning to smart with unshed tears at the unfairness of Una's story. She blinked hard to ward them off.

'Leo and Aisling waited until I was back to full health before they said anything.'

It was no good the blinking didn't work, and a tear rolled down Aisling's cheek. It was as she'd feared. She swiped it away, feeling a surge of anger for this woman, a virtual stranger whose life she now knew intimately, at the events that had unfurled fifty years ago.

'It was Leo who told me it was Aideen he'd loved all along. He called for me a week or so after I got home. The fresh air would do me good, he said, suggesting a stroll alongside the canal. It must have been a Saturday because Aideen wasn't home. I can remember seeing Mam's face, pale and anxious, as she told me to be sure to do my coat up. I put it down to her worrying about my health, but I think she had an inkling that things weren't as they'd been between Leo and me. There was tension between us as we set off. A sudden awareness on my part that something had changed between us over the course of my hospital stay. I wondered why he didn't reach for my hand like he always did, but I didn't say anything. When he suggested we sit down on a bench not far from the spot where we'd shared that first kiss, I was grateful for the opportunity to rest. The short walk had left me breathless, and my limbs felt like dead weights. I'd been told to expect this; it would be a long time before my physical health returned to what it had been. It wasn't just my physical self that had been damaged, though; my brain, too, seemed to struggle to process things for a long time after I left the hospital. I couldn't hold onto thoughts for any length of time. Words I wanted to say would be right there, and then they'd dissipate like smoke. Such a strange time.' She shook her head and toyed with the tie of her dressing gown for a beat before continuing.

'Once I was settled on the seat, Leo took my hand, and I felt a weight lift because I thought to myself that everything would be alright now. It was then he explained in a matter-of-fact manner he'd made a mistake. His voice was steady, measured, as though he'd practised what he was going to say to me. I couldn't make sense of it. This wasn't the Leo I knew, and I thought it must be me not processing things properly. I'd misunderstood because his words were nonsensical. Him and Aideen? It only sank in when he took his hand away from mine. This was how things would be from now on. It would be my sister's hand, not mine he'd be holding.'

'Oh, Una!' Aisling got up and put her cup and saucer down on the buffet. She wanted to hug the older woman, but Una held her hand up to silence her. She needed to finish. She needed to share this story. She'd never breathed a word of it to anyone since the day Leo Greene had shattered her heart into pieces so small she'd never managed to put them back together again.

'It was my personality, you see. I didn't understand what he meant, and he tried to explain, saying I was so strong-willed. He'd gotten swept along by the sheer force of what I wanted. It was only when I was convalescing that he'd had time to clear his head and think properly, to understand his feelings. It had been Aideen all along. Quiet, gentle Aideen. I don't remember much of what he said after that. They were words that tumbled on top of each other rather like clothes in a washing machine. What needed to be said had been said, and the rest was just that, words. It had become clear that Aideen, too, had been in love with him just as I had from the time she was ten years old. I'd chosen not to see it because then my feelings for Leo would have been impossible. I was hurt, yes, and I might have been able to move on from the pain eventually, but not the humiliation. That and the sense of betrayal was the worst of it, Aisling. I was a proud woman, foolishly proud.'

'I know a little about what that's like,' Aisling murmured, her heart going out to this woman huddled inside her dressing gown on the chair next to her. Her story was far more wounding than Aisling's. She'd been hurt by the two people she was closest to in the whole world. Heartbreak was heartbreak, though, and she did know how deep that pain cut. Her words had echoed those of Marcus too. He'd said he'd gotten swept along by what she wanted.

Una nodded. 'Yes, I suppose you do.'

Aisling got up and took the cup and saucer from Una's, whose hand was shaking. She placed it on the buffet next to her own before sitting back down. Una began talking again. 'I couldn't get the thoughts out of my head of how I'd prattled on about the wedding to them both. How I'd told them it was all I thought about while I was in the hospital, and all the while, they'd nodded and smiled, told me how good it was I well again. How great it was I was home. All that time they'd known my talk of getting married was farcical. How could Aideen, whom I'd confided all my hopes and dreams in, do that to me? It ate away at me for the longest time.'

'What did you do, you know, after Leo told you how he felt?'

'It was a little like being sick again, there are chunks of time I can't recall, but I do remember shouting at Aideen and grabbing at her hair; where that strength came from, I don't know. Mam pulled me off her. It was Aideen who bore the brunt of my anger. I couldn't carry on living under the same roof as her, so I packed my bags. Mam and Da begged me to stay. Time would heal, Mam said, but I wouldn't listen. I only made one stop after I left the house that day, and that was to Mr Hart. I thanked him for his kindness in holding my job open while I was ill and for allowing me the extra time to recuperate at home, but I wouldn't be coming back.' Una's laugh held no mirth. 'Oh, the look on his studious face when I told him I was leaving due to the fact my sister, my twin sister no less, had stolen my fiancé. Thus, rendering my life in Dublin intolerable.'

Such was the picture Una was painting Aisling could almost see the small middle-aged man with thinning hair sitting behind his desk. The scandalised expression he'd have worn at what his young secretary was telling him.

'I took all the money Leo and I'd saved for our wedding out of the bank and closed the account. There was no guilt in the act. I felt I was owed it after what he'd done. I said goodbye to Mr Hart and made my way to the train station. I boarded the first train out of Dublin. I didn't care where I wound up so long as it was miles away from the city.'

'And you wound up in Waterford.'

'Yes. I made a new life for myself there.'

'But what about your mam and dad?'

'I think I regret the pain I caused them the most. My poor dad somewhat ironically was killed in an accident in his beloved Anglia not long after I left. But something had happened to me in the aftermath of Leo and Aideen. It was like my heart had been hardened. I couldn't feel like I felt before. It was like nothing would ever cut quite so deep again. I wrote to Mammy and told her where I was. She came to visit me, but things between us were always strained because of my refusal to hear any news about my sister. I would not and could not forgive her or Leo.'

'And you never saw either of them again?'

'I saw them twice, both times at funerals, first Dad's and then Mam's. I kept my distance from them and their sons both times; they had three boys all close in age. Aideen tried to make amends, she wrote and asked to be forgiven, but I couldn't get past what had happened. Leo tried to put things right, he approached me after Mam's service, but I gave him short shrift. He got rather angry and called me a selfish woman.'

It was unfair of Leo, Aisling mused because she could see how hard it would be to mend bridges that had been blown to smithereens. But it also seemed, listening to her tale, that despite the wrongs done to her, it was Una who'd lost out in the end. Her life had never been whole since she left Dublin because of her refusal to bend in her emotions. She'd lost not just her fiancé; she'd lost her family too. It was just too sad. She swiped another rogue tear away with the back of her hand.

Una glanced at her sharply. 'Don't waste your tears on me, Aisling. What's done is done. It was my foolish fault not to at least try to find some forgiveness in my heart. If I had, I might have been able to open myself up to the possibility of someone else, but I was too stubborn for that, and I'd lost the ability to trust in others.'

'You never met anyone else?'

'Oh, I had a few suitors over the years, but I wouldn't let them close enough to hurt me. One by one, they got tired of being held at arm's length and moved on.' Una reached over then and took hold of Aisling's hand, giving it a brief squeeze. 'Don't let pride stand in the way of happiness, my dear. If you're sure of your feelings and you still love this man, then find a way to put that wedding business behind you and give him another chance.'

Aisling shifted uncomfortably. She didn't know how she felt. Marcus's sudden appearance had her in a spin. She did know she was scared of making the wrong choice and regretting it in years to come. She didn't want to be like Una living a life in bitterness. She deflected the subject from herself, curious as to why Una had come back to Dublin now, after all those years. What had changed? 'Why are you here now?'

Una didn't answer the question right away; she still seemed lost in the past. 'Do you know I used to walk past O'Mara's on my way to work for Mr Hart?' It wasn't a question rather a statement, and a small smile played at the corners of her mouth. 'I dreamed of what it would be like behind the grand brick facade, and I used to imagine the stories that had played out inside these walls. It's funny to think my story's part of the fretwork now, too, isn't it?'

Aisling smiled gently. 'Una, I hope your story's going to have a happy ending.'

'You asked me why I've come back?'

Aisling nodded.

'Aideen wrote to me not long ago. It was the first letter I'd received from her in years. She'd long since given up on contacting me, and I suppose I was curious as to why she was getting in touch after all this time. I felt compelled to read it, and once I had, well, I had no choice but to come back.'

Aisling was on the edge of the seat.

'Leo passed a few years back, a heart attack. It was a terrible shock, by all accounts. No warning. One minute he was standing in the kitchen talking to her about the early peas in the garden, the next, he'd keeled over, and that was that. It's strange to imagine him gone. To know, I'll never see him again. I suppose I always thought I might one day, that somehow, we'd all come back together, but time marches on. That wasn't what she wrote to tell me, though. She wrote to say she's sick herself. It's breast cancer.'

'Oh, I'm sorry, is she having treatment? What's her prognosis?' She might never have met Una's twin, but she felt now as though she had, privy as she'd been to the sisters' past.

'She didn't get into any of that. She didn't write so as I'd feel sorry for her or anything like that. She got in touch because she wanted to tell me to go and get checked myself.'

'You should, Una, things like that can be hereditary, and if it's caught quick enough, well, the doctors can work wonders these days.' She shivered, thinking of her own dad's fight with stomach cancer. It was still an open wound. She knew he'd been unwell for a long time before he'd gone to the doctor. He'd always had an aversion to medical practitioners. There was no reason for this so far as Aisling knew, other than he thought he knew better. A glass of Guinness could fix anything. *Sure*, he'd say, *the black stuff is a meal in a glass. It's loaded with goodies.*

Aisling couldn't help but wonder if he hadn't been so pig-headed whether his cancer might have been caught sooner. Things may have had a different outcome.

She knew right enough that the disease was hard to detect in the early stages. She'd heard all the jargon, but they'd never know for sure whether it might have been picked up had he been checked. She'd never voiced these thoughts out loud, and she didn't know if anyone else in the family shared her sentiment. It would be pointless to bring it up now, achieving nothing because he was gone and, as Una had just said, that was that.

'I started thinking after I read her letter, and I couldn't stop thinking about what Aideen was like when we were young. She looked out for me. I was the wilful one who skirted the edges of trouble, but she always had my back.'

Her eyes, Aisling saw, were glazed with faraway memories of the past.

'There was an occasion I couldn't get out of my head. It was the day we met Leo for the first time, and I insisted on wearing my new cardigan despite Mam specifically telling me not to—not when looking for eels. She'd knitted identical blue cardigans with the prettiest of flower trims for Aideen and me. I knew I should do as I was told, but I didn't. I wore it because I wanted to impress him; even then, there was something about Leo Greene. Somehow as we were getting up to go home, Leo's stick got snagged in it, and when he freed it, there was a gaping hole. He told me the day he broke it off between us. He'd felt so terribly bad all those years ago about that. There he'd been homesick and missing his mam, going to the canal with Aideen, and I was the tonic he'd needed. He said he'd been grateful I'd taken the time to talk to him, and then he'd gone and spoiled it. He'd been making it up to me ever since.' Una shook her head. 'Fancy him feeling like that; I had no idea. At the time it happened, I was sick to my stomach because it meant I'd miss out on our annual trip to the zoo. Aideen said she didn't want to go without me and took the cardigan from me, wearing it home herself. She told Mam it was hers and that she'd been showing off to the lad who'd come to stay with Mrs Greene down the road. I don't think Mam believed her—she knew me too well—but she had no choice, and you see, that's the way Aideen was. She wasn't cruel and spiteful or selfish, as I tried to convince myself. The enormity of all these lost years hit me then.' Una's voice cracked for the first time. 'So, that's why I came back.'

Aisling got up and put her arm around her shoulder. They stayed like that for a few minutes, and she couldn't help but think what an incongruous sight the pair of them made in their nightwear, spilling their secrets in the dead of night.

'Have you been to see Aideen, Una?' Aisling asked, assuming that this was where the woman had gone each day since she'd come to stay at the guesthouse.

'No, not exactly.'

Aisling was puzzled. 'But I thought that was why you'd come to Dublin?'

'It is, and I've caught a taxi to the street where she lives every day since I arrived, but I haven't been able to walk up her front path and knock on her door. I've been sitting across the street on a bench in the park opposite.'

It was a good job the weather had behaved itself, Aisling thought. Then again, maybe if the heavens had opened, Una might have been forced to shelter inside Aideen's house.

'I don't know how I'll be received; you see. She never asked me to come back. She might hate me, Aisling. She might be angry with me for leaving and not trying to work things out. She might think me a selfish old fool, and I have been.' Una's voice rose several notches, and she looked small and vulnerable, absolutely nothing like the cantankerous woman Aisling had encountered each morning.

'I don't think so, Una. You said she was your other half.'

Una nodded.

'Well, I think you'll find she understands why you couldn't stay. You were hurt badly by her and Leo. What they did, even if it was done out of love for each other and not with the intent of hurting you, is not something most people would find easy to forgive.'

Una wasn't listening. 'I've come to realise I'm a coward. I ran away when I couldn't face what had happened, and now, I can't summon the courage to knock on my own twin's door.'

Aisling didn't need to compose one of her letters. The answer was simple. 'You're not a coward, Una! I think you're very brave for coming here. You've just got to take the next step. Do you think it would help if we went to Aideen's house together?'

Una looked at the pretty young woman opposite her. That glorious red blonde hair of hers was sticking up here, there, and everywhere, the result of all the tossing and turning she must have done before making her way downstairs. 'You'd do that for me?'

'I would gladly come with you, but I'm afraid you're going to have to do something for me in return first.'

Una felt her guard go up. She should have known there was nothing for nothing in this life.

'I want you to tell Mrs Flaherty how much you enjoy her white pudding. She's a little temperamental, our cook, and a little praise goes a long way with her. It's her day off tomorrow, but she'll be back on-board Monday morning, and it would get the week off to a good start!'

Una looked at Aisling in disbelief and her lips curved into a smile, mirroring the girl opposite her. 'I think I can do that.'

Chapter 28

O n Sunday morning, the run of good weather decided it had had enough, and when Aisling woke, she could hear the rain pelting against her bedroom window. The sound of it hitting the panes of glass was something she'd always loved. To lie in bed, warm and cosy, knowing outside was cold and wet, was a snuggly treat, and she burrowed down under her covers.

Marcus's handsome features floated in front of her, and she conjured up the warmth of his body and the way in which he used to press himself up against her. She could almost feel his breath on her neck and the tingles it would send up and down her spine. They'd fitted together, slotted into place like pieces in a jigsaw puzzle.

He's a selfish eejit. A spoiled only child used to getting his own way, and when he doesn't, he throws his toys out of the cot. Moira's words reverberated in her ear. Would he flounce off to another city the next time he felt she didn't have his best interests at heart? People did make mistakes, though. Listening to Una's sad story last night had opened her eyes to that. Nobody was perfect, but did people change?

The birds had been chirping by the time she and Una had made their way back to their beds, exhausted and spent. Neither woman had any wish to be caught out in their nightwear by an early-rising guest, so they'd said goodnight or good morning, unsure what was appropriate. They'd arranged to meet in the guest lounge once more. This time however it would be at the respectable hour of eleven am, and with that, they'd hugged each other tightly. Aisling had climbed the stairs, let herself quietly back into the apartment and fallen into bed, drifting off into a dreamless sleep almost straight away.

It was quite amazing, she thought, enjoying the weight of her bedding on her, that she should form such a strong bond in such a short space of time with a woman she'd dreaded bumping into these last few mornings! Who would have thought?

Still, waters run deep, she mused, then realising that was exactly the sort of thing Mammy would say changed the sentiment to you could never judge a book by its cover. That was worse! She decided to abandon the train of thought and risk a peek at the clock. It was nine forty-five, and she felt a stab of guilt at having lain in so late.

Normally she would have been up and about making sure O'Mara's morning routines were playing out as they should be. The guesthouse under her watch ran like a well-oiled machine, or at least she liked to think it did; Ita's face floated to mind—the exception to the rule. Still, she was off today, and it would be Geraldine humming as she stripped beds and vacuumed.

It was a pity Geraldine and Ita didn't swap places. Geraldine had no interest in working more than the four hours she did on a Sunday morning, though. Not with three littlies running around at home. Her Sunday morning job, she'd confided in Aisling, was a welcome break from the routines of being Mam to her trio, but by the time one o'clock rolled around, she was ready for the off, eager to see them all again.

James would have been stationed at the front desk for well over an hour now, too, Aisling knew. He'd have already demolished the enormous plate of eggs, bacon, and sausage Mrs

Baicu foisted on to him every Sunday morning not long after he let himself in. She had sons herself, she said and knew how much they loved to eat. She'd come to Ireland with her husband from Romania many moons ago and would be in the kitchen cooking up a storm. Her roots might not hail from here, but she could still whip up a full Irish fry-up to rival Mrs Flaherty's with her eyes closed. Not that Aisling would ever tell Mrs Flaherty that!

They were all more than capable of doing their jobs without Aisling peering over their shoulders. And while they might wonder where she was this morning, O'Mara's would not grind to a halt without her. Nevertheless, it was time she got up if she were going to be ready in time to meet Una. She needed a strong cup of coffee after her broken night.

She hoped Una had managed to catch a few hours solid sleep too. She'd need it. They had a big afternoon planned. This time Una would walk up the front path and knock-on Aideen's door. She tossed her blankets aside and shrugging into her dressing gown and slippers once more, padded through to the kitchen.

Moira was already up. Her dark hair was tied back in a loose ponytail, and she was lounging on the sofa in her pyjamas; the television tuned into a soap opera where everybody on the screen looked hard done by. She was engrossed in their problems and didn't hear Aisling enter the room as she spooned cereal into her mouth.

'Good night, was it?' Aisling called as she set about making herself a cup of coffee. 'You were snoring like a train. I could hear you through the walls.' At least she was up and about and looking a lot brighter than she had yesterday morning, she thought as she retrieved the coffee jar.

'I don't snore, and yes, it was a good craic. We met up with some friends and carried on until late. Copper Face Jack's was going off,' Moira mumbled through the sugary frosted flakes she insisted on buying. 'Oh, before I forget, Roisin rang earlier.

Mammy's been on to her with the breaking news Marcus fecking coward McDonagh's sniffing around. Anyway, she said she'll ring back just after ten. How come you're not downstairs telling everybody how to do their jobs?'

'I fancied a lie in for a change.'

'You haven't got anyone in there, have you?' Moira put her spoon down and turned her narrowed eyes in her sister's direction.

'No!'

'Just as well, because if you did, then I'd have no choice but to ring Mammy and tell her you had Marcus fecking coward McDonagh holed up in your bedroom. Then you'd be for it.'

'Ha-ha.' Actually, it wasn't funny. The wrath of Maureen O'Mara, if she had indeed spent the night with her ex, would not be a pleasant thing to bear witness to at all. She sighed; it was clear, even if she decided to give Marcus another chance—perhaps take things slower this time around without the pressure of a big white wedding looming—her family weren't going to let him off the hook lightly.

Aisling poured the boiling water into her cup, stirring it as she debated confiding in Moira. She wouldn't tell her about her conversation with Una last night. That was between the two of them, but she decided she might as well own up to Marcus, having been here where she got back yesterday. If she didn't, Moira would hear it through the O'Mara's grapevine anyway and be suspicious as to why Aisling hadn't said anything. 'Marcus called around yesterday.'

The cereal bowl was placed down on the coffee table and the television muted as Moira swivelled around to stare at her sister; she was all ears.

'And?'

'He wants us to put the wedding business behind us and start again.'

The noise Moira emitted would have been more at home in a farmyard than in the apartment of a Georgian manor house.

'Charming,' Aisling muttered, taking a much-needed swig of her coffee.

'What did you say? I hope it began with an 'f' and was followed by an off.'

'No, not exactly.'

'Ash!'

Aisling banged her cup down on the bench, sending a slop of the brown brew over the side of her mug. 'He's genuinely sorry, Moira! Not everything's black and white in life; sometimes, there are shades in between. It's alright for you. You're twenty-five; you've got plenty of time left to make mistakes and meet Mr Right. I'm nearly thirty-five, and I wanted to settle down and hopefully start a family in the not-too-distant future. What if Marcus was the 'one'? What if I send him packing once and for all and, down the line, realise it was the worst mistake of my life?'

'He's not.'

'How do you know?'

'Because the 'one' would never do what he did to you, and the worst mistake of your life would be taking him back. What would Mammy say?'

'I don't know!'

'Yes, you do.'

'Don't.'

'Do too.'

Aisling knew she wasn't going to win. 'A leopard doesn't change his bloody spots,' she muttered.

'Exactly, and Mammy'd be right. You get back with him, Ash, and somewhere down the line, when the going gets tough, he'll leave you in the lurch again. Only this time around, you might have a couple of kiddies to worry about too.'

The sisters glared at each other, and the phone ringing was a welcome diversion. Aisling pounced on it.

'It's me. You're up.'

Aisling rolled her eyes; she'd forgotten Roisin was calling back. She'd had more than enough familial lecturing for one day as it was without her bossy older sister getting on the bandwagon. She sighed down the line, 'Hi, Rosie, how're ya keepin?'

'Grand here. You could at least sound pleased to hear from me though, Ash.'

'She's all mardy because she's had feck face around!' Moira shouted from the sofa. Aisling wasn't quick enough to cover the receiver.

'You never!'

'She did!'

'Shut up, Moira.' Aisling hissed, carrying the phone out of the room and into the privacy of her bedroom. She pushed the door shut with her foot before flopping down on her bed.

'He was here when I got back from lunch with Mammy yesterday, Rosie. I didn't ask him to come.'

'Mammy says he's been writing to you for months. You kept that quiet. Noah, go and do some colouring or something. You can have a word in a minute; I'm talking to Aunty Aisling first.'

'Because I knew what you'd all say, that's why.' Aisling caught sight of herself in the dressing table mirror and grimaced. Her eyes were like two pee holes in the snow. She was in desperate need of mascara and getting up; she rummaged through her cosmetic purse sitting beneath the mirror.

'You can hardly blame us, Ash. We saw the state you were in when he left. It was us who had to pick up the pieces. I tell you; he's got some nerve thinking he can waltz back into your life. Mammy says he wants you to give him another chance.'

The O'Mara women's bush telegraph was in fine fettle; it would seem. Aisling retrieved her tube of Lustrous Lash.

'He does, and I think he means what he says. He made a mistake. We're all only human, Rosie, and he felt like he was being steamrolled by me where the wedding was concerned.'

'Bully for him. Colin had to deal with Mammy hijacking ours, but he still stuck around and said I do. You remember, Ash, the poor man, had to watch me walking down the aisle looking like I was wearing one of those crochet toilet-roll cover dresses Nanna Dee used to make. She crocheted eleven of the bloody things, one for us and one for every loo in the guest house. Mammy would only put them out when she came to stay. Ugh, they used to give me the willies, horrible doll eyes staring at me while I was sat on the throne.'

Rosie was easily side-tracked, so Aisling got back on the subject. 'No, you don't get it. I've been thinking about it a lot, and I did turn into bridezilla. It was only because I was so determined to give us all a day to remember, a happy day after everything we'd been through with Dad. I wish Marcus had tried talking to me about how he was feeling at the time, though, because things could have worked out differently if he had.' She swapped the phone over to her other side, cradling it between her neck and shoulder before unscrewing the mascara and pulling out the wand.

There was a click, followed by heavy breathing. 'See, I told you she was wavering where feck face was concerned, Rosie. I could see it in her face at lunch yesterday, and honestly, you want to have heard her going on this morning. She's over the hill, blah blah, and Marcus could be the 'one' blah blah, and what if she misses her chance? You'd think her ovaries were shrinking as we speak. She needs to toughen up and be like your woman; what's her name? The one battling the big monster alien in that film.'

'Sigourney Weaver.'

'Yeah, her. She wouldn't take Marcus fecking coward Mc-Donagh back, ovaries or no ovaries.'

'Moira get off the phone,' Aisling said. 'Now!'

She waited until she heard the click. 'She's going to be the end of me, so she is.'

'She's right, Ash, not about Sigourney Weaver—you're way too short to be like her. You do need to toughen up, though and sure, you've loads of time to be worrying about your eggs and whatnot. Us O'Mara's we're from good childbearing stock. Look at Mam. She was nearly forty when Moira came along. Noah, put that back! He's only after helping himself to the chocolate biscuits because I'm on the phone and his dad's out for a run. And you know what she'd have to say on the subject.'

'Who?' Aisling was struggling to keep up with the conversation. She peered into the mirror and ran the wand under her lashes.

'Mammy, of course.'

Ah, God, here we go again, Aisling thought, blinking and cursing to herself as a flurry of black dots appeared beneath her eye. 'What?'

'Marry in haste repent at leisure.'

'Ow!'

'What happened?'

'I stabbed myself in the eye with my mascara. I look like I'm heading off to an audition for KISS. Damn it.'

'You don't learn the fine art of multitasking until you've had a baby, Ash. And I'm done. I've said all I'm going to say to you on the subject of Marcus McDonagh.'

And pigs might fly, Aisling thought, blinking furiously.

'Listen, if I don't put Noah on to say hello, he'll burst a blood vessel.'

Aisling grinned, 'Well, we don't want that. Stick him on.'

Chapter 29

♥

Aisling made it down the stairs with fifteen minutes to spare before she was due to meet Una. The weather looked fierce outside, and she'd decided to wrap up warmly. It had been hard going, but she'd managed to squeeze into her black jeans, throw on a sweater and wrap a scarf around her neck. Lastly, she'd pulled her black boots with the silver buckling detail on over her jeans. She'd fallen in love with them after spotting them in the window of Debenhams in last year's sale. A quick check in the mirror that all those pesky mascara dots were gone, and she was good to go.

It was a relief to escape the apartment and her sister after the morning's debacle. Moira didn't look as though she intended rushing off anywhere; she was still in her pyjamas and in her happy place watching the EastEnders weekend omnibus. She'd barely looked up from the screen when Aisling said she'd catch her later.

'Morning, James, everything under control?' she said, descending the stairs to reception.

'Hi.' He swivelled around in his seat, looking fresh-faced, his dark hair artfully styled. Aisling wondered if he'd even started shaving yet. 'Grand, Aisling. It's been quiet so far.' He looked at her for a beat but was too polite to ask why she was late down. It was, after all, completely out of character for her. 'Nobody's checked out yet, though Room 3 is due soon.'

'Yes, the Petersons are on the move today, and the Prestons are leaving too.' She wondered idly whether the company had sold the young couple on relocating.

James brought up the screen on the computer and nodded, 'Mr Walsh's checking out too.'

Of course, he was! Aisling had nearly forgotten he was going back to Liverpool today. It would have been dreadful if she hadn't said goodbye to him in person. It wasn't like her not to know the comings and goings of O'Mara's guests off the bat and especially a regular like Mr Walsh. It was this business with Marcus. He wasn't good for business!

'He'll be down having his breakfast. I'll go and say cheerio to him now. I'll take that downstairs, shall I?' She picked up the plate beside the computer. There was nothing left on it save a piece of bacon rind. Mr Fox would enjoy that later she thought.

The phone began to ring, and James grinned giving her a thumbs up. 'Cheers, Aisling. Tell Mrs Baicu it hit the spot.'

Aisling smiled back. His mam probably sorted his breakfast at home before he left to come here, and then he no sooner sat down to do some work, and Mrs Baicu served him up a second great helping. Ah well, look at the Australian brothers staying with them at the moment, the Freeman boys. Mrs Flaherty had been in seventh heaven seeing their heaped plates hoovered up each morning.

Branok and Emblyn Nancarrow were making their way gingerly down the stairs. Aisling paused at the foot of them as they reached the landing above her and called out a good morning. They both looked rather crumpled and still half asleep, relics from a bygone era in their flowing tie-dyed ensembles. She hoped they had layers on under all that garb, or they'd freeze today.

'Thank you for your recommendation of Quinn's, Aisling. We had the most divine Irish stew followed by a slice of gateau, but I don't feel guilty,' Branok patted his middle, hidden beneath his loose shirt, 'because we worked it off after dinner by putting our dancing shoes on. The chap playing the fiddle had everybody up.'

'Branok forgets he's not in his twenties anymore, and he was throwing himself about the floor like he was at Glastonbury or Woodstock. His body brings him up with a short shrift reminder the next day, though,' Emblyn said. 'We're both in need of a good strong cup of coffee, I'm afraid.' She yawned to demonstrate her point.

Aisling laughed, 'Well, you'll find a pot brewed downstairs. Mrs Baicu hails from Romania, and her coffee is thick and strong. A bit like Turkish coffee.'

'Just what we need, Emblyn.' She nodded her agreement.

'A cup of that and a plate piled high with bacon and eggs will see you both right.' Aisling flashed them a smile before glancing at Una's door on her way past Room 1. Perhaps she should knock in case she'd slept in. She hesitated but then decided to leave it and carried on down the stairs. She was more than likely getting dressed, or she may even be downstairs having breakfast. Either way, if she wasn't in the guest lounge at eleven, she'd tap on her door.

The dining room was busy, and Aisling smiled and greeted the guests, pausing to check in with Mrs Baicu, who had Geraldine beavering away buttering toast. They were a well-oiled machine, and she'd only get underfoot were she to linger in the kitchen, so she made a beeline for Mr Walsh.

He was ever the gentlemen, dapper in his suit. There was no such word as casual in his world, and getting up, he pulled the seat out for her.

'That colour's becoming on you, Aisling.'

She glanced at the maroon scarf draped over her sweater. 'Thank you. It's a sad day to be sure, Mr Walsh, what with you leaving us again to cross the water,' Aisling twinkled. She sat down opposite him shaking her head and putting her hand over the cup to signal that she was alright, when he gestured to the teapot. 'The weather certainly thinks so. It's tipping down outside.'

'Ah, Aisling, as much as it pains my heart, I have to leave. I'm a man with commitments. I've a dog needs picking up from the kennels and a garden that will be due some attention,' he bantered back.

'We'll miss you.'

It was true. Aisling had a lot of time for Mr Walsh. She could tell he had a kind heart. She wondered about his life in Liverpool. She had a vague idea he'd been a salesman or something like before he'd retired. He certainly had the necessary charm for that line of work. Her eyes strayed to his left hand, and she wondered if he had a lady friend. There was no ring on his finger to signal he'd ever been married and was perhaps widowed. Then again, he could be divorced; the ring tucked away in a drawer forgotten about. It was none of her business either way.

'Be sure to tell Bronagh I said goodbye now, won't you. She's a good woman that one.'

Aisling might not have had much in the way of sleep the night before, and her brain may have only been running at half capacity, but there was something in his tone of voice. It was the way his expression seemed to lighten and lift when Bronagh's name rolled off his tongue. It had her matchmaking antennae all a quiver. She did the maths. Bronagh had never married; she lived with her ailing mammy. Mr Walsh would appear to be something of a bachelor. If she were a few years older, quite a few years older, she'd have him pegged as a catch. One plus one equalled three! It was a match Moira would wholeheartedly approve of.

'I'll pass it on to her, Mr Walsh. You know we're only a phone call away. Keep in touch, won't you? Don't leave it a whole year until we hear from you again.' She wanted to add that Bronagh's hours were eight am until four pm Monday to Friday. She was single so far as Aisling knew, and if he wished to correspond with her, Aisling would happily forward all mail on. She thought that might be a little obvious, however, and refrained. She caught sight of his watch face; the time had ticked over to eleven o'clock. She couldn't sit here any longer pondering subtle ways in which to orchestrate further contact between this dapper gent and her receptionist, but as she made to get up from her seat, she had a brainwave.

'Mr Walsh, I've got to dash. I'm due to meet a friend but, you know, I just realised you're not on our Christmas card list. That's a sin, so it is, what with you being our favourite guest and all. Why don't you leave your address with James at the front desk?'

Mr Walsh nodded, and at that moment, Mrs Baicu, her dark hair silvered with grey scraped back in a bun, burst through the kitchen doors and marched toward them. An efficient, angular woman who always reminded Aisling of a Liquorice Allsort, she put this down to her multi-coloured voluminous peasant skirts. She wore the same style of skirt no matter what the season and, if it was cold, she pulled on woollen tights. Today was definitely a woollen tights day. Her accent still echoed strongly of her Eastern European roots. 'Mr Walsh, you can't leave without this.' She thrust a glass jar at him, its contents a dark and syrupy jam secured by a twist-top lid. 'It's what we Romanian's call magiun, plum jam. A speciality of mine. It would give me great pleasure to know you were enjoying this on your toast each morning once you are back in Liverpool. You spread the word the Romanian jam is good, yes?'

Aisling's mouth twitched. It was a good job Mrs Flaherty wasn't here. The two cooks were fiercely competitive over their jam making skills. If she were to get wind Mrs Baicu was giving their regulars samples of her traditional plum jam to take home, there'd be a good deal of fecking. It would be followed by a shortage of oranges in Dublin as she set about whipping up her marmalade for all and sundry staying at O'Mara's.

Aisling wished Mr Walsh all the best for his journey home, and leaving Mrs Baicu fussing over him; she made her way up the stairs and through to the guest lounge.

Una was perched on the same chair she'd been sitting in only a few hours earlier. The green quilted dressing gown, however, had been replaced. She was wearing the same cardigan and skirt combo as yesterday, along with the blue blouse Aisling had complimented her on. Somehow, she looked less severe this morning. It was down to the splash of subtle colour from the lipstick and blush she'd applied, Aisling realised. For a woman who'd been up half the night, she looked surprisingly well, although her anxiety was palpable. Her hands were clasped so tightly in her lap her knuckles were white. Aisling tried to put her at ease.

'Did you manage to get a little more sleep, Una? You certainly look rested.'

'I did, thank you, I went out like a light. I'd still be asleep now if I hadn't set the alarm. Yourself?'

'Me too. Have you had time for breakfast?' It dawned on her she'd been too busy battling Roisin and Moira off earlier to grab anything. She could have helped herself to what was on offer in Mrs Baicu's kitchen, but she'd gotten caught up chatting to Mr Walsh. Ah well, it wouldn't do her any harm, and her stomach was beginning to churn on Una's behalf, anyway.

'No, I couldn't, dear, not this morning.'

They were a right pair. Aisling gave her a smile to say she understood. 'I'll get James to call us a taxi, shall I? Oh, and if you've got a coat with you, it might be an idea to put it on. It's a miserable old Sunday out there.'

Una nodded, 'I'll go and get it now, shall I?'

'Grand.'

Chapter 30

♥

Aisling was sitting in the back of the taxi, Una in the front. She glanced at her profile. The hood of her rain jacket was bunched around her shoulders. Her gaze was fixed straight ahead, and her mouth set in a firm line. She looked away to stare out the window. Rivulets of water were running down. It was bucketing down; they were getting a taste of the winter to come today for sure.

Their driver, she'd seen when he strode cheerily into O'Mara's announcing his arrival, had a bulbous red nose. He also had the tell-tale broken capillaries of a man who was partial to a glass or two—they formed a network to rival the London Underground across both his cheeks.

Now he began intrepidly trying to engage his two passengers in cheerful patter about the gloomy day and where they might be off to on a wet Sunday morning. Neither Una nor Aisling replied with more than the bare minimum of conversation necessary so as not to appear rude. They were both worn out from the talking they'd done through the night and were content to sit in silence, lost in their own thoughts.

The driver heaved a sigh and gave up as he drove them over the Liffey. All they could hear as they reached the red brick suburb in which Aideen lived was the ticking over of the meter, the sluicing tyres as they rolled through the puddles, and an annoying jaw-clicking sound the driver was making. It was painful to listen to.

'It's just up there. If you pull over beside the park, that will do nicely, thank you.' Una gestured to the wedge of dull green grass up ahead on the left.

'Are you sure? You'll get soaked, so you will. Can I drop you to the door of wherever it is you're going?'

'Thank you, no. We'll be fine.' Una was curt, her voice tense. 'What do I owe you?'

Aisling opened her purse, but Una was insistent she pay as the driver idled the car. There was no point arguing, and, getting out of the car; she popped her umbrella. The street was quiet, with a row of cars parked along one side nose to nose. There were no signs of human life, but she wasn't surprised; they weren't a country of early risers. Her eyes flitted over the deserted park. The play area stood in the middle, empty and forlorn. She saw a tree, its branches drooping under the rain, a bench seat beneath it, and surmised that was where Una had been whiling away her days since she'd been in Dublin. The sight of it saddened her.

Aideen's house was one of the houses in the row of smart terraces across the road. How would they be received? Aisling hoped the sight of her sister standing on her doorstep after all these years didn't prove too much of a shock for Aideen. She wasn't well after all. Aisling was nearly as anxious as Una, who appeared beside her a beat later. Her face was pale and apprehensive as she peered out from under her rain jacket's hood. Aisling held her umbrella up over both of them while they waited for the taxi to drive away. Then she linked her arm through Una's—to offer reassurance and make sure she didn't try to change her mind as they crossed the road.

The house Una halted outside was opposite the park.

'This is Aideen's, number eighteen.'

Aisling opened the gate and, keeping a firm grip on Una, walked up the front path. Despite the time of year, the garden was neatly kept, the foliage trimmed back for winter, and the path led them to a cheery red door. It had the shiniest brass knocker she'd ever seen. Aideen was obviously house proud, and before Una could protest, Aisling lifted it and rapped three times. Aisling could feel Una's body ramrod and rigid next to her as they waited. The seconds stretched long.

'She's not home. We'll come another time.'

'Una, she'll have barely had time to get out of her chair. Give it a minute.'

Aisling crossed her fingers that Aideen was home. She didn't fancy her chances of getting Una back here again. Her gut told her if the sisters didn't reconnect today, it wouldn't happen. Una would get back on the train and chug away for good.

They should have gotten the driver to wait even if that jaw clicking thing was annoying. It was not the day to be standing on the side of the road waiting for taxis. She picked up the knocker and rapped it twice more, willing Aideen to open the door. She'd count to twenty slowly, and if no one had answered by then, they'd have to go. They couldn't loiter on her front doorstep all day, the neighbours would get suspicious, and they'd wind up with pneumonia.

'I think we should leave.' Una shifted impatiently.

Aisling had counted to fifteen. She sighed; maybe Una was right. Hang on; she could hear movement. She squeezed Una's arm in nervous anticipation.

'Someone's coming.'

She heard the sharp intake of breath next to her as the door opened.

Chapter 31

The sisters stared in open-mouthed silence at each other, and Aisling stared from one to the other. She knew, of course, that Una and Aideen were twins, but the reality of seeing Una's double standing in the entrance of her home was still a shock. They were identical twins, but the difference between them was glaringly obvious. Aideen's face had a puffiness to it, and her eyes were hollow with dark shadows beneath them. Her head was covered by a scarf, and Aisling noticed it was the exact cheerful shade of cornflower blue as Una's blouse. She was dressed in a pretty lilac jumper with grey trousers with fluffy pink slippers on her feet.

'Una,' Aideen whispered finally, clasping the door as though frightened she might fall. 'Is it really you?'

Una nodded and then launched herself on her sister, who nearly did fall backwards as she was wrapped in a soggy embrace. Aisling could hear Una's sobs mingling with her muffled, 'I'm sorry, I left it too long, I'm so sorry.'

'So am I. Shush, it doesn't matter now. None of it matters anymore. You came. That's what counts.'

Aisling wasn't sure if it was droplets of rain or tears running down her face as she watched the sisters embrace. She suspected the latter. She couldn't imagine not having seen either of her sisters for so many years. Oh, they drove each other to distraction most of the time, but they were always there for each other when it mattered. Aideen looked over her shoulder at Aisling questioningly. It dawned on her that she might assume she was Una's daughter, and she quickly jumped in before there could be any misunderstanding.

'I'm Aisling O'Mara. Una's staying at my family's guesthouse, O'Mara's.'

'The guesthouse on the green?'

'Yes.'

'You always wanted to stay there, Una.'

Una broke away and turned toward Aisling. 'I did. Aisling and I haven't known each other long, but she's been a good friend to me, Aideen. I don't know if I'd have had the courage to come today if it wasn't for her.'

'When did you arrive in Dublin?'

'Midweek, I've come every day to see you. I've sat over there,' she gestured to the park, 'trying to pluck up the nerve to knock on your door, but I couldn't. Not on my own.'

'I'd have never turned you away, Una. You must have known that.'

'I was frightened. Scared I'd left it too long to put things right.'

'Never. Una. My door's always been open for you.' Aideen registered that they were all standing in the doorway. 'Come inside both of you before you catch a chill. Una, we'll hang that wet coat up, and I'll put the kettle on.'

'That sounds lovely, thank you,' Aisling said. She'd stay awhile to be polite, besides which a cuppa would go down a treat. She was freezing! She closed the umbrella leaving it to stand on the doorstep as she followed behind Una. Aideen closed the door and fussed around, taking Una's coat and hanging it on a hook. Aisling took the opportunity to look around her. They were in the hallway, stairs leading off it to the upstairs where the bedrooms would be. There was a room off the hall on either side—a living room and a dining room, no doubt. Aideen must have been in the kitchen Aisling surmised seeing the light was on at the end of the hall. It explained why it had taken her a while to answer the door.

Photographs lined the walls, and a quick glance proved them to be family portraits. A montage of Aideen and Leo's boys over the years. How boisterous Aideen's life would have been bringing up her boys compared to her sister's. They were mischievous looking little lads who'd grown into handsome young men. There were grandchildren too, she saw. Six of them if the photograph of them looking angelic in a formal garden setting was anything to go by.

Her eyes settled on a wedding photo, curious to see what Leo looked like. He was handsome in his suit, and Aideen was a beautiful bride, but she fancied she could see a sadness in her eyes lurking beneath the surface. Maybe she was being fanciful. As for Leo, he was just a man, rather ordinary, truth be told, but both sisters had seen so much more in him. Who would have thought his love could cause so much distress? The same could be said about Marcus, she supposed.

'Do you remember Mam's friend, Maire Reynolds,' Una was saying.

'Of course. She liked her tea strong enough for a mouse to trot on!'

The sisters smiled at the mutual memory.

They had so much shared history, and so much they didn't know about each other's lives, Aisling thought. It would be a day full of chatter as they desperately tried to catch up on their lost years. A light glowed invitingly in the kitchen, and she followed Una and Aideen toward it.

'I keep the heating on high in here.' Aideen was saying.

The room was indeed toasty, and Aisling enjoyed the tingling warmth spreading through her cold limbs. It was a small kitchen in need of updating but functional, nevertheless. The window over the sink overlooked the garden, where an empty washing line spun around in the wind.

I hope it's not too much of a sauna for you. But I feel the cold these days since I began the chemo.'

Una made an odd sound.

'It's alright, Una, everything's going to be alright now you'll see,' Aideen said, going through the motions of making a pot of tea. 'Because you're here.'

Chapter 32

♥

Aisling drank her tea, enjoying listening to the sisters' animated conversation as they talked overtop of one another. Their eagerness to fill each other in on their lives meant the plate of digestive biscuits Aideen had set out along with the tea were ignored. Just one more, Aisling told herself. She was partial to a tea biscuit, and she gave it a brief dunk before chomping into it watching the sisters' shared gestures and mannerisms with fascination. They were mirror images, peas in a pod.

She let herself be transported along with them back to their childhood as they relived their younger days. She could see where those boys she'd peered up at in the photographs in the hallway got their mischievous streak from. She'd happily while away the rest of the afternoon in Aideen's snug kitchen drinking tea and polishing off the biscuits, listening to their tales, but that wouldn't be fair. She was a third wheel even if she had been made welcome. A yawn escaped unbidden, and she was aware of being lulled by the warmth and the lilt of their voices. It was time she made tracks and stopped earwigging.

'Aideen, Una, I'm sorry to interrupt, but I should be getting back to O'Mara's.'

They looked at her startled, pulled from their reminiscing. It was as though they'd forgotten she was even in the room with them. They probably had, she realised, asking Aideen if she'd mind if she borrowed her phone to call a taxi.

'Of course not, dear. It's on the table in the hallway. Help yourself.'

Aisling rang the number she knew by heart, having called it a thousand times before for guests. She spieled off the address and was told the taxi wouldn't be long. She glanced up again at the wedding photo that had caught her eye earlier as she hung up the phone. It was nice to think Leo was looking down on Aideen and Una, a silent witness from up there in heaven to their reunion. He'd be happy, she thought, studying his face. It was kind, and she knew he'd have had no wish to cause the rift he had by misplacing his affections on Una. She could see the devotion on Aideen's face as she smiled up at him frozen in time, but yes, there was a definite sadness there too. What a choice they'd had to make, and their happiness had come at a high price.

She hoped, as she made her way back to the kitchen to say her goodbyes, that Aideen and Una had plenty of time left together. That this chapter of their lives would be happy. Perhaps Una would prove to be the tonic Aideen needed to overcome her illness.

Aideen was telling Una of all the different ways in which she'd learned to tie her headscarf since her hair had begun to fall out as she entered the room, and Aisling inadvertently raised her hand to her own hair; despite the umbrella, it had gotten wet and had dried in ratty spirals.

'My taxi won't be long, so I'll say cheerio to you both now and thank you for your hospitality, Aideen.' She was on the receiving end of warm hugs when a horn sounded from the street outside. She would see Una again and hear what her plans were from this point forward. Who knew, she might even see Aideen again—she hoped so. She wished her all the very best and left her to catch up with her sister. She was looking forward to doing some catching up of her own tonight with Leila and Quinn. It had been ages since she'd had a good laugh with her old pals, and she was well overdue to catch up on all their news.

The driver having tooted his arrival was a clue, Aisling thought five minutes into the journey home, as to his sullen, uncommunicative manner. She stole a sideways glance at him. His surly expression said he was clearly not living his dream. Bring back the jaw clicker! She focussed her attention on the road ahead, not really seeing it though as she pondered Marcus. Her head was spinning with all that had happened in the last forty-eight hours. She wouldn't call him today. She wasn't ready. Seeing Leila would give her another perspective, and she'd hash it over with her tonight. Leila dealt with the business of love on a daily basis, so hopefully, she could offer some advice that would help her decide whether giving him another chance might lead to her happy ending. One thing she knew for certain was she couldn't cope with having her trust shattered a second time.

Quinn's face floated before her. He had such an infectious grin. An old memory fought its way through. They'd gone ten-pin bowling, and he'd let her win. As the victor, it had been her responsibility to buy chips on the way home. A grand debate had been waged in the chipper over drowning them in curry sauce or eating them plain with salt and vinegar. Aisling was partial to the curry sauce. Quinn said it was sacrilege. They'd had such a laugh that night. She quashed the familiar pang but not before remembering how he'd let her have her way with the curry sauce.

The taxi pulled up across the road from O'Mara's, and Aisling paid him. She wasn't a tipper, but even if she was that way inclined, he didn't deserve one. As if he'd read her mind, he sped off, spraying her with water much to her chagrin, though she managed to refrain from giving him a rude finger sign. She waited impatiently for a break in the traffic and ran across the road, keen to get out of the weather. Evie was on the desk and looked up, startled when she barrelled in through the door, shaking herself off like a dog.

'You look like a drowned rat.'

'Cheers.'

'Have you been out with yer man, Marcus, then?'

Straight to the point. She really was a nosy madam. Aisling toyed with the idea of telling her that she'd had a delightful morning riding her ex, and the cobwebs had well and truly been blown away. It would almost be worth it to see the shock on her smug little face. It was on the tip of her tongue, but she held back. A lie like that, however satisfying, would be cutting her nose off to spite her face and God help her if it got back to Mammy!

'I've been out with one of our guests, actually.' And that was as much information as she was going to give her. 'Right, I'd best get into some dry gear.'

She left Evie pondering who the guest might be and why Aisling had ventured out on such a miserable day with them. That morsel of information would keep her amused all afternoon as she tried to solve the mystery—a regular little Nancy Drew.

Moira was sitting where she'd left her, still glued to the television, although her favourite show would have finished by now. She called out a cursory greeting. This time her sister switched the set-off and focussed her attention on her. 'Where've you been? Mammy called. Her sailing lesson got cancelled, and she wanted to chat. I told her I couldn't cos EastEnders was on, but seeing how it was an ad break, I'd go downstairs and nab you instead. I didn't know you were heading out.' Her tone was accusatory.

It was like she was a wayward teen and Moira was the mam desperately trying to keep her in line. 'You wouldn't have heard me if I'd told you where I was going, anyway. You were too involved in whatever was happening in Albert Square this week.' The soap opera was almost a religious experience for Moira, and you did not interrupt her when she was watching it. 'Give me ten minutes to have a shower. I need to warm up; then I'll tell you what I've been up to. Oh, and by the way, it doesn't involve Marcus if that's what you were thinking.'

Aisling clambered out of her wet gear and put her dressing gown on. She carried the damp clothes through to the kitchen and left them to whir around in the dryer before sitting down next to Moira. As there were two mugs of tea on the coffee table, she decided the hot shower could wait a little longer, and then she could think about getting ready for her date with Leila and Quinn.

'I made you one.' Moira stated.

'Thanks.' Aisling picked hers up. It was out of character for her sister to get off her arse and make her a cuppa, but she wouldn't look a gift horse in the mouth. She realised what had just run through her mind and shuddered. She really was morphing into Mammy with all her little sayings—a gift horse in the mouth; what did that even mean, for goodness sake? She had a sip and felt the sweet hot liquid warm her right through. 'Oh, that's good.'

Moira looked pleased with herself. 'So come on then, where've you been.'

'Well, you know the guest in Room 1, Una Brennan?'

'The battle-axe who's got a face on her like someone farted. You should have seen her giving me the hairy eyeball the other morning when I was under the weather.'

'Jeez, Moira, you come out with it. Yes, her, only she's not such a battle-axe, listen to this.' Aisling didn't think Una would mind her sharing her story with Moira, not with how things had worked out today. She filled her in on the Brennan twins' story, and Moira listened wide-eyed. She wasn't as hard as she liked to make out. Aisling saw her eyes well up when she got to the part where Una hadn't long been out of the hospital, and Leo had told her he'd realised it was Aideen he loved.

By the time she'd finished her tale, Moira was reaching for the tissues. 'Jaysus, that was worse than when Tiffany Mitchell got run over by Frank Butcher.'

Aisling assumed she was referring to an EastEnders plot but didn't dwell on it further because the phone began to ring. It was probably Mammy ringing back. A beat later, hearing the familiar voice, she knew she'd guessed correctly.

'Aisling, is that you?'

Mammy always sounded surprised when she answered the phone. It probably stemmed from all those years working abroad. You'd think she'd have gotten used to her being home by now, though. 'Yes, it's me. How're ya keepin', Mammy?'

'Ah grand, although I'm at a bit of a loose end. My sailing got cancelled, and I can't very well go and play golf in this weather unless I want to put my bathers on and have a round with the ducks.' She sighed as though the weight of the world rested on her shoulders.

Maureen O'Mara was a people person. She didn't like rattling about on her own and was in her element when her social calendar was full. The idea of a day at home by herself followed by more of the same in the evening would fill her with fear. Mother and middle child were different like that. Aisling enjoyed her own company and hated having a social calendar that was full to the brim—not that there was much chance of that these days. Musings aside, she got what her mammy was hinting at. 'Did you want to come over this evening for some company?'

'For dinner? Now that would be lovely. I'll be there by seven at the latest.' The phone went dead before Aisling could say that she wouldn't be home. Of course, Mammy would assume she'd be home for the night, given she hadn't been out for the evening in an absolute age. She got a glint in her eyes. It was payback time for Moira's behaviour this morning.

Moira, what're your plans tonight?'

She looked a little glum. 'I was hoping to hear from a friend.' She picked up her phone and eyed the screen before dropping it by her side. 'But I haven't, and it's not likely I will now.'

'What friend?'

'Oh, no one you know, just someone from work.' This was said quickly, and Aisling glanced at her sister sharply. She caught a glimpse of that secretive, closed Mona Lisa face once more, but Moira moved on before she could delve into what she was up to.

'How's about going halvesies on a takeaway?' said Moira. 'I'm starved with the hunger. How's about lemon chicken and maybe a black bean beef with fried rice.'

There it was again, the assumption she'd be sitting in. It annoyed Aisling. 'Actually, I'm out tonight, NOT with Marcus!' she shot back at her sister before she could open her mouth. 'I'm meeting Leila at Quinn's for your information. Mammy's on her way around, though; she'll go you halvesies. She's partial to black bean beef. I'd get out of those pyjamas, though if I were you, or you'll never hear the end of it.'

Aisling left Moira muttering under her breath and headed off to get ready. She planned to make her escape before Mammy arrived. The only person she wanted to talk to about Marcus tonight was Leila.

Chapter 33

♥

It was a little ridiculous calling a taxi to travel the short distance from O'Mara's to Quinn's, but there was no way Aisling was going to arrive at the restaurant soaked and looking like a bedraggled sea creature washed ashore. Not when she'd spent an age dolling herself up. Nor would she risk her Jimmy Choo glitter mules—a bargain so far as Jimmy Choo's went—bought in the sales several years ago, encountering a puddle. Truth be told, and puddles aside, she wasn't sure she could walk more than a block in the heels. They defied gravity even by her standards.

She'd made a special effort tonight, and she wasn't sure why. Leila and Quinn wouldn't care if she turned up in her pyjamas. Speaking of which, Moira had finally gotten dressed. The thought of the lecture she'd be sure to receive from Mammy on falling into slovenly ways was all the incentive needed.

Aisling had faffed with her make-up and hair before sliding into her little black dress—actually, she'd wriggled her way into it. She hadn't been sure if it would fit, but she managed to wrestle the zipper into place, completing her outfit with the crème de la crème pair of shoes in her collection. It was as though she were putting on armour; she'd mused, giving herself a final once over, proving to herself that she was in control of what happened next in her life. She sucked her tummy in and smoothed the dress down; she didn't scrub up too badly. It was nice to get dressed up. She used to all the time. She'd forgotten what a boost it always gave her.

'Give Mammy a hug from me,' she said before singing out a cheery 'Bye' to Moira. She had a face on her. A night in watching Ballykissangel with Mammy could do that to a girl. It was her habit of talking to the characters throughout the show, telling them what they should be doing. Ah well, Moira would cheer up once she had a helping of lemon chicken in front of her. Aisling pondered on what she'd order tonight, remembering the Irish Baileys cheesecake she'd spied on the menu board. Her tummy rumbled, reminding her all she'd had to eat today was tea biscuits.

Aisling gripped the banister tightly as she gingerly descended the stairs. It had been a long time since the Jimmy Choo's had had an outing. She was out of practice, but sure wearing high heels was second nature to her. Give her an hour, and she'd be up for a marathon. She tottered through into reception; head held high. It was deserted apart from Evie, who was eating a bowl of two-minute noodles with an unenthusiastic expression. Her face lit up when she spied her boss, though. 'Wow, Aisling, you look gorgeous—like a film star. I love those shoes.'

Aisling felt herself soften toward the younger girl, give her a compliment, and she was anybody's. 'Thanks, Evie.'

'You must be going somewhere special?'

Fishing, always fishing. 'For dinner with friends. Oh, there's my taxi. Have a good night.'

'Mind how you go.'

Aisling swept out into the night. Things were off to a good start, she thought, seeing the driver had the good manners to get out of the taxi to hold the door open for her. That surly fecker from earlier could learn a few tricks from him, she thought, sliding onto the backseat. Her hand reached up and patted her hair; it was still intact. Yes, a good start to the evening indeed.

Quinn's was heaving. She'd forgotten what a big night Sundays were. Alasdair didn't disappoint. He gave her a once over that from anybody else would be offensive, followed by a long slow whistle. 'Aisling O'Mara, I swear you're fit for the red carpet. Tonight, you have me in mind of Ginger Rogers when we featured in Swing Time together.'

Before Aisling knew what was happening, Alasdair was doing his best Fred Astaire tap-dancing impersonation and had grabbed hold of her, giving her a twirl. It was a dance move that would have ended in disaster had he not had a firm hold of her. 'Love those shoes, by the way. Divine!' He let her go. She was aware of other patrons looking on in amusement, and a few were clapping, but she was far too used to Alasdair's flamboyant ways to be embarrassed.

Quinn was standing in the kitchen doorway, giving her a slow clap along with a big grin. She could see he'd shaved even from where she was standing. She gave him a little bow before scanning the tables to see if Leila, ever punctual, had beaten her there. She had and was laughing at the display she'd just witnessed. She waved.

Aisling left Alasdair to accost the patrons who'd ducked in from the rain. They were making a show of rubbing their hands and stamping their feet as though they'd just escaped from a howling blizzard. She weaved her way around to the table in the far corner of the room. Alasdair had arranged for them to be as far away from the stage as possible, so they could hear themselves speak. A solitary amp and microphone were the only clues there'd be live music later. Aisling hoped Quinn planned on joining them too and wasn't going to spend the evening slaving in the kitchen.

Leila stood up to greet her friend with a warm hug. She smelt gorgeous, Aisling thought, inhaling an unfamiliar scent. Leila looked down at Aisling's feet.

'Ooh, the Jimmy Choo's, my favourite. You look gorgeous, Ash. I love that dress.'

'Thank you, I wasn't sure if it would still fit, but I managed to squeeze into it. I'll be fine so long as I don't eat!' she laughed. 'You do too, but then you always do.' Leila, with her petite figure and lustrous blonde hair, didn't have to make much effort. She could wear a sack and look stylish. Tonight, she'd opted for a simple pale blue shift dress with bell sleeves. Her hair was loose, framing her pretty pixie face. 'And you smell divine, what is that?'

'I treated myself. It's a new Gucci fragrance called Rush.'

'It suits you.'

They sat down, and both began to talk at once, laughing at their eagerness to catch up. Aisling giggled as Leila relayed a tale about a recent wedding where the bride had gotten tipsy and called her new mother-in-law an old trout. They'd no time to move on to other topics before a waiter Aisling hadn't seen before made a beeline for their table. He looked like a student whose mam had told him to put on his good shirt, trying to earn a bit of cash on the side.

'Hello, there. I'm Tom, your waiter this evening. Now then, can I get you both something to drink before you check out our menu?'

'Hi, Tom. Yes, please. Leila, should we share a bottle of red?'

'Why not.'

'A bottle of your house red, please, Tom. Oh, and would you mind telling Quinn to get his arse out here and come and join us?'

Tom grinned and put his pencil behind his ear, 'I will. Shall I use those words exactly?'

'Definitely.'

He moved away to pass on the message.

'So, moving right along. Dare I ask, have you seen Marcus since I spoke to you?'

'I have. He was waiting for me when I got home from lunch with Moira and Mammy on Saturday afternoon.'

'And?'

'You can probably guess what he had to say for himself.'

Leila nodded. 'How did you leave things, or am I better off not knowing?'

'I promised him I'd think about what he'd said. He's staying with his mam and dad. As for any of that other stuff, it's been so long, I've forgotten how.'

'Sure, it's like riding a bike. Not that I'm encouraging you to get back on that particular bicycle.'

Aisling raised an eyebrow, glad to divert the conversation away from Marcus. She only went around in circles where he was concerned. 'That sounds like someone who's been doing a spot of pedalling recently.'

Leila smiled. 'I might have gone for a tandem ride after the third date with a photographer fella I met at a wedding. I have my standards, you know.'

'Glad to hear it, and what is this photographer fella's name then?'

Leila mumbled something, and Aisling strained to hear it but couldn't catch it.

'What was that?'

Leila sighed. 'Don't you dare laugh.'

'I won't.'

'Bearach, it means Barry.'

Aisling snorted before erupting into peals of laughter. 'Sorry, Leila, but Bearach?' She tried it out for size, 'Ooh, Bearach. Or, ooh, Barry! I don't know what's worse,' she choked.

'I knew you'd take the mickey.' Leila grinned. 'And for the record, I am not a moaner.'

Tom arrived with their glasses and a bottle of red which, for someone of his tender years, he opened with a flourish before leaving it to breathe.

'Bugger, all that breathing business, I need a drink after that.' Aisling poured them both a glass and raised hers. 'A toast. May you have warm words on a cold evening, a full moon on dark nights, and the road downhill all the way to your door.' They clinked glasses.

'Where did you get that from?'

'One of our guest's souvenir tea towels. I liked it.'

Quinn, having checked all was ticking over in his kitchen, made his way over. 'Hello, my two favourite ladies, may I join you?'

'Of course, sit your arse down.'

He grinned and did as he was told. Aisling, spying Tom about to move away from a nearby table, called out, 'Tom, would you mind getting us another glass, please?' She had to smile watching the young waiter, seeing it was his boss who required the vessel, virtually run to the bar. He returned a beat later, making a show of polishing the glass before pouring a generous amount of the ruby liquid into it. He stood back, cloth draped over his arm, waiting for approval. It was too late for Quinn to do a tasting, given Aisling had already drunk half the contents of her glass. Leila had had a good go at hers too. Nevertheless, Quinn played the game. He held the glass up to the light and swirled it before sniffing the contents and finally taking a sip.

Aisling's heart skipped a beat as a memory of Marcus came to the fore. She knew wine connoisseurs did this to get a sense of the wine—at least, this what Marcus had told her. He was a spitter and insisted on performing the ritual whenever they ate out. She hated it, finding it a seat-squirming, pretentious show—especially if he waved it away for whatever reason. It had taken the enjoyment out of the evening for her on more than one occasion. Funny, she mused; she'd forgotten that. Not to mention it was a waste of good wine!

Quinn swallowed, and Aisling exhaled.

'Cheers, Tom. That hit the spot. Bottoms up, ladies.' He raised his glass and clinked with Leila and Aisling. Tom asked if they were ready to order.

Quinn picked the menus up off the table and passed them up to Tom. 'There's no need for these. These two are old friends of mine, and I've prepared something special for them.'

Aisling and Leila clapped their hands in delight—they were in for a treat.

'I hope you're hungry.'

'I could eat the back door buttered,' Aisling grinned.

Chapter 34

♥

True to his word Quinn had indeed produced something special. He disappeared into the kitchen, returning a few moments later with an enormous platter which he set down in the centre of the table. Tom materialised with a side plate for each of them before flapping napkins open to spread onto their laps. Aisling's mouth watered as she gazed down at the array of nibbles Quinn had created. It must have taken him hours to put together.

'This looks amazing, thank you! How spoilt are we?'

Leila uttered the same sentiment.

'Ah well, you know me. I never miss a chance to show off in the kitchen. It's just a little something I threw together.' It was tongue in cheek. Aisling knew how to throw something together. It usually involved retrieving whatever was left over from last night's dinner from the refrigerator and reheating it. This, sitting on the table ready for them to tuck into, was art on a plate.

'Of course, if we were doing the proper degustation dining experience, then I'd be bringing these out for you to sample plate by plate and pairing each dish with a complementing wine. I wanted to join you, though not keep running off to the kitchen, besides I figured I'd be wasting my time walking you two lushes through the different wines.'

Leila waved the near-empty bottle, 'Ah, the cheek. But you figured right. Another bottle of the house red will do us nicely, thank you very much.' She caught Tom's eye, and he gave her the thumbs up. 'I'm almost frightened to eat anything; it looks so pretty,' Leila said, her attention returning to the platter of food in front of them.

'Well, now that would be a waste. Here why don't you begin with this,' Quinn used the tongs and placed one of the dainty, colourful morsels he'd selected on a side plate for each of them. 'My personal favourite. Seared scallop drizzled with pea puree on a cauliflower rösti.' He popped his in his mouth. 'That's good,' he mumbled through his mouthful, 'if I do say so myself. Come on, you two. It's not like you to hold back.'

'Don't mind if I do,' Aisling grinned before demolishing hers, Leila following suit. Aisling had worked her way around to a generous sliver of smoky maple pork belly by the time Quinn, in between bites and wiping his mouth with a napkin, had finished regaling them with a kitchen disaster story involving an exploding pressure cooker. She made a mental note never to dig out Mammy's old one. It could stay tucked away down the back of the cupboard.

As they began to make short work of the food, they laughed over their student days and the things they used to get up to. Aisling leaned back in her chair, taking a breather from stuffing her face. She was feeling relaxed and merry. It was a tonic sharing wine and good food with her two most favourite people in the world, family aside.

Quinn, she thought, feeling a warm glow as she looked at him across the table, had been such a good friend to her, especially during those awful weeks before Dad had passed. Leila, too had stepped up above and beyond the call of duty, both when Dad died and after Marcus left. She resolved there and then to get the three of them together more regularly from thereon in. 'So,' she twinkled over her glass, not wanting to get too sentimental. 'I've heard about Leila's latest fling with

Bearach, otherwise known as, *Ooh Barry*.' It earned her a kick under the table.

Quinn took Aisling's cue and began to chant, 'Leila and Bazzer up a tree—' he got no further before Leila threatened him with a Cajun-spiced chicken wing, and he held his hands up in surrender.

'You two are worse than children!'

They grinned across the table conspiratorially, and Aisling hoped her teeth weren't black from the wine. She picked up with what she'd been about to say. 'Like I said, Quinn, we know who's been parking his boots under Leila's bed, but what about you?'

'Did you just blush?' Leila squealed, eager for payback.

'I did not. I've nothing to blush over. You know me, married to my business.'

'Ah, but your business won't keep you warm at night.' Leila demolished her chicken wing and, wiping her greasy fingers on a napkin, said, 'There must be a lovely foodie lass out there for you. A girl who knows her rump from her sirloin. It's a waste a fine-looking chap like yourself being on his own. I think what you need to do is come along to one of my weddings. They're chock full of young ladies, all desperate to find Mr Right. We'll smuggle you in under the pretence of, oh, I don't know, being my assistant. We could call you Fabio or something like that,' she sniggered. 'What do you say?'

Aisling's insides twisted. How would she feel when Quinn met someone he was serious about? She didn't want to think about it.

'No fecking way,' he said.

Leila pouted. 'I think it's a great idea, and I seem to recall you saying exactly that to me once before.'

'When?'

'When I suggested we all give salsa a go.'

'I wasn't keen initially either. You were good at it though, Quinn, a natural,' Aisling said. 'You should have stuck with it.'

'So were you.' Their eyes met both, knowing why she hadn't continued. Salsa hadn't been Marcus's thing. It hadn't been Leila's either, but she'd have kept going for both their sakes. Quinn had called it quits when Aisling said she wouldn't be going back. The shine had gone out of it for him.

'What about you then, Aisling?' Quinn asked.

She shrugged and drained the dregs from her glass. 'What about me?'

'Any budding romances we should know about?' He reached over and filled her glass in an effort to busy himself.

'Marcus is back in town, and he wants her back.'

Quinn sloshed the wine over the side of Aisling's glass. 'Shit, sorry.'

'It's only a splash,' Aisling said, dabbing at the pink stain.

'What are you going to do?' Quinn sat back in his chair, finishing the rest of his drink too quickly.

'I don't know. I've had an earful from Mammy, Roisin, and Moira as to what I should do—all of it involving telling him to feck off. Oh, and I believe calling him a ballbag was mentioned more than once too. Come on, you two know me better than anyone else. What do you think I should do?'

'Ash, we can't tell you what you should do, you know that. You have to do what your heart tells you.'

'One of our guests—it's a long story—she said I should follow my heart and that there's a lot to be said for forgiveness.'

Quinn sat barely hearing as Leila replied; he was lost in his thoughts. The years had passed, other women had come and gone, but he still carried that same torch for Aisling. The flame had never even so much as flickered. He gazed into his empty glass at the deep red sediment. He should have laid it on the line when she came back from Crete, but it didn't seem right with her dad being so sick. He would have felt as though he were taking advantage of her when she was vulnerable. Instead, he'd tried to show her through his actions. The meals he'd cooked and brought around to O'Mara's during those dark days before Brian passed, and then after to try to tempt her into eating something. It had hurt him almost as much as he knew she was hurting to see her in so much pain. He'd felt incompetent because all he could do was make sure she knew he was there for her. He hadn't expected Marcus to happen along, but he had, and the window of opportunity had closed. He would have gladly knocked the bastard flat on his back for what he'd done to Aisling, especially when she was still so raw from her father's death.

At the same time, he'd hated himself for the relief he'd felt over the wedding not going ahead. He didn't wish that heartache on her, but any eejit could see Marcus and Aisling weren't right for each other. She'd latched onto him when she'd been lost and unsure how to get past her grief for her dad. They hadn't even been together a year when they got engaged. It had taken every ounce of Quinn's willpower not to tell her she was making a mistake. He'd distanced himself from her rather than say something she might not forgive him for.

Marcus held her back. She was a restrained version of the Aisling he knew when she was around him, her laugh not quite as loud. It had been a long time since he'd seen her throw back her head and laugh like she used to. It had been good to see her enjoying herself tonight. He watched the light play on the cascade of her hair, red and gold glints shimmering like fire. He wouldn't let that window close on him for a second time.

Chapter 35

It was after midnight when Aisling clambered into the taxi. Alasdair had called it to take her around the corner and home. She hadn't found herself in rags, her taxi didn't turn into a pumpkin, but her feet ached just as much as if they had been encased in glass slippers all evening. She couldn't wait to kick her shoes off and give her tender tootsies a massage. Her ears were ringing with the music they'd jigged along to with the best of them.

It was a miracle she and Leila had been able to get up from the table, let alone perform energetic dance moves after the dessert Quinn had produced. Come to think of it, Quinn had been a little subdued after dinner, and he'd barely touched any of the bite-sized sweeties he'd brought out to share. Instead, he'd sat back content to let them snaffle the lot. He hadn't wanted to join them either as they muscled in on the tiny dance area. He'd sunk the rest of the bottle of wine in their absence. It wasn't like him. She'd been having too much fun to notice anything amiss at the time, and, scrunching her toes, she felt a guilty pang. A good friend would have noticed.

Maybe he was worried about his mam. He'd said she was doing alright, but the stroke had given the family a shock. She should have asked him instead of twittering on like she had about Marcus. She'd pop around in the next day or so and thank him for a deadly night; she couldn't remember the last time she'd had such great craic. She'd be sure to ask him then if everything was okay. She settled on that as the driver slammed his door shut and performed a U-turn. His English was stilted, and he clearly wasn't in the mood to practice it, given the time of night.

It was a miracle she'd managed to dance in her Jimmy Choo's, but despite grievous risk to her ankles, she'd forgotten all about them as she threw herself into the mix. She never could resist a tin pipe and a fiddle. The music was catchy, and the atmosphere too infectious not to get in amongst it.

Aisling loved to dance; it made her happy. She'd briefly done ballet as a little girl, but she didn't have the physique to be a ballerina—too sturdy, and she'd joined the Brownies for a brief stint instead. Her dancing over the years had been relegated to sticky floors after dark with her friends until Leila had talked her into going along to salsa classes. She rested her head back on the seat and closed her eyes as the conversation between her and Quinn replayed. Why had she never gone back for a second class? She'd loved the initial one the three of them had attended. Not just because she'd met Marcus but because the music had made her feel carefree, like she was connecting with another part of herself. A part that wasn't sensible and bound by duty. Why then had she felt because it wasn't Marcus's thing, it couldn't be hers either?

She massaged her temples. She was knackered; last night's broken sleep had caught up with her. The second wind she'd been running on had well and truly blown itself out now. The taxi pulled up outside O'Mara's, which was in darkness. Aisling paid her fare, and the driver waited until she'd let herself in. She locked the door behind her and stepped out of her shoes, her sigh of relief an audible hiss in the deserted reception. As she tiptoed through the inky interior, she passed by Room 1 and wondered whether Una had come back. She might have decided to stay at Aideen's. She'd have to wait until the morning to find out. She was looking forward to hearing how the rest of the day's catching up had panned out for the sisters and what their plans were now they'd reconnected.

The stairs creaked as she made her way up them despite her best efforts to be quiet. Although fair play to her, she was getting quite good at this creeping about nocturnally business. She unlocked the door to the apartment, expecting to have to pat around the wall for the light switch, but Moira, uncharacteristically considerate, had left a lamp on for her. She would long since be tucked up in bed, Aisling thought, tempted to head straight for her own bed.

Her stomach rolled over, reminding her of the evening's excesses. What was it Mammy swore by for digestion problems? Bicarbonate of soda dissolved in warm water sprang to mind. She'd see if that would do the trick. It certainly wouldn't do any harm. So, she opened the cupboard where the baking things that hadn't seen the light of day since Maureen O'Mara had moved out were kept. There was a tin labelled bicarb—Mammy was a good labeller—tucked at the back, which she dug out. She hoped making up the potion it hadn't expired in 1990 or some other decade. It didn't taste flash, punishment for all the rich food she'd shovelled down earlier, but she got it down.

She forced herself into the bathroom to remove her make-up, not fancying waking up with her eyes glued together with the evening's mascara. At last, face washed and teeth brushed, she crept into her bedroom and, tossing back the covers, clambered in all set to snuggle down and visit the land of nod. Aisling's scream a second later as she felt a warm arm drape itself across her middle should have brought the Guards rushing to their door.

Chapter 36

♥

'Aisling, for the love of God, it's me, Mammy! Shut up.'
   'Jaysus, Mammy,' Aisling rasped, clutching her chest.
'What're you doing?'

'Having a heart attack, that's what. I'm getting too old for
shocks like that. I didn't know what was going on.'

'If anyone's having palpitations, it's me. I didn't know you
were there. You could have been anyone.'

'Who were you expecting to find in yer bed then?'

'Not you!'

Light flooded the room, and Aisling and Maureen blinked
at Moira, looking wild-eyed as she stood in the doorway
clutching her bedside lamp blinking back at them. 'What the
feck is going on? I thought one of you was being murdered.'

They both pointed at each other and said, 'It was her fault.'

'Why're you holding your lamp?' Aisling asked.

'It was the only thing I could find to clobber yer one with.'

'What one?'

'The one who was after sneaking into your room.'

'But it was Mammy.'

'For feck's sake, Aisling, I know that now.'

'Well, I wish one of you had thought to tell me what was
going on. Why didn't you go in Patrick's room, Mammy?'

'Ah, the bed's too hard for my back. Yours is nice and soft.'

'Who do you think you are? Goldilocks?'

'Shut up, you two,' Moira muttered.

Aisling began to calm down and rationale set in. 'I suppose we better check none of the guests were disturbed. We don't want anyone calling the Guards. We'll have everybody up then if they start hammering on the front door. Come on.' They could jolly well come with her, she'd done enough skulking about in the dark as it was, and her poor heart couldn't stand any more shocks like the one she'd just had.

Maureen borrowed Aisling's dressing gown, and she threw an oversized cardigan on over top of her nighty while Moira, in her pyjamas, once more led the way.

'If I break my neck getting about in the dark like this—,'

'Shush, Mammy,' Aisling threw over her shoulder. A beat later, she nearly smacked into the back of Moira, which would have sent her toppling down the stairs. She steadied herself, focussing on what it was that had brought her up short. A seemingly biblical apparition was illuminated by the light shining from Room 6's open door. At the sight of the wiry old man with the halo of silvery hair and wispy beard, Maureen began to cross herself.

'Jesus, Mary, and Joseph,' she whispered, peering around Aisling's shoulder. She could read Mammy's mind, and before she began reciting Hail Mary's, Aisling said, 'It's Branok Nancarrow, Mammy. He and his wife are staying with us. They're from Cornwall, not Jerusalem. Jesus Christ hasn't come calling.' She could almost feel the air go out of Mammy.

'I was thinking more Moses than Jesus, for your information.'

Branok looking decidedly rumpled, peered up at the three women huddled together near the top of the stairs. 'What's going on? We heard a scream.' From around the door peeped a bleary-eyed, Emblyn.

Aisling stepped forward. 'We're so sorry to have woken you and Emblyn, Branok. It was me you heard, and we're fine. Mammy here gave me a fright, that's all.'

Maureen pushed her way past Aisling and Moira and headed down the stairs. 'Maureen O'Mara, former proprietor, come to spend the night with her girls. How-do-ye-do?'

Branok shook her hand, a little taken aback by this bold greeting given the late hour. Emblyn stayed where she was watching the proceedings.

'The girls have always been prone to dramatics, but Aisling, well, she should have been on the stage.'

'Mammy! That's not fair you were in my bed.'

Branok looked from mother to daughter, bewilderment on his face. 'But everybody's alright, that's the main thing.'

Chastened, Aisling marched down and took hold of Mammy's elbow. 'We are, thank you, Branok, and again we're so sorry to have disturbed you and Emblyn.' She flashed an apologetic look at his wife. 'We'll leave you both in peace. Goodnight.'

Branok said there was no harm done and bade them goodnight.

'Don't pull my arm, so,' Maureen said as Aisling herded her up the stairs.

She was not apologetic, nor did she loosen her grip. This was not the time for polite conversation with their guests. She'd be asking what Branok did for a living next, and God help them all if she found out he and Emblyn were artists. There'd be no stopping her then; she'd be asking for tips on her latest watercolour. No, she needed to be taken back upstairs.

As she stepped back inside the apartment, Aisling wasn't sure if it was a good thing or not; only two guests bothering to get up. She could have been being attacked for all anyone knew. Ah well, she yawned; at least Moira and her lamp had come to her rescue. 'I'll take Patrick's bed tonight, Mammy,' she said, taking herself off to her brother's old room before there could be any argument.

———*ele*———

Aisling was asleep within minutes of her head hitting the pillow. It was a fitful sleep filled with dreams that made her toss and turn. Marcus was in their dining room. He was dressed in the suit she'd always hated. The one that didn't sit right around his bum, and he was holding a slip of paper. She was in the room too; only she was tall and willowy. She'd transformed into Maria Lozano. She strutted toward him, the most fabulous pair of pink Louboutin pumps on her feet, beckoning him to join her in a dance of love. He shook his head and waved the paper at her; he was angry. What was on the paper? She peered closer and realised it was her American Express bill. It had angry red circles on it. He threw the paper down, sat on the sofa, and picking up the remote, he switched the television on. The last thing Aisling remembered from the dream when she opened her eyes and realised morning had arrived was he'd been watching the Crocodile Hunter.

She sat up in bed, eyes wide with sudden clarity. She knew exactly what she had to do.

Chapter 37

M oira had left for work by the time Mammy made an appearance. Aisling was showered and dressed, sitting at the table eating her toast with relish. The weight she'd been carrying since Marcus's letters had begun arriving had lifted. She'd made her mind up as to what she was going to do where he was concerned, and the strawberry jam she'd dolloped on her toast tasted all the sweeter for it.

'I'll have a cuppa and get myself sorted. I'm looking forward to saying hello to everyone; then I'll be away. I've a painting class at twelve. I'm working on a representation of the pier. I think it'll look fetching in reception once I've finished it.'

Representation didn't bode well, Aisling thought.

'Now the rain's gone off; I might squeeze in a round of golf later, too. Derbhilla's getting about much better now. She's stopped hobbling about like a cowboy at high noon. Aisling, where've you gone and put the teabags?'

'Nowhere. They're in the cupboard where they always are. Put your glasses on.'

Mammy enjoyed breezing into O'Mara's. She was greeted like a retired Hollywood star each time, even if it'd only been a matter of weeks since she'd last called in.

Aisling finished her toast, debated another slice but decided that would be greedy, and, getting up, carried the plate through to the kitchen. She retrieved the sugar bowl and put the milk on the bench too before Mammy could ask where they were. 'I'm going downstairs now. There's a guest I want to check on. I'll see you in a while.'

Mammy was only half listening. 'I think I might see if Mrs Flaherty can spare me a nice sausage and egg. I haven't had a cooked breakfast for ages. Alright, if I borrow a pair of clean knickers? Moira's won't fit.'

Charming. She wasn't pinching her expensive Agent Provocateur panties. 'I'll leave a pair on the bed for you,' Aisling said—the old pair from Marks & Spencer she'd been meaning to chuck out should do the trick.

She headed down the stairs and called out good morning to Bronagh. She waved her cereal spoon by way of return greeting, and Aisling carried on to the kitchen. Room 1's closed-door gave no clue as to whether Una was in there or not, and she was eager to see if she was having breakfast. Mrs Flaherty had other ideas, accosting her in the doorway and blocking her view of the dining room.

'That fecking fox has been again.'

'Oh, dear.'

'Oh dear, indeed. The bin lid was lying on the ground, and he's left a trail of rubbish. I tell you, Aisling, I won't be responsible for my actions if I get hold of him.'

'Fair play, Mrs Flaherty. I'll see what can be done about him, shall I?'

They both knew full well this wouldn't happen, but Mrs Flaherty felt better for having sounded off. She leaned forward, giving Aisling a whiff of bacon fat. 'Oh, and, Aisling,' her voice dropped to a conspiratorial whisper. 'You'll never believe it.'

'What?'

'Yer woman from Room 1. Her, with the face that only a mother could love over there at the corner table, complimented me on my white pudding this morning. She said it was the best she'd ever had. Went so far as to say it was an art form getting the outside as golden and crispy as I managed to yet making sure the inside still stayed creamy and melted in your mouth. Well, I don't mind telling, you could have blown me down with a feather.'

It would take a lot more than a feather to knock Mrs Flaherty down. A bulldozer might do the trick, thought Aisling as she smiled, 'Compliments where compliments are due. Don't I always say you're a wonder in the kitchen?'

Mrs Flaherty's apple cheeks flushed with pride, and she toddled happily back to the kitchen, fox forgotten. The way was clear for Aisling to make a beeline for Una.

The older woman put her cup down as Aisling approached and beamed at her pushing her chair back.

'Don't get up, Una.' Aisling pulled out the chair opposite her and sat down. 'I'm so glad I found you. I've been desperate to know how the rest of your day with Aideen went.'

Una looked different, younger, brighter, and the pinched expression was gone. She looked how Aisling felt, and she wondered if she looked different this morning too.

Una reached across the table and took Aisling's hand in hers, holding it tight. 'I've got my sister back, thanks to you, dear.'

'Oh, it wasn't, thanks to me. I didn't do anything.'

'You did more than you'll ever know.'

'Well, you helped me too.'

They smiled at each other, and Una gave her hand a final squeeze before releasing it. 'It's been decided. I'm moving in with Aideen. I want to be there to help while she has the rest of her treatment. It will take a load off the boys' shoulders too. They've their own families to be thinking of, and I want to spend every second I can with my sister.'

'That's wonderful, Una. It means I'll get to see you again after you check out today too.'

'I'd like that. I'd like that very much. Now then, what's got you looking like the cat that got the cream this morning?'

'I've made my mind up where Marcus is concerned. It came to me this morning, clear as day. I had this dream, you see, and now I know what I've got to do.'

Chapter 38

♥

Aisling left Una to pack and headed back upstairs. There was no time for her morning check to see the cogs of O'Mara's were turning as they should be; she had a phone call to make. She heard voices as she reached the landing. It was Ita and Mammy; they were in Room 5, and she couldn't help peeking in on them. Mammy was perched on the chair by the window asking after Ita's mam while Ita whipped the sheets off and remade the bed faster than Aisling had ever seen her undertake any task before. Perhaps she should get a cardboard cut-out of Mammy and stand it in the entrance of the rooms she was supposed to be making up.

Carrying on up the stairs, she knew when Maureen ventured down to reception, she and Bronagh would embrace like it had been years, not mere weeks since they'd last seen each other. 'She's only come from Howth, Bronagh, not New Zealand.' Aisling had said the last time she'd witnessed this carry-on.

'Sure, look it, Aisling, you don't work for someone for thirty years without missing them when you don't see them on a daily basis anymore.'

'Fair play,' Aisling had said.

She let herself back into the apartment and, for a moment, only a moment, wished Mammy would move back in. The place was sparkling. She cast her eyes about before picking up the phone to dial the number she knew by heart.

~

The sky was a moody canopy as she followed the path through the Green. The grey clouds were left over from the downpour the day before, but there were patches of blue gallantly appearing. A duck quacked and waddled across the path in front of her, and Aisling shivered as a sudden gust sent leaves floating down around her. She was glad she'd thought to put her coat on as her boots crunched over the leaf laden path. Marcus was there already; Aisling saw as she approached the bandstand. A lone tourist was trying to capture an arty shot of it, her photo ruined by a man with a newspaper tucked under his arm striding in front of the line of her lens.

Aisling's resolve faltered momentarily at the sight of him. It would have been easier to do this over the phone, take the easy way out, but that wasn't her style. It was his. He waved out and began to walk toward her. The lightness in his step told her how he thought this conversation was going to go. Her insides tightened. *You can do this, Aisling.*

'Hi, you're a sight for sore eyes.' Reaching her, he leaned in and kissed her cheek. How formal, she couldn't help but think as he said, 'It's so good to see you.' He took a step back and thrust his hands in his pockets, eyeing her speculatively. 'You said you were ready to talk.'

She managed a watery smile but hesitated, trying to find the right words. She'd had no time to rehearse what she wanted to say.

Marcus cut to the chase, forcing her hand. 'Have you had time to think about what I said?' The anticipation of her expected response flickered in his eyes.

For a moment, Aisling wobbled. He'd hurt her, but she had no wish to do the same to him. This wasn't a case of tit for tat. 'I've done nothing but.' There was no point in playing games, and she breathed in sharply. 'Marcus, I'm sorry. We can't go back. It won't work.'

For a brief second, he looked as though he'd been slapped. It was clearly not what he'd expected to hear. 'But I love you, Ash.'

He looked like a lost little boy, and it wasn't easy to summon what needed to be said. 'I loved you too, but you don't love me, Marcus. Not properly. You love who you want me to be.' The past tense slipped easily from her mouth because she knew it was true. Somewhere along the line this last year, she'd moved on. She just hadn't known it.

She wanted to be the girl she'd been before Dad died and before she met Marcus. She wanted to be the girl who bought shoes on a whim again—okay, maybe not Louboutin's, but she'd find a compromise. She wanted to take dance classes and leave her inhibitions at the door. She wanted to throw her head back and laugh from deep down inside her belly. She'd never laughed like that with Marcus. He'd have found it loud and embarrassing. Quinn didn't; he found it infectious joining in with her. This wasn't about him, though.

There were no rewind buttons in life. She couldn't go back. She couldn't change Dad not being here. Nor could she undo the rippling effect grief had, but she could be a new version of her old self. The only way to do that was to keep moving forward.

'I don't get it.'

'I know, but you will. We weren't right for each other, Marcus. We're too different. You say *tomato*; I say *tomahto*.' She put her hand to her mouth. Where on earth had the Fred Astaire and Ginger Rogers lyric come from? Alasdair sprang to mind.

It had gone over Marcus's head. He was looking at the sycamore leaves settling around his feet. He raised his gaze to meet Aisling's. She didn't flinch. 'You mean it don't you?'

'I do. I won't be changing my mind, Marcus.'

'There's nothing else to say then, is there?'

She shook her head, a lump forming in her throat. 'Only that I wish you well.' She meant it. It felt good to finally let go of the anger she'd kept such a tight hold of this past year.

He reached out and touched her face, his fingers brushing the same spot where his lips had grazed her cheek in greeting. 'I wish you all the best too, Ash. No more saying I'm sorry.'

'No more.'

'Well, that's something.' His smile was sad.

'Goodbye, Marcus.'

She turned and walked away, not wanting him to see her tears as she strode back down the path.

Dear Aisling,

Today, I said goodbye to my ex-fiancé. He wanted us to try again, but I blamed him for calling our wedding off and leaving me in the lurch. I can see now he did me a favour. We weren't meant to be together. We're too different. So not going back was the right thing to do. The thing is, I don't know how to move on from the person I've loved all along. How can I switch off my feelings for someone who's only ever seen me as a friend?

Yours faithfully,

Me

~

Quinn marched up the stairs to the first-floor studio. He'd phoned ahead, and the Lozanos were expecting him. He was pulling out all the stops. He wasn't going to lose Aisling to Marcus a second time. If this all blew up in his face, at least he'd know he'd given it his best shot.

Chapter 39

♥

Reception was quiet when Aisling stepped back inside the guest house. There was no sign of Mammy. Bronagh, barely visible above the desk and with a custard cream halfway to her mouth, read her mind.

'Maureen left twenty minutes ago. She had a painting class she needed to get back for. Oh, and Quinn phoned while you were out too.' For no reason Aisling could fathom other than Bronagh having said his name, she giggled. 'He left a message, said it was very important you get it.'

Aisling was curious. She took the piece of paper Bronagh handed her and read it with a frown. He wanted her to meet him at seven pm at the Lozano's Dance Studio. There was no explanation as to why. She folded the slip of paper and sighed—what a day this one was turning out to be.

'Isn't that the place you did the salsa class, where you met you know who?'

'It is. I only went the once, and I have no idea why Quinn would want to meet there. Maybe I'll give him a call.' She wasn't in the mood for cryptic messages.

'Ah, well now, he also said if you mentioned calling him to try to find out what he was up to, I was to tell you not to. He said, and I'm quoting, *Tell her it's a surprise, and a surprise can only be a surprise if she doesn't know what it is.'*

Aisling's frown deepened. What was he up to?

Bronagh's eagle eye noted the smudge of mascara beneath Aisling's eyes, and she put her custard cream down. 'Is everything alright?'

'It's going to be, so long as you pass me one of those custard creams.'

'What custard creams?'

'Don't play innocent with me. The packet you keep in your drawer.'

'They're for emergencies only, but looking at the state of yer, I'd say you qualify. Pull up a chair and tell me what's been going on.'

Aisling did as she was told, thinking Bronagh must have an awful lot of emergencies as she helped herself to a biscuit. When she got to the part where she'd told Marcus there was no going back. Bronagh clapped her hands and said she could have the rest of the packet.

Somehow, she managed to fill the day, her eyes straying to the clock every so often, counting down the hours. Her mind kept drifting to the different scenarios of what Quinn was up to as she tried to run through the accounts. With a sigh, she put them aside. They could wait until tomorrow; she'd only make a mess of them if she kept at it today. In the end, she figured he'd booked them back into the dance classes after their conversation at dinner last night. It made sense, but what didn't make sense was the secrecy.

Moira, breezing in after work, was a welcome diversion.

'God, I was knackered today after your and Mammy's carry-on last night.' She flopped down on the sofa kicking her runners off. 'I kept putting calls through to the wrong person, and I got caught with my gob full of egg sandwich by Aiden O'Dwyer.'

'Aiden O'Dwyer's one of Mason Price's clients?' She had Aisling's attention; the man had starred in several Hollywood blockbusters. He was blue-eyed, square-jawed, dark-haired and always played damaged sort of people.

'Ah, he's not all that great,' said Moira. 'He needed a shave, and he was wearing green joggers. Green for feck's sake, and it's not even St Paddy's. But still, it was embarrassing the sanger got stuck on the roof of my mouth, and I couldn't get my words out properly. He'd have thought me a right eejit.'

Aisling grinned at the picture painted.

Moira was moving on in her usual hurricane Moira manner. 'You haven't seen the dress I bought to wear to Posh Mairead's bash yet, have you?' She didn't wait for a reply and bounced off the sofa. 'I'll put it on and give you a twirl.'

She reappeared a few minutes later and strutted her stuff through the living room. The dress was a clinging, deep cerise with spaghetti straps, which finished just above her knees. It was sexy but not in an overt way, and Aisling gave a low whistle.

'Wow, Moira, you look gorgeous.'

'Shelbourne gorgeous?'

'Savoy, Ritz, Four Seasons gorgeous.'

———

Dinner was a hit and miss affair of heated up leftover Chinese. Aisling wasn't hungry. The half pack of custard creams had seen to that. Besides, she was too fidgety and antsy to eat. She hadn't mentioned Quinn's message to Moira, knowing she'd be in for a derisive snort at the mention of salsa. She did, however, inform her as to what she'd said to Marcus earlier in the day.

To her surprise, Moira hugged her long and hard. 'I knew you weren't a total eejit.' Now, that was the Moira she knew and loved!

'I'm heading out to meet Quinn at seven. Will I leave it to you to tell Mammy and Roisin, Marcus won't be around anymore?' Aisling said as she headed toward her bedroom.

Moira looked delighted by the prospect as she nodded enthusiastically, then registering what she'd said about meeting, Quinn said, 'Do you know, Ash, I've always thought Quinn had the glad eye for you.'

It was Aisling who paused and gave the derisive snort. 'No way. We're friends, that's all.'

Moira let it be, eager to begin burning up the phone lines with her breaking news.

Aisling stared into her wardrobe. The red dress or the LBD? She held both out and opted for the red. Moira said it gave her a look of a short Nicole Kidman. As for the shoes, she chose her Valentino slingback sandals. They were made for dancing. Ignoring her sister's raised eyebrows, she swept through the living room and out the front door. She could imagine the turn the conversation she was having had just taken. *'Rosi, you want to see the state of her; she's in the red dress. Yes, the shag-me, short Nicole Kidman one. And... she's meeting Quinn!'*

Chapter 40

Aisling slammed the taxi door shut and stared up at the building. The first floor was in darkness. She knew she wasn't early, not by more than a couple of minutes. She'd left O'Mara's at six forty-five, and the traffic had been moving freely. Quinn wouldn't let her down; she knew that, so she crossed the street and opened the door. At least the light in the stairwell was on, and she climbed the stairs hearing movement above her. Someone was up there then.

Maybe it was a new thing, salsa in the dark? She pushed open the door expecting to find a few people at least milling about. The room, however, was empty, save for a table draped with a white cloth, a candle flickering in the middle of it. It was laid for two. Her eyes swung to the trolley next to it, not understanding. There were several silver tureens and a champagne bucket with a bottle on ice. What on earth was going on?

'Quinn?' she called.

Seemingly from thin air, a fast Latino beat erupted, and Quinn emerged from the shadows. It took a few seconds for her eyes to adjust to the dim light, and her jaw dropped. This was a version of Quinn she'd never seen before. He was wearing a black open-necked shirt and dress pants as he moved toward her in a cha-cha of triple step forward, right foot back.

Aisling stared in amazement before throwing her head back and laughing. She sobered a beat later as he reached her, and they stood in front of one another. His grin disappeared, too and was replaced by something she couldn't fathom.

How was she supposed to be? This was Quinn. The man she'd known since she was eighteen years old. The man she'd hankered after who'd never once looked at her the way he was looking at her now. She could see the question in his eyes as he held his hands out to her. The only sign he was laying it on the line in the slight tremor as she stared at them. They were strong hands, creative hands, and if she took them, she'd step off into the unknown. Aisling took a deep breath and grasped hold of them as tight as she could. He pulled her in toward him.

Surely, he must be able to feel her heart thumping, be aware of how the warmth of his chest against hers was liquefying her insides. She tilted her head to look up at him, searching for clues she was reading this right, and he was about to kiss her. She decided to be bold, and on her tippy toes, she sought his lips as he leaned down to find hers, grazing the side of each other's mouths by mistake. That's what happened when old friends crossed a line; Aisling's face was hot, but Quinn just laughed. It made her laugh. He made her laugh. He always had.

'Shall we try again?' he asked. 'See if we can get it right this time?'

She nodded.

This time their lips found each other, and as Aisling melted into him, she knew she'd gotten her happy ending, after all.

The End

Moira Lisa Smile

♥

By Michelle Vernal

Chapter 1

♥

1999

For as long as Moira O'Mara could recall, people had been telling her she was pretty. This was something which at times could be convenient. For instance, those occasions when she'd been naughty and the sight of tears welling in her big hazel eyes would get her off the hook. It could also be annoying.

She'd told Mammy just the other day she was still scarred from the little old ladies at the supermarket who'd peer at her when she was little. There she'd be, trapped in the trolley, kneeling alongside the meat, veg, and bread. She'd have been plopped in there having declared her legs were far too tired to walk any further. The temptation as those witchlike women cooed over what a wee dote she was, was to open her mouth and howl. She'd wanted to send them scarpering—stranger-danger and all that, but Moira had never been a silly girl, she knew which side her bread was buttered on, even at that age. There'd be no chance of a sweet treat at the check-out counter if she were to make a scene.

Twenty-one years later, Mammy was still not sympathetic to her plight. 'You're scarred Moira? Ha-now there's a joke. I was mortified the day you asked, at the top of your lungs mind, why old ladies had whiskers like Daddy and smelt like wet socks?'

She'd forgotten about that! Mammy always said, *For someone with a face like butter wouldn't melt, she had a gob on her like a sailor!* The memory of that conversation made her smile as she finished the last three strokes of polish on her big toenail before moving on to the next in line.

Sure, she thought, eyeing her handiwork, it was a compliment to be told she was pretty, but it was something she'd never really got. It wasn't as if it was a talent or an achievement, something she was responsible for. She was born with the face she was born with. It was not as if she'd had any say in the matter. If anybody deserved the compliment, it was Mammy and Daddy. It was their genetics that were responsible for the way her features had decided to arrange themselves on her face. So far as she knew, nobody had ever patted them on the back and said, 'Well done. You did a good job producing her.'

Her friend Andrea once said, *It's alright for you, Moira. It's easy to be blasé about being told you're pretty when you were born beautiful. Try going through life with a nose on you that makes Barbara Streisand's look small, and at least she can sing.* She'd launched into *Memories* then, making paws of her hands, as she sang the opening lines from the musical, *Cats*. It had made Moira laugh.

There was nothing wrong with Andrea's nose; it gave her a regal air, a bit like a Nefertiti bust. Moira had seen pictures of one of those in the encyclopaedia collection Mammy had been swindled into buying many moons ago by the smiling door-to-door salesman. He'd made her think her poor children would be missing out on the basics of education were she to close the door in his face. Her mammy had always been too nice for her own good; Daddy, too. It came from being in the hospitality business. As the hosts of O'Mara's Guesthouse, politeness was ingrained in them. Aisling was the same.

She dipped the brush back in the bottle before wiping the excess against the rim. Her gaze strayed over to the bookshelf, spying the neat rows of cherry-red leather spines with their gold embossed lettering. The way the internet was going those books would be relics from the past in the new millennium.

As for Andrea, well, she was right in that she couldn't sing. She sounded like the ginger tom who'd land on the roof at night, a heavy thud followed by a stealthy pitter-patter. He liked to fight with all the other cats in the neighbourhood. Her friend might not be able to hold a tune, but she did make Moira laugh. That right there was something worthy of comment—Andrea was funny. She made people laugh. It was an achievement. The thing she didn't get where Moira was concerned was, being told she was pretty didn't give her a sense of achievement or boost her self-esteem. It was her accomplishments that did that and she could count those on one hand. Her left foot done, she put the wand back in the bottle and leaned forward on the sofa to peer closely at her painted toes. They passed muster.

She had no idea where this contemplative mood had sprung from, but she'd roll with it. Her eyes flitted to the wall where the framed painting of Foxy Loxy used to hang. She fancied she could still see the outline of trapped dust it had left behind when Mammy took it down. She'd insisted on it going with her to her new apartment in Howth—what with the painting being one of the great highlights of her baby's childhood. Moira's sigh was audible in the emptiness of the apartment. It was mad how much had happened in the last two years. *Mad!*

The very idea of her mammy, living in a swish pad over-looking the harbour was mental in itself. She could picture her welcoming her golfing lady friends, or more to the point, her pals from painting class into her apartment. She'd only undertaken the art classes in the hope it would prove it was her who'd passed on the artistic gene to her youngest child. From what Moira had seen of her attempts so far, she'd concluded it wasn't. Mammy's *Howth Pier Sunset* which she'd insisted Aisling hang in the guesthouse's reception area was on a par with Noah, her five-year-old grandson's, daubs. His latest painting, a mish-mash of colours and stick figures sent over from London and titled *My Family*, was currently stuck to the fridge by magnets.

Mammy, Moira imagined would point out the profession-ally framed Foxy Loxy and tell her new friends, *Our Moira painted that when she was ten. It won the Texaco Children's Art Competition.* She'd pause waiting for them to ooh and aah over this accomplishment before continuing. *She was an unexpected surprise was Moira, and she's still surprising me. We always said she was gifted, her daddy and I, but she didn't take her talent any further when she left the high school.*

The latter would be said with a sad lament because Mammy had once had big plans for her youngest child. When she and Daddy accompanied her to the grand prize-giving at the Gresham Hotel all those years ago, Patrick, Roisin, and Aisling dragged along in their Sunday best, she'd been puffed up like a peacock. She'd worked the room telling anybody who cared to listen that Moira had a style similar to that of Georgia O'Keeffe. Where she got the comparison between the famous American artist with her penchant for big flowers and Moira's painting of the little red fox who liked to visit the bins at the back of O'Mara's was beyond her. 'So, there you go folks, my crowning achievement. Winning a children's Art competition,' she said. She did that when no one was home, talked to herself. She'd be bringing home stray cats next.

Aisling, Moira knew, called her chosen subject for the pres-tigious children's art competition, *Mr Fox*. The guesthouse cook, Mrs Flaherty, called him *that fecking fox*. Her con-niptions when she spotted the scraps from the bins scat-tered about the concreted courtyard in the morning were legendary.

'Conniption,' Moira said, as she set about beautifying her right toes. She liked the way it sounded and it was a word that perfectly described their roly-poly, apple-cheeked cook's be-haviour after Foxy Loxy, Moira's chosen name, visited. It was at those times; Mrs Flaherty could turn the air blue.

Moira knew the fox lived in the Iveagh Gardens behind the brick wall at the back of the guesthouse. She'd only ever got-ten shadowy, darting glimpses of him when she peered down from her bedroom window to the courtyard, three storeys below. He was O'Mara's secret visitor and some nights, she'd open her window and drop a piece of sausage, pinched from the kitchen, down to the courtyard below to tempt him out. Mrs Flaherty would have combusted had she known that! It was lucky for Moira that those wide eyes of hers filling with tears had always worked a treat on the cook.

The day she'd decided to enter the art competition she'd visited the library and found a book on foxes. Mammy had set her up at the dining room table, covering it with news-paper, and Moira had set about painting her picture from a photograph in the book. She'd learned a lot about foxes from that book. For instance, she knew that they were partial to hedgehogs, a fact she'd not been impressed by. She also knew they didn't live much past five years in the wild. This meant that the Foxy Loxy of her childhood was long gone. She liked to think it was his great-grandson who visited these days. Foxy Loxy Jnr.

By the time she'd turned fifteen, she'd stopped painting. She'd been too busy organising her social life and turning her parents' hair grey. She'd stopped dropping tasty treats out her bedroom window as well, too absorbed in her teenage self. The last time she'd had a tasty treat in her bedroom, Tristan Gallagher aside, was when she'd arrived home from a night on the lash clutching a kebab. She'd woken up the next morning with the half-eaten shawarma next to her. There'd been a piece of shaved lamb nestling in her hair and she'd reeked of the garlicky yogurt sauce. Not her finest moment. It was a good thing Mammy had moved out; she'd have had her bundled up and dropped on the doorstep of the Rutland Centre for rehab, had she laid eyes on her that morning.

Moira swore softly as the thought of her mammy's new abode made her slip with the polish brush. It was weird to think how much had changed in their lives in the last two years. It was like she'd been on an out of control lift with all these stops she didn't want to get off at. She picked up a cotton bud and wiped the rogue polish off the side of her middle toe. There was no room for error, she had to look perfect tomorrow night. She wanted to prove to Michael that she could move in the same circles as him.

The shade of pink she'd chosen was the perfect match for her new lipstick, purchased at the same time from Boots. They both complemented perfectly the dress she'd spent hours looking for with Andrea. It was cerise, clung to her in all the right places, and hit the right balance between sexy and elegant. The perfect dress for The Shelbourne Hotel, and the St Tropez tan she'd had applied at great expense two nights ago ensured no pasty flesh would be on display. How was she going to get through the day tomorrow? She'd be on tenterhooks, but at least she'd be busy. The phone barely stopped ringing from the minute she put her headset on and sat down behind Mason Price Lawyers' expansive reception desk.

Today she'd actually answered, 'The Shelbourne Hotel this is Moira, how can I help?' It was only when Gilly elbowed her, she'd realised what she'd said. Luckily the client on the other end was barely listening anyway as he demanded to be put through to Brendan Dockerill ASAP! Her mind had been on nothing but the party all week.

There was only one more sleep to go until the engagement party of Posh Mairead and Niall Finnegan, one of Mason Price's Senior Partner's, and as such, tonight had been set aside for a top-to-toe beauty treatment assault. She and Mairead weren't exactly friends, so it was a miracle they'd made the guest list given its limited numbers. She'd had to refrain from replying, *We'll be there with fecking bells on*, when Mairead asked if she thought they might be able to make it along to her and Niall's low key, little celebration. If the truth were to be told she'd been as stunned as Gilly that she'd received an invite. Her co-worker had gotten her nose right out of joint about it, and Moira had had to appease her with a bag of crisps from the vending machine in the staff kitchen upstairs.

For whatever reason, however, it would seem Posh Mairead had taken a shine to her and Andrea, and as such, Moira was trying to be big hearted about her impending nuptials. It took all sorts to make the world go round and perhaps Niall had a thing for girls with buck teeth. Sure, he was no oil painting himself. Moira was fairly certain Posh Mairead only worked at Mason Price because 'Daddy' had insisted she get a taste of mingling with the working classes at grass roots level. Perhaps she and Andrea were the token members of that working class on the guest list. She didn't care, the party had been circled on her mental social calendar ever since she'd received her invite.

Her eyes flitted to the fridge where the neatly printed gold embossed card was held in place by a magnet. Aisling must have brought it home from Greece given it was a donkey standing on top of the word 'Crete' and she felt a familiar frisson of excitement knowing Michael would be there.

The 'do' was to be an intimate soirée of around twenty guests in the hotel's Saddleroom. Moira had seen Niall in action and there was no doubt given his robust brown-nosing, he was a social climber. He was also in the top tier at Mason Price and as such the other high-level movers and shakers in the firm, including Michael, would be there. A bigger bash for the family and those that mattered in Dublin was being held in a month's time in the hotel's Great Room.

Moira's hair was wrapped in a towel turban, a deep conditioning treatment taking care of her split ends, and a pore minimising clay mask was beginning to tighten on her face to ensure she looked perfect tomorrow night. The word reverberated through her head, perfect, perfect, perfect; nothing less would do.

'Feck.' The phone rang banishing the word from her head. It was on the kitchen bench by the kettle where she'd left it when she'd said goodbye to Andrea. They'd run through their plans for tomorrow night and Andrea had confirmed she'd booked them both in for a shampoo and blow wave during their lunch break. Moira hesitated, torn between her toes and answering the call. She'd never been able to leave a phone to ring though, because she was far too curious by nature and besides the little voice in her head would always whisper, *what if it's something important?* She hauled herself off the couch and hobbled over, toes arched upward, and snatched the phone up.

'Hello.'

'Moira, is that you?'

She rolled her eyes. Mammy always sounded surprised. There was only the choice of two people answering the fecking thing, her or Aisling. 'Yes, Mammy, it's me. What's up?'

'Does there have to be something up for a Mammy to ring wanting to speak to her daughter?'

'Usually, yes. When the Mammy's social calendar is fuller than the daughter's.' Moira glanced down relieved to see her toes had survived their short journey from sofa to kitchen.

'I'm after some advice,' Maureen O'Mara huffed down the phone.

'Oh, yes?' Moira raised an eyebrow. Now, this was one out of the box. It was usually Mammy handing out the advice.

Whether it was warranted or not wanted, it never stopped her saying her piece one way or the other.

'I'm after booking a holiday.'

Moira could hear the rain lashing against the windows and accordingly felt a stab of envy at the thought of Maureen O'Mara stretched on a sun lounger somewhere hot and foreign. She'd probably gotten a late season week in the Costa del Sol, or maybe Tenerife; her and Daddy had gone there a few times. 'Good for you. Where are you off to then?'

'Vietnam, I'm going backpacking so I am.'

Moira dropped the phone.

Chapter 2

'Vietnam!' The sound of helicopter rotors whirring and a sixties musical medley began to play in Moira's head.

'Yes, I always fancied going there.'

'Since when?' Moira's voice rose as she cast her eyes around the empty apartment. She wished Aisling was here so she could shriek, *Mammy's after booking a flight to Vietnam and says she's going backpacking. She's officially lost the plot*! Her fingers itched to hang up so she could speed dial Roisin, her eldest sister across the water in London, with this breaking news. The toll rate was low this time of night so they could have a good old chinwag about it. This was too incredulous not to be sharing.

'I think you ruptured my ear drum, Moira.'

'Sorry, but, Mammy, come on, Vietnam? That's halfway around the world. What are you wanting to go there for?'

'Adventure, Moira. I want to have an adventure, and I want to sail on a junk.'

Ten minutes later Moira hung up the phone to her mother. She resumed her position on the sofa and finished painting her toes with swift, efficient brush strokes, her brain whirring. The advice Mammy had been seeking was whether she should spend the money on having a yellow fever jab as a precaution before she went. Apparently, it cost a small fortune, but it was advisable when getting off the beaten track. 'For feck's sake, Mammy you're not after jungle trekking or the like surely?' Moira had exploded. This was all too much to take in.

It would appear that Mammy was planning just that, and she was going on some rowboat down a big river too. Moira wasn't sure if they had hippopotamus's in Vietnam or not and the thought made her shudder. Only the other day she'd caught the tail end of a wildlife programme on when hippos attack. She was fairly sure they were only found in Africa but fairly wasn't one hundred per cent. She'd already lost her daddy; she wasn't going to lose her mammy too. And alright, maybe you couldn't call a short jaunt from some tribal village in the mountains jungle trekking, but still and all it was bad enough. Mammy had informed her she and her travelling companion, Rosemary Farrell from her rambling group, had been practising by taking to the hills around Howth.

Moira had latched on to this. 'Mammy, Howth is not a tribal mountain village and adventures aren't for women in their sixties.' They certainly weren't for mammies in their sixties! 'Sure, look it, why can't you and this *Rosemary*,' she'd already pegged her as a bad influence and she pronounced her name accordingly, 'have a nice walking holiday together down in Connemara or Mayo? Everybody knows there're loads of lovely trails around there you could explore. Listen, I'll even spring for one of those pole thing-a-me-bobs older people are so fond of hiking with if you change your plans.'

'Moira O'Mara, I've only just turned sixty and that was a non-event. None of us felt much like celebrating now, did we? This is my belated birthday present to myself and, for your information, young lady. I'm not a geriatric and there are no junks in Connemara or Mayo. I want to sail on a junk. I have done since I saw James Bond escape on one in *The Man with the Golden Gun*. It's on my list.'

She'd sounded like a belligerent two-year-old stamping her feet, and what was she on about? 'What list?'

'My list of things I want to do before I join your daddy.'

'Ah, Mammy, sure don't talk like that. You've years left in you. You don't need to start ticking things off a list.'

'Your daddy and I thought we had years left together. None of us know what's around the corner, Moira, and I don't intend to sit on my backside waiting for my number to be called.'

Moira chewed her lip, unsure what to say. They'd all handled Daddy's death nearly two years ago now, differently. Mammy had announced she wouldn't see her days out in the guesthouse without her husband at her side. Her ultimatum had been, either one of the O'Mara children step up to manage the business, or it would be sold. She'd then set about buying her apartment in Howth and joining the golf club, taking art classes, enrolling for sailing lessons, and putting her name down on every social committee the seaside community had to offer. In short, she'd gone completely round the twist.

It was Aisling who'd taken hold of O'Mara's reins. Her way of coping with her grief was by immersing herself wholly in the family business. Thank goodness she and Quinn had taken their blinkers off where each other was concerned; her sister had a much better work life balance going on since they'd hooked up. She'd been very bossy before, overly interested in what Moira was up to, and forever on at her to straighten her room up. Now she was all loved up, she was still annoying in a *my life is soo wonderful way*, but at least she left Moira to her own devices.

Moira didn't know how it was for Patrick and Rosie knowing Daddy wasn't in their lives anymore. Being away, they were removed from the day-to-day reminders of him. She still felt his presence in every room of the top-floor apartment of the Georgian manor house where she'd lived her whole life. Her breath caught, she missed her lovely, generous, kind father every minute of every single day. Mammy dragged her back into the conversation.

'I'll have you know just the other day Terry Lynch from the butcher's was after telling me I didn't look a day over fifty. He gave me an extra chop, too, so he did. And, Moira O'Mara, I'm the same age as yer Fonda woman and nobody'd bat an eye if she announced she were off trekking. So, as a grown woman, your Mammy no less—something you'd do well to remember my girl, don't be after telling me what I should and shouldn't do!'

She'd sounded very huffy and had hung up without saying goodbye. Moira was not in the mood to call her back. She knew from the tone she'd get the mortally offended version of Maureen O'Mara were she to do so and she'd be made to feel so guilty, she'd have to apologise. But if she apologised it would mean she approved of this trip to the wilds of Asia and she most certainly did not. No, she'd leave it for now and let Aisling or Roisin try to talk some sense into her. Mammy would not be going to Vietnam if Moira had anything to do with it.

Chapter 3

♥

M oira breathed a sigh of relief as she heard the front door open. Aisling was home, she'd know what to do about Mammy.

'Jaysus, it's wild out there tonight,' Aisling said, rubbing her hands as she came into the living room. Spying her sister, her eyes narrowed. 'Moira get your feet off the table.'

'Aisling, feck off, there're bigger things to be worrying about than my feet on the coffee table.' She felt the face mask crack as she spoke, a reminder that she should be in the shower by now.

'Such as?'

Moira removed her feet knowing she wouldn't get her sister's full attention until she did so. She glanced beyond Aisling checking to see if Quinn was behind her. He wasn't. She loved Quinn but a night off listening to the pair of them riding like they were trying to win the Grand National was welcome.

'Mammy's only gone and got it in her head to go to Vietnam for nearly a month with some rambling woman and she's going tribal and, and, and I don't know if there're hippos there or not.'

'Jaysus, it's like a sauna in here. Have you turned the heating up?' Aisling shrugged out of her jacket. 'No wonder you're babbling like a mad woman.'

Moira had adjusted the dial on the central heating but she wasn't going to admit to it. The two sisters had a constant battle over the setting. Aisling liked it to take the edge off while Moira preferred it hot enough to close her eyes and imagine she was somewhere like Spain, not fecking Vietnam! It was a country that had never been on her radar until tonight and Aisling wasn't giving her the aghast reaction she wanted.

'You're not listening to me!'

'Moira,' Aisling held her hand up. 'Stop and breathe.' She eyed her sister and shook her head. 'I don't how you expect me to take you seriously looking like that.'

If Moira could have scowled, she would have, but the face pack wouldn't stretch to that. She did, however, slow her breathing. She needed to be coherent.

'Right, now start at the beginning, only slowly this time.'

'Okay, what it is, I've not long got off the phone to Mammy. She told me she's booked a holiday to Vietnam with a woman she goes walking around Howth with. Rosemary something or other. I don't like the sound of her. I think she's trouble. Anyway, they're planning on doing a hill trek and sailing down some river and everything. She's got it in her head she wants to sail on a junk. Do they have hippos there?'

'No, you eejit, they're only in Africa.' Aisling frowned. 'Rosemary. That name sounds familiar.' She flopped down on the end of the sofa. 'Wasn't that yer woman who had her hips replaced? I'm sure Mammy told us a story about her setting the sensors off at the airport with whatever the doctors replaced them with. Kryptonite or something. No, hang on that's Superman; titanium, that was it.'

'Ah, Jaysus, it gets worse.' Moira rubbed her temples, the image of her mammy and this Rosemary Farrell getting patted down by airport security was too much.

Aisling slid her feet from her shoes and flexed them. 'Ooh, that's better. I'm sure I'll hear all about her travel plans on Saturday afternoon.'

Moira had forgotten about that; her head had been so full of the party. They were going to have afternoon tea at the Powerscourt Hotel, Mammy's treat. She'd have to apologise if she wanted her slice of cake.

'I don't know what you're making such a fuss about, though, Moira. Mammy's a grown woman. I was reading in one of our magazine's in reception that Vietnam is establishing itself on the South East Asia tourist trail. She'll be fine so long as she doesn't decide to befriend any strange men who ask her to carry their excess baggage through.' She rubbed her soles one after the other. 'I've been on my feet all day.'

'That's not funny and being on your feet all day makes a change from on your back.'

'Moira!'

'Well, it's true! You and Quinn are like rabbits.'

'We're making up for lost time.' Aisling got the daft look on her face she always got of late when Quinn's name was mentioned.

Moira had been gobsmacked the morning she got up to find Quinn, a chef who ran his successful bistro by the same name, sitting at their breakfast table. She still wasn't over the shock truth be told. Her sister had been good friends with him since her student days. Friends being the operative word, or so she'd thought. It turned out they'd both been in love with one another for years but it had taken the threat of Aisling going back to her ex-fiancé for Quinn to act on his feelings. Personally, Moira thought it was down to the salsa classes they went to; all that hip gyrating was bound to stir something up! She blamed the saucy Latin American moves on her sister having turned into a loved-up pain in the arse overnight. Speaking of which, she thought, tuning back into Aisling.

'But for your information, we've been at salsa class tonight and I had a mad day downstairs. One of the guests, Mr Rankin, missed his tour and I had to tee him up on another as he's only here for two days, then Mrs Flaherty had—'

'Conniptions,' Moira jumped in, eager to use the word once more.

'Yes, over the Ardern family's dietary requirements. You know she doesn't believe in such things.'

Moira smiled. Mrs Flaherty's idea of dietary requirements was a good stodgy Irish fry-up cooked in lashings of lard and woe betide anyone who disagreed with her.

'Then I had to give Ita short shrift. I caught her sitting on the side of the bath in Room 3 instead of making the room up like she was supposed to be, playing some game on her Nokia.'

'Snake,' Moira said knowledgably, having recently been caught doing the very same thing by Mr Price himself, Mason Price's fusty old senior partner. 'I don't know why you put up with Idle Ita.'

'Yes, you do.'

'Alright, but Mammy's not in charge any more, she's retired. You're O'Mara's manager which means you're no longer obliged to keep her friend's daughter on. Sure, if work was a bed that one would sleep on the floor.'

'I know but still—'

'You're a scaredy cat, Aisling O'Mara.'

Aisling couldn't argue, she was where Mammy was concerned. Moira was the only one who said her piece on a regular basis.

'But I still want you to talk Mammy out of this Vietnam business.'

'Moira since when has anyone ever been able to talk Mammy out of anything. Sure, look it, you know how it goes, Mammy tells us what to do not the other way around. It's the way it is. I can't upset the status quo.'

Moira tried to frown but couldn't. Aisling was right. The only person she might listen to was Patrick but her brother was too caught up in his new life over in the States to care much about what was happening here. She felt the familiar sting at his absence; she missed him and wished he'd make a bit more time for them. The last few times she'd called he'd been heading out the door to some function or other with that silicon-infused girlfriend of his, too busy to ask how she was doing since Daddy died. That left, Roisin. The odds were slim of her words holding any sway but given her seniority as the oldest daughter, she should at least try. It was her duty, Moira thought knowing it was too late to call her now. It would have to wait until the morning. She realised Aisling had moved on.

'Then I had to move Mr and Mrs McPherson from Room 8 because the shower was playing up. It was lucky we had Room 4 available and, to be fair, they were very good about it. Then, I spent the best part of the afternoon trying to get hold of a plumber, and you know how hard it is to get trades people these days.'

She did, Dublin was booming and as such trying to nail down a plumber, or any tradesperson was like trying to find that pot of gold at the end of the rainbow. It was also the reason why she had to listen to the headboard banging of a night. Accommodation was at a premium and she couldn't afford to move out and maintain a social life. For the time being she was stuck at O'Mara's with its memories of her daddy lurking around each and every doorway.

'I finally found an outfit who promised to send someone out for a look before lunchtime tomorrow so that means they'll be here around five o'clock. I'd no sooner hung up the phone than Tessa Delaney, who arrived yesterday—she's in Room 1—wanted to know what the kerfuffle in the middle of the night was all about.'

'Foxy Loxy?'

'Mr Fox,' Aisling confirmed. 'No doubt I'll get it in the ear from Mrs Flaherty. She's a bit of a strange one, I can't put my finger on it.'

'Mrs Flaherty is Mrs Flaherty, a heart of gold, a mouth like a sewer, a lover of food, and hater of foxes.'

'No, not Mrs Flaherty, Tessa Delaney.'

'Is she yer one from New Zealand? I overheard her asking Mrs Flaherty if she could have her *eeeg* served over easy. I made her say it again. I liked the sound of it.'

Aisling nodded. 'Mmm, although she's from Dublin originally. You'd never know it from listening to her; she's no trace of an accent left. I only managed to find that out because I suggested the open-top bus city tour was a good way to get her bearings. Her parents emigrated when she was a teenager. This is the first time she's been back.' She pursed her lips. 'I don't know what it is about her.'

'She seemed friendly enough to me. She'll find Dublin's not the backwater she left behind.'

Aisling nodded. 'It's a different city alright.' The influx of visitors since the Celtic Tiger had started roaring had been great for the guesthouse's business and the streets hummed with the vibrancy of its many visitors. 'And she's friendly enough. I got the feeling she wasn't honest about her reasons for coming back to Dublin that was all.'

Moira shrugged. 'Maybe she's jet-lagged. She has travelled from the other side of the world and she's in a different time zone. I had enough issues going to New York with Andrea last year; my poor tummy was telling me it was dinner time when it was bedtime for days. You know what you're like, Ash, you always see more in a situation than there is.' This was true. Aisling's imagination was prone to running away with itself.

'I suppose it's because she comes across as a closed book; I want to take a peek inside. There's definitely more to her coming back than a simple trip down memory lane. Besides, she had a week in London before coming here. That's plenty of time to get over the jet lag.'

'So, you know her parents left Dublin for New Zealand when she was a teenager and she's had a week sight-seeing in London? And, I just told you she likes her eggs over easy.'

'Mmm. What's your point?'

'You should have been a detective, Ash. What more do you want to know? How she likes her fecking steak? It's none of your business.'

Aisling poked her tongue out at her sister and picked up the television remote, 'The Late Late Show's on soon.'

'Ah, it's not the same without Gay Byrne.'

'He's only been gone a couple of weeks, give Pat Kenny a chance.'

'Not tonight, I've got to go and wash all this off.' Moira gestured to her face and the towel.

Aisling's gaze flitted to her sister's toes, back on the table once more. She let it slide. 'I like that colour.'

Moira pointed to the bottle of polish. 'I'll let you borrow it if you let me wear your red Valentino slingbacks with my dress tomorrow night.'

Aisling shook her head. 'Nope, no way.'

'Oh, please, pretty please. They'd be perfect.' That word again.

Aisling's eyes narrowed. 'So that's what this is all—,' she gestured to her sister's face and hair '—in aid of.'

Moira nodded. 'It's Posh Mairead's engagement party and you know how long I've been looking forward to it. Please, please, please. You're my favourite sister.'

'Liar, I heard you saying the same thing to Roisin not long ago and I still haven't forgiven you for wearing my Louboutin's without my permission.'

'You need to let it go. It's not good for you to hold on to stuff like that. I said sorry a million times. It was ages ago.'

'I'm not talking about when you got a scratch on the heel. I'm talking about when you sneaked out in them a month ago.'

Moira flushed beneath the clay. She'd thought she'd gotten away with that.

Aisling looked jubilant and Moira realised she must have stored the misdemeanour away, waiting for the right moment to use it. Feck it, she really wanted to wear the shoes.

'You could try splashing your cash on a pair of your own.'

'Sure, look it, Aisling, what would be the point? Not when I've a sister whose fashion sense is second to none.'

'Flattery won't work. I want something more.' Aisling hit the mute button on the television.

Moira pouted, 'Like what?' She was envisaging having to tidy her room like Mammy had always made her do of a Saturday morning when she was younger. Or worse, having to clean the bathroom, her most hated of all household chores. Housework was not her forte. What her sister said next took her by surprise.

Chapter 4

'I want to know why the secrecy every time I ask whether you have a new fella on the go?' Aisling said.

'There's no secrecy.' Moira's voice had a high-pitched intonation which she knew would not escape her sister.

'Do you want to borrow the shoes or not?' Aisling narrowed her eyes.

Yes, she did, but Moira hesitated. She was a truthful girl. There were some who might say she was too inclined to tell the truth, the whole truth, and nothing but the truth. There were some who might even go so far as to say that a little white lie for the sake of diplomacy wouldn't go astray here and there. It wasn't her style though. She'd never been one for subtleties or for unnecessary platitudes. She was what was known as one of life's blurters. It was the Mammy gene, and no course was needed to find out if it was inherited from the maternal side of the family. Therein lay her present dilemma. She wasn't prepared to tell Aisling or anyone else—Andrea being the exception of course. given her best friend status—about Michael.

It wasn't that she wanted to protect Michael, even if he had asked her to keep whatever it was happening between them to herself for the time being. She would of course. She'd do whatever he asked her to do because she wanted to be with him in a way she'd never wanted to be with anyone else before. Her reason for being discreet was for selfish reasons. She knew she'd get an almighty lecture. Her mask would be flaking off her face and her hair dry beneath the towel by the time Aisling had finished with her if she were to reveal Michael wasn't actually hers for the taking. It would be an understatement to say her sister wouldn't be impressed if Moira were to tell her the truth. She'd go mad, and then she'd ring Mammy. It was a given that this was what would transpire if Aisling learned her new love interest was married.

'You've gotten awfully furtive of late, Moira O'Mara.'

Aisling reminded Moira of Foxy Loxy at that moment with her reddish-gold hair and narrowed green eyes. 'I haven't.' She knew she had, but needs must.

'Yes, you have. It's little things, like the way you're so sneaky with your phone, and you never tell me who you've been out and about with.'

'I wouldn't call not telling you everything I do furtive, I'd call it my business, not yours. The only reason I don't mention who've I been getting about with is because nine times out of ten it's Andrea. There's no big secret.'

Aisling was undeterred. 'Sorry, I'm not buying it. It's that smile of yours. It gives you away.'

'What smile?'

'The one you always give me whenever I ask you who you're seeing. You'd have done it when I asked before only you can't move your mouth under all that clay. It's really annoying. Actually, it's more than annoying, it drives me potty.'

'I still don't know what you're talking about?'

'This, you do this,' Aisling attempted to demonstrate.

'Jaysus, you look constipated.'

She scowled. 'I call it your Mona Lisa smile, and like I said it's doing my head in. So, either spill the beans and look a million dollars in the Valentino's or, keep your little secret, whoever he is. It's no skin off my nose if you totter about your posh party in those high street heels of yours. The ball's in your court, sister.'

Moira weighed up the odds. This was one of those rare occasions when, for the greater good, she'd have to tell a half-truth. The very thought made her squirm but her moral code was being trampled all over by her desire to wear the perfect shoes with her perfect dress. 'Alright then,' she said licking her lips. 'You win.'

The smug look on Aisling's face irritated her as she leaned in to hear what she had to say.

'You're right, I am seeing someone.'

'I knew it.'

'I didn't mention it because it's early days, very early days. I don't know why you're making a thing about it. We're only just beginning to get to know one another. We haven't even done the wild thing yet, not even close.'

'There's nothing wrong with waiting, Moira.'

'Says the woman who ripped Quinn's clothes off the moment she realised he fancied her.'

Aisling ignored her. 'Tell me about him.'

'He's from London originally. Mason Price headhunted him from a rival firm over there and brought him over a couple of months ago as partner in the Aviation and Asset Finance Department.' She saw her sister fidget in her seat and read her mind. 'There's no point in you running off downstairs to reception to see if you can find him on the website, he's not on it. He's not been with the firm long enough for them to get round to updating it.'

Aisling looked disappointed but pushed it aside to demand, 'Name?'

'Michael.'

'Michael.' She tried it out for size. 'It's a respectable name, not like Leila's new man. Did I tell you he's called Bearach which she tells me means Barry?' Aisling snorted. 'She's getting serious about him so I'm going to have to get used to pairing them together without laughing.' She gave it a practice run. 'Bearach and Leila, Leila and Bearach.' Her mouth twitched with the effort to keep a straight face.

'Ah sure, give the poor girl a break. He's probably a really nice fella and you're in no position to laugh and point fingers. You've dated your fair share of eejits, one ex-fiancé included.'

'It's true alright. I had to kiss a frog or two to find my prince.' Aisling got that daft, dreamy look on her face again. It was the look that signalled she was having indecent thoughts about Quinn, and Moira made to get up from the sofa and make her escape.

Aisling blinked, obviously banishing Quinn for the moment as she wagged her finger. 'Uh-uh, I'm not finished yet. How old is he, this Michael fella?'

Moira paused, it suddenly mattered to her very much that her sister not disapprove of Michael.

'A-ha!' She slapped her thigh. 'I knew there was something. That's why you've been such a secret squirrel where this Michael is concerned. Come on then, is he ancient?'

'He's thirty-eight for your information, hardly ancient.'

'Old enough to be your father, though.'

'Not unless he was at it when he was thirteen, Aisling.' Moira decided to play the pity card. 'Sure, there are no decent fellas around my age, Aisling. They're all feckless tossers. Michael treats me like an equal and I love his confidence, his worldliness—,'

'His ancientness, and what's with the love word? I thought you said it was early days.'

'It is and I was speaking metaphorically. Thirty-eight is not old, Ash. He's the same age as Patrick. I bet you don't think of him as being old and his girlfriend, Cindy is only a year older than me.'

Aisling shuddered, 'Our brother and his choice in women isn't a good example, Moira. I don't think he asked Cindy out because he felt they were on the same intellectual footing and therefore would be able to engage in stimulating banter. Do you?'

Moira didn't, but now wasn't the time to concede. 'I knew you'd react like this, that's why I haven't said anything.' This time she stood up. 'You all treat me like I'm a kid in this family.' Sometimes the nearly ten years between her and Aisling felt more like twenty.

'A teenager at the very least.' Aisling grinned.

Moira muttered something rude before adding, 'Anyway the Valentino's are mine for the night because I kept my side of the deal and that's all I'm saying on the subject.' She flounced toward the door, turban wobbling, and paused as she reached the hall. 'And don't you dare tell Roisin or Mammy,' she threw back over her shoulder. 'I mean it, Aisling.' Her life would not be worth living if Mammy were to catch wind of the fact her prodigal daughter was dating an older man and if she found out he was married, well she might as well hightail it to Vietnam herself because she'd never hear the end of it!

Chapter 5

♥

Moira wiped the mask off with a flannel and eyed the grey residue before rinsing it out and holding her face towards the hot jets of water. It felt nice to be able to move her face properly once more. She stretched her mouth into an 'O' shape for good measure knowing her skin would be rosy, pink, and soft from the treatment. She closed her eyes for a beat and her mind drifted back over her conversation with her sister.

Mammy and her impending trip had been forgotten once they'd gotten onto the subject of Michael Daniels. Aisling had been aghast at his age. It was annoying given nobody in the family had batted an eye over Patrick's new plastic-fantastic being younger. This wasn't the dark ages it was 1999 for feck's sake. She was a twenty-five-year-old woman capable of forging her own path and making her own choices and way in life. I mean sure look it, here they were on the verge of a new millennium with the threat of Y2K and the like looming. The IT Department at work had been scrambling all year trying to put programming corrections in place to protect the firm's software. She'd heard talks of the bug having catastrophic effects like the banks going down; there could be widespread chaos. So, if Aisling were to look at the bigger picture, her new man being a little—alright over a decade older than her—was not a big deal in the grand scheme of things, not with the end of the world as they knew it nigh.

She never thought about Michael's age on those snatched rare moments they managed to be alone. It was irrelevant. What mattered was the way he wanted to hear what she had to say. He wasn't just listening with half an ear while thinking about how he could get into her knickers, he genuinely heard and cared about what she was saying. He made her feel special, worthwhile, in a way no one else had done before. She'd only known him a short while, and they'd only exchanged one proper kiss in that time, but oh, what a kiss. It had hinted at the promise of things to come. She'd never fallen this hard and fast for anyone, no matter what she'd said to Aisling about taking things slow.

She tried not to think about him being married and if she'd come clean with Aisling, Moira knew she would have rolled out the clichés in his defence. His marriage is in name only, he and his wife lead separate lives etc, they're only together for the sake of the children. At that point Aisling would have exploded, hand raised like an army sergeant as she shrieked, *Stop right there and back up. Did you say, children?* It would have swiftly been followed by finger pointing and the word homewrecker would have been wielded like a slap.

Moira wasn't proud of herself, or the situation she'd found herself in, far from it. She hadn't set out to fall head over heels for a married man but if that marriage was broken, irretrievably so, how could that make her a homewrecker? Surely the home was long since wrecked. She didn't know the answers and didn't want to delve too deeply in case she didn't like what she found because she was too far gone to walk away from Michael now. Her daddy's face flitted before her and she felt her eyes burn beneath her closed lids.

He wouldn't approve of what she was doing. She knew that, but then he'd always been protective of her, of all three of his girls but especially her being the baby. Mind you, he'd have struggled to approve of the future King of England when it came to his youngest daughter's choice of beaus. She grimaced, she didn't fancy Prince Charles in the slightest and had no idea where that weird comparison had come from. The fact of the matter was though, if her daddy was here now and knew what she was up to he'd be bitterly disappointed in her, and that would be worse than any histrionics or disapproval her sister could serve up. 'The thing is, Daddy,' she whispered into the steam, 'you went and died and the only person who's made me feel happy, made me feel anything at all since you left us, is Michael.' Moira tasted salt on her lip. 'Is it wrong to want to be happy?' She ignored the voice that whispered back telling her it was if it was at someone else's expense. The water continued to wash over her as she shook the maudlin thoughts away swinging her mind toward the night she first laid eyes on Michael instead.

Chapter 6

When she first saw him...

'I wish old Fusty Pants Price would buy a new suit. I'm sure he's owned that one since the year I was born,' Moira whispered out the corner of her mouth to Andrea as Mason Price's senior partner entered the boardroom. He was like the king on a Friday night walkabout to greet the commoners. It always amused her the way the partners all stood a little straighter when he appeared. The secretaries and the rest of the minions didn't bother, too focussed on making sure they got their quota of the free drinks chilling on ice that were on offer for the Friday night session.

'Mmm, the colour poo brown springs to mind and wait a minute—well, hellooo sexy, who is that?' Andrea's eyes widened over the rim of her wine glass and her hand froze over the bowl of potato crisps she'd been about to dive into as she checked out the stranger. 'There's a new boy in town.'

'I thought you only had eyes for Connor Reid.' Moira looked past Mr Price to the unfamiliar, handsome face that had materialised behind him. She didn't get much of a chance to check him out other than to note his hair was the colour of dark chocolate with streaks of silver around his temples, nothing poo brown about it in the slightest, and his eyes were blue. They made for a startling contrast against his dark hair she thought as he turned away. Fusty Pants was introducing him to John Bryant, eejit that he was, from Finance and she watched John Bryant's hale and hearty *I'm one of the lads* handshake with disdain.

It was unusual for her not to know a face given her front desk position. She knew everyone from the catering staff and IT gang, through to the secretaries and the solicitors they worked for, by name. It was her job to. She'd greet the various staff members as they breezed importantly through reception. It hadn't taken Moira long to realise it was part of Mason Price's job description to look as though you were on important business at all times even if you were just on your way to the loo. Perhaps this handsome stranger was a client whose meeting had run over and Fusty Pants had suggested he join them for a drink? Whoever he was she determined, looking at the way his elegantly cut navy suit with its faint charcoal pinstripe hugged his derriere—snuggly but not too snuggly—she'd find out.

She smiled a *no thanks* to Ciara from catering who had appeared in front of her and Andrea with a tray of sandwiches. Andrea, however, was not going to miss out and she nearly knocked Moira's drink from her hand in her eagerness as her arm snaked out and she helped herself to two of the triangles. Egg breath was not the order of the day, Moira thought with a sanctimonious glance at her friend's stash, even though she was partial to an egg sarnie.

'I do, but Connor's not realised he's only got eyes for me yet so I am allowed to browse elsewhere.' Andrea mumbled, stuffing the sandwich in.

Moira sipped her wine, all the while keeping her eyes trained on Blue Suit as she'd already nicknamed him in her head, while listening to Andrea's tale. It was a convoluted story about the injustice wielded upon her poor self that very afternoon by Nora McManus, the solicitor she worked for in the Tax Department.

'Up herself, unreasonable, self-important, cow. Honestly one of these days I'll tell her to stick her job where the sun don't shine.' Andrea had finished with the sandwich, so she turned and speared a meatball off the platter on the table behind them with a cocktail stick.

Moira shot her a sideways glance; they both knew this wasn't true. Andrea would stay right where she was. For one thing, Nora McManus was scary and it would take a stronger woman than Andrea to stand up to her, and for another, sometimes it was better the devil you know.

'It's not my fault she always leaves everything to the last minute and then expects me to type two hundred words a minute so she can file her stupid documents in time. I'm not bionic for feck's sake,' Andrea muttered, popping the meatball in her mouth and chomping angrily. 'I always eat when I'm stressed. Stress is not good for my figure. I'd be as svelte as Kate Moss if mealy-mouthed Melva would hurry up and retire. She must be fecking ninety if she's a day; then I could be Connor's right-hand woman.'

Moira knew she was her friend's sounding board. She need-ed to vent after having smiled sweetly at her boss all day as she told her she'd do her best to get the work completed in time. Listening to Andrea made her glad she didn't answer to one particular partner, she didn't think she'd last very long if she did, because she was nowhere near as diplomatic as Andrea.

'Ooh, ooh,' Andrea mumbled through her mouthful. 'He's turning around, we're going to get a full frontal. Wait for it!'

Moira noticed they weren't the only women in the room checking out Blue Suit. A new face, especially a handsome new face in the firm, was big news. The Property girls and Ciaron were huddled together in their usual cliquey manner, all gawping while trying to pretend they were fascinated with the painting hanging on the wall behind him. It was at that moment Blue Suit looked across the room to where she was standing. Moira felt as though someone had hit the mute button on the television; there was no sound, everybody else in the room faded out as though they'd never been there in the first place. It was just the two of them. Those electric blue eyes appraised her and when he smiled a sensation that made her blush pulsed through her.

'Smile back, you eejit,' Andrea muttered, and she did as she was told.

She watched, secretly pleased to note that Mary from the Litigation Department, who wore her skirts way too tight, was simpering up at him blissfully unaware of the piece of cress stuck to her lip. Served her right, Moira thought. She'd obviously not had the willpower to decline the egg sarnie.

Fusty Pants and his mystery cohort had worked the best part of the room by the time they finally reached their corner. Moira was hopping from foot to foot with impatience, waiting for an introduction. She leaned back against the boardroom table, feigning nonchalance. The realisation that there was a platter of half-eaten meatballs behind her, made her hope Blue Suit didn't think she was the greedy girl responsible. It was all Andrea's handiwork.

'Now then, Michael, this is Amanda. Michael Daniels meet Amanda. She works for Nora our Head of Litigation; you met Nora at the luncheon today.' Michael nodded giving Andrea a friendly smile as Moira willed him to look her way once more. She wanted to be pinned under his gaze. She rolled his name around in her head imagining herself whispering it in his ear and then she went a step further, trying out Moira Daniels for size.

'It's Andrea, Mr Price.'

Fusty Pants cleared his throat. 'Quite right, of course it is. My apologies, let's start again, shall we? Michael, this is Anna and this lovely young woman here is Moira. She's one half of the duo on our front desk. It's her pretty face that will greet you each morning.' He gave her a lascivious once over.

Oh, feck off you old perve, he really was stuck in the seventies, Moira thought, giving Michael, whose eyes twinkled seeming to tell her he had Fusty Pants pegged, her most beatific and beguiling smile as she took his outstretched hand. For the briefest of seconds, she thought he was going to raise it to his lips and she had to force herself to stay upright and not curtsey. *Get a grip, Moira.*

She flirted outrageously by refusing to be the first to lower her eyes which were locked into his. For his part, he held her hand a tad too long. If Ciara from catering had returned with the platter of cocktail sausages on sticks she'd breezed past with a few moments earlier, Moira knew she would have taken one and made an unashamed show of herself nibbling on it. A crude thought she knew, but there was something about this man that was making her so.

Fusty Pants droned on about how fortunate they were to have Michael on board and how he and his family had relocated from London. He would officially be joining Mason Price as Partner in the Aviation and Asset Finance Department as of Monday. Two things lodged in Moira's befuddled consciousness as Michael finally dropped her hand. The first being that that explained why she hadn't seen him around the place—he wasn't due to start work until Monday. The second and more important point being that Fusty Pants had referred to a family. She sought his left hand for confirmation as to the definition of what a family might mean. It was thrust inside his suit pocket hidden from view. She cast around for conversation not wanting him to be dragged away just yet, finally dredging up, 'How is our fair city treating you so far then, Michael?'

He smiled and she very nearly swooned, glad she was holding onto the side of the table she was leaning up against.

'What's the phrase you Irish use when things are going well?' He might have been London based but his accent had the rounded vowels of someone whose roots were in the north of England.

'Grand.'

'Dublin's grand, tanks, Moira.' He dropped the 'h' in a poor imitation of the Irish accent.

Fusty Pants laughed as though he'd said something exceedingly witty before hauling Michael on his way to where the gaggle of Banking girls were waiting their turn.

'Jaysus, Moira, the two of you needed to get a room. The sexual tension between you.' She flapped her hand across her face, 'hot!'

'Do you think he's married? Fusty Pants mentioned a family.'

'Sadly, my guess is yes. He'll be what, in his late thirties?'

Moira nodded.

'Definitely married then, sorry, Moira, but he's too fecking gorgeous not to be. You know as well as I do, how it goes, the good ones are always snapped up early on. So, if I were you, I'd go to the Ladies, splash some cold water on your face and refocus your affections on Liam Shaugnessy as per the plan you hatched at lunchtime today and I shall go dazzle Connor with my witty repartee.'

'Liam?'

'Yes, Asset Management Liam over there by Mary from Litigation who looks like she's about to attach herself to him like a limpet. Once she's latched on, he won't be able to get her off.'

Moira looked over at Liam. It was true she'd been making eyes at him this last while but she was ruined. Michael Daniels had ruined her for any other men—yes it was a dramatic thought but it was how she felt. The moment he'd caught her eye across the room, it was as though she'd been struck by lightning. All very clichéd but an accurate description nonetheless. Liam, she thought shooting him a second glance, came a sad second to Michael Daniels. Michael was a man, Liam a mere boy and Mary could have him. Just like a much-anticipated chocolate, unwrapped, and bitten into only to discover a nut in the middle, he'd lost his allure.

Michael turned and glanced over his shoulder locking eyes with Moira once more, and she felt herself begin to fall.

Chapter 7

T essa Delaney nibbled her toast. She was mouse-like in
the dainty way in which she was holding the triangle,
savouring each small mouthful with its miserly scraping of
marmalade. She'd opted for O'Mara's Continental breakfast
this morning and had enjoyed a bowl of cereal with a dollop
of yogurt, a treat given she was on holiday, before sliding
her bread under the grill. One slice would suffice; anymore
would be greedy, she'd told herself, tempting as it was. The
marmalade, she was guessing, was homemade and it was delicious. It had taken all her willpower not to slather it on.

She knew the cook, Mrs Flaherty as she'd introduced herself when she'd approached her yesterday morning, had been
perturbed by her previous day's breakfast order. It was why
she'd opted for Continental today. Yesterday she'd asked for
one egg to be served over easy on a slice of wholegrain
toast, nothing strange in that. It was the omission of all the
cook's lovingly fried trimmings, the bacon, sausage, and white
pudding that had disconcerted the older woman. Tessa knew
this because she recognised something in her as she stood
with her arms clasped around her generous middle, a frown
embedded on her forehead.

Mrs Flaherty was a feeder just like Tessa's mum. Her way
of showing she cared had always been to pile her husband

and daughter's plates sky high. Tessa had learned a long time ago to be firm, to not give in to the wounded look like the one plastered to Mrs Flaherty's face as she'd asked, *The white pudding's really rather good you know. I source only the best sweetbreads and are you sure I can't offer you a rasher on the side?*

Now, as she finished the last bite of her toast, she sensed movement out of the corner of her eye. A quick glance across to where it had come from near the entrance to the kitchen revealed it was Mrs Flaherty. She was waving her arms about as though in the throes of an energetic aerobics class. By the looks of it, she was engaging in a heated, one-sided conversation with Aisling, the establishment's manageress. Tessa couldn't hear what was being said in its entirety, their voices drowned by the clatter of knives and forks and general chatter from the other dining room occupants. She did, however, catch snippets of the words, *fecking and fox*, more than once. A strange conversation but it did explain the crash she'd heard outside her window in the middle of the night as she'd tried to get used to being in yet another strange bed. The culprit was obviously a fox getting into the bins on the hunt for scraps.

She didn't ponder the conversation further because her mind was otherwise occupied and her eyes swung to the clock on the wall near the dining room entrance. She did the maths; it was only nine hours until the ten-year school reunion of the pupils of St Mary's Secondary School in Blackrock. Nine short hours until she'd see Rowan Duffy, the bully who'd made her life, for what was ultimately only a short while in the grand scheme of things but at the time had seen interminable, almost unbearable. The wounds Rowan and her two awful friends had so carelessly inflicted hadn't been physical but Tessa still bore the scars of the taunts they'd tossed her way throughout her thirteenth year. She'd been unable to shake Rowan the ringleader—her nemesis had been with her ever since. The teenage spectre had clung on and become the whispering voice of self-doubt.

At the thought of what lay ahead that evening, her stomach turned over, a churning cocktail of nerves, excitement, and anticipation. She'd been waiting thirteen long years for tonight to roll around. It was thirteen years since she'd left Dublin and she'd been approaching the end of her thirteenth year at the time—half her lifetime ago. What was it about the number thirteen? It was supposed to be unlucky. Certainly, that year had been like the Queen famously once said, *annus horribilis,* but then one day, like a lighthouse beacon on a stormy night, her parents had offered her a way out.

The news that the family was to emigrate to New Zealand saw her set about reinventing herself. Once it had sunk in, she'd put her hand over her plate much to her mother's bewilderment, when she tried to ply her with a second helping. She'd gone without the lashings of butter she was partial to on her toast and cakes were off limits.

Her parents fretted and worried at first over her losing weight, putting it down to the impending move and unhappiness over leaving her friends. There'd been no time however in the flurry of packing their lives up to delve too deeply and in the end, they'd left Tessa alone. Her weight loss it was decided was due to the stress of moving and hormones. 'Sure,' she'd overheard her mother say to her father, 'aren't teenage girls supposed to be a mystery?' Through sheer bloody mindedness she'd arrived in New Zealand twenty pounds lighter and had never looked back until now.

She poured milk from the jug into her cup of tea, stirring it as she looked around the basement dining room. It was an elegant but functional space; in bygone days this would have been the servants' domain, she figured. The tables were laid with white cloths and set with silver cutlery. On the walls were various black and white prints of Dublin through the years. Her eyes settled on a shot of Grafton Street; judging by the street fashion it was taken in the twenties. A different world altogether she thought, sipping from her cup.

She turned her attention to her fellow guests, an eclectic bunch. There was an older couple each engrossed and apparently thoroughly enjoying the food in front of them. They'd be sure to get brownie points from Mrs Flaherty, she mused. A young couple were coaxing a small child who was vehemently shaking his head, into having another bite of his toast. If they weren't careful, they'd have a full-scale tantrum on their hands she thought, recognising the warning signs from her many nights spent babysitting. It had helped pay her way through university.

Her gaze fixed on the man she'd noticed at breakfast the previous morning. She'd seen him again when she dropped her key in at reception before heading out for a day's tripping down memory lane. It had amused her to see the receptionist, Bronagh, batting her lashes at him and talking in a girly voice. She was old enough to be his mother, but each to their own, she'd thought. One thing Tessa made sure she never did was sit in judgment of others.

She watched as he simultaneously sipped his tea and checked his Blackberry. A man who could multitask, now there was a sight to behold! He was clean-shaven, dressed for business not sight-seeing, and there was a shine on his shoes that would make any mother proud. She liked a man who took pride in his appearance, especially given how hard she worked to maintain her own. He looked to be around thirty at a guess and given the intensity of his frown she wondered what he had planned for the day. Was he brokering a make-or-break deal, or perhaps applying for a job in a career he'd been climbing the ladder toward since leaving school?

What would he think if he knew what her reasons were for coming back to Dublin after all this time? It was, after all, a long way to come for a high school reunion, especially given she'd only attended the school for a year. He'd think her strange, a little obsessed perhaps. She wondered if he'd read Stephen King's Carrie, because she knew the story would spring to mind. Her motives for coming back to Dublin weren't vengeful though. Oh, she couldn't deny it was going to be satisfying to see the look of shock on Rowan and the rest of her motley crew's faces when they saw how she'd turned out. She'd show them she'd succeeded despite them. Although, sometimes she wondered if her drive to be the best version of herself in every aspect of her life was *because* of them.

It was something she'd played out in her mind over and over again these last few months since she'd booked her plane ticket. She'd left *Ten Tonne Tessie* behind in Dublin when she and her parents left all those years ago. These days she was Tessa Delaney, Ms, by the way— that she was single was nobody's business but her own. A svelte Investment Consultant for a leading Auckland finance company with a personal assistant and an office overlooking the city and out to sea. She could see as far as the extinct volcano, Rangitoto Island, on a clear day.

Her home was a restored villa with a red Pohutukawa tree in the garden with a slash of blue ocean visible from her living room window. She'd grown used to watching the sea with its ever-changing moods and would find it hard not to have it in her line of sight. The villa had two spare bedrooms; it seemed she'd also inherited her mother's penchant for houses that were too big for their small family.

She'd kept in touch with her old school pal, Saoirse, over the years. They'd updated one another with the way their lives were panning out in the form of letters winging their way back and forth two, three times a year. Tessa would have liked to have come over for her friend's wedding but she'd been angling for promotion at the time and couldn't ask for time off. Saoirse would mention too from time to time that she'd love to bring her family out for a holiday in New Zealand, but financially, with young children and an enormous mortgage, it wasn't on the cards.

She told Tessa things from time to time. Like how she wished she'd been made of sterner stuff and had been able to stand up for her friend back when they were at St Mary's. Tessa told her she wasn't to blame; it wasn't up to Saoirse to sort her problems out. She should have had the sense to talk to her mother about what was happening to her. Hindsight was a wonderful thing and the choices her sensible adult self would make were very different to her frightened childhood self.

Saoirse would tell her things in her letters too, like how the only skill Rowan had learned during her schooling was how to light a cigarette on a windy day—a talent fine honed down the back of the school field. She'd been expelled at sixteen for one misdemeanour too many. Saoirse would mention how she'd seen her from afar on a trip to Dublin and how it seemed she had an ongoing penchant for wearing her skirts too short. The last she'd heard of her; she was working in a café. Tessa had felt just the teensiest bit gleeful as she'd read that it wasn't even one of the posh new cafés springing up about the city but a right old greasy spoon.

It was also Saoirse who'd mentioned the reunion. She'd written that the ten-year reunion of St Mary's class of 1989 was being held in the school hall this October and how she had no intention of going. For one thing, she lived in Galway these days and for another, there was nobody she was particularly interested in reuniting with! Tessa hadn't even been at the school in 1989 but it didn't matter. She knew as she sat reading and re-reading her friend's letter that she would be going. She'd talk Saoirse into going with her too because this was it, this was her chance for closure where Rowan and her two ugly stepsisters were concerned. It was her opportunity to confront her past and in doing so quieten that inner voice that still, even now governed how she felt others perceived her.

There were two Tessas—the outwardly confident version she'd perfected the moment she'd begun her new life in Herne Bay, Auckland and the Tessa who lived on inside her. The fearful, frightened Tessa who wasn't worthy of being loved.

Tessa blinked, she hadn't realised the man had looked up, bemused no doubt by the intensity of her stare. He was smiling at her and she glanced away, embarrassed at being caught out, feeling the pull to the past as she stepped back into 1987.

Chapter 8

1987

T essa burst through the front door of the large, too large for the three of them, detached house overlooking the sea where they lived in a leafy Blackrock Street. Mummy had always wanted a detached house, no matter that two of the four bedrooms remained empty and two bathrooms meant two bathrooms that needed to be cleaned each week—Tessa's loathed pocket-money job.

She'd slammed the door shut behind her not caring if she got told off and, resting her back against it, she willed her heart to stop racing. It was only then when she could feel the solid timber separating her from the outside world did she feel safe to let the tears that had threatened all the way home spill over.

'We're in the kitchen, Tessa darling.' Her mother's voice tinkled down the hall with no hint of reproach over her heavy handedness with the front door. Tessa swiped at her cheeks. She wouldn't let her see she was upset. It wouldn't do any good telling her what was going on. She'd only get a name for herself as a tattle-tale at school which would give Rowan and her gang of two more ammunition. She had thought about confiding in Sister Evangelista when she'd asked her if everything was alright last week. Tessa's overly bright eyes and flushed cheeks hadn't escaped her kindly, eagle eyes, but sure, what could the nun do? She sniffed knowing there was nothing for it but to keep ignoring them in the hope they'd get bored and leave her be.

It was only a ten-minute walk from the school gates to her front door but it was a journey that could be fraught with as much danger as navigating the Serengeti Plains on foot. They'd been learning about Africa in class that morning and as she'd stared down at the picture in the book Sister Mary Leo had passed around with its glossy photographs, Tessa had felt a kinsman ship with the beleaguered impala. Rowan, Teresa, and Vicky reminded her of the pack of wild dogs their teeth bared, caught on film as they hunted the poor creature.

She could avoid Rowan and the other two at lunchtime by taking herself off to the library with her friend, Saoirse, who was, if anything, even more timid than she was but Saoirse wasn't fat. There wasn't much of anything that stood out about Saoirse, she blended in with the crowd so they left her alone. It was as the clock on the classroom wall ticked its way ever closer to the final bell that the panic would begin to set in. Tessa would find herself unable to concentrate on her lesson as her heart beat a little faster, her breath sticking in her throat as the sick feeling in the pit of her stomach amped up. It was the worry, she knew this, whether the day would be a good day. She'd cross her fingers, the skin around her nails red from being nibbled at, under the desk and promise extra Hail Marys if today could please be a good day.

A good day was when she managed to race out the school gates and put a decent distance between herself and the trio lying in wait. Today she thought, her head still resting against the front door, hadn't been a good day. Sister Geraldine had continued to drone on, obviously enthralled with the partic- ular period in history she was informing her students of, and Tessa had felt like screaming. She'd wanted to stand up and yell at the nun, 'I don't give a flying feck about the Battle of the Boyne. I care about those ganky cows who'll all be waiting for me at the gate if you don't shut up and let me go home!'

Of course, she hadn't said a word. She'd sat at her desk clenching her fists so that the ragged ends of her nails dug into her palms. The seconds had ticked over into minutes and around her, her classmates had begun to fidget in their eagerness to be excused for the day. Still, Sister Geraldine waffled on. Tessa's gaze had flicked anxiously between the clock and the door until at last Sister Geraldine reached the part where King James II of England fled to France never to be seen in Ireland again. It was at this point Sister Geraldine gave the signal that they were allowed to slam their history books shut. There was a collective thudding as the heavy tomes were closed, followed by a mass scraping of chairs as the girls pushed past one another eager for the off.

As Tessa slid her bag's straps over her shoulders, she'd felt a small surge of hope. It was nearly ten past; surely they'd have tired of waiting for her and headed home by now. She'd walk extra slow so as to be sure to give them a head start. A few beats later her heart sank as she stepped outside and saw them milling about by the entrance. They'd elbowed each other as she came into sight. Their skirts were worn short enough for the nuns to frown upon and make noises about telling their mothers to unpick the hems, but long enough for them to be generally left alone. School ties had been loosened and socks were puddled around ankles. Tessa knew too that as soon as the bell had rung, their bags would have been hastily opened to retrieve stacks of multi-coloured jelly bracelets stashed at the bottom. These were then layered up their wrists in a school girl homage to Madonna for the walk home.

Tessa had looked straight ahead pretending she couldn't see them as she passed through the gates and out onto the street. If she pretended hard enough, surely they'd vanish. She made a silent phffing noise as she imagined them disappearing like a puff of smoke. She didn't even wince when Rowan called out in a voice designed to carry.

'Ooh lookout, girls, there she goes, Ten Tonne Tessie. Can you feel the ground shaking, Terry?'

Tessa had heard the snapping of gum and giggling.

'Fi, fi, fo fum, by gum, Tessa's got a big bum.'

'I can hear her thighs rubbing together from here!'

Titters and more gum popping.

Onwards she'd trudged, her eyes trained to the ground in front of her. One foot being placed in front of the other. Plodding, solid steps, befitting the solid, plodding lump she was. Her eyes burned and she blinked furiously, she would not let them know she heard them or that she cared what they thought. She pulled on her imaginary coat of armour and fended the taunts off like they were arrows—they were useless against her iron defence shield as they pinged off her and hit the ground.

It hadn't protected her from the pebble that hit her squarely in the back. 'Oi, we're talking to you, fat girl.'

'Tessa, is that you, love?'

Her mother's voice brought her back and she swiped her nose before calling, 'Yes, I'm coming, Mum.'

She pushed herself away from the door and, dumping her bag at the foot of the stairs to take up to her room later, she padded down the hall to the kitchen. It was her favourite room in the house. It looked out on the garden and to the sea and there were always comforting smells emanating from it. Her nose twitched at the aroma of something sugary and soft with a hint of spice and her tummy rumbled in anticipation. 'Hello,' she said, a flash of fear passing through her at the sight of Dad sitting at the table. He was in his suit which meant he'd been to work but he didn't usually get home until five o'clock. What was going on? She felt that familiar quickening of her heart and the sick feeling in her stomach. Nora Heatherington's father had been laid off last week and Nora said her parents had been doing a lot of shouting and whispering but not much proper talking ever since. She was reassured a little by his smile. He did not look like a man who'd received bad news. Mum, she noticed was wearing her new top, the one with the sparkles along the neckline that she'd helped her choose. Surely, she wouldn't be wearing a pretty sparkly top if something awful had happened.

'Hello, Tessa love, come on, sit down,' her mum said, patting her place at the table. 'I'll butter you a nice slice of brack.'

She sat down quickly.

In the middle of the table was the source of the aroma that had beckoned her in; a plate stacked with slices of fresh fruity, brack. Her mum smeared thick butter on the piece she'd put on a plate for Tessa and slid it across the table to where she sat. Tessa's gaze swung anxiously from one parent to the other.

'You're probably wondering why Daddy's home?'

She hated it when Mum called Dad, Daddy. She wasn't a baby but now wasn't the time to protest and she nodded because her mouth was too full to speak. She'd shovelled in as much of the loaf as she could fit, hoping it would quell the unsettled feeling that had descended the moment she stepped into the kitchen—homemade brack fixed most things especially when it had extra raisins in it.

'Well, Daddy and I, we've got some news. We think it's very exciting and we hope you do too.'

She was all ears.

'A grand opportunity's come our way. Daddy—'

Tessa wondered if they'd rehearsed this, whatever this was, as her dad cleared his throat and Mum picked up the knife to butter a second slice of loaf for Tessa.

'What it is, Tess,' her father continued. 'I've been offered a job in New Zealand. Auckland to be precise. It seems they need civil engineers there.'

Tessa's mouth fell open despite its contents—New Zealand! 'Are you taking it?'

'Tessa, finish your mouthful first.' Her mother frowned across the table ever mindful of manners.

She did so knowing she'd get the hiccups from eating too fast. 'Sorry,' she said after swallowing, feeling the loaf sitting solid like a lump of coal in her throat. 'But, New Zealand? Mum, Dad that's the other side of the world.'

They didn't seem fazed by her shock. If anything, their eyes flickered with amusement. 'We know where it is.' They smiled at each other and Tessa wanted to throw the piece of loaf her mother had now put on her plate at them. They weren't making any sense. You didn't just decide to move to New Zealand. It wasn't Cork or Galway or even the UK for that matter. It was about as far away from Ireland, her home, as you could go. And why hadn't they discussed any of this with her?

'It probably seems like a bolt from the blue to you, love.'

She nodded so furiously she felt at risk of dislocating her neck.

'*It is* rather sudden we know, but the opportunity for Daddy to put in for a transfer arose and we'd only ever heard wonderful things about New Zealand. We didn't want to say anything until it was definite in case it all fell through.'

It was definite, her mum had just said it was definite.

'And, Tessa, I'm always after telling you that to be successful in life you need to embrace opportunities and be open to change.'

It was true, she was always saying stupid stuff like that. She meant it to be encouraging and inspiring but mostly when she said it, it was annoying. Tessa's lips formed a mutinous line that caused her mum to babble on.

'Take my old school friend, Naomi, for example. She moved to New Zealand years ago when she got married—he was from there, her husband. She still sends me a Christmas card and her life in—' she looked to her husband for help.

'Christchurch,' Dad obliged.

'Christchurch sounds marvellous. In summer it's an endless round of picnics and barbecues. They live outdoors in New Zealand.'

What was her mother saying? They'd sleep under the stars? She wasn't selling her on the idea if that was the case. Tessa did not like camping. Her one and only experience had been with the Brownies. The heavens had opened and they'd all had to take cover. It had been the stuff of nightmares with Brown Owl trying to jolly them all along as they huddled together shivering.

'Then there's the Joyce family. You won't remember them; they lived a few doors down from us when you were a baby. They moved, all seven of them, to the capital.'

This time it was Tessa who piped up, breaking a piece of brack off with her fingers, the word tripping automatically from her tongue. 'Wellington,' she said, popping the morsel in her mouth. She'd learned a little about New Zealand in her geography lessons at school. She'd also learned it was a country that sat on the Ring of Fire. It had volcanos; most of them were extinct but you never knew *and* it was prone to earthquakes.

Mum took this as an encouraging sign. 'Yes, Wellington, and the last time I heard they were living in a great big house, overlooking the sea.'

A great big house seemed to matter a great big deal to her mother, Tessa thought. 'Our house is big and it overlooks the sea.' She knew her tone was belligerent.

This time her mother didn't tell her to finish her mouthful before speaking. Her eyes flitted nervously across the table to her husband. She wasn't giving them the response they'd been hoping for. He came to her rescue.

'Ah, but in Auckland where we're going, its warmer, almost tropical, and you'll be able to swim all summer long without catching hypothermia. You can eat watermelon every day too if you like.'

This Tessa knew had been tossed in because she'd developed a fondness for slices of the sweet fruit when it had been served up for breakfast on their all-inclusive holiday to Florida when she was nine.

Mum flashed him a grateful look but Tessa was only half listening now as her mind tried to wrap itself around this bombshell news. The word definite reverberated in her ears. Further evidence of their seriousness was in the nervous darting glances Mum kept shooting at Dad. She could tell too that they were holding hands under the table—moral support. They didn't think she knew they did this. It made her feel pitted against the odds, two against one. 'You said it's definite.' Her voice was flat.

It was their turn to nod and she was pleased to see they had the grace to look a little shame-faced at having made such a momentous decision without consulting her. Two against one, she thought once more. 'When? When will we go?'

'Just short of three months. I know it seems sudden, but this way we can have a good long holiday and settle in properly before you begin your new school. It will be their summer holidays so you won't start until the February. Imagine, Tessa you'll be sunbathing and swimming while everyone here will be in their winter woollies sniffing with coughs and colds. And, sure it's not as though you've been at St Mary's for years. You'll settled into your new school no bother.'

How would she know? Tessa pushed her chair back and ran from the room. She couldn't comprehend it and she couldn't take another second of their anxious expressions willing her to jump for joy at what they'd just laid on her. She heard her mum get up to follow her and Dad's voice saying, 'Leave her, Sheelagh. She needs some time by herself to get used to the idea. We knew it'd come as a shock to her.'

She took the stairs two at a time and threw herself down on her bed. She lay there staring at the ceiling and the boys from Duran Duran stared down at her from the poster she'd sellotaped above her bed. 'Can you believe it, John?' she whispered. John Taylor was her favourite band member; he had the most soulful of brown eyes and always looked like he understood when she confided in him. 'New Zealand. They want to drag me all the way to New Zealand. They've gone mad, the pair of them.' It was times like this Tessa hated being an only child. If she had an ally, things wouldn't seem so bad. Two against two.

She folded her arms across her chest and it was then it dawned on her. Her eyes widened because she herself had just said—it was the other side of the world. There would be no Rowan Duffy in Auckland. No Vicky, no Teresa. On the other side of the world, she wouldn't be Ten Tonne Tessie, she'd be Tessa Delaney, newly arrived from Ireland. She could be exotic, like Audrey from Paris, who'd spent the first term this year at St Mary's. All the girls had wanted to be friends with her simply because she was different—in a good way, not a fat way. The more she mulled it over the more she warmed to the idea. She was being given a clean slate. She could start over and suddenly, moving to the Southern Hemisphere seemed no bad thing at all.

Chapter 9

M ichael was on Moira's mind and as a result, she was tossing and turning, getting tangled in her sheets. She hated the fact she was alone in her bed; that he couldn't stay here with her. She didn't like to think about what his life was like at home. It was something she tried to store in the out-of-bounds compartment. It was where she stored the worst of her pain, her memories of her daddy's last days were tucked away in there too. Her mind, however, was a law unto itself and tonight it wouldn't stop straying there, determined to pick over all the details she'd filed away like an efficient secretary regarding Michael.

She knew he'd chosen to buy in Sandy Cove and he lived in the house they'd purchased with his wife and two children. The postcode meant their home would be expensive, more than likely detached, and for some reason she kept picturing an enormous rumpus room. 'Rumpus room,' she rolled the words off her tongue in a whisper, it sounded posh. There'd be no sitting on top of one another in a poky front room for the Daniels family, not in Sandy Cove.

His girls, he'd told her the first time they'd sat and talked, had started at a nearby private school. He'd looked pleased as he told her they'd settled into their new lives here in Dublin well. It was something that had clearly bothered him about making the move, given their awkward ages. He'd also confided they were the reason he stayed with his wife. The marriage, he'd told her earnestly, had been over for years but they'd agreed to do their best by their girls. They owed them that and their best meant staying together until the children both finished their schooling. It would be too disruptive, too selfish not to. Their happiness had to come before his. There'd been something in his eyes that had willed her to understand the situation he found himself duty bound to.

She'd felt a tug, her heart going out to him for the situation he found himself in. He was a good man, she thought. Despite what Andrea had told her when she'd heard what he'd had to say. 'That's the sort of thing all married men say to young women they want to cop off with. It doesn't make you special, Moira. Don't believe a word of it.' Moira had been annoyed because she knew Michael wasn't like most married men. She'd replied, 'But you weren't there. You didn't see the look on his face when he talked about his marriage. He looked trapped, desperate almost.' His eyes had begged her to understand and he had beautiful eyes.

'You're being played.' Andrea had rolled her eyes and shaken her head. It was the first time Moira had contemplated falling out with her friend but somehow, she'd bitten back a retort because she knew if the shoe were on the other foot, she'd be saying the same thing to her.

Michael's oldest daughter was fifteen and the youngest had recently turned thirteen. They weren't babies by any means, but she also knew what she'd been like as a teenager—independent yet fully dependent at the same time. A woman/child. She'd needed her mam and dad every bit as much as she'd protested she didn't. At a time of uncertainty and change, not to mention mood swings, they'd been her constant. Parents, she thought her eyes wide in the dark, should be like a solid brick wall. No matter how hard you pushed against them they remained there, solid. It was what made it so hard to accept her Daddy wasn't here anymore. Half her wall had crumbed down.

It wasn't too late to walk away. She could leave Michael to weather his marriage out to the end. It wasn't like they'd done more than talk and exchange a few kisses. She flexed her hand in the darkness imagining she could feel the solid warmth of his in it. There was no chance of them exchanging more than a few polite words at work and other than a few stolen hours over the course of these last few weeks their time was very much not their own. Despite this, she'd fallen for him.

He'd made his choices. She didn't need to be involved in them. She knew the reason Andrea had annoyed her was because she was right, in so much as she should step back. The problem was what she should do and what she wanted to do were two very different beasts. 'You're playing with fire, Moira,' Andrea warned the last time Moira had mentioned Michael's name. At the same time though, Moira knew her friend well enough to see she was on the edge of her seat waiting for the next instalment. *She* was on the edge of her seat waiting, too. She had been from the moment he'd cupped her face in his hands and kissed her. She hadn't seen it coming and she'd tried to pull away, but truth be told she hadn't tried very hard.

He'd confessed after that first kiss; he'd been unable to stop thinking about her since the night he'd seen her across the boardroom. She'd gotten under his skin, he said. The rest of the staff he'd greeted had paled and blurred after Noel Price introduced him to her. He'd not been able to get the impossible green and gold of her eyes out of his head. Moira sighed; her breath warm against the chill of the room. The central heating had clicked off hours ago. She couldn't wait five long years for them to be together properly. Her throat constricted as the thought of the days, weeks, and months stretching into years of what her sister would call furtive behaviour filled her with panic. She didn't want to be that girl. How had she got here? It was a pointless question; she knew exactly how she'd gotten here.

Chapter 10

How it began...

The poster in the window caught Moira's eyes and she came to a standstill. Standing in the shop frontage, huddled inside her coat she was oblivious to the corporate clad women who nearly walked into her. The woman sidestepped her at the last minute with a muttered, 'for feck's sake,' barely faltering in her frantic pace.

Moira was on her way home from work, in no great hurry to get there either given it was a Tuesday and nothing much happened at home on a Tuesday. Aisling was likely to while away her evening distracting Quinn in the kitchen of his bistro and it was her least favourite night on the television. She was too broke to suggest an impromptu night out to see a film or have a meal with Andrea. It would be a waste of time, anyway. Andrea was devoted to her soaps, Moira loved hers too but preferred to curl up on the sofa of a weekend, snacks to hand, to watch the omnibus on offer. At the very least it would take a Brad Pitt film to drag Andrea away from her viewing and, so far as Moira knew, he wasn't starring in anything at the Savoy this week.

So, there she was standing on the pavement outside the Baggot Street, Boots staring at the image of Elizabeth Hurley on display. The glossy poster was marketing at its best she mused, wrestling with the should she or shouldn't she question. Liz, all ethereal and lovely, boasted of a serum containing the latest miracle properties—it was packaged in a simple, sleek silver bottle. Her Visa card, with which she had a love-hate relationship, burned a hole in her pocket.

Serum, the word whispered to her, and Moira decided she liked the way it sounded. It wasn't quite on a par with conniption but it did sound exotic and full of promise. What the poster didn't mention though was what the undoubtedly eye-watering price for the magical properties contained in the silver cannister was. But sure, what price did you put on a miracle? She asked herself torn between a magical serum or the bottle of Allure—the new Chanel fragrance she'd had a spray of the last time she'd been in the chemist. She was nearly out of perfume. *What to do, what to do?* She was too busy wrestling with her dilemma to realise someone was standing alongside her until they cleared their throat.

'Moira, hi. I like your shoes.'

She hoped she didn't look like a total eejit as her mouth fell open and she wished she wasn't standing in front of such an enormous photo of Elizabeth Hurley as she gawped up at Michael Daniels. No woman could compete with Liz when she was doing provocative, and why oh why wasn't she in her heels all glamorous instead of her runners? She looked like Minnie Mouse. She gathered herself quickly as her heart began to hammer and her stomach danced to a fluttering beat. 'Ah well, now, Mr Daniels, I can't very well be trotting home in my stilettos now can? How're you settling in at Mason Price?'

He grinned and his smile lit his eyes. He had lovely teeth she thought randomly as she reminded herself to blink.

'Very sensible of you. The shoes I mean, although you do realise I'm going to have to start calling you Minnie Mouse.'

What was he she thought, a mind reader?

'And I am settling in thanks even if the weather has been awful since we arrived. But please don't call me Mr Daniels it makes me feel like my father! It's Michael, Moira. So, are you contemplating a spot of shopping or are you on your way home?'

We, she realised her heart plummeting, he'd used *we*. 'Both, and I probably shouldn't be contemplating the shopping. I should be saving for a deposit.'

He raised an eyebrow.

'For a flat, I live just across from the Green, in O'Mara's Guesthouse with my sister.'

'A guesthouse, that sounds interesting.'

Moira shrugged, she'd gotten used to people's curiosity when they realised she lived on the top floor of a busy, established old guesthouse. It wasn't the norm, but it was her norm. 'It's home. Well kind of, our mammy moved out recently and it's just me and my sister rattling around there these days. Aisling, that's my sister manages the place. We rub along alright so long as she doesn't tell me what I should be doing, but I'd still like my own place. It's not on the cards for a while though, not with rents being sky high and flats being so hard to come by.' She hoped she wasn't babbling. She was unused to the effect being in his presence was having on her, she was the girl who always played it cool.

'Supply and demand.' He gave her a rueful grin and her knees threatened to give way. She realised she'd zoned out the hordes of people buzzing past them when a man apologised for knocking Michael's shoulder.

'Well, it's a miserable evening and I'm sure you don't want to spend it standing around on the street talking to me! I'd better let you get on home. It was good seeing you, Moira.'

'Oh, I'm not in a hurry.' The short sentence popped forth unbidden, a bold invitation to talk longer.

That smile again and a slight hesitation. Moira looked at Michael expectantly. For his part, his expression was one of surprise but then he smiled again and rubbed his jawline; she could see the beginnings of a five o'clock shadow. 'Well, if you're not in a rush, then it would be great to get the low-down on my new hometown from a local. You know where to go, where not to go, that sort of thing. We could grab a drink, have a bite to eat? My treat.'

'Don't you have to get home?' She regretted the words as soon as she'd said them but she'd definitely heard that *we*.

It was like the sun went in behind the clouds. 'No, I'm not in a rush either but I didn't mean to put you on the spot so, if you'd rather not—'

Moira jumped in, 'You didn't. There's a pub not far from here, The Iron Bridge, they do a deadly Boxty if you're keen to try something traditional. We could call in there if you like?'

'I'd like that.'

They smiled at each other, pleased with the arrangement, and merged in with the tide of people walking up the street. 'Deadly Boxty?' he said a beat later, keeping pace with her. 'It sounds like some sort of mushroom. Should I be worried?'

Moira laughed. 'Boxty's an Irish staple, they're potato pancakes and where I'm taking you, they're served with a lemon and chive mayonnaise.' Under normal circumstances, Moira's mouth would have watered at the thought of the crispy, golden pancakes but this situation was anything but normal. She was too aware of Michael's proximity, hypersensitive to the brush of his arm against hers.

She spied Quinn's Bistro ahead and quickened her pace, casting a sideways glance as they passed by the cheery red door with its welcoming brass nameplate above it. Inside, she knew would be warm and inviting. The roaring open fire set back in the wall of exposed bricks would beckon people to sit down and take a load off. The low timber-beamed ceiling added to the cosiness and the atmosphere would be convivial and bustling. This would have been a great spot to introduce Michael to. Quinn's had a bar, live music, the food was great and so was the craic, but she wasn't risking bumping into Aisling. She didn't want her sister giving Michael the third degree as to who he was and what his intentions were. The odds of her sister being there at this time of the evening were slim but Moira's luck had never been great and even if she wasn't there, Alasdair the maître d' would be sure to pass on the news he'd seen Moira with a mystery man.

The thing was, she wasn't sure how she'd explain Michael if she were to bump into anybody she knew. It wasn't as if they were colleagues. They worked for the same firm, yes, but he held a senior position and ne'er the twain do mix. It was a sort of unwritten rule. Her step faltered, what was she doing? She was ninety per cent sure Michael was married and a man who was spoken for shouldn't be going for a drink with the receptionist at the law firm he worked at.

Her mammy's face flashed before her; with the same expression she'd had picking up Moira from school the day she'd gotten caught smoking in the girls' toilets. *Oh, go away, Mammy*, she gave her a mental shove and eyed Michael from under her lashes. There was still a ten per cent chance he was single. She was prepared to take a gamble even if the odds weren't good. Besides, she wasn't doing anything wrong. A drink, that's all it was. They were going for a drink not hotfooting it into the nearest hotel and asking for a room. As they reached the lights, the wind gusted down the road nearly cutting her in half, the sudden chill a welcome distraction from her thoughts.

'That's straight off the polar circle,' Michael muttered, shoving his hands deeper into his coat pockets. Moira nodded her agreement, shivering inside her coat as she wondered why, if it was all so innocent, she was so busy trying to justify her actions.

Chapter 11

♥

T he welcoming warmth from the blazing fire engulfed them as soon as they stepped inside The Iron Bridge. Michael shut the door after her, grateful to leave the chill wind outside and Moira smiled back at the barman who'd looked up from where he was pulling a pint to give them a welcoming grin. He was serving a middle-aged man and woman in the unmistakable casual clobber of cashed-up tourists.

The pub was busy given it was a Tuesday night and as Moira glanced around, she saw the majority of the patrons looked to be tourists, all after a taste of Guinness in an authentic Irish pub. Michael scanned the room and raising his eyebrows questioningly gestured to the only free table. It was in the far corner of the room by the stage. Moira saw there was a microphone and a stool in the middle of it but doubted there'd be live music tonight, and if there was, it wouldn't start until later. It would do nicely, and she nodded her agreement nearly tripping over the long stretched out legs of a man too busy loading his camera to notice her as she followed Michael over to it.

He pulled a chair out for her and helped her out of her coat. These were old-fashioned gestures the fellows she dated didn't bother with but which she'd observed her daddy do for her mammy many times. She liked it. It made her feel special she decided sitting down and waiting for him to drape his own wool coat over the back of his chair. He did so taking a moment to soak up the expansive use of timber throughout the cosy space, and the dim lighting of their surrounds before he sat down opposite her.

'There's no doubt about it, Moira, you Irish know how to do a good pub.'

Moira smiled pleased with her choice of venue.

'Now then, what can I get you to drink?'

'Well since we're being all traditional a pint of Guinness, please. The brewery's only down the road, you can do tours of it. You should put that on your list of things to do now you're in Dublin. You'll have seen the stacks?'

He nodded. 'I can't say I'm a stout man but when in Rome and all that.'

'That's the spirit.' Moira grinned. 'It's full of iron you know, it's a tonic more than a drink.' She said this tongue in cheek having experienced the morning after too much so-called tonic more than once. 'And my daddy always said it put hairs on your chest.'

'Did he now?' He looked amused getting up from his seat. Moira sat toying with a beer mat watching him make his way up to the bar. She itched to call Andrea and tell her where she was but she left her phone in her bag. There was no time for that; Michael was being served and he'd be back in a moment.

He returned with two pints both of which had a creamy head on them.

Moira picked hers up and held it toward him. 'Slàinte.'

He clinked his glass against hers.

'It's Gaelic for health. Now you say, slàinte agad-sa which means your health as well.' She looked at him expectantly.

'Slàinte agad-sa,' he repeated awkwardly, and Moira laughed.

'We'll make an Irish man of you yet.' They both took a sip, and she pointed to his upper lip as he put his glass down. 'That's the sign of a good pint, a Guinness moustache.'

He wiped it away with the back of his hand eyeing his glass. 'That's not bad, you know. Maybe it's a subconscious thing. It tastes better because I'm in Ireland.'

'Ah well now, pouring a Guinness is an art form and if it's not done properly you miss out on a lot of the flavours. I watched him, yer man behind the bar, and he knows how it's done. Slowly, that's the way. It can't be rushed.'

'You're very knowledgeable on the topic.'

'I'm Irish, aren't I?'

'You are indeed. Now, what about those potato pancakes you mentioned?'

'I'll get those.' She was up and out of her seat before he could protest. Her finances were not in good shape but she could stretch to two orders of Boxty. She didn't want to feel beholden to him in any way. She just wanted to sit and talk, get to know him a bit better and, she assured herself making her way up to the bar, there was nothing wrong in that.

When she returned, Michael asked her to tell him what it was like living above a guesthouse. She settled back in her seat enjoying the warmth that was settling over her both from the fire and the Guinness and began by telling him about the dumbwaiter. It ran from the basement kitchen, past the first, and second floors right up to their apartment. 'It was a great place to hide when I was in trouble with Mammy. If I could get in the thing—Aisling used to take herself off and sit in it reading. She's a bookworm, our Aisling and it was the best place to tuck herself away when she didn't feel like doing her chores.' She made him laugh filling him in on Idle Ita and Bronagh their receptionist who'd worked for the family so long she was a part of it. 'Bronagh's always on a diet, supposedly, but she has a permanent stash of custard cream biscuits in her top drawer she's forever eating her way through while blaming her belly on the menopause.'

'And you're the youngest you say?'

'I am, and the others never let me forget it. It can be very annoying. There's nine years between me and Aisling, then there's Rosie, and Patrick who's the oldest.' She gave him her parents backstory of how they'd taken over the running of the three-storey Georgian townhouse overlooking St Stephen's Green from her grandparents, who'd converted it into a guest-house many moons ago when the upkeep of the manor house got too much. 'A house like that always needs something fixing. It was the plumbing in one of the guest rooms this week. When Mammy and Daddy took over, it was tired, but Mammy set about doing the place up. It was a mammoth undertaking, but she has an eye for that sort of thing and they made a grand pair playing the convivial hosts. The guesthouse got a good name for itself. It's busy all year round although why anyone would want to come to Dublin this time of year is beyond me.'

'You said your mother moved out recently?' Michael asked, and Moira tried not to focus on the plain gold band in clear view as he raked his hair back with his fingers.

The sight of it threw her.

'Moira?'

'Erm, I did, sorry.' She forced herself to stop staring at the ring and meet his eyes. She saw the question in them. 'Everything changed after my daddy died.' Her voice caught.

'I'm sorry to hear that.'

'Thanks,' she managed to say over the golf ball sized lump that had formed in her throat. She didn't look up; her eyes were trained on the Guinness that had slid down the side of her glass to puddle on the table. She dabbed at it with a napkin as she tried to compose herself. 'It was cancer and it was the worst thing me, or any of our family have ever been through in our lives, watching Daddy waste away. He was always there for us, you know. He was like a big strong rock and none of us were ready to lose him. I still can't believe he's not here anymore.' She took a deep, steadying breath. 'It's part of why I'd like to move out and get a place of my own. I see him everywhere. It's why Mammy moved on. She said it was too hard living with his ghost and she didn't want to spend the rest of her days mouldering away in the guesthouse on her own.'

'I can understand that. I lost my dad a couple of years ago too and it was tough. Damned tough. He shaped every decision I ever made because I wanted to be just like him right from when I was a little lad. Then one day, he keeled over and that was that, he was gone. He'd had a massive coronary, no warning, nothing. It was a terrible shock.'

Moira looked up then and he reached across the table. His hand rested briefly on hers as he said, 'People tell you it gets easier.'

She nodded; it was a platitude she'd heard many times in the early days after Brian O'Mara's passing. 'They do, but I don't believe them.'

'It doesn't get easier. I don't think losing someone you love deeply ever can, I think what people mean is that the pain stops being raw. It's a bit like a scab healing over, that part heals but you're left with the scarring as a permanent reminder.'

Moira nodded, chewing her bottom lip. That, she could believe.

'It might sound crazy, Moira, but I believe my father's still with me. I feel him. I think he walks alongside me, watching over me and those that I love.'

'Like an angel.' It was a lovely sentiment; she hoped her daddy was with the angels.

Michael smiled, 'If you'd ever met him, you'd know it's hard to imagine him as an angel but yes, something like that.'

Moira felt something pass between them then as he held her gaze across the table. He understood her. He understood her pain. Nobody else did. She'd stopped talking to her sisters about the big black hole inside of her that she was frightened would consume her. They were moving on with their own lives. Aisling had Quinn, and Rosie, well Rosie had the chinless wonder and gorgeous Noah. Patrick was caught up in Patrick, and Mammy was always busy with all her different clubs and committees. And now she was off to fecking Vietnam! It was only her that seemed unable to get past her grief.

The arrival of the Boxty, golden and crunchy as promised, lightened the mood between them and Moira realised she was ravenous. They tucked in, making appreciative noises as to the deliciousness of the pancakes and the perfection of the lemon and chive mayonnaise they slathered them in.

'I'm sold,' Michael said, wiping his mouth with a napkin and pushing his chair back a little once they'd cleared their plates. 'Those were bloody fantastic. Another drink?'

Moira smiled hoping her mouth wasn't shiny with grease. 'Yes, please.' She was feeling very mellow in a happily satiated way.

'So, Moira O'Mara, tell me more about how you and your sister came to be in charge of the guesthouse,' Michael said, putting the foamy pints on the table and sitting down once more.

'Well, like I said, when Daddy died, Mammy couldn't face running O'Mara's on her own. She gave us an ultimatum. Either one of us take over the management of the guesthouse or she'd put it on the market. My oldest sister, Roisin, is married to a chinless eejit over in London; he was keen for it to be sold as was my brother Patrick. He's living in LA, he's very successful at whatever it is he does.' She waved her hand, 'He's an entrepreneur. I think he would have liked the guesthouse sold so he could free up some capital for investment. He wasn't very happy when Aisling stepped up and said she'd take over.' Moira paused, her drink halfway to her lips as she frowned at the memory. She adored Patrick even if he was proving to be a self-absorbed prick, and she hadn't liked the angst Aisling's decision had caused, but at the same time, she'd been secretly proud of her sister for sticking to her guns.

'You weren't keen to take over?'

Moira snorted and then flushed. 'Sorry, not very ladylike of me. But no, Aisling was the right person for the job. She's got a background in hospitality, she worked in resort management. I used to go pea-green over the places she was sent to. We'd get these postcards from the Whitsunday Islands in Australia, Fiji, the Seychelles. Places where the sun always seemed to be shining and the postman would always drop them in to us on miserable, rainy days. She was in Crete when she decided to pack it in and come home. Aisling's got a real way with people, whereas me, well my mouth would get me in trouble.'

'But you manage to smile and be polite on reception all day long. Mr Price speaks very highly of you.'

She suspected pervy old Fusty Pants spoke highly of her for reasons that didn't include her exceptional people skills but she wouldn't bring that up. 'Ah, but that's different. I can go home at five o'clock and switch off. Besides any arsey clients aren't really my problem; somebody else has to deal with them because it's not usually me they're arsey with. No, Aisling's got the patience of a saint when it comes to our guests. *The customer's always right,* she says, whereas I'd be after telling them they had a face on them that would draw rats from a barn.'

Michael laughed. 'Well, you can't have that I suppose.'

'No.'

They lapsed into a brief silence.

'Tell me more. I like listening to you. You've a magical way of talking, Moira.'

'What do you mean?'

'I mean every sentence is a story. You're like one of the talking books you can get out of the library. I could listen to you for hours.'

'Ah, Jaysus, is that polite of way saying I've been talking about myself non-stop for the last hour?'

'Not at all. I mean it.'

'No fair's fair, enough about me, it's your turn.' Her stomach tightened as she broached the elephant in the room. His eyes followed her gaze to his left hand.

'Well, I'm married but I think you probably guessed that?'

She nodded, busying herself with her pint glass, drinking too quickly from it.

'My wife's background is in law too, although she hasn't practised since we had the girls. We met at university and got married shortly after we graduated. It's an old story, but it happens to be true, we were too young when we got married, we had our children and grew up together. Then, somewhere along the way for no particular reason, we fell out of love.'

'Then why are you still with her?' Moira blurted out, the drink making her bold.

'We've two girls, Jasmine is fifteen and Ruby's just had her thirteenth birthday.' His face softened as he said his daughters' names. 'That's why. Once they're finished school, we've agreed we'll call it quits and go our separate ways.'

Given her own parents loving marriage, Moira couldn't understand staying in a loveless one, even for the sake of children. 'Isn't the atmosphere you know—' she didn't want to say toxic, but it was the word that sprang to mind.

'We don't hate each other, Moira. We get along well, we're great friends in fact. The way you are when you've known someone nearly half your life. It's just that we don't love each other the way a husband and wife should anymore.' He shrugged, 'I guess it's hard to understand why we're staying together if you haven't come from a broken home yourself. My parents divorced when I was a teenager and it was hard, all that toing and froing. I always felt like I was playing favourites if I asked to stay longer than the agreed arrangement with my dad like I was being disloyal to Mum. I wanted to spend my time with my dad though, I was a teenage lad after all but the wounded look on my mother's face, made me feel like a shit. I don't want that for my girls. It's not their fault the way things have worked out between me and their mother and they deserve a solid foundation to come home to each day.'

Moira was chastened.

'Sorry, I didn't mean to go on but I want to be honest with you.'

She was unsure why that mattered to him unless he wanted to take things further between them.

'Another drink?' he asked brusquely seeing Moira's empty glass. She wasn't fooled by his tone though. Moira could see the loneliness in his eyes tucked away behind the bravado.

'I'd like that, thank you, but I don't think I could fit in a Guinness, could I have a dry white wine instead?' There was something unspoken in his question and her response; an acquiescence that by accepting another drink after what he'd told her, she was accepting his situation. He looked at her for a long moment before giving her a smile she couldn't read as he got up to get her drink.

Chapter 12

♥

Moira watched as Michael navigated his way around the tables to the bar and decided to use the opportunity to visit the Ladies. The cubicles were all empty and ducking into the first in line she set about performing the balancing act instilled in her by Mammy, *Don't sit on the seat you can catch all sorts. Hover, Moira, like a helicopter.* The mantra always ran through her head when she used a public convenience. She flushed and exited the toilet, finishing her ablutions before inspecting her face in the mirror. Thankfully, there was no tell-tale shimmer around her mouth left behind by the Boxty but she could do with a touch-up. She dipped inside her bag and found her lip gloss, smearing it on before retrieving her phone.

'Andrea, it's me,' she whispered, not really knowing why she was whispering.

'Moira, I'm watching Emmerdale and I can hardly hear you. You sound like one of those obscene callers.'

'Sorry,' she spoke up a notch. 'But this is breaking news. Guess where I am?'

'Have you been drinking?'

'One or two pints of Guiness, maybe.'

'But it's Tuesday.'

'I know that, but guess where I am?'

'I don't want to. I want to watch Emmerdale.'

Moira ignored her. 'I'm at The Iron Bridge with...'

'Jaysus, spit it out would you.'

'Michael Daniels.'

There was a squeal and Moira held the phone away from her ear satisfied with her friend's reaction.

'How the feck did that happen?' Andrea asked a second later.

Moira filled her in. 'I've got to go. I'll see you tomorrow, alright?'

'Alright, but, Moira,' Andrea said before hanging up, 'be careful.'

'How long have you worked at Mason Price?' Michael asked, once Moira had sat back down at their table. They were back on conversationally neutral territory once more.

'A couple of years.' She tucked her hair behind her ears. 'I like it, the days fly by and they're a good firm to work for. When I left school, I started work for a smaller firm. My parents' solicitors, actually, which is how I got the job.'

'And you enjoy what you do?'

'Well, it's probably not challenging in the way your position is, although it can be.' She thought back to earlier in the day. The phone had been bleeping with incoming calls, a courier was tapping his foot as he stood, motorcycle helmet in hand, waiting for her to sign for a parcel. A po-faced woman in a business suit who looked like she needed a good meal was crossing and uncrossing her legs as she gestured to the clock and said, 'My appointment was for three o'clock, not ten past. We're all busy you know.' Why Gilly had picked that moment to swan off to the loo was beyond her and she'd felt like screaming, *Leave me alone the lot of you!* She hadn't of course, she'd taken a deep breath and dealt with the courier, the client, and the calls in a calm and efficient manner, as was her job. 'Did you always want to be a lawyer?'

'No, I wanted to be a commercial airline pilot but my father was a lawyer and I told you how much I looked up to him, so I decided to follow in his footsteps.'

'A commercial pilot? Wow.'

'Yup, Aviation Finance was the next best thing.' His grin was rueful. 'I did get my private plane licence a few years back. I belonged to a club in London and took a single engine Cessna 172 up whenever I got the chance.'

'Well, that's impressive. I've only ever been on Ryan Air.'

Michael laughed. 'It's quite different being in a four-seater like the Cessna, you're much more in tune with the plane. It's hard to explain, but you feel connected to it, I guess. You're missing out if you've never been up in a small plane. I've joined a local club here; I'll take you up sometime if you like.'

They were treading dangerous water, was he asking her on a date? Whatever his invitation was, Moira found herself breathing, 'Oh, I'd love that.'

'And what about you? What did you dream of being?'

'I wanted to be a famous artist. I was good at art, too. I won quite a prestigious competition when I was a kid with one of my paintings but I wasn't good at school. I didn't take instruction very well.'

He smiled and she grinned back at him.

'I couldn't wait to leave. I wanted money in my pockets so I could go out and about with my friends, to parties and on holidays, that sort of thing. So, much to my mammy and dad's disappointment, I announced I wouldn't be going on to any fancy art colleges, I was leaving school.'

'Do you regret it?'

'No, I would have messed about if I had gone, my heart wasn't in learning and I suspect that if I tried to make a living out of something I loved doing, like painting, then it would become a chore instead of my passion.'

'I can understand that.'

'I might go to college one day. I don't know, maybe I'll look into doing a night school course or something.' Moira shrugged.

The conversation was easy between them and Moira wasn't aware of time ticking on until Michael glanced at his watch. 'I don't want to leave but it's getting kind of late for a school night.'

Moira felt a flash of disappointment. She didn't want to go home; she didn't want this evening to end but she finished her drink and pushed her chair back. Michael helped her back into her coat and she followed his lead, calling out a goodnight to the bartender on their way out.

It was like stepping into a freezer she thought, bracing herself as they exited the pub. They found themselves on the deserted cobbles with the wind whistling past carrying a light misting of rain with it. The icy blast had a sobering effect and Moira felt her flushed cheeks cool.

'Come on,' Michael offered up his arm, 'We'll find a taxi.'

'There's a rank on the main road,' Moira said, plumes of white dispersing on the wind as she linked her arm through his. She was acutely aware there was no one else around as they made their way down the narrow street ,with its misty yellowish lighting of yesteryear, toward the brighter lights ahead.

'Tell me more about what it's like to fly a plane,' she said, and he did. She loved the passion she could hear in his voice and felt like she was soaring in the skies next to him as he described the sensation of being at one with the elements.

She came back to earth with a jolt as the taxi rank came into view. There was no queue waiting tonight and they walked up to the first in line. Michael, ever the gentleman, opened the back door for her and she clambered in, he shut the door and took the front seat. The driver indicated and cruised off once they'd told him where they were headed. The guesthouse wasn't far and she listened as Michael and the driver engaged in polite banter as to how each other's evening had been.

'That's me just there,' she said, as he pulled over outside the old Georgian manor house. Nina, the Spanish girl who manned the front desk from four pm when Bronagh knocked off would have gone home by now, and Moira would have to use the code to get in. She made a token gesture of rummaging inside her purse knowing there was nothing in there other than a few coins.

'I've got this, Moira,' Michael said over his shoulder before climbing out and opening her door for her. She tried to be graceful clambering out, no easy task, and once she'd alighted, she stood under the street light wondering if he would kiss her goodnight. She wanted him to but at the same time she was frightened. If he did and she kissed him back, then she would very definitely be crossing into unchartered waters.

He pointed across the darkened street, gesturing to O'Mara's. 'This is you?'

She nodded.

'Wow, that's some building.' Even against the street lights, O'Mara's Georgian grandeur was obvious. Moira was used to it, she saw it every day and it was home, but now and then she saw it through someone else's eyes.

'Yes, it is.'

He reached out and stroked her cheek, his touch warm on her cool skin. Then, he leaned down and kissed her on the tip of her nose.

'Goodnight, Minnie Mouse, I've had a lovely evening.'

'Me too.'

They smiled at each other until the taxi's radio rattling into life jarred them into action. Michael climbed back inside and the taxi idled on the street outside until Moira had punched in the code and entered the dimly lit reception area, locking the door behind her.

Chapter 13

♥

That kiss...

Moira wasn't used to dining in places like this. She was more often than not found shovelling a bag of chips down as she weaved her way home after a night on the lash. She wasn't a complete heathen though; she did up the ante from time to time, but on those occasions, Mammy was usually paying, or, she and Andrea were splitting the bill at Quinn's. Actually, now that she thought about it, she really must hit Quinn up about a family dining discount. It was only fair given the amount of headboard wall-banging she'd had to put up with of late.

The snowy expanse of crisply cornered cloth stretched between her and Michael, and she resisted the urge to run her hand over it. The cutlery was laid out in order of service and gleamed under the ambient lighting. Moira was certain if she picked up the spoon and held it aloft, she'd see her face reflected back at her. She left her spoon alone and picked up her wine glass instead. The waiter, Louis, who looked more like a Seamus or Padraig given his shock of red hair and stodgy middle—weren't French men supposed to be dark and lean?—had polished the glasses until they sparkled like an advert for dishwasher tablets, before pouring the wine. A mean little pour it was too she thought, eyeing the contents before taking a sip of the ruby liquid.

It was too dry for her taste but Michael had ordered it and therefore it really didn't matter that it tasted a little shitey.

'Do you like it?' he asked her, setting his glass down, and she liked the way his eyes sought her approval.

'It's gorgeous,' she beamed, pushing her hair back over her shoulder. He smiled back at her.

'I took a punt booking us a table here. I don't know my way around the Dublin restaurant scene but it got a good review in the paper.'

Moira's eyes darted about the room. It breathed with an understated elegance. It was the sort of place that made you feel you were somewhere special; that you were *someone* special. She liked that feeling, her daddy had always made her feel like that. Ooh and speaking of which, she was certain that was the model, Geena, and what's-his-face from that band sitting in the farthest corner of the room. Moira pinched herself under the table—wait until she told Andrea about this!

Louis glided silently up to their table, which was impressive given his girth, and handed them a menu each before spouting off about the fish of the day and gliding away again. Moira watched him go, wondering if he had some sort of special shoes on as she opened her menu and stared at it. It was in French she realised scouring the list. French! They were in Dublin not Paris for feck's sake. She squinted as though that might help her make sense of the words but they were gobbledygook to her. She didn't want to appear a total eejit but if she didn't own up to the fact she couldn't make head nor tail of what was on offer, then she was likely to wind up with frogs' legs or snails on her plate. She wished she'd paid attention in French class now.

'Do you want some help?'

Moira looked up and saw Michael had a twinkle in his eye as he watched her across the table.

'Am I that obvious?'

He smiled, 'Let's just say you have a beautifully expressive face.'

All she heard was beautiful. He thought she was beautiful.

'I'm going to have the Dublin Bay prawns to start and the venison loin with cauliflower puree.'

'Mmm, that sounds divine.'

'I can read through the menu with you if you like?'

'Do you speak French then?'

'Enough to get by.'

Jaysus, there was no end to this man's talents. The food was by the by though. She knew no matter how heavenly whatever was presented in front of her was, she wouldn't do it justice. She just wanted to sit here in this gorgeous place and admire Michael.

'I had the worst French teacher. He used to do this thing with his tongue where he made a clicking noise when he'd finished speaking. It was awfully distracting and it didn't take much to distract me so I used to file my nails under my desk instead of conjugating my verbs.'

Michael laughed and Moira was pleased.

'So, I take it that was a yes to me running through the menu with you.'

Moira smiled and nodded.

———*ell*———

By the time Moira finished scraping up the last of her crème caramel, she was a convert to French fine dining. So much for her earlier sentiment about the food being by the by, she'd managed to savour everything put in front of her *and* ogle Michael at the same time. She'd listened, her taste buds dancing with the flavour combinations she was treating them to, while he told her more about what his younger life had been like. His marriage was a subject that was skirted around as elegantly as the décor surrounding them. Now, she put her spoon down and settled back in her seat to announce, 'Michael, that was the best meal I've ever eaten.'

'I'm glad you enjoyed it.'

'I did, I really did.'

He reached across the table and wiped her top lip with his finger, 'Crème caramel.' He popped his finger in his mouth in a gesture so intimate, Moira felt an electric jolt shock her body. *Jaysus! What was this man doing to her?*

'That's good,' he said, licking his lips and smiling at her, seemingly oblivious to the sensations ricocheting around her body. 'I'm ordering that next time, although I have to say the profiteroles were a close second.'

It was a miracle Moira thought, trying to distract herself from the various X-rated scenarios currently live-streaming through her mind, she'd only managed to get the dessert on her lip. She'd been like a horse with a nosebag spooning the silky custard in. She drained the glass of Moscato that Louis had informed them was a good pairing with the caramel and profiteroles—he was right she thought.

'Coffee? Or maybe a digestif?' Michael raised an eyebrow.

Surely he didn't mean a digestive biscuit? Moira frowned. 'A digestive?'

He grinned, 'As much as I love a cup of tea and a digestive biscuit, to be dunked of course, I don't think they're on the menu here. A digestif is a liqueur or spirit. I might have a nip of Calvados, it's an apple brandy.'

She really was a prize eejit, but he seemed to like her naivety and his manner wasn't in the slightest condescending even if it was very much a Julia Roberts, Richard Gere moment. 'I'll try the Calvados too, please.'

The brandy when it came seemed to glow in the glass and she followed Michael's lead, sipping the spirit instead of knocking it straight back. She could feel the amber liquid's warm burn all the way to her belly. 'Perfect,' she murmured when the contents of the long-stemmed glass were a memory. 'You know, after tonight I think I might have to move to France.'

'Don't do that.'

She looked at him.

'I'd miss you.' He held her gaze for a long moment before looking away and gesturing to Louis that they were ready for the bill.

The bill was discreetly proffered a few moments later in a leather wallet sitting atop a white plate. Michael opened the wallet and without batting an eyelid placed his credit card in it. Moira was pleased Louis was presumptuous enough to have presented the bill to Michael, she had a sneaking suspicion had it been handed to her she would have shrieked, *Jaysus wept!* upon seeing the no-doubt eye-watering sum. She was guessing it was more than her week's wages.

'Thanks, Michael.'

'For what?' He looked surprised.

'For getting dinner.'

'It's me that should be thanking you, Moira, for coming.'

A brief silence hung between them. Moira wasn't sure what she should say to that and was pleased she was saved from doing so by Louis returning with his bank card. Michael waited until the waiter had left them alone once more. 'Listen, I know it's cold out, but do you fancy a stroll to walk off dinner?'

'That sounds a grand idea.'

They got up from the table and made their way to the exit, waiting a few beats for their coats to be returned to them. Michael took her hand, a gesture that made her feel safe and protected, and she followed his lead down the stairs to the street outside.

Normal everyday things looked different when you saw them through someone else's eyes Moira thought, gazing down at the shimmering black waters of the Liffey. They'd come to a halt halfway across the Ha'penny Bridge, pausing to look over the rails at the lights reflected in the river. She'd walked over this bridge a trillion times, she knew this city like the back of her hand, but tonight walking its streets with Michael, it had come alive to her with a certain magic. She spied the ghostly white outline of two swans, their posture regal as they floated toward the bridge, and pointed them out to him.

'Moira, I really want to kiss you right now.'

'Oh.' She hadn't expected that but while she processed his words, her body turned toward him of its own accord. She held her breath as he cupped her face in his hands, tilting it toward him. 'By God, you're beautiful, you take my breath away, do you know that?'

She didn't get a chance to reply as his lips settled over the top of hers, commanding a response. The sounds of the city's night life faded and the only thing she was aware of was the feel of his tongue as it sought hers to begin a slow, languid dance. At that moment, she knew she was lost to him.

Chapter 14

♥

Present

The alarm shrilled Moira into wakefulness and she reached over, fumbling around blindly for the button to silence it. The wind had begun to howl in the small hours and the sound of it rattling the old manor house's panes had distracted her from her thoughts of Michael. Now she yawned and rubbed her eyes. They felt gritty and raw as though she'd only been asleep for five minutes. It was going to take a supreme effort to get up this morning. 'You'll feel better after a shower,' she muttered aloud and then, with a groan, hauled herself out of bed before stomping down the hall to the bathroom.

'Feck!' she muttered seeing the door shut and the light shining out from under the crack. Moira had beaten her in there. They'd had this discussion before. Moira needed to be at work by eight thirty. While it was expected that she be seated, headset on, a cheery grin plastered to her face and her hand poised to hit the button for the morning's first call at that time, in order to fulfil her employment obligations and have any hope of her morning panning out smoothly enough for her to have that cheery grin on her face, she needed to be in the shower at seven fifteen on the dot.

Aisling could mosey on downstairs to see what was happening in the guesthouse whenever she fecking liked. Mrs Flaherty and Bronagh always had things under control of a morning and nobody would threaten her with dismissal if she decided to rock up at lunchtime! Moira raised her fist in readiness to hammer on the door, nearly falling into the bathroom as Aisling opened it, an apparition wrapped in a towel and shrouded by steam.

'Sorry, Moira, I didn't mean to hold you up but the McPhersons' tour bus is picking them up at seven thirty and I need to be downstairs to check them out.'

It was fair enough. Bronagh their receptionist who was as much a part of the guesthouse furniture as the antiques that littered it, didn't start until eight o'clock, but Moira was still half asleep and as such she didn't give a flying feck about the McPhersons checking out. So, with a scowl at her sister, she pushed past her and shut the door with the heel of her foot.

She used the few seconds it took for the water to heat up to peer in the mirror. A set of puffy eyes stared back at her and she wrinkled her nose in distaste before stepping into the shower. Puffy eyes she did not need, today of all days. At least they'd have gone down by the time Mairead's party rolled around and she could hide the dark circles with concealer.

Aisling had already gone down to reception by the time she'd finished her morning routine. And, after downing one coffee and having shovelled down a bowl of cereal, she felt ready to re-join the human race. The only sound breaking the silence was the tick-tock of the old grandfather clock in the corner of the room; an heirloom passed down on her daddy's side just like O'Mara's itself. She glanced at it to check the time and saw she had ten minutes before she'd need to slide her feet into her runners and head out the door for work. With the congested rush hour streets, it was faster for her to walk to work than to cadge a lift or catch the bus. Ten minutes was plenty of time to give Roisin a call and tell her what Mammy had planned. She'd need to keep the call short anyway, calling rates to the UK this time of the day were ridiculous.

Moira picked up the phone and hit the number saved to speed dial before cradling the phone against her shoulder to walk over to the dining room table to retrieve her cereal bowl. She wasn't in the mood for Aisling giving out about her slovenly ways, so she carried it back into the kitchen, dumping it in the sink. The phone kept ringing. 'Come on, Rosie,' she muttered as the seconds ticked by.

'Hello,' her brother-in-law answered.

She was surprised to hear his harried and self-important voice given he'd normally have left for work by now. 'How're you, Colin? It's Moira. Late start today is it?'

She half expected him to tell her to mind her own business, but he didn't, answering snippily, 'I've been working from home.'

Poor Rosie, Moira thought. 'I see. That's erm, nice. I was after a quick word with Rosie if she's about?'

There was a sigh. 'It's not a great time, she's got to get Noah ready for school. Is it urgent Moira? Or, can I pass on a message?'

He was such a controlling arse, she thought sparking with irritation. 'It is rather urgent, Colin, I won't keep her long.'

Another sigh. 'I'll get her for you.'

Moira pulled a face at the phone and drummed her fingers on the kitchen bench as she waited for her sister. What Rosie had seen in Colin was beyond her. The man had no chin for feck's sake and had earned himself the nickname Colin the Arse within minutes of meeting the family. No chin said a lot about the character of a person in her book. Then again, she thought as Noah's bright painting on the fridge caught her eye, if Rosie hadn't of met Colin there'd be no Noah, and Moira adored her nephew and his perfectly normal chin.

'Moira, what's happened? Colin said you told him it was urgent. Is Mammy alright?'

'Yes and no, Rosie. She's taken leave of her senses, but in the physical sense she's perfectly fine.'

'I don't have time for this, Moira, spit it out. Noah's got to leave for school in ten minutes and he's not being very cooperative. He won't eat his bloody cornflakes.'

She heard Colin in the background admonish his wife for swearing and Moira gave him a two-fingered salute down the phone on her behalf.

'She's only after booking a trip for herself and her friend, yer one who had the hip replacement, to go to Vietnam. She says she wants to sail on a junk.'

'Noah don't do that with your spoon.'

Moira frowned; she wanted her sister's full attention. 'Did you hear what I said, Rosie?'

'Something about Mammy going to Vietnam and having a hip replacement on a junk.'

'Rosie!'

'What?'

'She's not going to Vietnam for a hip replacement. Her hips are fine. It's her friend what's-her-name who had her hips done and she wants to sail on a junk. It's mad. The whole idea of it is bonkers.'

'Noah, eat your fe—,' her voice broke off and Moira heard her take a couple of rapid breaths. She'd probably been taught that in those breathing classes she was so fond of, she mused. Her sister had more money than sense sometimes. Sure, breathing was not hard. You inhaled, you exhaled and then you repeated the exercise. 'Noah, eat your cornflakes please, for Mammy,' Roisin said in a much calmer voice.

Moira, however, felt her blood pressure rise. This was hopeless. 'Rosie, did you hear what I said?'

'Yes, and I don't know why you've got your knickers in such a knot. Mammy's a grown up, Moira. She's perfectly entitled to go on holiday.'

'Yes, I agree, but not to Vietnam. Jaysus you know what she's like. She's liable to offer to carry some random drug smuggler's bag through customs, and she'll get busted because what's-her-name will set the sensors off with whatever it was they used to replace her hips with.' Andrea had filled her in on what happened to Bridget Jones in the Edge of Reason. Unlike her sister, Moira hadn't picked up a book in years but Andrea liked to read little excerpts out for her when they were on their lunch break. And, yes, she knew Bridget had been in Thailand at the time but sure the two countries were just around the corner from each other. 'That, or the junk she picks will have a rip in its sail, or she'll get fecking malaria or something.' Moira's breath caught in her throat; the varying scenes were playing out vividly in her head. She'd have a panic attack at this rate.

'What exactly do you want me to do about it, Moira?'

'I want you to talk her out of going. Why can't she be like normal mammies and have a week in the sun? I want her to go somewhere on the continent where she can complain the hygiene's dodgy, and the foreign food's upsetting her tummy.'

'But she can do that in Vietnam and you should know by now, Mammy is a law unto herself,' Roisin snorted. 'The way it works is she tells us what we should be doing with our lives and totally ignores any advice we give her about what she's doing with hers.'

It echoed Aisling's sentiment. 'I know that but *come on*, Rosie, please. You've got to try at least. If she goes, I won't sleep a wink for worrying the whole time, she's away.'

'What does Aisling say?'

'What you just said and it's different for Ash, she's well-travelled, Mammy's not. What if she got sold into slavery or something?'

'Ah, well now, Moira, they'd be asking for their money back once they realised how bossy she is.'

'It's not funny, Rosie. You didn't hear her, the way she was talking about wanting an adventure, it was very unnerving.' Moira had never much liked change, and there'd been far too much of it since their daddy had died.

'Moira O'Mara, you're being ridiculous.' Roisin's tone softened. 'It's not been easy for her, for any of us. This is her way of muddling through. You have to let her spread her wings if that's what she wants. She'll be fine. Now, I've really got to go.'

The conversation had not gone at all how Moira had wanted it to but she wouldn't hang up without hearing Noah's voice. 'Well, if you won't ring Mammy and talk some sense into her at least let me talk to Noah. I'll get him eating his cornflakes for you.'

'Good luck.'

A heartbeat later she heard familiar heavy breathing. 'Hello, Noah, its Aunty Moira. How're you doing?'

'I've been better, Aunty Moira. Mummy's trying to make me eat cornflakes and they taste like poos.'

Moira's mouth twitched; he was like an adult trapped in a child's body the way he spoke at times. 'Well, you know yer man who climbs up walls and catches bad guys.'

'Spiderman.'

'Yeah, him. I heard he has cornflakes for breakfast every single day.'

She could almost hear the cogs turning and the mouth twitching turned into a smile.

'No, he doesn't, because they taste like poos and milk is made from cows wees.'

'He does actually; it's the corn you see. It helps him climb up the side of buildings and the milk makes his bones strong. And just so you know, cows' milk is not wee-wee.' God, she was good she thought hearing the phone clatter down.

Roisin's voice sounded down the line. 'What did you say to him? He's hoeing into them like it's a bowl of fe— ice cream.'

'Ah, well now, that would be telling, but I will reveal all if you promise to ring Mammy and try to talk some sense into her.'

'That's bribery!'

'Blame Aisling.' Moira thought back to the deal she'd had to agree to in order to secure the Valentino's for tonight.

'Fine.'

A tick or two later, Moira hung up and after a few minutes of frantically trying to locate her runners—they were under the couch where she'd kicked them off when she'd gotten home last night, she picked up her bag and headed out the door.

Chapter 15

M oira's mood was vastly improved since she'd first opened her eyes. She'd pushed all thoughts of her conversation with Roisin and Mammy's impending trip aside because today was the day. Mairead's engagement party was only hours away. Sure, it was a whole day at the office away but that equated to hours, nonetheless.

Tonight, she would dazzle Michael when her arrival was announced at the Shelbourne's The Saddleroom. The images of herself swathed in all her finery, Aisling's Valentino slingbacks on her feet instead of glass slippers were all very Cinderella like, but then it had always been her favourite fairy tale.

'Morning, Ita, don't you be overdoing it now,' Moira called over as she reached the first-floor landing and paused for a moment. Her tongue was very much in her cheek.

Ita looked up from her phone, the bucket full of cleaning products by her feet. 'What was that?'

'Nothing, I just said you be sure to have a good day.'

Ita shot her a suspicious glance as she took the pass key for Room 3 out of her pocket. She never quite knew whether Moira was being serious or not. 'Sure, same to you.'

Moira carried on down to reception and perched on the side of the front desk as she did most mornings. Bronagh was on the phone taking a booking, tell-tale biscuit crumbs down her front. She was as much a part of the furniture as the plush cream sofa with its green stripes in the reception area, Moira mused. The three-seater was where guests could relax and read through one of the many brochures advertising everything from the annual Lisdoonvarna Matchmaking Festival through to Quinn's Bistro! Aisling always made sure her fella's brochures were well stocked just as she fastidiously plumped the sofa's cushions each morning before doing the same thing to the identical sofa in the guest lounge.

Moira couldn't see the point in cushions, they got in the way more often than not, and she couldn't be doing with all that plumping.

Bronagh finished the call, 'And how're you today?'

'Grand, Bronagh, or at least I will be when you give us one of those custard creams you're after snaffling.'

'Custard what?' Bronagh feigned innocence.

'A custard cream—ah go on, Bronagh, I need sustenance if I'm to walk all the way to work.'

'Sure, you're a fit young thing so you are, and besides I don't know what you're on about.'

'Don't play the innocent with me. The biscuits you've got hidden in your top drawer there.' Moira pointed to the drawer before thrusting her hand forth for a biscuit. Bronagh needed her hair doing she noticed, spying the zebra streak running through her jet-black hair as the older woman grudgingly opened the drawer,

Moira shook her head. Why their receptionist was one of life's flirts, especially when it came to men young enough to be her son, was a source of consternation to her. The way she used to carry on with Quinn before he and Aisling finally got it together was embarrassing. Aisling thought it was funny but to Moira's mind, Bronagh should be setting her sights on someone closer to her own age. She didn't let her mind dwell on the hypocrisy of that sentiment given the age gap between her and Michael as she helped herself to a biscuit.

'One mind. You and that sister of yours rob me blind, so you do. I've only got crackers for lunch I'll have you know.' Bronagh patted her middle and gave it a despondent look. 'And they'll hardly keep me going through the day. You've no idea what it's like to be peckish all the time, Moira, and never lose so much as a pound.'

Given Bronagh had just been stuffing biscuits in her gob, Moira very much doubted Bronagh had any clue either. As she chomped she remembered Mammy's news.

'I've something to tell you about my mad mammy.'

'Oh, yes?' Bronagh was all ears, she liked to be kept in the know. Moira filled her in on Maureen's plans for backpacking around Vietnam, pleased she wasn't interrupted mid-flow by the phone. She didn't know what she expected when she'd finished talking but Bronagh's wistful expression as she said, 'Good for Maureen, I say. She'll have a grand time so she will. Sure, I'd like an adventure.' was not what she'd had in mind.

'Ah now, Bronagh, come on, sure there's enough adventure to be had right here in Dublin so there is.'

'Not when you're battling hot flushes and a burgeoning middle, there's not.' Bronagh put the biscuits back in the drawer closing it with a bang as the phone began to ring. It was time Moira got on her way anyway and saying cheerio she psyched herself up for the blast of cold that would hit her as soon as she opened the door.

She could feel the air heavy with impending rain as she strode along the street. Well, it could rain all it liked this morning she thought, eyeing the bulging dark clouds challengingly. It had better not dare spit so much as a drop after she'd had her hair blow-waved come lunchtime. Her mind swung back to Bronagh as she weaved her way past the dawdlers dragging their heels on the walk to work. Aisling had mentioned she thought lovely Mr Walsh had his eye on Bronagh. He was a proper gentleman from days gone by who lived in Liverpool although he hailed from Dublin. He stayed at O'Mara's for a week every September visiting his sister on an annual pilgrimage home to Dublin. She still lived in the family home and he always maintained he got on perfectly well with his sibling so long as they weren't under the same roof!

It would be nice for Bronagh to meet someone special, someone kind—she deserved as much, Moira thought waiting for the lights to change. For as long as she'd known her which was most of her life, their receptionist had been on her own. She'd gone out with the odd fellow but that had been yonks ago now. She must be lonely with only her ailing mammy, who she looked after for company of an evening.

All thoughts of Bronagh dispersed as she pushed through the glass doors and pressed the button for the elevator. She smiled over at Hilary, a litigation solicitor with bad breath, and hoped she didn't want to strike up a conversation inside the lift. Her work day, she decided, was off to a good start when Hilary was mercifully silent as they rode together to the first floor. Moira called out, 'Have a good day,' to her as she stepped out of the lift onto the well-trodden carpets of Mason Price's reception area and headed toward the front desk. By the time she'd stashed her bag under the desk and got her bum on the seat, the phone had begun to ring.

It had been a busy morning and Moira felt herself relax now, well as much as she could given the current angle of her neck as her head arched over the basin. She was enjoying the tingling sensation across her scalp as Holly, Headstart's shampooist, massaged a conditioner into it that made her think of bubble gum. Andrea was positioned over the basin next to hers and she heard her friend give a contented little sigh that made her smile.

It would be hard going back to work after an hour's pampering here at the salon but she had high hopes the afternoon would pass as quickly as the morning had. Lunchtime had rolled around before she knew it and she'd said cheerio to Gilly before skipping down the stairs to the foyer to meet Andrea. They'd headed out the building's big glass doors pleased to escape for the hour and a half break afforded to them both. Sometimes having that long to twiddle your thumbs in the middle of the day was a nuisance but on days like this, it was a boon. The two girls had linked arms and dodged puddles as they chattered excitedly, affirming their plans for the impending evening all the way to the salon.

Holly began rinsing the conditioner out. 'Sing out now if the water's too hot won't you Moira? I don't want to be scalding you.'

'Mmm' The temperature was just right and she was enjoying the sensation of the warm water trickling over her scalp. It felt rather like a rude awakening when Holly told her to sit up a few moments later before briskly towel drying her hair. Andrea's hair was still being rinsed she saw, following Holly's lead over to a spare seat in front of the bank of mirrors.

'There you go, make yourself comfy. Can I get you a tea or a coffee?'

'A coffee would be lovely thanks, Holly. White and one, ta.'

'Madigan's just finishing with a client and she'll be right with you.'

Moira wouldn't let anyone other than Madigan touch her hair—the senior stylist had the magic touch. She watched as Holly scurried off as best she could in a black skirt that was strangling her legs. She wouldn't get any sympathy from Moira; it was the price of fashion she thought before picking up the latest glossy copy of *Hello*.

There was something a little decadent about sitting in the hairdressers flicking through *Hello* to see how the other half lived at lunchtime. She paused and eyeballed a photograph, imagining what it would be like to be called Tabitha or Tamara or something like while swanning about an old castle in a filmy dress for the day. She settled herself into her chair and was about to resume flicking through the pages once more when she spied the woman seated to her left. She looked different given her head was covered in foils but it was definitely her. She lowered the magazine. 'Hello, it's Tessa, isn't it? Fancy meeting you here.' The cliché rolled forth.

Tessa's eyes widened. She couldn't quite believe she'd wound up sitting next to the pretty girl from the guesthouse at the hair salon. What were the odds given how many million people were currently flitting about Dublin?

Tessa's eyes were an unusual shade of brown, almost amber Moira thought, they drew you in. She watched as a shutter went down on them. As much as Aisling was prone to dramatising things, she got what her sister meant. There was something furtive about this guest of theirs. Unlike Aisling though, Moira was not one for pussyfooting around. 'Are you off somewhere special tonight then?' Tessa's coffee cup still had its chocolate on the side and Moira fought off the urge to swipe it—she'd not had time for lunch. She'd pick up an egg sandwich from O'Brien's to munch on, on her way back to work. Their egg and mayo was the best. Her mouth watered and her tummy rumbled loudly at the thought of it.

'Ah, Jaysus, did you hear that? Sorry, but honestly I'm so hungry I could eat the balls of a low flying pigeon.'

'What did you just say?'

Moira put her hand to her mouth, 'Ooh, sorry, things just pop out of their own accord. It's the Mammy gene, so it is.'

Tessa's mouth twitched. She liked this girl, Maeve, or was it Moira? She had flashing eyes and a naughty grin. 'It doesn't bother me. My dad's favourite saying was, *I'm so hungry I could eat the arse off a nun through a convent gate.* Mum used to tell him off every time he said it but it never stopped him. He'd tell her he was keeping his Irish heritage alive.' She paused for a beat. 'I'm sorry but I don't think I ever got your name.'

Moira snorted, 'It's Moira and I'm with your dad, that's a good one. I'm filing it away for another day.' She rolled on with her conversation. 'I've an engagement party to go to. It's very posh and warrants a shampoo and blow-dry, that's why I'm sat here forfeiting my lunch.' She heard a throat clearing on the other side of her and realising Andrea had sat down next to her she swivelled in her seat and said, 'Tessa, this is my friend, Andrea. We both work at Mason Price Solicitors.' She leaned back so as Andrea could lean forward, explaining to her friend, 'Tessa's one of our guests.'

Andrea peered around her with curious blue eyes, her hair in dark blonde, dripping ringlets that grazed her shoulders. 'How're ya?'

Tessa smiled back. 'Fine thanks.' Both women were eyeing her curiously and she realised she hadn't replied to the earlier question. 'I've a school reunion to go to this evening, that's why I'm sat here looking like a visitor from outer space.'

Both Moira and Andrea giggled and Andrea piped up with, 'I love an Australian accent, I'm a big fan of Home and Away and Neighbours. I also think Danni has a better voice than Kylie and she's very underrated. I mean, sure, we could all swan around in gold hot pants if we were so inclined but it doesn't mean we can hold a tune now does it?'

'I'm from New Zealand actually, well Dublin originally but I've lived in New Zealand since I was a teenager so I couldn't possibly comment on the Minogue sisters.' Tessa bit back the smile, she'd forgotten what the banter was like in Dublin. She felt herself relaxing in the company of these two women.

'Ooh, sorry.' Andrea was dimly aware that New Zealanders didn't like to be mistaken for Australians. She'd learned this from Lisa the New Zealand temp to whom she'd also vented her feelings about the Minogue sisters.

'No problem, and off the record I'd give anything to look like Kylie in a pair of gold hot pants,' Tessa smiled.

'Ah sure, I'm telling you they're not what they're cracked up to be. They'd ride up your arse and the gardai would arrest you for your troubles if you paraded around the city in what equated to gold foil undies, so they would,' Moira said.

'Hmm, you're probably right and I'd get chafing,' Andrea lamented. 'I always do when I wear shorts.'

The three women laughed but then Moira sobered, 'You've a school reunion to be going to you said? What school? Jaysus, I could think of nothing worse.' She shuddered to prove her point. 'Everyone would be trying to out-do one another telling tall tales about how successful they've been since leaving year—at least the lot I was at school with would. That's not what you've come all the way from New Zealand for is it?'

'St Mary's and no! Well, sort of.' It sounded ridiculous hearing someone else say it Tessa realised as she explained herself. 'The reunion's part of why I came back. I think having a specific date to work around finally organised me into booking a holiday in Ireland. It's something I've been thinking about for a good few years now. I was thirteen when I left and I wanted to come back and see the city where I spent my childhood through adult eyes.' Tessa hesitated, should she tell them her real reason for going to the reunion? Would they think her ridiculous? Because she was going in order to do exactly what Moira had just said, only she wouldn't be telling tall tales. She *had* been successful and she wanted to rub Rowan Duffy's nose in it. She was spared from making a decision by the hairdresser, clad in top-to-toe black, sidling alongside Moira. She was wielding a comb and a hairdryer.

'Now then, Moira, what sort of look are you after today?'

Moira glanced down at the magazine still in her lap and jabbed at the picture of Jennifer Aniston grinning up at Brad

Pitt. Her hair was long, parted in the middle and hanging straight. 'That should do it, thanks, Madigan.'

Chapter 16

♥

Moira and Andrea stood in front of Moira's dressing-table mirror and struck a pose, hands on hips, heads tossed back. Moira's hair fell down her back in an iron-straight, dark curtain while Andrea's blonde Hollywood waves rippled to her shoulders.

'Will we do?' Andrea giggled over the top of *Livin' La Vida Loca*—Moira having declared a little of Ricky would get them in the party mood shortly after her friend had arrived. She'd shown up an hour earlier with her dress slung over one arm, toting a make-up case the size of a suitcase with her free hand.

'Come on,' Moira had said, dragging Andrea in through the door. 'I've got the champagne on ice.' Champagne was a stretch. She'd picked up the bottle of cheap plonk on her way home but it was cold and bubbly and would do very nicely she thought, cracking it open and turning the sound up. They had the apartment to themselves; as to where Aisling was, Moira didn't know. Quinn's at a guess. Her sister was in her good books given she'd remembered to leave the Valentino's outside Moira's bedroom door before she'd headed out.

'We're fecking gorgeous, so we are. Of course, we'll do.' Moira nudged the pile of clean laundry she'd meant to put away earlier over into the corner of her bedroom before picking up her champagne flute. 'Here's to a sweetheart, a bottle, and a friend. The first beautiful, the second full, and the last ever faithful, as my dear Mammy would say. Cheers!' She raised her glass.

'Jaysus, you come out with it, Moira, and honestly your room's a bombsite. I don't know how you manage to always look so well turned out. By rights, you should look like a crumpled wreck, but I love you anyway.' Andrea grinned, stepping over the jacket Moira had worn to work, so as to clink her glass against her friend's. 'You did well getting Aisling to loan you those shoes; they're a knockout with your dress.'

Moira glanced down at the red slingbacks, pleased. They did go well with the cerise sheath dress she'd chosen. She felt good, and she nudged the spaghetti strap back on to her shoulder before having a sip of her sweet fizz.

Andrea perched on the edge of the bed being careful not to crease her dress. It really did suit her Moira thought, eyeing her from where she was still standing in front of the mirror. She'd chosen a ridiculously pricey one-shouldered, black cocktail dress with a side slit but it was worth every single one of the pretty pennies, she decided. Andrea looked well in black, it wasn't a shade that did much for her serving to wash her out, but it highlighted her friend's fair colouring and gave her an old-school glamour.

'I wonder if Connor's going to be there?' Andrea's blue eyes were tinged with anxiety but hopefully wide.

Moira felt a pang, her friend had been hankering after Connor Reid forever but he never seemed to look her way, more fool him in her opinion. He didn't know what he was missing out on. She remembered the brief instructions Niall had tossed over to her as he waited impatiently for the lift. 'Well, he's quite friendly with Mairead's Niall, I heard they play squash together.'

Andrea sat up straight, 'You didn't tell me that.' Her tone was indignant, 'How do you know they play squash?'

Moira shrugged feeling a guilty stab, 'I forgot to mention it, sorry.' Her mind had been too full of Michael to remember to relay this nugget of information her friend had just pounced on. She could already see the cogs turning and knew it would only be a matter of time before Andrea suggested they invest in some whites and take up squash.

'Niall came out of a boardroom meeting that had run late and asked me to ring through and tell mealy-mouthed Melva that he was going to have to postpone his and Connor's squash game.'

Andrea looked wounded. 'And you didn't think to tell me.'

'I'm sorry, it just slipped my mind, I got busy with the phones, you know how mad the front desk can be and—'

'What do you think I'd look like in a pair of white shorts? Do you think the white would make my legs look chubby?' Andrea interrupted, her mind whirring ahead.

'Sure, you'd look grand in them,' Moira soothed, eager to appease her friend.

'Well, look at you two. You look fabulous so you do.' Aisling caused both girls to jump as she peered around the bedroom door. 'The shoes look fab, Moira.'

'Thanks.' Moira was grateful for the distraction now that her heart had returned to its normal rate of beats per minute. 'I didn't hear you come in.'

'I'm not surprised what with yer man Ricky blaring.' Aisling's eyes grazed the cluttered space. She pursed her lips and swallowed down the remarks that sprang to mind regarding the state of the room. She didn't want to be a spoilsport.

'I'll turn it down. You can't hear it downstairs can you?' The O'Mara children had grown up being told if they wanted to jump around then they'd best get outside because it sounded like a herd of wild African elephants stampeding overhead to the poor guests on the floor below.

'No, you're grand. How're things, Andrea? I love your dress.'

Andrea beamed and Moira was pleased to see Connor had, momentarily at least, been forgotten about. 'Fine, Aisling, for someone who's mammy keeps trying to set her up with her friends' sons. Honestly, the last fella she invited to tea had a face that looked like his head was on fire and it had been put out with a shovel.'

Aisling laughed, while Moira downed what was left in her glass. Her stomach was all aflutter. She tuned her sister and friend out as she thought about Michael. She knew he was going to be there having managed to corner Posh Mairead in order to subtly enquire whether the new partner in Aviation and Asset Finance was coming. She couldn't wait to see his expression when he saw her.

The Cinderella scenario she'd been envisaging all day played out in her mind once more and it was only when she saw the blinking red digits of her alarm clock that she realised it was time they got a move on. 'Ash, we've got to go. Come on, Andrea, we'll head downstairs and ask Nina to call us a taxi.' She shrugged into her coat and picked up her clutch. There was a brief moment of panic when Andrea couldn't locate her shoes but they were found under the bed and, doing her coat up as she followed Moira out the door, they called out their goodbyes. Moira shut the door of the apartment on her sister who was calling after her that the shoes had better come home in the same condition as they left.

They made their way carefully down the flights of stairs, Moira in the lead clutching the banister.

'You've got your invitation, haven't you?'

'Yes, you?'

'Yes.' They wouldn't be allowed across the threshold of The Saddleroom if they didn't produce them, Moira knew. They alighted into the cheerfully lit reception area where Nina was sitting behind the front desk on the phone. She looked up and mouthed 'Wow' at them both before gesturing she'd be with them in a minute. Moira liked Nina, they were around the same age and she often popped down of an evening to have a chat with her.

She'd listen to Nina tell her stories about what life was like in Spain hearing the homesickness in her voice. She felt sorry for her having to work so far away from her family. Nina had expressive hands when she talked and a rapid-fire way of speaking but she had sad eyes, Moira thought. Mammy and Aisling might drive her demented but she was grateful they were close by so she could lean on them whenever she needed to.

There were no jobs in the small town near Madrid where Nina came from and the family business, a restaurant was beholden to the tourist season. She'd had trouble finding employment in Madrid too and as such, she'd come to Dublin where there were jobs aplenty. In no time she'd secured two jobs, O'Mara's of an evening and during the day she wait-ressed. Her long hours meant she could send money home each week. It had made Moira feel a little mean hearing this. She'd carried on something awful about the injustice of it all when Mammy had announced that now she was working she could start contributing with a weekly board payment.

Nina hung up, 'You two look bello! Tonight is the party, yes? You want me to call you a taxi?'

'Thanks, Nina, yes, please.' The Shelbourne was only five minutes away on foot but neither girl was keen to brave the elements, not after the effort they'd put into getting ready.

Andrea and Moira sat silently in the back of the taxi hoping the smoky smell left behind by a previous passenger didn't attach itself to them. Their driver had driven at a snail's pace around the block in an effort to stretch the fare out. He'd muttered on, all the while, about it being a waste of his time. Yes, it was only around the corner Moira thought, mentally telling him to put a cork in it, but her hair had to come first. Still, given his head was a shiny bald dome she wouldn't expect him to understand. The drizzle that had set in since she'd left work would have been the ruin of her sleek locks and she was not subjecting herself to potential frizz, no matter what.

He pulled up outside The Shelbourne, wrenching the handbrake up with more gusto than necessary. Moira retrieved a fistful of notes from her clutch and handed them over the seat telling him to keep the change. She got out the car quick smart not wanting to hear what he had to say when he worked out, she'd tipped him about fifty pence.

He took off a moment later in a blaze of burning rubber. 'Arse,' Moira muttered, following Andrea's gaze as she looked up at the imposing five-storeyed brick facade that took up half a block. A doorman stood to one side of the entrance and a rich glow emanating from inside the lobby beckoned them forward.

'Wait a moment, Andrea.' Panic assailed Moira. 'Have I lipstick on my teeth?' She bared her lips and grimaced.

'No, you're grand. Am I?'

'Good to go.'

'Right then, best foot forward.'

They moved toward the door and Moira nearly tripped over herself when her friend yanked her arm. 'Jaysus, Andrea, what're you doing?'

'I just thought of something. Well, that's not exactly true. I've been thinking about it all day but I didn't want to put a dampener on your mood. I can't not say something though.'

'Spit it out.' Moira was impatient to get inside now they were here.

'What if Michael's wife's with him?'

Chapter 17

'Miss Moira O'Mara of St Stephen's Green, Dublin and Miss Andrea Reilly of Ranelagh, Dublin.' The tall, angular man with the peppermint breath announced the two friends as though they were royalty. A few moments earlier he'd inspected their invitations before relieving them of their coats. His coal-coloured hair was slicked back from a face as smooth as a baby's bum and he wore a tuxedo. It had taken Moira a beat or two to put her finger on who he reminded her of but it had come to her. Pee-wee Herman.

She felt like she and Andrea were starlets in an epic black and white Hollywood film as they stood there in the entrance of The Saddleroom. *What was that old film called?* It dangled just out of her reach as she stretched for the name. She knew it had been a book too, a famous one and the film version starred a dark-haired woman with a name not unlike O'Mara, and a genteel blonde. *Gone with the Wind*, she gave a mental cheer. She'd never in her life been announced at a party before but what a way to arrive! She looked out to the sea of approving eyes that had swivelled in their direction and felt a million dollars. There was only one man she was interested in seeing tonight though and her eyes scanned the room seeking Michael's. She wanted to see the admiration reflected in his eyes.

She couldn't spot his blue-eyed gaze amid the crowd of fifteen or so though and felt stabbing disappointment that he'd missed their grand entrance. She'd brushed off Andrea's words as to what she would do if he were here with his wife with a bravado she'd hadn't felt. Her back had stiffened as they'd made their way to the private function room as she made her rebuttal, 'Why would she be? I told you they're married in name only. They lead separate lives except when it is to do with their kids. Mairead's engagement party is nothing to do with his children.'

Andrea hadn't been convinced. 'I don't know—the more I think about it...' She shook her head. 'And, I've got one of my funny feelings, here.' She patted her stomach.

Moira knew her friend liked to think she had a touch of the 'sight' but she was sceptical. 'It's probably wind.'

'It's not. But even if he is alone, I just can't see what you expect him to do. He's hardly going to greet you with a kiss in front of all his colleagues now, is he?'

She knew that, she didn't expect him to. She'd told Andrea all she wanted was for him to acknowledge the friendship between them. Her resolve to prove Andrea wrong strengthened with each step she'd taken through The Shelbourne. Michael would be delighted to see her here. She was the shining light in his life, hadn't he said so after all?

Now, standing there in the entrance, she was distracted from that line of thought by Mairead stepping forth to greet them. Their hostess had a glass of champers firmly grasped in one hand a canapé in the other, and a welcoming horsey grin planted firmly on her face. 'Moira, Andrea so good to see you both, dahlings!'

She'd seen them both a few hours ago at Mason Price but Moira didn't point this out as she joined in with Mairead's enthusiastic air kissing.

'You look gorgeous, Mairead, absolutely stunning, so you do. Your Niall's a lucky man,' Andrea gushed, and Moira nodded enthusiastically. The bride-to-be had scrubbed up well. She'd chosen to wear copper which did look lovely with the auburn highlights in her hair. Her dress was almost 1950s in style with a sweetheart neckline and a full skirt cinched in at the waist. She blended rather well with the décor of The Saddleroom Moira thought, soaking in the opulent golds, browns, and bronzes of the room. As for the diamond on her finger which she was waving about as though she were teaching Girl Guides semaphore, it was enormous! Moira blinked, nearly blinded by its sparkle.

The tables in the room were laid with white cloths in readiness for the meal that would be served later and Moira guessed the coveted gold upholstered booths would be for the happy couple and their nearest and dearest. Clusters of people milled about the room between the tables clutching champagne flutes, and a handful were seated on stools at the bar. Their low buzz of conversation filled the air like bees humming around a hive.

Moira could almost smell the money in the room. The clues lay in the cut of the guests' clothes and the confident stances of the chosen few. There was an air of entitlement and of being at ease with their place in the world. A few of the faces were familiar from work but there were several people she was sure she'd never met before but who looked teasingly familiar. It came to her, she recognized them from the society pages.

Two young women, each dressed in the identical fashion of a chambermaid from the twenties, were passing around interestingly convoluted nibbles on a silver tray along with tall crystal glasses filled with the palest of yellow-orange bubbly liquid. She'd put money on the bubbles on offer tonight being Dom Perignon or Krug. There'd be no cheap plonk served here she thought, willing them her way.

Her mental powers worked and she helped herself to a glass and, well, she wasn't sure what the canapé was exactly but it had a sliver of smoked salmon on top of it. She popped it in her mouth and munched, only half-listening as Mairead filled them in on the plans for her impending nuptials. She heard the words 'castle' and 'designer' and nodded at the appropriate times. Her ears pricked up when she heard *Love Leila's Bridal Planning* mentioned. Mairead and Niall's wedding was a feather in the cap for Aisling's best friend since forever. Their big day was sure to make the papers and be fabulous advertising for her business. She tuned out once more, her eyes straying over to the entrance on the lookout for Michael.

'Will you excuse me?'

'Wha—, I mean pardon?' Moira corrected herself, flushing at being caught out not listening.

Mairead had that look on her face of someone scanning the room for important people to meet and greet. Her eyes settled on her soon-to-be spouse and she nodded. 'Sorry, girls, will you excuse me? I can see Niall signalling me. Time to play the dutiful fiancée and listen to the boring work talk.'

Moira hadn't known it was possible for human beings to bray until that moment. She managed to choke down the urge to giggle. 'Of course, better not keep him waiting.' Andrea's mouth was full of the latest snack being handed out. She squeezed out a chubby-cheeked smile, excusing Mairead as she wound her way over to where Niall was standing next to Fusty Pants Price and his wife Norma. The matronly Norma's grey coif looked as if it would withstand a tornado Moira thought, feeling a pang of sympathy for Mairead. Being from a fabulously rich family didn't excuse you from being bored silly by work talk or receiving the lowdown on Norma Price's housekeeper's slovenly habits. She'd been there, heard that, at the works Christmas party last year when Norma had cornered her in the Ladies.

It was only when she was safely out of earshot though that she turned to Andrea and muttered, 'Who'd have believed

Fusty Pants had a blue suit identical to his brown one. The blue one must be his party suit.'

Andrea sniggered but then as she saw whose head was visible behind Fusty Pants and Niall her sharp intake of breath was audible. Moira was glad she'd swallowed what she'd been chomping on or she'd have been in danger of choking. 'He's here.' She fanned herself as though having a hot flush. 'You were right.'

'Who?' Moira cast about, Michael hadn't arrived yet, she'd hardly taken her eyes off the door since they got here.

'Connor, of course. Oh, Moira, feck it, look he's talking to some brunette. I don't recognise her. Do you?' Andrea squinted over; her gaze intense.

Moira shook her head not wanting to state the obvious. Andrea did it for her. 'She's fecking gorgeous, too.'

'Ah well, that won't stop you from catching his eye. Sure, you look just as gorgeous.'

'I don't see how I'm going to catch his eye when he's just about got his nose buried in yer woman's cleavage.' Her friend's lower lip trembled but Moira was having none of it. 'Come on, get that champers down you and I'll get us another. We're here to have fun and you standing around with a face like a smacked arse is not going to win Connor over. You need to dazzle him with your wit. Go on over and introduce yourself. I bet yer one over there can hardly string a sentence together.'

'You think?'

'I know.' Moira affirmed, even though she hadn't a clue.

Andrea took a gulp of her drink and gave a little hiccup, 'Alright, wish me luck.'

'You don't need it.'

Andrea made a beeline for Connor and his lady friend and Moira wondered whether she should hunt down the canapés. She was starving. She'd not had time for the egg sandwich after her hair appointment and, she realised, her hand resting absentmindedly on her stomach, the last thing she'd eaten was the custard cream she'd managed to separate Bronagh from before she'd left for work. She was about to beckon the girl with the tray, refilled with what looked like a trumped-up version of vol-au-vents over when she felt a tap on her arm.

'You're looking even more gorgeous than usual tonight, Moira,' Liam Shaugnessy grinned wolfishly down at her.

She resisted the urge to tell him to feck off and pick on someone else. There was a time, not so long ago, that Moira would have embarked on some outrageous flirting with Liam. The smoothly handsome Asset Management Partner was a popular favourite amongst the female employees at Mason Price and indeed was slowly working his way through them. She'd fancied the pants off him herself until she'd laid eyes on Michael. Looking at him standing cockily next to her now, she thought he looked like an immature boy trussed up in a suit, by comparison. Still and all, she'd been raised with good manners which she managed to observe at least fifty per cent of the time, and as such she'd refrain from using bad language, for the time being at least.

'How're you, Liam?'

'All the better for seeing you.'

'Oh, for feck's sake.' It popped out of her mouth unbidden and she glanced around hoping she hadn't been overheard. Nobody seemed to be affronted by her outburst other than Liam.

'What?'

'You know what, Liam Shaugnessy. Honestly, that line's cheesier than a slice of cheddar.'

He managed a sheepish grin. 'Fair play to you but it usually works.'

'Not with me. I don't like cheese.'

'Ah, come on now, be nice. Sure, you can't blame a lad for trying.'

'I'll forgive you if you get yer woman with the canapé thing-a-me-bobs to come my way.'

'Actually, now that you mention it, she's a bit of a looker.'

She batted him on the arm and sent him on his way, and he passed by Andrea whose chin was just about scraping the floor as she made her way back to Moira.

'It didn't go well then?' Moira asked when her friend reached her a moment later.

'No, it did not. She's a fecking accountant. So, much for her not being able to string a sentence together.'

'I'll bet she's boring as anything and all she talks about is money.'

'They were discussing inequality and globalisation, actually,' Andrea said, fixing her with a look that told her she wasn't helping.

At that moment Pee-wee made an appearance in the doorway once more and Moira froze. 'Mr Michael and Mrs Adelaide Daniels of Sandy Cove, Dublin.'

She stared at the handsome couple, registering but not understanding that they were holding hands and smiling with that ease belonging to couples who've been married a long time. She felt her stomach fold over on itself as Michael's eyes met hers, his unwavering glance betraying nothing before it flicked away. She watched as his wife, a pretty, pixie-like woman with short black hair and enormous brown eyes, arched her neck up to whisper something in his ear, her hand resting proprietorially on his arm. He laughed delightedly at whatever it was she'd said and she planted a kiss on his cheek leaving her mark before he led her down the stairs. Moira couldn't look away. She felt like a child with her nose stuck to the sweet shop window, watching as they were warmly enveloped in Niall and Mairead's group as though they were all old friends. Her head began to spin and the last thing she heard was Andrea's voice as she said, 'What sort of name is Adelaide?'

Chapter 18

♥

Tessa sat in the tub chair in front of the Georgian sash window. The thick drapes were drawn tightly against the darkness of the courtyard outside. It was where she'd overheard the ruckus of the fox getting into the bin the night before. She'd have liked to have caught a glimpse of him. There were no foxes in New Zealand, so if she heard the clatter of the bin lid again, she'd be sure to take a peek. For now, though, all was quiet and she inspected her nails. Ten perfect shiny coral nails to match the bold, coral wrap-dress she was wearing.

Some might think coral was a colour that should be worn only in summer but Tessa disagreed. She thought colour was something that should be used to brighten the dull winter days and nights.

The Grafton Street fashion stores she'd meandered around this morning had been filled with sombre winter tones. What she was looking for was a statement dress and the wardrobe staples she'd seen in browns, greys, and blacks wouldn't do at all. The lack of colour hadn't deterred her from giving her credit card a good workout, though! A girl needed her wardrobe basics and she'd enjoyed checking out the latest styles. Dublin was a season ahead of New Zealand and it was nice to have a heads-up on what styles would be in fashion come winter time back home. She glanced at the bulging carrier bags she'd left inside the door and hoped she hadn't exceeded her luggage allowance.

Grafton Street had also brought back memories of shopping with her mother and she'd walked quickly past the children's wear department in Brown Thomas lest she catch sight of that unhappy child she'd once been. She'd dreaded their seasonal visits to the department store, wanting nothing more than to get the excursion over and done with so they could go and have tea and cake at Bewley's.

'You'd look well in this, Tessa,' her mother would say, holding a dress that had caught her eye up for inspection. Tessa would scowl and snatch it from her knowing that as she stomped off to the fitting room, her mother would be mouthing at the assistant, 'Girls can be very difficult, and she's at that age.' The assistant would give her an understanding smile.

Looking back, she'd been a nightmare but her mother had grinned and borne it. What she never understood because Tessa never told her was it didn't matter what she tried on—all she saw when she looked in the mirror was Ten Tonne Tessie. She should have said something, spoken out and explained why she was being so unpleasant. It wasn't that she was being intentionally difficult. It was because she was hurting. The truth of the matter though was she'd been too ashamed to breathe a word of what was happening every day on the walk home from school. So, she'd stayed quiet, unable to shake the sound of Rowan's nasally taunting every time she looked in the mirror.

Ten Tonne Tessie had been banished, at least on the surface, by the time they emigrated to New Zealand. Tessa's finicky appetite prior to the move had been put down to anxiety over the impending upheaval and as such her mother hadn't pushed her too hard to clear her plate. She knew her parents had pinned their hopes on her coming right once she'd settled into her new life. Indeed, six months later they were patting themselves on the back and putting their daughter's happier demeanour down to the outdoor Kiwi lifestyle. New Zealand agreed with them all. It had been the right move for the Delaney family they'd say, toasting one another as they waited for the sausages to need turning on the barbecue.

Tessa blinked the memories away returning her attention to her coral dress. It had beckoned her over like a beacon and she'd known she was going to buy it the moment she plucked it from the rack.

Coral was a colour, to Tessa's mind, that shouted the wearer's confidence in themselves and to the world. It was not a shade a timid girl wanting to blend into the shadows would choose to wear. It also happened to do wonders for her. She'd stood in the fitting room admiring the way the punchy hue brought out the natural peach tones of her skin and managed to make her brown eyes positively glow. It clung to her in the right places and turning this way and that, she'd known it was exactly right. Now, as she eyed the fabric, she hoped she'd made the right choice. It was awfully bright.

'Stop it, Tessa,' she spoke the words and they sounded loud in the empty room despite its cosiness. The guesthouse had been a good pick. It was central to everything but had a homelier feel to it than a hotel. Outside she knew a steady drizzle had set in, but her room here at O'Mara's was warm and snug. The bed in front of her was made with tightly tucked-in corners and plump pillows.

Tessa always thought there was something special about heading out of a morning leaving behind an unmade bed and wet towels dropped on the bathroom floor, only to come back of an afternoon to find the bed magically made and fresh towels folded on the vanity. She knew there was nothing magical about it whatsoever though. She'd seen the surly looking young woman exit what she assumed was a small staff kitchen to the rear of the reception area the other morning. She was carrying a bucket stuffed full of cleaning paraphernalia and had nearly bumped into her, barely looking up from her phone to apologise.

Her eyes flitted over to her bedside travel alarm clock, the one she could not leave home without. She had no time for the shrill bleeping of most alarm clocks and the first thing she'd done after dropping her bags on arrival was unplug the one on the bedside table. She'd placed it in the drawer, closing it firmly. The time she saw was getting on for six thirty. Saoirse should have well and truly been here now. It had been all arranged. Her friend was to have arrived on the three forty-five afternoon train from Galway. She was going to make her way to O'Mara's and they were going to get ready for the evening ahead together. Tessa had been looking forward to them catching up on one another's lives over a meal at the restaurant Aisling O'Mara had recommended, Quinn's.

Those plans had been scuppered earlier that morning by a phone message. Tessa had returned home from her shopping spree and various beauty appointments filled with a mounting excitement at seeing her old school friend again. 'You've been shopping then,' Bronagh the woman on the front desk had said. 'Sure, you're a woman after my own heart. Oh, and I've this to pass on to you.' She'd handed Tessa the piece of paper with the time of the call and the neatly written message relaying Saoirse's youngest daughter was running a high temperature and she couldn't leave her. Her face must have given her away because the receptionist asked, 'Is everything alright?'

'Yes it's fine, thank you.' Tessa knew she should have used the phone in the guest lounge and rung Saoirse back straight away to tell her she understood, and that these things happened. She would be going down to Galway anyway to stay with her old friend, it wasn't a big deal. Of course, Saoirse's priorities should lie with her baby and not in revisiting a time in their lives when neither woman had been particularly happy. She didn't ring her friend though. She'd felt a desperate need to get to the privacy of her room because she could feel a tell-tale burning behind her eyes. She'd been counting on Saoirse. There was strength in numbers and she didn't know if she could face going to the reunion on her own. The thought of it made her feel like that thirteen-year-old girl once more waiting for the bell to ring. Ten Tonne Tessie was always there, lurking beneath the surface, waiting to pull her back into the past.

Sitting in the tub chair eyeing her dress, she took a deep breath and repeated her go-to affirmation for when she felt the self-doubt set in. 'I have a healthy and positive attitude that glows through my smile.' She smiled beatifically feeling more than a little ridiculous but repeating the same sentiment again nevertheless before getting to her feet. She'd come all this way, the other side of the world for heaven's sake, and this was her opportunity to say goodbye to that hated version of herself once and for all.

She allowed herself one final check in the mirror. The caramel highlights she'd had put in at the salon that afternoon really lifted her and she shook her head watching the colours glimmer under the lights. Her make-up had been applied with a practiced hand so it looked like she was wearing a mere hint of colour on her lips instead of the works. As for the dress, well, she thought, smoothing the silky fabric; with its ruching in all the right places, it was perfect. She had no intention of being a wallflower and she looked nothing like that child who'd lived in fear of what Rowan and the others had to say. She *was* nothing like that child anymore and tonight she thought, taking a deep breath, she'd say goodbye to that girl once and for all.

Tessa picked up her purse and walked out the door.

Chapter 19

Tessa stood in the dark looking at the old wrought-iron gates with the neat gold signage: St Mary's School for Girls. The entrance, she could see from where she was standing across the road, was illuminated by street lights and the gates were wide open in anticipation of this evening's party. For a moment she visualised the child she'd been plodding through them of an afternoon. Her stomach would be in knots just like it was now, as Rowan and her crew pushed off from the wall against which they lay in wait.

She looked past that ugly scene, following the expanse of asphalt as black as the Guinness Lake tonight, to the main school building. The gates hinted at a grandness the building itself lacked. It was a bland, two-storey rectangle rather like a cardboard box with windows in it. It was fit for purpose and not much else. The seventies had a lot to answer for when it came to both fashion and architecture, Tessa mused, checking the building out. The spotlights dotted under the eaves lit her old haunt up enough for her to wonder at how much smaller it seemed, shrunken almost from the enormous and overwhelming school of her childhood. It was funny how that happened when you went back to places you'd been familiar with as a child.

She heard car doors slam across the quiet road followed by laughter and stepped further into the shadows. She didn't want whoever it was to see her loitering and think she was some sort of weirdo even if she was behaving like one. Two women passed under the street light a moment later. Their arms were linked and she strained to see if she might recognise them. The light was too dull to make out their features though and she watched them until they'd veered inside the school gates. It was time she went in herself but her legs, she realised, had gone to lead in the seconds since the taxi had deposited her here. She didn't know if she could manoeuvre them across the road and into the school grounds. It seemed an interminable distance to cover. Car lights sliced the night, reminding her she couldn't just stand here like a fool.

'Come on, Tessa. You're the woman who's invested millions of dollars of other people's money without batting an eye. You can face up to a few bullies.' It took all her strength, but she put one leg in front of the other just like she'd done all those years ago making her way home from here. She crossed over the road and walked in through the gates following the drift of music. It was a tune she recognised as an old hit by Tears for Fears—Sowing the Seeds of Love. The song made her smile conjuring up her and Saoirse in her bedroom under a canopy of Duran Duran posters. It hadn't all been bad times. The stereo was turned up as they sang along to it while her mother shouted up the stairs for her to turn it down. She'd always been worried about what the neighbours would think. She was the same even now.

Oh, how she wished Saoirse was here with her now. They'd be laughing at those silly memories together. 'One foot in front of the other, Tessa,' she muttered, rounding the side of the building and seeing the double doors of the gym, open ahead of her. The light pooled out and she was highlighted, there was no going back now. Shouts of laughter startled her as she drew closer. Her stomach rolled over and she breathed in to whisper, 'I have a healthy and confident attitude that glows through my smile.'

'What was that?' A woman's voice from behind her asked.

Tessa jumped, her hand flying to her chest as she spun around.

'Ooh, sorry I didn't mean to give you a fright.' The woman held out her hand and placed it on Tessa's forearm. 'Are you alright?'

She nodded. Her heart was beginning to return to its normal rate. 'Fine, you startled me. That's all.'

She got a glossy red-lipped smile by way of apology, the lips parting to reveal beautifully white, evenly spaced teeth as she peered closely at Tessa.

'Don't tell me, it will come to me.' The woman rested her thumb under her chin and tapped her cheek with her middle and index fingers, frowning.

Tessa stood there while the woman tried to place her. It had taken her a tick to realise who it was that had nearly caused her to wet her pants! Rose Gibson, only the girl she remembered had been shy and mousey with a mouthful of braces. Rowan, ever quick to pounce on points of difference had called her metal mouth, she recalled. She remembered how Rose would slouch low on the wooden chair behind her desk in the hope, Tessa had assumed, it would make her invisible. She'd done the same thing herself. This glamorous creature with her waves of chestnut hair and flashes of red hinting at the dress beneath her coat, however, was anything but shy and mousey! Faces didn't change though not really. They got thinner or rounder and, as the years stretched acquired lines and creases, but they were still fundamentally the same. It had been thirteen years since she'd seen Rose last and she had cheekbones now but essentially, she was still the girl she'd been.

'I've got it.' Rose took a step back looking pleased with herself. 'Tessa Delaney.'

Tessa nodded, 'Hi, Rose. It's been a long time.'

'Gosh, I'll say. You left St Marys when we were twelve didn't you?'

'Thirteen.' Tessa corrected. 'My family emigrated to New Zealand.'

'That's right, I remember now. I was terribly envious of you getting to go somewhere as exotic sounding as New Zealand. I should have picked it by your accent. You don't sound like one of us anymore. Did you move back to Ireland then?'

'No. I'm back for a holiday and I heard this was on—'

'So, you decided to swing by,' Rose finished for her, giving her the once over. 'Well, I for one am glad you did and, wow, you look fabulous.' Her smile was warm and genuine and Tessa felt herself begin to relax.

'Thanks, Rose. I said goodbye to Ten Tonne Tessie a long time ago. You're looking gorgeous too.' Tessa noticed the shade of red she'd chosen to wear was even bolder than her own coral dress.

Rose's grin was wry. 'Metal mouth disappeared when I was fifteen. And, for the record, I never thought of you by that name. Rowan, Teresa, and Vicky were bitches. I wish I'd done something to stop them but to be honest, I was terrified of them back then. I've often thought I should have stood up for you though, especially now that I have a daughter of my own. If anybody ever taunted her like they did us, well—.'

Tessa was taken aback; it had been her fight and hers alone or so she'd thought. 'I never stood up for you either.'

They smiled at each other in a silent understanding.

'Are you two going to stand around outside all night or are you coming in to join the party?' a voice called from inside the gym's entrance. There was something familiar about the bossy tone that tickled Tessa's memory.

Rose gave her a conspiratorial wink before linking her arm through Tessa's. 'Come on,' she whispered, 'Lets me and you show those nasty cows in there that we turned out pretty, bloody fabulous despite them.'

Chapter 20

Tessa had the feeling tonight was going to be fun now she'd bumped into Rose. The familiar old tense feeling in her stomach had dispersed as they approached the table in the brightly lit gym's foyer. A woman was seated behind it, obviously the source of the voice that had just called out to them both. On the table was a cash tin, a book like those used in a raffle, and an ice-cream container full of tickets the same as the one Tessa paused to open her purse and retrieve.

She'd downloaded her ticket once she'd registered her interest in attending from St Mary's website after Saoirse had told her about the reunion. Now, she handed it, along with the entry fee—she'd made sure she had the right change for earlier—to the woman. She was familiar enough for Tessa to know their paths had crossed before but she couldn't place her yet. She had an air of authority about her too, even though she looked to be around the same age as her and Rose. It emanated from her and Tessa wondered if she was a school-teacher.

She was wearing a simple black halter neck dress and her dark hair bobbed sensibly at her chin as she unlocked her cash tin before looking up to give them the once over. Tessa did the same and waited for the ding dong of recognition to toll while Rose rummaged around in her bag next to her. The woman's face was a blank in Tessa's mind as she looked from one to the other and back again, trying to put names to their faces. Rose having located the errant invitation and the tenner she needed to get in, beat her to it. 'Jill Monroe!' she exclaimed, sounding pleased with herself. Her voice was loud enough to be heard over the music emanating from inside the gym.

Ding, ding, ding, went the bells in Tessa's head. *Jill Monroe, of course!* The girl with the serious face sandwiched between dark plaits had always put her hand up to be monitor. Nobody else ever got a look in. She'd been an organising type who liked to be in charge and, from memory, she could also be prone to telling tales. It would seem she'd morphed into a serious-faced woman who'd no doubt put her hand up to be in charge of the door for this reunion fundraiser. In fact, if she was anything like what she'd been like as a child, she'd probably been the one who'd organised the whole event.

'It's Rose Gibson and Tessa Delaney, Jill. Or, you might remember us as Metal Mouth and Ten Tonne Tessie,' Rose explained, realising Jill hadn't twigged as to who they were.

Jill's jaw dropped as she stared at them both. Tessa took the opportunity to explain herself, unsure if Jill would remember her even having been reminded of that awful nickname. 'I wasn't actually at St Mary's in 1989. I left a few years earlier. My parents and I emigrated to New Zealand in eighty-six when I was thirteen.'

Jill nodded. 'Yes, I remember. We were all terribly envious of you jetting off to the other side of the world.' Her words echoed Rose's.

The grass always seemed greener elsewhere, Tessa mused.

'And, so you know, I reported Rowan and her awful friends to the head sister more than once over the way they treated you both, but they were a law unto themselves.'

'Really?' People had cared, Tessa realised; it came as a shock.

Jill nodded, 'I can't stand bullies.'

Tessa was uncertain what to say, so she reiterated Rose's thank you. 'Are they here then?' 'Rowan and the others?' She felt a wave of nausea as she waited for Jill's reply.

'I don't know. I've only been on the door for twenty minutes, Sherie Milligan was manning the fort while I dealt with a last-minute panic over the sound system. It's all sorted now. I'd be surprised if she is here, I doubt she's got very fond memories of St Mary's. She was expelled after all. Anyway, enough about her.' She gave a dismissive wave. 'Have you moved back to Ireland then, because New Zealand's an awful long way to travel for a school reunion?'

Tessa barely heard Jill's questions; her mind was on Rowan. She'd be here, she had to come because she hadn't travelled to the other side of the world for her to be a no show. Besides, she told herself, a reunion was just the sort of thing someone like Rowan would go to. Like the old Bruce Springsteen song, she'd want to relive her glory days when she ruled the roost.

'Tessa?'

'Oh, sorry. No, I haven't moved back to Dublin. I live in Auckland. I'm here on holiday, revisiting my old haunts and I plan on travelling around for a week or so. Saoirse Hagan and I have kept in touch over the years and she knew I was going to be here at the same time as the reunion and wrote to me about it. I thought it would be fun to come along and catch up with some old faces.'

'Well, I'd never have recognised the pair of you! You're both looking very well on it. What is it you're doing with yourselves these days?'

Rose went first and Tessa listened, curious to find out what she was up to. 'I've a four-year-old daughter, Ella, and I work in PR,' she said, and Tessa wasn't surprised. She looked like the sort of self-assured woman who would work in what she'd always perceived to be the glamorous world of public relations. Good for her rising above the slights of her childhood. 'Yourself?' Rose asked.

'I'm a primary school teacher, here at St Mary's believe it or not. I can tell you, ladies, your money is going to a good cause, a new computer for the library, and it's Jill Ferris these days. I'm married to Phil and we have a little girl as well, she's two, called Molly.'

Tessa held back the unladylike snort. *She knew it!* She was a teacher.

'Congratulations. Molly's a lovely name.' Rose carried on, 'I'm raising Ella on my own. Her father was a dead loss and I'm happily single again after giving my last squeeze the flick, he had the most annoying habit of leaving the loo seat up. Spot the woman who's gotten used to living on her own.'

Jill looked unsure whether to laugh or not so she turned her focus back to Tessa.

'I'm an investment consultant. The hours don't leave me much time for dating.'

'You always were top of the class in maths and dating is overrated, anyway,' Rose said.

Jill smiled that smug smile of the happily married before asking, 'Is Saoirse coming?'

'No, she had planned to, but her youngest is poorly. She lives in Galway with her husband, Tom, and their two children. The baby, Tarah, is one, and Luke's two and a half. They keep her busy by all accounts.'

'They would indeed. One of each, lovely,' Jill said, before calling over her shoulder into the room behind her. 'Linda, what are you doing in there? You won't believe who's here!'

If Tessa's memory served her correctly, the room was a cloakroom.

'She only went in to hang up a few coats. The reunion was my idea, we're in desperate need of that computer and I thought it would nice for all us old girls to re-connect. Find out where we're all at in life. Do you remember Linda? Linda Stagg?'

They both nodded, and Tessa thought some things never changed. Linda had always been Jill's second in command—a girl who'd been so skinny she'd seemed to be all angles, always eager to do her friend's bidding. She remembered her shock of black ringlets. They'd sprung madly from her head and had been a source of fascination to Tessa. She'd had to resist the urge to pull one just to watch it ping back into place whenever Linda walked by.

'Sorry, Jill. I was calling home to tell James his dinner was in the oven.' A woman appeared in a dress not dissimilar to Jill's only in navy. There was no mistaking it was Linda. Her hair still sprang madly from her head but these days the ringlets were longer and could be called her crowning glory. She'd grown into her gawky body too, to emerge a pretty, if a little understated—who wore pearls at their age? woman.

Linda's deep brown eyes flicked from one face to the other before she put a hand to her mouth. 'Tessa Delaney and Rose Gibson, well I never. You two look fabulous!'

Rose and Tessa smiled their thanks and returned the compliment. Tessa was about to ask what Linda was doing with herself these days when Jill interrupted. 'Ladies, like I said, Linda's on coats.' It was Jill's way of telling them they couldn't be standing about making small talk, not when they had a job to be getting on with. Tessa's mouth twitched as she did as she was told and shrugged out of her coat, just like people's faces never really changed their core personalities never did either.

'You two aren't going to be stuck here all night, are you?'

'No, doors shut at eight o'clock sharp and then Linda and I shall be helping ourselves to a well-earned glass of punch.'

'Fair play to you,' said Rose, shedding her own coat as she spoke.

Linda scribbled Tessa's name on the stub before ripping off the ticket. 'Don't lose that now will you?'

'I won't.' She tucked it away in her purse and waited for Rose. Her dress was stunning, a statement dress just like her own she thought, seeing it properly now she'd taken her coat off and handed it to Linda. For the first time, she felt a frisson of excitement at what lay beyond the foyer.

Chapter 21

♥

Neneh Cherry was rocking as they walked into the gym. The lights were dimmed, but it wasn't dark, and all signs of equipment of torture, such as the vault Tessa used to have to be helped over, had been hidden away. She was hit by a wave of nostalgia, not necessarily a fond nostalgia but rather the sensation of having passed many hours here. There was a band of women shaking their groove thing in the middle of the floor and her eyes raked over them trying to see if she knew anyone. One or two faces were easily recognisable but neither Rowan nor the other two she concluded, was in their midst.

Around the edges of the designated dance floor, old friends had clustered, paper cups in hand and heads bent as they strained to hear what one another was saying over the music. Balloons and streamers hung from the rafters and a trestle table had been set up in the corner of the room. It was bow-legged thanks to the enormous punch bowl weighing it down. There were paper cups laid out in neat rows next to it and the rest of the cloth was covered with paper bowls filled with crisps. The ticket had mentioned a light supper was being served at the end of the night. Tessa had a strong suspicion it would be the stuff of children's parties, the little red cocktail sausages that always made an appearance alongside a bowl of tomato sauce to dunk them in, and a few savoury sausage rolls.

'Let's get a cup of that punch.' Rose made a beeline for the table and Tessa followed her lead, keeping her eyes peeled for Rowan. She couldn't spot her as they passed by the huddled, chatting groups. A few heads turned to look their way, checking them out to see if they'd been classroom pals but nobody waved and the faces didn't look familiar to her. Rose did the pouring honours ladling the ruby coloured punch into the paper cups. They carried them over to the side of the dance area, surveying the scene.

'Jaysus,' Rose shouted over the music after a beat. 'All this place needs is a giant glitter ball. It takes me back to some of the awful school dances I went to as a teenager, only there's no spotty lads in sight.' Tessa laughed in agreement; it was all rather tacky.

She blinked as her eyes watered following her first mouthful of the punch. It had a kick to it, she thought. Jill had been very generous with the rum. 'I hope they didn't serve this stuff up at those school dances.'

'Would have given the spotty lads more of a chance if they had,' Rose laughed.

Jokes aside, Tessa thought, she hadn't had any dinner so she'd better watch herself. She'd not been in the mood to go out and grab a bite to eat after Saoirse cancelled, but now feeling the alcohol burn her stomach she wished she had.

Rose raised her cup. 'A few more of these and we'll all be hugging one another like we're long-lost family.'

The familiar guitar chords of *Sweet Child o' Mine* began to play and Rose shouted again. 'Oh, I used to love this song, I wanted to marry Axl Rose, he was such a bad boy.'

'I was a Jon Bonjovi girl,' Tessa shouted back, grinning. The grin faded as Rose elbowed her and gestured at the entrance.

'Look who's here.'

She felt herself getting pulled back in time as she saw Rowan saunter in through the doors, her henchmen, Teresa and Vicky flanking her on either side. The trio were an advertisement for satin in blue, green, and pink, each wearing a different style—baby-doll, slip, and tube. The longer Tessa stared at them the more she could see the subtle differences of time. They were all thinner of face, the pubescent plumpness having dispersed, but looked harder around the edges.

Rowan would have been a pretty girl when she was younger if her favourite expression hadn't been a sneer. She was only twenty-six but the years since Tessa had last seen her hadn't been overly kind she decided, finishing her inventory. The blue shimmery fabric of her dress was stretched tight across her middle, the tube style an unflattering mistake. It looked, she cast about for the right word, tawdry, that was it. The sneer she saw had been replaced by a thin mean little line of a mouth. It hinted at a life that wasn't turning out the way she'd thought it would.

Tessa hadn't known what she'd do or say when she saw Rowan. Oh, she'd had plenty of one-sided conversations with her inside her head in the months since she'd booked her ticket back to Ireland. Now she was here though, her mind had gone blank, but her feet seemed to have taken on a life of their own. They began to carry her across the gymnasium floor. She barely registered Rose asking her what she was doing. How could she answer when she didn't have a clue herself?

Rowan was leaning in to Vicky's ear and whatever she was saying was making her laugh, Tessa saw the flash of a silver stud in Vicky's open mouth. It was Teresa who nudged Rowan as Tessa came to a halt in front of them. She could sense Rose behind her, hovering uncertainly, wary perhaps of a scene reminiscent of WWE women's wrestling.

'Hello, ladies. Do you remember me?' She had to shout but her voice was strong and steady as she eyeballed each of them in turn.

Three blank over-made canvases stared back at her. Rowan spoke up and her tone was a little belligerent as she sensed from Tessa's body language this was someone they hadn't been pally with. 'Should we? I don't have a clue who you are, sorry.' She looked to each of her friends to see if they were any the wiser but they were shaking their heads, too.

She was still the ringleader, then, Tessa thought at the same time as she wondered who this confident woman in a coral dress was. This woman wasn't in the least intimidated by the trio. They were like the Three Stooges, and the analogy made her smirk. Looking at them now, she wondered how she'd ever let them have the power to hurt her. Well, never again. She liked this version of herself she decided, before enlightening them. 'It me, Tessa, Tessa Delaney or you'd probably remember me as Ten Tonne Tessie. You lot made my life at St Mary's hell.'

Rowan's gob fell open revealing a piece of gum moulded to her bottom molars.

'Feck, I'd never have recognised you.' She closed her mouth and the muscle in the side of her jaw moved rapidly as she chewed her gum, trying to gather herself. 'Ah, well we're all grownups now. Sure, that stuff was all just a bit of fun.' She waved her hand as though dismissing Tessa.

'Yeah, it was a laugh, that's all. We were kids we didn't mean anything by it,' Teresa added.

Rowan nodded and made to move on as she swivelled her head toward each of her friends. 'C'mon, let's get this party started.'

'Fun?' Tessa squared up in front of them.

Rowan looked uncomfortable and very, very small as her eyes darted toward Vicky and then Teresa making sure they were still there, on side.

'Look, it was dumb kids' stuff that's all. Move on.'

'Oh, I have. I've well and truly moved on. But I came here tonight to tell you that you don't matter. None of you matter.' Tessa looked each of them in the eye and as they looked everywhere but at her, she held her gaze steady. 'I turned out pretty darn good despite your best efforts and I just hope if you've got kids or when you do, that they never have to go through what you put me, or Rose here, through.' Then and only then did she step aside and let them scuttle past.

Rose came and stood alongside her, she clapped slowly. 'Well done, you. If I had pom-poms, I'd be waving them about.'

'Thank you. I have to say that felt pretty, bloody amazing and it was long overdue. You know what, Rose? I'm going to go. It was great seeing you again, but I've done what I came here to do.' She gave her old classmate a tight squeeze and then walked out of the gymnasium with her head held high.

Chapter 22

'**Y**ou should have stayed. It's not fair you missing out on a slap-up meal, because I made an eejit of myself,' Moira muttered, although she was glad her friend was by her side. Andrea had her arm linked firmly through hers as they walked down the darkened pavement toward O'Mara's. 'And these bloody shoes are killing me.' She didn't add that she felt as though she'd been slapped. The shock of seeing Michael with his wife hadn't worn off. She doubted she would ever wipe the image of the intimate exchange she'd witnessed between them from her mind. She felt—what did she feel? Angry? Sad? No, not one, not the other, both. She wanted to cry and she wanted to kick something—not that she'd dare to in Aisling's Valentino's.

'Ah, sure it could have happened to anyone,' Andrea soothed, and not for the first time since they'd left The Shelbourne. 'And you'd do the same thing for me. Besides in case you didn't notice I wasn't exactly having the time of my life. It wasn't my idea of fun watching Connor and the accountant getting up close and personal.'

Oh yes, the beautiful accountant. She'd forgotten about her. Poor Andrea. And she was right, she would do the same for her but she wasn't mollified. 'It didn't happen to anyone though did it? It happened to me.' Moira had felt like Cinderella arriving at the party earlier and she'd behaved exactly like Cinderella in the end too, fleeing the ball. In her version of the fairy tale, however, Prince Charming hadn't come running after her. Oh, no, he'd stayed at the party with his wife. He'd shown her precisely where his loyalties lay. The bastard hadn't even checked to see if she was alright. She could have hit her head or anything when she passed out for all he knew.

She glanced down. At least she had both the Valentino's on her feet, small mercies and all that, because she didn't fancy having to answer to Aisling if she arrived home missing a shoe.

'How're you feeling now? The fresh air's got to be helping.'

'It is. That will teach me to drink on an empty stomach. I'm absolutely starving now.' That was something that could always be counted on. She might be angry and sad but unlike Michael Daniels, her appetite never let her down.

'Me too. Have you plenty in the cupboards at home or will we order a takeaway?'

'Things were grim last time I checked. Aisling's always after sniffing around Quinn's kitchen these days. I think we might have to get a Chinese.' Her mouth watered at the thought of lemon chicken and she marvelled that she could summon up such enthusiasm at the thought of food despite her heart being broken.

'Fine by me.' Andrea squeezed her arm. 'You know, Moira, it could have been worse. I bet Michael was bricking it when he saw you there because you could have made a scene. You could have outed him as the cheating, lying bastard he is, in front of his wife and colleagues. All you did was faint and you even managed to do that gracefully. I didn't see so much as a flash of knickers as you crumpled to the floor.'

'It's not quite all I did, Andrea. I was sick all down the front of my new dress,' Moira reminded her friend, shooting her a look. She was unsure if she was trying to be funny and make light of the situation. It might be something she'd look back on in ten years' time with a giggle and a, *Do you remember that night I made a holy show of myself at The Shelbourne?* And yes, the look of horror on snooty Mrs Price's face should have been caught on camera. Right now, though, passing out at Posh Mairead's engagement party in front of the senior partners of the firm she worked for, and—oh Jaysus, the shame of it—throwing up down the front of her dress when she came to, was not in the least bit humorous.

It had all been too much. The pre-loading party fizz getting ready and the classy bubbles at the party with nothing to bounce off except a solitary canapé. Then she'd seen Michael and his wife. The look they'd shared flashed before her and she felt scalded by the memory of it. She'd felt like a voyeur as she gawped over at the entrance where they were standing. It was such an intimate exchange and there'd been nothing about it that suggested they were a couple who were married in name only. If that were the case then they deserved a flipping Oscar. It had dawned on her then that she'd been played and the room had begun to spin in a twirling mass of golds and browns. She'd felt as if she were in the midst of a washing machine's spin cycle as everything faded to black.

She'd felt such a fool coming around to a sea of concerned faces only to hurl the bubbles she'd been quaffing down her front like a silly little girl who couldn't hold her drink. She was a silly little girl. A stupid, naïve cliché. Thank goodness for Andrea. She'd given Mairead and Niall their apologies, blaming a dodgy imaginary egg sandwich she'd had for lunch on her being unwell, before hustling her out the door. Could you even get food poisoning from an egg sandwich? she wondered. As for Michael, feck him. It was his fault she'd been necking the champers in the first place. Alright, he hadn't literally forced it down her throat but the jangling anticipatory nerves she'd felt waiting for him to arrive had been a good incentive. It was an incident she had no wish to take any personal responsibility for whatsoever.

A taxi was pulling up outside O'Mara's as they approached and Moira checked to see her coat was buttoned up. She didn't want any of the guests seeing the mess down the front of her dress. The door of the cab opened and out climbed a woman who she recognised as Tessa Delaney, their Kiwi guest. She heard her thanking the driver before closing the door and taking the few short steps to the guesthouse entrance.

'Isn't that yer woman we met in the hairdressers at lunchtime?' Andrea asked. 'I thought she had a school reunion to go to?'

'She did,' Moira answered non-committally. She'd enjoyed her chat with Tessa at lunchtime but was hoping she wouldn't look their way now. She wasn't in the mood to make small talk with anyone, even if she was a little curious as to why her evening appeared to have been cut short too.

'I liked her, she seemed fun,' said Andrea, and before Moira could stop her, she called out. 'Hello, there!'

Tessa's hand was on the door knob and she dropped it seeing Moira and Andrea making their way toward her. 'Hi,' she smiled at them. 'You're not back from your engagement party already are you?'

She looked different Moira thought on closer inspection, and it wasn't because she was all dolled up. It was something else, her eyes maybe? Whatever it was, she was too hungry to analyse it further.

'We could say the same about you. Your reunion can't have been much of a knees up. It's not even nine o'clock yet.'

'I'd caught up with the people I wanted to see and couldn't see the point in hanging around. Your turn.'

Andrea glanced at Moira who threatened her with a black look. It didn't deter her. She put her hand up to her mouth as though whispering a secret. 'She had a little whoopsie and we had to leave, quick smart.'

Tessa nodded in understanding although she hadn't a clue what a whoopsie was. A drink or food spillage, perhaps? And speaking of food she was ravenous. Suddenly the thought of going back to her empty room to order something in seemed very unappealing. 'Listen if you two haven't eaten yet do you fancy heading out for a bite. You said yourselves it's only nine o'clock.'

'We were going to order a Chinese but sure, look at us, we're all dressed up. It would be a shame not to make the most of it. Though my hair's probably doing a Shirley Temple with this drizzle.' Moira felt like kicking Andrea.

'It looks lovely.'

Andrea flashed Tessa a grateful grin, 'And Moira here would have to get changed obviously.'

She couldn't be arsed arguing and she did not want to be left to her own devices, wallowing in an empty apartment while stuffing her face on Lemon Chicken. 'C'mon then you two, get inside. You can wait for me in reception, I'll only be a tick.'

Tessa opened the door and they bundled in. Nina looked up from her filing.

'Hi, Nina,' Moira said, rubbing her hands at being back in the warmth.

'You're back so early!' Nina shook her head. 'In Spain, the party does not start until at least ten o'clock.'

'We're not stopping. I'm just racing upstairs to change my dress; I had a little spillage.'

'Your beautiful dress, you can—how you say?' she mimed wiping at it.

'Sponge it?'

'Yes, sponge it.'

'I hope so, Nina.' Actually, she thought, she never wanted to see this dress ever again after tonight. She wouldn't be sponging it or, or getting it dry-cleaned, she'd be balling it up and binning it.

Tessa shrugged out of her coat revealing an eye-catching coral dress. 'It's lovely and warm in here,' she said, picking up one of Quinn's brochures from the rack and waving it. 'I'd planned on going here for dinner with my friend Saoirse before the reunion. It sounds great.'

'Quinn's?'

'Mmm.'

'It is but I'm biased. Quinn and my sister are doing the wild thing.' Moira looked up the stairs, 'Hopefully not as we speak.' She'd be sure to knock loudly on the door before entering the apartment. It wasn't likely they'd be there, not with Saturday being the restaurant's busiest night but Aisling had thought she was out for the evening. Jaysus the sight of the pair them swinging naked from the rafters would finish her off. She couldn't be doing with that on an empty tummy.

'She's not biased, Quinn's is well worth a visit,' Andrea said, taking her coat off and sitting down on the sofa to wait while Moira sorted herself out. 'The food's gorgeous and the craic's always great. I say Quinn's it is.'

Tessa looked at Moira who had her hand on the banister. 'What do you think? Does it get your vote too?'

Moira nodded, and as she took to the stairs she called down, 'But if Aisling's there and asks any awkward questions as to why we're not living it up at the Shelbourne, you're both to lie and say it was full of boring old farts.' It was a half-truth at least, she thought.

Chapter 23

♥

The foot-stamping beat of traditional Irish music could be heard and a warm glow was visible through the windows of Quinn's as they approached the bistro. It beckoned the trio in. They'd had no choice but to walk around the block to the restaurant as the wait for a taxi was ridiculous. It wouldn't do them any harm they decided, rugging back up in their coats once more, before setting forth. Moira and Andrea had long since given up on their hair anyway. The persistent misty rain had already done its worst and Tessa couldn't care less what she looked like. She felt very free and easy. A load she'd been carrying around for an awfully long time had been lifted tonight.

'I hope we can get a table,' Tessa said, frowning. They didn't have a reservation after all.

'Oh, don't worry about that, Alasdair will make room for us even if they're fully booked.'

Tessa was reassured by the confident tone as Moira pushed the door open.

Alasdair's greeting as the three women barrelled in the door was effusive. He came out from behind the counter where he'd been scanning the reservation book and made a beeline for Moira. A kiss was planted on both her cheeks before he took a step back, a delicate hand rising to rest on his chest.

'Moira O'Mara, I do declare, be still my beating heart. Two O'Mara women under the same roof.'

Aisling was here then, Moira registered as Alasdair carried on. He was only just warming up. 'What have we done to deserve to be graced by the presence of the two most beautiful girls in Dublin town, tonight?'

He missed his calling, he really should have been on the stage Moira thought, watching as his eyes fluttered briefly shut. He held on to the counter as though fearful he might swoon and then fixed her with a wide-open gaze. 'I'm remembering a time when it was you and I against the world, Moira. I was a poor, struggling writer, you my American bride. We lived in a Paris apartment and survived on nothing but love. I worked on my masterpiece during the day while you kept house. Come the night time we attended intimate soirées with other artistic souls where we partook of intellectual discussions and enjoyed a tipple or two.'

Moira giggled while Andrea jostled her from behind, eager for her turn to hear what she and Alasdair had done in a past life together. It was always the highlight of a visit to Quinn's. Tessa stared goggle-eyed at the maître de who was parodying Hemingway. She was unsure what to make of him. Was he bonkers? By the time he'd clicked his fingers and asked the waiter, Tom, to seat their very special guests at the best table in the house, he'd won her over. Who knew she'd once been Mata Hari and he a handsome Russian pilot?

The three women followed Tom as he deftly ducked around the seated guests to a table in the corner. It was indeed a good spot, Tessa thought. It afforded them a good view of the cosy space which was heaving with happy looking diners chatting over the music. Once they were seated, Tom handed them each a menu before spieling off the specials of the day. They smiled their thanks as he told them he'd check back with them in a few minutes once they'd had a chance to look through the menu.

Tessa opened her menu, she'd check it out in a moment knowing tonight, for the first time in a very long while, she was going to order whatever she wanted. Her days of calorie counting were over. Her days of self-doubt were over. For now though, she looked over the top of the glossy card to the musicians seated on the slightly raised stage area. There was a grisly looking man with a Father Christmas beard playing the accordion, his foot tapping along to the beat. A younger, serious-looking man was perched on a stool next to him. He had enormous owl glasses and was earnestly blowing into his flute. Tessa watched the woman on the fiddle for a few beats, marvelling over the speed with which her bow was skimming over the strings. She'd have loved to have played an instrument, but she didn't have a musical bone in her body. Her eyes took in the rest of their surroundings; the exposed brick wall, roaring fire, and heavy ceiling beams, gave the bistro a rustic and homely feel. She loved it.

'What do you think?' Moira asked.

'Wow. I mean, I love New Zealand. It's home, but when I come somewhere like this—,' she cast around for the right words and Moira jumped in laughing, 'I meant what do you think of the menu. I'm thinking the smoked salmon on soda bread for a starter and I liked the sound of the special of the day, the Beef and Guinness stew for a main.' It was the mashed potatoes it was served with that had swayed her toward it. A big mound of fluffy, buttery, mashed potatoes was the best sort of comfort food.

'Oh, I see.' Tessa laughed. 'This place is pretty cool though. We have a lot of good stuff going on at home, but we don't have this.'

'What? Restaurants?'

Tessa laughed again and Andrea elbowed Moira, 'You're an eejit sometimes.'

'The sense of tradition and history. We're a young country. I get the same shivers that music being played now is giving me when I walk in the door of O'Mara's. There's this sense of lives having been lived; stories having been played out within its walls. We don't have that. Well, not to the same degree, anyway.'

'Tessa, that's just a very romantic way of saying we have a lot of old shite in this country,' Moira laughed. Although as she looked around, seeing Quinn's through Tessa's eyes, she felt a sense of pride. The atmosphere *was* buzzing and the ambience just right. It wasn't down to luck either, she knew how hard Quinn had worked for this bistro. This place was his dream. O'Mara's had been her parents dream and they'd set about modernising the amenities while keeping the charm of a bygone era, and they'd brought the struggling guesthouse into the twenty-first century and turned it into a successful family business. It would be nice to have a dream, a passion she felt strongly about. Something other than Michael. It dawned on her; she didn't have any real interests. She'd loved art, but that was back in her schooldays and it had been so long since she picked up a pad and pencil to do anything other than write down messages at work.

Tessa grinned at her. 'Seriously though, how long has the guesthouse been in your family?'

The history of the house she'd grown up in was a story Moira knew well. 'Oh, it's been part of our family for a long time, ever since it was built back in the Georgian era. It was my grandparents who converted it into a guesthouse. With the building's high maintenance costs, it had to start paying its way, or it was going to go rack and ruin, and it's been a family business ever since.'

'You've lived there your whole life then?'

She nodded.

'It must be lovely to have that connection with a building.'

She supposed she was lucky, even if she didn't feel it at times. It was easy to take the things around you for granted.

She shrugged, 'Its home.' All this talk of home reminded her that Aisling was lurking about the place somewhere. She scanned the tables but couldn't see her sitting at any. She must be out the back in the kitchen distracting Quinn from his work, she surmised. Perhaps she wouldn't spot Moira, Andrea, and Tessa tucked away in their corner table setting. She hoped so, she'd be spared having to embellish the night's events then. She crossed her fingers under the table. Aisling was hawk-eyed when it came to her younger sister's activities. She never managed to get much past her. Sure, look at the way she'd known about her borrowing the Louboutin's? There was no way she was telling her that Michael had fronted up to the party with his wife in tow. She'd be liable to march on over to The Shelbourne to sort him out.

'What's everyone thinking of ordering to drink? Shall we share a bottle of wine?' Andrea looked up from the drinks' menu. She turned to Moira, 'Sorry, you probably don't feel like it after earlier. I didn't think.'

Moira waved the comment away. She wasn't missing out. 'Ah, sure I'm grand, or I will be once I get some food into me. Tessa, are you a red or a white girl?'

They agreed on a bottle of the house red and when Tom appeared a few minutes later, they placed their drink order. Moira followed Tom as he made his way over to the bar. He was a bit of a fine thing. Not in the silver fox way Michael was, mind you, he was too young to qualify for that status.

She wondered what he did with himself when he wasn't working nights at Quinn's. A student maybe? He looked a couple of years younger than her so it would make sense for him to be doing shifts at Quinn's to pay his way through uni. That shirt didn't quite sit right on him she thought, even if he did fill it out nicely. It was just that he looked like he'd be more at ease in a singlet with a surfboard tucked under his arm or, better yet, no singlet and a surfboard under his arm. It was down to the honey colour of his skin, and hair that was a cross between blond and brown knotted back in a ponytail at the nape of his neck. He had a cute bum too she noticed before glancing away. Feck Michael Daniels, Moira thought, feeling a surge of righteous anger. He might have strung her along but there were plenty more fish in the sea.

Chapter 24

'Jaysus, Moira, have you no shame? The poor boy didn't know where to put himself. If you'd given him any more of an eyeful, he would have been inside your bra,' Andrea muttered over the top of her wine glass.

'He's not a boy. He's well and truly over the age of consent.' Moira was unrepentant.

Andrea recognised her mood; she was going to be trouble tonight.

Tessa looked bemused. Moira had laid it on rather thick when their waiter, Tom, had come back with an open bottle of red. She'd made a big show of sampling the small amount he poured in her glass for her approval, before holding her glass out for more. She'd managed to convey, without actually saying so, that she really did want more, and if he was up for more, then so was she. The poor chap had been terribly flustered she thought, her eyes flicking to the stain on the cloth where he'd managed to spill a few drops thanks to his shaking hand.

'I know how you operate, Moira O'Mara, and copping off with him won't make you feel any better about Michael.'

'It might.' Moira took a greedy slurp of her wine. It certainly couldn't make her feel any worse than she did right now. At least the acid burn left in her tummy by the bubbles had dissipated. 'And, I didn't do anything. I just wanted to make sure he poured me a decent glass.' She turned to Tessa, 'I can't be doing with miserly measures.'

That much was obvious Tessa thought, watching her swig the full glass. She'd lost the thread of the conversation and asked, 'Who's Michael?' She watched the two friends exchange a look. 'You can tell me to mind my own business if you want.'

Moira spoke up, 'No, it's fine. We're talking about Michael Daniels. He's the feckiest, fecker to ever walk the planet.'

'Ah, right. He's the whoopsie then?'

'The what?'

Tessa looked to Andrea for assistance. 'You said Moira had had a whoopsie earlier and that's why you left the party early.'

'Oh, well, what I meant was she passed out and then she threw up down the front of her dress when she came round.'

'I see. I think I'd make a get-away too.'

'It was Michael's fault.' Moira defended herself. 'In a round-about way.'

'So, this feckiest, fecker, he's your ex, right?'

Andrea jumped in. 'Kind of.'

Tessa raised a quizzical brow. Now, she really was confused.

'He told me he was falling in love with me, Andrea. I think that makes him my ex.'

'I know, but he wasn't free to tell you that, now was he?'

'Life's not always black and white.' It was a phrase that had been thrown at her by her sister but it was true. There were times when feelings overrode common sense or what was right and what was wrong.

Tessa was at risk of a neck injury so fast was her head swivelling back and forth as she tried to make sense of what the pair of them were talking about.

'He told me the marriage was in name only and they lived under the same roof for the sake of their kids.'

'It didn't look like that tonight.'

Andrea was right and Moira couldn't think of a comeback. She carried on knocking back her wine.

'And,' Andrea continued, 'he wouldn't be the first man to trot that line out. Michael Daniels wants his cake and he wants to eat it too. I told you that.'

'Andrea Reilly, don't you dare tell me I told you so.'

Andrea pursed her lips for a moment, before turning to Tessa, 'I did tell her so.'

Moira glared at her.

Tessa was busy digesting the conversation. Moira, she was piecing together, had been seeing a married man. She wouldn't have thought it of her. She came across as having a toughness about her as though she had street smarts and knew her way about the world. She would've given her more kudos than to fall for a married man and especially not to have swallowed the age-old lines he'd trotted out.

'For the record, I didn't sleep with him, Tessa. It wasn't about the sex for me.' Moira didn't want their new friend thinking badly of her.

Andrea snorted. 'Don't believe a word of it. He's gorgeous, Tessa. I'm talking drop dead. Of course, it was about sex.'

'Alright, yes, he is sexy as hell and I did want to ride him. I'd have ridden him all the way to Belfast and back if the opportunity had arisen but it didn't and obviously after tonight, I'm glad it didn't. It was deeper than the physical stuff though. I liked the way he made me feel about myself—like I was worth cherishing. The only other man that ever made me feel special like that was my daddy.' Her eyes burned and she stared hard at her wine glass, willing the tears away.

Andrea rested a hand on her friend's forearm and Tessa wondered how it was someone as beautiful and seemingly self-assured as Moira could be so insecure. You never could tell what was going on beneath the surface; she of all people knew that. She'd never told anyone how Rowan, Vicky, and Teresa had made her feel. She'd been ashamed at how she'd allowed a stupid, cruel name from her childhood to be imprinted on her psyche. For so many years she'd worn that name like a tattoo she hated but wasn't brave enough to get lasered off. Seeing the three of them tonight had given her a perspective she'd lost by moving to New Zealand. In her mind, they'd loomed large and menacing in the background of her day-to-day life. She'd never had the opportunity to work through her fear and stand up to them. To see them for what they were. A pathetic, small group of girls with little lives, who took pleasure out of belittling others.

Tom interrupted her train of thought as he appeared to take their order. He was like a moth to the flame with Moira. Tessa watched in amusement as he hovered next to her while she ordered her starter and main. How Moira managed to make soda bread sound like an inuendo was truly a thing of wonder she mused, her amusement turning to annoyance that he might forget to ask herself and Andrea what they fancied, so enamoured was he by her order of Beef and Guinness stew. By rights, he should have asked them first because it was obvious what Moira fancied and by the way the young waiter was puffing up like a peacock, it was definitely on the menu. He turned his attention reluctantly away from Moira and her query as to whether the stew was 'hot'? He was too well trained to forget the other guests sitting at the table and with their orders hastily jotted on his pad, he headed off to the kitchen. Hopefully to cool down, Tessa thought.

Once he was out of earshot, she spoke up. 'So, I take it this Michael showed up at the engagement party tonight with his wife and you weren't expecting her to be with him. Is that what happened?'

Moira nodded. 'I went to so much trouble to look my best. I wanted to wow him. I wanted to look like the kind of woman he wanted on his arm when he walked into functions. Stupid, huh?'

Tessa shrugged, 'We've all done our fair share of being stupid when it comes to men, or at least I have.'

'Me, too.' Andrea agreed.

'It's just that I never thought she'd be with him. I know, you tried to warn me, Andrea, but I honestly took him at his word. I thought leading separate lives meant just that. I s'pose I believed what I wanted to believe.'

'What *he* wanted you to believe,' Andrea interjected.

'He didn't know I'd be there and when he saw me, he looked right through me. It was really confronting that's when I lost it.' She rubbed her temples. 'I think I will be cringing at the memory of my performance at Mairead's engagement party for a very long time.'

'We'll stick to our story. It was food poisoning. Sure, it will all be grand,' Andrea soothed. 'Remember he's at fault too, don't put it all on yourself.'

Moira managed a grateful smile, her earlier irritation at her friend dispersing. She'd only been serving up a few home truths because she didn't want her getting hurt. It was a pity she hadn't listened to Andrea in the first place. Now it was too late.

'It probably doesn't feel like it now, Moira,' Andrea continued. 'But I think you've had a lucky escape. Imagine if you'd slept with him? And his wife found out about it. Affairs always have a way of coming to light. You know who'd get their marching orders at work if Adelaide Daniels was to have a quiet word in Fusty Pants Price's ears, don't you? Because I can tell you right now, it wouldn't be her husband.'

'Adelaide?' Tessa piped up.

'I know,' Moira said.

'And imagine if his children had spotted the two of you together. How would that make you feel?'

'Ugly.' She didn't want to be the other woman. It was not a role she'd ever thought she would play. She didn't want to feel the way she did about Michael, but it was all beyond her control. It had been from the moment she'd seen him. So, while Andrea was right, there was nothing she could say that was going to make her feel any better. She did not feel like she'd had a lucky escape. She was in pain. She wished she was a child again so Mammy could kiss the hurt better before sticking a plaster on it and magically making everything alright. The pain she was in was very much an adult one though and she'd immerse herself in it tomorrow. For now, she planned on enjoying her meal and sinking enough red wine to anaesthetise any emotion. And she'd had quite enough of talking about Michael.

Chapter 25

'Hello, there.' Aisling appeared at their table seemingly from thin air. 'I was in the kitchen helping Quinn. Alasdair sent word you were here,' she explained, shooting Moira a quizzical look, 'I thought you had the posh engagement party tonight?'

Andrea leaped in. 'Oh, we did.' She gave a casual wave of her hand. 'It wasn't much craic though. They were all stuffed shirts so we left and when we got back to O'Mara's we bumped into Tessa here.'

Tessa lifted her hand in acknowledgment. 'I'd been to a high school reunion which wasn't up to much either so I left early.'

'Oh, what school?' Aisling was curious, still convinced there was more to this girl than met the eye.

'St Mary's.'

'Ah, I was a St Teresa's girl.'

Tessa smiled and nodded.

'Anyway,' Andrea carried on, 'It was far too early to call it a night and Tessa fancied trying Quinn's.' She shrugged, 'So here we are.'

The story seemed to sit well with enough with Aisling but if Moira thought she'd gotten off scot free she was mistaken. 'I thought this party was a big deal because yer man, Michael was going to be there?'

'I never said that.'

'You didn't have to.'

'Well, he wasn't there if you must know. He's poorly.' She couldn't look her sister in the eye. Moira did not lie and she had just told two of them.

'That's a shame, what with you pulling out all the stops.' She checked out Moira's silky handkerchief top. 'What happened to the gorgeous cerise dress you were going to wear?'

Moira half expected her to look under the table to see if she still had the Valentino's on.

Nobody did the Spanish Inquisition quite like Aisling. 'I feel like I'm on Prime Suspect and you're that Tennyson character. I did wear it for your information, but I dropped a blob of crème fraîche from one of the canapés down the front so I got changed before we came here. Your shoes are back in your wardrobe in case you were wondering.' Moira glared at her sister, not liking all the stories she was making her tell. She had turned into a regular Pinocchio.

Aisling eyed her speculatively for a moment before deciding to let it drop. 'Grand. I'm staying at Quinn's tonight but I'll be back in the morning and don't forget about tomorrow afternoon.'

Moira had no idea what Aisling was on about and her sister reading her expression, rolled her eyes. 'Mammy. She's picking us up at half past twelve. We're going to Powerscourt for afternoon tea remember?' She shook her head exasperatedly.

'Of course, yeah, I hadn't forgotten.' With everything that had happened, she had forgotten. 'Don't *you* forget to tell her she's a mad woman booking this trip of hers to Vietnam.'

Aisling shook her head, her hair dancing under the light like flames. 'I don't fancy an ear bashing over my petit fours thanks very much.'

Tom brought the end to that conversation as he appeared with a starter balanced on the palm of both hands.

'Right, I'll leave you to it. Enjoy your meal.' Aisling smiled at Andrea and Tessa before mouthing, *Don't forget tomorrow* at Moira.

Moira was too busy looking up from under her lashes at Tom to pay her sister any mind. He leaned over her to place her appetiser down and she felt his breath, warm on her neck. 'Could we have another bottle please, Tom?' she simpered, waving the empty red as he deposited Andrea's crispy-skinned chicken wings.

'Sure thing.' He locked eyes with her for a tension-filled beat, only breaking away when Tessa coughed. A deliberate move on her part to get him moving.

Moira managed to hold off tucking in while they waited for Tessa's starter to arrive. 'So,' she said averting her eyes from the slivers of smoked salmon, 'Tell us about the reunion, then.'

'Oh, it's a long story. And don't wait for me,' Tessa said gesturing to their plates.

Moira didn't wait for her to tell her twice and she began to eat as though she'd just completed the forty-hour famine. Despite her mouthful she managed to mumble, 'We're not going anywhere. So, talk.'

Tom returned with Tessa's bowl of scampi before taking himself off to the bar to procure another bottle of the house red.

'I used to love scampi when I was a kid. Whenever we ate out, Mum and Dad didn't have to ask what I was having.' Tessa avoided the subject of the reunion as she picked up one of the plump, breaded Dublin Bay prawns and dunked it in the thick, creamy tartare sauce. She popped it in her mouth flapping her hand at how hot it was. It seemed right that she order her childhood favourite given how she'd revisited her past tonight. She saw Tom making his way toward them with the wine and while he refilled their glasses she looked from Moira to Andrea. She didn't know either of them very well but what she did know she liked. Moira had been open and honest with her, so she'd return the favour. She waited until Tom had gone, having been beckoned over to a table near the windows by an older couple, before she began to talk.

'You asked me about the reunion?'

Moira nodded.

'Well, I only went because I wanted to show three women, who made my thirteenth year a complete misery, that I turned out alright, despite them. I hated every moment of my time at St Mary's because of them. Rowan—she was the worst—Teresa, and Vicky used to wait for me by the gates every afternoon. They'd follow me home, throwing stones and calling me names. I lived in terror of them.' She surprised herself with how matter of fact she sounded about it and not wanting her scampi to get cold, she paused to snaffle a prawn. Moira's mouth, she saw with amusement, was agape and she'd yet to wipe away the breadcrumbs stuck to her lips. Andrea meanwhile had frozen with a chicken wing raised halfway to her mouth.

'Ten Tonne Tessie, that was what they called me.' She wondered if they'd think her ridiculous holding onto something like that for so many years. It sounded a ridiculous name when she said it out loud. 'It probably sounds funny now, such a stupidly childish thing to taunt someone with, but I could never laugh it off.'

'No, it doesn't sound funny at all,' Moira said, and seeing Andrea tap her lip picked up the napkin and wiped her mouth.

'I used to get teased something rotten about my nose,' Andrea said.

'What's wrong with your nose?' Tessa eyed it, failing to find any anomalies.

'There's nothing wrong with her nose, it's all in her head,' Moira spoke up.

'Moira, you've no idea, you're stunning. Do you know, Tessa, she once got asked for her autograph, this woman and her daughter thought she was Demi Moore.'

'You do have a look of her about you.'

Moira was non-plussed it didn't mean anything. What she looked like was irrelevant. It didn't stop her from hurting just like everybody else.

'And that's what Tessa's getting at I think, isn't it?' Andrea said. 'Words, when you're young and have one hundred and one insecurities anyway, can be hard to unhear. Especially when they're constantly thrown at you. They get inside your head and when you look in the mirror, they're all you hear and all you see.'

'Exactly,' Tessa said. 'And there is nothing wrong with your nose by the way. It is a perfectly respectable nose.'

'And you're hardly a Ten Tonne Tessie.'

'Not now I'm not. I was chubby when I was younger though, not that I'm excusing them their behaviour. I lost my puppy fat before we emigrated to New Zealand. I left that girl here in Dublin. Or, at least I thought I did. It took me years of self-doubt to realise it was never about the weight, it was about how they'd made me feel about myself. Tonight, fronting up to them, it dawned on me that I don't have to prove anything to anyone. I'm me, big, small, whatever, and I finally think that person is pretty cool. That all sounds very deep doesn't it?'

'A little yes,' Andrea said.

'Well, on a not so deep note. It also felt damned good to rub those three bitches' noses in it tonight.'

They all laughed.

'I'd have liked to have been a fly on the wall for that,' Moira said, and Andrea agreed. 'Did you say anything to them about the way they behaved back then and how it affected you?'

Tessa repeated what she'd said, and Moira and Andrea clapped just as Rose had done earlier.

'Serves them right, nasty cows.'

'You know, seeing them tonight, I couldn't believe that I'd let those three pathetic women with their cheap perfume, shiny dresses, and awful gum-chewing habits, affect me for as long as they have. Well, no more. I shut the door on them once and for all.'

'Good for you.' Moira raised her glass and they clinked.

They all had stuff going on beneath the surface, Moira thought, feeling her throat constrict as she thought of Michael.

Chapter 26

♥

By the time the threesome's mains had been cleared away, they'd put the world to rights. They'd also sunk enough to wine to keep the grape growers in Bordeaux in business for a year. A crowd was bopping to the music, which had gotten decidedly jiggy, in front of the stage area, and Andrea suggested they work their dinner off by joining in. A scraping of chairs later they stood up, before ducking and diving around the tables to join in. Aisling who'd poked her head out the kitchen was watching the dance floor shenanigans with a smile as she clapped along. She gave them a wave and Moira beckoned her over. Her face lit up and she made her way over to join them. 'I can never stand still when these guys really get going,' she grinned.

Tessa looked at her shoes, 'You deserve a medal for being able to dance in those. Prada?'

Aisling nodded, 'Years of practice.'

'They're gorgeous. I have shoe envy,' Tessa shouted back.

The tempo was contagious and they found themselves with their arms draped over one another's shoulders as they kicked their legs up. It wasn't clear whether they were attempting Irish or Greek dancing as they got jostled by other enthusiastic patrons. Whatever it was, it was fun and they were all laughing. Moira kept a watchful eye on Tom. He was working the bar and, after a few songs, she disentangled herself announcing all that jumping up and down had made her need a wee.

She went to the loo and after she'd washed and dried her hands, paused to inspect herself in the mirror. Did being heartbroken make you look different? Her eyes looked a little bloodshot and a tad puffy, but that was probably down to the wine. Her mouth too she saw, the longer she stood there staring at herself, had a downward tilt. It was a funny thing how when you looked at yourself, really looked at yourself, you became almost unrecognisable. Your features broke down into individual segments like a jigsaw puzzle. She pulled her facial muscles up until she was grinning. Her teeth had a purple tinge to them and she ran her tongue over them before rubbing her index finger back and forth in a futile effort.

Bloody red wine. It might have stained her teeth, but it had also made her bold. What was Michael doing now? A knife-like pain twisted in her stomach. Was he home from the party and, buoyed from a successful night's networking, making love to his wife with a passion, Moira had thought was reserved for her? The thought sickened her.

The door opened and she stepped away from the mirror as two women crowded in, giggling. She'd do and, pushing past them, she felt the noise of the humming restaurant wash over her as she re-entered the crowded space. Tom was still at the bar and she honed in on him.

He nearly dropped the bottle he'd just taken from the fridge as he turned and saw Moira draping herself across the bar.

'What time do you finish?' She wasn't going to beat around the bush.

'One. Why're you asking?' A playful glint lit his eyes. Blue like Michael's she noticed but wider, more innocent. She licked her lips. Feck you, Michael, feck you.

'I'll wait until one thirty for you in the foyer of O'Mara's, the guesthouse across the road from St Stephen's Green. Do you know it?'

He nodded, momentarily chastened by the reminder this was his boss's girlfriend's sister but simultaneously not quite believing his luck. Tom had never been one to look a gift horse in the mouth.

'If you're not there by then I'll take it you're not interested.' She moved off, not quite believing she'd just said what she'd said. She'd sounded like a brazen hussy. She was behaving like a brazen hussy but she was spared further analysis as Andrea dragged her back into the throng.

elle

It was Tessa who gave up the ghost first, announcing her feet hurt and she was shattered. It was after twelve Moira noted. She looked around and spied Tom, clearing the tables. He caught her eye and gave her a mischievous grin. It told her odds were he was going to take her up on her offer. He was definitely a fine thing, but still, what on earth did she think she was doing? Before she could delve any deeper, she felt Aisling squeeze her arm. 'I'll see you tomorrow.' Aisling turned to the other two. 'Thanks girls, that was great fun.' She gave them both a brief goodnight hug and trotted off to find Quinn.

The trio gathered up their things and made their way over to the entrance to Alasdair. He tallied up the bill and presented it with a flourish. Moira and Andrea peered over Tessa's shoulder and both tried not to gasp. Moira knew her friend would be thinking exactly the same thing she was. The evening would bankrupt them but it had been worth it.

'This is my treat, girls,' Tessa said, placing her bank card on the wallet and handing it back to Alasdair. They protested and made a show of opening their purses but Tessa was adamant. 'I've had a brilliant time. It's my treat.'

'Settled?' Alasdair asked, 'Or will we be having fisticuffs?'

Tessa grinned and nodded, 'No, it's settled.'

'Thank goodness for that.' He set about swiping the card while the two girls thanked her.

He handed the piece of plastic along with the receipt back to her a second later. 'You fabulous females will be wanting a taxi, I assume?'

'Yes, well Andrea will. Tessa and I can walk but we'll wait with her at the rank down the road.'

'No, no, no. I've a friend, he'll drop you all home.' He tapped the side of his nose. 'Let me make a quick phone call. I'm not having you waiting around at a rank or walking home on a night like this.'

True to his word a yellow and green taxi pulled up outside the restaurant ten minutes later. Alasdair herded them out after making them promise to come back and see him soon. He stood on the pavement blowing kisses until the cab had indicated and pulled away.

Chapter 27

♥

Not wanting to leave Andrea to travel alone, they agreed
to drop her home first, and as the taxi swung back in
the direction of O'Mara's, Moira asked Tessa what her plans
were for the rest of her time in Ireland.

'I've ten more days here, so I thought I'd head south. My
friend, Saoirse, who lives in Galway, wants me to go and stay
with her and her family so that will be my first port of call after
I check out tomorrow. Then, I'd like to hire a car and explore.
I've never been to Kerry, so that's definitely on the itinerary,
and I want to kiss the Blarney Stone, do something properly
touristy.'

'You're not really a tourist, though are you? I mean you were
born here that makes you Irish.'

'It does, yes, but I fancy being blessed with the gift of the
gab, so the Blarney Stone it is.'

'Fair enough. I got carsick all around the Ring of Kerry,'
Moira lamented, recalling a rare family holiday from O'Mara's.
They'd all been jammed in the back of the rusty old Beemer,
Daddy at the wheel. Mammy had been driving him mad in the
passenger seat with her habit of pretend braking with her right
foot whenever she thought he was teasing the wrong side of
the speed limit. The icing on the cake had been her throwing
up all over poor Roisin. 'The scenery from what I remember

was lovely, though in a wild, rugged sort of way,' she quickly added, not wanting to put a dampener on Tessa's plans.

Alasdair's contact in the cab world, whose name was Big Jes, an anomaly given his small stature behind the wheel, chimed into the conversation. He told them a no-holds-barred tale of a wild night he'd spent in Killarney on the edge of the Ring of Kerry. By the time he pulled up outside O'Mara's both Tessa and Moira were shell-shocked by his candid sharing. Moira insisted on covering the fare, it was only fair with Tessa having picked up the dinner tab and she hastily handed it over, keen for the off.

'Well, that was interesting,' Tessa said as Big Jes drove off and Moira punched in the afterhours code which would let them in.

'I'll say,' Moira said, hearing the click that signalled the door was unlocked. She opened the door and stepped into the reception area. It was lit by a solitary lamp for late guests and the light pooled weakly across the carpet.

Tessa shut the door behind her and instinctively dropped her voice to a whisper that sounded loud to her ears in the night-time silence. 'Well, thanks again for a brilliant night.'

'*Thank you* for suggesting it. Quinn's was a great idea and much better than being left to drown my sorrows in a Chinese takeaway and whatever wine I could lay my hands on.'

Tessa gave her a quick hug. 'Try to forget him, Moira. You deserve better.'

It was easier said than done and she flashed her new friend an unconvinced smile before asking her what time she'd be away in the morning.

'I'll get the eleven twenty-five train from Heuston to Galway, so I'll leave here around ten thirty.'

'Well, I'll make sure I'm up to see you off.' She followed Tessa past the reception desk. Her room was situated around the corner near the top of the stairs leading to the dining room area and Moira waited until she'd let herself in before taking the stairs. She was mindful of every creak echoing around the sleeping house as she made her way up the three flights to their apartment.

The old grandfather clock told her it was a quarter to one when she flicked the lights on in the living room. The detritus from her and Andrea's party for two that had moved from the bedroom through to the living room was littered about the space. She'd deal with that tomorrow, then realising it *was* tomorrow resolved to clear up later in the morning. She headed into the kitchen. Right now, she needed an Alka-Seltzer and then she'd better tidy herself up a bit.

Once the fizzy antacid was sorting the contents of her stomach, she made for the bathroom. Her legs, she noted were a little unsteady, she had downed a lot of red, but they were keeping her upright and that was the main thing. The smell of hairspray still lingered on the air as she set about brushing her teeth. She wiped a flannel under her eyes to remove smudges of mascara and lastly picked up her hairbrush, running it through her hair before flicking it back off her shoulders. She'd have to do. She ducked into her bedroom and picked up the pile of clean clothes, chucking them in the wardrobe and shutting the door on them before kicking the other flotsam cluttering her floor under her bed. She didn't want him thinking her a total slob the living room was bad enough. The only thing left to do was to turn the main lounge light out. The softer glow of the lamp was much more flattering and she switched it on before leaving the door ajar and creeping back down the stairs.

She felt like a teenager, sneaking about the place the way she was, only this time there was no Mammy waiting to catch her out. Her hand flew to her chest as a sudden burst of coughing emanating from the room closest to the stairs on the second floor erupted and she waited a couple of counts before carrying on down to reception. There was no glimmer of light peeking out from under Tessa's door and she was hoping she'd gone straight to bed. The amount of food and wine they'd poured down their throats should have been enough to tranquilize even the most hardcore of insomniacs. Speaking of which, she stifled a yawn, trying not to think of her own bed for purposes other than rolling around with Tom, and carried on through to reception. She perched on the edge of the sofa in the soft lamplight glow, to wait.

The self-doubt began to creep in as the minutes ticked by and a silent conversation with herself ensued.

'What are you doing, Moira?'

'I'm proving I can ride whoever I like and flipping the birdy at Michael fecking, feckiest, fecker ever Daniels, for lying to me that's what.'

'Do you think it will make you feel better?'

'Did you see the arse on Tom? Of course, it will make me feel better?'

'You ate an awful lot of mashed potatoes and the stew was very rich. Are you sure you're up for all that giddy-upping?'

'I took an Alka-Seltzer remember; sure, I'll be grand.'

The conversation came to close as she heard a tap on the window. Ah, Jaysus, he'd come. She stood up and opened the door before he decided to knock on it. She held her finger to her lips indicating he needed to be quiet and he nodded his understanding. His hands were thrust in the pockets of a bomber jacket and his hair now hung shaggy and loose to his shoulders giving him even more of a surfer-boy look. For the briefest of seconds, she imagined telling him she'd changed her mind. She could close the door on him and walk away but the uncertainty on his face stopped her, and she pulled him inside. She pointed upwards and then turned and made her way up the stairs, hearing them creak behind her.

'This is where you live?' Tom whispered once Moira had closed the door to the apartment behind them. 'It's pretty cool.'

'You don't have to whisper now, and yes, it is.' She felt awkward and suddenly very sober. Was she supposed to just launch straight into things and jump his bones or should she offer him a drink? She couldn't see herself lunging at him. The cocky, assertive woman who'd leaned over the bar an hour ago and invited him to her place seemed to have deserted her as sobriety sank in.

'Do you want a drink?'

'No, I'm grand.'

'Here, let me take your jacket.'

He shrugged out of it and handed it to her. He was still wearing his work shirt she saw taking the jacket from him and trying not to ogle his broad shoulders and chest as she draped it over the back of one of the dining chairs.

'Have you worked at Quinn's long then?'

'Four months, nearly five. I'm into my fourth year at med school. Waiting at Quinn's helps pay the bills.'

'You're studying to be a doctor?' She wouldn't have guessed that, you really couldn't judge a book by its cover. She hadn't realised it had been that long since she'd last been to Quinn's either.

'Yeah, it's all I've ever wanted to be since I was eight years old and broke my leg, I fell out the treehouse. I was in awe of somebody being able to put it back together for me again.' He laughed. 'What about you, what do you do?'

Moira felt the familiar pang of envy she always felt when she met someone who knew what they wanted to be. It always seemed to her people with that kind of focus were always sure of who they wanted to be too. 'I'm a receptionist at Mason Price, they're a solicitor's firm,' she shrugged. 'I don't mind it. It wasn't the dream, but then I never really knew what that was anyway and it keeps me in the style I'm accustomed to which is living with my sister in the house I grew up in.'

He grinned, 'You're funny.'

It was a compliment, and one that made Moira feel good.

Tom chewed his bottom lip for a second as though making his mind up about something. She could almost see him deciding it was now or never as he took a step toward her and pulled her to him. 'You're also bloody gorgeous, do you know that?'

She didn't get a chance to return the compliment before his lips settled on hers. Her mouth opened slightly and his tongue found hers. He was a good kisser and closing her eyes she tried to lose herself in the moment. Michael was a good kisser, too. She felt Tom's hardness against her as his hand crept under the hem of her handkerchief top and her skin tingled where his fingers began caressing the bare skin of her back.

A delicious sensation coursed through her core and she pressed herself against him. She'd done that with Michael too, wanting to take things further but knowing the timing was wrong. His fingers fumbled with the catch on her bra and as it pinged free, she felt reality crash down on her. She couldn't do this. She disengaged herself from his embrace and took a step backwards.

He blinked his eyes, heavy-lidded with drowsy arousal as he registered the look on her face. 'Did I do something wrong?'

'No, you didn't. You were doing everything right. It's me. I'm a fecking eejit, behaving like I'm some sort of femme fatale. I shouldn't have invited you back here, I'm sorry.'

He looked like a child who'd been told Christmas had been cancelled.

'It's a long story, but it's not you.' She felt awful leading him on the way she had. 'Truly it's not. It's just I've been seeing someone and well, he let me down badly tonight.'

'So, you were planning on using my body for revenge sex? Is that it?'

She tucked her hair behind her ear, feeling her face flush with shame, 'That's pretty much it. I'm sorry, Tom, you seem a nice guy. You don't deserve to be treated like that.'

'Listen, I don't have a problem being used, you are more than welcome to treat me like that.' He was so earnest she had to laugh and he grinned back at her.

'Well, I do.' She picked up his jacket and passed it to him. A signal he should leave. She was suddenly exhausted and all she wanted to do was clamber into bed and sleep. He took the jacket and slid back into it. 'Do you want me to call you a taxi?' It was the least she could do. It wouldn't be fair to turf him out on the street at this hour.

'No, you're grand. I don't live far. I can walk. It might help take my mind off things.' He gave his crotch a mournful glance.

'Tom, I really am sorry.'

'So am I. Listen—feck I don't even know your name. I mean I know your Aisling's sister but that's as far as it goes.'

'Moira.'

'Well listen, Moira, whoever it was that let you down tonight, he's the eejit, not you.'

'Thanks.'

He gave her a rueful smile.

'C'mon then you'd better see me out.'

She led him back down the stairs opening the door to the misty night outside. 'Goodnight, Tom. Thanks for being so understanding.'

'Like I said, he's an eejit.' He gave her a smile tinged with regret before shoving his hands back in his pockets and striding off down the street. Moira watched him for a few seconds before closing the door quietly. All she wanted to do was fall into bed and sleep. She locked the door one last time and crept back upstairs.

It was too much effort to wash her face, she'd barely managed to clamber into her pyjamas as it was and pulling back her covers she was all set to dive in when she heard a distant clatter. It was a noise she recognised and she moved to pull back her curtains. She pushed her window up feeling the blast of cold air as she peered down into the inky well of the courtyard. It took a moment for her eyes to adjust but when they did, she could see the shadowy outline of the culprit. It was Foxy Loxy. 'Hello, you. Long time, no see,' she breathed and saw two eyes glowing back at her. She couldn't recall them ever having locked eyes before. He'd always been too intent on his covert mission. 'Remember me?' He flicked his tail and turned away, darting off into the darkness. She didn't know how she'd expected him to, not when she barely remembered who she was herself.

Chapter 28

♥

Moira knocked on Tessa's door. It opened a minute later and Tessa stood there looking fresh and rested for someone who'd seen the wrong side of midnight the night before. On the bed was an open case.

'Good morning, come in. I'm just packing the last of my things.'

Moira did so and flopped down in the tub chair. Tessa looked over, hardly able to believe all that had happened since she'd sat there herself last night, a bundle of insecurities and nerves in a coral dress.

'So, you're off to Galway today then?'

'Yes, I'll be gone a week and a half and then I'm coming back here for a night before I fly to London. From there it's the long-haul home.' She grimaced. She wasn't looking forward to that flight, but it was a means to an end. 'And, Moira, you'll never guess what happened at breakfast.'

'What?'

'I was asked out to dinner.'

'Really, who by?'

'His name's Owen. He's from Waterford, but he's been here in Dublin these last few days on business. I saw him the other morning and thought he looked tasty but I wouldn't have done anything about it. He asked me if he could join me this morning so we could compare notes on whether Mrs Flaherty does the best full Irish in the country. Unfortunately, I couldn't find out because she wasn't cooking this morning.'

'No, Mrs Baicu's on of a weekend. She does a fantastic fry-up by the way, not that I'd ever let on to Mrs Flaherty.'

'I can vouch for that. I had the works.' Tessa had succumbed and placed her order with the skinny woman. She'd been dressed in what looked like a national costume for wherever her strong Eastern European accent hailed from and was as intimidating as Mrs Flaherty. Tessa had been sure to compliment her when she'd banged the plate down in front of her. 'He was so easy to chat to, Moira. I told him I planned on visiting Waterford on my travels and he asked me if I'd have dinner with him when I do.'

'Go you,' Moira smiled.

Tessa paused halfway through folding a sweater. 'And how are you feeling today?'

Moira's head had been thumping that morning and she'd sworn off the red wine for the foreseeable future. She wasn't going to say anything to Tessa about Tom either. When she thought about how she'd behaved, she felt a searing flush of embarrassment. 'I'm a bit rough around the edges, but I've felt worse. I'm going to head downstairs for a Mrs Baicu special myself in a moment—her bacon and eggs are a cure for most things.' She sighed. 'I could do without being mammified this afternoon but on the other hand afternoon tea at Powerscourt is always good and it's her treat.' She wasn't looking forward to having to say sorry for going on the other night with regard to Mammy's trip to Vietnam either but she'd manage it for the sake of the fresh, warm scones with strawberry jam and the scrumptious Chantilly and lemon curd they were served with. She was drooling already.

'I mean about Michael.'

'I know you did, I just opted to pretend otherwise.' They grinned at each other and Moira's phone burned a hole in her pocket. She'd switched it off and left it to charge overnight and this morning when she'd staggered bleary-eyed into the kitchen where she'd plugged it in, she'd seen Michael's name flash up. He'd left voice messages and texted her.

'He's left messages for me, but I haven't listened to or read any of them.'

'Good, don't. You know exactly what they'll say. Delete them, Moira. Come on, do it now while I'm with you.'

Moira pulled her phone reluctantly from her pocket and looked at Tessa.

'You can do it.'

Under Tessa's watchful gaze, she hit delete until his name was wiped from her phone. 'I don't feel any better.'

'You probably won't for a while yet, but you did the right thing.'

'Maybe.'

'Definitely.'

'So, I'll see you in just over a week?'

'You will.'

'Have a fantastic time, don't catch herpes off that old Blarney Stone and try not to think about what Big Jes got up to in Killarney when you reach the Ring of Kerry.'

Tessa laughed. 'I'm glad I've eaten; you'd have put me off breakfast reminding me of that.'

'Oh, and have a super, hot date with your man in Waterford.'

'I'm planning on it.' Tessa winked.

Moira got up then and gave her a squeeze. 'I'm glad I met you.'

'Me too.'

Chapter 29

'Jaysus what is she wearing?' Moira muttered as she came around the front of the red Ford Focus Mammy had replaced the Beemer with not long after Daddy passed. Aisling joined her sister giving their mammy the once over.

'They're fisherman pants, you know the sort people wear in Thailand on their hols. You don't normally team them with a black polo neck and boots though,' Aisling informed her sister. She'd not be holding her hand up to having once worn baggy elephant pants on a Bangkok stopover. 'All she needs now is one of those conical leaf hats and a scooter.'

Moira shook her head. The wide-legged pants might look the part in a tropical climate but on a freezing day beside the South Lough in the Powerscourt Estate's car park, they looked bizarre. 'I'd got only just gotten used to the nautical look.' Since she'd moved to the seaside village of Howth, Mammy had taken to wearing nautical striped tops, white pants, and boat shoes. Moira had never thought she'd say it but they'd at least looked the part.

'I can hear you,' Mammy said as the car bleeped and, satisfied it was locked, she stuffed the keys in her bag before joining her daughters.

The sisters were unabashed. 'Where did you get those pants, Mammy?' Aisling asked. 'They're very ethnic looking, so they are.' She eyed the green and gold swirls on the fabric dubiously.

'Shirley from golf gave them to me when she heard Rosemary and I had booked to fly to Vietnam. She got them on her holidays in Thailand last year.'

Aisling shot Moira an *I told you so look*, before saying, 'Do you not think you might have been better saving them for your trip to Vietnam?'

Mammy suddenly lunged, left leg forward. Moira was reminded of the Warrior pose she'd once done in a yoga class Andrea had dragged her along to. Her favourite pose had been Corpse. It had been great, lying there like she was dead, listening to swishing tides and seagull cries, very relaxing, her kind of exercise. Andrea hadn't wanted to go back though, she said yoga wasn't for her, she was after more of a cardio workout.

'What are you doing?' Aisling asked as they made their way toward the palatial entrance of the hotel.

'I'm showing you why I'm wearing them.'

'Right.' Aisling was bewildered but Moira just shook her head once more—and Mammy had the nerve to say *she* took things too far!

'See, I can do all sorts in them.' She squatted to prove her point.

'Mammy!' Moira hissed, fearful she might demonstrate the Downward Dog next, here in the regal grounds of the Powerscourt Estate. She cast around for CCTV cameras but couldn't spot any.

Mammy was not chastened, although she contented herself with taking giant strides instead of striking any more unusual poses. 'They're the comfiest pants I've ever owned, girls. Although I did manage to get myself into a bit of a tangle trying to do them back up after I'd been for a visit.'

'Jaysus, Mammy, that kind of visual could put a girl off her cakes.'

'Moira, I'd be quiet and quit while I was ahead if I were you or you won't be getting any cakes. You're still in my bad books.'

Moira did as she was told. She kept her mouth zipped all the way to the Sugar Loaf Lounge. The Georgian-styled lounge bar was busy. It was a popular destination with locals and tourists alike, and she was surprised Mammy had managed to secure them a table over by the windows. She relaxed into the mustard upholstered chairs and couldn't help but admire the glorious, albeit overcast view of the rolling Wicklow country-side. 'This is a lovely treat, Mammy, thanks.'

Maureen O'Mara looked appeased. 'So, we'll not be having any more of you carrying on over me booking myself a nice holiday? Because I had a phone call from Roisin asking what I thought I was up to. She told me you put her up to it.'

Moira chewed her lip; her sisters were both tell-tale tits and she still had plenty to say about Mammy's trip but the fight had gone out of her today. She felt like a vacuum-packed bag that had had all the air sucked out of it. 'I shan't say another word.' Today at least she thought watching the staff scurrying back and forth with the three-tiered serving trays piled high with edible works of art. Mammy was chattering on about the plans she and Rosemary had been making for their trip with Aisling commenting in all the right places. She let their voices wash over her as her mind strayed to Michael. She wished she could get that intimate moment she'd seen him and his wife share in the entrance to The Saddleroom out of her head.

The arrival of their afternoon tea was a timely distraction from replaying the scene yet again. It seemed to get worse each time she ran through it. They'd be having a fecking grope in the entrance at this rate she thought, helping herself to a scone. It was deliciously light and fluffy and the dollop of strawberry jam along with the Chantilly and lemon curd that had had her taste buds in an anticipatory tizz earlier was divine. Except, today it wasn't. Today, it tasted dry, like cardboard, and the cream seemed to have a tang as though off. It wasn't the food, it was her because Mammy and Aisling were tucking in, pigs at a trough, making annoying little *mmm* noises, and *is yours good? because mine's lovely* remarks. She put the half-eaten scone back on the plate. It seemed Michael had broken her heart *and* killed her taste buds.

'What's up with you, Moira? It's not like you to let your sister get the rainbow-coloured tiramisu cake.'

She looked over at Aisling who gave her a triumphant smirk. The said cake was on her plate and her fork was raised ready to do its worst. Mammy was right, it wasn't like her. Once she'd even rapped her sister hard over the knuckles with her teaspoon to prevent her from getting it. There was only ever one slice amongst the other delectable bites and if she didn't get it, things could get ugly. It was her favourite, and as such, she wasn't prepared to consider going halves.

'Nothing's wrong. I'm fine.'

Mammy put her fork down and swivelled in her chair to face her youngest daughter before pushing Moira's hair away from her face.

'What're you doing, Mammy, you've Chantilly cream all over your hands, you'll get it in my hair.'

Mammy stared hard at her through narrowed eyes. 'You've not been out doing the binge drinking again have you?'

'Jaysus, Mammy.'

'What? You drink too much, in my opinion, Moira. Every time I see you, you're green around the gills, so you are.'

'I'm not.'

'You are. I remember telling you the last time we went for lunch you looked like your Shrek woman, the Princess Fiona.'

Granted, that had been a particularly big night.

'I think it's man troubles, Mammy,' Aisling piped up, and at the word man, Maureen O'Mara's eyes lit up and she put down the shortbread she'd decided to nibble on next.

Moira glared at her sister and decided she'd pin the poster of Bono she'd had hidden on the shelf at the top of her wardrobe, waiting for the right moment, to Aisling's bedroom door when she got home. Her sister couldn't stand the Irish rocker, and a dose of Bono is what she'd get for landing her in it. It was a close-up shot of him too she thought, with a modicum of short-lived satisfaction, because Mammy was like a dog with a bone when it came to the man subject.

'Have you a man then, Moira?' The hope on her face made it shine and she looked almost angelic. Almost.

'No.'

'She does, or she did. His name's Michael.'

'Shut up, Ash.' Moira got her foot ready because if Aisling mentioned Michael's age, she was going to get a kick under the table.

Mammy looked at Moira questioningly.

'We had a fight,' she said limply. 'It's over.'

'A-ha! I knew it. He wasn't sick at all. You left your posh engagement party early because you'd had a barney.'

'Engagement?'

Moira almost laughed. Aisling had done it now. She'd said the 'e' word. Served her right. Her sister sat back in her chair sensing the error of her ways.

'Shirley from golf who gave me these pants, her daughter, she's younger than the both of you, by the way, is after getting engaged to a lovely young man. Shirley never stops talking about the wedding.' Mammy directed her attention to Aisling. 'How are things progressing with you and Quinn?'

'We're grand,' Aisling replied, feigning great interest in her cake.

Chapter 30

♥

I t was four o'clock by the time Mammy dropped Aisling
and Moira back at O'Mara's. She pulled up outside the
guesthouse and told them she couldn't come in. 'I've joined
the yacht club and there're drinks being held in my honour at
five. I need to get home and get changed.' Her foot was idling
over the accelerator in readiness to take off.

Aisling opened the passenger door with, 'Are you expecting
us to drop and roll, Mammy?'

Moira was guessing the nautical gear would be getting an
airing once she got home. She clambered out the back and
had barely got the door shut before she was gone. A flash of
red disappearing down the road. Her head spun sometimes
she thought, making her way to the door, with the volume of
activities her mammy involved herself in. It was her way of
filling the hole Daddy had left behind in her days, she guessed.
She wished she could do the same, but she wasn't of a mind
to take up golf or join a rambling group and she certainly
wouldn't be seen dead in boat shoes. She heard her phone
bleep the arrival of another message from somewhere in the
depths of her bag and gritted her teeth. If it was from Michael,
she didn't know if she'd be strong enough to ignore it this time
around. She pushed open the door, Aisling close behind her
and ventured inside.

Evie who came on at four was settling herself down behind the computer in the reception area while James, his shift finished, was slinging his backpack over his shoulder. Moira knew there'd be an empty lunch box and nothing else inside it. She marvelled over the amount of food the boyo could put away. Whenever she breezed past the front desk of a weekend, he'd be sitting there eating. Mrs Baicu, the mother of sons herself, had a soft spot for James and never failed to present him with a full Irish, more often than not he got a second helping, too. Bronagh had given him and him alone, permission to help himself to the custard creams and his mammy sent him off to work with a packed lunch fit for a king. She caught Evie eying him from under her lashes. He was a good kid, Moira thought. Give him another year and he'd be a proper heartbreaker.

James engaged Aisling with a brief run down on how his shift had gone. He'd only had one glitch when Mr Rochester in Room 5 came downstairs blustering about not being able to find his watch. James had located the Rolex down the side of the bed for him and everybody had been happy. 'Apart from that everything's been grand. I'll catch ya.' He gave a wave and pushed the door open ready to head home. For his tea, no doubt, thought Moira as Evie, a mournful look on her face as he shut the door behind him, took her headphones off.

The tinny sound of a Boyzone's hit *Everyday I Love You* rattled from her MP3 Player before she turned it off. She'd be deaf by the time she was thirty listening to it that loud, Moira frowned. It was a very odd, old sort of thing to have thought. She wasn't in her right frame of mind, she needed to get upstairs and check her phone in private. She also had a desperate urge to swap the dress she'd worn, knowing Mammy thought she looked well in it, for her pyjamas. She wanted to burrow in for the duration of the day and night.

Aisling moved beside the fax machine as it whirred into life, waiting to see what it would spit out. 'I'll check Ita's made up all the rooms on the list before I come up. We've a tour group arriving in the morning.'

'Hello, goodbye,' Moira said to Evie, who gave her a grin having forgotten about James—out of sight out of mind—young love could be fickle she thought, taking herself off up the stairs.

—*ele*—

The message was from Andrea. Moira eyed it as she lay prone on the sofa with her striped pjs on. She didn't want to call her back. She'd done enough hashing through the events of the night before as it was. Her hand snaked inside the family pack of Snowballs and she popped one in her mouth. She'd discovered the half-eaten bag tucked away behind the tins of spaghetti. It was where Aisling always hid things she didn't want Moira getting hold of. Snowballs were Aisling's premenstrual go-to. She was adamant there were hormonal balancing ingredients to be found in the chocolate and coconut marshmallow balls. Moira didn't know about that, Aisling was always a snappy madam around that time of the month, but she was finding comfort in them.

She tossed her phone down next to her not knowing if she was disappointed or relieved that Michael hadn't tried to get in touch with her again. She was spared dwelling on it further by the front door opening and she leapt into action shoving the bag under the cushions in the nick of time. Aisling wouldn't be happy when she discovered her sister had been helping herself to her Snowball stash. There were times though when a girl had to do what a girl had to do to survive and right now Snowballs were hitting the spot—that was all there was to it.

Chapter 31

There was someone was knocking on the door, Moira realised, opening an eye. She'd been dreaming she was hammering on the bathroom door shouting at Aisling to hurry up, the way she did sometimes when she needed a wee. Her subconscious mind's way of waking her up. The knocking sounded again. Whoever was there was determined she thought, trying to rouse herself and wishing Aisling were here to answer it but knowing she'd be downstairs. The tour group from America was arriving this morning; she'd have her hands full settling them in. Feck it, she murmured out loud tossing the covers aside. She clambered out of bed and slid her feet into her slippers, which for once were easily located beside the bed. Her eyes were bleary as she made her way to the door, sure it was Andrea on the other side. That girl got up far too early on a Sunday morning. No doubt she was annoyed because she hadn't returned her call last night.

She better have bought croissants with her Moira thought, flinging the door open and blinking stupidly. Surely, she was still dreaming? She closed her eyes firmly this time and counted to three before opening them again. He was still there. It wasn't a holy vision backlit by the landing lighting but Michael. He was dressed in the casual weekend clothes she'd only glimpsed him in a couple of times and he was only just visible behind the enormous bunch of red roses he was holding out to her. She looked at the spikey, delicate blooms, registering at the same time that she must look like a wild woman in her Marks & Spencer's flannelette pyjamas. Moira took the term bedhead to a different level most mornings and she instinctively raised her hand to smooth her hair.

'What are you doing here?' Jaysus, she was such a mess.

'You haven't returned my calls. I needed to know you were okay.'

'I'm fine apart from being caught out in my pyjamas.' She wasn't fine, far from it, but for once the lie tripped easily from her tongue.

His smile was wan. 'You probably don't want to hear me say you look beautiful right now, but you do and I uh, I brought you these.' He was still holding the roses out to her she realised and, against her better judgment, she took them from him without comment.

'Can we talk?'

She was glad Andrea was not here. Had she been lurking in the vicinity she would have snorted and told her the man was a walking cliché and to tell him to sling his hook.

'I don't think there's anything to say, Michael.'

'Please, Moira. Let me explain.'

She should shove the roses back at him, call him a fecker, and shut the door in his face but she hesitated and that was all he needed.

'Five minutes, Moira, please, that's all I ask. Five minutes to explain and then I'll go if you want me to.'

It was the earnestness in those twin, ocean-coloured pools that swayed her. She stepped aside allowing him past, 'It's through to the left,' she said as he hesitated and followed him into the living room. Aisling had drawn the curtains and she caught a glimpse of an uncommonly clear sky. It was going to be one of those bonus winter days where the sun shone and you could almost fool yourself into thinking spring had arrived early. She went into the kitchen and placed the flowers down on the bench unsure as yet what she'd do with them. Put them in water? Or perhaps they'd be better in the bin in the courtyard downstairs away from her sister's twitching nose. She wouldn't want Foxy Loxy scratching his nose when he poked inside it, though.

Michael took in his surrounds, his anxiousness made visible by restless hands. 'This is a great space,' he said, for want of something to say, and Moira nodded before gesturing him over to the sofa. She had no intention of joining him, she'd be staying right where she was thank you very much with the kitchen bench top serving as a barrier. He removed the empty pack of Snowballs peeking out from behind the cushion, looking at them bemusedly before putting it on the coffee table. He perched on the edge of the sofa, not quite at home, not yet. Good, Moira thought, staying right where she was. She could smell the coffee Aisling had made for herself this morning and she felt a pang for caffeine but it would have to wait, she wasn't going to let Michael stay any longer than the time it took for him to say his piece.

'I had no idea you were going to be at the party,' he offered up, seeing she was waiting for him to get on with it.

'Clearly. I wanted to surprise you and I obviously did.'

'Adelaide only came because Noel Price would frown on a spouse not attending. He's old school, but he's also my boss, Moira, and I have to play the game.' He massaged his temples.

Adelaide. Moira realised it was the first time she'd heard him say his wife's name.

'God, what an awful night. All I wanted to do when you left was run after you and make sure you were alright.'

'Like Prince Charming.'

He looked a little mystified. 'I've never had that comparison made before, but yes, I guess so, like Prince Charming.'

'Only Cinderella had made a holy show of herself and you stayed right where you were by your wife's side.' The word 'wife' resounded like a verbal slap.

'I wanted to go to you, Moira, believe me, I wanted to but I couldn't show Adelaide up like that. It wouldn't have been fair.'

'Ignoring me the way you did wasn't fair.' Her voice climbed an octave and she didn't like the note of hysteria in it. 'And I saw the way you looked at each other.'

He looked at her beseechingly. 'You saw a couple who've known each a long time, Moira. That's what you saw. We're good friends, I told you that, but that's where our relationship, apart from a piece of paper that says we are married, ends.'

She wanted to believe him; she really did. She also bloody well, really wanted that cup of coffee and she turned her back on him to give herself a moment to think. 'Do you want a tea or a coffee?' She flicked the kettle switch.

'I'd love a coffee.'

She knew how he liked it. White with one. They'd sat nursing a cup of coffee each only a week ago, talking about how they'd both like to visit New Orleans one day. Moira wanted to go there because her daddy had loved the Dixieland jazz—she'd grown up to the sounds of his Louis Armstrong records. It would be a homage to visit the Big Easy as he'd called the river city. It had floated unsaid between them that perhaps they might stroll the French Quarter together. The café's smell of warm baking and cinnamon that afternoon had permeated the part of her brain where she stored the things she wanted to hold on to. Those moments she could pull out and relive when the lid on the painful compartment wouldn't lock properly. She set about making the drinks, banging and clattering the cups and the teaspoons to fill the silence.

'Thank you,' he said, as she handed him his cup his eyes searching hers. 'My car's parked outside. There's somewhere I want to take you, if you'll let me.'

Chapter 32

♥

'Thanks for agreeing to come, Moira.' Michael held the passenger door of his silver car, with its sporty undertones, open and she clambered into the bucket-style black leather seat, glad she'd had the foresight to wear jeans. This car was not skirt friendly unless you wanted to share your smalls with all and sundry who happened to be walking down the road. Nor was it a car for family outings she thought, feeling comforted by the fact, even if her arse did feel as though it were inches away from scraping the tarmac. She pulled the seatbelt across her chest buckling in as he got behind the wheel. He opened the glove box and produced a tape.

'Do you like Moby?'

Moira nodded and while he messed around with the CD player, she glanced back at O'Mara's. It had been a relief to make it out the door without bumping into Aisling. She was grateful too that James was more interested in dipping his soldiers into the yolk of his fried egg to care who she was going out and about with. It would have been a different story had gossipy little Evie been manning the fort.

Michael gunned the engine as the familiar beat of *Why Does my Heart feel...* reverberated around the interior. The traffic was light and he zipped his way through the city streets. Moira leaned her head back against the seat, content to let the music wash over her. It was only when the housing began to disperse giving way to wide open spaces that she finally spoke up. 'So then, are you going to tell me where we're going?'

'We're nearly there, you'll see.'

Moira stared at the plane they were walking toward across an expanse of green field purporting to be a runway in disbelief. 'You're not planning on taking me up in that are you? It's tiny. It looks like something my nephew, Noah, would play with.'

'That there, is the Cessna 172. She's a four-seater work-horse. One of the safest planes ever built.' Michael waved over to the handful of people milling about inside the hangar to their left. There were two other similarly small aircraft housed inside it and they were faffing around the planes the way a man going through his mid-life crisis might his new Ferrari. Boys and their toys Moira thought, beginning to drag her heels. She could feel her boots sinking into the winter-soft ground, but Michael was having none of it. He reached out behind him for her hand and pulled her along. She liked the feel of hers cocooned protectively inside his. She could do this.

'You said it yourself, you've only ever flown Ryan Air. You'll love it. Although I can't promise any in-flight service.'

'Neither can Ryan Air,' Moira muttered, and he laughed.

'Touché. Afterward, if you fancy it, I thought we could go and check out Lough Tay, it's supposed to be nice right?'

He seemed confident all was forgiven; indeed, Moira could feel herself unpicking the knot of doubt as to what he'd told her about his other life with every step they took. 'The Guinness Lake, yes it's gorgeous.'

'Does it really look like a pint of the black stuff, as you say?'

She nodded, picturing the lake viewed from the hilltop. Its black waters were deep and mysterious and with the white sands of the beach on the northern side it really did look like a pint of Guinness.

'A good spot for a picnic?'

She nodded. It would be busy. It was always busy there because it was on the tourist trail but there was safety in numbers. She wasn't ready to take the next step with Michael, not yet.

'Good, because I'll have you know I slaved over the rolls and cakes I packed.'

'Did you?'

'No, I stopped at Tesco's, I thought it best to leave the picnic preparation to their bakery department experts.'

She laughed, the confusion and upset of yesterday was beginning to dissipate like slowly dissolving bubbles in a bath—almost a forgotten memory.

He really was pulling out all the stops, but what had she let herself in for Moira wondered a second later as she hoisted herself into the passenger side of the plane. She eyed the panel of knobs and dials with mistrust as Michael settled in behind the controls. 'Relax, Moira, the conditions are perfect. I wouldn't take you up otherwise.'

'Have you taken Adelaide flying before?' She hadn't expected to ask that question and it felt strange acknowledging his wife out loud to him by saying her name, but his answer suddenly mattered very much to her.

'No, she doesn't like heights. She won't fly unless it is an absolute necessity.'

Moira's shoulders relaxed and she let him help her on with her headset and microphone, pushing her hair away from her ears. His touch sent an electric shiver through her and she was certain her pupils had just dilated to twice their normal size. Michael didn't appear to notice; he was intent with getting on with the job at hand. 'You won't be able to hear me otherwise,' he said, checking she was belted in before doing the same himself.

She gritted her teeth as the plane rumbled into life and the propeller spun around. It began to bump down the grassy runway and she closed her eyes. If she'd had her rosary beads with her, she would have begun reciting Hail Marys. Instead, she contented herself with clutching the seat, knowing without looking her knuckles were white. The last time she'd felt like this was when she'd had her wisdom teeth out and at least then there'd been gas.

'Here we go!'

Moira peeked at Michael in time to catch the slightly mad gleam in his eyes. It was the look of someone who thrived on speed, on danger, she thought clenching her buttocks for good measure too, as the plane picked up speed. She squeezed her eyes shut again not enjoying the sensation of the ground slipping away beneath them as the plane juddered into the air.

'You can open them now,' Michael said, his voice sounding tinny in her ear.

She did so and squealed. The sky was the road ahead and she peered out her window and watched in wonder as the fields became a patchwork quilt, each segment a different shade of green, the livestock on the ground mere specks. It took her a beat to realise the fear of the unknown had shifted and given way to a new sensation. She was aware of a surge coursing through her and realised it must be adrenalin. It swiftly liquified to fear as the plane buffeted up and down. She was sitting in a tin can with a propeller stuck to the front of it and the sudden jerking served to remind her that can was no more than a tiny blip in a vast sky.

She side-eyed Michael to see if she could pick up on any panic on his face but he was completely chilled, obviously enjoying himself. He must have sensed her eyes on him. 'It's fine, Moira. You feel the turbulence more in a smaller plane than you would in a larger one. They're just air pockets.' Her nerves began to untangle themselves as the seconds passed and they didn't begin a sudden nose dive toward the ground like a seagull honing in on a fish. She grew used to the plane's movement and as the time ticked by was aware of a big grin she couldn't have wiped from her face even if she'd wanted to. So, this was what it felt like to be a bird she thought as Dublin stretched out beneath her like toy town. She, Moira Lisa O'Mara, was flying.

'What did you think?' Michael asked as they made their way back to his car. The time had passed swiftly and Moira had no idea how long they'd been in the air.

She felt like yelling, 'I'm alive!' but it brought Frankenstein to mind so instead she said, 'It was incredible, thank you.' She wanted him to hold her hand like he had before.

'It's addictive.' He flashed her a grin, and if there'd been any angst or doubt left inside her where he was concerned, it melted like the last of the snow in spring.

'I can see why.'

She felt like they'd shared an intensely personal experience. Something that no one else could understand. A bit like when you had really fabulous sex, she mused. It had been just them up there in that big blue sky, alone in the world. She could see why people did crazy things now. Why they threw themselves out of planes with nothing but a modified sheet to keep them from hurtling to the ground, or why they leapt off the side of tall buildings with a piece of elastic tied to their ankle. That sensation of the blood rushing through your veins as your heart pumps wildly—it was thrilling because you knew in that moment you were alive, properly alive. Not that she had any plans to sky dive or bungee jump! No, this morning's adventure had been enough living on the edge for her. Or had it?

Michael held his hand out to help her step over the crater-sized puddle beside the gate to the car park entrance. She'd only narrowly avoided it on the way in and she took his hand, holding on tightly for fear he'd let her go once she'd jumped over it. A Land Rover that hadn't been there earlier was parked next to his car but nobody was in it. There was a van too, but again it was empty. The car park was deserted. It was just the two of them and Moira decided it was her turn to take charge. She tugged at his arm to stop.

'What's up?'

'Nothing.' She didn't want to think, she just wanted to act and she snaked her free hand around the waist of his jeans sliding her fingers inside the belt loop in order to pull him in to her.

He opened his mouth to speak, but she silenced him, standing on tiptoes and covering his mouth with her own. She kissed him with the intensity of someone who'd thought her heart had been broken only to find it miraculously mended. He groaned and she felt his arousal. She didn't want to go picnicking she wanted to go somewhere where they could be together, properly together.

'Do you know somewhere we could go?' She didn't have to explain herself, he understood her meaning.

'Are you sure?'

'I'm sure.'

Chapter 33

♥

M ichael navigated the winding lanes back to the main road deftly, with one hand on the steering wheel. Moira's hand rested on top of his as he changed the gears. Neither spoke, and the air in the car hung heavy with anticipation of what was to come. The silence was only broken by the bleep of a text message arriving. It was Michael's, but he didn't pull over to check his phone. He was in a hurry to get where it was they were going and the realisation sent a thrilling tremor through her.

Where would they go? Moira wondered as the green belt gave way to suburban houses. Where was it people who had to be discreet went, a hotel? She supposed so. It hadn't mattered when they'd met for drinks or dinner. Those outings could be easily explained away but visiting a hotel in the middle of the afternoon was another matter altogether. Dublin was a small city on a world scale, three degrees of separation and all that. The odds were if they were to check in somewhere edgy and cool like The Clarence, U2's hotel, they'd see half of Mason Price on a Sunday team-building excursion at the pub across the road or something like. She didn't fancy a seedy alternative down a back alley much either. They didn't head toward the city though; they were moving in the direction of the airport and for a fleeting moment she allowed herself a fantasy whereby they flew to Paris and lost themselves in the city of love.

Michael was indicating she realised, hearing the steady tick-tick-ticking as he waited to turn in. She looked past him and saw, not the Eiffel Tower but the perfectly respectable looking Crowne Plaza Airport hotel. A transient place where people went when they needed to put their heads down between flights. It was ideal. There would be no knowing looks from an Evie type on reception because it was reasonable to assume they'd flown in from somewhere far away and couldn't face the long drive back to their little village down south. She was getting carried away with her different scenarios she realised, putting it down to a cocktail of nerves and excitement.

'Will this be alright?' He looked concerned that she approved. 'I mean it's not where I'd choose to take you had I time to arrange things but—'

She silenced him by leaning over to kiss him. 'It's fine. Next time you can take me to Paris.' She smiled to let him know she was joking.

'I would love to take you to Paris.'

His phone began to ring as they got out of the car. He retrieved it from his pocket and looked at the screen. She wondered whether he would ignore it again but he flashed her an apologetic smile, 'I won't be long, you go ahead and wait for me in reception.'

She walked toward the entrance trying not to think about who might be on the other end but the sound of his voice carrying toward her on the snappy afternoon breeze stopped her.

'Is she going to be alright? The words burst from him like a gun being rapidly fired. 'What happened?'

Moira turned around and saw his ashen face, hearing him say, 'I'm on my way.' He disconnected the call and shoved his phone in his pocket as Moira ran back to him

'What is it? What's happened?'

He was already moving to unlock his car. 'Ruby's been knocked down by a car. She's being taken to St James's, now.'

'My God, is she alright?'

'I don't know, Adie, said she's unconscious; that's all she knows. I'm going to meet them at the hospital.'

'Here, give me your keys. You've had a terrible shock, I'll drive you.' She held out her hand, but he didn't toss her his keys. Moira felt something shift and change between them in that split second of hesitation before he climbed behind the wheel. Of course, he didn't want her driving him, he couldn't have her dropping him off at the hospital. How could he explain that while his and Adelaide's daughter had lain in the road broken and possibly dying, he'd been caught up in his own lusty emotions with her? She heard him say he was sorry before he slammed the car door shut and gunned the engine, leaving her standing in the hotel's forecourt.

Moira paid her fare and sat down in an empty seat near the back of the bus. She stared out the window at the grey high-rises of Ballymun, seeing but not seeing as the bus rumbled back toward the city. She hadn't stopped praying for Ruby to be alright since Michael had driven off. She didn't think she could live with herself if she wasn't. As the bus lurched to a stop to pick up more passengers, she chewed her bottom lip in contemplation of everything that had happened since those fateful boardroom drinks when she'd first seen Michael.

Had she read too much into their relationship if it could even be called that? Had she built him up to be more than he was in her mind because she'd been trying to fill the gaping hole in her life? She'd thought the times they'd spent together, although snatched, were special, but she was wrong. The realisation sat heavily on her shoulders. What he had with his family was special. Just like the relationship she'd had with her Daddy had been special. Who was she to muscle in on his family? And yes, she knew it wasn't all down to her, but had she chosen to hear and believe what she wanted? It was all tainted now, the more she thought about him the more what they'd had become skewed like the image in a funfair mirror.

It seemed to take an age but, at last, she pushed the bell and clambered off the bus. She'd call in to Tesco's and pick up a couple of bottles of red. She very much wanted to drown her sorrows.

Chapter 34

M oira clinked in the door of O'Mara's and Evie looked up from her phone. Curiosity was stamped to the young girl's forehead as she called out a hello. It was swiftly followed by, 'Have you got company coming tonight, then?' She eyed Moira's shopping bag. The temptation to tell her to mind her own business was great but she couldn't be dealing with Aisling wanting to know why she'd gone and upset their young receptionist, even if she did agree she was a nosy madam.

'Just stocking up, Evie.' Her tone made it clear she wasn't up for a chat and she took to the stairs, hoping as she made her way to the third floor that Aisling wouldn't be home and she could be left with her Tesco's specials, three for the price of two Chilean reds in peace.

The apartment was empty and Moira put the bottles of wine down on the kitchen bench before moving to switch the television on. The silence, only broken by the monotonous ticking of the grandfather clock, would make her feel like she was going mad. She wanted some mindless background noise. She also wanted to get out of her jeans and into her pyjamas which seemed to be getting a good innings of late. She went to get changed, sitting down on the edge of her bed to check her phone in case she'd somehow managed to miss an incoming message from Michael. She was desperate to hear how Ruby was doing but the screen was blank.

Her pjs were where she'd stepped out of them that morning. She'd felt so buoyant and hopeful of things working out after all as she'd thrown her clothes on while Michael waited for her in the living room. How could things change so fast? she thought, pulling the bottoms on before buttoning the warm flannelette top. She paused as she made to leave the room to look in the dressing-table mirror. She half expected to see someone she didn't know staring out at her because she felt different, numb yet raw. All her nerve-endings were flayed and exposed. The wine would help calm her she thought, amazed to see the face in the mirror was pale but apart from that exactly the same as it had been that morning.

ele

The silence from Michael was deafening Moira thought, knocking back her fourth or was it fifth glass of wine. She was onto the second bottle she knew that much. She'd left three messages asking him to call her, concentrating on not slurring the words together as she'd asked how Ruby was. The room had taken on a softer glow, the familiar shapes of the furniture blurring so she was uncertain whether there were two armchairs or one, one grandfather clock or two. She was still on edge, but the panicked thoughts as to the state the teenager might be in had grown muted, and fuzzy around the edges like the furniture, with each mouthful of the claret liquid.

Moira pulled herself up from the sofa and wobbled her way over to the bench—she'd just have one more glass.

Chapter 35

'Moira Lisa O'Mara, this is your mammy speaking, wake up.'

A nightmare? Moira thought she was having a nightmare whereby Mammy was about to rip open her curtains and tell her she was sleeping her life away, the way she'd done when she was a teenager. She opened one eye seeking verification it was all a bad dream and squeezed it shut again as the light sliced through her retina and pierced the part of her brain that had shrunk to the size of a dehydrated pea. Her tongue, she realised, was stuck to the roof of her mouth. She didn't want to wake up fully and suffer the hangover she knew was lying in wait, preparing to smother her the moment she acknowledged she was compos mentis.

'Moira, I will drag you out of that bed if you—'

She opened her eyes and groaned. It wasn't a dream; it was horribly real. Mammy's face was inches from hers and as she inhaled, she wondered if she was about to be put out of her misery with an overdose of Arpège perfume. 'I'm awake, please go away.'

'Good, that's a start and I'm not going anywhere. There's a cup of coffee and two Panadol on the cabinet here for you. Now do as you're told and sit up.'

Moira was too weak to argue and she dragged herself up to a sitting position. She leaned her head against the wall. She really did feel like she was dying and she had no idea what she'd done to deserve to be woken by her mammy when she felt this terrible. She reached over for the coffee, her hand shaking as she picked up the mug. She heard Mammy tut something about the 'state of yer' before she scooped up the Panadol and holding them out to her, told Moira to swallow them down with her drink.

She did so and slowly the coffee penetrated the fog in her head as she pieced together what had happened yesterday with sickening clarity. Had Michael phoned? She knew she'd left messages on his phone asking him to but she'd have slept through a freight train crashing through her bedroom given the state she must have been in. She cast around frantically for her phone. It was on the pillow next to her and she snatched it up to see if there were any missed calls or messages to check. There was nothing and she tossed the phone back down in frustration. She would ring the hospital herself she resolved. She'd say she was a relative, so they didn't block her with their silly privacy laws.

She couldn't remember going to bed and assumed she'd staggered off of her own accord when the wine ran out. Her eyes flitted to her bedside clock and she nearly dropped the mug. 'Mam, it's after ten! I should have been at work an hour and a half ago.'

Mammy paused, the pile of clothes she'd picked up off the floor in her arms. 'Calm down and finish your drink. The coffee will sort you out so it will. Your sister had the foresight to call in sick for you when she couldn't wake you up.'

So, she had Aisling to thank for Mammy being here to administer her unique brand of TLC. Her face must have given her thoughts away because Mammy said, 'And don't you be giving out to Aisling about telling tales. She phoned me because she's worried about you. I don't blame her either. I don't blame her at all. I mean just look at you, Moira, look at the state of yer, and you a grown woman not a teenager who doesn't know when to stop.' There was no muttering this time. Her message came across loud and clear.

Moira didn't say a word as she drained the cup and hoped she didn't bring the strong black liquid back up again. It swilled uncertainly in her tummy for a moment but then decided to stay where it was. Mammy finished putting the clothes away in the drawers and took the mug from her. 'Right-oh, my girl, in the shower.' She shook her head. 'I could get drunk just off the smell of yer, and those sheets are for the wash. You're a disgrace, so yer are.'

Moira wasn't looking forward to being upright but she could tell by Mammy's face she wasn't messing. There was nothing for it, she'd have to get up. She threw the covers aside and stood up. The room spun around her and it took a few seconds for her to feel steady enough to make her way to the bathroom. The sheets were already being ripped from the bed before she reached the door. She didn't hang around and once safely inside the bathroom she wet a flannel and held it to her face.

A glimpse in the mirror as she dropped the flannel into the basin a minute later revealed a horror show of roadmap eyes and dry chapped lips, and she grimaced before brushing her teeth. She turned on the shower, looking forward to letting the hot water wash over her sore head and, leaving her pyjamas in a heap, she stepped under the jets. It did help ease the throbbing behind her eyes and as she shampooed her hair, she wished she could wash away the events of yesterday as easily as she could the soapy suds. How was Ruby? she wondered for the hundredth time, reaching for the bodywash. By the time she stepped out of the shower she knew she smelled a lot sweeter than when she'd stepped into it. She could have stood under the spray until the hot water ran out but didn't want to further incur the wrath of Mammy.

Spying her smelly old pyjamas, she turned her nose up; she didn't want to put them back on and so, wrapped in a towel, she made her way to her bedroom. It was like a fridge she thought, shivering and seeing her bed had been stripped. The sheets were undoubtedly spinning around in the machine right at this moment. The curtains billowed out startling her, no wonder it was freezing, Mammy had yanked the window up to let some fresh air in.

She took her time getting dressed despite the chill air because she didn't want to face the music and she knew, without having to look, Mammy would be in the living room tapping her foot impatiently. She'd be sitting in Aisling's favourite chair over by the big windows like a judge presiding over her courtroom waiting for the accused to be brought before her. Moira had been there before, not for a good long while but it was all coming back to her including the feeling of trepidation knowing she was in trouble.

She checked her phone again and this time her heart leaped as she saw she'd had a call. It sank immediately as she was it was from Andrea. Her message said it was urgent and for her to call her back on her mobile as soon as she could. She held the phone in her hand for a moment, should she call her back? She probably just wanted to find out if Moira was bunking because of what had happened at the party on Friday night, too embarrassed to front up. She hit speed-dial before she could change her mind and stood by the window, huddling inside her oversized sweater, waiting for Andrea to answer.

'Where are you?' she demanded after three rings.

'I'm at home and I *am* sick; self-inflicted but believe me I'm sick.'

'Moira, you know Sunday sessions are the work of the devil come Monday morning,' Andrea chastised.

'Don't go on at me. Mammy's here and she's on my case.'

'Oh dear, you're in big trouble then.'

'I sure am.'

'Have you heard about Michael?'

'What about him?' The drama in Andrea's voice made her stomach clench and her innards threatened to liquefy as she sent up a silent plea for the news not to be bad.

'His youngest daughter's after being in an accident. He's not in work either and the news has been going around the office like Chinese Whispers all morning.'

'I know she was hit by a car and I'll explain how I know in a minute, but please, Andrea, just tell me is Ruby going to be okay?'

Andrea must have picked up on the desperation in her voice because she didn't argue. 'She will be. She fractured her leg and her pelvis and I did hear something about internal bleeding but she didn't have any head injury which was the big worry, apparently. She was lucky. It was her fault so everyone's saying. She didn't look just stepped out on the road and the poor man driving the car had no show of stopping. At least he wasn't speeding.'

Moira didn't know if a fractured pelvis and leg could be called lucky but she was alive and she was going to be okay. That was the main thing. She collapsed on to the bed needing to feel something solid underneath her as the news-soaked in.

'Are you still there, Moira?'

'Yes. It's a relief that's all. I was with Michael when it happened.' Andrea listened in silence as she filled her in on the events of yesterday finishing when she reached the part where Mammy had woken her up.

'At least you didn't sleep with him, Moira, and what happened to his daughter is not down to you. Don't you start blaming yourself. Her accident is not some form of karmic retribution.'

'I know that, I do, but I can't stop thinking about how while she was lying there on the road injured, I was thinking about having sex with her dad.'

She heard a sound in the doorway and her heart flew into her mouth, she'd done it now. 'Andrea, I've got to go.'

'I think you and me need to have a chat about what exactly you've been up to, Moira O'Mara.' Mammy said.

Chapter 36

M oira didn't know where it came from but as she sat statue-still on the bed, the phone warm in her hand, something bubbled its way up inside her. It erupted into a sob and once it had escaped the floodgates opened and a torrent followed. She dropped the phone and held her head in her hands as her body racked with violent unstoppable shudders. She felt herself getting pulled in to an Arpège embrace but this time she gulped in the scent desperate to cling on to her mammy. The hole she'd been skirting around since her daddy died had just widened into a chasm and she was teetering on the edge terrified if she fell in, she'd never be able to clamber back out.

'I'm scared, Mammy.'

'Shush, now. I'm here. Whatever it is we can fix it.'

'Mammy, what's going on?' Aisling's voice sounded from the doorway. 'Moira, what's happened?' Moira felt her sister sit down on the other side of her and her arms wrap around her so she was cocooned between her mammy and her sister.

She choked out the words she'd been holding inside, 'I miss Daddy.'

'Ah, sweetheart I do too. He was one in a million your daddy. I miss him all the time. It's like an ache that won't go away.' Mammy's voice was choked.

'That's how I feel too,' Aisling sniffled, joining in.

They stayed like that for an age until Moira's crying began to abate to small kitten-like hiccups.

'Come on,' Mammy said. 'I'll make us all a nice cup of tea. Aisling, go downstairs and ask Bronagh for a packet of her custard creams, tell her it's an emergency.'

Moira was sprawled on the sofa; the blanket Mammy had tucked around her threatening to slide off as she leaned over and dunked her biscuit. She quickly popped it in her mouth before it could collapse into her tea. She instantly felt better for the sugar hit. She'd held nothing back, she'd told Mammy and Aisling all about Michael and was grateful that, for once, they'd just sat and listened. They didn't pass judgment until she'd reached the bitter end. Then, there'd been some debate whether the relationship could even be deemed a relationship given it hadn't been consummated—Mammy's word—it had made both Aisling and Moira cringe. It was decided that it didn't matter if any riding—Aisling's word—it had made Mammy blanch, had taken place or not. The intimacy of the conversations, the feelings they'd shared, the kisses, they all amounted to an affair, of the heart at least, and if they were Adelaide—what kind of name was that?—they'd see it as a betrayal—both their words. The main thing was, Mammy said, fixing Moira a no-nonsense gaze, was that it was all over and done with now.

It was, Moira had told her. She meant it too. This time there'd be no going back. She'd seen it in Michael's eyes when he'd taken Adelaide's call. It had dawned on him in those awful seconds he could lose his family. She didn't want to be responsible for that. She'd mend. People didn't die of a broken heart, or at least she didn't think so. Ruby would heal too. It would just take time that was all.

Aisling had cocked her head and sighed. 'I'm going to check on Ita. I asked her to hoover the second-floor landing but I can't hear anything. The last time I saw her she was sitting on the stairs on her phone. I don't know what we pay her for, I really don't.'

'Ah, sure don't be giving out. I've known her mammy for years, she's like an aunt to you so she is. Ita's a good girl, Aisling, she just needs a prod here and there.'

'Foot up the arse, more like.'

'What was that?'

'Nothing.' Aisling rolled her eyes in Moira's direction before heading off in search of their Director of Housekeeping, leaving her sister to the remainder of the biscuits. Mammy was transferring the wet sheets into the dryer.

'I think going to see someone you can have a chat to about how you've been feeling might be a good idea, Moira.'

'What do you mean, see someone?' Her hand hovered over the last two biscuits as she visualised lying on a sofa. Much like she was now come to think of it, only in a darkened room with a wizened old man with huge glasses on, writing notes on a pad as he asked her how she felt. No, not a good idea she concluded.

'A grief counsellor. I should have suggested it after yer daddy passed but it was all I could do to get out of bed each morning. I went and had a few sessions with a lovely lady. I think it helped, a little anyway. But hitting the bottle the way you've been isn't the answer, Moira.'

'Did you have to lie on a sofa?'

'No, I sat in a chair.'

'Did she wear big owl glasses?'

'No.'

'I'll think about it then.'

'Now then,' Mammy said, setting the dryer to run and heading in Moira's direction. 'Scrunch up, I've something else to tell you.' She sat down next to her with her hands clasped in her lap as she told Moira that Rosemary had cancelled her trip to Vietnam.

'Are her hips not up to it?' Moira feigned sympathy. It would seem she could scratch her plans to employ good cop, bad cop tactics with Aisling where this holiday was concerned.

Mammy gave her a funny look. 'Nothing to do with her hips and all to do with the new fella in our rambling group she's got her eye on. She's frightened if she goes away Breda McGrath will get her hooks into him. It's a blessing in disguise, Moira because I've had an epiphany this morning.'

Moira could feel her headache returning as Mammy picked up her hand and held it in hers, giving it a squeeze for good measure. 'I still think grief counselling is worth a go but a change of scenery after well, all this other Michael business will do you the world of good. We'll make it a mother-daughter, trip. You and me against the world, kiddo.'

Moira cringed at her faux-American accent but it went over the top of her head.

'A break from hitting the sauce won't do you any harm and then when we get home, we can reassess your drinking see if we need to look at getting you some professional help.'

'But Mammy—' This was a waking nightmare.

'But Mammy nothing. We'll have a grand time, so we will.'

Chapter 37

Tessa hefted her bag on to the wooden luggage rack at the foot of the bed. She was back in Room 1 of O'Mara's and arriving here this afternoon had felt like coming home. Bronagh on reception had greeted her like a long-lost friend and Aisling had appeared from the guests' lounge with a cushion in her hands to ask her how her road trip had been. She'd chatted with the two women until the phone had begun to shrill and she decided she'd better let them get back to their work. Before she let Aisling return to her cushion plumping though, she asked her if she'd mind booking a table for three at Quinn's for seven that evening. Aisling had beamed—it was business for her boyfriend after all—and said she'd be delighted to.

Tessa opened her case and eyed the neatly packed contents. Was it worth unpacking for the sake of a night? No, it wasn't, she decided. Instead, she pulled out her coral dress and shook it out. She'd worn it to dinner with Owen and he'd told her she looked stunning. The memory of the lovely evening they'd shared made her smile. She'd really liked him and hoped they would keep in touch because, you never knew what could happen. The world had suddenly opened up with possibilities for Tessa and she marvelled over how much more enjoyment there was to be found in life once you stopped letting negative thoughts and feelings weigh her down.

Next, she retrieved her toilet bag which she put in the bathroom and then she dug down in the bottom of the case for her travel clock. The time was just after four she saw opening it and setting it down on the bedside table. Moira wouldn't be home until at least six and she'd surprise her with the dinner reservation she'd made then. She hoped she and Andrea could make it, otherwise she'd be dining alone and she desperately wanted an update on all that had happened in the time she'd been away. A yawn escaped her lips. It had been a busy day. She'd been on the road early in order to get the car back to the hire place at the agreed time. There'd been a lot of faffing around when she got there over the mileage but it was sorted in the end. She deserved a little afternoon siesta she decided, lying down on the bed and enjoying stretching out on the soft covering.

ele

'This was a grand idea, Tessa,' Andrea said, still smiling over Alasdair's ebullient greeting of them as she sat down. They had a table near the window tonight and could either watch rugged-up Dubliners getting from A to B under the glow of the street lights or turn their attention to the fireplace and be mesmerised by the dancing flames in the fire. Paula, their waitress, passed the menus out and informed them that today's special was a hearty slow-cooked Irish stew. It was the sort of meal that would warm you right through after being bitten by the cold evening air and Tessa remarked that's what she planned on ordering.

Moira had been anxious about bumping into Tom, not that she could tell Tessa and Andrea this. She also knew she couldn't avoid Quinn's forever and now they were here and he was nowhere to be seen she felt a little let down.

'Wine?' Tessa asked. 'This was my idea and it's my farewell dinner treat so order what you like.'

'No, be fair, you paid last time. Andrea and I are getting this, and I'm off the sauce but don't let that stop you two having a drop.'

Tessa raised an eyebrow. 'I can see I've some catching up to do.'

They sorted the drinks, a homemade lemonade for Moira and the house red they'd enjoyed the last time they'd been here for Tessa and Andrea. It didn't take them long to make up their minds as to what they wanted for dinner and once they were all comfortable, Moira took a deep breath and launched into her tale. Andrea was abreast of all the goings on and she sipped her red quietly while Moira filled Tessa in on what had happened in her absence. She interrupted when Moira told her how she'd dreaded going back to work with the likelihood of bumping into Michael.

'Awkward,' Tessa murmured.

'Yes. He's politely reserved when I do see him, and if he can avoid passing by reception he will, which I'll admit stings a little, well a lot. Feelings aren't taps. You can't switch them on and off, but it is the way it has to be. I get that and I accept it, it's just hard that's all.' She stirred the ice in her drink around with her straw. 'On the bright side, the egg sandwich food poisoning story seems to have been taken at face value. Mairead told me she's sticking with cheese sarnies from now on.'

Tessa laughed and then her face grew serious, 'Your mother's right, you know. A break away will do you good. It will help you get some perspective.'

'Yes, but I could get some perspective on a sun lounger in Spain, not backpacking around Vietnam with my mammy.' Moira shuddered; she still couldn't believe that in a week's time she was going to be winging her way to Asia. The thought of sitting on a plane, London to Ho Chi Minh, for fourteen odd hours with Mammy, well, she didn't know what she'd done to deserve it. Actually, that wasn't true—she knew exactly what she'd done to deserve it. She hadn't even been able to play the *I can't get time off, Mammy* card. Work when she broached it with HR, had been surprisingly understanding about the sudden request for time off and she'd start showing Amanda, the South African temp, the ropes tomorrow.

'Ah, sure it's quality bonding time for the pair of you.' Andrea's snigger didn't escape Moira and she poked her tongue out at her before turning to Tessa.

'So that's me, how was your holiday, or more to the point, how was dinner with yer man Owen?'

They ordered their meals while Tessa told them about Owen. 'Typical isn't it? I finally find a man I'd like to take things further with than a first date and he lives on the other side of the world.'

'How did you leave things?'

'We agreed we'd like to keep in touch and who knows?' She shrugged. 'He might pay me a visit in Auckland. He said he's always wanted to visit New Zealand and now he's got the perfect excuse to. Failing that, I'd love to come back to Ireland again at some point in the future. I thought I'd moved on, that my life was in Auckland, but I've loved being back; it's home too, you know?'

The two women nodded although they couldn't imagine living anywhere else than Dublin.

'What about you, Andrea? Is there anyone you've got your eye on?' Tessa asked, realising she knew the ups and downs of Moira's love life but had no clue as to Andrea's.

'I've had my eye on Connor Reid at work forever but he's got his eyes on an Amazonian accountant. Unrequited love is a bugger.' It was said lightly but Moira knew her friend found it tough. She saw him every day of the week; she hankered after him and spent her lunch breaks reading things into nothing where he was concerned. He never looked her way and, in her opinion, it was time Andrea moved on in her affections too but that was easier said than done. She knew that first-hand.

'You need to cast your net wider,' she told her friend. 'Give somebody else a chance, sure there're loads of fellas who'd love to take you out.'

'Who?' Andrea demanded.

'Well, there's yer man in IT, Jeremy wotsit.'

'He doesn't fancy me.'

'He does so, he always makes fixing your computer a priority.'

Tessa smiled listening to them banter back and forth.

By the time their mains arrived, steaming piles of deliciousness, the topic of conversation had moved on to long-haul flights.

Moira was listening as Tessa recommended using a mineral water spray to stop your skin drying out and not to drink alcohol.

'Fat chance of that anyway,' Moira muttered. 'I've promised Mammy I won't touch a drop between now and when we get home from our trip. I suppose I was knocking it back any opportunity I got. It had become a bit of a bad habit and it won't do my liver any harm to have a breather. I must say it's been nice waking up in good form too.' She'd had to explain to Mammy that yes, she was prone to drinking too much, but she wasn't an alcoholic. She could stop, it was just she hadn't wanted to because she liked the fuzzy, numb feeling she got when the hard knocks life had delivered after her daddy's passing got to be too much. It was a fine line she was walking; Mammy had said with her finger wagging and so Moira had decided to prove to her that she didn't need to drink. It was her choice whether she did or she didn't. To be fair, she was finding it strange not having her customary glass of something or other bolstering her, but she'd get there. Habits were hard to break.

She was about to fork up a mouthful of the cottage pie she'd opted for when she saw Tom. He was crossing the restaurant and making for the kitchen. Her heart began to race. He hadn't seen her so, what should she do? Ignore him and hope he didn't notice her on his way out? Or brazen it out and go over and say hi. Without the red wine egging her on she was shy and embarrassed but she still felt she owed him an apology.

She wiped her mouth with the napkin and pushed her seat back before she could change her mind. 'Excuse me a moment, I've just seen someone I need to say hello to.' She could feel Andrea and Tessa's eyes on her back as she called out to Tom before he pushed the door open into the kitchen and disappeared.

'Moira.' He grinned seeing her. 'How're ya doing?'

'Oh, I'm grand enough. Listen I wanted to apologise again for, you know,' she knew her face was strawberry pink.

Tom looked surprised. 'Ah, sure you're grand; forget about it. So, how is he? The eejit you were seeking revenge on by using my body?'

Moira's mouth curled upwards. 'We called it quits before it even began really. I'm going off on a bit of a compulsory adventure for a while with my mammy to Vietnam. We leave next week.' She realised she sounded like a child off on her hols with her mammy. 'It's a long story as to why I'm going with my mammy. I didn't have much say in it, and to be honest I hope we don't murder each other. We'll be joined at the hip for nearly a month.'

He laughed. 'I'd love to hear that long story some time. Vietnam, though, wow! I spent six months backpacking around Asia. Thailand, Vietnam, Laos, and Cambodia, it was fantastic.'

They grinned rather inanely at one another.

'Well...' Her cottage pie would be getting cold but for some reason, she wasn't in a hurry to get back to it. He had kind eyes and she liked the way they were appraising her. 'It was nice seeing you, Tom. I'll get back to my dinner then.'

'I only called in to pick up my pay; it was a bonus bumping into you again.'

Moira hesitated but wasn't sure what to say or do.

'I'd love to hear all about your trip when you get back. You know relive my backpacking glory days vicariously. Maybe we could go for a meal? Not here, obviously, somewhere where I can sit and eat, too.' His eyes twinkled invitingly as he added, 'Now that the eejit is history.'

Moira looked at his expectant handsome features. She needed to work on herself before she went out with anyone else. Would it be fair to say yes only to realise she wasn't ready; she wasn't over Michael? She'd be leading him on a second time. Then again, he'd made her smile and there was that cute bum of his to take into consideration. Oh, for goodness' sake, Moira, she admonished, he's not asking you to marry him, it's only dinner. 'I'd like that, Tom, thanks.' They grinned stupidly at one another once more before Moira turned and walked back to the table. She knew the big silly grin was still plastered to her face but she couldn't help it.

She realised as she sat down and Andrea and Tessa chimed, 'Well, what was all that about?' that the fugue she hadn't known she'd been walking around in since her daddy passed had lifted a little. Through the grey fog there was a pocket of bright blue. The future, once she got this ridiculous trip with Mammy out the way, might just hold rainbows and sunshine after all.

The End...Almost

T he red fox set about his familiar night-time routine. He padded stealthily over to the gap he'd dug under the bricks that separated the park that was his home and the courtyard beyond. He poked his nose through the hole and sniffed the air. It was damp and filled with all the usual scents of chimney smoke and late suppers that would make a poor winter-starved fox's nose twitch. It was silent at this time of the night unlike the daytime when the gardens he lived in were filled with life and he burrowed down deep to sleep. This courtyard that was home to his favourite bin was a dangerous place in the daylight hours and he stayed away knowing the round, red-faced woman who meant him harm with that rolling pin she wielded lay in wait.

For now, though, he was safe and he eased his bristly body through the cavity, his ears pinned back as he listened out. The only sounds were far away from him and his beloved garbage bin. He began his pitter-patter march toward it. The scraps had been sorely lacking of late; it had been an age since he'd tasted the sweet creaminess of white pudding or the savoury tang of its black cousin but he never lost hope that the bin would yield a feast. A sudden noise, the sound of a window squeaking open made him freeze and his yellow eyes darted upwards to its source.

She was there again, the girl who used to toss him treats until one day she'd stopped. She was bigger now her face sharper than it had been but her hair still hung long, the colour of the night. Her face was ghostly in the light from her room as she smiled down. 'Hello again, you. I've brought you something.' She shook what was wrapped in a napkin out and it landed with a soft thud by his front paws. His heart soared, his luck had turned, it was a large sliver of his beloved white pudding! He snatched it up, and marched with his tail held high back to his hole in the wall. As he squeezed through, he heard her call down, 'I'll see you tomorrow night, Foxy Loxy.'

These humans were a funny lot he thought, melding into the darkness on the other side of the wall.

The End

What Goes on Tour

♥

By Michelle Vernal

Chapter 1

Dublin Airport was a hive of activity, full of people with places to go and people to see. A sea of bobbing heads striding around importantly, hefting bags about, wheeling cases behind them or pushing luggage-laden trolleys. There was a buzz in the air and it was infectious making Moira feel important as she strode toward the check in desk or rather shuffled toward it. She was bent double by her backpack, a turtle with its house on its back. How those poor creatures carted that weight around day in day out was beyond her and she was beginning to wonder if she'd overdone it on the packing.

Moira had packed for every possible climatic event. The guide book Mammy had bought and given her to read said it was cooler in the north of Vietnam than the south. She hadn't wanted to take any chances with the retail outlets on offer once on foreign soil. She didn't know much about the shopping situation in Vietnam but she was fairly certain there'd be no Marks and Spencer or Penneys finest where she was going. Hence, she'd opted to stuff her pack with everything from bikinis and flip-flops through to thermals and hiking boots. The hardest decision had been not packing one single pair of heels, not even her casually, dressy ones. She didn't think she'd gone a whole day in flats since she was at school but this definitely wasn't going to be a high-heeled sort of a holiday.

The backpack wasn't hers either. This encumbrance weighing her down belonged to Lisa the no-frills Australian legal secretarial temp at Mason Price where Moira was employed as a receptionist. She'd offered her the loan of it when she'd gotten wind of Moira's upcoming trip assuring her she'd find it much easier to manage getting on and off buses than lugging a suitcase about. It had been very generous of her and Moira had felt quite intrepid laying it open on her bed deciding where to put what in its many compartments. She'd left her packing to the last minute as per usual.

Now, feeling the straps pinch her shoulders she'd put money on Lisa not being a subscriber to the O'Mara family travel policy. Mammy was a firm believer in not being caught short. She'd drummed it into her four children to always take two pairs of smalls for every single day they were away and then a few extra sets just in case. Lisa, Moira had decided, was likely to be one of those practical types who'd wash her knickers out at the end of the day, leaving them to dry overnight.

The art of travelling lightly was not something any of the O'Mara's had mastered, not even Patrick. Mind, he had a suit collection that put Aisling's designer shoes to shame and more in the way of hair products and skin potions than any of his sisters. Having said that Moira *had* packed a giant bottle of Evian mineral water spray in her carry-on; her friend Tessa had recommended it to stop her skin drying out. It wasn't that she was vain, it was just she couldn't be doing with flaky skin. Patrick was a vain man. Not a ray of sunshine was allowed to caress his handsome features unless he'd slathered on his SPF 30.

It rankled that Pat hadn't been in touch to wish her and Mammy a good trip. For Mammy's sake as much as hers. He was her golden boy, after all. Her only boy come to that. Fair enough he was in LA but a phone call wasn't too much to ask—five minutes of his precious time. She'd taken off the rose-tinted glasses she'd always worn where her elder brother was concerned these last few months. She'd not liked the way he'd behaved when Aisling had told Mammy she'd take over the running of O'Mara's. It had been obvious he wanted the family guesthouse sold; the proceeds divvied between them so he could focus on whatever it was he was actually doing over there in the city of Angels. Most of all though his lack of contact at a time when she'd needed him most had hurt.

Vain git. She gave him and his obsessive SPF habit a metaphorical flick as she heard Mammy's strident cry behind her. 'Aisling, Moira! I'm after forgetting my passport.'

Christ on a bike, the holiday was off to a grand start.

Chapter 2

M oira swore softly under her breath and came to a halt.
She teetered forward as she swung around, narrowly
avoiding taking Aisling out in the process.

'You're a menace, with that thing so you are,' Aisling muttered, putting out a steadying hand as she glared at her sister
before turning her attention to Mammy.

Maureen O'Mara was patting down the pockets, of which
there were many, in her new travel pants. She too had a pack
strapped to her back, only hers was brand new and a more
compact design than Moira's; it also had a lot of compartments. Plenty in which to lose a passport. Unlike, Moira's pack
though, her mammy's wasn't bulging at the seams. Watching
her now, Moira couldn't stop thinking of the musical Joseph
and the Amazing Technicolour Dream Coat, only it had morphed into Mammy and her Pants of Many Pockets.

'Breathe, Mammy, breathe,' Aisling soothed. 'C'mon now
it'll be somewhere on your person. You checked it off your
list before we left, remember?' The checklist had been gone
through twice to avoid dramas precisely like this one.

'So I did.' Maureen O'Mara took big gulping, calming
breaths like Roisin had shown her on her last trip home. *Like
you're eating the air, Mammy.* She'd needed to attempt this
particular breathing exercise after she'd gotten the bill for the

lunch she'd treated her eldest daughter to. She had expensive tastes did Roisin. It came from living in London—the big smoke.

'Mammy have you checked your bum bag?' Moira was impatient, keen to join the line. The sooner they checked in the sooner she could get this pack off her back.

'Moira, I wish you wouldn't call it that, it sounds so undignified.' Nevertheless, Maureen lifted her new quick-dry top to reveal the black bag strapped around her waist, unzipping and thrusting her hand inside it to triumphantly hold the little book aloft a beat later.

Moira cut her off before she could launch into the Thanksgiving prayer and they were mistaken for travelling evangelists. 'Jaysus, Mammy, would you cover yourself! I can see your tummy and that's undignified, so it is,' she hissed before carefully turning to make her way over to the ever-growing British Airways queue.

They were flying with the airline to Heathrow where they had to pick up their bags and check in with Thai International for the long haul through to Ho Chi Minh. It meant hanging around Heathrow for a few hours but it had been their cheapest option. By the time they reached the smiley check-in woman with her pillbox hat tilted just so, Maureen O'Mara had told twenty-five strangers she was after having a Mammy and daughter adventure in Vietnam. She'd also informed them that she had six pockets in her travel pants—*six pockets, sure wasn't that a marvellous thing?* Moira knew it was twenty-five people because she'd counted.

Now, she began going through the motions of checking in, cringing at the sight of her passport photo. It was a mug shot, not a photograph. She couldn't blame the smiley woman with a name badge that said she was called Ciara for narrowing her heavily made-up eyes as she glanced down at the photo and then back up at Moira. She did look guilty in it. Whatever her thoughts though, she let it go and passed the little book back to her.

'You look very smart in your uniform,' Maureen beamed pushing past her daughter to take her place at the counter. Moira moved aside watching as her pack was swallowed up by the rubber flaps, satisfied it was on its way to being loaded aboard the plane. Aisling helped her mammy off with her pack and put it down on the scales. Ciara beamed back at Mammy.

She had lipstick on her teeth Moira noted, ignoring the sharp-eyed glance she got as Mammy compared her youngest child with the glamorous woman busy stamping her boarding pass. Moira had thrown on joggers and a sweat top, going for comfort over fashion for their journey. She might have a reputation as the last of the big spenders in the O'Mara family but even she drew the line at forking out shedloads for travel pants. So what if they could be dried in a couple of minutes? Sure, they were bound to have a laundromat somewhere over there and she'd been adamant she did not need six pockets. Nobody needed six pockets! Mammy begged to differ but more to the point the pants were fugly (fecking ugly) in Moira's humble opinion.

'That's a lovely photo of you,' Ciara said to Maureen before snapping her passport shut and handing it back.

Maureen puffed up peacock-like and looked set to launch into a long and involved story as to how she'd managed to get such a fetching passport photo taken. Moira, however, was having none of it and she linked her arm firmly through her mammy's, smiling her thanks at Ciara as she dragged her away.

'Don't rush me, Moira.'

'There's other people waiting, Mammy. Yer woman doesn't need to hear about how if you hold your chin up just so it makes you look younger in photos or whatever it was you were going to tell her. She's a job to be getting on with. There was a queue a mile long waiting to check in.'

Mammy made a tsking noise. 'Well let them wait, I say. People are in too much of a hurry these days, so they are. The art of polite of conversation is being lost and I for one think it's a crying shame.'

Moira cast an exasperated glance over at Aisling who was smirking. She didn't need to be able to read her sister's mind to know it was at the thought of Moira and Mammy sharing a room for nearly a month. The thought made her shudder! Three and a half weeks alone together and not one drop of alcohol was to pass her lips during that time either! There'd be no fuzzy glow to hide behind because she'd be, had been, stone cold sober since Mammy had more or less ordered her on this trip and put the kibosh on her drinking. It was her penance; not in so many words but Mammy was a woman whose face said it all, for the pickle she'd gotten into with a man she'd no right to be carrying on with.

She felt the familiar pang of loneliness mingled with long-ing she always felt when she thought of Michael. One thing she'd realised though was Mammy was right in so much that hitting the bottle was not the answer. All the things she didn't want to think about, Michael, Daddy not being here anymore, they didn't magically disappear with each drink, they were still there the morning after. The pounding of her head only serving to make her pain worse.

It had been nice to wake up clear-headed this last while. For the first time in a long while she felt like she had some semblance of control over her life. She'd have to survive this trip with Mammy though because she had her date with Tom to look forward to when she got home. She liked him and wanted to see where that took her. He also got two very big ticks in the potential new boyfriend department. One on account of his outstanding bum and the second because he was a nice guy. He had to be because only a nice guy would bother to ask a girl out who'd led him on only to turn him down because her head was all over the place.

Right now, though, a meal with Tom to tell him all about this mental trip she was going on, seemed ever such a long way away. Oh yes, it was going to be a tough test getting through this tour of duty with Mammy. Speaking of whom, she noticed she was delving into one of her pockets. A tick later she produced a crumpled tissue and gave a tell-tale sniff. 'Go now while you can,' Moira mouthed at Aisling. Mammy was not good at goodbyes. They were only going on holiday, not emigrating, but she knew from past experience Maureen O'Mara would look like a panda bear, thanks to the non-waterproof mascara she insisted was the only one that didn't make her eyes itch, by the time she disappeared through those gates.

Aisling should know better too than to wait around, what with the number of goodbyes she'd said over the years. Her job in resort management had taken her all around the world until she'd put her roots back down in Dublin to take over the running of the family guesthouse, O'Mara's. Instead of wishing them a happy holiday and saying a quick goodbye however, she was busy rummaging in her shoulder bag.

'I've something for you,' she said to Moira.

Chapter 3

'Is it drugs?' Moira asked receiving the sharp end of Mammy's elbow. She rubbed at her ribs. 'What was that for? Sure, it was only a joke.'

'It's not funny, Moira. You never know who's listening.'

'It's not drugs, Mammy.' Aisling rolled her eyes before retrieving a scrunched-up bundle of material and thrusting it at her sister.

'Yes, but the walls have ears and we might be targeted by the Custom's man if they hear the 'd' word.' She made the inverted comma sign with her fingers.

'Oh, for fecks sake, Ash, you loaned her the film, didn't you? After I said not to.'

'Bangkok Hilton's a great film, so it is.' Aisling was defensive. 'And, neither of you are exactly worldly. I let her watch it for educational purposes. Jaysus, Mammy would be the first to put her hand up if someone asked her to carry their bags or a stuffed toy through customs for them especially if they were nice to her.'

'Oh no, I wouldn't, not after seeing that film. Yer Kidman woman deserved an Oscar so she did.' Maureen piped up momentarily distracted from the tears she was working up to by the turn the conversation had taken.

'See.' Aisling shot her sister an 'I was right' look and then re-membering what she held in her hand she jiggled the bundle. 'C'mon take them. Don't leave me standing here waving them at you like an eejit.'

Moira did so shaking the fabric out and holding it up. She stared uncomprehendingly at a pair of baggy elasticized waist and bottomed pants. They had elephants all over them and looked like something a clown might wear. 'What the feck are these?'

'Elephant pants,' Aisling said. She'd debated whether or not to give them to her sister. They were the sort of thing that would look ridiculous if she were to strut down O'Connell Street in them but in the middle of Asia, they'd look right at home. 'I bought them when I was in Thailand. Everyone wears them and they're super light and comfortable.'

'Like my fisherman pants,' Maureen piped up. She'd opted not to wear them on the flight deciding on her six pocket, trav-el pair instead. It wasn't just because they wouldn't crease but because she didn't fancy her chances of getting the fisherman ones done up in the airplane toilets. It would be too much of a challenge in such close quarters and she'd decided the odds were too high of her smacking her head on the toilet door as she bent down to pull the back bit up through to the front—a complicated business. A concussion was not on the cards for this holiday, thanks very much!

'They have elephants all over them.' Moira screwed her nose up. 'And I'm going to Vietnam not Thailand. They don't have elephants there, do they?' She'd been wary when Mam-my had first informed her she was heading to Asia of hip-popotamuses. They were, according to the television show she'd seen recently, among the world's most deadly creatures. She now knew there was no chance of bumping into one of them but elephants? Well, she wasn't one hundred per cent. She'd have to look it up in the guide book.

'Look, Moira, you won't care whether they're covered in teddy bears once you hit the tropics. Those pants are light enough to wear despite the heat and they'll stop your thighs rubbing together and your legs getting eaten alive.' Aisling was indignant her gift wasn't being well received, although she knew she shouldn't be surprised; graciousness was not one of her sister's stronger personality traits.

'My thighs do not rub together!'

'Believe me, Moira, in that heat your thighs will slap together. Kate Moss's thighs would rub together.'

'Girls, stop bickering. I've brought the Lanacane gel, nobody's thighs will be rubbing or slapping together under my watch.'

Moira shook her head; it was one of those surreal life moments. Here she was in the airport discussing elephant pants and chafing. It was hardly the stuff of Hello Magazine, where the celebs, ie aforementioned Kate Moss, all strode out of Arrivals looking amazing, a pair of big black glasses covering their faces and the kind of tight-fitting jeans sprayed on that Mammy always said would give a girl a nasty bout of thrush, especially if she were to sit in them for thirteen hours straight.

'Take the pants, Moira, and say thank you to your sister. It was very thoughtful of her so it was.'

Moira grudgingly did as she was told even though she knew she wouldn't be seen dead in them. She shoved them inside her carry-on bag while Mammy yanked Aisling toward her quick dry top. She hugged her daughter to her ample bosom and began to sniffle.

'Mammy, stop that.' Aisling's voice was muffled. 'I'll be fine. I've got Quinn to look after me remember?'

'Ah, he's a lovely lad, so he is.' The words and a grand son-in-law he'd make hung in the air.

'Don't you be moving him in while I'm away,' Moira muttered pulling her sister from her mammy's arms to give her a hug goodbye. 'Because I plan on coming back.'

'I plan on you coming back too.' Aisling squeezed her sister back, although, it would be nice spending each and every night with him for the next month, because moving him in while her sister was away was exactly what she was planning on doing. She knew he was at his mam's this very minute packing his bag. 'Look after each other,' she called as Moira hauled Mammy toward the sliding doors. 'And keep in touch. Promise me you won't be riding on any of those scooters over there, Mammy?'

'I promise. We promise, don't we, Moira?' Maureen paused to call back.

Moira gave her sister the Girl Guide salute. 'I promise to do my very best.'

Aisling didn't grin, another panicked thought had sprung to mind. 'Mammy you remembered to sort your insurance out, didn't you?'

Mammy gave her the thumbs up and a final wave before the doors slid shut behind them.

Aisling stood there for a moment feeling odd. That was it then, they were gone. It had always been her that had done the leaving. This was a first and, sending up a silent prayer that her mam and sister travel safely, she turned and made her way toward the exit. Quinn would be waiting at home for her. The thought warmed her and chased away the feeling of trepidation watching them walk though those doors had left her with. Five minutes later as she eyed the ticket under the windshield wiper, she was too busy cursing the parking warden to worry about Mammy and Moira. There went the new pair of Manolo's she'd had her eye on.

Chapter 4

♥

M ammy dabbed at her eyes with the tissue that looked like it had seen better days as she stood on the other side of passport control. They'd emerged in the glitzy duty-free area having passed inspection without incident despite Moira's dodgy picture. Moira suspected this was down to the customs officer man's sixth sense. An ability to size people up must be in their job description because she was sure he'd known were he to give Maureen a conversational opening he'd live to regret it.

As it was Mammy had drawn breath, her chest puffing up magnificently beneath that quick-dry fabric. She was all set to tell him why she was teary over leaving the country even if it was only for a holiday, how it was a mammy's lot in life. He must have guessed too it would be followed swiftly by questioning along the lines of how it was a nice young man like himself, had come to be working on customs and did he catch many drug dealers? Hence, he'd slammed her passport shut, thrust it back at her and waved them both through, Mammy sniffing all the way, partly from indignation and partly because it was just what she did.

Now, Maureen O'Mara's tears miraculously dried as she spied the perfume section. A child in a sweet shop. Mind, thought Moira, a certain serum she'd been unable to justify the price of at Boots might just be affordable tax free. Oh, and there was that bottle of Allure by Chanel she'd been hankering after. She'd had to make do for months with a sneaky spray of Aisling's Gucci. Personally, it wasn't Moira's favourite but needs must. Where was the harm in checking them out? Hadn't her credit card just received its minimum repayment? Sure, it was raring to go.

'Ooh, I do like a free squirt so I do, come on, Moira.'

She was like a bee to honey, and Moira followed her as she honed in, her nose twitching as she sought out her go-to fragrance.

'Mammy, why don't you try something new? Live dangerously, come on. Look at them all, there's hundreds to choose from.' To demonstrate her point she picked up the bottle of Jean Paul Gaultier that was closest to hand. Maureen blinked at the womanly shaped bottle with its gold cone bra, corset embellishment.

'I don't think so, Moira. I couldn't be doing with that. I'd think of what's-her-name every time I picked it up.'

'Madonna?' That's who'd inspired it after all.

'No not her. I don't mind a bit of Madonna. I like that song you know, the Virgin one. I'm thinking of Patrick's friend.' She had the lemony lips she always wore when Patrick's girlfriend Cindy was mentioned.

Moira couldn't quite make the connection herself but she put the bottle down. She'd had a better idea. Perhaps she could talk Mammy into buying a bottle of Allure. That way she could uses hers and she'd be able to splash out on the serum. It was smart thinking if she did say so herself.

Maureen however, had other ideas. 'I'm an Arpège woman, Moira, you know that. It's my signature fragrance so it is.'

'You're not Coco Chanel, Mammy.'

'Now listen to me, Moira O'Mara. If for some reason you found yourself in a dark room, lost and needing your mammy, would you or would you not be able to follow your sense of smell and find me?'

Moira shook her head slowly. On the one hand Mammy was right. She would indeed be able to sniff her out but on the other hand it was an out and out weird analogy to come up with. She sincerely hoped she'd never find herself in a darkened room trying to hunt her mammy down by smell alone.

Maureen O'Mara however had moved on and her eyes were darting around the dust free shelves. They were simply laden with gorgeous bottles yearning for a place on her dressing table but there was only one that would be given the honour. She spied the familiar stylish black and gold canister, by Lanvin. Classy, that's what it was, not like that pornographic thing Moira had been waving about. Maureen was an extremely loyal woman when it came to her scent. She harboured a secret fantasy that somehow Lanvin would get wind of this loyalty of hers and offer her a free lifetime supply of Arpège in exchange for her squirting it daily and spreading the joy. She picked up the bottle and stroked it lovingly for a beat before, ignoring the cardboard strips in the plastic container alongside it, she sprayed a heady cloud around her and closed her eyes to inhale the floral symphony.

Moira wafted her hand back and forth coughing. 'Jaysus, Mammy, I feel like I'm standing inside one of the glasshouses in the National Botanic Gardens.'

'Indeed, madam, Arpège is the fragrance of one thousand flowers,' cooed the consultant whose own eyes were watering with Maureen's heavy handedness. She'd seemingly materialised from thin air, lurking and ready to pounce from behind one of the shelves. A bony, hard-faced woman who was testing various lipsticks on the back of her hand nearby began to splutter and putting the tube back in the slot she flat-eyed Maureen. Moira didn't blame her. The odour wafting off her mammy was akin to walking into the toilet after the prior occupant had gone berserk with the air freshener. Still, it would take more than a lick of colour to soften that face she thought, defensively glaring back at her. It was like a blind cobbler's thumb.

'One thousand flowers you say?' Mammy squinted through the perfume atoms floating in the air to the consultant's badge. 'Eva. Now that's a pretty name so it is.' And just like that, she was away.

Moira smirked and left her bending Eva's ear while she went in search of her magical serum. She found it tucked in alongside a glorious selection of eternal youth potions and picked it up. The bottle was smooth and cool in her hand as the battle between the little common sense she had when it came to money and her conscience began.

'Moira, you are a woman in her mid-twenties do you really need an age-defying serum?'

'Yes I do. It's never too early to start planning for the future. I do believe the phrase is "future proofing". And, I like the bottle.'

'Sure, you pinched that from a building society advert, so you did.'

Moira sighed; it was true she had. Her conscience had played a blinder and she put the bottle down backing slowly away from it. It was time for a compromise and she made her mind up that if she had any credit left on her card at the end of the trip, she'd buy it on her return.

Eva, she noticed, approaching her and Mammy, was wearing a glazed smile that didn't quite stretch to the perfect liquid eyeliner flicks on either side of her eyes. She was, Moira guessed desperate to get a word in edgewise. Her chance came as Mammy was momentarily distracted by Moira's return. 'I hope you haven't been spending money you don't have.'

'I haven't.'

Eva jumped in. 'Madam we also have the fragrance in, erm,' she cleared her throat, 'Eau de Parfum. This stays on the skin longer and mellows throughout the day. Or, if Madam prefers, we have the concentrate perfume.' She eyed Maureen meaningfully. '*One* dab is all one needs.'

Moira had had enough; she wanted a cup of coffee and something to eat. She only had so much willpower and it was wavering. Time to put some distance between her and the serum. 'Don't encourage her,' she said to Eva. 'Would you want to sit next to one thousand flowers in a tin can with no windows? She'll be setting my hay fever off as it is.'

'Excuse my daughter, she forgot to pack her manners,' Maureen tutted. 'Thank you for your time, Eva. I won't be buying today because I have a bottle to tide me over on my holidays. Now then, did I tell you Moira and I are off to Vietnam?'

'Erm, you did, yes.' Eva looked like a mouse cornered by a cat and Moira felt a pang of sympathy. She'd been that mouse many times and as such she turned to her mammy and said, 'Mammy I just heard a lady over by the Elizabeth Arden stand saying she'd seen Daniel Day Lewis buying a slice of mud cake from Butler's Chocolate Café.' It was a total fib and Moira was normally a very truthful girl but desperate times called for desperate measures. Her rather enormous white lie would move Mammy over to where she wanted to be. Besides the chocolate café was a highlight of any trip to the airport and she wasn't about to miss out on a visit.

It worked a treat because at the mention of her favourite heartthrob, Mammy was off like a racehorse at the starter gate as the flag dropped. 'She loved him in Last of the Mohicans. It was the loin cloth that did it,' Moira said to an open-mouthed Eva, before following the trail of burning rubber, Mammy had left behind.

Chapter 5

♥

'I know what you're going to say and it wasn't me,' Maureen shouted at her daughter. 'And don't interrupt me, I'm watching Entrapment. That Catherine Zeta Jones is very bendy, so she is. Sure, you wouldn't believe the limbo dance she can do to get under those laser beam thing-a-me-bobs.' Maureen might have added that Moira had a look of Catherine about her but she didn't feel like giving her daughter a compliment. She still hadn't forgiven her for her little Daniel Day Lewis trick. It wasn't nice to get a woman all het up like that over nothing.

She turned her attention back to the screen in time to catch Sean Connery attempting some bending of his own. It didn't impress her; she'd never been a fan of his. Roger Moore was the Bond for her ever since she'd seen him in The Man with the Golden Gun. It was that film that had set this whole adventure in motion. The scene with Roger on the romantic old boat with its venetian blind-like sails had cemented a desire in her to one day sail on a junk. Preferably with Roger but Moira would have to do.

It had happened that one day she'd been out shopping for good quality walking shoes with her friend Rosemary—they belonged to the same rambling group—when she'd seen a poster of Ha Long Bay. She'd stood outside the Grafton Street

Thomas Cook, mesmerised by the glossy photograph of lime-stone islands soaring out of emerald waters. That alone was breath-taking but it was the red-sailed junk that had captured her imagination and seen her drag Rosemary inside the travel agency.

Moira lifted the headphone away from Mammy's ear. 'Stop shouting,' she hissed. 'And it was so you. I told you not to eat the cheese.'

'It's not my fault. I think I may have a little intolerance problem.' She definitely wasn't going to say kind things to her daughter if she kept that up. Maureen folded her arms and tried to ignore her.

'Then why did you eat it? And such a great big wedge too.'

'Sure, what else was I supposed to have with the crackers?'

'You could have left them; nobody twisted your arm to eat them.'

'Moira, it was complimentary and the O'Mara family does not turn their nose up at complimentary.'

'Well, I'm turning my nose up now, aren't I?' Moira let the headphone ping back against Mammy's ear and glanced past her to where the gentleman who'd told them he was in the importing and exporting business was asleep. He looked to be around his mid-fifties with a big head of badly dyed hair and the kind of girth that would make long haul flights uncomfortable. His importing and exporting, whatever that entailed, couldn't be doing that well, she thought, not if he couldn't stretch to a business class ticket.

He was late boarding and Moira was sure she'd caught a strong whiff of whisky coming off him as he'd squeezed into his seat muttering an apology. Once he'd managed to adjust his seatbelt he turned and offered up a brief greeting before, to Mammy's disappointment, putting his headphones on and closing his eyes. He hadn't so much as stirred since, not even when dinner was doing the rounds. Mammy was most con-cerned about him missing out on the beef noodle stir fry but

Moira had managed to convince her that he wouldn't thank her for waking him.

She felt a stab of envy watching his chest heave with a contented snore. Oh, to be sound asleep like that. He must have taken something because while she was knackered, completely banjaxed in fact with her poor old body clock telling her it was way past her bedtime, she felt wired. There was too much going on around her and she shouldn't have had so many coffees. Lucky so and so she thought, screwing her nose up as she turned away, and not just because he had the aisle seat.

She normally loved the window seat but next to Mammy she felt trapped, squished in, and she twisted for the umpteenth time in her seat. She couldn't get comfortable and crossing then uncrossing her legs she mused that the lack of leg room was punishment for being economy passengers. Sure, it was torture the way you had to walk through business class when you boarded. Trying not to stare at them all spread out like they were on their sofas at home, blankets already tucked in around their laps. She'd been about to nod off an hour or so back when she'd been startled awake by a kick in the shin thanks to an unapologetic Mammy doing her ankle rotations. Now, she let out a huffy sigh and glanced at her watch. Jaysus, five more hours of this! It seemed an interminable amount of time and leaning her head back against the seat rest she closed her eyes and let her mind drift off.

Heathrow had been a nightmare; the busy hub was heaving due to a swirling fog that had plonked itself squarely over the London airport causing delays. She and Mammy had fought their way through the swarms of disgruntled travellers to collect their bags and had checked in with Thai Airways without drama. They'd been left with enough time for another cup of coffee, and to have a wander in order to stretch their legs before boarding their plane.

Moira was grateful for small mercies, like Mammy refraining from dousing herself in Arpège at the duty free this time round. She was sure she'd only gone without a free top up because of the little boy who'd had the misfortune to sit in front of them on their short British Airways hop. He'd announced in that loud and proud way of the under-fives that he reckoned Nana must be hiding on the plane because he could smell her stinky flower smell. Moira had elbowed Mammy but she'd pretended she hadn't heard.

Thanks to the fog, it was well over an hour before the plane that would take them on the last leg of their journey to Ho Chi Minh had been cleared for take-off. It was just long enough for her and Mammy to get edgy with one another. There they were trapped in their seats thinking about those feckers in business class as they sniped at one another—beholden to Mother Nature waving her wand and banishing the pea-souper. By gosh, at that moment in time, Moira would have loved a drink. Her mouth had watered at the thought of an icy cold glass of crisp, white wine.

She'd imagined the dry fruitiness smoothing out her ragged edges. Instead of imbibing she doused herself in Evian and as the pilot's voice finally crackled over the tannoy system, he'd come as a welcome distraction. The sound system was dodgy but she'd managed to string together enough of what he was announcing to know they were expecting to be airborne in the next half an hour or so. She'd sat digging her nails into her palms thinking unkind thoughts about the woman who'd birthed her sitting next to her.

Moira blinked, coming back to her present situation. Her eyes were dry from the air-conditioning; the Evian wouldn't do anything for that and she was beginning to feel a little cold. She retrieved the blanket from under the seat in front of her and ripped the plastic off before draping it over herself. Mammy she saw was still engrossed in her film. They'd stopped niggling at one another once dinner was served. All those foil sealed containers had broken the boredom as they'd peeled the lids back excited to see what was inside. Mammy had been most impressed with her meal as she said the last time she'd flown, a budget airline to Tenerife with Daddy, the meal had been so small 'it t'wuldn't fill the holes in yer teeth.' Moira jammed her pillow up against the window and leaned her head on it feeling the vibrating motion of the plane as she thought back on her going away dinner with Andrea.

They'd met at Zaytoon in Temple Bar for a chicken shish, too skint to stretch to anything fancier but both agreeing the Mediterranean food was to die for. Andrea had been trying to keep a straight face over her glass of Coke, the restaurant wasn't licensed which suited Moira just fine, at the thought of her friend backpacking around strange and exotic Far Eastern shores with her mammy.

'It's not funny.'

'Sure, you'd be falling about the place if the shoe were on the other foot.'

It was true she would have been. 'No, I wouldn't, friends are supposed to support and sympathise with one another.'

Andrea had snorted. 'Ah well, on the bright side it's a good thing you're off for a bit because Friday night drinks are rolling around at the end of the week and someone is sure to shag someone they shouldn't. You and Michael will be old news by the time you get back.'

'But I didn't shag him.' Moira had defended herself.

'*I know that* but you can hardly make a public announcement to say that while you seriously entertained the idea of finding out what lay beneath that suit of his and taking him for a few laps around the race track you didn't actually pass the start line. And if he is after having extra marital affairs it's not with you.'

'He wasn't like that.'

'He was exactly like that Moira.'

Moira refused to believe *her* Michael, no scratch that he wasn't hers, never had been, made a habit of sleeping around on his wife. Andrea however had him pegged as a middle-aged cliché and would not be swayed from her way of thinking. It had been time to deflect the conversation away from herself. 'I wish you'd hurry up and give yer man one. That would give the Property girls something else to talk about. They're the worst so they are.'

'Conveyancing will do that to you, it's boring as shite. As for me and Connor, there's no chance. He's still dating the Amazonian Accountant.' Andrea had gotten that daft dreamy look at the thought of Connor Reid. It was the same expression she wore when she tucked into her bag of hot chips after a night on the lash.

'No, not Connor, you need to move on from that eejit. You do not want a man who fancies himself more than he fancies you, Andrea. Sure, you'd spend the rest of your days fighting for mirror space. I told you I caught him gazing at his reflection in the lift doors the other day. I'm talking about Jeremy from IT. He's cute in a computer man sort of a way.'

'I don't know why you seem so sure he fancies me.'

'Because of his exorbitant interest in your box that's why. He's forever after tinkering with it.'

Andrea's Coke had gone down the wrong way and as she coughed and spluttered, she sent tiny pieces of chopped lettuce flying off her plate. A couple glanced over alarmed, watching Moira get up to give her friend a few whacks on the back before fetching her a glass of water.

'Are you alright now?'

Andrea had nodded.

'I was talking about your computer by the way. You need to get your mind out of the gutter.'

The memory of that conversation made her smile but the smile faltered as an unpleasant smell wafted her way again. Mammy was shifting tellingly in her seat but had her eyes glued to the screen. Moira scowled at her even though she was oblivious. She felt bullied into this trip. It wasn't on her bucket list. She didn't have a bucket list for fecks sake, she was only in her twenties and as such never in a million trillion years had she thought she'd wind up where she was right now.

Ah she knew well enough it wasn't Mammy's fault she was here, not really. She'd gotten herself into a mess and Mammy was just trying to get her away from the pig's ear she'd made of her life for a while. That and fill Rosemary of the recent hip replacement's place. Why, oh, why couldn't Mammy have booked herself a lovely long holiday in Sydney where there were lots and lots of shops and beaches or, or, she cast around, Hawaii, she'd always fancied Hawaii. But no apparently, Mammy had a dream—a dream to sail on a fecking junk, and had decided that since you never knew what was waiting for you around the corner, the time had come to fulfil that dream.

Thinking about it, if anyone was to blame for her present predicament it was Mammy's so-called friend, Rosemary Farrell. It was her who'd left Mammy in the lurch. She'd decided she couldn't possibly go to Vietnam for a month with Maureen, not when Bold Breda was making eyes at the new fella in their rambling group. This was despite already having booked. She didn't want those bionic hips of hers going to waste. She hadn't actually said that last bit and Moira pushed the thought of Rosemary getting up to shenanigans aside only to find the space instantly filled by Michael Daniel's handsome face. She felt the familiar pang as she conjured up those beautiful eyes of his. Eyes she'd lost herself in. What there'd been between them had ended before it really began which was a blessing because she was not the sort of girl to have a fling with a married man. Although, she'd come close, too close for comfort.

In that respect it would be good to put some distance between herself and Michael because it was hard seeing him at work. There was part of her that longed for a glimpse of him, while the other half found it crushingly painful when she did catch sight of him. She'd never been the sort of girl to get red in the face and flustered when it came to men either but each time she set eyes on him she turned into a gibbering, scarlet faced imbecile. It wasn't professional and people had noticed. She didn't much like being the subject of office gossip and felt guilty for the times she'd gleefully listened to a juicy morsel being whispered over the top of the reception desk before repeating it to Andrea over lunch.

As for Michael he was seemingly unaffected by her presence and unfailingly polite when he spoke to her, which was only when strictly necessary. The consummate professional with his head held high around the law offices where he was a partner in the Aviation and Asset Finance department. The tattle about him and Moira was circulating like a virus travelling through the air conditioning ducts but it didn't seem to touch him. Whereas her face ignited every time she walked into the tea room and the conversation came to a halt. Her sudden sabbatical would only add fuel to the fire but it would soon sputter away to nothing when she wasn't sitting at her reception-desk post serving as a reminder to those with nothing better to talk about.

She thumped the pillow. Perhaps if she put some classical music on it might clear her racing thoughts and soothe her off to sleep. She dug out the headphones and plugged them in before fiddling with the remote until she found something suitable.

Chapter 6

M aureen watched the credits roll down on the small
screen in front of her. It hadn't been a bad sort of a
film even if Roger wasn't in it. It had served its purpose and
successfully whiled away a couple of hours. The man next to
her was still sound asleep and taking off her headphones she
could hear his raspy snores. Moira she saw had dropped off
too. She'd always looked like she was catching flies when she
was asleep, she thought with a fond smile as she caught sight
of her daughter's open mouth. The poor love was exhausted,
she always got snarky when she was tired—had done since
she was a baby. She was the same when she was hungry.

The poor love had been a lost soul since her daddy had
died, Maureen thought, feeling the pangs of maternal guilt at
not having been there for her youngest daughter. Her bottom lip quivered and she resisted the urge to reach out and
stroke her dark hair. She'd been an ostrich where Moira was
concerned. She knew she'd developed a strong liking for the
sauce. The girl was greener around the gills each time she
saw her than a frog, and she should have put her foot down
long before she'd gotten herself involved with *that* man. Sure,
she'd been a neglectful Mammy but, she'd prayed hard and
look what had happened. They'd been given a chance to
reconnect. Maureen yawned, she was bone tired too but she'd

never been one for sleeping on planes or in cars, or anywhere for that matter, unless she was lying horizontal. She'd just have to catch up when they got to their hotel.

She caught sight of the presentable young woman with her hair slicked back in a glossy bun making her way down the aisle with her trolley. How did the cabin crew all manage to look so groomed? The girl didn't have so much as a hair out of place and her make-up was perfect whereas she felt like a crumpled auld wreck. Reaching Maureen's row, she offered her a glass of water with a beatific smile which she accepted gratefully. It dehydrated you flying so it did and she'd never understood people who filled themselves with drink like Mr Whisky-a-go-go next to her. She could get tipsy off the smell of him alone.

Maureen nursed her water as the trolley rattled off and marvelled over the fact she was on her way. Who'd have believed it? She, Maureen O'Mara, the girl from Ballyclegg, was over half way to Vietnam! When she was young just going to the capital constituted an overseas trip. Ah well now, maybe that was a bit of an exaggeration but it wasn't all that much of a stretch. She wondered what her mam and da would make of what she was up to if they were still alive. They'd never approved of much when it came to their only daughter, and they'd probably think she was mad, just like they had when she'd run off all those years ago. Life had a funny way of working out though because if she hadn't of gotten on that bus to Dublin, she'd never have met her Brian.

At the thought of her husband her eyes burned and she bit down on her bottom lip to stop the tears from spilling over. She was prone to being tearful but she didn't cry over Brian in public. That was her cardinal rule and she'd not broken it, not once in the two years since he'd passed. She could cry over waving goodbye to her daughter for a month, or a scene from Ballykissangel—mind, Sunday evening's episode had had her wanting to bang that Assumpta Fitzgerald and Father Peter's heads together. Sure, the sexual tension between the pair of them would have you on the edge of your seat shouting at the television for them to just get on with it. Other weeks watching the show, she'd cry buckets. When it came to Brian though, well those great big ugly sobs that would rack forth at the thought of however many years she had left without him, well now they were best left for when her front door was firmly shut.

People said time healed. This was true on some levels because Maureen knew by the tight fit of her clothes that she no longer wore the signs of grief physically. One's appetite could only disappear for so long! Emotionally however it was a different matter. Some folk dealt with grief by wallowing while others were stoic, choosing to soldier on. Maureen had always had to fight for what she wanted in life and she was no wallower.

Instead of retreating inside herself like a snail into its shell which is exactly what she'd wanted to do, she'd launched into action by announcing she was moving out of the family home. She hoped to leave the daily reminders that Brian was no longer by her side, sharing the load and decision making when it came to the day to day running of O'Mara's, and make a fresh start by the sea.

So, she'd bought an apartment, not a flat because apartment had a much more sophisticated ring to it, in Howth. She'd gadded about, joining every committee and social group for retirees on offer, with the energy of a girl half her age. Thanks-be-to-God, Aisling had refused to let her sell the guesthouse and had taken over its running; a grand job she was making of it too. To offload the old girl as she thought of O'Mara's would have been a decision made in haste, and one she knew now she'd have lived to regret.

O'Mara's was a family business and it was important it stayed in the family. Had she sold the resplendent Georgian home, Brian would have surely turned in his grave. Not everybody had been happy with Aisling's decision though; Patrick had huffed off to America. It had hurt Maureen to think her oldest child, and only son had no interest in carrying on the business despite her protestations that the O'Mara children had the right to follow their own dreams and not step into those that had belonged to their parents.

Patrick had wanted his share of the cash from the business so he could invest it in whatever scheme he was involved with over there in La La Land as she thought of Los Angeles. Sure, it wasn't where his real life was and look at the state of his lady friend, Cindy, or was it Cynthia, and that enormous bosom of hers? What woman in her right mind would pay good money to stand in the shower and not be able to see their toes? Sure, that came around soon enough as it was. She cast a baleful glance at her midriff. Moira was right; she shouldn't have eaten the cheese she was awfully bloated as a result. Cynthia or Cindy was a woman who clearly wore her brains in her bosom, Maureen had her number.

Patrick was a good boy but he clearly had his brains somewhere else too when it came to his girlfriend. He was all about the money was Pat. He hadn't always been like that but these last few years he'd become like a shark. Money, he would learn, could you buy a lot of things but it couldn't buy you the love of a good woman and a happy life. Still in all it was no good her telling him that, he'd learn the hard way. You had to step back where your children were concerned, like she'd done in the end with Roisin. She wasn't one for meddling, well not much anyway.

Maureen sighed, you never stopped worrying about your children from the moment they came kicking and bawling into the world. No matter if they were two years old or pushing forty, you still worried and it had been easier to bear the weight of that worry when she'd had Brian to share it with.

His passing had changed them all. Her life had been tootling along nicely, their children were all grown, they ran a successful guesthouse, and they were as much in love with one another as they had been from the moment they'd met. Then Brian got sick. It hadn't been part of their plan and she'd refused to face it for the longest time, refused to accept her big strong Brian wouldn't be there for her, until he began to wither before her very eyes.

The fall-out from his illness was plain to see where their children were concerned too. Poor Moira had bounced from mistake to mistake. Aisling had gone and gotten engaged to that eejit but at least she'd seen sense and was with lovely Quinn now. Maureen had high hopes of welcoming Quinn into the family fold before too long and she smiled at the thought of it. Rosi was the one who'd probably coped the best out of all them, removed as she had been from the daily indignity of illness by distance. Besides, she couldn't fall apart, not with Colin and little Noah to look after.

The thought of her grandson warmed her. She'd promised to send him a postcard from every place they visited on their travels. He loved getting mail. She could picture him abandoning his breakfast to run to the front door as he heard the mail get pushed through the slot. As for Pat, well he'd decided the grass was greener in Los Angeles. A silly analogy because the grass was most definitely not greener. There was nowhere in the world with grass as green as Ireland as Brian used to say each spring when St Stephen's Green came back to life.

She winced, half expecting to taste blood where she'd bitten her lip this time. *Mustn't cry, mustn't cry.* She couldn't very well do what she normally did which was keep herself busy. She was stuck in this seat for the next few hours. At home she had her rambling group, her art classes, and sailing lessons to while away the days. The thing was, none of those things filled her long, lonely evenings. There were times she'd be sitting in her living room on her new sofa in her new apartment and if she stared at the four walls around her long enough, she could conjure Brian up. All of a sudden, he'd be there standing in front of her, so real she'd reach out to trace her finger down the lines and crevices of time etched on his beloved face but her finger would slice through the air. She'd blink and the image before her would disperse like tiny granules of coloured sand running through her fingers. She'd never breathed a word of that to anyone; they'd think she was mad but that's when she'd let herself cry those ugly sobs.

Ah, Brian. What would he think of her and Moira winging their way to Vietnam? They'd had grand plans of travelling the world together when they retired. Mind they'd always thought Patrick would be the one to take over O'Mara's when that day came. They'd been wrong about so many things. They'd kept a list, her and Brian, of places they'd visit one day. They'd had a curiosity about the world outside their guesthouse, which perhaps was due to their guests. They'd met so many interesting people from so many different places over the years. They'd both loved nothing more than to listen to the stories their visitors had to tell about the places they called home. Vietnam hadn't been on that list and Maureen suspected that's why it had held such appeal. It was somewhere different, somewhere she might just be able to stop and breathe. She wasn't a proponent of what she called Oprah phrases—words like journey and the such irked her, but in this case, she'd make an allowance because that was exactly what she was embarking on. A journey to try and reconnect with who she, Maureen O'Mara, was without Brian.

As she drained her cup, she realised she needed the toilet. It wasn't good for a woman who'd borne four children to hold on she thought eying the snoring lump next to her. What were her chances of waking him, she wondered? She gave him a tentative tap on the arm, 'Excuse me,' she said and then again in a louder voice with a much firmer tap but to no avail. He didn't move so much as a muscle. Maureen pursed her lips; it was no good. She couldn't hang around waiting for him to come out of his alcohol induced slumber. There was nothing for it, she'd have to go over him.

She unbuckled and got out of her seat, turning around in the cramped space so she was holding the back of her seat. The man in the seat behind her gave her a weary smile, before tuning back into his screen. The passengers either side of him were asleep—the woman on his left resting her head on his shoulder. It was now or never she thought attempting to swing a leg over Mr Whisky-a-go-go. He was a big man and she was a little woman. Her leg wouldn't quite stretch to the aisle floor, not unless she propelled herself nimbly over, like a sideways attempt at the vault. She'd been good at gym as a child. Sister Abigail had said she plenty of spring in her. *On the count of three, Maureen*, she could almost hear Sister Abigail's voice as she counted, 'One, two, and three, up and over.' Only this time she didn't quite make it across, landing instead in an undignified heap spread-eagled on Mr Whisky-a-go-go's lap, her bosom pressed firmly against his lolling head. That was when she heard a voice.

'Mammy, what the feck are you doing?!'

Chapter 7

♥

'For the tenth time, Moira I was not straddling him!' Maureen's eyes never moved from the carousel. They were in the arrivals hall of Tan Son Nhat Airport. There was only one bag left winding its way around on the belt in front of them and it wasn't hers. The black shiny case shuddered past once more teasing her as Moira, who was leaning against the trolley upon which she'd heaved her pack, refused to let the incident on Flight TG485 go.

'I saw you with my own two eyes, Mammy, and it did not look good. They have laws about that sort of thing on aeroplanes you know.' Okay, she was taking things a bit far but it had been a long flight and the drama that had unfolded as Mr Whisky-a-go-go nearly choked in Mammy's cleavage had been too much for her fuddled brain to take.

'Jesus wept, Moira, that's the mile-high club so it is and all I was doing was trying to get to the toilet for a wee! Was it my fault the drunken eejit wouldn't wake up?' Maureen's patience too was wearing thin and her voice had gone up several octaves. She'd had enough.

'Shush would you.' Moira furtively glanced around her. 'Everyone and their mammy doesn't need to know your business.' Actually, the crowds had thinned out considerably and she wasn't fancying Mammy's chances where her bag was concerned. It had been a good five minutes since the last of their fellow passengers had retrieved their bag from the carousel and gone on their way. She supposed they should go and find someone to tell.

———ℓℓ———

Forty-five minutes later, minus one bag but with assurances from a most apologetic Thai Airways that it would be delivered to their hotel sometime tomorrow, a disgruntled Maureen followed Moira's lead. They were following the signs to the exit that would take them to the taxi rank. The helpful woman on the Tourist Information desk had booked them into a very reasonable hotel for the night, before gesturing in the direction of the exit where they would find the metered taxis. One thing mother and daughter had whole heartedly agreed on was that neither was up for hostels. There would be no dormitories, six to a room, drunken bunkmates on this trip. Two to a room was going to be struggle enough, thank you very much.

Maureen spied the Foreign Exchange desk and subconsciously rested her hand on her bum bag where their funds were tucked safely away. They had enough money to tide them over in the meantime. She'd organised it through the AIB at home and had both Vietnamese dong and US dollars. She was more partial to the dong because her couple of hundred punt had officially made her a millionaire in Vietnam.

The name of their hotel was, Dong Do and their Tourist Information lady had neatly printed it for them on the piece of paper Moira, not trusting Mammy and her pants of many pockets, had put in her pants of only two pockets. She pushed her trolley through the sliding doors to the waiting night outside and gasped as the heat and hordes of shouting people descended on them. Sweatpants and joggers were a mistake she thought, because it was like someone had thrown an electric blanket over the top of her and hundreds of strangers had decided to crawl underneath it with her. She felt momentarily panicked by the foreign scene and her last coherent thought before Mammy took charge was this humidity would be murder on her hair; she was justified in packing her hair straighteners.

Mammy was magnificent, a warrior woman, Moira admiringly pushed the trolley after her as she blazed a trail through the hotel touts with their flapping brochures to the white airport taxi at the front of the line. The little man got out of his car and with a superhuman strength hauled her pack into his boot, while someone, Moira never saw who whisked the trolley away. She and Mammy collapsed into the back seat of the cab shutting the doors on the chaos outside. The air-conditioned calm was blissful and they sighed their relief simultaneously. Their driver got behind the wheel and Moira passed him the paper with the name of the hotel. He nodded and Mammy watched hawkeyed to see he set his metre before deftly weaving his way out of the busy hub.

A few minutes later Moira and Mammy had exhausted polite conversation with their driver. His English was limited and Moira was too tired to pick out phrases from the guide book. As for Mammy, well she was still sulking over her errant pack. Both women peered out their respective windows as they moved away from the airport and out onto the main road. Their eyes widened at the cacophonous horns mingling with shouts but it was the sights swarming around the vehicle that made their jaws drop. On either side of them a veritable ocean of mopeds and motorcycles whizzed around, behind, and in front of them.

'Mammy, look.' Moira stabbed at the glass; her exhaustion momentarily replaced by wonder. 'There were four on that bike, two little ones and their mammy and daddy. None of them had helmets on either.'

Maureen peered around her daughter, watching in amazement as families went about their business. Youngsters were indeed sandwiched between their parents on mopeds. Their small faces taking what, to the uninitiated, seemed like mayhem in their stride, some were even sleeping. Teens flirted with one another in an age-old ritual only instead of sidling alongside one another at the dance as they had in her day, they rode alongside one another on their mopeds. Pretty girls two to a scooter with flowing black hair smiling back at grinning lads determined to keep pace. 'Mother of God it's like watching Blind Date on scooters,' she muttered. Her eyes caught those of their driver who was watching their reaction to the scenes around them with amusement.

'Only without Cilla,' Moira echoed.

Maureen didn't know she'd been holding her breath until they pulled up outside a respectable looking hotel on a leafy street. Their driver deserved a medal in her opinion for dealing with those roads, he must have nerves of steel because hers were shredded. 'Dong Do,' he grinned over his shoulder before getting out and opening Moira's door. The taxi drivers back home could learn a thing or two about customer service, Maureen thought sliding across the seat to exit.

The heat after the cool of the car came as a shock and she stood on the cracked old pavement blinking in wonderment at the busy, neon-lit scene around them. Their driver retrieved Moira's bag from the boot and bent double, staggered with it toward the hotel. Moira scurried after him and Maureen watched as a smartly dressed night porter opened the door and relieved him of it, placing it on a trolley.

She was reluctant to head inside just yet and a frisson of excitement penetrated Maureen's jet lagged torpor, tomorrow she'd get to explore this place. She could already see it was like nowhere she'd ever been in her life. A horn blared and a pair of young men roared past on their Hondas making her jump. She realised the porter was holding the door waiting for her and so smiling her thanks at him she went inside.

'Make sure you tip him well, Mammy,' Moira whispered nodding at their patient driver before making for the smiling receptionist. She wondered whether this young woman kept a stash of biscuits in her top drawer like their receptionist, Bronagh. Did Vietnamese people even eat biscuits? She hadn't a clue. The only thing she was certain was a national staple was rice.

Maureen made the driver blush as she flashed her midriff once more attempting to find the right notes, stashed inside her bum bag. He'd set his price in American dollars and at this moment in time she was grateful as it was easier to fish out two five-dollar notes, she was tipping him generously, than to sort her thick wad of Vietnamese dong. He seemed pleased with the tip and there were lots of nods and smiles and little bows on both their parts until Moira having had enough called her over.

'Mammy, c'mon, we need to check in.'

Maureen didn't ask for a lot when it came to her accommodation but it wasn't too much to ask for a soft bed, hot water and a flushing loo. Oh, and cleanliness was next to godliness in her book. You should be able to run a finger down the skirting board and have it come up clean, so you should. This was a test she'd often employed at O'Mara's and not once, in all her years of running the old place had anyone ever complained that their room was not up to standard. Sure, a clean room wasn't too much to ask when you were paying good money to stay in an establishment now was it?

So no, she wasn't a woman of fancy tastes. She'd never had champagne tastes on beer money—mind she wasn't sure about Moira. She cast a cursory glance in her daughter's direction as they rode the lift to the third floor in silence. Moira seemed to subscribe to the theory that it was better to spend money like there was no tomorrow than to spend tonight like there's no money. Maureen's lips tightened; she was a spendthrift that girl of hers. She shook her head as the lift groaned ominously. It was down to that ridiculously overstuffed pack. If they wound up stuck in the elevator for the night it would be her five pairs of shoes, fifteen outfit changes and God only knew what else that would be to blame.

This line of thought made her think of her own missing backpack and that made her frown but she was distracted from dwelling on it by the lift juddering to a halt and the doors sliding open—thanks be to God. The porter trundled off down the tiled corridor, the wheels of the trolley echoing loudly in the silence as the two women dutifully followed. He stopped outside room 310 and unlocked the door, wheeling Moira's pack inside and lifting it onto the luggage rack before standing to one side to let Moira and Maureen see their room.

Maureen clapped her hands in delight. It was very, well, exotic Far East. The décor was a montage of rich reds and dark, ornately carved wood. It was the polar opposite of O'Mara's with its Georgian grandeur and it was perfect. She caught Moira's eye and remembered to tip their porter before going through the smiling, nodding, bowing process once more until as if they were playing rock-paper-scissors, he conceded and left them to it, closing the door behind him. Outside they could hear the faint sound of the horns and rumbling roar of motorbike engines. A fluorescent glow emanated from signage across the road. Maureen moved over to the window and closed the blinds shutting the foreign world below them out. It could wait until tomorrow.

'We made it,' Moira announced, flopping down on the bed closest the door. 'Bags first shower.'

'Five minutes and no longer, Moira. I'm shattered so I am, I want to get to bed.' Maureen watched her daughter as she got up and moved toward her pack. A minute or so later as she'd finally located her toilet bag and pyjamas she muttered, 'I could have been in and out of the shower in the time it took you to find those.'

'They were right down the bottom.' Moira marched into the bathroom and closed the door firmly behind her. She eyed the dish by the sink with its array of tiny tubes and bottles, tempted to inspect them all but thought better of it. Instead, she turned the handle on the shower around to hot and stepping under the jets had a quick wash. She felt one hundred times better by the time she reappeared in the bedroom. A flannel, soap, and hot water was a marvellous thing she thought, retrieving an oversized T-shirt from her pack and tossing it at Mammy. 'There you go, you can sleep in that tonight.'

Ten minutes later the luxury of stretching out in bed was wearing thin, Moira wanted to turn the light out. Her body was crying out for sleep but Mammy was still faffing around in the bathroom. 'What are you doing in there?'

'I'm just drying myself off. I had to wash my knickers so I've a pair for the morning.'

'Sure, you can borrow a pair from me. I've plenty. Just hurry up would ya, I'm knackered.'

'I will not wear a pair of those wisps of string you call knickers.'

'G-string, Mammy and they stop VPL.'

'I don't want to know what VPL is when it's at home, sure it sounds like some terrible disease down yonder.' The door opened and Mammy appeared in a T-shirt that came down to the middle of her thighs, her chest was emblazoned in red with the words 'Red Hot Chili Peppers – One Hot Minute Tour 95. Her face was shiny, scrubbed clean.

Moira's eyes narrowed. 'You used my Elizabeth Arden exfoliating cleanser, didn't you?'

'No.' Maureen fibbed. She had and her skin felt marvellous.

Moira wasn't convinced. Mammy better not have used her toothbrush or there'd be trouble she thought, but she was too tired to pursue it further. 'Hurry up and put the light out.' She curled up pulling the sheets up under her chin. The air-conditioning was keeping the room at an almost chilly level but she suspected if they turned it off the room would soon be stiflingly, stuffy.

Maureen pulled back the red coverlet and clambered into bed. The mattress was firmer than she was used to but sure, it would be good for her poor auld back. The sheets however were crisp, cool and fresh smelling as if they'd spent the day snapping in the breeze, just the way she liked them. Although, if they had been snapping on the breeze outside, she suspected they'd smell more of petrol fumes than the clean starched smell of laundry currently pleasing her nostrils. She reached up and flicked the light off.

'G'night, Mammy.'

'G'night, Moira, love.'

Chapter 8

♥

Mammy's Travel Journal

*H*ello from Ho Chi Minh! What an eye opener our first day's been. It's just after five o'clock and mine and Moira's feet are in bits from all the walking we did this morning. You wouldn't believe the things we've seen but I'm getting ahead of myself. I'll start at the beginning.

We slept for ten hours solid. I'll admit to feeling a bit like the back end of a bus when I woke up and yes, I used Moira's mascara even though she says sharing eye make-up will give you the pink eye but what she doesn't know won't hurt her. Sure, as it was, I had to put up with itching eyes all day and kept rubbing at them. By the time we got back to the hotel I looked like yer man Alice Cooper. I learned my lesson. I do like that exfoliating scrub of hers though.

The restaurant where we could get breakfast, it's included and is very good value, is on the top floor of our hotel. We had a grand view over the Saigon River and we sat watching all the activity on the streets below. I was a bit worried as to what would be on offer but we ate very normal breakfasty things, you know eggs, toast and the like but, the gentleman at the table in front of ours was slurping up some sorta broth. It had big, fat white noodles in it that reminded me of worms. Honestly, it was like that old Jerry Lewis recording of The Noisy Eater and him in a suit too. Moira said it was making her feel sick which I thought was a bit pot calling the kettle black. You'd want to have heard the racket she used to make sucking her spaghetti noodles up when it was Monday night, Spag Bog. I told her this and it didn't go down well.

I think I was feeling outa sorts because I'd slept heavy and because of my missing backpack. It's not a nice feeling knowing your smalls and other personal items are in the hands of strangers. I felt much better once I'd had a cup of coffee and as we walked back to our room, I resolved to be nice. No more sniping. God works in mysterious ways you know because not two minutes after we'd shut the door behind us there was a knock. I opened it, to be greeted by a different but equally noddy, smiley porter as the one we encountered last night and, he had my backpack on his trolley! I could have kissed him.

I didn't of course but I did send up a quick prayer of thanks and, of course I tipped him generously. I felt a little bad because even though I was eternally grateful to him for returning my bag to me, I had to shut the door on him in the end. He wasn't playing the rock-paper-scissors game like the other fella had and we'd have been there all day with the smiling and nodding.

I don't mind telling you it was a load off my mind to have my luggage and the first thing I did was put on a fresh bra and change my top. I treated myself to a blue one and a green one in the quick drying fabric. They were pricey like but to my mind well worth every penny. I put the blue one on and washed the green one I'd worn on the plane in the bathroom sink. I hung it over the shower rail and would you believe it? It's bone dry now. Sure, it's marvellous stuff. Moira says they might be quick drying but they're a fashion affront. I ignored her, because I'm being nice.

Anyway, we decided we'd explore the sights on foot. Although Moira quite liked the look of those cyclo thing-a-me-bobs. They're a sorta three wheeled bicycle taxi but I told her no. I'd feel awful sitting there like Lady Muck, so I would, while yer poor wee man pedalled away looking like he was about to expire at any minute.

Stepping outside the hotel was like wading into warm soup and there were even more motorbikes zooming the streets than there'd been the night before. They're a menace so they are. Moira and I agreed there must be at least a million of the things buzzing about the place and from what we could see there are no road rules. It's a case of survival of the fittest.

Moira was in charge of the guidebook because she has a better sense of direction than I do and I've never been any good at reading the maps. Brian used to say road signs were like a foreign language to me. So, Moira took the lead and we set off admiring the grand old buildings. They reminded me of a film I once saw. It was set around a big white hotel in Singapore. I remember a fan rotating lazily around and people lounging about in cane chairs sipping cocktails. It might have been a Bond one if there were cocktails involved but I can't remember for certain.

In between these smart buildings there were tall, narrow shops with shuttered windows. There was lots of silk for sale too, jewel bright fabrics decorating the shop windows, and it was like a magnet pulling me and Moira in through the door so as we could stroke and admire them. I bought a pashmina for myself and each of my girls, excluding Moira because she's getting the trip and the other two aren't. Moira bought herself a pretty black sleeveless top with a band of red silk around the hemline. We had to remind ourselves it was the first day of our holiday and not to go mad with the spending.

The noise is like nothing else, the constant sounding of horns, shouts and construction work which is going on every-where. It wasn't long before we happened across Notre Dame

Cathedral, not the Paris one obviously. This Notre Dame was built with red bricks and had twin spires. I felt right at home when I set eyes on it the way I always do when I see God's House. Moira says she feels like that when she sees the McDonald's big yellow arches. They comfort her because she knows there's food, drink, and a toilet close at hand. The women trickling in and out of the cathedral clutching their rosary beads were wearing silk tunics in all the colours of a bird of paradise, and black pants, not at all the sort of getup you'd see back home. Moira and I lit a candle and I said a prayer. I'm not telling you who I prayed for though, that's private.

Outside the cathedral there were lots of men shouting at us 'would we like a ride in their cyclo?' No, we would not. There were groups of children vying for our attention too, they were selling postcards. There was one little lad whose smile reminded me of Noah's, he looked to be around the same age as him too. Imagine, five years old and already out contributing to the family coffers. I'll have to tell Rosi. She can't even get Noah to put his pyjama pants under his pillow of a morning. I wanted to buy cards off all of them but Moira pulled me away after I'd bought my tenth.

We were grand, Moira and I, as we carried on with our exploring until we came to the intersection we needed to cross in order to visit the Ben Than market. There was no nice green man to bleep and let everybody know it was our turn to cross the road and so we stood by the kerb watching all those millions of scooters pass by like a pair of lemons. Of course, the longer we stood there the more frightened of stepping out into all that chaos we became. Then would you believe it? A little old lady happened upon us. She spoke to us but of course we couldn't understand a word, and she couldn't understand a word we were saying but you know sometimes you don't need language to communicate. She gave us a big toothless grin, took us both by the arm and steered us out into the traffic. Well now let me tell you, she was like Moses parting the Red Sea. She trotted across that road dragging us along with her, and every single one of those scooters whose path we were stepping into weaved their way around us.

We did the noddy, smiley thing once we'd made it to the other side and then we went our separate ways. The market was undercover and very hot and cramped. It had all sorts of things in it from teeny tiny shoes to teeny tiny tea sets. We were fascinated by the fish market at the far end. Every kind of fish was flapping around and the crabs, well, you'd want to see the size of the pincers on them. If one of them got hold of your toe at the beach you'd know about it. There were even rogue frogs making a bid for freedom. I suppose the frogs is down to the French influence on the place.

We had a sit down once we'd had a good look around. It was time for a cool drink along with a cheese baguette, lovely and light the bread was too with a crispy crust. Nature called after that.

It was no easy feat to find a public convenience because Moira couldn't find the word for toilet in our guide book. In the end I did a knock-kneed demonstration and we got pointed in the right direction. Like I said sometimes you can communicate without language. It was one of them squat toilets and we had to pay a lady for a piece of toilet paper. I was dubious as to whether I'd get back up again and I was terrified I'd lose my footing and slip or something, but sure I was grand. It's a blessing Rosemary didn't come with me because she's been making noises about her knees giving her trouble. Moira whose knees are perfectly fine made an almighty fuss about the cleanliness of the facility and I told her to cop on to herself. Sometimes that girl doesn't know she's born. Sure, when I was a girl, we had an outhouse down the bottom of the yard. It was dark and full of spiders with hairy legs just waiting to get you.

I think Moira was tetchy because she was in pain. She said she'd had enough walking and asked me if I'd brought the

Lanacane gel with me. I said no but I did have hand sanitizer. Well, she ate the head off me. I told her not to take that tone with me and that if she'd worn the elephant pants her sister had given her instead of a silly short skirt, she'd be grand. She still says she won't be seen dead in the elephant pants and I said that she's not to come crying to me when she's red raw. I don't know where that one gets her stubborn streak from.

As it happened, I'd had enough of the walking too so we caught a taxi to the tourist office because we needed to buy our tickets for the hop on, hop off bus we're going to take to Hanoi. Would you believe our ticket only cost twenty-eight American dollars each? I tell you Bus Eireann are running a racket. I think I might have to write a letter to the man in charge when I get home. We're being robbed so we are. We've also booked a day trip tomorrow to the Mekong Delta, $14.00 with lunch, inclusive. Now, if that's not good value I don't know what is.

We visited the War Remnants Museum next. It was very upsetting so it was and I don't really want to talk about it. All I will say is there are never any winners in war not when you're a Mammy. I did have my photograph taken by a fighter plane though, and Moira posed by a US helicopter.

My observations from today are that this country has come through a terrible time and despite hardship the people are lovely. They're ever so smiley and noddy and always keen to help you. It gives you faith in the human spirit. Oh, and I like the Buddhist monks too, they have a gentle manner about them, not at all fierce like Father John can be if you miss the mass. And I think their robes are very sensible given the hot weather.

$$\sim\!\!\ell\ell\sim$$

Postcard

Dear Noah,

It's your nana here. Aunty Moira and I have been having a grand time in Hoi Chi Minh or Saigon which is what the people who live here call it. It's very confusing, so it is. It's a big, busy city even busier than yer man Richard Scarry's Busytown in those books of his you love. I've never seen so many motorcycles in my life. There are thousands of them on the roads. There's lots to see here and it's a very interesting city. The sounds and the smells are very different to home. It's also the hottest place I've ever been. Noah, I hope you're being a good boy for your mammy and dad give them a hug from me and have one for yourself.

Love Nana

Chapter 9

♥

Sally-Ann

S ally-Ann Jessop inhaled sharply, it couldn't be, could it? Surely it was too much of a coincidence that she should smell that particular smell, here, now. She'd definitely caught a strong whiff of that soft flowery scent she'd once adored though. It had made her look up sharply from her guidebook and she was certain it was the dark-haired woman who was wearing it. She looked to be around her age, only with skin that hadn't baked under a hot, unforgiving Australian sun. She was making her way in a bustling manner down the narrow aisle, a younger woman—she had to be her daughter—was following behind her.

The daughter appeared to be having a spot of difficulty, Sally-Ann noticed, the nurse in her concerned to see she was walking quite bow-legged. The poor girl had a nasty eye infection taking hold too, she hoped she had some antibiotic drops for it. Despite the puffy eye she couldn't help but notice she was lovely looking. She reminded Sally-Ann of an American actress, and she wracked her brain for the woman's name *Dee or Dina,* but it wouldn't come to her. She was identical to her mother, the Arpège wearer, just younger.

Sally-Ann would know that fragrance anywhere although she hadn't worn the scent herself in well over thirty years. Not since she'd last set foot on Vietnamese soil. It held too many memories. Smells were a powerful tool for triggering the memory she'd learned. They were every bit as powerful as sounds. Even now, all these years later a sudden bang like the back firing of a car or a tardy Guy Fawkes cracker would send her diving for cover but the smell of Arpège, well that took her right back in time to what was another world now.

It never left you, the fear and the instinct to survive. Poor Robert had suffered terribly with nightmares for the rest of his life once he'd returned home. He'd cry out in his sleep and she'd know he was reliving things no young man should ever have to live through. Her breath caught in her throat as she thought of her husband, and the familiar lump that warned her that tears weren't far away formed. She swallowed hard and took a few steadying breaths becoming aware that the two women, a few seats behind her now, were bickering, and eager for distraction she tuned in.

'Mammy, I get the window seat. Sure, it's only fair.'

'Why? You had the window seat on the plane and it's not my fault you've got the pink eye.'

'That was no picnic, squashed into the corner I was for thir-teen hours. And it is your fault. I know you used my mascara.'

'I wouldn't do that, Moira, but sure, I haven't even had a cup of coffee yet and the sun's only just after rising. It's too early for arguing. Take the window seat, and I want to hear no more about it.'

'Aha, I knew it. You do feel guilty.'

Sally-Ann's mouth twitched as, glancing over her shoulder, she was in time to see the younger woman wag a finger at her mother before sliding into the seat. She wasn't going to give her a chance to change her mind.

She'd always been one of life's people watchers, happy to sit back and listen and tuning in now she liked the sing-song quality of their Irish accents. To her ears the Irish always sounded like they were telling a story even when they were just wrangling over who sat where. You couldn't say that about the Australian accent with its lazy, drawling vowels. She knew it sounded brutal and harsh to delicate ears but then you had to be both of those to survive the conditions in the dusty old sheep farm she'd always called home.

She admired their dark Celtic looks too, they were both dainty, petite women. It was a category the feminine kernels beneath her sun-worn exterior had always yearned to fit into. Ha, she thought to herself glancing down at the age spots decorating the back of her hands, thanks to that damned sun, there'd never been any chance of that. She'd tipped six foot by the time she was sixteen and had filled out into the sort of solid build that had people describe her as a strong Sheila. A strong Sheila was not something she'd wanted to be at sweet sixteen but it had served her well over the years because if she hadn't of been strong, inside and out, she wouldn't have survived. Yes, these hands of hers might be worn and coarse to touch, the hands of a worker, but they were also healing hands. She was proud of them.

The mother flopped down into her seat and looking up caught Sally-Ann watching them. She smiled and shrugged in that universal way women do when it comes to their offspring. Sally-Ann smiled back. She'd been there done that with her own kids. Jeff and Teagan were both off living their own lives now though and she could imagine their faces if she'd suggested they make this a mother, daughter, son trip to Vietnam! She was intrigued as to why these two were travelling together. It wasn't the norm, she thought, her attention flickering to the front of the bus. A young woman with matted hair on the verge of forming dreadlocks had just boarded. She was cutting it fine Sally-Ann thought, watching as puffing and panting she showed the driver her ticket.

Jeff and Teagan had both been uncertain about her heading away so soon after Robert's passing but she'd told them it was something she had to do; she'd promised their father she would. They'd accepted that. They'd not wanted to delve too deeply into her reasons for coming back to Vietnam. They'd heard Robert crying out from his nightmares through the years and she'd embarrassed them both during their awkward teenage phases more than once by shielding her head at a sudden noise or inexplicably crying at the smell of lemongrass in the supermarket.

Sally-Ann didn't want to tell them why she was going back either. It was always hard to imagine your parents having had a life before you came into it and sometimes your children were better off not knowing the ins and outs of that life.

She'd sensed their reticence at being back on the farm while they waited for the deed of sale to finalise. It was a place they'd both been eager to leave and see beyond. She understood. She'd felt the same once, too. The world was a big place and the boundaries of life on a rural sheep farm could feel as restricting as the electric and woven wire fencing used to keep those sheep in. So, with Robert's funeral done and dusted, she'd driven them to the airport and hugged them close, her kiss goodbye her blessing. They'd been quick to accept her assurances that she'd be fine and she'd watched them board the plane that would take them back to their big city lives on the other side of the country waving until she thought her arm would drop off. She'd stayed to see the plane take off and as it taxied down the runaway, the speed growing until it was airborne, she'd felt very alone.

She startled as the bus rumbled into life and the travel weary looking backpacker who'd obviously overslept stumbled down the aisle, her pierced midriff on display. She grasped hold of the seat in front of Sally-Ann's with an apologetic smile. She managed to smile back at the young woman as she steadied herself before continuing down the aisle. Hers was a freedom she and Robert had never known in their youth although they'd both sought adventure. How naïve she'd been back then.

She felt a pang for those lost years. The innocence of youth had been snatched from them by the reality of war and they'd both had to grow up brutally fast here. The dewiness of early adulthood had dried up in this place just like the lush green jungle of the countryside had withered and died. She'd seen the brown arid land burnt by Agent Orange spraying and fields filled with moon like craters from the B52 bombs dropped like rain from her vantage point in an old workhorse Hercules. Now her eyes flitted to the window opposite her. The glass was smeared with dust giving the world beyond a sepia tone. She stared but didn't see as they began to nose their way down the congested streets and as the smell of Arpège wafted up the aisle teasing her senses, she found herself back at the beginning.

Chapter 10

1967

'But why, Sal, I don't understand?' Terri's eyes, violet-coloured mirrors of Sally-Ann's were wide. She stopped nibbling on the cheese sandwich letting it drop on the brown paper bag on her lap. Its crusts would curl in no time in the dry heat of this particularly hot summer's day, despite the shade from the gazebo under which they were sitting. Sally-Ann, on a rare weekend home from the Royal Perth Hospital where she was soon to complete her nurses training, had whisked her sister away from her Saturday morning job at Woolworths for lunch. She'd slapped together a hastily made picnic of Mum's tangy sheep's milk cheese sangers, apples, and a thick slab of homemade pound cake for afters. The scent of the roses wilting under the hot sun drifted by and Terri waved her hand in annoyance at the buzzing flies keen to investigate what was on the menu. 'Is it Billy?'

Sally-Ann made a choking sound and she too abandoned her sandwich even though she adored Mum's cheese. It was buttery soft and creamy, and one of the best things about coming home in her opinion. 'Billy Brown? No! He only had one thing on his mind and I wasn't interested. He's not the settling sort, Terri, and besides I'm not ready to settle.' Billy worked on the railway and she'd met him at a dance. He had a cheeky larrikin way about him that told her he'd be fun and he was, but he wasn't the sort of man you'd want to get serious about.

'Then why? You said you'd come home to Katanning to work in the hospital here when you finished your training.'

'And I will, just not yet.' Sally-Ann felt guilt poking its finger at her. Her sister was five years younger. It was a big gap when you were little but that gap had closed over the years and now at twenty-one Sally-Ann considered her sister her best friend. Mum had told the story often enough of how she'd refused to have anything to do with baby Terri when she'd brought the swaddled bundle home from the hospital. Her nose had been properly out of joint having had five years of Mum all to herself. Terri, however had adored her big sister from the get-go. Her enormous eyes, the exact same unusual shade of indigo as her own, a source of comment and compliments all their lives, would follow Sally-Ann's every move. As she got bigger, she'd howl of a morning when her sister banged the fly-screen door shut behind her, on her way to get the bus for school. She didn't know when it had changed. Mum reckoned it was when Terri began teething and the only person she'd be comforted by was Sally-Ann. She'd been her little sister's protector, confidante, and partner in crime ever since.

Should she tell her sister about Elsie the lovely old nurse who had taken a shine to her when she'd first arrived at the Royal Perth? Elsie had recognised her homesickness, and taking her under her wing, had assured her it would pass. Sally-Ann hadn't believed her at first; leaving home was an unexpected wrench she'd felt physically. She missed the wide, open expanse of flat land from her bedroom window and the sunsets she'd taken for granted each evening. She even missed Bessie's incessant barking of a morning as she waited for Dad to take her out on the rounds of the farm.

Elsie was right though and she'd soon made friends with the other nurses settling in to the new routines of life in the nurses' hostel. She'd even begun to enjoy the buzz of being in the big city. Of course, she missed Terri, and Mum's cheese! She went home whenever she could manage it, knowing it was harder for her sister. Sally-Ann was busy having new and exciting experiences, she was learning and being challenged whereas for Terri life was exactly the same only her sister wasn't there to talk to at the end of each day.

It was Elsie who'd told her the world was bigger than Katanning. She'd nursed in Japan during the war and Korea too. She suggested given the intensive care experience Sally-Ann was gaining from her training she should put it to good use and join the army. Elsie said that she'd be married with children wrapped around her legs before she knew it and that she should go, see a bit of the world first. At first Sally-Ann had thought the idea was ridiculous. The army wasn't for the likes of her she'd told Elsie. She was a country girl whose home was where her heart was. Elsie had argued that she was strong, kind, and compassionate, exactly the sort of girl the army would be glad to have.

Elsie's words gnawed at her and each time she went home to Katanning, to the familiar rhythms of life on the sheep farm, she knew were she to leave nothing would change. It would be as it was when she returned. Nothing would change in the town either. The heritage rose gardens across the road from the town hall where she and Terri were sitting now, the Pioneer Women's clock tower, the familiar shops and main street, they wouldn't change. It would all be here just the same when she got back, only she wouldn't be the same because she'd have done something different, seen new things. Her feet grew increasingly itchy until she found herself sitting here now trying to explain to her sister why she'd enlisted.

She was desperately trying to put all of this into words for Terri who was nodding like she understood but whose trembling bottom lip told a different story.

'It's not forever, Terri, I just need to spread my wings for a while. I'll be back before you know it.'

The bus swerved violently jolting Sally-Ann back to the present. The driver slammed his hand on the horn letting the man behind the wheel of the minivan veering too far over into their lane know what he thought of his road skills. If only she'd known what had lain ahead of her she thought, knowing that even if she had she still wouldn't have done things any differently.

Chapter 11

♥

Present

Maureen did feel bad; no Mammy likes to see their daughter with a sticky pink eye. They'd go to a pharmacy and get some antibiotic drops as soon as they got to Nha Trang. Her own eyes were like sandpaper but that was from lack of sleep. She wasn't a natural early riser and neither was Moira. It was a good job they'd had reception give them a wake-up call or they'd both still be sound asleep. She glanced around her, catching the eye of a woman who looked like she'd spent a lot of time in the sun over the years. Her skin was a weathered, freckled brown which made her cornflower blue eyes all the more startling. Maureen liked cornflowers and she shrugged and smiled her 'Kids, who'd have em' smile at her'. The woman smiled back before turning away and Maureen settled herself into her seat before opening her day pack to retrieve her travel journal.

The bus was around three-quarters full now she noted, looking up to see a young woman clambering aboard mumbling her apologies and flashing her ticket. Her hair was terribly matted and could do with an introduction to a hairbrush. The bus juddered into life and the girl nearly went flying, reaching out and grabbing the seat in front of the woman with the cornflower eyes to steady herself. That was when Maureen noticed what she was wearing. She elbowed Moira.

'Ow, what was that for?'

'Look,' she fizzed excitedly.

Moira peered around her mammy to see a girl a year or two younger than herself. A bit of a hippy type she mused unsure what she was supposed to be looking at. She liked her nose piercing, not that she'd ever be game to pierce anything other than her ears. She had her belly button pierced too. Andrea had had that done. She said it wasn't the needle that hurt but the clamp used to hold the skin firm. It had made Moira feel sick just thinking about it. It was then her gaze drifted down and she saw what had Mammy all worked up. The woman was wearing identical elephant pants to the ones Aisling had shoved at her and fair play to her, they looked class. She could feel Mammy's eyes gleeful and triumphant on her.

'Do you think I'd look good with the dreadlocks then? It would save a fortune on shampoo and visits to the hair salon, so it would.'

'Don't be obtuse, sure they're an invitation for the mice to move in, so they are.'

Moira's lips formed a thin straight line. The insides of her thighs were still stinging and yer hippy one had managed to rock the pants. It wasn't as if she'd see anyone she knew while she was here, either. 'Alright then. What goes on tour stays on tour, yes?'

Maureen's nod was emphatic.

'Shake on it.'

'Shake.' She shook her daughter's hand. 'What am I shaking on?'

'I'll wear the fecking pants. When the bus pulls in for a comfort stop, I'll change into them but you are not—read my lips, Mammy—NOT to tell Aisling I wore them. I won't have her saying I told you so, understood?'

'Understood.' Maureen was already mentally penning her postcard to Aisling. In the meantime, though, she'd update her travel journal. They'd gone to bed early last night what with the ungodly hour they'd had to get up this morning and she'd not had a chance to write in it. She wanted to fill it in while things were still fresh in her mind because one day when this trip seemed like it had all been a dream, she could pull it out and relive it all though her own words. She pulled the tray on the back of the seat down and set about writing.

_ee_

Mammy's Travel Journal

Well now here I am sitting on the hop on, hop off bus. It's bit of a ramshackle old thing as though it should have been retired to wherever it is retired buses go a while back. It runs though and we're going to be hopping off at Nha Trang. We've another long day ahead of us as we're not due to arrive until dinnertime but sure we can put our feet up for a good few days once we get there. We had a grand day yesterday on a tour we booked at the same time as we bought our bus tickets. The minivan picked us up outside the Dong Do at eight o'clock and our driver, Duc, took a shine to Moira and insisted she sit up the front with him. I think he felt sorry for her because she's walking a bit bow-legged at the moment and what with the pink eye, she's a sorry sight. Serves her right, the bow-legged bit anyway, I say. At least she's seen sense and agreed to wear the elephant pants.

It took a long time to get out of the city. Hoi Chi Minh, Duc told us is home to over six million people. Imagine that, the whole of Ireland has less than four million people living in it! The sprawl just went on and on and once we were on the highway the potholes in parts were spine jarring. I'm glad I brought a sturdy bra with me but I will have to have a word with Moira. It might be hot but she'll regret it when they're down around her middle in another ten years. Perky is as perky does.

My first glimpse of the mighty Mekong River was a little disappointing. Sure, it was a big sea of a river but it looked about as clean as the Liffey only there were no shopping trolleys in this one. An American woman, she had enormous teeth—I kept thinking of the wolf in Little Red Riding, told me it's because of the sediment from the surrounding countryside and the rocks that sit along the bottom of it. It's the colour of stewed tea being poured from a pot. We got on a long boat next. There were no life jackets that I could see but I forgot all about that once we motored off. Wooden stilt houses were dotted all along the banks and we passed lots of boats with lone fishermen casting their nets. Moira took loads of photographs. It was very peaceful although I did wonder how they get on with toilets and the like because I couldn't see any signs of plumbing under the houses.

We got off the boat at a market. I tell you nobody would ever go hungry here not with all the fruit and vegetables for sale, there was lots of shouting and bartering going on. All the women were wearing the conical hats. I quite fancy buying myself one because they'd keep the sun off your head a treat but at the same time, they're as light as a feather which would save you from the hat hair at the end of the day. Moira said I'm on my own if I do. We shared some fresh pineapple and had a stroll around, well she swaggered more than strolled. I don't think I'll be eating much in the way of chicken not after seeing all those birds, freshly plucked, sitting out in the heat with the flies paying them a visit.

We got back on the boat and motored across to a place called Turtle Island where we trekked through the bush. I told Moira I was delighted my rambling training was already coming in handy. We came to a clearing where lunch was laid out and so we sat surrounded by mangroves and under a canopy of banana trees and had the tofu with noodles followed by fruit. I'm not really a tofu sort of a person but it was quite tasty. I kept saying 'Can you believe we're sitting under a banana tree, Moira,' because I really couldn't believe it. I don't think she could believe it either.

After lunch we got back on the boat and putted down a stream. It was very pretty with the sunshine dappling through the bamboo. We made a stop to visit a shop making banana wine and coconut sweets. I bought a packet of the fudgy sweets which was a mistake because I couldn't stop eating them. Very moreish they were but I felt sick once I'd finished the bag. A little further on we came to a village where we had honey tea and listened to traditional music.

Now, I'll be honest here, I thought Aisling's musical attempts as a child were appalling. I had to resort to bribery to try and get her in to the St Teresa's choir but not even my Porter Cake could sway those nuns. This, however, was something else it was like listening to a classroom full of children playing the recorder for the first time. Of course, I smiled away and tapped my foot the way you do and even though it hurt my ears all the different musical instruments were very interesting. Oh, and there was a snake in the café too. Two of the braver members of our group posed for photographs with it. It was green and yellow and kept hissing. Moira and I both said, NO thank you very much when it was waved our way.

It was a long, sleepy ride back to our hotel and over our early dinner of Vietnamese pancakes which didn't cause me any intolerance problems, although the chilli sauce was a bit hot for my liking. Moira and I agreed our day trip had been very good value. I thought we were rubbing along quite nicely, Moira and me, but then she woke up this morning with the pink eye and got very angry, accusing me of helping myself to her eye make-up. I've let her have the window seat on the *bus and I think she's forgiven me. I'm not sure if it's a good idea writing this on the bus because it is very bumpy and I'm beginning to feel bilious.*

———*ell*———

'Look, Mammy.'

Maureen must have nodded off because she started awake at the sound of Moira's voice. 'What is it? Are we there?'

'No, but look out there at the rice paddies it's so pretty and over there, see, I think it's some sort of cow.'

'It's a water buffalo, so it is.' Maureen sat up shaking off the drowsy fog of being on the road. The colours outside were glorious shades of green and gold and as they bounced through a village, the children, their faces bright with smiles came and stood in their doorways waving out to them.

'Ah bless.' Maureen wasn't sure that it was a good idea Moira peering out the window at the wee dotes the way she was, she'd frighten them with that eye but she decided it might be wise to hold her tongue on the matter. A particularly deep pothole saw her cross her legs. 'I hope we stop soon; I need to pay a visit. It's all this bouncing around.'

It was another twenty minutes before the bus rumbled into a lay-by. There was a restaurant with a toilet off to the side. Maureen did a silent head count of those ahead of them through narrowed eyes. 'Moira don't mess about getting off and when you do make a run for it.'

Chapter 12

♥

T he waves shushed up the beach in an almost hypnotic manner. Maureen and Moira were sitting at a table beneath gently swaying palm trees beside a breezy restaurant. On the other side of the restaurant was the promenade where, Moira had read in their guide book, American soldiers used to hold cyclo races. A postcard Maureen had just written to Noah was leaning up against the plastic napkin container and Moira had abandoned her good intentions of penning the promised cards to Andrea and her New Zealand friend, Tessa, in favour of watching the sunset.

The sky was awash now with hazy purples and pinks and the sun, a giant orange orb slipping slowly beneath the line where the silver sea and sky merged. The sticky heat of the day had dispersed and the light wind wafting in from the water gently caressed them. 'This is bliss so it is,' Maureen sighed happily waiting for her order of baked baby clams to arrive before taking a sip of her fruit juice. She'd have quite liked a Pina Colada but didn't think it would be fair to wave it under Moira's nose. 'I always feel like I'm on holiday when I see a palm tree.' *And sip on a Pina Colada*, she added to herself.

'Mmm,' murmured Moira soaking up the scene spread out before them. Her eye was already beginning to feel better thanks to the drops they'd picked up as soon as they'd gotten off the bus. Although she still had to resist the urge to rub at it. She stifled a yawn, it had been a long day and the roads in parts on the journey here had been bad, nerve-janglingly so, but they'd made it and she'd seen things along the way she'd never seen before. Sugar cane plantations, rice paddies, water buffalo, and houses with tin roofs that looked like they'd tumble down with one good gust of wind. What had struck her though was how all the people they'd seen as they'd rumbled alongside their farms or through their villages, had looked so content. Happy with their lot. People didn't look like that in cities she'd realised. They were always striving for more as they rushed off to somewhere important they had to be. It had felt, sitting on that bus today, as though time itself had slowed down.

She gazed out toward the beach. Ah, Jaysus but it was beautiful and she wondered briefly what Andrea was doing back home now. She'd tried but couldn't wrap her head around the time difference and had no idea if she'd be at work or fast asleep. Her mind drifted to Mason Price; had anybody done anything gossip worthy at the work's drinks she'd missed on Friday? To her surprise, she found she didn't really care. If people had nothing better to talk about than who was riding who, then they weren't really living were they? This was living she thought, and it dawned on her that for the first time in a very long while she felt as though she didn't have a care in the world. Well not quite, she did still have the pink eye and she'd have to make sure to hide her Elizabeth Arden exfoliating wash from Mammy for the rest of the trip. Oh, and she would like to know if Andrea had given Jeremy from IT the glad eye after a wine or two. She'd done her best planting the seeds where he was concerned in an effort to sway her friend away from her unrequited love. She'd seen a few internet cafes around Hoi Chi Minh there was bound to be one here somewhere to check her e-mail.

One thing was certain, whatever Andrea was up to right now she wouldn't be sitting by the seaside sipping coconut juice fresh from the shell in a singlet top with a pair of elephant pants on. She glanced down at them and ran her hand over the soft cotton fabric. They'd grown on her since she'd slipped them on in that nightmare of a toilet stop on the way here. She'd had to do a veritable Irish dance just to get the fecking things on without touching anything. The chaffing was a forgotten nightmare now and she liked how the pants made her feel ethnic, like she wanted to go get her belly button pierced and let her hair clump together in big knotty dreads. The idea of forgetting your real life and spending months tripping through Asia like that girl who'd been on their bus today was an appealing one. Of course, yer hippy woman didn't have Mammy by her side. She might not have looked so laid back if she had.

Moira had earwigged on the girl as she'd compared travel stories with the guy sitting across from her. The pair of them were kindred spirits, she'd thought, because his hair, having automatically checked him out as he'd boarded the bus also looked like it could do with a jolly good wash. She'd dismissed him with a big red cross when she caught sight of the wispy tufts of fluff protruding from his chin.

This poor attempt at a beard instantly reminded her of the old Ladybird book story Rosi used to read her, The Three Billy Goats Gruff, and she'd found herself doing the trip, trap, trip, trap bridge crossing bit in her head. Leather bracelets were wrapped around his wrist and somewhat disturbingly, she noted he had a pair of fisherman pants on just like Mammy's only his were orange. Mercifully Mammy was too busy rummaging in her pack to notice him otherwise she'd have felt obliged to let him know she too owned a pair only hers were green with gold swirly bits on them. She'd yet to break the pants out, too enamoured of her quick dry pants of many pockets.

Tom had mentioned when he asked her if she'd like to catch up when she got home, that he'd spent a lot of time backpacking around Asia. Had he worn pants like that fella's? Jaysus she hoped not, they wouldn't have done that lovely bum of his justice and he just wasn't the type to do the chin fluff thing. If he was, he wouldn't be her type at all. A scenario whereby she was in the throes of passion with him ensued, only for some reason he was wearing fisherman pants and she couldn't figure out how to get them off. It killed the moment and turning scarlet at the fact Mammy was sitting next to her and had always had an uncanny ability to read her mind, she'd diverted her thoughts by concentrating on the conversation going on behind her instead.

She'd heard them bandying words like full moon and the best beach ever about and envied them their carefreeness.

Now, a thought occurred to her. 'Mammy they have palm trees outside the Bloody Stream pub by the station in Howth. Is that why you like living there? Do you feel like you're on holiday whenever you wander around the harbour?' It would go a long way to explaining why her mammy had opted to move to the seaside village after Daddy died. There was something cathartic about palm trees; the sea and holidays, they were good for the health.

'No, I like being by the sea but sure those trees aren't proper palm trees like these.' She gestured to the spiky fronds above her head.

Moira spied a clump of coconuts and hoped that wind didn't get up. It wouldn't be a good look, being flown home on their travel insurance after being hit on the head by falling coconuts. 'Yes they are.'

'No, they're not, Moira. It's not a proper palm tree if you have to wear your Aran sweater and a vest to sit under it.'

They were diverted from pursuing this line of conversation by a lone woman, her face hidden by her conical hat, who was making her barefooted way up the beach toward them. Across her shoulders rested a stick, a basket dangling down either side. From where they were sitting and with the deepening dusk it was impossible to make out what she was on her way over to offer them.

'Say no, Mammy,' Moira muttered under her breath. 'N. O. It's not hard and sure, you've enough postcards to send Noah one once a week until his twenty-first and I do not want another coconut,' she gestured to the shell with the straw poking out of it, 'or a whole pineapple or papaya. Too much fruit gives me spots.' Spots she didn't need, not on top of the pink eye.

It was true, Maureen knew. She did find it hard to say no but the hawkers were very entrepreneurial in her book and it was so little to give and it obviously meant so much. She didn't have a tough streak like Moira. 'No' was a word she only used freely when it came to dealing with her children.

The woman reached them, her brown eyes twinkling and her smile broad as she relieved herself of her burden and gestured to the half full baskets. Moira didn't even look to see what was in them as she shook her head and said firmly, 'No, thank you.'

The arrival of Maureen's clams saved her from having to shake her head and the woman moved on. Moira eyed the open shells with distaste and wafted her hand back and forth across her face. 'They stink, Mammy.'

Maureen speared a crustacean with a fork and waggled it in her daughter's face. 'Do you want one?' Moira's face was shiny from the heat but she looked well she thought, eye aside of course. It was doing her good laying off the drink.

'No, I do not.'

It had been a stroke of genius on her part insisting Moira join her on this trip, Maureen congratulated herself before popping the sweet, plump clam in her mouth.

Moira looked over at the restaurant pleased to see her omelette was on its way over.

'You'll turn into an egg the rate you're going,' Mammy said as the yellow omelette was placed in front of her along with a dish of chilli dipping sauce.

'I know where I'm at with an omelette even if it does have those beansprout things in it.' Some of the things she'd seen at the market in Hoi Chi Minh were unidentifiable and some like the rat kebabs were all too identifiable. No, an omelette was a safe bet and she tucked in, suddenly starving.

They cleaned up their plates in no time and decided to visit the night market. Maureen was mesmerised by the brilliant colours of the lacquerware boxes and vases on display, one stall stocking much the same as the next while Moira was like a moth to the flame with the lanterns. In her mind she was already turning her bedroom into a moody boudoir lit by deep purple and pink lanterns.

'Over my dead body,' Mammy stated as Moira put voice to her interior decoration aspirations.

As it happened neither woman was up for the haggling involved with making a purchase and Moira knew she was going to have to offload some of the gear she'd carted with her if she wanted to bring anything home. She'd only just sneaked in under the luggage allowance as it was. They were both beginning to yawn their heads off and in mutual agreement set off down the bustling streets to the hotel the bus had dropped them at.

Vietnam, Moira had noticed, came alive after dark. It must be down to the heat; hot countries were like that; look at Spain. They all napped in the middle of the day and didn't eat their dinner until ten o'clock at night. Music was pumping out onto the street as they passed by bars spilling over with young backpackers. She felt a strong urge to abandon her mammy and join them, especially as a fine young thing with shaggy blond hair grinned over at her. He reminded her of Tom. If she'd been here with Andrea, she knew she'd have been in the thick of all that, holding court. Her days would be spent lounging on the beach sipping cocktails, proper ones not kiddie style mocktails, and getting the odd massage. There'd be none of this chafing business, not because she was getting attached to the elephant pants but because she'd be relaxing not being herded about by that make-up thief Mammy of hers.

She trudged along as Mammy twittered on about whether the electric blue lacquered vase she'd been particularly drawn to would suit her sideboard or whether it might look a tad garish. 'Sure, that was the problem wasn't it? It was class alright but sometimes something that looked wonderful on holiday could look ridiculous once home.' Moira had bitten her tongue as she flashed back to the fisherman pants worn for high tea at Powerscourt. This wasn't right, she huffed to herself. She was twenty-five years old and willingly heading back to their hotel room for an early night—hanging around a person of sixty was making her act like one.

Chapter 13

♥

Postcards

D̲ear Noah,
The picture on the front is of the beach here in Nha Trang. You'd like it here because the beach is sandy and perfect for building sandcastles.

Moira paused, pen in mid-air. What would interest a five-year-old boy? Sure, he wouldn't want to know about gorgeous sunsets and cute, shaggy-haired backpackers. She thought for a moment longer and then it came to her. Little boys liked revolting things.

I have seen lots of things since we arrived in Vietnam. Rat kebabs for one thing! Can you imagine that? I've also had my photograph taken by a helicopter and your Nana had hers taken by a fighter plane. Tonight, I drank from a straw straight from a coconut. It was delicious. Your nana ate seafood straight from the shell. It was gross. Tomorrow I'm going to go exploring and swimming. Be good for your mam.
Love Aunty Moira
Dear Aisling,
It's your mammy here. Moira and I are in Nha Trang by the seaside. We're getting along surprisingly well and had a

grand time exploring Hoi Chi Minh once we got the hang of crossing the roads. It's very busy so it is, there's ten million registered motorbikes in Vietnam and the traffic is terrifying. It was nice to get away from the busyness of it all to visit the Mekong River. The tour we booked was very good value and I enjoyed seeing the stilt houses along the banks of the river. Poor Moira's struggling with the heat and she had a terrible bout of the chafing. Don't tell her I'm after telling you but she's wearing the elephant pants and thinks they're the best thing since sliced bread. She's always been the same, won't listen to advice and has to learn the hard way but sure, that's Moira. Tell Bronagh and Mrs Flaherty I've cards in the post to them too.

Love Mammy

Maureen put her pen down on the bedside table and flexed her fingers. They were cramping from all the news she had to write. She slid the postcards back into the brown paper bag before stuffing it in her pack, away from Moira's nosy gaze, ready for posting in the morning.

Their accommodation was nothing flash but it was neat and tidy and there was an en suite. She'd told Moira as they'd inspected the room that she'd stayed in a guesthouse in Italy once with a shared bathroom and it had been a nightmare. This room, she'd said, looking for dust balls under the bed and finding none, would do them nicely. Moira with that ridiculously oversized pack of hers had just been grateful to dump it on the bed.

Now, she heard the shower turn off and set about digging out her pyjamas, she was looking forward to a nice cool shower to freshen up before bed.

Moira carefully put the drops in her eye before exiting the bathroom. Her mood was somewhat improved now she'd washed the stickiness of the day away. There was nothing wrong with retiring early. Sure, it wasn't a crime to be sensible just because she was young. She wasn't missing out on anything she hadn't done hundreds of time before and she was worn out after the ridiculous time she'd fallen out of bed this morning. An early night was just the ticket, she told herself pulling back her sheets. She clambered into bed to wait for Mammy to finish her ablutions and a short while later she appeared, smelling of toothpaste as she yawned widely. By mutual agreement they flicked off the lights.

Moira lay in the darkened room listening to the honks, shouts, and revving engines below. The walls were paper thin and she didn't know how she was supposed to drift off with all of that going on. When she was little a story had always helped send her off. What was the harm in asking? She rolled over on to her side propping herself up by an elbow. 'Mammy?'

'Mmm'

'Are you awake?'

Maureen smiled, as the memory of her youngest daughter standing silhouetted in the doorway of the bedroom she and Brian had shared at O'Mara's for most of their married life sprang to mind. Only back then when she'd appear, she'd be frightened having heard a creak or a groan she couldn't explain away. 'There's no monster under the bed, Moira. Old buildings make lots of night time noise, go on back to bed.' Maureen would murmur knowing it was pointless even as she pulled back the covers so her baby could clamber in beside her.

She could remember the feeling of that warm little body spooned into hers and how she'd tried to imprint the feeling of it on her memory. She knew too well how fast the time went. You blinked and your children were nearly grown, too big for middle of the night sleepy cuddles.

'Mammy,' she whined now. 'I can't sleep will you tell me a story.'

'Moira you're twenty-five.'

'I still want a story, c'mon tell me how you met Daddy.'

'Ah sure, you've heard that old chestnut a hundred times.'

'Ah, please, Mammy, it's been ages.' Moira liked the story. Hearing her mammy tell that particular tale was like that feeling you got sliding into bed in the middle of winter when the electric blanket had been warming it. '*Please*, I promise I won't mention you stealing my make-up ever again.'

'I didn't steal it. I borrowed it.'

'Pretty, please with a cherry on top.'

'Ah, go on then.'

Moira snuggled down under the bedding in anticipation.

Chapter 14

'Things were very different back then, Moira, you're talking the nineteen fifties.'

'The dark ages when you were lucky to get an orange in your stocking come Christmas and nobody knew what a computer was.'

'The cheek of it.'

'Sorry, carry on.' She liked hearing about where Mammy had grown up and her grandparents because they'd both passed on before she was born, not that they'd been a big part of their daughter's life once she'd left home. Moira had gleaned this from the bits and pieces she'd strung together over the years. Mammy didn't have much to do with her brothers either. This made Moira a little sad. She'd always thought it would be nice to be a part of her uncles' lives and to get to know all their cousins properly but it had never happened.

'Well as you know I grew up in the village of Ballyclegg in Connemara and my da was a farmer. He was a stern man, with the blackest of eyes and when he'd fix you with a certain look you'd quake in your boots. I don't recall him smiling very often, nor Mam for that matter. They were an arranged marriage, but I don't think that was the problem.'

'I can't believe that used to go on, arranged marriages and in our family too.'

'I'm sure there's loads worse gone on if you dig deep enough. Most families have all sorts of skeletons hiding in their cupboards. Sure, look at my friend, Kate, she found out her mammy's youngest sister, whom she'd grown up thinking had passed on was locked away in one of those awful Magdalene laundries.'

It was true enough, what Mammy said, Moira supposed.

'I don't think it would have mattered who my mam and da married, they still wouldn't have smiled a lot. They just weren't smiley sorta people, so, I suppose in that way they were well suited. And you know, as a Mammy myself I can see the benefits of sorting out your children's spouses for them. I'd have saved you all a lot of messing so I would. I'd have found you a man with pots of money to keep you in the style you seem to think you should be accustomed to and I'd have had Aisling and Quinn together years ago. There'd of been none of that shilly-shallying around each other. Oh, and I'd be giving Pat's Miss Pneumatic Bosoms the heave-ho.'

Moira giggled. 'What about Rosi and Colin then?' She pulled a face in the dark at the thought of her chinless eejit of a brother-in-law. Their pairing was one Moira had never understood. There was Noah's arrival eight months after the wedding, but sure in this day and age getting pregnant didn't mean you were named and shamed if you didn't have a ring on your finger. Mammy was silent for a beat obviously not wanting to put her foot squarely in it which made a change, Moira mused.

'No, I don't think I would have picked him for our Rosi, but they muddle along well enough and if she hadn't of met Colin, then we wouldn't have Noah.'

There was that, Moira thought thinking of her nephew's chubby and highly kissable cheeks. 'But I don't want to muddle along.'

'Don't be all sanctimonious now. You were doing a grand job of it not long ago.'

'Ah, Mammy, just get on with the story.' Moira didn't want to think about Michael.

'Alright then. Now, where was I? Ah yes, well in our little cottage where the air was always smoky from the turf fire there was one rule growing up for my four brothers and another for me. I was expected to help Mam with the housework and the cooking while those lazy eejits didn't lift a finger about the place other than to eat or to fight.'

'Like Patrick then, Mammy?'

'No, not like Pat, he did his fair share.'

'Of not a lot.' Moira mumbled.

Maureen ignored her she was getting into the swing of her story now. 'Mam was a firm believer that a woman's place was in the kitchen. Whereas, I was not. It caused many an argument between us which usually resulted in me being made to wash my brother's dirty football togs in water from the rain barrel. I hated that. Can you believe that, Moira? No running water in the house. Things were so different back then. Children, especially girls, were seen as possessions of their parents and weren't expected to be independently minded. I don't think Mam knew what to do with me and all my opinions.'

'It sounds awful, Mammy.'

'No, not awful. It was just the way it was. I wouldn't say I had an unhappy childhood just not a particularly happy one. I don't remember an awful lot of laughter in our house. And you know all the children in Ballyclegg, apart from the family in the big house on the hill, we all came from not a lot. If I were to stick my head in the cottage next door and the one next to that to see what they were having for their tea it would be the same as ours. It was stew on a Monday, leftovers Tuesday, and bacon and cabbage on Wednesday—you could smell the cabbage as you wandered up the road from school and if you'd any doubts as to what day it was, you'd know it was Wednesday— and so it went. We all had the same so no one ever felt hard done by. I think it's probably why I spoiled you children.'

'We weren't spoiled.' Moira was indignant as she thought of every injustice ever served up by her parents growing up. Admittedly she could count them on one hand but still, spoiled? No way. Sure, hadn't she begged her mammy for the boots from Korky's to no avail when she was fifteen years old, an age when the kinda boots you wore really mattered.

'You'll see what I mean, when you have babies of your own, Moira. I mean didn't we take you on a grand family holiday around the Ring of Kerry when you were small? And we had some lovely weekends in Rosslare. In my day we had to walk everywhere and the only place Mam and Da ever took us was church on a Sunday.'

Moira remembered the trip around the Ring of Kerry. She'd been violently carsick all over poor Rosi. Patrick was about to move out and goodness knows what her parents had bribed him with to make him join them, but come along for the ride he had. Her sisters too were at an age where it was friends first, family second, and so Mammy and Daddy did the unheard of and took time off from running O'Mara's in order for them to have one last hurrah all together as a family.

'The only time I left Ballyclegg growing up was on a school trip to Dublin and I had to beg and beg to be allowed to go. I was so excited about it I threw up half an hour before I had to leave for school to get the bus and Mammy very nearly didn't let me go. I always felt bilious when I got too excited as a child. It was a terrible thing because sometimes I'd miss out on whatever had me in such a state altogether on account of being sick. Anyway, I knew the moment we arrived in the city and I saw the busy streets all bursting with life that I'd live there one day.'

'And you did.'

'And I did, but it wasn't an easy path I chose to take. My future was mapped out for me like Mam's had been. I mean they hadn't gone so far as to find me a match but I knew they had their eye on the Doyle family's son, Gerry. I can tell you, Moira, I certainly didn't. He was a right eejit of a fella, as thick as a plank, and Jesus, Mary, and Joseph you'd want to have seen the teeth on him.' Maureen was silent for a moment lost in her memories. 'You know, I knew deep down that if I didn't leave the minute my schooling was done then I'd never leave and my life would play out exactly like Mam's only under a different roof. So, one day, Moira, I did something very bad.'

Moira knew what she'd done but she still had to ask, it was all part of the story telling. 'What did you do, Mammy?'

'I stole the fare to Dublin and enough for a couple of nights lodging from Mam's tin and I got on that bone-rattling auld bus to the big smoke and I never looked back. Sure, when I thought about all those years toiling after my brothers with not so much as a word of thanks from them, it was only what I was owed anyway.'

Moira knew her mammy had sent the money back as soon as she'd earned it but what she'd done had soured family relations and things had been very strained between them all as a result. She couldn't imagine what it would be like to be estranged from your family. To not speak to Aisling every day when she was home or not to roll her eyes at something her mammy said at least twice a week. She took it for granted that she could pick up the phone and chat to Rosi and Noah whenever she wanted. Sure, Patrick was hit and miss these days but still she liked to think if she'd actually come right out and said to him she needed him, he'd have come. 'You were very brave.'

'I was, wasn't I? Although, Moira, when I look back now, I can't quite believe that I was that bold young girl. Risk taking is for the young.'

Moira didn't need the light on to know her mammy was shaking her head at the memories. 'It all worked out though,

Mammy, and if you hadn't of left Ballyclegg you'd never have met Daddy and had us.'

'True enough I might have married Gerry Doyle and had a tribe of children all with teeth you could eat an apple through a tennis racket with.'

They both giggled at the image that conjured.

'What was it like arriving in Dublin? It must have been frightening not knowing anyone or having anywhere to go.'

'It was but I'd made my decision and I was determined I'd make a success of it. Although lying awake most of that first night in the awful lodging house I'd found, I wondered if I'd made a mistake. It was the first time I'd slept in a bed that wasn't my own and I didn't like the smell of the sheets. They were coarse too and made my skin itch. The noises of the city outside were so different to the noises of the country and I was full of the fear.'

Moira tried to visualise it but she always found it hard to equate her sensible, bossy Mammy with the free-spirited young woman who'd run away to Dublin, that she was describing.

'Everything looks brighter in the light of day though and come morning I resolved to find myself job. I set off with quite a spring in my step but by lunchtime my feet hurt and I found myself sitting in the middle of St Stephen's Green wondering what I was going to do. I hadn't counted on needing telephone experience or typing skills and I didn't even know what book-keeping was.'

Moira held her breath. This was her favourite bit in the story. When Mammy first met Daddy. She was fairly sure she embellished bits and pieces but didn't care a jot.

'I sat there in the park watching the ducks swim lazily around for an age before I told myself that it was no good sitting on a bench feeling sorry for myself. All I'd accomplish was a bout of the piles, sitting in the cold like that. Watching the ducks wasn't going to find me work. So, even though there was a hole in the sole of my shoe and a blister on my heel, I got up and I made myself walk out the gates. Something, and it must have been fate, made me cross the road. It was as I was walking up the street admiring the tall, elegant manor houses I spied a sign in the window of a guesthouse.'

Moira found herself mouthing the words, 'Live-in house-keeper position available, only hard worker's need apply.'

'It was the answer to my prayers. I'd been housekeeping from the moment I could hold a broom in my hands. So, I opened the gate and marched up to the front door. I didn't see the peeling blue paint as I lifted the lion's head which was in need of some Brasso and elbow grease, and I rapped on that door. A young man opened it, he was very smartly turned out, and I stood there for a moment staring like the culchie I was because he was also the most handsome fellow I'd ever seen.'

'You weren't exactly spoiled for choice in Ballyclegg by the sounds of it though, Mammy.'

'Shush, Moira, you're ruining the moment.'

'Sorry.'

'Right then, where was I?'

'He was the most handsome fellow you'd ever seen.'

'He was, and a fine set of teeth he had on him too. My stomach began to behave very strangely when he smiled at me and when he asked "Can I help you?" I hardly heard him. He had to repeat himself before I managed to say, "I'm here about the job in the window." Then I remembered to put on my brightest smile and my best foot forward. It was all well and good behaving like a love-struck fool but I needed a job. "Ah right," he said opening the door wider. "You'd better come in and meet my mam."'

'And then he went and fetched Granny O'Mara and you became her right-hand woman running O'Mara's and you and Daddy fell in love, got married and lived happily ever after in the Guesthouse on the Green,' Moira finished off the story feeling very satisfied with it all. She thought she might just be able to fall asleep now.

'Eventually, yes.'

No that was not how it went. Her eyes popped open. 'What do you mean, eventually?'

'Well, I went to Liverpool first.'

'What?' Moira pulled herself upright. This was news to her. So far as she knew Mammy had never left Ireland without Daddy and she'd had no idea she'd spent time in Liverpool. 'You never said.'

'I didn't see the need. You always liked the story to end when I met Daddy and moved in to O'Mara's. It was your fairy-tale ending.'

'But I thought that *was* where it ended.'

'Oh no, Moira, I hadn't left home to settle down. Sure, I was only seventeen. I wanted an adventure first.'

Chapter 15

1954

Maureen Nolan closed the door on the lodging house behind her and set off down Parliament Street. The purposeful confidence to her step belied the uncertainty she was feeling. She'd only been in Liverpool three days and the busy streets were new and unfamiliar and more than a little exciting! She kept her brisk pace up, passing by the imposing Liverpool Cathedral before heading down Upper Duke Street, as per her landlady's instructions, not daring to dawdle and risk being late for her interview.

She'd landed on her feet with her lodgings, and was grateful to Mr Drinkwater, a travelling salesman with a roving eye who'd spent a few nights at O'Mara's, for his recommendation. A few years older than her he'd seemed rather worldly to her inexperienced eye as he leaned against the wall in reception while she manned the front desk. He'd been in no hurry to head up the stairs to his room as he stood gloating about the talent competition, he'd taken part in at the Grafton Ballroom in the heart of Liverpool. The hall was apparently a popular nightspot in the Merseyside city, a regular port of call of his, and one he made certain to visit each time he parked his shoes in Liverpool. The girls, he'd told her, smoothing his quiff, had flocked around him upon hearing his version of Sinatra's *New York, New York*. Ol' Blue eyes had nothing on him he'd winked before offering to demonstrate his singing prowess but Maureen had told him, there was no need, she'd take his word for it.

He might have been an arrogant so and so but his banter got those feet of hers itching again. The wanderlust had lain dormant while she'd being working at O'Mara's. Her days had been full as she beavered alongside Mrs O'Mara learning the ropes of running a guesthouse. She'd not sat around twiddling her thumbs on her days off either. Brian was always on hand, seemingly happy to take her out and about even if it was at his mammy's suggestion. She was half in love with him, she knew that. She had been from the first moment he'd ushered her inside his enormous family home the day she'd come knocking about work but if the feeling was reciprocated then he'd yet to play his hand.

She would spend those afternoons when they were together imagining what it would be like to have his brown eyes with their flecks of gold gaze into hers before his soft lips descended on hers. He hadn't given her any sorta sign that he saw her as anything more than, well, than a kid sister, apart from the time he'd held her hand. She hadn't known whether it was because he thought she needed help crossing busy Dame Street or whether he'd wanted to feel her hand in his and he'd dropped it when they got to the other side.

That was the problem with Brian, nothing was clear, nothing at all, and perhaps she was wasting her time. Maybe he was just being kind by showing her the delights of old Dublin town. A girl couldn't wait around forever. She'd resolved to ask Mr Drinkwater where she could stay were she to want to spend time in Liverpool and perhaps visit the Grafton Ballroom herself.

Mrs Murphy's house he'd said, while in a colourful area, was safe enough so long as she kept herself to herself. It was a clean, central, and reasonably priced establishment and she could do a lot worse than staying at the home of the affable widow who cooked a damned good fry-up. Brian had come in from work then, smart in his suit and tie, and there was something about his bristling manner that had seen Mr Drinkwater peel himself off the wall and make himself scarce.

For Maureen though the seed had been planted. She'd left Ballyclegg determined not to moulder away her youth there and now she was feeling equally determined not to waste it by not going and seeing a bit of the world because she was too busy waiting for Brian O'Mara to decide whether he was half in love with her too. She'd handed her notice in, much to Mrs O'Mara's consternation, and tried not to be upset by Brian's silence where his feelings for her one way or another were concerned. He'd had his chance she resolved, clasping the worn old leather case that contained her worldly belongings to her chest as she tried to keep her lunch down while the ferry rocked and rolled its way across the Irish Sea.

Moira had liked Mrs Murphy immediately. She had a warmth about her that invited you in and made you want to stay. She'd told Maureen, she had a soft spot for the Irish given the late Mr Murphy could trace his roots back to County Clare. The older woman had taken her under her ample wings, recognising how green around the gills she was. She called her young Mo and this morning had filled her up on toast and porridge insisting she needed fattening up because if she wasn't careful a gust of wind off the Mersey would pick her up and blow her back to Dublin. It was Mrs Murphy who'd directed her to the Labour Exchange the day before which had resulted in her being handed a card to give to the Personnel Manager this morning at Lewis's Department Store where she was headed now. 'You'll know you're at Lewis's,' Mrs Murphy said clearing her plate, 'when you see Dickie Lewis.' She'd laughed at Maureen's expression and with a wink said, 'You'll see what I mean.'

She recited the directions in her head, right onto Berry Street, then follow it down to the end before veering left on to Renshaw Street, this would take her to Ranelagh Street where the store was. Maureen had worn her best white blouse and new burgundy skirt with the tiny daisy pattern, she'd bought just before leaving Dublin. She'd parted with her carefully saved pennies in a last desperate bid to catch Brian's eye. It hadn't worked, though she was certainly catching a few eyes this morning, she thought, as a fella tipped his hat at her. She'd cinched her waist in with a black waspie belt and had a matching handbag. It pleased her to see she looked as fashionable as any of the young women she'd seen thus far. She held her head high nearly tripping over a loose paver in the process!

There'd been so many different sights to see since arriving a few short days ago. On her first morning venturing out she'd bumped in to the first black person she'd ever seen. The spiced smells drifting from open doorways had left her curious as to what was for dinner and the sounds emanating from the houses as she'd apologised to the man and gone on her way had danced to a different beat too. It was one she'd never heard before and she liked it.

'Ah now, that would be calypso or perhaps jazz you heard, young Mo,' Mrs Murphy had said tossing the tea towel down on the bench before taking her hand and doing a little jive right there in the kitchen. 'I'm partial to a capella myself.' She'd had to explain what that was to Maureen.

The streets were alive this morning too, with men in suits and shoes you could see your face in, all checking their watches, briefcase in their other hand, as they strode to their offices. Young women in the latest fashions minced along and matronly head-scarfed early morning shoppers keen to secure a bargain joined in with the throng. A newspaper boy was doling out copies of the Liverpool Echo and a double-decker bus was disgorging its passengers on time for them to get to work and clock in. The air was a curious mix of diesel fumes, cigarette smoke and, if you inhaled sharply enough, you could detect a tang of salt from the nearby Mersey. Maureen felt dwarfed by the smog blackened buildings, seagull droppings adorning their ramparts either side of her. She shivered at the biting wind somehow sneaking its way in through the nooks and crannies of those buildings and was grateful for the white cardigan she'd thrown on at the last moment.

Her mind strayed to Brian, and she wondered what he was doing now. She tried not to think about him, she tried really very hard not to, but he'd creep into her thoughts unbidden more often than she liked. It was just after eight thirty so she supposed he'd be sitting at his desk now. He'd shown her the rather bland building where he worked as a draughtsman, a job he said he'd been steered into by his father who didn't want him reliant on the whim of holidaymakers. Had she been in Dublin she'd have been helping Mrs O'Mara with the breakfasts before setting about making up the vacated rooms. She'd liked the people side of the guesthouse business the best, had loved listening to their stories about the places they called home.

She supposed she could have sought hotel work or a house-keeping position here in Liverpool but she wanted to try her hand at something different. It was all part of her grand adventure. So, she was pleased when the po-faced man at the Labour Exchange had said that since she was obviously adept at dealing with the public, he'd put her forward for a position that had just become available at Lewis's.

She realised she was nearing Ranelagh Street and as she saw the imposing nine-storey building looming ahead of her, her mouth stretched in to a wide grin. She'd just spotted Dickie Lewis and she sent a silent thank you to Mrs Murphy because she was too busy giggling to herself to pay attention to the nervous flutterings of anticipation. There above the entrance to the department store was the statue of a man, his naked body there for all to see, arms flung wide as he stretched forward from the prow of a ship.

Maureen had been employed in the haberdashery department at Lewis's for exactly two weeks and was, thanks to her predecessor, now an authority on all things handbags, scarves, and stockings. She arrived to work each morning pinching herself at the elegance of her place of work enjoying the way her heels tip-tapped across the Italian marble tiled entrance floor.

As promised, she'd written to Mrs O'Mara full of news about her lodgings with Mrs Murphy and her new job. She'd filled a page telling her how, come Easter, her new friend Mary who worked in the food hall at the rear of the ground floor had told her the toy department would be transformed into a springtime wonderland. A farmyard was to be created for the children to come and admire with bales of hay and daffodils. There were to be chicks and miniature ponies and everything. Sure, the whole thing sounded just magical, she'd written. As for the Christmas grotto she'd heard tell of, well that was a whole other letter.

This particular morning, Maureen looked up from her discussion over the merits of different deniers to see a man standing at the top of the steps leading down to her floor. He had a hand thrust in his wide-legged trousers pocket as he stood with a casual nonchalance surveying the departments below for a few ticks. Then, cutting a dashing swathe past a woman with an impressive bouffant, he made his way toward the perfume counter where prim Miss Mottram was busying herself with a counter arrangement.

He looked like Rock Hudson, Maureen decided, assuring the woman in her coat and headscarf that the nylons she was hemming and hawing over wouldn't ladder easily.

'They'd better not for the price, luv,' she said but Maureen barely heard her as she placed them in a bag and handed the woman her chit. She was too busy watching Miss Mottram fall all over herself. She positioned herself by the handbags so she could better observe their interaction.

Miss Mottram had sprayed a sample of something on to a card and was wafting it under his nose. He shook his head and she cocked her head to one side listening before retrieving another for him to sample. This one he seemed to like because she looked very pleased with herself as she retrieved a bag in which to place his purchase. Maureen sighed so wistfully a woman with a small boy clutching her hand asked her if she had the weight of the world on her shoulders. Maureen had laughed the comment off, but oh how she'd have loved a bottle of the French perfume and especially if it was given to her by a man with movie star good looks! She thought of Brian and pushed him away. It wasn't the sort of thing he'd ever do; he'd never even told her she looked well when she'd worn her new skirt. He just wasn't a French perfume sorta man.

At clocking off time, she and Mary, twins in their matching black and white uniforms, picked up their bags and linking arms left the building to join all the other workers making their way home at the end of a busy day. They crossed over Ranelagh Street and Mary cheekily blew a kiss at the Adelphi's doorman but his dour expression didn't change nor did he tip his top hat at her. She was a live wire, Maureen thought fondly before launching into her tale about the dreamy fella who'd bought a bottle of French perfume for his girlfriend. Mary agreed whoever she was, was one lucky lady and she laughed at Maureen's description of Miss Mottram giggling and carrying on like a schoolgirl and not a forty-something spinster.

'My feet are killing me, it's like little needles stabbing at them,' Maureen moaned. 'I thought I'd be used to being on my feet all day by now but they're aching, so they are. I don't know how I'll manage tonight, Mary.' They were meeting later at the Locarno Dance Hall where a skiffle band contest was being held that evening. A fella Mary was sweet on who was handy with the washboard was going to be taking a turn on the stage with his band.

'Soak them in vinegar and warm water. It works a treat, Mo, and you'll be good as new by eight o'clock, I promise.' The two girls veered down the lane that would take them to the little Chinese restaurant they'd discovered did a tasty Thursday special of chicken and rice. It would do nicely for their dinner. Maureen wondered fleetingly what her parents would make of her frequenting a Chinese restaurant and the thought of the look on their faces made her smile. The smile vanished though as she recalled the curt letter she'd received in reply from her mam after she'd written to her enclosing the money she'd borrowed. She'd wanted to let her know she was safe and well and enjoying herself in Dublin, but her mam had told her she was a selfish mare who needn't bother showing her face in Ballyclegg again. It was what she'd expected but it still stung.

Maureen tapped her red kitten-heeled shoes along to the beat; the vinegar had indeed rejuvenated her poor tired feet and she was itching to take a turn on the dancefloor. The six-piece band on stage might be amateurs, but they had rhythm and they were playing her favourite, Buddy Holly's *That'll be the Day*. The lad on the banjo was fantastic. The Quarrymen as they were called would go far, she thought fanning herself with her hand.

It was hot and crowded inside the dance hall. Maureen had lost sight of Mary half an hour ago when she went in search of her washboard player leaving her to stand on the side-lines soaking up the electric atmosphere. This was her first visit to the Locarno and she'd been in awe of its Tardis-like interior as Mary, giggling with excitement, had pulled her inside. She'd gushed that the elephants and other animal carvings adorning the walls were due to the ballroom having started life as a circus venue. She'd even said that hidden underneath the wooden dance floor was an elephant pit that had been home to the lions and elephants starring in the circus. Maureen's gaze fell to all those stamping feet on the dance floor and a feeling of trepidation stole over her lest the floor cave in. Ah, sure you're being silly Maureen Nolan, she told herself turning her imagination away from collapsing dance floors to Brian O'Mara. What would he make of it here? Did he like to dance? She didn't know.

'The perfume was for me ma in case you're wondering.' A broad scouse accent sounded in her ear sending a shiver ricocheting down her spine and she swung around startled. It was him, Rock Hudson, only instead of an American accent he had an unexpected Liverpudlian intonation. It was at odds with the picture she'd had of him in her head but she forgot all about that as he gave her a wink, 'I saw you today over by the handbags in Lewis's, luv.'

She could smell the minty gum on his breath as he chewed and eyed Maureen cheekily. She was glad of the dim lighting as she felt her face heat up at having been caught out.

'Are you dancin'?' he asked running his fingers through an Elvis like quiff.

Maureen kicked the door shut on Brian O'Mara as she replied, 'Are you askin'?' Just like Mary had told her she should before letting him take her by the hand to lead her into the melee.

Chapter 16

♥

Present

'Mammy, stop right there. If this new version of the story finishes with you telling me that Patrick was in fact the secret love child of you and this Rock Hudson fella with the Elvis hair, I don't think I need to know.' Moira was feeling a little short of breath now sitting up in bed, her back pressed up against the wall. She couldn't believe the twists and turns of this story she'd thought she'd known from start to finish. 'What I want to know is where does Daddy fit? Because I'm beginning to wonder from the way you've been describing him if myself, and my sisters were conceived by immaculate, conception.'

Maureen laughed. 'I was a good girl I'll have you know, Moira. I kept my legs firmly crossed until my wedding night. You're always in such a hurry to get to the end of things. And the end is the best bit, you should savour it not hurtle along towards it.'

'Mammy, get on with it!'

'God Almighty, Moira, I'm getting there.' She cleared her throat. 'Yer man Rock, whose name was in fact, Len.'

Moira snorted, 'Len?'

'Yes, Len. Short for Leonard. What's wrong with that?'

'Nothing, Mammy, nothing at all.'

'Good, then stop interrupting. *Len* and I became an item. I was his bird as they say over the water and I was smitten. I forgot all about your father. Len worked for the newspaper as a machine manager and he knew all the fun places to dance away the weekend. Then, one day, ooh it would have been three maybe four weeks after we started courting, I arrived home from work. Mrs Murphy greeted me at the door with a peculiar look on her face and said, 'There's someone come to see you.' Well, standing there in the doorway I went hot and cold at the thought of it being my da come to fetch me back but when I went through to the kitchen, I couldn't believe my eyes because there, larger than life, was Brian. He was sitting at the table sipping a cup of tea with one of Mrs Murphy's teacakes in front of him.'

This was more like it thought, Moira. 'He'd come to whisk you back to Dublin.'

'He had, although he told me it was his mammy who sent him because she hadn't found anyone half as good as me to help out around the old place and would I please come back.'

'So, you packed your bags and sailed off into the sunset with Daddy.'

'I did not.'

Moira, humphed in frustration.

'I told Brian, I had a good thing going on here in Liverpool and that I would be staying where I was thank you very much. I told him I was courting and he couldn't just bowl on up and expect me to leave my job, my fella, and my new home on the word of his mammy. No, I sent him off that evening with a flea in his ear although I did tell him to tell Mrs O'Mara I was sorry I wasn't coming back. It wasn't her I was angry with after all. She was a lovely lady, your nan.'

Moira's Nana had passed away before she was born. She'd always felt cheated listening to the others reminisce about her. 'He can't have given up on you though, not unless we're all Len's love children and Daddy adopted us.'

'Would you stop harping on about love children? I told you I was a chaste girl; I didn't get up to any shenanigans until I was a married lady unlike you lot today. We weren't all free n easy in the fifties dropping our drawers willy-nilly. We had morals, so we did.'

'Nothing wrong with trying before buying, Mammy.'

'I'll pretend I didn't hear that, Moira O'Mara. Now then, do you want to know what happened next, or not?'

'Of course, I do.' It was like reading a serial in a magazine, Moira thought with all the painful long breaks in between instalments.

'It was Mrs Murphy who brought Brian and me together in the end. She wasn't overly taken with Len. She didn't think he was right for me, too much of a wide-boy in her book. A flash Harry was the term she used I believe. She liked Brian though from the moment he complimented her on her teacakes. She reckoned she could see the pair of us were smitten with each other but apart from banging our heads together she wasn't sure what to do about it, and then it came to her. She recalled me telling her about the first time I saw Len. She stopped Brian at the door that evening as he made to leave with his tail between his legs. I'd flounced off to my room by then and before he went on his way, she told him how she thought I was the sorta girl who might be swayed in her thinking by a bottle of French perfume and how if he were to make a grand gesture along those lines he might persuade me to go back to Dublin with him.'

Moira felt a shiver of anticipation.

'When I arrived home from work the next night Brian was sitting at the kitchen table. At first, I thought he'd come back for more of Mrs Murphy's teacakes because I'd made it perfectly clear as to where I stood the day before. That wasn't why he'd come, although if I recall rightly, he did have a teacake in front of him when I—'

'Mammy!'

'Alright, alright. This time around, he'd come bearing a gift. He presented me with a beautifully wrapped box and what do you think was inside it, Moira?'

'A ring?'

'Jesus wept are you not listening to what I'm telling you. We hadn't even had our first kiss. No, it was a bottle of French perfume, you eejit. Arpège. Brian took hold of my hand and said, 'The woman on the counter told me it was a bold and beautiful floral fragrance and that made me think it was perfect for you.' And I melted right there on the spot. So, there you go Moira, that's when I packed my bags and sailed back to Dublin with him. You know the rest.'

'Are you crying, Mammy?'

'Happy memories, Moira, happy memories.'

'What about Len? He must have been heartbroken when you left.'

'I don't think so. Len moved on pretty smartly. I kept in touch with Mrs Murphy until she passed and she told me she'd heard down the line that he married a girl called Shirley. She said he'd got her in the family way which meant she'd been right about him all along, a wide boy, and hadn't I made the right decision by breaking up with him. The End. Now then, do you think perhaps we could try and get a spot of shut eye?'

Chapter 17

♥

The sunlight sneaked in through the cracks in the curtains and on the street below Moira and Maureen's window, a street that had only gone to sleep a few hours ago, some arse was revving his bike. *Did these people never rest?* Moira thought opening her good eye. Jaysus, she muttered to herself, you'd think whoever it was, was about to take off in the Isle of Man TT with that carry-on.

Moira knew about motorcycle races, not because she had a love of speed but because at sixteen, she'd had a boyfriend who did. Callum or was it Ciaron? She couldn't remember now but either way he'd been obsessed with motorbikes and everything to do with them. It was at the end of their three months together that he'd shown up outside the guesthouse one Saturday morning on the only bike his motor mechanic's apprenticeship wage could afford—a gutless Yamaha. The relationship's death knoll had sounded because Moira had refused to be seen on the back of what she told him had less grunt than her hairdryer. He wasn't a keeper, she'd decided, as he'd revved his engine in her direction one final time before taking off in a blaze of backfiring exhaust fumes.

'Feck off, would ya,' she said now in response to the revving below. Mammy had begun to make those annoying little lip-smacking noises that signalled she was on the verge of waking up. Moira wondered how she'd be feeling when she did rise and shine; not too bright she guessed. She lay there a few beats longer, a seething mass of irritability as she debated whether she could summon the energy to get up and hang out the window to repeat the sentiment. She was not in fine fettle this morning. It had been a terrible night.

It had taken her forever to nod off, what with the ruckus coming from outside, but even if it had been silent, she knew she'd have had trouble getting to sleep. Mammy's story had unsettled her. She'd been unable to shake the 'what if's' of which there were many. They'd trotted themselves out one after the other as she'd lain there stewing.

What if Mammy had stayed in Ballyclegg and married yer bucktooth man? Or, what if she'd walked out Fusilier's Arch when she left St Stephen's Green that day and headed down Grafton Street instead of leaving through the south gates? She'd never have seen the sign in the window of O'Mara's and she'd never have met Daddy. She'd felt very peculiar at that point because it had occurred to her that if Mammy had been drawn toward the busy shopping street, instead of wandering past the row of Georgian buildings, she and her siblings wouldn't exist. It also occurred to her that she was reliving the film she'd seen last year with Andrea, the one with yer Paltrow woman in it. *Sliding Doors*. Very good it had been too.

Most of all though, she'd been disturbed at the twist the familiar old story of how her parents met had taken. It was a bit like listening to *Beauty and The Beast* only Beauty takes off from the big mansion where she's staying with yer Beast, goes and has a bit of a thing with the village blacksmith before coming back and marrying the Beast. Not that Daddy was a beast he was the handsome prince at the end of the story.

The very thought of her mammy being torn, she refused to say between two lovers because, well the 'l' word was not a word used when thinking about Mammy, typically indecisive was a better fit, well, it had shocked her. She knew what she was struggling with. It was trying to equate, Mammy, her mammy who'd always been part and parcel of the furniture at O'Mara's, ready to kiss a grazed knee better or hold out a hanky with which to blow a runny nose, with the young woman she'd been before she turned into Mammy. A young woman who'd been unafraid as she boldly went adventuring into new cities. A young woman who had men fancying the pants off her. I mean, it was *Mammy* for fecks sake! Yes it was all very unsettling, there was no other word for it she'd thought rolling over and thumping the rock of a pillow for the tenth time. That was when the groaning had started from the bed next to her.

'Mammy, what is it? Are you alright?' she'd hissed into the darkened room. She was annoyed with her for changing the story on her, she realised, finding it hard to muster up sympathy for whatever it was had her moaning. Sure, it was probably just indigestion or wind. She could be very dramatic at times.

'Oooh, Moira, my tummy's after doing some very unnatural things.'

She heard an unearthly rumble and grimaced. 'Jaysus, was that your stomach?'

'I can't talk. I've got to go.' Her tone was desperate and Moira heard her stampede to the bathroom, the light flickering on and illuminating her white face briefly before she kicked the door shut.

Moans, groans, interspersed with mutterings about fecking clams and never again, drifted out from under the door. You'd have to be inhuman listening to that and not feel sympathy, Moira thought clenching her cheeks in solidarity at the other sounds that surely the whole hotel would be privy to. She hoped nobody thought it was down to her when she ventured forth, that would be mortifying. It seemed to take an age but finally there was a flushing sound and she could hear the tap running as she washed her hands before the handle turned and Mammy reappeared.

'Ah, Moira, I'm just after losing half my bodyweight.'

'I'd believe it. Go back to bed and try to get some sleep. I'll get you something to settle your tummy from the pharmacy when they're open.'

'You're a good girl.'

The room had the hazy half-light that signalled daylight was on its way and Moira had watched as her Mammy buried herself under her bedding, before shutting her own eyes and finally drifting off.

That must have been around five o'clock, she thought now. Then, with one final humph in the direction of the window she kicked the sheets off and sat up. There was no point lying here, she'd be better off having a shower and then going in search of a cup of coffee. She made her way with trepidation to the bathroom which she'd already nicknamed the clam-room hoping Mammy had had the foresight to open the window. She eyed the hump under the bedclothes that was just beginning to stir, before pushing open the door. Her gaze flicked around the space checking it out like the gards with a warrant but all was as it should be apart from the trio of geckos who'd taken up residence on the ceiling thanks to the open window. She could feel their beady reptilian eyes on her while she showered. It was most unnerving.

The water revived her and she was pleased to see on inspection that her eye was much better today. She put the drops in and waited for her vision to clear before checking on Mammy. Maureen's tousled head was just visible above the sheets she'd wrapped around herself.

Moira laid her hand on her forehead which was reassuringly cool. She'd live. 'I'm going to go and find some breakfast, and I'll pick you up something to settle your stomach while I'm out. You'll be alright here for a bit.' There was a mumbling she took to be a thanks and, pausing only to open the window a crack to let some fresh air into the room, Moira headed out.

She felt quite adventurous. It was the first time she'd been on her own since they'd left Dublin and she should make the most of it. Be bold, like her mammy had been and explore. There was plenty of time for that though, first things first, coffee, food, an internet cafe and a visit to the pharmacy in that order.

The sun cleared away the last vestiges of her broken night and feeling invigorated she strode up the street toward the road where she knew she'd find everything she needed. Her nose wrinkled as she tried to ignore the pungent sewage smell that wafted up, seemingly from nowhere, stagnating in the humid air. She was determined it wouldn't put her off her breakfast. Across the street she saw a woman, her face hidden beneath her conical hat, crouching beside a street cart. She was washing a wok out in the water that was running down the gutter. Moira gave whatever was being fried up on the street cart a big fat red cross and carried on until she came to an airy café on the bustling road. *This was more like it.*

She ordered and arranged herself at one of the tables so she could watch the street life. As she did so she caught a darting movement out of the corner of her eye. Swivelling her head, she was just in time to see a fat brown rat scarpering from the kitchen. It skittered across the café floor, out the door, over the pavement, and disappeared down into the deep gutter. Moira wished Mrs Flaherty were here, she'd have made short work of that fella with her rolling pin she thought shuddering. She tried to put the rat out of her head as her steaming coffee arrived, dark and sweetened by condensed milk. It was reviving and she sipped on it trying not to think about whether Roger the Rat was running solo or if he'd left his extended family behind.

A little boy who looked to be around the same age as her nephew shyly inched his way toward her while she waited for her omelette and she smiled, receiving a dimpled grin by return. He was selling chewing gum and postcards. She already had a pack of gum in her pocket and Mammy had bought enough postcards to make a mural when they got home but his brown eyes were looking at her so beseechingly. Sure, she thought even the most cynical of tourists would struggle to say no to that face. She was glad Mammy wasn't here to bear witness to her handing over her money. She could almost hear her saying, 'That's the pot calling the kettle black, so it is, Moira.' It would be fair play to her to given it was only last night she'd told her how hopeless she was at saying no.

She watched him stuff the notes in his shorts pocket before scarpering off, full of energy, and wondered what life had in store for him. He should be at school not hawking his wares to the tourists but then what right did she have to judge. This wasn't her country. Her mind flitted to Noah with his orderly, routine filled, pampered life. How different the two boys' lives must be but she was guessing if you sat them next to each other and rolled a ball over to them they'd soon be kicking it around like the best of mates.

The omelette arrived a moment later and when she looked up again the little boy was gone. She tucked in hitting Roger the Rat away with her imaginary hammer as he kept popping up, only he'd morphed into more of a grinning mole type of a thing like that old arcade game you found at fairs. The omelette was tasty despite Roger's best efforts to put her off but she had to concede there were only so many omelettes a girl could eat. She might have to branch out and try something different. She glanced at the postcard lying face up on the table she'd chosen. It was a glossy picture of a big white Buddha resplendent against a blue sky. She flipped it over, and read *Lon Song Pagoda, Trai Thuy Mountain, Nha Trang.* She wouldn't mind checking that out today, it looked very impressive, but first things first, she fancied a bit of beach time.

Feeling comfortably full and considerably perkier than she had an hour ago, Moira set off again in search of a pharmacy. It didn't take her long to find one and the transaction was surprisingly straightforward. The chemist was well used to tourists and their delicate tummies. His English was good too and he'd suggested she buy a bottle of Coke for her mammy as the sugar and caffeine would help perk her up. She made a pitstop at an internet café, scrolling through the messages. Aisling was checking in to make sure she and Mammy hadn't murdered each other and Andrea's email was annoyingly vague. She banged off quick replies to say that postcards would be on their way and not to worry if they didn't hear from them because she wasn't sure how easy internet access was going to be to find from hereon in. Then armed with her supplies she made her way back to the hotel.

Mammy was in the shower when Moira pushed the door open and she flopped on to the edge of the bed flicking through the guide book to find directions to the White Buddha. It wasn't too far she thought, her finger tracing the route; she could walk it. When Mammy appeared a few minutes later, her swimsuit on beneath her fisherman pants, Moira could see that despite her attempts at brightening herself up she was still pale. There was no way she'd be up to anything strenuous today. It looked like she'd be visiting the pagoda on her own. She handed her the pills and the bottle of Coke and then kicked back on the bed for a bit reading up on the local sights to wait while the fizz and tablets worked their magic.

It was odd, she mused, keeping one eye on the text she was reading and one on the rogue gecko on the ceiling above her; yesterday she'd felt out of sorts because she wasn't baking in the sun sipping cocktails or hanging out at a bar chatting up her fellow backpackers. Today, she wanted to explore. She'd done plenty of hanging out in pubs chatting up the fellas and she could lie out in the sun and bake at home—well at least three times over summer any road! She'd come all this way, and it had just dawned on her she didn't want to waste a moment.

'I'm feeling better now, Moira, that Coke helped thanks. Marvellous stuff the Coca-Cola. I'm not up for a marathon but I think I could manage a sun lounger in the shade with my book.'

'I'll join you for a while but I wouldn't mind having a wander about.'

———ℓℓℓ———

The beach was a hive of industry as hawkers in full force patrolled the waterfront sun loungers, smiling and offering their wares to pink-faced tourists. Moira surveyed the shore until she spotted two free sun loungers off in the distance in the shade of a palm tree. That would do nicely she thought, marching off in that direction. She placed her towel on the spare lounger while Mammy arranged herself on hers. 'Another Coke?'

'Grand.'

Moira returned with a drink for them both and settled herself on her seat. The surf was white and frothy and she lay back listening to it crash along the beach. It was such a soothing sound; she could see why Rosi liked playing those beach music tapes of hers. The whale song she didn't quite get but the sound of the sea was lovely. She lay there until she was good and hot and couldn't face turning down another smiling face offering her a paperback book or tropical fruit, before going for a dip. Mammy, mercifully, was snoozing and hadn't seen the woman with her steaming tin pots of shellfish approach them. Moira had shaken her head vehemently and she'd carried on her way. There must have been some weight in those pots, she thought watching her pad toward a huddle of skimpily clad sunseekers, her shoulders stooped. She plunged straight into the surf and the water cooled her off as she floated around, bobbing with the waves until she'd had enough. It was time to go and explore.

ele

Moira fanned herself with the guidebook and gulped down the cold water she'd bought at the base of the steps. It was so, hot, she could feel the shirt and shorts she'd pulled on over her bikini sticking to her. She gave the guidebook one last wave for good measure, managing to swat a lazy, humming dragonfly away before retrieving her camera from her pack. She crouched down and angled it upwards, overwhelmed by the scale of the Buddha as she craned her neck and tried to fit it in its entirety in the frame. She wouldn't do it justice she knew that; you wouldn't get a feel for the scale of it in a photograph but it would make a stunning picture nonetheless with that brilliant blue sky behind it.

She spied a shady corner in the pagoda and made for that. The climb up all those steps had been worth it she decided as she saw Nha Trang spread out like a roll of carpet below. It was very peaceful up here which surprised her. She'd assumed it would be mobbed like the beach but the only hawkers were in the car park below. Then again, she'd chosen the hottest part of the day to come and visit. She was beginning to fall a little in love with this country, she realised, wiping her face with her shirt sleeve. When was the last time she'd stood somewhere silently and just let the scene wash over her? She was thinking clearly for the first time in a long while too and had stopped being frightened of where her thoughts might take her because standing here now thinking about her daddy it didn't feel like a dark place with no hope.

Moira remembered how he used to sit playing the spoons at the table come teatime. She had no idea why he did that; it was just something he did while they waited for Mammy to put dinner on the table. It always made her smile even when it was fried liver and onions on the menu—*it's full of iron for young girls, Moira*, Mammy would say. She smiled now too recalling how he'd stick the tea cosy on his head when he went to pour from the pot. He was silly her daddy and she loved him for it. He was part of her, *her* story and he always would be.

Her recollections were broken by a tour bus group materialising through the hazy heat waves at the top of the stairs. Their faces peered out from under umbrellas in an attempt to shield the midday sun. It was time to go and check on Mammy, Moira decided.

—*ell*—

'Jaysus, Mammy! I was only gone a couple of hours. What have you done?'

'Don't you like it?' Maureen sat up and swished her hair back and forth, the beads in the tiny woven braids decorating her head clacking.

'Mammy, you look,' Moira was momentarily speechless. 'You look—'

'Like yer Bo Derek in that film, Ten?'

'No, Mammy not Bo Derek. She was blonde, tall, and tanned, not short, Irish and sixty when she starred in that.'

'You're never too old to try a different look I say, Moira, and you'll be wishing you'd had yours done when all I have to do of a morning is rinse and go.' Maureen pointed across the rows of sun loungers that had been filling up the empty sand in Moira's absence. She followed the line of her finger to where a tiny bird-like woman was crouched over a lobster woman, her deft fingers weaving her frizzy blonde hair into cornrows of braids.

'She's no feckin Bo Derek either,' Moira muttered. 'She should know better.'

'I could call her back over when she's finished. Her name's Chau, it mean's like a pearl. Isn't that lovely? She could do yours too if you like, Moira? We'd look like sisters, so we would.'

'Over my dead body, Mammy. One of us looking like they're about to burst into a Boncy M song is more than enough.'

'I like a bit of Boney M, especially around Christmas time. And I'll have you know, yer man at the bar over there, him in the scanty pants, has been sniffing around while you've been gone.'

Moira turned toward the beach bar from which the strains of Bob Marley's One Love drifted. She saw a ruddy faced man who was indeed in scanty pants leaning against the bar, a cigarette smouldering in the ashtray beside him. His chest looked as though it had one of those shag pile rugs glued to it and as for the rest, well, she was trying not to look. He caught her staring over and raised his can in greeting.

Mammy elbowed her. 'Don't be after gawping at him or he'll think I'm interested and I don't know how to say feck off in German.'

They looked at each other and burst into a fit of giggles.

Chapter 18

♥

Postcards

Dear Rosi,
   The pictures on the front are of Po Nagar Cham Towers, the White Buddha and the Cai River. Cham Towers are really, really old and were used by the Buddhist monks for worship. We visited them as the sun was setting and the stones almost looked like they were on fire. I enjoyed the White Buddha too and the Cai River with all the blue fishing boats was pretty. We've had a grand time in Nha Trang apart from Mammy getting the trots. I've found it very peaceful. There's something about these Buddhist temples that makes me feel calm. I can see why you do yoga and all those breathing exercises. Mammy's on at me not to forget I'm a Catholic but I can't take anything she says seriously at the moment. She's after having her hair braided and looks like a geriatric Irish version of Bo Derek. Honestly, Rosi, you want to see the state of her. If I catch her jogging down the beach in a one-piece then I'm on the next plane home.
   Love Moira
   Dear Andrea,
   Have you and Jeremy, you know? I can't be too specific in case the postman is the type who reads people's postcards

but you'll know what I'm getting at. I've seen a few rideable men here but I think the fact I'm travelling with my mammy is scaring them away. It seems to be having the opposite effect for Mammy—a German man in his underpants took a shine to her today. Honestly, Andrea, I could hardly see his thing for his belly, not that I was looking! It disturbed me to think of Mammy being chatted up too. I haven't been thinking about Michael too much since we left. I've been focussing my thoughts on Tom, his bum in particular. It's therapeutic. Mammy and I haven't murdered each other yet although once or twice I've been tempted. Vietnam is very hot and sticky but it is surprisingly interesting and we've seen and done a lot since we got here. It's been nice kicking back and enjoying the beach here in Nha Trang but we're moving on again tomorrow to Hoi An. Hope the weather back home is not too shite.

Love Moira

Mammy's Travel Journal

Hello from Hoi An. Well, today was the longest bus ride of my life, thirteen hours we were on that auld rust bucket on wheels and I don't mind telling you there were times I wasn't sure we'd make it here. Moira said she felt like she was engaged in a never-ending game of chicken, what with all the trucks not keeping to their lane. Their constant honking hurt my head. The roads off the motorway were a nightmare too. The tar seal was non-existent in parts and we did more jigging in our seats than yer Michael Flaherty fella in Riverdance. I had to have words with HIM upstairs asking HIM to get us there in one piece.

HE is good, so he is, and here we are but I tell you a lovely thing did happen along the way. I made a new friend. Her name's Sally-Ann and she lives on a sheep farm but not for much longer as she's sold it, not far from a town beginning with K, in Western Australia. I keep thinking it's called Kangaroo but sure, that can't be right. I recognised her from our journey from Hoi Chi Minh to Nha Trang and when I saw her getting on the bus I waved out. She sat down across from me because Moira pinched the window seat again and wouldn't budge. I warmed to her straight away not just because I liked her eyes, they're such an unusual shade of blue but because she said she liked my hair. I wished Moira had heard her say that but she had her headphones on.

Sally-Ann told me to call her Sal because everybody does. We chatted a bit about our homes, hers she said is a dusty, dry place in the summer but that she loves the wide uninterrupted sky and would struggle to live anywhere else. She said she's going to find it hard moving into the town but that it's time and she's looking forward to being a stone's throw from her sister. I told her about O'Mara's and how I've downscaled to an apartment, not a flat mind, I was quick to point that out, near the sea in Howth. It turned out she's a widow too. Her husband died earlier in the year. It was the cancer. I reached across and gave her hand a squeeze when she told me that because she got a little teary and I could see her grief was still raw.

We talked a little about that, how hard it is to find yourself on your own after so many years spent with someone else. Especially, if they were good years. And how some days you just don't want to get out of bed but with your children keeping their beady eyes on you, you somehow manage to. It's a hard thing, Sal said, having to put a brave front on for the sake of your kids. I told her that's just a mammy's lot and she agreed.

It's not the big romantic stuff you miss either, not that my Brian was a flowery sorta man. Although he did buy me a bottle of Arpège on our wedding anniversary, all our married years— never missed. Praise where praise is due, I say. No, it's not the sweeping sentimental gestures on anniversaries or birthdays it's the everyday things. The sitting on the sofa together dunking your biscuit in the cup of tea he's made you. The way he always agrees with you when you moan about some eejit on the television. It's those sorta things and I said to Sal you think your life is going one way and then it picks you up and throws you on your arse. She said that's exactly how it is. Our chat was a good distraction from all those trucks.

She and her husband, Robert, had grand plans of getting someone in to manage their farm in a couple of years so they could be freed up to travel. They fancied Europe because you couldn't find anywhere else more different to the K place she comes from. She told me it was always something they'd planned on doing one day. The thing is we both agreed, 'one day' doesn't always come.

She wanted to see the Leaning Tower of Pisa and her Robert wanted to see the Eiffel Tower. She wasn't much interested in seeing either now. She said her kids talked her into selling up and buying in town where her sister lives. It would give them peace of mind because she couldn't manage on her own and they had no interest in coming home to help run the farm. A farm was a tie, she said, and if she hadn't of done what they wanted and sold up she wouldn't have been able to travel here. It broke her heart to let it go because of all the memories it held, not just her and her husband's but of growing up and her parents too. I told her how it was the memories that made me leave O'Mara's. They were suffocating me. We all handle things differently.

We moved on after that and I asked her what had brought her to Vietnam. She told me she nursed here in the war and that's how she met Robert. She hadn't thought she'd ever come back but he'd wanted her to. He'd made her promise she would because he thought it would help her make peace with the past. She said her kids thought she was mad coming back on her own but they hadn't pushed it too much, not after getting their way with her selling the farm. She was glad she'd come because it was comforting to see that life even after a catastrophic war, carried on. It was hopeful, she said.

She asked why Moira and I had come and I felt a bit funny telling her it was because I've always wanted to sail on a junk after seeing James Bond do it in a film. And, Moira's come with me because she was getting herself in bother at home and needed a break. I mean there's Sal busy saving all those poor people's lives in terrible circumstances and there's me hankering after Roger Moore and making sure my daughter doesn't fall off the wagon.

Moira's moaning on at me to turn the light out as she wants to be up early to have a look around in the morning. I can't believe this is the same girl I left Dublin with; I mean this is Moira. I just about had to put a rocket under her bed to get her up most mornings!

Chapter 19

♥

S ally-Ann inspected her room. It would do just fine she thought, dumping her pack at the foot of the bed. She liked the arrangement the bus company had with the local hotels because she'd been perfectly happy to stay at the first one it had stopped at. Everybody had their hand in somebody's pocket but sometimes that worked and if it meant she didn't have to trawl around a strange town in the dark quibbling over a few dong for a bed then she was all for it. She'd venture out and find something for dinner shortly but first she'd just stretch out for a few minutes, she decided, kicking her shoes off and flopping down on the bed. It was comfortable and she knew after the long journey today she'd sleep like a baby later.

It had been a boon Maureen introducing herself on the bus. Sally-Ann would have smiled at her, recognising her of course from their journey to Nha Trang. She doubted she'd have initiated a conversation though. She was too reserved for that. She'd always been one of life's observers whereas Maureen was an outgoing woman. The kind of woman who'd start a conversation with strangers waiting at the check-out in the supermarket. Or, for that matter, strangers on a bus.

Sally-Ann had warmed to her immediately, and they'd clicked over their common ground. It had been nice talking to someone who understood how she was feeling. She was sure to bump into her and her daughter again given they were staying here in Hoi An at the same hotel and following a similar itinerary north as far as Hue, any road. Their reasons for coming here couldn't have been more different though, she mused, her eyes feeling heavy. The memories of the bloodshed she'd seen here was scored on her brain but there had been good things that had happened here too and that was why Robert had wanted her to come back. He'd hoped she'd find resolution. It was here after all that they'd met and here she'd sat holding little Binh's, whose name ironically meant peace, hand all through the night. It was also here she'd stopped being that wet around the ears girl from Katanning.

Maureen had smelt of Arpège again today. The soft floral fragrance tugged at Sally-Ann's memory and as her lids drooped shut, she found herself remembering a different time.

ele

1967

Strewth it was hot, Sally-Ann thought, not for the first time, as she went about her rounds of the ward here at the No.4 Hospital, Butterworth. The beds were filled by a mix of Brits and Gurkhas, the young Nepalese men serving in their brigade of the British Army. Their reputation was that of being fierce fighters, something she found at odds with the gentle natured men she was enjoying looking after.

She could feel her white veil wilting in the heat despite the starching it had received and felt ridiculously overdressed for the infernal heat, it would be the end of her she was sure. Not for the first time she shook her head, the cursed limp material sticking to the back of her neck with the movement. It was

1967 for heaven's sake and she was wearing a veil. Ridiculous, Sally-Ann huffed silently.

Still, she shouldn't complain. What was a bit of discomfort compared to what these poor diggers had been through, were still going through? How strange it was to think that one short year ago her biggest worry had been how to stop Billy Brown and his persistently wandering hands from reaching their end goal. She'd dealt with that pretty swiftly by accidently on purposing upending her drink in his lap, and she'd deal with feeling like she was permanently paddling about in a hot bath too.

Sometimes Sally-Ann had to pinch herself that she wasn't the star of a peculiar dream when she ventured out to explore with her new friend, Margaret, on their day off. The sights and sounds were so different to home and she was soaking up all of those differences. She'd never been on a plane in her life either, until she'd decided to volunteer and then things had happened very quickly. A few signed papers and much wringing of her mum's hands when she'd made the call to tell her what she'd decided to do, and she'd found herself on a Qantas flight bound via Singapore for Malaysia.

The humidity when she'd disembarked had been oppressive and had been unrelenting ever since. She couldn't imagine a time when she'd get used to this cloying tropical climate. The air was so heavy and thick it weighed her down. It made mundane tasks feel like hard work and she was perpetually tired though it wasn't surprising given the long shifts she was rostered on, ten hours at a time six days a week. Now, she stifled a yawn, giving herself the hard word. It was her job to put on a bright and cheery face as she bustled about looking after these boys, who were such a long way from home and some of whom looked like they were barely out of school. She hadn't come here to stand around looking like she was ready for bed!

Oh, but she was finding things tough. So much tougher than she'd expected but then she didn't know what she'd expected, her experience of life outside Katanning being somewhat limited. Not that she admitted any of this when she wrote her weekly letters home. She was upbeat and full of the sights she was seeing, not dwelling on the heart-breaking side of her nursing role. For someone who'd always struggled to keep a secret she was getting adept at keeping things from her family. It wasn't just the heat; it was the unexpected Britishness of her posting that had thrown her off kilter. She'd barely gotten her head around the Australian Army's jargon in the short time since she'd enlisted and been sent to Ingleburn Army Hospital, let alone even attempt to decipher the unfamiliar ranks here at Butterworth.

That cocky girl with her brand-new title, Lieutenant Sally-Ann Jessop who'd left Australia four short weeks ago with a certainty that after her practical experience at Ingleburn she was going to be a brand-new shiny asset to the army, had had an awakening as rude as a bucket of cold water being thrown over her upon arrival here at Butterworth.

'How are you today, Liz?' an accent she'd been informed came from the Midlands of England asked. Twinkly blue eyes with sandy lashes peered up at her, the rest of his face hidden beneath a swathe of bandages but the tufts of hair protruding from the top giving away his red-headed genetics.

She'd gotten used to the banter of the soldiers. It was harmless and she'd soon come to realise if they were capable of mustering up a bit of cheek then it should be taken as a positive sign. The spirit of some of the lads after what they'd been through amazed her. They epitomised brave in her opinion. 'That's enough from you, Edward. You know full well its *Sister* to you.' Sally-Ann tutted, the smile she gave him belying the stern tone as she set about checking his bandages. He'd decided her eyes were the colour of Elizabeth Taylor's and had taken to calling her Liz. Not very cheeky on the scale of things. He was only nineteen and he was going home with one leg missing. It broke her heart.

She finished her rounds and with her shift finished, made her way down the corridor heading toward the nurse's quarters. A senior, more experienced nurse, Eileen Wilson, who had an intimidating air about her, one that didn't lend itself to cheeky banter, materialised from one of the wards and called her aside. She steeled herself for a dressing-down unsure what misdemeanour she'd committed but Sister Wilson wasn't one for idle chit-chat.

'I'd like you to assist me on the next medevac flight to Vung Tau, Sister. Do you think you're ready for that?'

'Oh,' she hadn't expected that and she hesitated, momentarily on the back foot, until the impatient question in Sister Wilson's no-nonsense grey eyes galvanised her. 'Yes, Sister, definitely.' Sally-Ann breathed, feeling that urge to pinch herself once more. She would be flying into Vietnam to bring their wounded boys back to the safety of Butterworth until they could be flown home. Her stomach flipped and then flopped with a mixture of fear and excitement at what lay ahead.

'Goodo.'

Sally-Ann was being dismissed and she nodded at Sister Wilson, 'Thank you, Sister,' before continuing on her way.

'Sister Jessop.'

She paused hearing her call after her and turned, 'Yes, Sister?'

'Do you have any perfume here with you?'

It was the strangest of questions Sally-Ann thought as she nodded.

'Wear it, I find it helps.'

Sally-Ann puzzling over what she'd taken to be an order from Sister Wilson, went back to the nurse's quarters. The stuffed koala bear she'd brought with her from home and nicknamed Lily for no reason other than she liked the name, was perched on her pillow and she said, 'Hello, Lily' as she always did before opening the top drawer in the chest next to her bed. Her prized bottle of Arpège was tucked away in there, it being the coolest place she could find to store it. She'd been told or had read somewhere that sunlight and heat were not good for fragrance, they'd change the notes of the perfume.

She opened the drawer to retrieve it, the sight of the black and gold canister instantly conjuring up the memory of her twenty-first birthday. There'd been candles and cake and even a small glass of champagne to celebrate her coming of age, followed by her favourite dinner. Roast lamb with Mum's mint sauce and new potatoes. Afterwards she'd taken Dad's car and driven to the dance in town, allowed for the first time to take Terri who'd reminded her of a skittish lamb in her excitement. The perfume had been a gift from Mum, Dad, and Terri, her first bottle of French fragrance. She was officially a grown woman.

'Off somewhere nice?' Alice a nurse with a cockney twang from London winked at her. Sally-Ann hadn't heard her come in. She thought Alice was very glamorous, one of those girls who always managed to look put together without seeming to make any effort to do so. She even managed to give her nursing uniform a certain joie de vivre, although, she constantly bemoaned the humidity denouncing it as no good for her mane of thick dark hair. She seemed very worldly to Sally-Ann, London a far-off cosmopolitan place she could barely imagine, and Alice with her huge brown eyes and penchant for bold lipsticks, always brought Natalie Wood to mind. She'd loved *Splendor in the Grass*.

'I'm going to Vung Tau with Sister Wilson.'

'Oh, well, good luck.' She looked at her bemused, but Alice was the sort of girl who always had some place to be and with a smile that said she didn't have time to enquire further as to why she was sitting on her bed holding a bottle of perfume, she said 'I'm more of an Estee Lauder girl, myself,' and swished past and out through the doors at the bottom of their dormitory to the gardens beyond.

Sally-Ann took the lid off the bottle and sprayed generously behind each ear and then on her left wrist holding her right against it for a beat. Susan, with whom she'd done her training, had worked on the perfume counter of her local department store before deciding nursing was her vocation and had told her that rubbing your wrists together bruised the fragrance. As the scent teased her nostrils, she closed her eyes. It made her think of twirling skirts at the dances, stolen kisses in the car park outside the dancehall, and lazy Sunday boat rides down the Swan River. She sat there like that for an age waiting for the word that it was time to go.

Sister Wilson strode ahead, her medical kit banging against her thigh, Sally-Ann scurrying behind her to where the hatch of the Hercules yawned open ready for them to board. Her mind whirred as she thought about the dangers ahead. More than fear for herself though, she was frightened of what she would see when they arrived. The diggers they were going to retrieve would be in a bad way, she knew that. It was their job to get them safely back here to Butterworth from where they'd be flown home within the next couple of days. She'd see horrors she'd never be able to un-see. 'You can do this Sally-Ann, you're a nurse. It what's you're trained to do,' she whispered silently before sending up a prayer to ask for the strength she knew she was going to need to help these boys.

'Arpège?' Sister Wilson asked once they were strapped into their seats. The question pulled Sally-Ann from her reverie. She nodded.

'That's my sister Bet's favourite,' Sister Wilson said offering the younger nurse a smile. She could sense the nervous energy coming off her in waves.

The smile softened her somewhat austere features and it emboldened Sally-Ann to ask, 'Sister, why did you suggest I wear perfume?'

'It's for our boys, Sister, so even if their injuries mean they can't see they at least know they're safe when they smell our perfume.'

Chapter 20

Present

Moira was still half asleep and was grateful for the steaming brew that had just been put in front of her. She'd successfully ordered her and Mammy's morning beverage the local way asking for two cà phê sua nongs. It had made her feel a little bit proud and very intrepid when the woman had nodded her understanding straight away. It made for a pleasant change not to have to listen to Mammy ask for two, holding her fingers up invariably the wrong way (Moira had told her more than once she was actually giving the poor restauranteur the fingers), café au lait coffees please. She enunciated this slowly and in a very loud voice as though that would make what she was ordering clearer.

Now she sipped away on the hot sweet drink. They were sitting under the awning outside the restaurant attached to their hotel. Hoi An remained a surprise for them to discover today because they hadn't seen much from the bus last night. It had been dark when they'd finally rumbled into the city. Their driver had done a quick circuit past rows of fluorescent bulb-lit shops with screeds of colourful fabrics for sale, machinists toiling away in the background before veering off down a labyrinth of side streets and depositing them here.

They'd ordered a club sandwich from the restaurant each but had been too tired to venture out, opting instead for another early night. Moira would not be relaying how many early nights she was having on this holiday in any of her postcards home.

She took in their surroundings as curiosity kicked in along with the caffeine. A row of bikes was parked across the street and a few doors up from them a group of men were sitting on upturned crates, noodles dangling from the chopsticks they were expertly handling. Street dogs snuffled around or lay snoozing in doorways. She watched a woman cycle past with a basket full of fresh greens. Nobody, not even the dogs, seemed to be in any hurry.

'Where you from?' A little girl bobbed up from nowhere, her grin wide, revealing baby teeth pearly white against creamy skin as she grinned up at her.

'Ireland,' Moira smiled back at her, her grin infectious, before putting her cup down.

'You buy?' She produced a selection of colourful bracelets.

'No, not today thanks.' She had an armful of the things as it was.

'Can I have Ireland coin? I collect.' She widened her brown eyes to gaze beseechingly up at her.

She was a pro at this Moira thought feeling a tug at her heartstrings. She dutifully retrieved her wallet from her shoulder bag and opened the flap where she'd put the coins she'd been handed back at the airport. Dublin seemed like another world and retrieving the fifty or so pence she had left she handed the money over. She was rewarded with another smile that made her feel happy inside. The child stuffed the coins in her pocket. 'Bye, Ireland,' she shouted haring off down the street, another hotel with more tourists sitting around in the morning sunshine already in her line of sight. Mammy, Moira realised was smirking over the top of her coffee cup.

'Just say 'No' eh, Moira? N.O. isn't that how it went?'

It was the children she struggled with Moira thought simultaneously poking her tongue out at her mammy. Their little faces, so bright and eager were impossible to say no to. It would feel, well it would feel unnatural to ignore them. She could see that little girl wasn't going hungry but she was spending her days trying to make money and not going to school and that made her sad. It wasn't as though she hadn't seen people in need before. At home there were always hunched mounds sitting on pieces of cardboard as you crossed over the Ha'penny Bridge but they weren't children.

Maureen was unaware of the deep thoughts her daughter was having because she'd spied Sally-Ann. She waved over to where she was standing in the foyer and the Australian woman smiled her recognition before heading over to their table. Maureen gestured to the empty seat. 'Come and join us. We've just ordered.'

'Thank you,' Sally-Ann sat down and smiled at them both before offering up an apologetic, 'I'm starving,' as she picked up the menu. 'I'd planned on heading out to find some dinner last night but I fell asleep as soon as my head hit the pillow. That was some bus ride.'

Maureen and Moira nodded their agreement.

'Maureen, I hope you don't mind my asking but that's Arpège you're wearing isn't it?' She looked over the top of the menu.

'It is, it's my favourite. My husband, Brian, used to buy me a bottle on our wedding anniversary. I'm going to treat myself to a big bottle when we go through duty free on our way home.'

'It was my favourite too. It was the first bottle of French perfume I was ever given. My family gave it to me on my twenty-first birthday.' The two women smiled at each other.

Moira observing the exchange was struck by how different they were. There was Mammy with her ridiculous beaded braids and quick dry T-shirt which she'd teamed with her fisherman pants and sandals, and there was Sally-Ann. She reminded Moira of a scout leader, all she needed was a whistle around her neck. She was decked out in a plain T-shirt, knee length khaki shorts and sensible walking shoes. Her hair was a no-nonsense cropped grey and her demeanour was that of a practical capable, woman. It was her eyes that caught your attention, they were quite startling.

'My husband,' Maureen was saying now. 'Well, he wasn't my husband back then, he wooed me with a bottle. It was the first French perfume I'd ever owned too.'

'It's special isn't it? That first bottle. It symbolises womanhood, or at least that's how I felt.' Sally-Ann smiled she'd been about to ask Moira what her favourite scent was but the woman who ran the hotel approached with her pen and pad at the ready and the conversation halted.

'Chào buổi sáng,' Sally-Ann smiled looking up. The woman looked pleased and repeated the sentiment before Sally-Ann added, 'I'll have báhn mi hòa mã please.'

Moira had no idea what she'd just said but she'd just put her cà phê sua nongs to shame.

'Sal told me on the bus yesterday that she nursed here during the war, Moira.' Maureen explained in that irritating tone she used when she was 'in the know'.

'Oh.' Moira had seen plenty of films about the war, hadn't everyone? 'That must have been tough.' It sounded lame given what this woman must have seen and done during that time. She was embarrassed that it was all she could come up with in response but was saved by the arrival of her and Mammy's baguettes along with a selection of jams. She chose grape just because she hadn't had it before and peeling back the seal she listened in as the two women chatted about their plans for the day.

Mammy rattled off all the sights they were looking forward to seeing, the wooden Chinese shop houses and the covered Japanese bridge in the ancient town being top of their list.

'I read in my guide book that Hoi An is the tailoring capital of the world.' Sally-Ann's food arrived, eggs sunny side up with a baguette and she thanked the woman before sprinkling a little chilli sauce over her eggs and continuing. 'Apparently there are over three hundred of them in the city. It's a great place to get clothes made to measure especially custom-made suits. Super cheap.'

Moira received a kick under the table and she sent crumbs flying as she protested.

'Did you hear what Sal just said, Moira? You can get clothes made to measure here. That's what they were up to in those shops we saw from the bus last night. Sure, you could get yourself a whole new work wardrobe.'

Moira was surprised Mammy wasn't already up and out of her seat stampeding up the road to where they'd seen the rows and rows of dressmaking shops. The thought of a whole new work wardrobe wasn't inspiring her to get moving, she didn't want to think about work full stop and she carried on eating her jam and bread.

'I thought I'd see about having something made for my daughter's graduation while I'm here. She's at university in Sydney,' Sally-Ann said. 'I'll need something smart for that.'

'Ooh, you've just reminded me.' Maureen's beads clacked as she jiggled in her seat with excitement. 'I could get a dress made for the Yacht Club Christmas dinner. It's quite formal or so I've been told. Did I tell you, I'm learning how to sail, Sal?'

Sal shook her head, dipping her bread in her yolk, 'No, I don't think you did, Maureen.'

'I took it up recently. It's something I always fancied doing but never had the time when we ran the guesthouse.' And with that she was away. Moira tuned out as she prattled on about her painting classes, the politics of the ladies who golfed, and her rambling group. She informed Sally-Ann she'd learned the key to surviving grief was keeping yourself busy. 'Don't give yourself time to fall into that big black hole.' She wagged her baguette at her. 'And talk about how you're feeling don't let it fester, like Moira here was doing.'

Moira scowled at her mammy. Nothing was sacred with her. She switched off again as Mammy began talking about the counsellor she'd gone to see and how she was hoping Moira might use her services when they got home. Ignoring the one-sided chatter, she polished her breakfast off and wished Mammy would shut up and finish her food so they could go and see what the city had to offer.

Chapter 21

♥

'Well, what do you think? Is the colour me?' Maureen was standing next to a headless mannequin in a figure-hugging Chinese styled blue silk dress. 'This fabric in that style.' She held up the piece of vibrant red silk she'd plucked from the table where they'd been browsing the stacks of sample fabrics and struck a hands-on-hip pose next to the mannequin.

'Jaysus, Mammy, it's very China Beach. Yer boatie men might think you're touting for business,' Moira said.

Sally-Ann who was feeling a little overwhelmed by the selection, choked back a laugh.

'Don't be rude, Moira, it's lovely and bright so it is and sure, who wants to be a wallflower?' Maureen was holding the material tightly to her chest looking ready to play tug-o-war should her daughter try and take it off her. 'What do you think, Sal?'

'I think life is far too short to be a wallflower, Maureen.'

Mammy shot a triumphant look at her daughter before casting around for assistance. Moira sighed. It looked like the red silk would be making an appearance at the Howth Yacht Club's Christmas do.

'Have you seen anything you like, Moira?' Sally-Ann asked.

'Lots. Too much really, I don't know where to start.' She didn't and she wished she had Andrea with her. She'd help her pick just the right fabric and decide on a style. She always took Andrea shopping with her.

'Me either, although I do like the look of this.' Sally-Ann's hand settled proprietorially over a folded bolt of sea-green silk.

'Oh, that's gorgeous. It would really set your eyes off,' Moira encouraged. 'Do you have a style in mind?'

'I'm not sure. Maybe something like this?' She moved over to another headless dummy only this one was wearing a more sedate, and much more age appropriate in Moira's opinion, black dress. It was sleeveless, the cut simple and stylish.

'I like that, you could get a jacket made in the same fabric too.'

'I could, couldn't I.' Sally-Ann's eyes danced and Moira left her and Mammy to be measured up while she decided to see what was on offer next door. The shops were all much of a muchness, she thought, determined to order something. Although this one she saw, looking around and making a mental note to steer Mammy in the opposite direction when she was finished with her order, had an abundance of baggy ethnic pants on display.

'I've really enjoyed today. Thanks for letting me tag along,' Sally-Ann said. The trio were perched on stools outside a street café in the Ancient Town. They were waiting for the bowls of pho, Sally-Ann had insisted they try. The chicken noodle broth with its plump white noodles was a Vietnamese staple and she'd said they'd be doing themselves a disservice if they didn't at least try it. Mammy had been gung-ho, keen to impress her new friend with her worldly palate but Moira had pursed her lips and taken a bit more persuading. She'd kept flashing back to Roger the Rat from Nha Trang. It made her tummy tighten with apprehension. She was outnumbered though and pho it was. What was the worst thing that could happen? It was the wrong way to think because then she flashbacked to the nightmare of the clam-room.

A whiff of lemon grass and something else she couldn't put a name to, wafted past her on a plate and her nose twitched appreciatively. Maybe it would be alright after all.

'Not a bother. It was a grand day,' Maureen said. 'Wasn't it, Moira?'

'A grand day, Mammy.' She grinned at Sally-Ann.

It had been too. They'd spent an industrious morning trawling the tailors' shops and buying up large. Moira was going to have to be on her best behaviour where Mammy was concerned and not make any more cracks about the red silk—as hard as that would be. She'd no room in her backpack to cart home today's haul and was reliant on Mammy unless she wanted to pay for excess baggage. For someone who'd started off looking about the shops reticently she was now the proud owner, or would be tomorrow when the garments were ready to be collected, two new dresses, a pair of black trousers, and three new tops. She'd thought about ordering Andrea something because they were more or less the same size but then she remembered the way she'd sniggered at Moira going on her hols with Mammy and changed her mind.

She'd also bartered her way into buying three lanterns, in purple, pink, and red, on their way here for dinner too. Mammy had huffed at the lantern purchases saying they'd look ridiculous in the bedroom of a Georgian manor house. Moira had told her that it was debatable whether a Chinese styled dress in red silk would look at home mingling with the stuffy yachting set. They'd begged to differ not wanting to squabble in front of their new friend.

The street they were sitting on was illuminated by lanterns strung across the cobbled lane. If Moira closed her eyes, she could imagine how it would have been when the Japanese, Chinese, and European merchants were here pedalling their wares. The lanterns had looked pretty by day but now, lighting up an inky sky, they were positively magical. They'd all agreed there was something very special about this place. There'd been photo opportunities around every corner and she'd soon whipped through a whole roll of film, looking on enviously at those travellers with up to the minute gear and the new digital cameras that were starting to make an appearance.

The first of the fragrant bowls of soup arrived and Sally-Ann indicated Moira should have it. She inhaled the aroma and decided so far so good, then, with all eyes on her she wielded the chopsticks to the best of her ability and fished out a fat white noodle. She slurped it up, feeling it flick against her chin before she caught the rest of it in her mouth. She took a moment to savour it and then looking up gave Sally-Ann the thumbs up.

Postcards

Dear Aisling,

The picture on the front is of the Japanese covered bridge in Hoi An. The old town here is beautiful. Mammy and her new friend, Sal, and I explored the Chinese quarter which was very quaint with ornate architecture (pinched that description from travel guide book). I loved the lanterns hanging every-where and I liked the sampan boats on the waterfront too. I used a whole roll of film up just wandering around. You'd love it here because it's got these amazing tailors' shops where you can get clothes made to measure and yes, there were shoes for sale too, lots of shoes. I'm after getting some lovely things made up. To give you a heads-up, Mammy has had a dress made in red silk, think yer red-headed, prostitute woman in China Beach but with Bo Derek braids. She's also had one made for you in blue, and purple for Rosi. I tried to talk her out of it but you know what she's like when she's got her heart set on something. I can't wait to see the three of you in them though. Laughing already.

Love Moira

Dear Roisin

It's your Mammy here. Hoi An is very good value and we've had a grand time. We especially enjoyed looking around the old town. It's another world, so it is. We visited a Chinese merchant house called Tan Ky House. It was very dark and atmospheric with lots of lovely antiques. After that my new friend, Sal, Moira, and I shopped until we dropped. You know those Faraway Tree stories you used to love? Well, if this place was a land at the top of the tree it would be the land of get whatever clothes you want made. How it works is you choose the fabric and the tailor takes your measurements and you're away. I've had a dress made for the Howth Yacht Club's Christmas Dinner in red silk. It's very elegant. Moira suggested I get dresses made in the same style for you and Aisling. You can't afford to put any weight on because I used Moira's measurements. I think you girls will love them, they're both in your colours.

Love Mammy

Dear Noah,

It's your nana here. We are in Hoi An. It is very nice here with lots of shops with colourful things for sale. Your Aunty Moira has bought lanterns like the big white paper shade you have in your bedroom except hers are made of material and are the sorta colours that would keep you wide awake at night not send you off to sleep. The streets here are decorated with them and a long time ago Hoi An was a port town and people came from Japan and China to sell things. I had a soup called pho which had noodles as fat as worms in it. It was very tasty. I hope you're being a good boy for your mammy and dad give them a hug from me and have one for yourself.

   Love Nana

Chapter 22

♥

Mammy's Travel Journal

*H*ello from Hue where we have just had a very interesting meal of rice paper rolls stuffed with pork and I'm not sure what else but it was tasty and very good value. The rolls were Sal's suggestion, she knows her way around a Vietnamese menu, so she does. I liked them but Moira said the texture reminded her of a— well, I knew what she was going to say and it wasn't appropriate for sharing around the dinner table. I kicked her under the table before she had the chance to say the word. Sal doesn't need to hear my daughter's uncultured response to rice paper rolls and for the record there was nothing rubbery about the rolls whatsoever.

I was sad to leave Hoi An but the drive here through the Hai Van Pass was very beautiful. I could have been excused for thinking I was in County Clare what with all the greenery, spitty rain, and rainbows. It was more jungle-like than Clare though and we had magnificent views down to crescent shaped white sand beaches. They don't have those in Clare either. I was worried for a while there that history would repeat itself with Moira. She's not good on the winding roads *and I had a paper bag at the ready but Sal came to the rescue. She gave her a ginger sweet to suck on and it did the trick.*

Sal was very quiet on the journey here. I did ask if everything was alright and she said she was fine, just a little lost in the past which is understandable. Although as I always say, it doesn't pay to bottle things up. I'll be sad to go our separate ways but we travel up to Hanoi from here and she's going to visit some unpronounceable village in the hills. I'm not sure why. She didn't say and as much as I'd have liked to have prodded for more information there was something in her face that stopped me from prying.

This morning we were up bright and early and I have to say the cooler weather here was a shock to the system but I'd come prepared. I have one long sleeved quick dry top; it's got a little pocket on the front and I think the orange looks well on me. I'm very impressed with the versatility of my travel pants. I can zip them off at the knees and wear them as shorts in the hot weather, then zip them back on in the cool, like I did this morning. I think Moira was secretly impressed especially as it means I didn't have to pack all manner of shorts and trousers. I had plenty of room in my pack when we left Dublin but the way she's been going we're going to have to buy an extra bag to cart all the gear home. Moira's turned into a bit of a haggle monster; she loves it so she does. The thrill of bartering.

Sal announced she needed to organise how she was going to get to this village she's set on visiting after breakfast so we arranged to do our own thing for the day. We agreed to meet up later for dinner and went our separate ways. Moira and I set off to visit the Forbidden City first. Doesn't that just sound delicious? We agreed it made us feel like we were visiting somewhere very cutting edge you know like Eastern Germany or the likes when the wall came down. I remember watching that on the news and feeling all sorta fizzy inside.

Inside the city walls it was a ruin but the Imperial Palace has been restored. Splendid is the word that comes to mind.

Splendid and opulent, but sure, that's two words. We headed back to town after that and wandered down to the Perfume River, isn't that a lovely name for a river? I don't know how they came up with it because it was brown like the Mekong. I was impressed by Moira's negotiating skills as she organised for us to go by dragon boat to the track that would lead us to Tu Duc's Royal Mausoleum. The boat was home to yer man steering us down the river, his wife, and five children. No privacy in their household. I had to wonder how they get on. I mean I was mortified the time Patrick had a bad dream and barged in on me and Brian engaged in the, you know what.

It was very relaxing sitting on that boat watching the world go by. We saw people working in the fields, children riding on buffalos with kites flying behind them, and women washing their clothes in the river. Sure, you wouldn't want to be doing your whites in that water. We were on the boat about an hour before we docked. It was a four-kilometre hike to the mausoleum and from what we could see it looked very muddy. Moira looked at me and I looked at Moira and we both looked at the man with the scooters for hire. We made a pact, that neither of us would tell Aisling.

Moira drove the thing and I sat on the back and we were grand until she got cocky and wasn't looking where she was going. She rode right through a puddle and we got covered in mud. She really is ruing the day she didn't invest in some quick dry gear now.

Yer man Tu Duc was a one. We read in our guide book that he was only 153cm tall. He had 104 wives and countless concubines. I said to Moira he was suffering badly from the short man's disease. The funny thing is he went to all this trouble to have the tomb built and then he wasn't even buried there. No one knows where he wound up buried along with all his treasure because the two hundred servants who put him in the ground all had their heads cut off to keep it a secret from grave robbers. Charming, he obviously didn't believe in rewarding loyal service.

Chapter 23

M oira was making short shrift of her breakfast as Mammy and Sally-Ann nattered on in between bites. She was only half listening but her ears pricked up when she sensed their conversation was about to get interesting.

'So, come on then, Sal, tell us about this village you're off to.' Maureen had decided there was nothing else for it, she'd have to pry. It was obvious Sal wasn't going to be forthcoming without a nudge. Sometimes in life people needed a good nudge.

'It's a long story.'

'Ah sure, we're not in a rush to head off are we, Moira?'

Moira looked up from her eggs. 'No, no rush.' She was curious to hear what Sally-Ann had to say. It was a bit weird her going off on her own to some village out in the middle of nowhere.

Sally-Ann looked from one to the other. They'd think her mad if she told them. Then again maybe she was. What was the saying? A problem shared is a problem solved was that it? Or was it a problem halved? Well, either way they wouldn't be able to solve this for her but perhaps talking about why she'd come all this way might help to make some sense of it. She took a deep breath and put her knife and fork down.

ell

1968

Sally-Ann was more tired than she'd ever been in her life. She now understood what it meant when people said they were 'bone tired'. Her bones did indeed ache with weariness. There were days she was sure her body was fuelled by adrenalin and not much else. She'd just come off a ten-hour shift, the sixth in a row here at the Vung Tau 1st Australian Field Hospital and her plan was to sleep, sleep, and sleep! Maybe tomorrow she'd see if she could borrow Lynn's tape recorder and microphone instead of putting pen to paper. She owed them a letter back home.

She felt the familiar pang for home. Terri had herself a young man now and from the last few letters her sister had written to her, she was in those heady throes of first love. She was describing things in greater detail as though all her senses had suddenly come to life. There was an underlying joy to her words that made Sally-Ann wistful; it wasn't something she'd ever experienced. You could hardly count Billy Brown and his wandering hands as a grand passion. Terri and Terry though, she shook her head and smiled, you wouldn't read about it. She couldn't have met a Henry or a John she had to meet a Terry. One of them would have to revert to their full name. Teresa had always been Terri though and as for Terry she had no clue whether he'd answer to Terence. It must drive their friends mad!

It would be nice to be lying on her bed at home as Terri chattered on. To be hearing first-hand about her life. She missed her but she steeled her resolve as she always did when the homesickness tugged. She was needed here. Terri was perfectly happy and one day, before too long, this awful war would be over and she'd be back home probably shaking her head over the ups and downs of her sister's new romance.

She kicked off her shoes and collapsed on her cot not bothering to get out of her uniform. Her own senses had gone into overdrive when she'd first been deployed into this dirty, dusty, chaotic place. She'd spent the last three months assisting on the medevac flights having proved herself more than capable to Eileen as she'd come to call Sister Wilson. It was a process she'd grown comfortable with despite the dangers and even though she was familiar with Vung Tau, a port city, this latest three-month deployment had tried her. She was one month in and being tested to her very limits.

The hospital was tucked away by the beach behind the sand dunes but it was no holiday camp you'd ever want to come and stay at. The South China Sea seemed a pale, washed out version of the beaches from home and even the sand had an ashen tinge. Rubbish choked the gully ways and the lack of sanitation and stink of the place had been a slap in the face for this girl from Western Australia. Their base had been positioned strategically so that the Aussie diggers battling it out nearby were only thirty minutes away from medical care which meant their chances of surviving the horrors they were enduing was far greater. They were horrors Sally-Ann had seen first-hand.

The bloodshed on both sides was like a never-ending newsreel of carnage. Young bodies destroyed, and for what? It was a question she couldn't find an answer for and so she'd stopped asking it.

The shrilling siren penetrated her fug competing with the familiar beating whir of a chopper coming into land. She forced herself into consciousness before staggering down to triage to see how bad it was. The doors slammed open and the stretchers were carried in. The team of nurses on duty swung in to their well-honed routines cutting the wounded men's clothes off to check them over as the medics inserted drips.

Sally-Ann rolled up her sleeves and set to work. She didn't know how many hours had passed before she saw the local boy lying on a gurney in the far corner of the resuscitation area. He stared back at her with glassy eyes.

'Poor kid, an orphan, I think. He was brought in on a rickshaw before this kicked off. He's lost his leg from the knee down.' Sister Healey had followed Sally-Ann's gaze.

'A landmine?'

'Mm.'

'Jesus, he can't be more than ten years old.' It wasn't anything Sally-Ann hadn't seen before but there was something in this boy's eyes as they'd locked on hers. They seemed to be pleading with her. She knew too, the day she failed to be shocked that people could do this to one another was the day she had to go home.

'You're rostered off, aren't you?'

'Yes.'

'Go then, get some rest. We can manage now.'

She looked over at the boy once more and felt herself being pulled over as she realised what else she'd seen in those desperate eyes. It was fear. She smiled reassuringly at him as she took his hand in hers holding it gently. He gripped hers back. 'My name's Sally-Ann, what's yours?'

He looked at her blankly for a moment but then seemed to register what she'd said. 'Sally-Ann?' he said in heavily accented English.

'Sally-Ann, but you can call me Sal.'

She thought she saw the faintest of smiles. 'Binh.'

'Well, I'm here now, Binh. You're going to be okay because I'm going to watch over you.' He squeezed her hand tightly in understanding.

'You stay?'

'I won't leave you; I promise. I'm staying right here. Now try and sleep,' she said pulling up a chair to sit alongside him, listening as his breathing began to slow and calm as he drifted off to sleep. Sally-Ann fell asleep in her chair, her body hunched over with her head resting on the side of the bed and she was still there holding his hand when Binh next opened his eyes.

———ee———

'Ironically the name Binh means peaceful.' Sally-Ann finished her story and Mammy and Moira both blinked as they came back to the present. 'To cut a long story short I received a letter from Binh not long after my husband, Robert, first got ill. It was completely out of the blue, I never expected to hear from him again. He'd sent it to the Royal Australian Army Nursing Corps who'd forwarded it to me. All he wanted, he said in it, was to let me know he was okay and he had a good life. He said he'd never forgotten me. The nurse with the blue eyes who stayed with him.' Her eyes shone suspiciously bright and she blinked several times before carrying on. 'I told you he was orphaned?'

Maureen and Moira nodded; they were entranced.

'Well, it turns out Binh was part of Operation Babylift.' She registered their blank faces. 'The US government's response to South Vietnam's pleas to the United Nations and other humanitarian organisations was to put money into airlifting orphans out of Vietnam. There were nearly three thousand babies and children in total who were flown to the US, Canada, Europe, and Australia to be adopted by families eager to help. It wasn't without controversy though because some of the children were taken from poor families who thought they'd be returned to them. And, of course it wasn't easy for these children growing up either. Some were subject to racism and felt they were neither one nor the other, not Vietnamese or American, Australian, Canadian or wherever they'd found themselves transplanted to.'

Maureen made a choking sound; the world was full of sad stories and sometimes the lines blurred between good intentions and what was right and what was wrong. There were no simple fixes when it came to human life. Sure, she'd read enough in the papers at home over the years to understand that. There'd been some terrible things done under her church's watch but they'd been done with the conviction that what they were doing was right. Just because you believed you were doing the right thing didn't always make it so, though. Moira simply shook her head.

'Binh was taken to Canada where he received rehabilitation treatment to learn how to manage the loss of his lower leg. He was adopted by a family with two older sons and he wrote he'd had a happy upbringing with them. He'd always told them he wanted to go back to Vietnam one day though. It had never stopped being home, as much as he loved his new family. I think perhaps he was lucky; his mother and father must have loved him very much to agree to let him go and he said in his letter that they come and visit him often here in Vietnam.

He finished university in Canada and just as he'd said he would, he came back here. He decided to travel first wanting to see his country and he met his wife on his journey. They settled in Hanoi and four years ago with three children now, they decided they'd had enough of city life. They moved back to the village where she came from and built their farm-stay accommodation with a dream of being self-sufficient. He said they're extremely happy and that it was important to him that I know that because he'd never forgotten me and the kindness I showed him.' Sally-Ann's voice cracked. 'Sorry.' She chewed her bottom lip blinking back the tears that had returned. 'It's just he'd written in that letter that he'd wanted to die that night. He'd lost everything but that I brought him back.'

'Don't be sorry,' Mammy was swiping at her own eyes and the two women exchanged a watery smile. 'It's a wonderful thing you did.'

'I did what any nurse would do. Robert, my husband made me promise before he died that I'd come back to Vietnam and visit Binh. He said I needed to see for myself that he's happy and that the country has moved on. He thought it would bring me some closure.' She shrugged, 'It never leaves you; you see. I mean they have a fancy name for it now PTSD.'

'What's that?' The term tickled Maureen's memory cogs but she couldn't recall what it stood for.

'Post-traumatic stress disorder. When I came home to Australia it wasn't a diagnosable condition. We weren't allowed to talk about our experiences, we just had to go back to our lives as though the war had never happened.'

'See, Moira, bottling it up, it doesn't do anyone any good.'

Sally-Ann fixed those piercing eyes on her. 'She's right, dear, it doesn't.'

This wasn't about her though, Moira thought. She'd been enthralled listening to Sally-Ann and she was seeing the woman sitting across from her very differently. She wasn't Mammy's rather staid looking new friend; sure, she was an angel.

'You were his angel, so you were,' Mammy said to Sally-Ann and Moira looked at her in surprise that they'd been thinking the exact same thing.

'No not an angel, just a human being,' Sally-Ann said, but what she said next took them both by surprise.

Chapter 24

♥

'Come with me.' Sally-Ann's piercing gaze swung imploringly from mother to daughter. The idea of these two Irish women she might not have known long, but whom she liked immensely, accompanying her had just occurred to her. She seized hold of it ferociously, surprised by how much she wanted them to join her. She was anxious, she realised, as to how she'd be received. It was one thing to write and tell a woman who'd sat with you through a long night over thirty years ago that your life had turned out well. It was quite another for that woman to turn up on your doorstep to see for herself.

Binh's letter had brought the war crashing back because for so many years it was his face that had haunted her dreams. He'd become her poster boy, that terrified little boy who'd lost both his parents and whose body had been brutally maimed in a fight that wasn't his. It wasn't hers either but she wouldn't have changed her time at Vung Tau. Those men, boys really, and the locals whose lives were in unimaginable turmoil had needed her and the other women she'd worked alongside. She'd grown to love her fellow Sisters as much as she loved Terri. She knew they'd agree too; it had been a privilege to nurse in Vung Tau.

Then, there was the fact she might never have met the digger who'd lost the sight in one eye and whose leg the medic had only just managed to save. Despite his wounds he'd still mustered up a cheeky grin as he asked her if his crown jewels had survived the mortar attack. They'd formed a friendship during his stay in the hospital. A friendship that had developed into something more. She and Robert had married six months after she arrived home. She'd gone back to nursing and he'd taken over the running of her family sheep farm with Mum and Dad happy to pass the mantle and take things easier. Together, they'd built themselves a good life.

Robert had known her better than she knew herself and he'd been right. It was time she put what had happened here to bed. Life could be fleeting or, if you were lucky, it could be filled with stages. She'd been lucky and for Robert's sake as much as her own she needed to embrace whatever this next stage would bring. In order to do that she needed to see Binh with her own eyes.

She realised Moira and Maureen were looking a little taken aback by the insistence in her tone and she flushed, feeling foolish. She barely knew them after all but she couldn't seem to stop herself. "I looked it up on the internet, Mui Ha the village where they live. It's about a two-and-a-half-hour drive from Hue and sits on a popular backpacking trail for those heading further into the mountains.'

Moira could feel a tingling excitement. There was nothing to stop them going with her, they weren't on any fixed itinerary. Maureen however was less certain. 'Ah, but sure, we wouldn't want to be intruding. It's a pilgrimage of sorts you're undertaking. A personal thing.'

'Yes,' Sally-Ann said slowly. 'It is. But to tell you the truth I'm a little scared. I never replied to Binh's letter. He doesn't even know I got it for certain. I booked my flight to Hoi Chi Minh on the spur of the moment and I didn't think about what I was going to do until I got here. I went down south initially.

I needed to lay old ghosts to rest in Vung Tau.' She closed her eyes for a moment. She'd visited the Martyr's Memorial taking her life in her hands as she'd weaved across the busy road to the enormous roundabout in front of the Pullman Hotel. The city was unrecognisable to the one in which she'd lived and worked. Life, however brutally interrupted, never stood still, she'd thought, sitting on a bench and finally letting the memories of her time here wash over her. The good, the bad, and the ugly.

She opened her eyes. 'Vung Tau was nothing like I remembered but I paid my respects and came back to Hoi Chi Minh where I bought a hop on, hop off bus ticket. I'd decided to work my way here to Hue having a look at the country along the way. I thought it would all become clear to me what I was going to do once I got here but I'm no more certain now that I'm doing the right thing by landing on him out of the blue than I was when I bought my ticket.' She shrugged, 'I keep thinking I've been foolish. I should have written back to him, waited for a reply but the thing is, I've made it this far now. I can't leave without seeing him. So, you see you'd be doing me a favour by coming with me. Strength in numbers and all that.'

'Mammy?' Moira looked at her expectantly. She wanted to go. Sally-Ann's story had moved her. 'She needs us.'

Maureen leaned over and rested her hand on top of Sally-Ann's, just like the Australian Nurse had Binh's all those years ago. 'Of course, we'll come with you, Sal. It would be an honour, so it would.'

Chapter 25

Moira was sat in the front of the minivan on account of her car sickness tendencies and Maureen and Sally-Ann were strapped into their seats behind her. They were driving through an area lush with leafy green tea plantations and the road was quiet except for the odd motorbike passing them. It was a different pace altogether to what they'd grown used to in the bigger towns and cities. Their driver, Danh, was a jovial sort with a gold tooth which he flashed every time he grinned. He was armed with a toothpick which he used sporadically, steering with one hand when he felt the urge to dig around. Moira looked out the side window when he did this, partly because she didn't want to see what he'd unearth, but mostly because she couldn't bear watching him drive fast enough to leave a cloud of dust behind them down roads that were barely sealed with only one hand. She felt a tap on her shoulder and turning to look found a bag of ginger sweets being waved under her nose.

'Oh, thanks,' she said, helping herself and unwrapping a sweet. She sucked away on it wondering how they'd be received when they got to where they were going. Would this Binh fella know Sally-Ann on sight? It had been over thirty years since they'd met and given the circumstances it was amazing he could recall the nurse who'd stayed with him all through what must have been a horrific night at all. Her kindness above any call of duty had obviously had a profound effect on him.

Sal was a very strong sort of a person, Moira thought, in all senses of the word. Mammy didn't look strong physically but she was fierce on the inside too she'd come to realise. They were both brave women in different ways.

It must be nice to have a vocation, a calling to do something worthwhile, she mused, feeling her kidneys or something like hit the top of her rib cage as they hit a particularly deep pot-hole and bounced out the other side. Nursing was definitely that, sure it wasn't the sort of thing you decided to do just because you were fed up with being told what to do all the time at school. Her mind drifted to the children she'd seen here. Delightful faces that never stopped smiling flashed in front of her. Their world, while beautiful, was narrow and little would be handed to them along the way. They'd have to fight hard for everything that came their way. To break any moulds would be a battle.

She could have done anything she wanted when she left school. She was lucky but that luck wasn't down to anything she'd done. She hadn't earned the right to have a wealth of opportunities available to her, it was simply down to the circumstances of her birth. And what had she done with all those endless possibilities? She thought of Mason Price and frowned. There was nothing wrong with her job. It was a good job, a respectable job, and it paid well but it wasn't a calling or a vocation at least not for her. It wasn't, if she were honest with herself, what she wanted to do.

She'd never admitted that before and she shifted in her seat aware of a restlessness building. It was a restlessness that had been gnawing at her for a while now but she hadn't known what it was about and she'd put it aside upon arriving here. The question she'd been unable to face was staring her right in the face. If she didn't see herself at Mason Price then where did she see herself?

Danh honked his horn shooing her confusion away and a cluster of children, their school bags dangling from small shoulders, waved out. Moira smiled and waved back as enthusiastically, seeing their beaming faces as they jostled to be noticed. A beat later a bike went past and she did a double-take. 'Did you see that?'

Danh laughed. 'No big deal.'

She craned her neck to see Mammy and Sally-Ann. 'There was a man and a woman on that scooter with a live pig squashed between them.'

Mammy peered behind to see if she could see them but they were gone and besides she wouldn't have seen much through the brown dust anyway.

'I once saw a calf being transported on one,' Sally-Ann smiled at the memory.

'Mui Ha, not far now,' Danh announced, and true to his words it wasn't long before they began to see more signs of life in the rice paddies on either side of them where workers laboured. The gates denoting the entrance to a village appeared ahead of them and Danh slowed. They were elaborately adorned with Vietnamese script along the top of the bricked arch and down either side. The leaves of a gnarled tree grazed the windows as they passed through them. 'Banyan tree, very old. It's traditional in Vietnamese village. It watches the good times and bad times of the peoples,' Danh explained. 'Mui Ha famous for carpentry and grapefruit. Very good.'

Moira assumed he meant both were very good. She could already see it wasn't the blink and you'd miss it village she'd envisaged but rather a sizable place and as they wound into its heart, she saw numerous alleyways spidering off. They were filled with houses packed tightly together in the same brick as the gates and clad with the weathered clay tiles of the north. A woman cycled past and without the incessant roaring motorbikes it felt relaxed and laid back although the street was bustling with activity. There were several tourists meandering down the main drag pausing to inspect the impressive wood carvings on display. Moira watched a young couple unloading backpacks from the back of a flatbed truck. A food market appeared ahead and Sally-Ann leaned forward and passed across a piece of paper on which she had written Binh's address.

Danh pulled over and wound his window down to call out to a man unloading a container of ripe golden grapefruit. They spoke to one another in rapid fire Vietnamese and then with a nod, signifying he was satisfied he knew where he was going, he wound the window up once more before veering out onto the road.

Moira could sense without seeing Sally-Ann's growing tension as they grew closer. It was palpable and she would have liked to have reached over and held her hand but she wasn't a contortionist. She'd put money on Mammy doing exactly that right now though.

The denser living of the village gave way to the neatly gridded rice paddies once more, the verdant hills a backdrop. It was only a few minutes before Danh slowed once more at the entrance to a driveway. A wooden handmade sign announced they'd arrived at Ben Trang farm. They turned in and parked in an open area where a couple of motorcycles had been abandoned. A house was just visible through the green growth, almost hidden alongside a row of banana trees. Sally-Ann leaned forward tapping Danh on the shoulder. 'Do you mind waiting here with our bags while we go and see whether they have room for us? I didn't book ahead you see.'

'No problem.' He flashed his gold tooth at them all and fished out a packet of cigarettes.

He was probably gasping for one, Moira thought clambering out and inhaling the hint of citrus floating on the breeze.

The trio made their way toward the path leading to the house as a dog, so hairy its eyes were barely discernible, ambled out to greet them, tail wagging with the lethargy of age. Moira stopped to pat him briefly, 'Hello, boy,' she said before scurrying to catch up with Mammy and Sally-Ann. The door to the house was open and the area they ventured into was clearly a reception room. The space was cool, and dark from the shade afforded by the foliage outside. A fish tank gurgled away beside the desk upon which a book lay open with handwritten entries. The sound of a television or radio could be heard emanating from deeper in the house. There was also a cacophonous chattering of birds but it wasn't clear where that was coming from.

'Hello!' Sally-Ann called above the din. They all listened out for movement even though it was unlikely they'd hear a thing over the birds.

Moira realised her own stomach had begun to do flip-flops; how must Sally-Ann be feeling? She glanced over at Mammy who gave her a funny sort of a smile that told her she was anxious too.

Sally-Ann didn't have to call out twice because a sweet-faced woman who made Moira and Maureen seem tall appeared from where they'd just come. She was carrying an empty dish. 'Sorry, I just feeding the birds. Welcome to Ben Trang farm,' she said, nodding at them as she went to stand on the other side of the desk. She placed the dish down next to the book and picked up a pencil before smiling expectantly up at them. Her English was good.

'We don't have a reservation.' Sally-Ann explained. 'But we would like to stay. First though we wondered if Binh might be here? I'd like to say hello to him.' She spoke slowly and clearly but she didn't shout like Mammy was prone to do, Moira thought, knowing if she were a nail biter, she'd be making short shrift of all ten of them about now. 'I knew him a long time ago.' Sally-Ann left the words 'in the war' hanging.

'He's my husband.' The woman nodded her smile never faltering although a flicker of curiosity was clearly visible on her face. 'Yes, one moment, I go get him.'

Sally-Ann was feeling sick with apprehension. Was she doing the right thing? Would seeing her again conjure up the horror of what had happened to him as a child? Perhaps she was being selfish by coming here. She was trying to help herself after all. What benefit was it to him to have her materialise here at the home he'd built for himself and his family. To distract herself she stepped outside looking around at their surroundings.

The farm she'd seen from their approach down the road was surrounded on one side by pancake flat rice paddies and on the other an orchard of what she was guessing were grapefruit trees. From where she was standing now, a path stretched away from the house and she followed it with her eyes. It snaked around a large pond to a row of bungalows. They were very rustic looking and each had a veranda yawning out over the pond with a hammock on which to while away the day if one so wished. Tucked away down the side of the house was an aviary; the birds it housed still in full conversation. To her right Sally-Ann could see an area fenced off by chicken wire, on the other side of which hens bossed each other about. Beyond that there was a large patch of green which she guessed was a vegetable patch. Behind her, just inside the entranceway, was a bike rack with several ramshackle bicycles. She gazed at them for a few beats unable to remember the last time she'd ridden one of those before turning back, thinking she'd head back inside.

A man had appeared on the path ahead, he walked with a slight awkwardness that was only really detectable if you were looking for it. The woman they'd just met was beside him. Sally-Ann's legs took on a life of their own as, just like they had all those years ago, they propelled her toward him.

Chapter 26

♥

M oira and Maureen had stepped outside and they hung back watching as Sally-Ann drew level with the man. They couldn't see her face but they could see his as he peered at her from beneath the brim of his hat. He frowned for a moment and then as he looked closely at her, his face erupted into a wide incredulous grin. It was as though the sun had come out and both women found themselves exhaling. He held out his arms and Sally-Ann stepped into the embrace. They made a strange pairing, her being a head taller than him. They stayed locked together for the longest time while his wife stood to one side clueless but her smile said she understood that whatever it was that was happening, it was something good. Mammy nudged Moira and she took the tissue she was proffering gratefully, unaware that the tears were running down her face until she tasted their saltiness on her lips.

Less than five minutes later introductions were underway as Sally-Ann half crying and half laughing introduced Moira and Maureen to Binh and his wife, Hoa. Their three children had also appeared wanting to see what the fuss was all about and Binh had hugged them to him providing his mystified family with an explanation as to who Sally-Ann and her friends were.

Hoa was holding Sally-Ann's hand tightly as though frightened she might evaporate, her face a picture of wonder.

Now, Sally-Ann, Maureen, and Moira were sitting in Binh and Hoa's living area on a long, low wooden bench seat, which Maureen was not entirely sure she'd be able to get up from without assistance. Moira had been charged with settling the fare with Danh and telling him that they wouldn't be needing a ride back to Hue. He didn't mind, he'd been paid for a return fare and gracing her with one last flash of gold he ground his cigarette out and got back behind the wheel. Binh was seated across from the three women and Hoa was knelt on a woven mat, upon which stood a dark wooden table separating the group, pouring tea. She kept looking up and smiling at Sally-Ann beatifically. The couple's three children, who ranged in age from fourteen to five, were also kneeling on the mat, chocolate eyes wide, and as quiet as mice lest they miss any of the unfolding story.

'I recognised Sally-Ann's eyes straight away,' Binh said now, his voice still holding traces of his Canadian upbringing. 'So blue. I'd never seen eyes that colour before and I never forgot them, they were so kind. It seemed to me that compassion radiated from them. Eyes never change. You can see a person's soul through their eyes.'

'Unlike the rest of me.' Sally-Ann laughed; her body language relaxed as she accepted the tea from Hoa with a smiling thanks. She told the family about her life in Australia. How she'd married an Australian soldier and that she'd returned to nursing in Australia while he ran the sheep farm they'd bought from her parents. They'd had two children who were now grown-up and had left the family fold for the delights of big city life. She told them how her time in Vietnam had haunted her for many years and how she'd often wondered what had become of Binh. She spoke of her wonder at receiving his letter and how happy it had made her to know he was happy.

She explained that it was Robert, her husband, who'd insisted she come back to Vietnam to see him.

Binh reached across the table and took both her hands in his. He looked at her intently as he said, 'I think your Robert must have been a very wise man. And I'm very happy you are here.'

'He was,' Sally-Ann agreed, trying to hold back those pesky tears. This was a happy reunion there would be no more tears.

Moira and Maureen helped tidy away the remains of the meal. For unexpected guests they had been treated to a feast and were feeling full and more than a little sleepy when Hoa gestured they should follow her. They left Sally-Ann and Binh talking and followed their diminutive hostess through the reception area where she paused to pick up a torch. The glow from the front room illuminated the bicycles lined up in the rack. 'These are for our guests; you are very welcome to make use of them tomorrow.'

Both women murmured their thanks. Moira thought it might be fun to cycle into the village tomorrow for a look around. Mind, she'd seen the hammocks on the verandas of the bungalows earlier when they'd arrived. It was equally as tempting to lie in one of those reading her book for the day. Hoa led them around the side of the now silent aviary to an outbuilding and opening the screen door she flicked the light on. 'This is the breakfast room, please help yourself in the morning,' she said smiling. There was a fridge humming and a small electric stove top for frying but most importantly there was a kettle with a jar of Nescafe next to it along with a container which presumably held teabags. All was good in her world, Moira thought, as she followed Hoa's lead, turning the light off on her way out.

They scurried behind the sweeping torch as she led them down the path toward the bungalows. 'You are in number three. Be careful there is a step.'

Voices called out hello in the darkness and as Hoa opened the door and the light flickered on they spied a couple sitting wrapped in a blanket on the adjacent veranda. They were stargazing as they sipped from their bottles of beer and Mammy, never one to miss an opportunity, introduced herself and Moira. The brief ensuing chat revealed them both to be Swedish.

'Mammy, you're letting all the bugs in standing out here, say goodnight,' Moira whispered, seeing Hoa waiting patiently inside for them.

Their bags were already miraculously in the room, leaning against the far wall of the cosy space, and Moira guessed the kindness would be down to Sang, Hoa and Binh's oldest child. She made a note to self to thank him in the morning. 'It's lovely, so it is. We'll be very comfortable in here won't we, Moira? Thank you, Hoa.'

'Yes, it's grand, thank you, Hoa.'

Their hostess looked pleased. 'I say goodnight now.' She beamed.

'Goodnight.' Moira and Maureen chimed.

Mammy and daughter did their ablutions and then turning the light out clambered in to the bed they were to share. It creaked under their bodyweight as they snuggled down under the blankets. They lay, eyes growing used to the darkness, talking over what a wonderful night it had been until Mammy yawned. 'I think I'll have to shut my eyes now, Moira. Keep to your side of the bed do you hear?'

'It's not me who thinks she's a starfish,' Moira replied before partaking of her nightly routine of plumping her pillow and twisting and turning until she was satisfied this was as good as it was going to get. She lay listening to the silence which was absolute apart from Mammy's snuffly breathing and the odd plop of a fish. She was, she realised, giving a contented little sigh, feeling very Zen. The world was a wondrous place. It was then she heard a high-pitched whine buzz past her ear. 'Oh, for feck's sake,' she muttered hauling herself upright.

'I was nearly asleep then, Moira. What's the problem?'

'There's a mosquito buzzing about.' She got out of bed and padded the short distance across the wooden floors to the door where the light switch was. The room flooded with light and Maureen squinted into it none too pleased at the sudden brightness. She made a guttural grumping sound.

'What? I can't sleep with that thing buzzing around.' Moira's eyes flicked wildly around the space trying to locate the culprit.

'Sure, there's nothing here it probably flew out through the bathroom window. Put the light out, I'm knackered so I am.'

'Mammy,' Moira's tone was indignant, 'have you forgotten the time you left Aisling and Rosi in charge and you, me and Daddy went to Rosslare for a weekend by the seaside? I got bitten on the eye and it swelled up something terrible. It was awful and I'm not long getting over the pink eye.'

Maureen hadn't forgotten. She could remember it clearly. Moira had been very dramatic about it all, as was her way, refusing to leave the bed and breakfast unless her parents provided her with a pair of Jacqui O sunglasses to hide behind. Thirteen was a trying age so it was, she and Brian had muttered, setting off to find a shop that sold oversized black sunglasses. Now she sighed heavily. There was something about that girl and her eyes when she was on her holidays. She also knew what her youngest daughter was like when she got a bee in her bonnet. If you can't beat em, best join em.

A flickering movement caught her eye and she clambered out of bed picking up her paperback. The sooner the thing was dealt with the sooner they could put the light out and get some sleep. *Aha, there it was.* Maureen crept stealthily over to the wall and thwacked her book against it. She missed and the spindly creature twirled teasingly, up out of her reach. She used bad language as did Moira after her ensuing near misses. The minutes passed with the pair of them leaping and thudding about the room. This was getting personal. Until Moira in a rage leapt up onto the bed clutching a flip-flop and swinging blindly.

'I think you got it.' Maureen cried; she was as invested in getting the beasty thing now as Moira. It was a matter of pride; she wouldn't be beaten by a four-legged, flying bug.

Moira stopped swinging and inspected the sole of the flip-flop, 'Yes!' She held it out showing Mammy the splayed mosquito embedded on its sole. 'Got the fecker, she said thudding down to the floor. 'Don't mess with Moira O'Mara.'

'The poor Swedes will wonder what's going on in here,' Maureen said, half expecting a knock on the door as she put the light out and climbed back into bed.

They slept like babies after that.

Chapter 27

Maureen and Moira found Sally-Ann once they'd showered and dressed the next morning. She was setting about making a pot of tea in the building Hoa had shown them the night before and seeing this Moira could have kissed her. She'd kill for a brew. Pouring the boiling water into the pot, Sally-Ann told them she'd spent the night in the house with the family, Binh, having assured her there was room, had been insistent she stay with them. 'He said I was part of the family,' she said smiling from mother to daughter. 'Thank you for coming here with me.'

'Not a bother. Sure, it's a lovely part of the world from what we saw yesterday. And we were very comfortable in our bungalow last night weren't we, Moira.'

Moira put the grapefruit she'd been inspecting back in the bowl and agreed.

Their Swedish neighbours were just finishing clearing up their breakfast things. 'Good morning,' they greeted in their clipped, precise English. They had some serious looking hiking gear on and the admiration shining in Mammy's eyes made Moira smile to herself. She was developing a thing for outdoor, active wear. Morning pleasantries were exchanged before the tall, athletic looking couple headed off to tackle their action-packed plans for the day.

An assortment of fresh fruits; melon, papaya, bananas and grapefruit had been laid out for the guests to help themselves. There was a loaf of bread for toasting and fresh eggs could be fried on the stove top if so desired. Moira settled for banana on toast and sat down to enjoy it at the little wooden table in the corner along with her cup of tea. Sally-Ann and Mammy busied themselves frying eggs. She could detect, in between bites and sips, the genuine happiness in the Australian woman's voice as she told Mammy she hadn't gone to bed until late because there'd been so much to talk about. She was overjoyed, she said at how welcome the family had made her feel. It was unexpected and it was a joy.

They sat down with Moira and ate their food to a background symphony of birds before washing up.

'Moira and I thought we might cycle into the village today. Would you like to join us, Sal? We think we'll stay tonight, if the bungalow isn't booked—I'll check with Hoa and Binh on our way out. And I know Binh said we were his guests but we'll be paying our way.'

Moira nodded her agreement.

'Moira wants to pick up some more mosquito repellent and I'm eager to have a look at the handicrafts on offer. We'll sort out a way of getting back to Hue when we're in the village too and, if it all goes to plan, make our way back there tomorrow for a night before getting the bus to Hanoi. Do you know what your plans are yet?' Maureen finally stopped to draw breath and Sally-Ann leaped into the opening.

'If you don't mind, I'd like to stay around here today and help Hoa, repay her for her hospitality and get a feel for this place. They farm organically and I'm curious to see how it all works. I haven't thought any further than that.' Sally-Ann shrugged.

'Fair play to you.' Mammy, who was on drying, said before wiping the last plate and popping it back into the dish rack.

'Ooh I haven't been on one of these in years,' Maureen shrieked, she'd had a bit of difficulty cocking her leg over the bar initially but now she was happily wobbling her way around the area where Danh had parked yesterday. She was doing a few practice circuits, ringing her bell a couple of times for good measure. She liked the bell. The big, hairy dog whose name was Wag was sitting in the shade of the banana trees watching her antics his tail thumping sporadically.

'Come on, Mammy, let's go. You'll be grand.' Moira was impatient to get moving. 'Just follow me and keep in to the left if you hear anything coming.' She pedalled toward the entrance.

Maureen drew alongside her. 'I should go in the lead, I think, Moira. What with me being older.'

'That's exactly why I should go in the front. Besides I know what I'm doing.'

Maureen gave a snort. 'You do not! Sure, you're all knees on that thing.'

'At least I can ride in a straight line, you're steering it like you're on your way home from a night on the lash.'

There was a stand-off as they eyed one another and if they'd had engines, they would have revved them. Their matching hazel eyes challenged one another until Moira broke away to pedal up the road as fast as she could, her dark hair streaming out behind her.

'That's not fair,' Maureen cried, frantically pumping her legs to catch up. 'Slow down, Moira, I can't keep up.'

Moira looked back over her shoulder. 'I'll go in the front on the way there and you can be in the lead on the way back, alright?' She knew a compromise was going to have to be reached because she wasn't fit enough to keep this pace up all the way to the village.

Maureen seemed to accept that, slowing to a more leisurely pace so she could enjoy the unfolding scenery.

Moira stopped pedalling and coasting along, she too looked around her. A light mist still clung to the rice paddies giving the fields a mystical, lost in time aura. The lone water buffalo she could see appeared as a ghostly spectre plodding along with birds hitching a ride on his knobbly back. A large black-winged hawk, or at least that's what she thought it was, soared starkly against the cloudless sky. The only sound was that of her own puffing breath as she tried to catch it. It was broken a few beats later by the familiar labouring sound of an approaching moped and she called back over her shoulder for Mammy to keep in.

'I know what I'm doing thank you, Moira,' Maureen shouted back veering dangerously close to the verge which dropped down into the waterway. She righted herself in the nick of time, pleased Moira hadn't witnessed her near miss and, as the children on the scooter passed by, the one on the back waving to her, she rang her bell.

They passed the vegetable plots Moira recalled seeing from the minivan yesterday which signalled they weren't far from the village. She saw the farmers with their heads shaded by their conical hats, baskets on their back as they went about their tasks. She also saw a bridge up ahead and a flash of red in the middle of it. She looked closer.

'Look over there.' Moira gestured to the stone bridge. It led away from the edge of the village and across to the rice paddies. A minivan pulled up and idled while a group of sightseers piled out. They formed an orderly line beside the stone walkway and Moira guessed they must be British. Nobody knew how to wait in a queue quite like the Brits. She cycled closer before braking to see what it was they were waiting for. An older woman, her silvered hair pulled back into a bun, was sitting on a mat in the middle of the bridge. She was wearing a red padded jacket and it was this that had initially caught

Moira's eye as she rode along. A rangy young blonde woman, wearing pants not dissimilar to Moira's elephant ones but in blue, was crouched next to her and the old woman held her upturned palm in her hand; she was tracing a finger along it.

Mammy pulled up alongside Moira and they watched the interaction, along with the huddled group waiting their turn, curiously. The driver of the van came and stood alongside them. 'What's going on?' Maureen asked him.

'Her name is Mother Bui, she's the Love Fortune Teller of Mui Ha Bridge. Very popular with the tourists. She tell you what is going to happen with you in the future for a donation.' He grinned, no gold tooth on display but he did have an impressive hole where one of his front teeth should have been. 'You want your fortune told?' He grinned at Moira who was listening intently and gestured to the back of the line. Moira nodded eagerly; she liked the sound of this. She liked the sound of it a lot and getting off her bike, she kicked the stand down. Maureen did the same and they stood at the back of the short line.

It wasn't long before the blonde woman stood up and they watched while she unzipped her bum bag retrieving a wad of notes which she placed in the dish next to the old woman. The old woman rewarded her with a gummy smile and a nod and the blonde made her way back across the bridge. Her face was flushed pink and a smile was playing at the corners of her mouth.

Moira collared her as she walked past. 'What was it like?'

'Mother Bui? She was great. I mean wow—she, like, knew so much.' The girl looked to be around the same age as Moira with a Californian valley-girl inflection. 'She mentioned the guy who broke up with me recently straight off, and then she told me there's someone else waiting to meet me but first I need to get to know what's in here.' She tapped her white singlet-clad chest and Moira thought she really should have put a bra on, what with the slight chill the sun had yet to ward off. 'And you know, like, that's why I'm here. I realised I, like, had no sense of who I was after my ex and I split. I'd spent so long trying to be the kind of girl I thought he wanted that I, like, didn't know who I was anymore.'

Moira smiled and shifted a little uncomfortably, too much, like, information. 'Well, I'm glad things are going to work out for you.'

The girl smiled, she was very pretty in that wholesome no make-up, beachy kind of way. She reached out and rested her hand fleetingly on Moira's forearm. 'I hope you, like, hear whatever it is you want to hear, too.' And she went on her way.

Mammy who'd been listening dropped in, 'They're very forthcoming, the Americans. They like to share.'

Moira thought this amusing given Mammy would tell a lamp post her life story if there was no one else about. 'Are you going to have your palm read?' she asked.

'I am.' Maureen's nod was emphatic. 'Sure, I want to know what's on the road ahead of me as much as the next girl.'

Moira side-eyed her mammy. It was disconcerting to think of the possibility of her with anyone other than Daddy. On the other side of the coin, it was sad to think of her on her own for the rest of her days. Come to that, neither option was something she liked to think about. Mammy wasn't over the hill just yet though; this holiday had reinforced that. Sure, look it, she'd had a beer-bellied German give her the glad eye and taken to her bicycle like a duck to water. She was beginning to understand that Mammy wasn't just her mammy, she was a woman in her own right. It was quite a startling thought. Referring to herself as a girl was a bit of a stretch though.

She wished the middle-aged man with the combover flapping in the gentle breeze would get a move on—surely his romantic future couldn't be that involved. A thought occurred to her. 'Mammy you're not to be earwigging on what she has to say to me.' If she were to overhear whatever this Mother Bui revealed it would hit the O'Mara women's telegraph faster than a speeding bullet. Her sisters would read far more into what was divulged than was healthy, especially Rosi with her being into all that new agey stuff, she'd take it as gospel. No, Moira decided, she'd listen but she'd take whatever she was told lay ahead for her in the love department with a pinch of salt. Especially if she didn't like what Mother Bui had to say.

Maureen shot her a withering glance, 'Back at yer. I don't want you listening in on what she tells me either, thank you very much.' She knew if Moira's big ears were flapping then whatever this Mother Bui had to say would be communicated to her daughters faster than the speed of light *and* they'd all read far too much into whatever it was she was told. No, she resolved, she'd be sensible and take whatever she heard on this bridge in the next while with a grain of salt. Unless of course she was told yer man, Daniel Day Lewis, was going to be making an appearance in the near future.

The line eventually shortened as the last of the happy customers clambered back into the van, assured of their romantic destiny and ready to head to their next port of call. Moira looked at her mammy. 'You can go first.'

'No, after you.'

A brief skirmish in the reverse order of their earlier discussion over the bikes ensued before Moira, receiving a push in her back from Mammy, set off toward Mother Bui. She checked over her shoulder to make sure Mammy wasn't following her. The old woman had watched their exchange with amusement, and her face was lit up in welcome as she gestured for Moira to sit down in front of her. She knelt down and as she looked into Mother Bui's eyes, she found herself thinking of raisins; they were crinkled, dark, and sweet, but more than that they held the kind of wisdom gleaned from a long life led.

She held out her hand seeking Moira's who placed hers trustingly in Mother Bui's. The fortune teller stared at her palm for a long time and Moira was beginning to get antsy, *this couldn't be good.*

'Your heart it has been broken.' She tapped her chest with her spare hand. 'Not long, yes?'

Moira nodded, her English was very good, she got brownie points for that, but she wasn't handing any out for her summation just yet, even if it was on the mark. It was, after all an easy guess. Sure, half the people who walked across this bridge to see her were bound to have had their hearts broken at some point. It was the stuff of life.

'He married.'

Moira shifted uncomfortably now; this she couldn't shrug off.

Mother Bui traced a finger down one of the lines on her palm and shook her head, a silvered wisp escaping and floating around her face. 'He no good for you.'

Moira found herself nodding her agreement, she was holding her breath.

'I see a man. He much better, you will have much happiness together.'

Moira sat back on her haunches breathing out in a long, slow hiss. *Did she have his phone number?* Her nerves had abated now she knew she wasn't destined for spinsterhood and she smiled at Mother Bui unsure whether she'd finished her reading.

'He a healer. A man of medicine. A good man.'

Moira thought of Tom, *please let her mean Tom,* her insides grew warm and fluid as she conjured up his surfer boy good looks. They'd have beautiful babies, so they would.

'He have very nice,' Mother Bui patted her rump and she grinned her gummy grin. Moira looked at her in surprise and then her face split into a wide grin.

'He does.'

A few minutes later, and five American dollars poorer, she made her way back across the uneven cobbles of the bridge to where she could see Mammy waiting chomping at the bit for her turn. She was a prophet that Mother Bui, Moira thought, unable to wipe her smile from her face.

'It obviously went well,' Mammy said seeing Moira's inane grin.

'She knew things, Mammy. She's the real deal.'

Maureen looked at her daughter for a second; she'd dearly love to know what she'd been told. Now would be the moment to squeeze it out of her too, while she was all starry-eyed and full of it. Two women around her age in the unmistakable clobber of tourists came into her line of vision. They were making their way from the village toward the bridge. She'd not have them pushing in, she decided, and with that she lolloped over the bridge toward Mother Bui, eager to hear what she would say.

Chapter 28

♥

Maureen walked back to where Moira was waiting for her. She still had a sappy look on her face. She, however, was feeling rather odd. She hadn't known what she wanted to hear, not really. She supposed she'd wanted to know that she'd be alright. That one day the awful aching void inside her, that no amount of filling every waking moment helped ease, would abate. If it did though, would that mean she was letting go of Brian? It was the fear of losing the part of him she carried with her that made her cling to that ache. Mother Bui had seemed to know all this. She'd certainly known her heart hurt and she'd told her that the pain would stop and it wouldn't mean she'd stopped loving her husband. She said she had a very big heart and could love more than once. She'd also told her to watch for a man with grey eyes and hair. She'd tapped her own hair and then she'd made a swimming motion with her hand as she said he was a man of the water. It was this man who would bring back her smile but only if she let him.

Obviously, Maureen thought, ignoring Moira's questioning gaze as she asked what took her so long, that meant he enjoyed sailing. She was pleased she'd had the red dress made for the Christmas party just in case this man with grey eyes and hair happened to be there. She wasn't ready for any sort of a thing with anyone. She didn't know if she ever would be.

But sure, that didn't mean she couldn't look her best, now did it? She kicked the stand up on her bike.

Both women were quiet as they cycled the short distance to the main street they'd passed through the day before. They parked their bikes on a spare bit of pavement, confident nobody would try and pinch them, as they set off to have a look around. There were wooden artefacts on display everywhere and piled up pots, varnished to a high gloss spilled out onto the pavement they were wandering down. If a pot wasn't up your alley then there was furniture for sale of a similar style to that which they'd admired inside Binh and Hoa's home. Maureen ran her hand over an occasional table. That would look lovely in her living room. She refused to call it a sitting room. Her apartment was far too modern to have a sitting room. She looked at it longingly but knew she'd never get it home. An intricately carved wall hanging caught her attention. 'Whoever's after making this is very clever. Look at the detail in it, Moira.'

'Mm,' she replied. It was very busy, lovely if you liked grinning gargoyles and lots of them. 'What's going on over there?' She pointed to a shop across the road with an open frontage. Three men were cross-legged on woven mats surrounded by wood shavings as they chipped away at lumps of wood. A handful of curious observers stood around them watching or snapping photos as they worked.

'Come on, we'll go and see for ourselves.'

'Mammy, look where you're going!' Moira yelped, pulling her mother back from the path of an oncoming scooter.

'I saw it, Moira, thank you.'

Moira shook her head knowing full well she hadn't, she had tunnel vision at times, like a toddler with their destination in sight, oblivious to what was going on around them. So, mumbling words beginning with f and liability under her breath she trailed behind her.

They joined the huddle and watched as hunks of wood were shaped into religious deities, elephants, and dragons. They were artists these men and it was fascinating to observe their deft actions as they chipped something from nothing. One of the men picked up a chunk of wood, a piece that would nicely feed a fire, and held out his chisel gesturing for one of the onlookers to have a turn. Maureen just about fell over herself in her eagerness to push the gentleman, clad in travel pants just like hers only with fewer pockets, out the way.

Tunnel vision, Moira thought to herself once more, trying not to laugh as Mammy took hold of the chisel. She knelt there on the mat for a moment observing how the other two carpenters were holding theirs. Then, tongue poking out the corner of her mouth in concentration, she began to gouge lumps out of her wood.

The minutes ticked by and a few of the group dropped away. They'd clearly decided they didn't want to stand here until teatime when the woman with the beaded braids finally finished whatever it was she was trying to do. 'C'mon, Mammy, you've been ages and it still doesn't look like anything.' Moira shifted from foot to foot; she too was growing impatient. We all have talents in life, she thought to herself, and woodwork was not one of Mammy's.

'Don't rush me, Moira.' She brandished the chisel at her, brow furrowed, before getting back to work. Finally, she sat back on her heels and proclaimed she was finished.

Moira half expected a cheer to go up.

'Very good. Very good.' The man whose chisel it was snatched it back before she could change her mind.

There was a polite round of applause from those that had hung in there for the duration as Maureen held her creation aloft for them to admire. It looked to the untrained eye like a banana and Moira asked for confirmation of this as she hauled Mammy from the shop. 'Is it one of those wooden fruits you display in a bowl?' It would look rather on odd all on its lonesome but she didn't fancy Mammy's chances of being allowed to sit down again in order to chip out an orange or an apple.

'No, it is not. It's a canoe.' Maureen's tone suggested this should have been obvious. She would've liked to have tried her hand at a junk but she didn't think she'd be able to manage the complicated sails so she'd settled on a more straightforward but still seaworthy vessel.

'Jaysus, Mammy, it's just come to me what it reminds me of.' Moira almost snorted her tonsils up through her nostrils.

'If you're going to be rude—'

'A man's bits. I'm telling you right now, Mammy, you're not bringing that home with us. Sure, if you get stopped at customs, they'll think you're after trying to import some sort of fertility effigy.' She eyed the offensive looking lump of wood in her mammy's hand and began giggling.

Maureen huffed. 'You've a dirty mind, so you do. I'm sure I don't know what company you've been keeping but it's not like any man's privates I've ever seen.'

—— *ell* ——

Postcards

Dear Patrick,

It's your mammy here. Moira and I are in the village of Mui Ha which is a few hour's drive from Hue where we got off our hop on, hop off bus. I'll telephone you to tell you the story of how we came to be here when we get home. It's like something from a film so be sure to make time in your schedule to talk to me. We're staying on a farm with a main house and bungalow accommodation for the guests, it's gorgeous. We've been made to feel like family by the owners. Our bungalow has a veranda which overlooks a pond, and there's a hammock which Moira's spent a lot of time today swinging on. She likes listening to the fish plopping about. I haven't had a look-in but sure that's no bad thing. I don't think I'd be able to get back out of it. Yesterday we explored the village. The wood carvings which are a local specialty are beautiful and good value but sadly mostly too big to bring home. I had a go at the carving and made you something. I'll give it to you when we see you next.

Love Mammy

Maureen couldn't bring herself to ask after his big-breasted girlfriend, besides she'd run out of room, her writing had grown so tiny as she'd tried to squeeze all she wanted to say in that it was barely decipherable. She put the card aside and set about penning the next one.

Dear Rosemary,

It's Maureen here. Moira and I are having a grand time. We're two and a half hours from Hue in a village called Mui Ha. We're staying in a very nice bungalow on a farm-stay which is down to my new Australian friend, Sally-Ann, and we're being treated like royalty. I can't wait to tell you how we came to be here but it's a long story and it will have to wait until we get home. It's very beautiful here. Very peaceful. The sun is beginning to set and I am sitting on the veranda of our bungalow. Moira is swinging back and forth on the hammock; she won't let me get a look-in. There's a pond in front of me and it's like glass apart from ripples now and again from the fish swimming about in it. I can see the mountains behind us reflected in the water. It's a mirror image and everything around us is bathed in a golden light, even Moira. She looks like yer woman from Goldfinger. I hope the weather is not too grim at home.

Yours, Maureen

Ha! Eat your heart out, Rosemary. She hoped it was raining cats and dogs in Howth today. It would serve her right for cancelling on her the way she had. Still and all, if she hadn't then Moira and her, wouldn't be here together and that was something she wouldn't swap for all the tea in China. She looked at her daughter fondly for a moment before setting to writing her last card.

Dear Noah,

It's your nana here. Aunty Moira and I are having a grand time. We're staying in the village of Mui Ha on a farm-stay where there are chickens and fish, real ones not crumbed like the fish fingers and chicken burgers you're always asking your mammy for. It's not a farm like how we think of one though, more a place to stay in the country. They grow grapefruit, vegetables and rice here. The village is well known for its woodwork and we watched the carpenters turning pieces of wood into all manner of things. I got to have a turn and I made a canoe. Aunty Moira has been very rude about it but I'm very pleased with it. We were only going to stay for one night but we liked it so much we stayed for three. I hope you are being a good boy for your mammy and dad - give then a hug from me and have one for yourself.

Love Nana

Chapter 29

♥

Mammy's Travel Journal

*H*ello from Hanoi. We've been here two days and are
now fully recovered from the journey here. We travelled
through the night from Hue and didn't get a wink between us.
The bus was bursting at the seams and we were jammed in
like sardines. On the bright side the roads were a lot better so
we weren't in fear for our lives. It was our last leg on our hop
on, hop off tickets. We're on our own from here on.

It was hard saying goodbye to Sal but it was time for us
to move on from Mui Ha. We'd stayed an extra day as it was
because it was so relaxing. I thought Moira's bottom had been
welded to that hammock. Sal has decided to stay with Binh
and Hoa for a while. There is plenty she can do to help earn
her board and I think she feels she's found another home with
them. I told her she has a home with us too whenever she
wants to come and visit the Emerald Isle. She promised me
she would come and see us one day soon. She's a golfer so
we'd have a grand time on the Howth fairway so long as she
decides to come in the summertime.

We didn't know what to buy the family to say thank you for
their hospitality and saying thank you alone when they'd made

us so very welcome wasn't enough. I thought about giving them my canoe but I'd already promised it to Patrick in the postcard I'd sent him and besides I don't think Moira would have let me. In the end we took the whole family for dinner at the restaurant in the village and we had a lovely time. There was lots of laughter around our table and the food was very good. I especially enjoyed the rice dumplings Hoa suggested for dessert. It's a funny thing saying goodbye to people you feel so warm towards. It's not easy either to leave somewhere you've felt so, peaceful, is the only word I can think of to describe it. Moira and I were both reluctant to leave for Hue but we'd arranged a driver.

His name was Phuc—I had to have words with Moira when we had a toilet stop because she kept repeating his name. It was all Phuc this and Phuc that. I told her she wasn't being clever if that's what she thought. She was exactly the same the time we had a guest stay with the surname Condon. I told her off back then too. Anyway, I think Phuc might have got a bit tired of her talking in the end because he put his radio on loud and my ears were ringing by the time we got to Hue.

The sun had been up a couple of hours by the time the bus dropped us at a hotel in Hanoi's Old Quarter. It was the first one on our trip that was not up to standard. I didn't need to run my finger along the skirting to see that. It was a disgrace so it was and whoever their Director of Housekeeping is, she should be ashamed of herself. We said we wouldn't be staying to the girl on the desk who was too busy eating her pot noodles to care and as we stepped outside the touts were like a school of fish swarming us. It put me in mind of famous people when they're being mobbed by the paparazzi. It was not a nice experience especially because we were dead on our feet.

In the end we followed a man who assured us his hotel, was very clean and only a short walk away. It took ten minutes to get there, he took my bag for me which annoyed Moira no end. She moaned all the way there. I told her what doesn't kill you will make you stronger and that it was her own fault for packing her bag with enough gear in it to immigrate to Australia. She needs to wash her elephant pants too, I noticed, she's sat on something on the bus and I didn't have the heart to tell her she looked like she'd had an accident.

The Red River Hotel was an improvement on the last place but after checking out the shower I told Moira to be sure to wear her flip-flops in there because she didn't want to be going home with verrucas. Moira thought we should try and stay awake but I told her I was a woman of sixty who'd just survived an overnight bus trip, I needed an hour's sleep before venturing out again at least. Well, let me tell you, she was snoring before me. We'd set the alarm so as not to sleep the day away and got up at lunchtime.

There was plenty going on in the Old Quarter. It was hectic but not as busy as Hoi Chi Minh. Still and all we decided to visit Hoàn Kiếm Lake to escape the crowds. It wasn't far away and it was very pretty. Moira and I took turns having our photographs taken on the red bridge which leads to Jade Island in the middle of the lake. There's a pagoda there with lots of incense burning. The smell was a bit much for me but Moira said, sure it was no worse than me with the Arpège at Dublin airport. She's very taken with all the Buddhist temples and shrines we've seen. I'm beginning to wonder if the elephant pants were a good idea after all.

We slept for twelve hours solid that night and packed in a full day sightseeing given how bright eyed and bushy tailed we were the next morning. We visited the French Quarter which was very French and yer man Hoi Chi Minh's museum, partly because you can always find a toilet in a museum and partly because we thought we should. We also saw the Presidential Palace. Tonight, we went to a water puppet show at a very beautiful theatre. I wasn't sure if I was going to like it as Punch n Judy always frightened me but it was a gas. I loved every minute of it and I gave those puppeteers a standing ovation.

Moira's after buying a puppet to bring home with her—at least it wasn't another lantern. I said she could supplement her income by doing a puppet show on Grafton Street.

We've booked a day trip tomorrow to Ninh Binh which we were told is like Ha Long Bay but on land. The trip's very good value too with lunch included.

<hr />

Postcards

Dear Tessa

I said I'd send you a postcard so here it is. The picture on the front is of the view from Bich Dong, a pagoda built into a cave over three levels where Buddhist monks once lived. We climbed up there today before going on a sampan boat ride through the waterways which was very relaxing after all those stairs. I have thigh burn now. This trip with Mammy is not turning out how I thought it would. I thought we'd drive each other mad but we haven't. Well not much anyway. Mostly we've had a good craic and I never thought I'd say this but there's no one else I would have wanted to come away with. Not that I could have come with anyone else because I didn't have the airfare. Still and all, I feel like I've got to know another side of her since we've been here. We've seen and done some incredible things together including today's trip. I hope you're enjoying being back home. Has your man, Owen, made any noises about visiting you? I'd like to come to New Zealand one day soon. This trip has made me want more.

Your friend, Moira.

Dear Noah

It's your nana here. Aunty Moira and I are in Hanoi which is the second biggest city in Vietnam. We've had a good look around and have decided we like it. It's an interesting city. You don't actually have to do anything. You can just find somewhere to sit and watch everything going on around you, because there's so much happening. We went to see a puppet show last night which was performed on water, can you believe that? We also explored a big cave three storeys high and I thought my knees might give out before we got to the top but they didn't. That was in a place called Ninh Binh where the landscape was like going back to the dinosaur era. Tomorrow we go to Ha Long Bay and I get to sail on a junk. I feel like you feel on the night before Christmas. I hope you're being a good boy for your mammy and dad give them a hug from me and have one for yourself.

Love Nana

Chapter 30

♥

'I can't walk down that. Sure, it's like walking the plank. Where are the hand rails?'

'Give the man your pack, Mammy, and then walk towards him. Sure, you'll be grand.'

Maureen swung her pack at the crew member waiting for her at the other end of the gangway. He caught it, staggering back before placing it on the deck and holding his hand out to indicate Maureen should walk toward him. There was still a good few yards between where she was and he was. No man's land and this was what had her in a state. 'I'll wind up in the water for sure.'

'No, you won't. It's only a few little steps, you can do it.'

'I can't.'

Moira's softly, softly approach wore thin. 'Listen to me, Mammy, you have to. How else are you going to get on the boat? They can't airlift you in.'

'Junk, Moira, it's called a junk. Look at the sails.' She pointed at the red concertina sails. 'I didn't come all this way just to go on a boat, now did I? Sure, I can do that at home whenever I like.' Her voice went up an octave as she eyed the wooden plank dangling over the water as it stretched from the wooden vessel in front of her to the wharf on which she was standing.

'Shall I go first? Would that make it easier?'

'No, I'm not after having you standing there looking at me like the cat that got the cream. I'll do it. Just give me a minute.' She shook her wrists like she was limbering up.

Moira heard an impatient cough. 'There's a queue behind us Mammy c'mon you can't be holding everybody up.'

Maureen's head did an exorcist style swivel and she only just missed slapping herself in the face with her beads as she turned to glare at the line behind her. 'Well,' she turned her attention back to Moira and said in a voice designed to carry, 'they can fecking well wait.' Fear was making her maniacal and Moira turned around and mouthed 'sorry' to her fellow passengers. They were being very understanding she thought, given the circumstances.

Maureen looked upward before crossing herself and following it up with a quick word with HIM upstairs before looking at Moira one last time. 'If I don't make it, I want you to know—'

'Jaysus, Mammy just get on the boa-junk, would ya!'

The very air itself seemed to hold its breath as she took a tentative first step onto the plank. She wavered for a moment before holding her hands out either side, then placed one foot daintily in front of the other like Roisin used to do on the balance bar at gymnastics when she was a child. One step, two steps, three steps. Her hand reached out and was clasped by a strong male grip as the crew member helped her down onto the deck.

A round of applause went up and Maureen preened before shouting across to them, 'It's alright once you're on it, just don't think about it too much and don't stop.'

Moira tossed her pack over and eyed the plank. 'Mammy, stop shouting you'll distract me.'

'C'mon, Moira, if I can do it, you can. On the count of three now.'

'Mammy, shut up!' Moira was terrified, not that she'd admit it, but there was a nasty drop either side of the plank into the oily swirling water below. What happened to health and safety? That's what she wanted to know. She heard that same cough again and, knowing she couldn't stand here all day she did what Mammy had said, counted to three and across she went.

She too got a smattering of applause but she refrained from shouting any helpful hints over to the beanpole in a light rain-jacket who she was fairly certain was the cougher. Instead, she said, 'Let's go up there.' She pointed to the upstairs deck, 'and find somewhere to sit.' They passed through the main cabin filled with empty seats, and their bags, Moira saw, were already being stacked in an alcove. The stairs leading to the upstairs deck were at the rear and they made their way up them to a covered open-air seating area. They slid along a bench seat and took a moment to soak in their surroundings.

'Is it what you thought it would be like?' Moira asked.

Maureen sighed happily. 'It's better, the only thing missing is Roger.'

Moira thought of Roger the Rat; she was sure there were plenty in the hull below. It took her a moment or two to twig Mammy was referring to her favourite Bond actor. They both scowled, watching people lithely skip over the plank and leap onto the boat. It was unnatural, Moira thought, as Maureen stood up. 'Take my picture, Moira, with the sails in the background would you, before that bunch of prancers comes up here.'

Moira obliged, snapping away as Maureen struck different Bond girl poses until the first of the other passengers appeared at the top of the stairs. They sat back down as the seats around them began slowly filling, not wanting to lose their spot. The scene around them was a hub of activity as boats, cruise ships, and junks of varying sizes and shapes vied for space against the industrious wharf area. It was just as chaotic on the water as it had been on the roads in Hanoi, Maureen mused. She watched a crew member on the boat next door nimbly navigating his way from one end of the timber deck to the other. Down the way she could see fishermen checking over their nets. A thought popped into Maureen's head. 'Moira you don't get seasick, do you?'

'No, well at least I don't think so. The last boat I went on was the ferry in New York and I was grand on that.'

A couple were sitting in front of them and the man turned around; he was wearing a cap back to front and looked to be in his early twenties. 'I've got something if you're worried you might get sick.' His accent was peculiar, Moira thought, frowning as she tried to place it. *Australian maybe?* 'We're from South Africa,' he said reading her mind as he opened his satchel and while he was looking inside it his girlfriend glanced back.

'You don't want to be sick and miss the cruise,' she smiled. 'The scenery is going to be fabulous.' Her partner produced a glass vial. 'Just take one, it might help.'

Moira took the bottle thinking she'd be doing him a favour because if she was sick it was his back that would wear it. 'Thanks.'

'Oh no, you don't.' Maureen snatched the glass bottle from her daughter's hand and holding it out tried to read the label before giving up and retrieving her reading glasses.

'What are you doing?' Moira asked out the corner of her mouth, giving an apologetic smile to the South African man.

'Listen Moira it could be anything in here.' She shook the bottle. 'Bangkok Hilton *remember?*' This was said as though it were code between them and Moira had had enough, she took the bottle back.

'Yer man here is not after asking me to take it home through customs he's offering me a tablet to help settle my stomach for fecks sake.' She rolled her eyes at the man who was now looking from mother to daughter as though they'd just come down from Mars.

Mammy remained unrepentant. Moira helped herself to a tablet and swallowed it dry. 'Thanks for that, and sorry about—' she tilted her head toward her mammy. 'She watched a film before we left. You might have seen it. Nicole Kidman gets set up as she leaves Bangkok by a fella who comes across as being all nice and that and she winds up in prison. My mammy's very impressionable.'

He nodded as though he totally understood before elbowing his girlfriend. 'We might go and sit downstairs, I think. It's a bit cold up here.' And off they went.

'See what you did? He thinks we're mad.'

'Well, if you start seeing enormous spiders climbing up the walls don't come crying to me.'

The boat juddered as the engine grumbled from deep within its bowel. Maureen clutched Moira's arm. 'We're off!'

At first all the two women could see ahead of them were mist shrouded monoliths rearing up from the dark, mysterious water. Behind them the skyline of high-rise hotels was growing smaller and the cruise ships that had looked so enormous while they were berthed had taken on a Lilliput-like quality. As they bobbed gently over the calm body of water it was as though they were looking through a camera lens and the subject was slowly coming into focus. The oily seawaters lapping the wharf were forgotten as the mists dispersed and they found themselves surrounded by an emerald sea. It was like a bolt of rippling silk, Moira thought, pleased with the analogy. The limestone pillars with their carpet of green came into sight and she overheard an English couple seated behind them talking. There were one thousand six hundred islands in the bay, and they were entering the first cluster of them.

Houseboats with waving families dotted the area and Moira found herself staring upwards in wonder at a Buddhist pagoda on top of a sheer, soaring column of rock. It defied belief as to how it had been built. She got up and moved to the railings, snapping away with her camera. Maureen came and stood alongside her. 'Mammy, I think this is the most beautiful sight I've ever seen.' Maureen linked her arm through her daughter's.

'Me too, Moira. I won't forget this for the rest of my days.'

Chapter 31

♥

Mammy's Travel Journal

*H*ello from Cat Ba Island in Ha Long Bay where Moira and I are spending the night. Tonight, I am a happy woman. I sailed on a junk today and it was everything and more I thought it would be. I felt like I'd stepped back in time. The journey through the island groups of limestone rocks and the emerald waters here to Cat Ba was breath-taking. We saw houseboats bobbing about, home to several generations. I got a bit uptight when Moira wouldn't stop harping on about your Buddhist temple plonked on top of a big rock. I was pleased when we moored up so we could explore a cave called 'Amazing Cave'. It got her off the topic. Walking into the cave was like having landed on the moon, it was a lunar landscape. We'd entered another world with razor sharp stalactites dripping from the roof, we walked deeper and deeper into it and saw caverns that looked like fairy grottos. The cave must have been underwater at some point because we could see the wave patterns worn into the ceiling.

We watched the sunset from our junk, a magical experience, before mooring at Cat Ba. Even though the light was dusky we could see as we trudged to our hotel that it isn't an island *paradise. There's construction going on everywhere and road works. It's a work in progress and I think if we were to come back in a few years we wouldn't recognise the place. We enjoyed our dinner which was included in the price of our hotel for the night. It was very good value. We get breakfast too.*

Afterward to work off our meal Moira and I went for a stroll down to the water. The moon was out and it was lighting a path across the black waters. The shadowy outlines of the junks that had brought us and all the other tourists to the island were moored for the night, waiting to take us back to the mainland in the morning. Above us millions of stars danced and we sat on a rock and just let it all wash over us.

I felt very grateful to HIM upstairs and I told him so. Something else too, I felt hopeful. This was new. I've not felt hopeful in a good while. The thing is I knew sitting there on that rock with Moira skimming pebbles that whatever happens next, I'm going to be grand. What's ahead of me is not what I thought it would be but I have to accept that because I can't change things. I don't think I understood that before we came here to Vietnam, not properly anyway. I realised I've so much to be grateful for in my life and at that moment as I saw a shooting star streak across the sky, I felt overwhelmed by gratitude.

Oh, and I've decided I'm going to get a dog too. Not a big one, a little one I can sit on my lap. It's not healthy sitting alone and imagining Brian's still with me. I've not been helping myself and sure, he'd have been the first to tell me if I'm not careful I'll send myself doolally. I think he'd approve of a dog. We can go for walks along the pier together. It will be good company so it will.

Tomorrow we're getting the bus to Sa Pa. It's our last destination before heading back to Hanoi to fly home. This holiday's after going awfully quick all of a sudden. Moira and I have been reading in the guide book and we decided that we will do an independent trek. I'm looking forward to it and told Moira she's to take lots of photos because I will be giving a talk

on our Vietnamese rambling experience for my fellow Howth
ramblers when we get home.

Postcard

Dear Noah,

It's your nana here. Aunty Moira and I are on an island called Cat Ba in Ha Long Bay. We sailed here today on a junk which is a ship with big red sails like a fan. It was a dream come true for me. I hope when you're grown up your dreams come true too Noah. There were mountains rearing up out of the water which was a very unusual shade of green. We saw families living on houseboats. Big, extended families, the mammy, the daddy, the children and the grandparents on both sides sometimes too. Imagine living with me, your mammy, daddy, and your granny and gramps! Sure, one of us would get pushed off the boat. We also explored an enormous cave which had very sharp stalactites (ask mammy what they are). It looked like somewhere magic that fairies might live. I hope you're being a good boy for your mammy and dad give them a hug from me and have one for yourself.

Love Nana

Chapter 32

M oira breathed a sigh of relief as the bus pulled up outside Sa Pa's main post office. The last leg of their journey here as the bus wound its way higher and higher into the mountains until, looking at the swirling mists, she'd thought they were in the clouds, had seemed interminable. Her stomach had behaved itself thanks to Sally-Ann having insisted Mammy take what was left of the ginger sweets but she'd still felt it roll ominously around every hairpin bend. They pulled their day packs down from the overhead luggage holder and shrugged into jackets before following the rest of their weary travellers as they exited the bus. Their backpacks were already unloaded by the time they set their feet down on the pavement, and they helped one another on with them. 'We don't have to go far do we, Mammy?' Moira asked, stooped over as she eyed their fellow passengers marching down the street.

'God Almighty, Moira, you wouldn't last five minutes with one of them milkmaid's yokes.' The beads clacked as she shook her head.

It was cool enough here for a hat, Moira thought, sniffing the air. It'd be a relief if Mammy wore one and she didn't have to look at those braids. They hadn't grown on her. There was a definite alpine bite to the air, a sharp contrast to what it had been like when they began their trip in the south and she'd felt like she'd be smothered by the heady humidity. Come to think of it, she thought, jiggling the pack, one of those carrying poles would probably be a better option. It felt like the weight was all on one side of her pack and she was sure by the time she took it off she'd be like Quasimodo. She followed in Mammy's wake looking around her as she went.

'The book says the main centre is only down there, Moira, and that the place is overrun with hotels, we'll decide what we like the sound of when we get there.'

This wasn't the quaint little town in the hills she'd envisaged, Moira thought. The place was heaving with tourists from all destinations and the touts were out in force. Here and there through the teeming chaos, she caught a glimpse of a colourful local. The buildings, while not high rises by any means, still closed in on the street they were on and she was sure when darkness descended the place would be awash with flickering neon lights. They came to a square and if they'd had any doubt they were in the right town it was assuaged by the wooden monument in the middle of it. The bottom circular tiers were filled with greenery and on the triangular centrepiece the words Sa Pa had been laid out in a vivid yellow flower of some sort.

Maureen leafed through the guide book while Moira looked about. It was a strange sorta place. Not one thing or the other. From what she could see, some of the buildings in the distance spreading down the hillside were like those you'd find in a French Alps ski resort while her closer surrounds were a maze-like concrete jungle, a miniature version of Hoi Chi Minh or Hanoi. It felt, she thought, as though it had spread rapidly to accommodate all its visitors but with no town planning or thought to how it would look when it all came together.

Maureen read her expression. 'It's a base, Moira, people come to visit the villages nearby and to trek. We're going to have a grand time here, so we are.'

A light rain began to fall and Moira eyed her mammy. The last time she'd used that cajoling 'It's going to be jolly good fun' tone on her was when they'd set off on their epic O'Mara family road trip around the Ring of Kerry. It hadn't reassured her then and it wasn't reassuring her now.

'I've my eye on a hotel, it sounds like it's very good value. C'mon it should be down that road over there. Let's get out of this rain.'

ell

Postcard

Dear Noah,

The picture on the front is of Ta Phin Village in Sa Pa where the Red Dao people live, they're famous for their red dao leaf bath salts. The village is full of massage spas with bathtubs full of the stuff. They're sorta like the bubbles your mammy puts in your bath only these ones make the water red and the smell off them or whatever else goes in with it is gorgeous. Nana and I sat in a tub together and even though it was weird to sit in a bath with her it was also very relaxing because we were looking out over the rice terraces. I think Nana was responsible for the bubbles in our bath too. She said she felt like a girl of twenty again when she got out. I don't think she'll be saying that when we get back from our trek tomorrow. I have run out of room so I am going to write another card.

Love Aunty Moira.

Dear Noah,

The picture on the front is of the rice terraces here around Sa Pa. The villagers in Ta Phin wear bright colourful layers of clothes and are very smiley even though they don't have television. Imagine that Noah? No Thomas the Tank or Postman Pat. There were lots of handicrafty things for sale too. I had to stop Nana from buying a coat in the local brocade. It's a handmade fabric the people here wear like on the other card I'm sending you which looks grand on them. She did buy lots of cushion covers though and a hat which she is going to wear on our trek tomorrow. I don't know why she went on at me about my lanterns because her living room is going to look like an ethnic minority village by the time she's finished. It's quite cold here and I didn't like Sa Pa much when we first arrived. It wasn't what I expected but having seen more today, I've changed my mind. Be good for your mam.

Love Aunty Moira.

Chapter 33

♥

'Mammy I don't know if I'm able for this.' Moira's head spun as she leaned over to tie the laces of the walking boots she'd lugged the length of the country.

Maureen pulled the little black hat with the band of brocade around the bottom down low over her ears and inspected herself in the mirror. She was pleased with her purchase; she looked the part so she did. She had thermal leggings on underneath her quick dry pants and a special thermal insulating top she'd invested in under her rain jacket. She looked at Moira's reflection, she was sitting on the bed with a face on her that could curdle milk. 'Sure, we've come all this, we're not going home without rambling. I trained for months for this, Moira, you know that.'

Traipsing around the hills and calling in at the local pubs for a refresher along the way with a few old faithfuls like Rosemary Farrell and the rest of the Howth Ramblers wasn't what Moira would call training. 'But I've not had a wink of sleep.' She really hadn't. There'd been a non-stop row of door slamming and loud drunk sounding indecipherable voices echoing throughout the hotel for the best part of the night. At four am, fed up, Moira got up and stuck her head out the door, set to have a go at whoever was behind the current ruckus. There'd been no one there and she realised it wasn't even coming from their floor. The sound was carrying from somewhere below. She'd wished nasty things on the arse responsible along with the builders for not soundproofing the place before slamming their door shut.

'Neither have I but once we get out there amongst the rice terraces in that lovely fresh air, we'll forget all about it. You've a good breakfast in you to see you through. C'mon, Moira, you'll be grand. And I've got scroggin.' She held up the bag of seeds and nuts she'd put together at the market yesterday.

'Oh, feck off with your scroggin, Mammy,' Moira said standing up. Chocolate might have seen her muster some enthusiasm but scroggin was obviously as good as it was going to get.

Her boots, never worn, were stiff on her feet and she hoped she wouldn't get blisters. Mammy had assured her the trek she'd picked for them to do would be a picnic, but sure, who'd trust a woman who looked like that, Moira thought, shooting the hat a look of disgust. It looked grand on the local people, but it looked ridiculous on the short Irish woman presently warming up in her active wear. 'C'mon then, let's get this over and done with.'

'That's not a very sporting attitude, Moira,' Maureen chided as she locked the door behind them.

Moira eyeballed every guest they passed as they made their way down to the reception area just in case they were one of the noisy arses from the night before.

'Right,' Mammy flapped the fold-out map she'd picked up from the reception clerk yesterday and on which she'd circled their route. 'We head down the main road and veer off down Muong Hoa Street and that's where we'll come to the ticket booth to pay our entry fee into the rice fields. Easy-peasy.'

'A rambling we will go, a rambling we will go, hey ho a derry-o, a rambling we will go.' Moira had found herself singing this silently as she put one boot in front of the other. Mammy was a few steps ahead of her, whistling as she traversed the terraced paths on their itinerary. She reminded Moira of one of Snow White's little helpers and she half expected her to have grown a white beard by the time she turned around next. She was in her element, map in hand, a natural leader and it would have been really annoying if she hadn't shaken off her foul mood just as Mammy had said she would. The clean, sharp air had cleared her head half an hour or so back and their surroundings were far too beautiful for anyone to stay grumpy for long.

They wound their way through the fields, the terraced ridges splaying down the hillside in a mosaic of green and gold. They'd passed by lots of small walking groups all of whom had a guide leading the way. Mammy had whispered to Moira that they obviously weren't ramblers if they needed someone to show them the way. Moira didn't want to burst her bubble by mentioning that her clueless tourists probably kept whole families here fed and clothed with the fee they'd paid their guides. When they came to a fork on the trail the cluster of water-bottle toting people they'd been shadowing turned left.

'We'll head off to the right, Moira, get away from the crowds and according to the map there should be a village we can visit an hour or so from here.' She took her reading glasses off and popped them back in her jacket pocket before folding the map up and putting it away too.

Moira felt the left heel of her boot beginning to rub. She thought this walk was going to be a picnic, that's what Mammy had said. An hour or so away did not make for a picnic in her book but first things first. 'Mammy, have you got plasters because I'm after starting with a blister?'

'Sure, you'll be grand, Moira.'

If she heard that one more time...

'We'll crack on a little ways further and then have a rest; I'll sort you out with one then.'

There was no point arguing so Moira took a moment to click away with her camera at the vista of picturesque wooden houses dotted in the distance before, trying not to think about her sore heel, she hurried after her mammy.

It was beginning to get quite warm she thought as they wound their way up higher and higher into mountainous countryside. Mind that could be down to the exercise as much as any change in the actual temperature. She gave a grateful sigh when Mammy at last held her hand up and announced they would have a scroggin break. A few ticks later Moira snatched the plaster from her and tended to her reddening heel. She followed it by drinking deeply from her water bottle and helping herself to a handful of the scroggin. The way Mammy was talking it up she was expecting a surge of renewed energy as she munched on the superfoods but five minutes after swallowing, she felt exactly the same. She hoped she didn't wind up constipated from the peanuts, they were good for that.

'How much further to the village, Mammy?'

'Ah sure, it's not far away now.'

'Will it be uphill all the way?'

'It's only a little slope, Moira, you'll be grand.'

Famous fecking last words, Moira thought, eyeing the black clouds that were banding together overhead. The sun had disappeared and in the few minutes they'd been resting the temperature had dropped too. 'Look up there.' She pointed to the ominous sky. 'It looks like it's going to pour. Maybe we should turn back?'

'What's that thing you're wearing?'

'A jacket.'

'What sorta jacket, Moira?'

'A rain jacket.'

'I rest my case. Now c'mon the sooner we get moving the sooner we'll get to the village. We can shelter there for a while if it gets heavy but I don't think it will come to much and anyway you won't melt. A bit of rain never hurt anyone. Anyone would think I was in my twenties and you had sixty-year-old bones the way you're carrying on.'

Moira did a rude finger sign behind her mammy's back.

By Moira's reckoning they'd been walking for at least an hour and the air had been growing steadily heavier and cooler. Her blister had erupted too despite the plaster. She was convinced they'd taken a wrong turning somewhere along the way because surely, they should have been at the village now. There were no signs of life around them and the terrain had changed. They'd long since moved away from the rice terraces and onto a track fit for a mountain goat. The foliage had thickened on either side of them too. It was madness to keep going she thought as a fat drop of rain splatted on her head. It was swiftly followed by three more. 'Right, that's it, Mammy I'm making an executive decision. The heavens are about to open and this track will turn to mud when they do. It's been a glorious walk.' That was overdoing it, she'd had enough an hour and a half ago. 'But it's time to turn back.'

Maureen frowned. She was a determined woman and as a proud rambler she was struggling to admit to herself that there was a strong possibility she had indeed misread the map. The rambler motto was 'Not all who wanders is lost,' but in this case she thought they might well be.

There was a hissing as the rain began to sheet in earnest. It dripped off Maureen's nose as she conceded that yes, this was ridiculous. It was time to go back to town. It was hard to believe now that they'd begun the day with glorious sunshine, she thought, silently setting off back the way they'd come. Her shoulders slumped with defeat. It was going to be a long and sodden walk back to town.

Moira felt the track liquefying beneath her feet and as her boots squelched deeper with each step, she poked her tongue out at Mammy. She'd only worn these boots once and they'd be destroyed by the time she got back to the hotel. Not that she had any intention of doing anything that might require hiking boots ever again. She'd toss the fecking things out when they got back to the hotel. And, she was definitely getting first shower. Trust Mammy to have to go against the grain and turn the opposite way to every other tourist on the mountainside.

Maureen was not happy either. This was not what she'd had in mind. Nor was it anything remotely like she'd envisaged all those times as she'd tramped around the Howth hills. By now she and Moira should have been sipping tea in the village and munching on something hot and tasty. She'd hoped to buy a bit more of the brocade too. She'd planned on timing their return to town through the rice paddies so that they'd be bathed in a photographer's dreamy, late afternoon glow. Instead, here they were bumbling about in the pouring rain, getting soaked to the bone, miles from any signs of life. She was so busy huffing with the injustice of it all that she didn't see the rut in the track. Over she went, landing with a sickening crunch.

'Jaysus, Mammy! What did you do?' Moira's voice was shrill as she skidded toward her. She knelt down beside her. Mammy was sitting at an awkward angle, her face white and her eyes huge in her face with shock.

'Oh, Sweet Mother of Divine, Moira, I think I'm after breaking something.'

Chapter 34

'**D**o you think you can walk if I help you?' Moira didn't like the way the beads of sweat had broken out on her mammy's face or how she was shivering, her teeth chattering. The rain kept pouring and opening her pack she retrieved the T-shirt she'd brought in case she got too hot. Fat chance of that she thought wiping the rain from her mammy's face. 'Put your arm around my shoulder and I'll see if we can get you up on your feet.'

Maureen did as she was told and Moira tried to ease her upright but she fell back against the sodden earth with a howl of pain. 'I can't do it, Moira!'

Moira's breath was coming in short steamy puffs as panic began to set in. *This was bad, this was very bad. If Mammy couldn't walk how were they going to get back to town?*

'You're going to have to go and get some help,' Maureen rasped, the pain leaching into her voice.

'I'm not leaving you here alone in this.'

'Moira, you have to. I can't walk and we can't just sit here. We could be here all night if we don't do something.'

Moira knew she was right. Nobody would be out looking for them because nobody knew they were here. She didn't know much about surviving in the great outdoors but she did know hypothermia was a very real risk if they didn't get off this mountainside before the temperatures plummeted, as they would do once it grew dark. She shivered and it wasn't from the cold it was from fear. They were in a right mess and it was up to her to get them out of it.

'Go, Moira. Fast as you can.'

Moira kissed her mammy on the forehead and said somewhat inanely, 'Don't move. I'll be as fast as I can. I love you, Mammy.' She felt her throat closing over and she swallowed hard. This wasn't the time for dramatics, she had to stay focussed and get moving. She didn't look back not wanting to see Mammy so small and vulnerable as she raced off down the path. She could do this. Just follow the path all the way back to the fork where they'd made the mistake of turning right, and then the path through the terraces back to town. *Be brave, Moira, be fearless for Mammy's sake. C'mon, girl, you can do it!*

She jogged along thinking about the story Sally-Ann had told them and how brave she must have been. Mammy too had been brave leaving the family fold and going far afield. Brave women. She was brave too, she told herself just before she slipped over, feeling her shoulder burn as she hit the ground.

She sat up and took a second to catch her breath. Whatever she'd just done it was only on the surface. Nothing was broken and giving her shoulder a quick rub, she got up. As she carried on, she made a promise to HIM upstairs that if she got her mammy out of this okay then she would do better. She'd be a better person. A kinder person. She'd help others. Something else too, she decided as she ploughed on through the mud and the rain, she'd go to college and do the Fine Arts degree she should have done all along.

Moira heard the voices before she saw who they belonged to and finding her voice she bellowed, 'Help!' before picking up her pace and racing toward where they'd come from. The rain had eased and through the mist she saw a small group of trekkers. She'd never been so grateful to see anyone in her life and that's when she began to cry.

Chapter 35

♥

Mammy's Travel Journal

*H*ello from Noi Bai International Airport, Hanoi. We're on our way home and me with my foot in plaster because, let me tell you, what a dramatic end to the trip we've had. I'll spare you some of the detail but Moira and I set off on our trek through the Sa Pa rice terraces three days ago and somehow found ourselves halfway up Mount Fan Si Pan—only the highest mountain in the country! The weather changed all of a sudden and one minute we'd been happily moseying along in the sunshine, the next it began to pour down. It got very dark too. We'd decided we'd better head back and it was only a few minutes later that I was after taking a tumble. So, there we were in the torrential rain up the side of a mountain and me unable to move up or down the track because I'd managed to break my ankle.

It was all a bit of a worry and the only thing for it was for Moira to run off to find help. I didn't want her to leave me on my own but we didn't have a choice and when she'd gone it crossed my mind that I could die there all alone, and that's not one word of a lie. The pain was horrendous, even worse than the childbirth just in a different location obviously. But you know a funny thing happened, I was frozen to the bone so I was and very afraid when all of a sudden, I felt as if someone had tossed a thick blanket around me and that I was wrapped in a warm embrace. I knew it was Brian he'd come to keep an eye on things until Moira could find help. Everything would be alright, and it was.

I have to say I was very proud of Moira. I know she was frightened to leave me but she did what she had to do. She proved herself a brave and able girl when it mattered. The thing with Moira is she underestimates herself and her abilities she always has. It's a frustrating thing to watch your child who has so much potential shy away from it instead of striding toward it with both arms wide open. I think knowing she saved the day has given her more confidence. The silver lining in a cloud and something else very good came out of it all. She's decided to go to the college and do her Fine Arts degree. She made me a very happy Mammy when she told me that and it took my mind off the nurse at the hospital taking to my travel pants with a pair of scissors. I'm getting ahead of myself though.

Moira happened upon a group of strapping Danes who came to our rescue. Two of the men made a queen's chair with their hands and carried me back to the town. It's all a bit of a blur but Moira tells me I kept telling them they were fine young fellows. She thinks I must have been delirious. We went to the local hospital but they couldn't set the cast there so we were driven to a hospital some 38km away in Lao Kai. I'd been given pain relief by then so everything was rosy until we got there and the nurse snipped away at my pants. I was disappointed about that but it was the only way they could get the cast on. Moira was marvellous sorting out all the travel insurance. She says we'll claim for the pants.

I spent the night in the hospital and we went back to Sa Pa the next day and spent one more night there before getting the bus back to Hanoi. I've been told we're going to take up *a whole row down the back of our plane as I have to keep my ankle elevated. It doesn't hurt so much now more of an ache but I've been keeping up with the pain medication just in case. I can't wait to see Rosemary's face when I tell my story at rambling group, she'll be agape so she will. At least too if it had to happen then at least it happened at the end of our tour.*

I don't mind telling you it's been a marvellous trip, broken ankle and all. I am a lucky woman so I am.

Moira looked across at where Mammy was sprawled across the four seats, plaster cast resting on a pillow. She'd already written 'you're a Ten in my book Mammy' on it. The braids were fanned out on the pillow on which her head was resting at the other end of the row. For someone who said she never slept on planes, she was doing a grand impersonation of being out for the count, right down to the soft, contented snores. It was probably the pain medication she was on, Moira mused. She too had the three seats over from Mammy to herself and was enjoying the luxury of stretching out. She couldn't complain with how they'd been treated since Mammy's accident. Everybody had been wonderful right from the moment she'd stumbled across the Danes. She couldn't fault anyone, not even the nurse who'd snipped mammy's pants, and now the cabin staff were giving them the royal treatment too.

What a trip it had been Moira thought glancing down at the elephant pants. She felt different to the girl who'd left Ireland. She was making plans for herself and settling back into her seat she thought about what it would be like going back to college as an adult student. How would she manage? She didn't know for sure but she wasn't frightened. One thing she did know was she'd pay far more attention to the course work than she would have done when she was fresh out of school. Art was her passion; she'd just lost sight of that for a few years. Life, she'd learned on this tour was too short not to follow her dreams. It was a lesson her mammy had taught her because if she hadn't of followed her dream, she could very well be married to yer buck toothed man in Ballyclegg.

ell

The red-carpet treatment continued through duty free where Maureen splashed out on her Arpège and Moira threw caution to the wind and what was left on her credit card by splurging on a bottle of Chanel's Allure. There'd be no treats when she became a poor student. Maureen made noises about how it would have been nice to receive a little extra discount on account of her injury, all the way to Irish customs. It was as Moira handed over their declaration cards that the proverbial carpet was pulled out from under them.

'You've ticked this.' An officious, ruddy-cheeked man stabbed at a box on one of the cards. Moira peered closer; it was to do with wooden products.

'My wood carving, Moira.' Maureen piped up from her wheelchair. Her crutches were resting across her lap and the patient assistant who'd been there to greet them with the chair when they'd disembarked was standing with his hands resting on the handles waiting for them to clear customs. Moira was standing behind the trolley on which their packs were stacked. 'It's in the top of my pack. Moira, don't just stand there. Yer man, here wants to see it.'

Which would be on the bottom of the trolley, Moira thought, her patience wearing thin. Mammy had no right to go on at her for not waking her when the dinner trolley came around; she'd not stopped going on about missing out on her chicken curry with rice for the last hour. The lack of discount from the duty free had been a welcome break from the topic. She heaved her pack onto the ground before crouching down to unlock and unzip Mammy's.

'Moira.' Maureen hissed. 'These two gentlemen do not want to see my smalls.'

'Well, you shouldn't have put your canoe inside a pair of them then should you?' Moira unwrapped the offending piece of wood and handed it over. 'It's nothing to do with me,' she said as he took it in his gloved hand and began to inspect it. She hastily did the bag back up and lifted hers back onto the trolley. She was keen to get this last bit over and done with so they could get home now that it was within sniffing distance. Mammy was going to stay with her and Aisling, who was in the dark as to the accident. They'd figure out a way to get her up the stairs, maybe Tom and Quinn could do the Queen's chair lift thing.

The officer held the carving out in front of him, turning it this way and that, a frown forming between his bushy black eyebrows. 'What's this when it's at home then?'

'It's a canoe of course.' Maureen pulled a face at Moira who was biting her lip in an effort not to giggle at the officer's bewildered expression. 'I made it myself.'

'At least you didn't pay for it.' He handed it to Maureen before waving them on their way.

So it was, a strange man wheeled Mammy through to the arrivals area where Aisling who'd been waiting impatiently for them was beginning to wonder if they'd missed their flight. She stopped her anxious fidgeting as she saw a woman in a wheelchair with braided hair like a member of Boney M being pushed through the doors. On her lap she was holding something proudly erect and dear God, thought Aisling surely it wasn't a—

'Aisling.' The woman waved the offending wooden item and the penny dropped as Moira appeared behind her in the elephant pants. She rushed forward to greet them both. 'What's happened, Mammy? Are you alright? And what is that on your lap?'

'It's her wooden p—'

'Moira! That's enough of that. It's a canoe, Aisling, sure, what do you think it is?'

Aisling and Moira's eyes met and they exchanged a look that said they were in mutual agreement as to exactly what it looked like!

'Now then, we'd better let this young man have his chair back, Moira.' She shot her a look which Moira correctly interpreted as give him a little bit of cash which she did, while Mammy ordered Aisling to help her out of the chair. 'I'll tell you all about what we've been up to on the way home. Ooh I'm gasping for a cup of good ole Irish tea and one of Bronagh's custard creams if she'll let us have one.'

The End

Bonus Content

Character Profile

O'Mara women character profiles

Maureen O'Mara – Mammy

Age:
Sixty years old.

Place of Birth:
A fictional Irish village called Ballyclegg.

Current location:
An apartment in Howth.

Children:
Patrick who lives in LA, Roisin, Aisling and Moira.

Grandchildren:
Noah and Kiera.

Relationship Status:
Widowed.

Occupation:
Semi-retired with a finger in many pies in the Howth community. Mammy is also an entrepreneur and sells the Mo-Pant (yoga-pant) as a side-line.

Physical appearance:
Maureen is short with brown eyes and hair which she wears in a swishy bob which she likes to swish around a lot. She takes pride in her appearance and is a well-groomed woman who loves Arpège perfume and is heavy handed with it. She has a penchant for the nautical look and has taken to wearing navy and white stripes along with boat shoes. She's also sported numerous dodgy hair do's over the years.

Childhood:
Maureen was put upon by her mammy and da along with her tribe of brothers, known as the Brothers Grimm by her daughters. She left home at a young age seeking a bigger life than Ballyclegg.

Dream job as a child
To work in the films.

Jobs:
Maureen's first job was as a live-in housekeeper at O'Mara's the Guesthouse on the Green and this is where she met Brian O'Mara. She went on to work in sales in the haberdashery department of the iconic Lewis's in Liverpool. Eventually she married Brian and they took over running the guesthouse.

Closest friends and hobbies:

Rosemary Farrell from her rambling group. Kate Finnegan is an old friend whose daughter, Ita (Idle Ita) is employed at O'Mara's as a housekeeper. She has also been friends with Bronagh Hanrahan, O'Mara's receptionist for more than thirty years.

Personality:

She is an optimist with her biggest strength being her love for her family. Maureen is a tiger mammy. She's also extremely bossy but has a big heart.

She is the sorta woman who, in an elevator, would push the button more than once.

Bucket List:

To meet Daniel Day Lewis as she has a penchant for the loin cloth he gadded about in in The Last of the Mohicans film. She'd also like to sail on a Junk having seen one of these boats in a Bond film.

What does she do on rainy days?:

Drives her daughters demented.

Story Motivation:

Maureen is lost without her husband, Brian and is trying to find her way as a woman now on her own. She's opted for a fresh start with an apartment by the sea. She keeps busy with all her activities and involves herself in her daughters lives in an effort to distract herself from her grief.

Roisin – the oldest daughter

Roisin Deirdre Quealey nee O'Mara. Her middle name was chosen for Nanna Dee the cantankerous great gran on her father's. Her name is pronounced Row-sheen. She's mostly called Rosi.

Age:
Thirty-six.

Childhood:
Rosi had a happy childhood but was a teenage rebel with her bolshie attitude which had her mammy and daddy tearing their hair out. She wanted to be a rock star when she grew up.

Current location:
London.

Occupation:
Stay at home mammy but in her past life she had a brief, disastrous stint hairdressing, she also sold alco-pops around Dublin nightspots and worked on reception in a car sales yard. Her last job was as a bank teller temp in London.

Relationship status:
Unhappily married.

Children:
Noah aged five.

Physical appearance:
Rosi is short and slender thanks to all the bendy yoga she does. She doesn't spend much time on her appearance and her favourite outfit is casual yoga pants (Mo-pants). Rosi with her dark eyes and hair which she wears any which way, takes after her mammy and she scrubs up well when the occasion calls for it.

Personality:
Rosi is the quietest of the three sisters. She can be a little introverted. She's a strong woman but unaware of the inner strength she possesses. Her biggest flaw is her lack of staying power and tendency to be, as mammy puts it, airy fairy.

Closest friends and hobbies:
Her sisters. Rosi has lost touch with her old pals and doesn't have any particular close friend in London. Her favourite past time is yoga.

Bucket List:
To visit an ashram in India.

What does she do on rainy days?:
She plays Lego with Noah and practices the bendy yoga.

Story motivation:
Rosi has come to a crossroads in her marriage and has some big life decisions to make. She's lost sight of herself as an individual in the years since she became a wife and mammy. Now Noah's at school it's time she figured out where she fits in the world.

Aisling – the middle daughter

Aisling Elizabeth O'Mara otherwise known as Ash is pronounced Ash-leen.

Age:
Thirty-four.

Occupation:
Manger of O'Mara's Guesthouse on the Green in Dublin.

Education:
College Diploma in tourism.

Jobs
Resort manager at various beauty spots around the world before coming home after her father's death to take over the running of the guesthouse.

Children:
Not yet.

Physical appearance:
Aisling is the changeling in the family with her fair colouring. She is a girly, girl when it comes to makeup and her dress sense. She LOVES high-heels on account of being short and will wear them no matter where she's off to. Her pride and joy is her designer shoe collection. Her eyes are green and her hair colour is reddish-gold, she has wavy hair she wears long. Aisling is prone to being curvier than she'd like.

Childhood:
Aisling was a dreamy child with her nose permanently stuck in a book. When she wasn't reading she enjoyed following her parents around and learning the ropes of running the guesthouse.

Dream Job as a child:
Librarian.

Closest friends and hobbies:
Leila who is a high-end wedding planner and Quinn owner of a local bistro. They all met in college.

Personality:

Aisling is kind and compassionate with an ability to sort other people's problems out. She struggles to sort her own out however and has a tendency to bury her head in the sand. her biggest fear is being stood up on her wedding day.

Bucket List:

A big white wedding.

What does she do on rainy days?:

She curls up with a good book and eats snowballs. Her favourite chocolate marshmallow treat.

Story Motivation:

Of all the siblings, Aisling is the most passionate about the guesthouse which is why she takes over the running of the guesthouse when Maureen makes noises about selling. She feels attached the Georgian Manor house in a way the others don't. She also thought she had her future all mapped out but it didn't pan out the way she thought it would. She's having to start over and might find her happy ever after in the unlikeliest of places.

Moira O'Mara – the baby of the family

Moira Anna O'Mara – Moira's not a nickname sort-a girl.

Age:

Twenty-five.

Occupation:

Receptionist at Mason Price Solicitors, a large Dublin firm.

Relationship status
Single and about to embark on an unfortunate relationship.

Children:
Not yet.

Physical Appearance:
Moira is annoying, effortlessly beautiful. She bears a strong resemblance to Demi Moore and Andrea Corr. She also has champagne tastes on a beer budget and is always stylishly turned out. She, like her sisters is short and has hazel eyes with long dark, straight hair. She's slim of course.

Childhood:
Moira was spoiled as the baby of the family with her siblings, mammy and daddy all running around after her. She had a very happy childhood indeed!

Dream job as a child:
Artist.

Jobs:
A receptionist in a small Dublin law firm before moving to Mason Price.

Closest friends and hobbies:
Andrea whom she works with at Mason Price. She doesn't have hobbies apart from socialising.

Personality:
She is street smart and can be a prima donna. She is also extremely loyal and fun.

Bucket List:

Moira lives in the here and now, she doesn't have one.

What does she do on rainy days?:

A face pack while drinking wine and eating stolen snow-balls.

Story Motivation:

Moira's been burning the candle at both ends. She's drinking too much and has fallen in love with the wrong man. She's a train wreck emotionally after the death of her father.

Final Note:

All of the O'Mara women like to Jaysus a lot. Mammy and Moira are the two who come out with the real clangers. The word 'feck' also features in their vocab but it's not meant in a bad way. They are all grieving the loss of their husband/father and their stories reflect that. They are also fiercely loyal to one another. They'll argue over anything and everything!

Excerpt from Rosi's Regrets

♥

Book 4, The Guesthouse on the Green

I very much hope these stories made you smile. Thank you for reading about the O'Mara women. If you're keen to find out what happens next in their lives then read on for an excerpt from Rosi's Regrets:

———ell———

Prologue

The black nose poked through the gap under the bricks, twitching as it sniffed the frosty night air. A bristly red head popped through the hole, eyes sweeping the courtyard to check the coast was clear. A strip of light illuminated the familiar path to the rubbish bin; his bin. The beam was shining through the gap, where the curtains hadn't quite been closed in the room directly over this outdoor area. It might only be a short distance across the concreted ground to his destination but it was one fraught with potential landmines. One big one in particular who waved a rolling pin and screamed louder than he could! Satisfied the cook who had it in for him was long gone for the day, the little red fox squeezed his body through the hole. It was harder work than usual; he'd been eating well of late. But he was nothing if not determined and after one good push, out he popped.

He padded across to the bin, a sniper with his target in sight, a bin where a myriad of treats added a splash of variety to a fox's diet and a layer of padding around his middle. A noise broke the silence and he froze, statue-like, ears pricked on high alert. He didn't move, prepared to wait it out until he knew what had made the sound. An acrid smoky smell danced over the high walls surrounding the courtyard. It would be the man next door; he would be puffing on that smelly stick he so loved while the woman in the house shrieked it was high time he gave the things away. She would tell the man he'd catch his death standing around in the cold and the man would reply, 'If a man who'd worked hard all his life could partake of the one pleasure he had left inside, then he wouldn't catch his death.' She'd shout back that he could 'Fecking well freeze.'

The little red fox didn't like their backyard, it wasn't worth visiting. There was never anything worthwhile in their bin. Not like here; this was the piece de resistance of rubbish bins. His tongue poked out as he carried on his stealthy path to where, if he was lucky, he might find a sliver of black pudding, or even better white pudding, bacon rind, and soda bread. If there was an award for rubbish bins this one would get the Oscar. He reached it and began to salivate as he stretched up to nose the lid off with well-practised ease, and as it clattered to the ground he worked fast. His luck was in, white pudding! It was a night to celebrate, indeed! He nose-dived gleefully into the bin and retrieved it, snaffling it down. There was bacon rind too, oh yes he was fine dining tonight. He was about to go in for seconds when the window above the courtyard squeaked open. A man, with a mean thin face which looked angrier than the rolling pin woman's, peered out.

The fox didn't like the look of him. He meant business and although it broke his heart to leave, he scarpered across that courtyard to the safety of the gap under the wall. A splash of icy water hit his tail as he pushed his way back through from where he'd come, the midnight garden beyond the wall.

The man with the thin, pinched face shook his head and wrenched the window back down. Vermin, no better than rats those things. He put the empty glass down on the bedside table and got back into bed. He'd have words with the manager in the morning. The girl with the mane of red-gold hair and silly shoes. Oh yes, he'd be telling her: for the ridiculous sums of money he was being charged for the dubious privilege of staying in this establishment, O'Mara's needed to up its standards.

Chapter 1

♥

London 1999

Roisin twisted the plain gold band on her finger and stared at the statement lying open in front of her. There were two sharp creases across the piece of paper where it had been folded inside the envelope and she smoothed them hoping that the action might magically erase the information neatly set out before her. It didn't of course and she blinked trying to convince herself she hadn't read what was laid out in neat, black font but when she re-focused the words were the same as they'd been a split-second ago.

The table at which she was sitting still wore the debris from breakfast—from normal day to day life. A puddle of milk left behind by Noah who'd been craning his neck trying to catch sight of the cartoon he'd left blaring in the living room as he shovelled in cornflakes. Dirty dishes waited to be cleared and toast crumbs kept the puddle company as they waited to be wiped up. The postcards Noah had received from Mammy and Moira sent from their Vietnam holiday were resting against the salt and pepper shakers.

Speaking of Noah, he'd left the television on and it was almost but not quite drowned out by the kitchen radio which Roisin had tuned to BBC 1. It was her routine to change the station over from the newsy BBC World Colin preferred of a morning the moment he shut the front door behind him.

She was dimly aware of an annoyingly preppy pop hit, currently storming the charts, playing. It seemed at odds with what she'd just discovered. Beethoven's classic da-da-da-du-uum from *Symphony No. 5* would have been more appropriate.

She stopped twisting her ring, only to find it felt like the precious metal was branding her. The sensation, she knew was in her head but it felt real and unable to stand it she wrested the band from her finger before dropping it on the table. She watched as it rocked and rolled like a penny piece before finally giving up its dance. Her finger looked naked without its gold adornment. She'd stopped wearing her engagement ring eons ago. The marquise cut diamond had been a stunning choice but it had proven to be an impractical one. She'd constantly snagged her tights, pulled sweaters, and in the end, when Noah had been born, terrified she'd scratch him with it she'd put it back in its box and tucked it away down the back of her knicker drawer. If Colin had noticed she'd stopped wearing it he'd never commented.

Roisin didn't know where the impractical gene she'd been bestowed with had come from but making fanciful decisions was the story of her life. Not once in her thirty-six years had anyone said, 'Gosh that Roisin O'Mara is a practical girl,' or 'Sure, Rosi O'Mara's full of sensible ideas, so she is.' She'd never been the girl people turned to for sage advice or the person you'd rely on to hold you steady through one of life's storms. It wasn't that she was unreliable as such, and she was fiercely loyal when it came to family and friends, it was just she was what Mammy liked to call a little bit airy-fairy.

If you were to ask Maureen O'Mara to sum up her three daughters, Rosi knew exactly what she'd say. Moira, her baby, was a prima donna who thought she'd been born with a silver spoon in her mouth. She hadn't, although in Roisin's opinion she was spoilt and got away with a lot more than her three siblings ever had. Aisling, the changeling with her red-gold hair was one of life's peacemakers and she spent far too much time sorting out other people's problems while ignoring her own. A bit of an ostrich was Aisling. As for Rosi, her eldest daughter, well, Mammy would say, she'd been a pain in the arse teenager—all attitude and such but, one thing was for sure, she'd been born with her head in the clouds. Anyone would think the milkman had had a hand in things when it came to her girls, she'd lament laughingly to anyone listening, if it weren't for the fact Aisling took after her father's side of the family, God rest his soul. Rosi and Moira were the dark haired, olive skinned spits of their dear mammy.

Annoyingly, and a little unfairly in Roisin's opinion, Mammy never included her only son and eldest child, Patrick in this equation because to her mind, she could sum him up on one word, 'perfect'. It irked all three of the sisters because he was far from it but she of all people knew love was blind. She also knew, since becoming a mammy herself, that you'd forgive your children anything, even for being an arsey, vain, eejit like her brother was.

Roisin thought she'd made a proper, practical, grown-up choice when she'd said yes to Colin's proposal. It had come about after a very impractical decision—forgetting to use a condom. He'd been very old-fashioned about the whole business, quietly ringing her dad to ask if he'd give his daughter's hand in marriage before popping the question. Seeing as Roisin was over thirty and pregnant, Brian would have bitten his hand off had he done this in person, or at the very least thrown a dowry at him, but it had been done over the telephone and so far as she knew no money had exchanged hands. So, with her father's permission and unbeknown to her, the rest of the O'Mara clan were eagerly awaiting a further telephone call to confirm her engagement; Colin had taken her out for a meal in a posh London eatery.

It was somewhere in between the main and dessert he'd gotten down on bended knee. At first she'd been unsure what he was up to. He'd leaped out of his seat, crouched down and looked very red in the face. She'd wondered if he'd been seized by cramp and contemplated getting down beside him and rubbing his leg to try and ease it but then dessert had arrived as he simultaneously asked if she'd like to marry him.

In hindsight Roisin didn't know if she'd been so quick to say yes because she wanted to get stuck into her crème brûlée. She was four months pregnant and dessert really, really mattered to her. She'd managed to hold back long enough for Colin to open a red velvet box and found herself blinking at the sparkle. Inside the box nestled a diamond ring. It was exactly like the one she'd pointed out in the window of the jewellers as being the sort of thing she'd like *were* they ever to get engaged. She didn't trust Colin's taste and had a feeling if she wasn't clear about what she wanted she could very well wind up being offered his great granny's hideous heirloom opal if he decided to make an honest woman of her.

The thing was though, she'd thought, torn between the glittering stone and the golden sugary crust of her brûlée, saying yes wasn't just about her. There was little bean too. This was not the time to be flighty and act on the spur of the moment, nor, she told herself sternly was it the moment to crack that gorgeous crust so she could tuck in. Oh no, this was the time to behave like a sensible, pregnant women. Accordingly, she'd paused and taken a moment to run through a mental marriage checklist.

Would Colin be a good husband and father? *Yes, she thought he probably would.*

Would he make a good provider? (Yes, okay it was old-fashioned, but Rosi fully intended to stay at home throughout little bean's formative years and make lots of wholesome, whole foods) *Yes, he was a hard worker and liked to think of himself as one of life's movers and shakers.*

Was he trustworthy? *Well, if he'd lied to her, she didn't know about it.*

Did he love her? *He must do, mustn't he? Just look at the enormous blingy ring he was offering her.*

Did she love him? *Yes, she thought she did, not that she had much experience of being in love but he made her feel safe and while it wasn't the grand passion she'd seen in films, he was steady and reliable and there was a lot to be said for that when you had a little bean on the way.*

Accordingly, as Colin began to grimace from spending so long balancing on one knee, Roisin had accepted the ring and beamed that yes she'd love to marry him. All the while she'd been eyeing the crème brûlée and thinking to herself *righty-ho, let's get this show on the road.* The custard dessert had been delicious too, when much to her relief he'd finally slid the ring on her finger and she'd been able to thwack that toasted sugar with the back of her spoon.

That had been nearly six years ago. She hadn't eaten crème brûlée since, she realised wondering how she'd gotten it so wrong? She picked up the bank statement that had thrown her morning into a complete tizz. Without thinking she screwed it up into a ball and threw it at the wall.

Available from your favourite Amazon store.

Michelle Vernal lives in Christchurch, New Zealand, with her husband, two teenage sons, and attention-seeking tabby cats, Humphrey and Savannah. Before she started writing novels, she had a variety of jobs:

Pharmacy shop assistant, girl who sold dried-up chips and sausages at a hot food stand in a British pub, girl who sold nuts (for 2 hours) on a British market stall, receptionist in an Irish guesthouse, and legal secretary... Her favourite job, though, is the one she has now – writing stories she hopes leave her readers with a satisfied smile on their face.

If you'd like to be kept up to date with the O'Mara family series you can sign up for her no spam newsletter by visiting her website at www.michellevernalbooks.com . You'll receive a free O'Mara novella. to say thanks.

Also, by Michelle Vernal

♥

Printed in Great Britain
by Amazon

32974707R00367